Without a Trace

Beyond a Doubt

COLLEEN COBLE

THOMAS NELSON
Since 1798

NASHVILLE DALLAS MEXICO CITY RIO DE JANEIRO BEIJING

Published in Nashville, Tennessee, by Thomas Nelson. Thomas Nelson is a registered trademark of Thomas Nelson, Inc.

Thomas Nelson, Inc., titles may be purchased in bulk for educational, business, fund-raising, or sales promotional use. For information, please e-mail SpecialMarkets@ThomasNelson.com.

Unless otherwise noted, Scripture quotations are taken from the HOLY BIBLE: NEW INTERNATIONAL VERSION®. © 1973, 1978, 1984 by International Bible Society. Used by permission of Zondervan Publishing House. All rights reserved.

Publisher's Note: This novel is a work of fiction. Names, characters, places, and incidents are either products of the author's imagination or used fictitiously. All characters are fictional, and any similarity to people living or dead is purely coincidental.

ISBN: 978-1-59554-581-7

Printed in the United States of America

08 09 10 11 12 RRD 6 5 4 3 2 1

Without a Trace

For my wonderful, supportive family:
my husband, David, my son, David Jr., and my daughter, Kara.
I love you all very much!

Acknowledgments

The joy of working with Ami McConnell, my editor at Thomas Nelson Fiction, has been a dream come true. Thanks for believing in me, Ami! Her fabulous eye for character and my editor Erin Healy's plot suggestions helped mold the story in many ways. Thanks, gals!

Every writer ought to have an agent like mine. Karen Solem sent me back to the drawing board when it was needed and encouraged me when I wanted to crawl into bed and pull the covers over my head. Karen, thanks for the handholding and the equally necessary swift kicks! I thank God for bringing you into my life.

Kristin Billerbeck and Denise Hunter read and reread every word I write. Thanks, friends, for all the hours you put into helping to make my writing better.

My husband of thirty-two years, David Coble, helps keep me straight on time lines and other necessary things. Thanks, honey, for your faith in and constant prayer for me.

My "grandpup" Harley was the inspiration for Samson. His constant love and happy smile for all of us exemplify the very best of canine friendship.

A special thanks to Harry E. Oakes Jr. Harry founded the International K-9 Search & Rescue Services & Consulting Firm. He and his team are often called in when amateur teams fail to find missing persons. Harry sent me all kinds of training materials and sample cases. His information was invaluable. Harry's dog Ranger was the first of Harry's SAR dogs to hold an International SAR Dog Record of 370 missions with 157 documented finds. Ranger was the only SAR dog to win the Higgens and Langley Swift Water Rescue Award. He jumped into the Pacific Ocean and saved a drowning child while Harry jumped in and rescued her brother. Ranger died in 1994, and Harry's current award-winning dog, Valorie, is an eight-and-a-half-year-old Border collie–schipperke-mutt mix. Valorie was saved from the dog pound at age five months and trained for SAR. She has documented 2,348 missions with 924 documented finds and assisted finds of people, pets, suspect identifications, and evidence. This is a world record. Thanks, Harry! I owe you!

And, finally, my thanks to Pete Connor, Yankee Aviation Services in Plymouth, Massachusetts, for answering my questions about small planes. Thanks for your patient answers, Pete!

I fled Him, down the nights and down the days;
I fled Him, down the arches of the years;
I fled Him, down the labyrinthine ways
Of my own mind; and in the mist of tears.

—"The Hound of Heaven"
(FRANCIS THOMPSON, 1859–1907)

*I*t was days like this, when the sun bounced off Lake Superior with an eye-squinting brilliance, that Bree Nicholls forgot all her qualms about living where the Snow King ruled nine months of the year. There was no other place on earth like the U.P.—Michigan's Upper Peninsula. With Keweenaw Peninsula to the north and Ottawa National Forest to the south, there could be no more beautiful spot in the world. The cold, crystal-clear waters of the northernmost Great Lakes stretched to the horizon as far as she could see.

But she'd never find those kids by focusing on the seascape. Pressing her foot to the accelerator, she left the lake behind as she urged her old Jeep Cherokee forward along the rutted dirt track. Bree's best friend, Naomi Heinonen, steadied herself against the door's armrest and looked over her shoulder at the two dogs still safely confined in their kennels. The Kitchigami Wilderness Preserve lay to the east, past Miser, a drive of only fifteen miles or so, but on this washboard road, it took longer than Bree liked.

"Don't kill us getting there," Naomi shouted above the road noise.

Bree didn't reply. These lost children weren't some vacationers without ties; they were residents of Rock Harbor, two of their own. And night would be here soon. If Naomi were driving, her foot would be heavy on the accelerator too. The preserve was a formidable tract that could swallow up two kids without a trace.

The wind churned autumn's red and gold leaves in eddies and blew them across the road like brightly colored tumbleweeds. Equally colorful trees crowded the hills like giant banks of mums. The U.P. in autumn was Bree's favorite time, except when ever-shorter days put strangleholds on their search efforts.

M-18 headed on east, but Bree made a sharp turn onto Pakkala Road, which would take them into a heavily forested area. In the spring, motor homes and SUVs pulling campers plied the road on their way to experience some of the last wilderness left in the Midwest. Today the road was practically empty.

"Fill me in on what we know," Bree said.

"Donovan O'Reilly reported Emily and Timmy missing three hours ago. They were on some outdoor nature thing with their school," Naomi said.

Bree knew Donovan O'Reilly—he owned the local Ace Hardware store. His wife had left him and the kids nearly two years ago, and now his eyes had a haunted look, as though he wondered what fate would hand him next. Bree often stopped by Ace to pick up supplies for the ongoing renovation of her lighthouse home, and a friendship of sorts had developed between them.

"One of the students said she heard Emily talk about seeing a raccoon," Naomi continued, "so that might be what caused the kids to wander off. It's not much to go on, but they've started searching." She chewed on her lip. "You remember Timmy has diabetes? I wonder when his shot is due."

"I was thinking about that." Bree imagined Donovan was out of his mind with worry. "Donovan asked me out last week; did I tell you that?" she asked. She'd been tempted to tell him yes. Her lighthouse echoed with silence, but she had realized it wasn't fair to use someone like Donovan to ward off her loneliness. "I said no, of course."

Naomi didn't reply, and Bree looked at her curiously. "What? You don't like him? Didn't he used to be your brother's best friend? You probably know him and the kids pretty well."

A flush moved to Naomi's cheeks, and she looked out the window. "That was a long time ago. I only see him at the hardware store now, and I like him fine. Why did you say no?"

"I'm not ready. Maybe I never will be." Bree tapped the steering wheel with impatient fingers, wishing the Jeep could go faster over the bumpy, rutted road. Instead, she slowed and turned onto the access road that would take her back to the campground parking lot.

As she pulled in, Bree saw people fanning out in a search grid. There was an assortment of searchers, ranging from teenagers like Tommy Lempinen to professional types like Inetta Harris, who was still dressed in her business suit. When one of their own was threatened, Rock Harbor residents pulled together.

Bree and Naomi got out, attached leashes to the dogs, and shrugged their arms into their ready-kit backpacks, fully outfitted with first-aid kit, small plastic tarp, energy bars, flashlight, flares, bug repellant, towelettes, compass, Swiss pocketknife, radio, topographic map of the area, canteen, sunglasses, sunscreen, and every other item one was likely to need on a search. A young woman in a brown National Park Service uniform was Bree's first target.

"We're the Kitchigami K-9 Search and Rescue team," Bree told her, though that much was printed on the bright orange vests that both the women and the dogs wore. "I'm Bree Nicholls. Who's in charge?"

The young woman pointed toward a group of people nearly hidden by a stand of sycamore. "The lead ranger is over there." Bree looked and recognized Donovan's ink-dark hair among them.

Bree and Naomi headed toward the group. Donovan saw Bree and broke away. Pain contorted his handsome features. With his black hair and dark blue eyes, Bree had always thought he looked a bit like Pierce Brosnan, though today he was too upset and pale to carry off the James Bond sang-froid.

"Please, you've got to find the kids!" His hands trembled as he thrust two small jackets toward her. "They don't even have their jackets on, and it's supposed to get to near freezing tonight." The torment in his eyes spoke of his fear of loss more clearly than his words. "Timmy's shot is overdue now."

His voice quavered, and Bree put a comforting hand on his arm. She knew the anxiety he felt. "We'll find them, Donovan. The dogs are well trained, and Samson has a special radar for children."

His head snapped up as if mounted on a spring. A dawning hope filled his face. "I'll come with you."

How well Bree remembered that overwhelming desire to help. The waiting was the hard part. When her husband's plane went down, taking their son and all her hopes for their future with it, she had felt a crushing need to *do something*. In her case, there had been nothing to do but try to move on. With any luck, Donovan probably would not be in that situation.

She shook her head as she took the jackets from his hand. "You have to stay close to base, Donovan. The kids will be scared when we find them, and you'll need to be in a position to get to them quickly when they're found. Try to stay calm. We still have several hours before sunset. We'll find them."

Donovan nodded, but his gaze flickered from Bree to Naomi with a naked appeal in his eyes. "I want to do something."

"Pray," Naomi advised.

His eyes squeezed shut. "I started that as soon as I learned they were gone," he whispered.

Naomi's answer to everything was prayer. Prayer had done little for Bree's own desperate pleas. What use was a God like that?

"Let's go," Bree said.

As they approached the tree line, a slim, feminine figure stepped out of a stand of jack pine and came toward them. Bree lifted a hand in greeting. She should have known her sister-in-law wouldn't be far from the action. She craved media attention the way the mine owners craved cheap workers.

Hilary Kaleva pushed aside the branches barring her way into the clearing as though they were a personal affront. Hilary, Rock Harbor's mayor, was having the mother of all bad-hair days. Her hair, blond like her brother Rob's, was swept up in a formerly elegant French roll, but strands loosened by tree branches now clung damply to her neck. Streaks of mud marred her navy suit, and bits of pine needles clung to the fabric.

"It's the poodle," Naomi muttered to Bree. "I'm out of here. I'll wait with the rangers."

"Coward," Bree murmured. She wished she could laugh. Rob used to call Hilary his "poodle sister," which Hilary found less than amusing, but Bree and Naomi had always thought the description apt. Hilary could be sweet and loving one moment then turn and bite without provocation. And she talked until Bree grew weary of listening. But she could be just as endearing as a poodle when she wanted to be. From the expression on her face, today wasn't one of those days.

Samson woofed at Hilary in greeting and strained at the leash to meet her. The mayor flinched at the sniffing dog, pulling away with a moue of distaste. As if sensing Hilary's animosity, Samson lurched toward Hilary then came alongside Bree and rubbed his nose against her knee. Bree tugged him farther away from her sister-in-law. No sense in upsetting her.

Hilary's scowl eased when Bree pulled the dog a safe distance away. "What are you doing here? I thought you were searching the northeast quadrant today."

Bree's smile faltered. Hilary always managed to drain her confidence with a relentless determination to bend her to her will. "I was home when the call came in. The brick is crumbling on the tower, and it seemed like a good day to repoint it. I was just about to mix the mortar when Mason called." Bree stopped and chided herself for babbling like a kid caught playing hooky. Maybe it was time they both realized

Rob's plane might never be found. Not in the northeast quadrant or any other. The forest had swallowed the Bonanza Beechcraft like Superior could swallow a sinking ship.

Hilary's eyes flashed. "You have more important things to do than to repoint the brick on your lighthouse. Let a professional do it."

"The last time I checked, my bank balance was screaming for mercy, Hilary."

Hilary sighed, and she gave a smile that seemed forced. "I'll pay for it. You promised you'd find them, Bree. It's been nearly a year. Rob's birthday is the day after Thanksgiving. I'm counting on giving him a decent burial by then."

Bree wanted to run away from the admonishment. The graves at Rock Harbor Cemetery were as empty as her heart. Even if she found the bodies to fill those graves, it wouldn't change things, but at least maybe then she could bring herself to go there to mourn. Besides, Bree was tiring of Hilary's constant harping on her failure to find them.

"Samson and I are doing the best we can, Hilary. But they could be anywhere. Here in the Kitchigami or maybe even down in Ottawa."

"My patience is running out."

Bree had trained her temper to stay on its leash when she was around Hilary, but some days were harder than others. "I want to find them just as much as you do, Hilary. But I'm not Superwoman." A muscle in Bree's jaw jerked. Hilary didn't understand how hard a task Bree had set up for herself. At least there was still a chance for Donovan's kids. "Look," she finally said, "I need to get on with the search for the O'Reilly children."

She turned and rushed into the woods then hurried along the pine-needle path toward Naomi and the group of rangers under the trees. The rush of cool air soothed her hot cheeks. Would she never find them? *Never, never,* her footsteps answered.

A dark-haired man was giving directions. About six feet tall and stocky, he gestured with broad hands that looked tanned and capable.

When Bree approached, he stopped talking, and his gaze settled on her. Bree smiled and nodded a hello as she stepped forward with an outstretched hand.

"You look like the man I need to see," she said. He looked vaguely familiar, and she wondered if she'd seen him around town. His brown park service uniform matched his hair, and his blue eyes were as keen and intelligent as an Australian shepherd's. She guessed him to be in his early thirties. "I'm Bree Nicholls with my dog, Samson, and this is Naomi Heinonen and her dog, Charley."

The blue eyes narrowed when they saw the dogs. "Who called in the SAR?"

"The sheriff did," one of the men said.

The man pressed his lips together then nodded with obvious reluctance. "I'm Ranger Kade Matthews. I wouldn't have called you in yet, but since you're here we'll try to use you."

Kade Matthews. Bree had heard talk of him at the coffee shop. Rumor said he'd given up a promotion that would have taken him to California when his mother died and left him as guardian of his sixteen-year-old sister. It was to his credit that he'd followed his mother's wishes to have his sister finish school here, though Bree pitied the poor girl. Who would want him as a guardian? She'd run into his kind before, law-enforcer types who wanted to run the show their way even if it cost lives.

"Has anyone found a trail yet?" Bree's gaze wandered toward the gloom of the thickly wooded forest, and she shuffled her feet. The setup always took too long, in her opinion. While people stood around discussing where to start and how to begin, Samson could be homing in on the scent. She knew organization was important, but there was a limit.

Ranger Matthews shook his head. "Not a hint of one. But we're down to the wire here. The little boy's diabetes is a bad case. I've divided the search area into quadrants. The board is over there." He pointed to the trailer set up as a command post. "You and your team can take quadrant two."

"We find our dogs more effective if they're allowed to scent on an article of the victim's then follow where the scent leads. Donovan already gave us—"

The ranger interrupted with another shake of his head. "It's not an efficient way to search. I need to know who's where."

Bree hunched her shoulders and gave Naomi a helpless look. Why did she find it so impossible anymore to speak her mind? When she had first met Rob, her nickname at school was "Brassy Bree" because she had the nerve to do anything she was dared to do. Now she wavered when asked what she wanted to drink. She wanted to argue, but her mouth refused to open.

"We've only got a few more hours of daylight left," Ranger Matthews said. "The sheriff is in the camper briefing the searchers. Please join them."

Thank goodness Mason was here. Bree left the arrogant ranger and went to find her brother-in-law in the camp. Naomi trailed behind her, pausing to say something to Donovan, and Bree wondered at her friend's reluctance to leave him.

The camper sat along the side of the parking lot. It hadn't been leveled and tilted heavily to the right. The silver siding bore scratches and gouges from its many brushes with tree branches and thorny shrubs. The door to the camper opened as Bree approached and Mason stepped out.

"Oh good, you're here," Mason said. Sheriff of Kitchigami County, Mason was thickly built and good-natured, a mellow, golden retriever sort of man instead of the pit bull some in Kitchigami County thought a sheriff ought to be.

"Who's Attila the Hun?" Bree asked.

Mason frowned. "Who?"

"The ranger honcho. Kade Matthews."

"He's a good man. You have a problem with him?"

"He's insisting on a grid search. That will take forever," Bree said. Naomi joined her finally, and Bree thought she looked a little flushed.

Mason shook his head. "I'll handle Kade. You two take this insulin for the boy and find those kids." He handed Bree a syringe.

Bree took the insulin and tucked it into her ready-pack. The hormone was a stark reminder of the urgency of the search. Tomorrow wouldn't be good enough—they had to find those kids tonight. She knelt beside Samson and Charley and held the jackets Donovan had given her under their noses. The jackets had been contaminated with other scents, but Samson had worked under these kinds of adverse circumstances before, and she had confidence in her dog. To help the dogs, she had them sniff the insides of the jackets where there was a greater likelihood of strong scent untainted by handling.

Samson whined and strained at the leash. Bree released his lead and dropped her arm. "Search!" she commanded.

Samson bounded toward the trees. Charley plunged his nose into the jacket again then raised his muzzle and whined. Naomi unclipped Charley's leash, and he raced after Samson. Both dogs ran back and forth, their muzzles in the air. The dogs weren't bloodhounds but air scenters. They worked in a "Z" pattern, scenting the air until they could catch a hint of the one scent they sought. Samson's tail stiffened, and he turned and raced toward the creek.

"He's caught it!" Bree said, running after her dog. Naomi followed Charley. Bree heard the ranger shout as he realized they were disobeying his instructions, but then the sounds of people and cars fell away as though they had slipped into another world. The forest engulfed them, and the rustling of the wind through the trees, the muffled sounds of insects and small animals, and the whispering scent of wet mud and leaf mold all welcomed Bree as though she'd never been away. In spite of their familiarity, Bree knew the welcome was just a facade. The North Woods still guarded its secrets from her.

*A*fter nearly two hours, Bree was hot and itchy. She started to sit on a fallen log, then the drone of honeybees inside alerted her, and she avoided it, choosing instead to rest on a tree stump to catch her breath. Though the bees were sluggish this time of year, she didn't want to take any chances. Naomi thrashed her way through the vegetation as she rushed to catch up with Bree and the dogs.

Samson had lost the scent about ten minutes ago, and he crisscrossed the clearing, searching for the lost trail with his muzzle in the air. Bree unfastened a canteen from her belt and took a gulp of water. Though warm, the water washed the bitter taste of insect repellant from her tongue. She dropped her backpack onto the ground and pulled out a small bag of pistachios. Cracking the nuts, she tossed the shells onto the ground. She munched the salty nutmeats and took another swig of water.

Naomi came up behind her, short of breath. "Anything?" She pushed away a lock of hair that had escaped her braid. Naomi was like a cocker spaniel with her soft brown hair and compassionate eyes—and like a spaniel, just as persistent. Her spirit never flagged, and she always managed to transfer her optimism to Bree.

Bree shook her head and held out the bag of nuts to Naomi. "Want some?"

Naomi wrinkled her nose. "I don't know how you can stand to eat those things. Give me walnuts or pecans, not those funny green things. You eat so many of them, we'd never need search dogs to find you; we'd just follow the shell trails."

Bree grinned and put the bag of nuts back in her bag. She screwed the lid back onto the canteen and fastened it to the belt around her waist. "Time to get moving again."

"Charley's lost the trail," Naomi said. Charley nosed aimlessly among a patch of wildflowers while Samson thrust his head into the stream running to their right.

"Maybe the other searchers are having better luck." Bree snapped her fingers, and Samson came to her. He shook himself, and droplets of water sprayed her jeans. She knelt and took his shaggy head in her hands and stared into his dark eyes. "I know you're trying, buddy," she whispered. "But can you try just a little harder?" Samson's curly tail swished the air, and he licked her chin as if to say he'd do what he could. And Bree knew he would. As a search dog, Samson was in a class by himself.

Bree knew dogs. From the time she could barely toddle, she'd had a dog. When she and Rob had lived in Oregon, she'd been introduced to K-9 Search and Rescue, and she knew it was what she was meant to do. Margie, her first dog, had been a pro too, but she'd had a stroke three years ago, about six months after Samson had come along.

She'd never seen a dog with as much heart as Samson. His markings and size betrayed his German shepherd lineage, but his curly coat was all chow. Since the day she'd found him in a box by the river, barely alive and not yet four weeks old, his gaze had spoken to her more clearly than any human words could. When he'd turned his head that day and tried to lick her hand, she lost her heart. There was a special bond between her and Samson, and he loved search and rescue as much as she did. Together they'd been on search missions all over the country as part of the FEMA team.

He whined and sniffed the air as if determined not to let her down.

"If Samson can't find the kids, we might as well all go home," Naomi muttered. "He could find a flea in a hay field."

Bree grinned. "The fleas seem to find him." But she knew Naomi was right. Samson was special. She wanted him to prove it today.

Up ahead, Samson began to bark and then raced away. Bree's adrenaline kicked into overdrive. "He's found the scent again." Her fatigue forgotten, she followed the dogs.

Twilight cast deep shadows in the little clearing in the woods, but Rachel Marks had no trouble picking out the shack with the stack of split logs beside it. She could find everything in this meadow with her eyes closed. As she shuffled through the thick carpet of leaves and pine needles toward the woodpile, her feet kicked up the sharp scent of pine. Sam limped along beside her, and she slowed her pace to match his.

She frowned. His thin arms stuck out from the sleeves of his blue jacket, and his pants didn't even come to the top of his socks. He could barely squeeze into them anymore. Thank goodness he was almost well enough to take to town. Otherwise, she'd have to buy him some new clothes. His pinched white face beneath the blue stocking cap he wore showed a tinge more color than it had last month. Day by day he grew stronger.

He was quiet, as always. Too quiet. Of course, there was no one for him to talk to but her and his pet squirrel, Marcus. She couldn't put off the inevitable much longer.

But not yet. He'd only been walking for twenty minutes, yet his limp had grown more pronounced over the past few yards. He needed to rest. She beckoned to him, and he followed her toward the cabin.

Just outside the door, he stopped and tilted his head to one side. "I hear something." Sam's hushed voice seemed unnaturally loud in the still night.

Rachel stopped, her booted feet settling into the soggy leaves on the ground. Had they been found out? Her adrenaline surged and she tipped up her head and listened. "It sounds like a little kid crying," Rachel said.

Sam turned his face up to hers, his eyes glowing. "A kid like me?"

"You stay here, Sam. Let me check it out." She'd heard of cougars sounding like a child, but this sounded like no painter she'd ever heard. Just to be safe, she grabbed the ax as she passed the woodshed. Stepping cautiously toward the sound, she hefted the ax to her shoulder.

She caught her breath as the sound came again. That was no wild animal; it was a child. A crying child. She pushed aside the brush and peered into the tangle of shrubs then stepped into the fir grove. It was darker here than in her clearing but still bright enough to see the two children who sat on the ground. The little girl was weeping, her arms around a smaller child, a boy. Her woebegone face was streaked with mud, and she rocked back and forth, shudders wracking her small frame.

"I'm sorry, Timmy. It was my fault," the girl sobbed. "Now you're sick, and it's all my fault."

Rachel looked around warily until she was sure there was no danger of discovery. Could these children possibly be alone this far from town? "Hello," she said, stepping near the children. "What's your name, little girl?"

At the sound of her voice, the little girl whipped her head around and stared up at Rachel through saucer eyes. Twigs and debris matted her dark curls. She looked about seven or eight.

Rachel saw the fear in the child's face and realized how frightening she must seem to the children, a fifty-year-old woman with braided gray hair topped with an old leather fedora.

"It's all right; I'm not as mean as I look." Rachel stepped closer. "Is this your brother?"

The little girl wiped her face and nodded. "His name is Timmy, and he needs his shot. I'm Emily. Daddy is going to be awfully mad at me." Her voice was doleful. "We just wanted to see the raccoons."

"I'm sure your daddy will be too glad to be angry when he gets you home safe and sound." Rachel surveyed the little boy and frowned. He looked about Sam's age, maybe four or five. She needed to get him inside where she could see him better.

She slid her bony arms under the little boy and lifted him up. Heat radiated off him like hot coals, and he shook like the few leaves still clinging to the trees above her head. She hoped he was as tenacious. His sister had mentioned a shot. Could he be diabetic? Rachel's nurse's training kicked in, and she leaned forward and sniffed. A fruity scent issued from his open mouth, and she winced. Yep. Poor kid. She had no insulin here, and town was miles away.

"Come with me," she told Emily. "We'll get you something to eat and drink." Then she had to get them out of here. Without drawing attention to herself. The last thing she needed was the law on her tail.

Emily followed her into the clearing. "Is that your house? It's sure little."

"It suits us," Rachel said shortly.

Sam was still standing where she'd left him. Motionless, he watched her come toward him. His gaze darted from her and the child she carried to the little girl who followed them.

"Sammy, open the door for me," she said. He limped to the cabin and fumbled at the latch then swung the door open. He held it wide while Rachel carried the little boy inside.

The cabin wasn't much, but it had been home for over a year. Only one room, but they made do. Sam's cot was pushed up against one wall, the colorful log cabin quilt she'd made for him now faded but still serviceable. A battered table, four chairs, and a braided rug, faded and worn, completed the furnishings.

It was all scrupulously clean. She might live in the back of beyond, but that was no reason for slovenliness. Laying the little boy on the bed, she studied him. His face was flushed beneath the numerous scratches, and his breathing was labored. This little guy needed his insulin, now. Looking at the sunken areas under his eyes, Rachel saw he was dehydrated as well. A saline IV would come in handy, but that wasn't something Rachel kept on hand.

"There's a pitcher of water on the table," she told Emily. "Pour some water for you and the lad. I'll fix you a peanut butter sandwich, and we'll get you back to that daddy of yours."

Emily looked weary, but she stepped to the table and poured two cups of water. She drank thirstily from her cup, but Timmy turned his head and closed his eyes when Rachel offered him a drink.

As quickly as she could, Rachel slathered some peanut butter on slices of homemade bread. The law would be searching for these kids, and she had to get them out of here before the rangers found her cabin. Timmy refused to eat, and Rachel waited until Emily finished her sandwich. "You ready to go back to town?"

The little girl didn't answer. She was too busy inspecting Sam. The food and drink had calmed her, and her eyes were inquisitive. "Are you his grandma?" Emily gave Sam a tentative smile.

Rachel searched for an answer. "I'm his mother," she said, struggling against the irritation she felt at the girl's assumption. It wasn't only twenty-year-olds who were blessed to be mothers. She'd seen plenty of women who'd waited until later in life to have children. Her own grandmother had given birth to her last child at fifty-two. Thank goodness Sam wasn't as inquisitive as this child.

Emily sidled closer to Sam. "What's your name?"

Sam ducked his head and didn't answer.

"He's shy," Rachel said. She fought the panic clawing at her belly. All these questions! She could only hope the kids would remember little of what they saw here. Luckily the stocking cap still covered Sam's hair. The children wouldn't have much of a description.

"Sammy, you hop into your pajamas, and I'll be back soon."

"I want to go too." Sam stared up at her, his green eyes pleading.

"You're not strong enough, Sam. I'll have to carry Timmy—I can't carry you too." He knew to stay inside and keep the door latched until she came back. She'd had to leave him often over the past months.

Sam's lower lip trembled, but he didn't argue with her. It was no wonder the poor little guy wanted to go along. These children were the first contact he'd had with other people in months. Rachel gnawed her lip. She wished she could do better by him. But sometimes you just had to play the hand you were dealt. He would learn soon enough how life threw you punches and you had to stiffen your backbone and fight back, just as she did.

Giving Sam a little push, she went toward the little boy. "I'll be back soon. You rest."

Sam nodded and watched with wistful eyes as she picked up Timmy then took Emily's hand and led her out the door. "Wait!" he cried suddenly. He limped toward them and thrust his beloved stuffed koala bear in the little boy's hand.

Rachel frowned. "You don't want to do that, Sam." The kid had few enough toys. He didn't need to be giving them away to strangers. From the looks of these two, they were middle-class and probably had bedrooms full of toys.

Sam's lip protruded farther. "I want to give it to him," he said.

Rachel shrugged. "Just don't come crying to me tonight when you miss it."

"His name is Pooky," Sam said, ducking his head.

The little girl took the bear from her brother's unresponsive hand and cradled it in her arm. She gave Sam a brilliant smile. "Thanks. I'll give it to Timmy when we get home." She fumbled in her jeans pocket and pulled out a yo-yo. "Here, you can have this."

Sam stared at the yo-yo then back up at Emily.

"You play with it like this." Emily took the toy back, slipped the string over her finger, and threw it. Sam's eyes grew wider as the yo-yo returned to her hand. "Here, you try it." She thrust it back into his hand and showed him how to put the string on his finger. He awkwardly tried to throw it, but it only came partway back.

"You'll get the hang of it," she told him. "Just practice. Thanks for the bear." She leaned over and kissed Sam on the cheek. With Pooky in her hand, she scampered out the door behind Rachel.

Carrying Timmy, Rachel led Emily across the yard and entered the forest. Stumbling over branches and brambles, they wound their way through the thick trees. Rachel's back ached from the little boy's weight.

*O*ver an hour later, Rachel set Timmy down to rest her arms then stood and stretched. The road wasn't far now, another fifteen minutes maybe. It was still light enough to see. She could park them by the side of the road, and someone would be along shortly. It was the best she could do.

Leaning down to retrieve her burden, she froze at the sound of voices. People—more than one. And dogs. That could be trouble. She set Timmy back on the forest floor.

"You're safe now, kids," she said hastily. "I've gotta go."

"Don't leave us!" Emily scrabbled for her hand, but Rachel evaded her, cursing herself for ever getting involved. She hoped she didn't regret this day, but she was a sucker for kids.

Flipping her braid over one shoulder, Rachel took off at a run. "You'll be okay," she called behind her. "There are people coming. They're probably looking for you." The safety of the forest beckoned her, and she plunged into its sheltering depths. Emily's wails followed her.

*K*ade's temper was short as he organized the teams and finally got them on their way. The K-9 team he'd worked with before in

Yellowstone had represented the height of ineptitude, scattering evidence and leading searchers in the wrong direction. He knew all teams were not that bad—the media reported plenty of success stories—but this search was his responsibility, and those kids were depending on him. Bree Nicholls had deliberately disobeyed his orders. Worse, the sheriff had made it clear his sister-in-law was to be allowed to have her own way. Typical of the nepotism in a small town like Rock Harbor.

He saw the mayor talking on a walkie-talkie and stalked her way. "Anything?"

Hilary clicked off the device. "None of the dogs has picked up the scent yet," she said.

Kade leaned against the truck. "I thought this was a hotshot K-9 team."

"Samson has been written up in more magazines than you can count," Hilary said. "But even he isn't perfect. They still haven't found the plane that went down with my brother and their son."

An awkward silence passed between them. "Your family issues are none of my business," Kade said. "But I don't like the way Bree Nicholls disobeyed my orders and put those kids in jeopardy."

"She knows what she's doing," Hilary said. "You haven't been here long, but she and Samson have found quite a few lost campers since she and Rob moved here."

Before Kade could reply, a familiar red car slid to a halt in a cloud of dust. The door on the battered Plymouth spilled open, and his sister, Lauri, got out, her face its usual mask of petulance. He'd often thought of taking her picture and showing her that expression. Would she want her face to take on those lines for the rest of her life? He hadn't done it, because he knew it would just make her mad. Everything was his fault these days.

"We've already missed the movies," she said with her hands on her hips. Her gaze traveled to the two young rangers standing near the path to the pavilion. Straightening at their looks of interest, she preened and gave them a sultry smile.

Kade gritted his teeth. She was way too young to be flirting like that. At sixteen, his sister was a budding Lolita, using the power of her beauty in ways he probably didn't want to know about. "What are you doing here?" he asked abruptly.

Lauri turned from her silent flirtation with the rangers and gave her brother a smoldering glare. "You didn't even phone. If I hadn't called headquarters, I'd still be wondering where you were."

"I should have called, but things developed too fast for me to remember. There are two children lost in the woods, and one of them is sick. I forgot all about the movies. Sorry, kid."

"Don't call me 'kid'!" Lauri tossed her head again. "I'm sick and tired of always taking second place to your job. If you don't want me around, just say so. I could go stay with Grandma and Grandpa."

Kade sighed, weariness settling over him like a suffocating wave from Lake Superior. "We've been over all that, Lauri. You are not going to our grandparents. You'd run over them inside a week. Besides, I promised Mom you'd finish school here, and I intend to keep my promise."

Lauri gave him a calculated look far too mature for a sixteen-year-old. Where did she get that manner? He wanted her to enjoy her remaining years of school, to be a normal teenager, but he didn't know how to ensure that, how to reach the vulnerable child he still sometimes glimpsed in her eyes. She refused to go to youth group at church. It was all he could do to get her to go to church at all.

"Fine," she said through gritted teeth. "I'll see you later." She slung her long legs under the wheel and slammed the car door shut.

"Lauri, come back here!" he yelled. Her face set as though she didn't hear, she tore off down the road, dust spitting from the tires. He clenched his jaw.

"Why don't we drive along the access road?" Hilary asked. "It would be better than sitting around here doing nothing."

Kade nodded, thankful the mayor had the tact to ignore Lauri's little scene. He felt the need to be doing something. Otherwise, he might go find his sister and strangle her. He opened the truck door for the mayor then slammed it shut and got in on his side. He started the truck and drove into the dark forest.

Hilary cleared her throat. "Kids can be a trial, can't they? I was a lot like Lauri at that age. It was an admirable thing to take on her care."

"I'm regretting it daily," he said grimly. The mayor's sympathy surprised Kade. In their few encounters, he'd always thought her all business. "You have any kids?"

She turned to look out the window. "Not yet."

That was a stupid question and clearly none of his business. When would he learn to keep his mouth shut? The radio attached to his belt crackled to life.

"Ranger station, come in." Bree's voice cut out then surged stronger. "We've found them, and I'm sending up a flare. We're in sector four."

Kade grabbed the radio. "Ten-four. What kind of shape are they in?" Only a crackle of the radio answered his question, then a light shot from the forest and illuminated an area to their left. He gunned the truck down the rutted track. Hilary clung to the door as the truck pitched from side to side. He tossed the radio to her.

"Call an ambulance!" When the truck finished grinding to a halt beneath the spreading light, he jumped from the vehicle, grabbed his first-aid kit from the back, and ran toward the cluster of people huddled at the base of a giant sycamore.

Bree and Naomi were kneeling beside the two children. The little girl's face was streaked with mud, and tears had left blotches on her face. She held her younger brother's hand. Kade's gaze dropped to the little boy cradled in Bree's arms, and his heart sank at his condition. Even in the fading twilight, Kade could see him shaking. The sour smell of vomit lingered in the air, which didn't bode well.

"Timmy is sick," Emily sobbed. "Is he going to die?"

"We just gave him his shot," Bree said. She pulled the little boy closer to her and wrapped her coat around him. Timmy visibly relaxed at her tender touch. He turned his face into her chest and sighed.

Bree appeared oblivious to everything but Timmy, and Kade wondered if holding the little boy brought back memories of her own loss.

Kade opened his canteen and knelt beside the children. He poured a few drops of water into Timmy's open mouth. The little boy coughed but managed to swallow it, then Kade gave Emily a drink too. Running his hands over their arms and legs, he was relieved to find nothing broken.

"Just insect bites," he said. "They seem to be all right. But we need to get them to a hospital. The mayor is calling the ambulance."

"I already did," Naomi said. "It should be here any minute."

Kade whipped off the jacket of his uniform and knelt beside Bree. He wrapped the jacket around Emily like a blanket. "The ambulance won't get here any too soon. I think we'd better run them to the hospital in my truck. Some of you will have to ride in the back of the pickup or wait for the ambulance." He took Timmy from Bree and moved toward the road without waiting for an answer. Timmy's head lolled against Kade's chest, and his small feet dangled from the folds of the coat. Kade didn't like the boy's limpness.

Bree took Emily's hand, and they started toward the dirt access road. As they reached the road, Kade heard the shrill wail of the ambulance in the distance. Relief left him almost lightheaded. Timmy and Emily would soon be under medical care. Moments later the flashing lights came into sight, followed by the headlamps of two other vehicles.

Putting her radio away, the mayor came toward them. She reached out a hand and touched Timmy's hair. "You're safe now, sweetheart." She stroked his face then reached down and touched Emily's head. "You're both going to be just fine."

Emily took her hand, and Hilary's face softened. Kade turned away from the naked longing in Hilary's face. He felt he was intruding on something private. His eyes connected with Bree's, and he saw sorrow in them. All this motherly angst made him put his hackles up, and he tensed.

Kade signaled with his flashlight in case the driver had trouble seeing them in the twilight. Crunching gravel under the tires, the ambulance came to a stop and two paramedics leaped out. One of the men took Timmy from Kade and rushed him to the back of the ambulance. The second paramedic led Emily to the back as well. The other two vehicles stopped, and two men got out of the battered Dodge truck, its paint a dull orange-red in the light of the full moon.

"Daddy!" Emily dropped the paramedic's hand and ran to Donovan. He dropped to his knees and folded Emily in his arms.

"Thank God you're safe. Where's your brother?" He gave her a little shake. "What have I told you about wandering off by yourself?"

Emily gave a little hiccup. "That I was never supposed to leave without an adult. I'm sorry, Daddy."

The man looked around wildly. "Where's your brother?" he repeated. Hilary reached out her hand but let it drop when the distraught father made no move to take it. "Your children are going to be fine, Donovan. Timmy is in the ambulance."

Donovan let go of Emily and ran to the ambulance, where he stood watching the paramedics work on his son. An occasional groan issued from Donovan's mouth. Kade could only imagine how he felt.

"Daddy's mad at me," Emily said, tears making her voice tremble.

Bree held out her hand. "He's just worried, sweetheart. Come with me, and let's see if I can find you a candy bar or something to eat."

"I'm not hungry. The witch in the woods gave us some peanut butter sandwiches."

Kade frowned. "Who's that, Emily?" No one had been with the children. His gaze met Bree's, and he saw the same confusion in her face.

"The witch in the woods. I was afraid she was going to eat us like the witch in the woods in the Hansel and Gretel story, but she gave us a peanut butter sandwich. Timmy wouldn't eat his though."

"There was no one with you," Bree said.

"She ran away when she heard you and the dogs," Emily said.

The little girl may be more stressed than they thought. Either that or she had quite an imagination. "Better get her checked out," Kade mouthed softly to Bree.

She nodded. "That's fine, but let's get you back to town," Bree said. "You'll get to ride in the ambulance. Won't that be fun?"

Emily's lip trembled, but she nodded. "Is Timmy going to die?"

"No, he'll be okay in a few days. But the doctors are going to want to look at him, and at you, just to make sure you're okay," Kade said. He took her other hand, and they led her toward the ambulance.

Her head haloed by the light from the ambulance, Emily stopped and looked up at Bree. "What's your dog's name? Will you bring him to see me?"

Bree smiled at Emily and touched her head. Kade dropped his gaze and wondered how old her son would be now. As young as she was, he couldn't have been very old. Sometimes Kade had to admit he wondered how the Almighty chose who to save and who to take.

Bree nodded at Emily. "This is Samson. Samson, say hello to Emily." The dog thrust his nose into the little girl's hand. Emily giggled as the dog licked her face. "We'll check on you tomorrow," Bree told her.

Kade had trouble keeping his eyes off Bree. Though not really beautiful, she was arresting. The cut of her short red hair emphasized the delicate column of her neck and the fine bone structure of her face. Large green eyes that seemed a bit sad tilted up at the corners. It was no wonder, considering what she'd been through, what she was still going through. Though she looked fragile, Kade had seen her heft a heavy backpack with ease and knew she was stronger than she appeared. He guessed her to be a little younger than him, maybe late twenties.

Within minutes the ambulance, trailed by the kids' father in the pickup, tore back the way it had come, leaving only dust and the fast-fading echo of the siren in its wake. "I'll run you home," Kade told Bree and Naomi. He could see both women visibly wilting. The day had been grueling, even for him, so they had to be exhausted. The dogs lay panting on the side of road, spent as well.

"My Jeep is at the parking lot," Bree said.

"I've already arranged for your vehicle to be left at your home," Kade said. "I'll take you straight there."

Bree stared at him. "Without asking me?"

He shrugged. "You left the keys in it. I figured you'd be too tired to drive."

Bree motioned for Samson to jump into the back of Kade's pickup. The dog moved slowly on sore feet. Charley followed him. "You were wrong," she said. Her gaze dropped. "I had things I needed to attend to before going home," she said softly. She bit her lip like there was more she wanted to say then headed toward the passenger door.

His lips tightened. She had been no saint today in spite of her success. "And you disobeyed orders!" Kade snapped. Bree just looked at him, and the calm confidence in her face irritated him even more.

Naomi jumped into the fray. "You have no idea who you're talking to, do you? Bree and Samson are one of the top search teams in the country—in the world! Those kids would still be out there if we'd followed your orders."

"I've worked with some bad teams in my time," he snapped.

"Well, we aren't one of them!" Naomi said hotly.

Kade compressed his lips. This was getting them nowhere. "How about we call a truce? I made a mistake and so did you. Sorry, Miss Nicholls, Miss Heinonen."

Naomi opened her mouth, and from the fire in her eyes, Kade expected a scathing reply, but Bree shot her a quelling look and held out her hand. "Truce," she said. "But it's Mrs. Nicholls. And the only mistake was yours."

He gritted his teeth but held his tongue. "Let's get you home." Naomi opened the door and slid in first, then Bree scrunched in beside her. Suddenly anxious to be free of the whole prickly mess, Kade slammed the door behind them and crawled behind the wheel.

They rode in silence to town. As they rounded the last curve, the twinkling lights of Rock Harbor came into view. Part of the town's special flavor came from the setting. Surrounded by forests on three sides, it had all the natural beauty anyone could want. Old-growth forests, sparkling lakes where fish thronged, and the brilliant blue of that Big Sea Water called Superior along the west side.

They drove through town, down Whisper Pike to Houghton Street and past the businesses that comprised Rock Harbor's downtown. "You'll have to direct me," Kade said.

Bree pointed toward the far light. "The lighthouse is mine. Naomi lives in the Blue Bonnet Bed and Breakfast right beside me—the house that used to belong to Captain Sarasin."

Kade knew the house. Built by a famous captain of the area so his wife could watch for his return, it was the last house on Houghton Street before it curved into Negaunee, the road out to the lighthouse. He hadn't realized it was a bed-and-breakfast until now. He rarely drove to that side of town. The lighthouse was perched just behind it at the end of Negaunee on a sliver of land that bravely faced Superior's fury.

"You live in the lighthouse?" he asked. "I haven't been to town much since I returned two months ago. When I was a kid, I used to prowl around that deserted lighthouse. I figured someone had turned it into a museum by now."

"It's not a lighthouse anymore. The Coast Guard replaced it with the offshore automated light years ago," Bree said. "I'm in the process of restoring it. I'm on the last room now."

"How long have you owned it? I figured someone from out of state bought it—someone with more money than sense." He grinned to take the sting out of the slur.

"That might have described me and Rob at one time." Bree laughed. "When we bought it, the chimney had fallen through the roof, and the porch boards were all decayed. Rob had inherited some money from his grandmother and a plane from his uncle. The lighthouse was just another piece of Rob's dream. Our dream," she amended.

"You've done most of it yourself," Naomi said. "I don't know how you've managed all alone."

Bree smiled. "I plan to reinstall the Fresnel lens and light the tower, someday." Her gaze softened and took on a faraway look. "I'd like to think my light might save a ship someday."

Kade wondered what had triggered her obsession with rescuing people. It was admirable, but surely something had caused it. Did it start with the deaths of her husband and son, or had she always been that way?

Kade stopped in front of the bed-and-breakfast and let Naomi and Charley off. Naomi waved at them from the front porch then went inside. Kade drove on down Negaunee to the lighthouse.

Gravel crunched beneath the pickup's tires, and Kade stopped the vehicle in front of the lighthouse. The brick building's pink paint gleamed in the glare of the porch light, but the light tower was dark. Bree opened the tailgate for Samson and followed him to the front door. Kade lowered the windows. The smell of boat exhaust hung heavy in the moist air blowing in from Lake Superior. A ship's horn bellowed a lonely note in the middle of the bay. The Ojibwa called the lake *Kitchigami,* which meant "giver of life," though right now he felt that meaning was erroneous. It was more a taker of the life he wanted. At one time he thought he'd left this place for good, only to find he was trapped in it as easily as a rabbit in a hunter's snare.

The slap of the water against the pier carried across the water. "Thanks again for all your help. I'll call again if we need assistance."

"You're welcome," Bree said. "Let's hope you don't have more lost campers anytime soon."

"We both know that's not likely," he said with a wry grin. "People are pretty foolish when it comes to the wilderness. They think diving into the forest is no more dangerous than taking a stroll in the city park."

Bree grinned. "I guess I'll see you around then, Ranger Matthews."

"Call me Kade," he called through the window as he pulled away. The few businesses open in Rock Harbor's three-block business center spilled enough light onto the sidewalk to make it appear quasi-welcoming. The neon still shimmered above The Coffee Place. He pulled into the café parking lot.

The rich aroma of espresso took the edge off the day's frustrations. He'd been as surprised as everyone else in town when The Coffee Place got a newfangled espresso machine. It had proven surprisingly popular with more than just tourists. Milt Granger's boy, Brad, was behind the counter, but he was too busy talking to a sweet young thing with three studs up each ear lobe to pay much attention to Kade. Kade coughed several times before Brad took his order. Kade finally succeeded in getting his latte and a turkey club sandwich with a piece of chocolate pie.

"Mind if I join you?"

Startled, he nearly spilled coffee down the front of his shirt. "Hello, Fay," he said. Just what he didn't need. Fay Asters stood behind him with one hand on a slim hip. He pushed out the chair opposite him with his foot. "Have a seat."

"You seen Eric around?" she asked, sliding into the chair. Her slim fingers played with her hair then slid down to fidget with the chain around her neck.

"I've told you to stay away from him. He's trying to straighten his life out. You'll just muck it up again." It was hard to keep his gaze from the quick movements of her hands.

"You're not his keeper."

"No, but thanks to you, he had one of those for three years." He'd never understood what Eric saw in Fay. Slim to the point that she had none of the womanly curves most men admired, she didn't even wear makeup unless she was in her femme fatale mode. It must be that innocent, little-girl way she had about her, a facade that hid the truth of her real nature.

She laughed, a silvery, tinkling sound that drew his gaze to her mouth. Okay, so that was attractive too.

"If you see Eric, tell him I have important news," she said.

She slid away from the table with a grace that reminded Kade of a sleek cat. He drummed his fingers on the tabletop and wondered what he could do to keep her away from Eric. Whatever her news was, it would likely bring trouble.

*T*he Blue Bonnet Bed and Breakfast might not have been the most popular lodging spot in the Keweenaw Peninsula, but Naomi and her mother were beginning to get some repeat visitors. Naomi closed the register with a sense of satisfaction then stretched out the kinks in her back. The scent of lemon polish and the faint aroma of pine cleaner in the air were worth the soreness in her muscles. Six thousand square feet of house, and every inch of it polished and shining. The new crop of weekend visitors would arrive later in the morning.

The registration desk stood at the end of the entry hall. They'd opened the wall between the office and the foyer, and now an antique marble counter separated the two. Naomi sneaked a book from under the counter. Maybe she could get in a few pages before her mother came down. She flexed the spine, and, as if on cue, her mother floated down the curved walnut staircase. She disappeared momentarily into the parlor before hurrying toward the office in the room behind the entry.

Though fifty-eight, Martha Heinonen's skin glowed a pink, healthy hue of fresh air and hard work. Strands of silver were just beginning to highlight her hair, and her consistent exuberance made her even more attractive. Dressed in a pink-flowered dress with a soft skirt that swirled around her still-shapely calves, she looked every inch the lady. Someone had once told her she looked like England's reigning monarch, Queen Elizabeth, and since then she'd played up any resemblance to the hilt, a fact Naomi found amusing.

Naomi guiltily tucked away the book before her mother could see it and level her usual litanies about ruining her eyes and how men weren't interested in a bookworm. Maybe her mother had a point. The men weren't exactly beating a path to the door.

"There you are, darling. I peeked in the parlor on the way down. It looks lovely. I see you managed to get that stain out of the piano scarf. You are such a treasure!" She disappeared again, this time in the direction of the kitchen, and emerged a few moments later carrying a heavy tea-and-cookie-laden tray as though it weighed nothing.

"Come along before the tea gets cold," Martha said.

Naomi followed her to the parlor. Martha set the tray on the coffee table and sank into the plush armchair upholstered in pink cabbage-rose chintz. "It's nearly time for our guests to arrive. Are you going to greet them dressed like that?" She wrinkled her nose at Naomi's faded jeans and oversized T-shirt.

Naomi often wondered how she had been born to such a woman. She preferred denim while her mother craved silk. Her mother teetered daily on two-inch polished pumps, while the footwear on Naomi's shoe rack looked like castoffs from the Salvation Army: scuffed boots, flats with eroded heels, and ragged tennis shoes. Still, Naomi and her mother got along well. Naomi did the heavy cleaning; her mother prepared the elegant teas and made small talk with the New York businessmen and the bored Connecticut housewives. Her mother's pies were famous throughout the peninsula.

Naomi had been gearing up to deal with the subtle guilt her mom would try to impose. "I'll change my top to something nicer." It was as great a compromise as she was willing to make today. Some days she wished she could let the real Naomi come out in full view, but it just took too much energy to confront her mother. Compromise had led her to a placid state of living with her mother at nearly thirty-two. She found small victories like this one hollow, knowing the battle had been lost long ago.

The doorbell pealed. "I'll get it." Naomi made her escape and stepped into the long entry hall. She opened the door and found Bree standing on the front porch.

Naomi grabbed Bree's arm and drew her inside. "You're just in time to save me from strangling my mother."

Bree chuckled and followed Naomi into the parlor. "You may not be so thrilled when you hear what I've come to tell you."

"Mom just put out some tea and cookies. Come tell us all about it."

Bree followed Naomi into the parlor.

"Bree, dear, I was just thinking about you." Martha smoothed her flowered skirt and leaned over to pour the tea. "You look like you could use something to drink."

Bree plopped onto the sofa and curled one denim-clad leg under the other. "You two are my sanity. Oops." She fished around under her and pulled out a book. "This has to be yours." She handed it to Naomi.

"I was wondering where I put that one," Naomi said with a surreptitious glance at her mother. She'd managed to hide the book she'd been reading in the office from her mother, but not this one.

"I don't know why you tote a book everywhere you go; you're always losing them. I could stock a library with the books you've lost." Bree took the cup of tea with a smile of thanks. "I have a summons from the mayor," she said with a dramatic flourish of her hand.

Naomi wrinkled her nose. "The poodle has issued a decree?"

"Girls, that isn't respectful," Martha murmured.

Naomi felt a shaft of shame. But Hilary got under her skin in the worst way. She bossed Bree around, and Bree let her. Naomi didn't understand the hold Hilary seemed to have on her friend. She pushed away her unspoken censure of Bree, who had been through so much. It was no wonder she craved peace at any cost.

"What for?" Naomi asked.

"Hilary's reelection campaign kickoff dinner is tonight. Mason's too, of course, but since he coasts on Hilary's coattails, his campaign is immaterial as far as she's concerned. I thought maybe I could evade an order to appear, but my luck ran out. So did yours." She looked over her teacup at Naomi and raised an eyebrow for effect. "She wants *us* to come so she can show off yesterday's successful search like her latest trophy." Bree took another cookie and bit into it.

Naomi groaned. "Not a dinner party! Anything but that!"

Martha smiled, her eyes lighting with pleasure. "That means a fancy dress, Naomi dear."

Bree grinned. "I'm afraid your mom is right, Naomi. It's pull-out-all-the-stops, knock-'em-dead time."

Naomi fell back against the couch in an exaggerated posture of despair. "And here I thought you were my friend."

"Hey, that's what friends are for," Bree said with a trace of smugness. "For that and chocolate-chip cookies." She took another bite of cookie and grinned.

*B*ree studied the large topographic map that decorated the wall in the lighthouse's spare room. She needed to get an updated copy. This one had some inaccuracies. She was almost done with sector fifteen, which was smack in the middle of the southern half of the Kitchigami Wilderness. Should she move east or west? Or keep pushing north? The Rock River Gorge wilderness lay east of sector fifteen. She hadn't even begun to search there. The monumental size of her task felt almost suffocating.

Saturday was not normally her preference for a search day. Hunters and fishermen were out in force on weekends, and they tended to try to engage her in conversation when their paths crossed hers. But October's Indian summer wouldn't last long, and she needed to take advantage of every hour.

Though she knew she should spend the day preparing for Hilary's party, she decided to finish sector fifteen, on the west side of the gorge.

She pulled her backpack and rescue vest out of the spare room's closet, found her cell phone, and headed for the woods.

*S*ix hours later, the only thing she'd accomplished was closing the door on sector fifteen. No sign of a crash anywhere.

Weariness gripped her as she drove home. A party was the last thing she felt like attending. Driving up Negaunee Street, the light tower of her lighthouse seemed illuminated from within by the last shafts of clear sunlight, and she was reminded again of the repair that needed to be done. Yet one more thing to attend to. Suppressing a sigh, she parked the Jeep, let Samson into the backyard through the gate, then went inside to get ready.

She took a quick shower and washed her hair then cinched her robe around her waist. The thick terry cloth felt warm and comforting after schlepping through the cold forest mist all day. She sat at the dressing table with her makeup bag in hand. Dark circles marred the pale skin under her eyes. It would take some major paint to pass Hilary's critical inspection. Bree made a face at herself in the mirror. If Hilary didn't like the way she looked, she'd be glad to go home. She finished dressing and drove to Naomi's.

Bree pulled up outside the Blue Bonnet and honked the horn. Naomi came out the front door almost immediately. Dressed in a classic black dress with pearls and heels, she looked every inch a lady. A gold lamé shawl reflected light into her elegant upswept hairstyle.

"Looks like your mom got hold of you," Bree said with a grin. "You look great though."

Naomi rolled her eyes. "I wanted to wear my red dress, but Mom said it made me look cheap. *Cheap.*"

"You couldn't look cheap no matter what you wore," Bree said comfortingly. "Hop in and let's go wow them all."

Naomi managed a faint smile. "You always know how to make me feel better," she told Bree.

Naomi fastened her seat belt then leaned forward to fiddle with the radio. "How do you listen to this stuff?" she complained. "No one listens to Elvis anymore." She punched the search button until Houghton's country station came on. Singing at the top of her lungs, Naomi belted out the lyrics to a Reba song.

Bree grinned. "You've missed your calling."

Naomi smiled back. "You have any idea who all will be there?" Her bejeweled fingers played idly with the fringes of her gold shawl.

"Everyone who can help Hilary. Business owners, other politicians, ordinary people with a tad of influence. The guest list will read like a *Who's Who of the Upper Peninsula.*"

"Do you suppose Donovan will be there? That's pretty cool he asked you out. He'd make a good husband," Naomi said.

The diffidence in Naomi's voice struck a wrong chord with Bree, who glanced at her friend sharply and said, "I'm not interested in Donovan, but it sounds like you are. I hope you know what you're letting yourself in for. He'll find it hard to trust another woman after his wife ran off like that. And two small children can be a handful, especially when they aren't your own."

"It's getting to where a girl can't ask a question without risking her ring finger," Naomi complained. "I didn't say I was interested. I was just wondering if he would leave the children for something like this. That must be the worst thing about being a single parent."

A chuckle bubbled out of Bree's throat. "Cut the outraged spinster act, Naomi. This is me, remember? I know the difference between casual interest and something more, and this is something more."

Naomi compressed her lips and looked away. "Mom will have me married by the end of the month if she finds out. I'm sure there's no hope anyway. If you're his type, I'm obviously not. Besides, you've got an advantage: Emily likes you. Did you notice she tagged after you right up to the time the ambulance took her away?"

Bree would allow no man to come between her and Naomi. Men were as plentiful as salmon, but a best friend was a freshwater pearl. "She's just a kid enamored with Samson. Give her time. I have no intention of dating him. When did this interest of yours start?"

"When I was fifteen." She chuckled, but it was only halfhearted. "I was just a pesky little twerp back when he was my brother's best friend."

"Bat those big brown eyes at him, and he'll be a goner."

"I'm not very good at flirting." Naomi sighed and twisted her bracelet around and around on her wrist.

"What is it about Donovan that's kept you hooked all this time?" Bree turned into the parking lot of the community center.

"He's real," Naomi said. "And he loves God as much as I do. I don't know how to explain it, but it's like God is telling me he and the children belong with me, that I need to take care of them. They need me."

Bree hunched her shoulders at the God talk. Fortunately, they'd arrived. Any conversations about God and his expectations would have to wait.

Built by Rock Harbor's early residents during the heyday of the Copper Queen mining era, no expense had been spared in the construction of the beautiful community center. It stood in stark contrast to the rough wooden buildings in other parts of town.

Inside, the patina of age and old money gave an elegance to the central hall that newer, more expensive buildings couldn't match. Crystal chandeliers glittered with prismatic color and light while men and women arrayed in every imaginable style of dress milled around the floor. Some wore suits and brightly colored dresses, while others came dressed in jeans and flannel shirts. Hilary wouldn't turn away anyone who could cast a vote. Glassware tinkled while laughter and conversation formed a constant background hum.

Bree felt as out of place as a starling in the ocean. "We should let Hilary know we're here." What she really wanted to do was find a corner to hide in until she could slip back to the lighthouse. Though she called Rock Harbor home, many in town still regarded her as a newcomer, even after nearly five years as a resident.

"You go ahead," Naomi said, looking past Bree. "I want to talk to Donovan."

So he was here. Bree watched Naomi move to Donovan's side and smile up at him. If that man hurt sweet Naomi, she'd make him regret it. How Bree intended to protect her friend, she wasn't sure, but she'd lay down her life for Naomi. First, though, she needed to let her presence be known to her sister-in-law.

Hilary and Mason were talking with Jacob Zinn, an older man who ran a fishing resort on the edge of town. Mason gave Bree a smile.

"Bree, how nice you look," Hilary said. She leaned forward and touched her lips to Bree's cheek. "You know Jacob Zinn, don't you?"

Bree nodded and shook hands with Jacob.

"Mrs. Nicholls." He pressed her fingers briefly. "I had thought you would have headed back to Oregon by now. There's not much in Rock Harbor to interest an outsider, eh?" His dark eyes flickered over her then just as quickly dismissed her. He spoke with the familiar Yooper cadence, punctuating his sentence with an "eh" and ending with an upward lilt that made the statement almost a question.

How long would she have to live here before people like Jacob accepted her? Twenty years, fifty? If she took out an ad in the newspaper and proclaimed her intention never to leave, he still wouldn't believe it. "This is my home, Mr. Zinn. My family is here."

He snorted and waved his hand in a dismissive gesture. "They will never be found, Mrs. Nicholls. The North Woods guards her secrets well. I suggest you pick up your life and get on with it." Without waiting for a reply, he nodded to Hilary and strode away.

"That man is so rude," Hilary said. She linked arms with Bree. "We're your family, not just Rob and Davy. Come with me. The Asterses just arrived, and I want to say hello."

Though Jacob Zinn's invective had made Bree reel, Hilary's words made her heart sing. Words of approval from her were as rare as a Michigan monkey flower. If she could freeze this moment, the next time Hilary bit her head off she could remember this and savor it. She walked arm in arm with Hilary to greet Fay and Steve Asters, with Mason trailing at a distance.

Hilary dropped Bree's arm and held out a hand to Fay. "I'm so glad you could make it," she said, her gaze on Steve.

Bree knew Fay and Steve Asters fairly well. As manager of the Rock Harbor Savings and Loan, Steve had been forced to handle the mortgage paperwork on the lighthouse when the loan officer quit. Rob had trusted Steve, and Bree found him quite charming. She and Fay met for coffee once in a while, though Bree found the other woman's intense need for attention somewhat off-putting. An hour at a time was the most she could usually stomach being with her.

Hilary launched into easy conversation with Steve. Bree sometimes wondered if there was more history between Hilary and Steve than a simple high-school romance that ended when Steve fell for Fay.

"How goes the search?" Fay asked with a flip of her palm while Steve chatted with Mason and Hilary. Fay's fingers fluttered in the air to punctuate every word. Her dark blue eyes glittered with avid interest in everything around her.

"Nowhere," Bree said. Just once, she wished people would talk to her about something else. But the search was always the first topic. Did they ever stop to think she might be interested in the weather or politics?

"Maybe I could join you one day," Fay said, twisting the gold hoops in her ears. "I saw something the other day that needed checking out. There was a woman outside a cabin. In the ravine beside it, I thought I saw an old airplane seat."

Bree had learned to take everything Fay said as the bid for attention it usually was. Six months ago, Fay had told everyone in Anu Nicholls's shop that she'd seen a jacket like Davy's along the river near Ontonagon. Bree had rushed there only to find a man's red parka rather than a child's blue jacket. "An airplane seat?" she asked, measuring her interest. "Are you sure?"

"Not totally sure, but it looked odd sitting there. I just can't remember what sector I was in. I'll try to remember."

"Can you think of any identifying landmarks?" That would be one way to see how much truth was in Fay.

"Oh, let's talk about this later," Fay said, waving away her earlier comments. "It's probably nothing."

Almost certainly it was nothing. Still, what did she have to lose by looking? There were no other clues clamoring for attention. She just needed to know where to look. "Why don't we meet at the Suomi for coffee in the morning?"

"Fine." Fay stretched with ferretlike grace then tugged on her husband's arm. "As long as I don't have to eat anything."

Fay normally ate like Samson. Bree lifted an eyebrow. "Dieting?"

"Hardly." Fay gave a little laugh. "I'm going to look like a tub by the time the next seven months are up. Steve and I are going to have a baby!"

Bree didn't miss the triumphant smile Fay tossed at Hilary. Hilary's face froze for several long moments, then she managed a brittle smile that didn't include her eyes.

"Congratulations. When is the . . . the baby due?" Hilary asked.

Bree heard the pain underneath the lighthearted voice, though she didn't understand it. Did Hilary still really care for Steve? Poor Mason. Her gaze lingered on the sheriff's face, but he seemed unperturbed.

"Not until May. I'm just barely knocked up." Fay's tinkling laugh came again.

"How . . . how wonderful," Hilary managed. "You must excuse me."

Bree watched her rush away then excused herself and followed her to the rest room.

The ladies' room was a luxurious space with marble floors and counters, gold-plated fixtures, and mauve wallpaper in a subtle acanthus pattern. Hilary stood at a counter in front of the mirror, her eyes too bright in her white face.

"I couldn't stay another minute," Hilary said. Her chest heaved in small pants. Her fingers darted into the picture-perfect coiffure of curls piled atop her head.

"What's wrong, Hilary?" Bree went to her and touched her shoulder.

"Why, nothing, of course. What could be wrong? My reelection is a shoo-in, Mason's job is going well, and he'll certainly be reelected too." She stopped, and chagrin spread over her face. "I didn't mean that the way it sounded. But really, I need to count my blessings."

"What's wrong? Is it Fay's announcement? Did something happen today? You can tell me." Bree's unease grew. Whatever ailed her sister-in-law, it was something major.

Hilary's lips twisted, and she began to tremble. She leaned forward and gripped the edge of the marble counter with both hands.

"I'm never going to have a baby, Bree." She sobbed. "You can't imagine the money we've poured into the fertility clinic in Marquette the past weeks as they've run all those tests. But today another disappointment. I was sure I was pregnant," she whispered. "I was nearly two weeks late, my stomach was bloated, nausea—all the symptoms. I'd hoped to announce it tonight. I finally got up the courage to buy a pregnancy test. It was negative. Then the doctor called with all my test results, and . . . and . . ." Hilary leaned against the wall for support. "He says Mason has a low sperm count. We may never have a baby. Now Fay flaunts her pregnancy in front of me like a war trophy. I could have had Steve, you know. He was mine before she moved to town. I hate her; I hate her! That baby should have been mine."

"You don't hate her. Come sit down." Bree embraced Hilary and led her to a wingback chair positioned against the wall. "Sit here. I'll get you some water." The marble counter held crystal glasses with cardboard covers in a neat pile on a mirrored tray. Bree's hand shook as she held a glass under the faucet and filled it with water.

Hilary took the glass Bree offered and gulped it down. "I haven't told Mason yet. I can't bear to disappoint him again; he'll blame himself. We intended to have at least four, you know. And here we are ten years later with just the two of us rattling around in that great mausoleum that was built for a family."

"What about adoption?" Bree said tentatively. She'd thought of adopting a child herself. None could ever replace Davy, but maybe another child, one who needed a home as desperately as she needed a reason for living, would fill the empty void in her heart.

Hilary shook her head. "I want a child of my own, a baby I carry in my body."

"I see." Words of advice rose in her throat and died there like a cake gone flat in the oven. Rob's family was all she had left, the only safe haven left to her. Hilary's rage could rise like Vesuvius, and Bree didn't want to be caught in the lava flow. Not now.

As Bree predicted, anger quickly replaced the sorrow on Hilary's face. She rose and grabbed a tissue from the counter. "I should have known you wouldn't understand! Everyone would know it wasn't my baby. I don't want their pity! Oh, why am I even talking to you about it? You never say anything that matters. I don't know what's wrong with you lately."

Bree couldn't explain it to her sister-in-law any more than she could explain it to herself. Hilary brushed past Bree and began to repair the damage to her makeup. Dabbing at her face, she tested a smile, then her face crumpled again. She dabbed at the tears until she finally succeeded in putting on a serene face.

"It will be all I can do to even speak to that cat Fay. I hate her!" She swept out the door without looking back.

Bree followed at a distance. Hilary melted into the festive crowd with a laugh that seemed to fool her friends but pierced Bree with dregs of sorrow as bitter as old tea. Hilary was right. Since Rob and Davy had died, she'd lost hold of who she was, and she didn't know how to find herself again.

"Bree, *kulta,* I have looked everywhere for you."

The soft sound of her mother-in-law's voice was enough to ease Bree's tension. Anu Nicholls always knew what to do. Bree turned to greet her with a smile. "How lovely you look!" Bree told her.

Dressed in a creamy gown overlaid with exquisite Finnish lace, Anu Nicholls wore her fair hair high on her head in a coronet of braids. Though nearly sixty, Anu boasted shining hair that held no trace of gray, and her face was as unlined as Bree's. From the moment Bree had married Rob and became a Nicholls, Anu had claimed her as one of her own, though the same couldn't be said for the rest of the family.

As Anu embraced Bree, her mother-in-law's subtle perfume slipped over Bree like a caress.

"So *kumoon* you look. Slim and so beautiful." Anu linked a graceful arm through Bree's and strolled toward the pastry table. "Come with me. You know how wonderful Hilary's thimbleberry tarts are. Even when I know my hips will pay, never can I resist."

"Like you have to worry about your figure!" Bree eyed Anu's lithe, long limbs with envy. She hated being short. If she could pick someone to look like, it would be Anu Nicholls. In fact, Bree wished she were like Anu in all ways. They had a lot in common even now, especially in love. They both had loved and lost. Anu's husband had run out on her after five years of marriage, leaving her to raise Rob and Hilary alone. He'd never so much as written to let her know he was still alive. The abandoned woman had never remarried, though not for lack of admirers.

Rob's father never knew the way the town looked up to Rob. The night he was appointed fire chief, Bree and Rob had lain in bed and talked far into the night. Rob confessed he'd always worked hard in his profession so that maybe someday he could make his dad proud enough of him to come back. Bree had held him as he cried that night, and it made her hate Rob's father for more than just abandoning Anu.

Anu had bounced back though. She'd opened Nicholls's Finnish Imports nearly twenty years ago, and it had grown into one of the finest Finnish shops in the country. Bree loved to touch the shop's beautiful items, treasures like Arabia china and colorful Marimekko linens. Working there was a joy, not a chore.

"Something has caused that long face, eh?"

Bree came back to earth and managed a smile. "Did you find anything new in Finland for the shop?" Bree said, knowing shop news should distract her.

Anu brightened. "Some lovely wool sweaters. And a new line of saunas I will carry." She wagged her finger under Bree's nose. "Do not change the subject. You were about to tell me what hides that lovely smile. And do not tell me 'nothing.' I know you too well."

Hilary would be livid if she revealed something she didn't want her mother to know. "I was with Hilary," she began, trying to think of a way to deflect the question.

Anu held up a slim hand. "That is enough of an explanation. I suppose she was badgering you again. I'm sorry, my Bree. I have tried to talk with her, but she refuses to listen to reason."

Bree took the invitation to drop the topic and switched to another. "I'm still having no luck finding any trace of the plane crash," she admitted.

Anu was silent for a long moment, her gaze pensive, then her eyes grew luminous with tears. "I spent much time thinking at the Puulan Lake cottage," Anu said. "The time has come to let it go, Bree." Anu's blue-eyed gaze gently traveled over Bree's face. "When Abe left me, I clung to the hope he would return. At holidays, the children's birthdays, I was sure he would call or write, or show up at the door. I spent my life imagining how I would act, what I would say. Then one day I woke up and knew he wasn't coming back. He was as dead to me as if he were buried in Rock Harbor Cemetery." She rubbed her forehead.

"It is time we all faced facts. Rob and Davy are gone. It is time for you to move on with your life. We must cease asking the impossible of you. They are gone. Let them rest in peace."

Bree's throat clenched, and she felt the beginning flutters of a panic attack, an experience she hadn't had in nearly six months. She couldn't let go of Rob and Davy, not quite yet.

"Soon," she whispered. "But not yet, Anu. Not yet."

Anu laid a hand on Bree's cheek. "I know it is hard, *kulta*. But you will grow stronger when you let go."

Bree shook her head. "I'm giving myself until the first of the year. It seems appropriate, don't you think?" Anu shrugged in acquiescence, and Bree wondered if she would give it up even then. The search was the only connection she had with her son and her husband, faithless though he was. Without that search to give her life meaning, what else was there?

— 4 —

*B*ree dutifully made the rounds through the room, shaking hands, smiling until her face hurt, and garnering all the goodwill and votes she could manage for her sister-in-law. Most folks had heard of the latest rescue and congratulated her. In spite of such kindness, events like this emphasized her presence as an outsider even as she slogged on in her quest to be accepted.

One family, however, loved Bree in the way she craved. She spotted Palmer and Lily Chambers from across the room and went to join them. Their friendship was birthed in the context of misery loving company, since they were outsiders to Rock Harbor themselves. Lily and Palmer had opened a fitness center after Palmer's stint as an airplane mechanic in the military was over. Today, two years later, the fitness center still barely limped along, a fact not too surprising, considering most of Rock Harbor's residents believed true exercise could only be had outdoors. Fishing, swimming, hiking, hunting—all these were acceptable forms. The Chamberses' high-tech machines were viewed with suspicion that was lifting only little by little.

Lily turned as Bree approached. Her round, homely face was wreathed in smiles of welcome. "Bree, I've been meaning to call and invite you to dinner. What are you doing tomorrow night? Or is that too late of a notice?"

"Let's see, dinner at your home or macaroni and cheese from a box? That's a no-brainer, I think." Bree laughed. "What time, girlfriend?"

Lily turned to Palmer. "Six sound good?"

Palmer nodded. "I should be done with my meeting by five." He hugged Bree with one arm around her shoulders. "You've been too much a stranger lately. Bring Samson; the girls have been yammering to see him."

Slender with fine blond hair and green eyes, Palmer's good looks seemed incongruous next to Lily's plain features. The fact he'd seen beyond Lily's plain exterior to her beautiful spirit endeared him to Bree. And she adored their two-year-old twins, Paige and Penelope.

"There are some darling puppies at the shelter," Bree said. "Why don't I pick up the girls one night next week and take them over to pick one out?"

Palmer wagged his finger at her. "I haven't decided to get one yet."

"Oh, Palmer, you know perfectly well you'll give in sooner or later. You might as well do it gracefully now," Lily put in.

"We'll see," Palmer said, smiling. "Now we'd better go. The sitter will need to get home."

"We'll see you tomorrow at six," Lily reminded Bree.

Bree watched a moment as Palmer and Lily wove their way back through the crowd. A warm contentment settled in her bones. It was nice to have friends like that, friends who cared about her in tangible ways.

Around nine o'clock, her feet throbbing, Bree slipped into a corner and found a chair by the curtains that formed a small hallway between the main hall and a smaller room. Scooting her chair partially into the other room and away from the crowd, she eased out of her shoes and rubbed her feet. Another half an hour and she could go home. She'd look for Naomi next.

Moments later Fay joined her. She sat in the chair beside Bree then opened her purse and took out a cigarette. She lit it and blew a circle of smoke in the air.

"Smoking isn't good for the baby," Bree said, knowing Fay wouldn't care if she spoke her mind.

"I'm not about to give up my life for this baby," Fay said. Her gaze roamed the room.

Such disregard for her baby's well-being made Bree want to get up and walk away. "Aren't you happy about it?" she asked.

Fay shrugged. "I'm not sure yet. Ask me again after it's here and I can tell whether the changes are good or bad."

A movement across the empty room caught Bree's attention. The side door opened, and a man stepped in. Bree had never seen him, though he reminded her of someone. Then she realized he looked like a younger version of the pictures she'd seen of Elvis before booze and drugs had marred his good looks. Though "the King" had died when Bree was a child, she'd been fascinated by articles she had read about him in old *Modern Screen* and *Photoplay* magazines she'd found in the back of her mother's closet.

The same petulant expression crossed this man's face as he scanned the room from his partially hidden position in the curtains. When his gaze settled on Fay, the smoldering look deepened, and he swaggered across the room toward Fay as though adoring fans screamed along the sidelines. Fay saw him approach and scowled. He stopped in front of her and stood with his hands on his hips, looking down at her.

"You said you'd meet me at nine." The man made no attempt to lower his voice.

"What are you doing here, Eric?" Fay hissed. "Get out before Steve sees you. He's already asking questions."

"Then tell him the truth!"

"Don't tell me what to do. We're playing this my way." Fay ground out her cigarette on the floor and stood to walk away.

Eric grabbed her arm. "You think you can snap your fingers and I'll follow at your heels. Don't make that mistake. I'm not a lap dog like your husband."

"Take your hands off me." She jerked her arm away, but he grabbed it again.

Bree rose, and Eric glared at her. An older man materialized from the main hall. Bree recognized him as Fay's uncle, Lawrence Kukkari.

"This man bothering you, Fay?" he asked.

"No, he's just leaving," Fay said. "I'll meet you later," she said softly to Eric. "Now please leave before Steve comes looking for me." She smiled prettily, but Eric's scowl just deepened.

"I won't wait forever, Fay."

"I'll meet you later," Fay whispered. "Please, don't make a scene."

"One hour. Then I come looking for you again." With a muttered oath, Eric spun on his heels and stalked away.

Bree's gaze followed him as he made his way through the crowd. Kade Matthews put out a hand to intercept him, and Eric stopped to talk to him. Bree frowned as she saw them talking. Kade appeared to be as angry as Eric. At one point he stabbed his finger in Eric's chest for emphasis. How did he know this guy?

Lawrence's voice drew her attention back to Fay. "You know better than to get mixed up with him again."

"Don't start, Uncle." Fay's voice was soft with weariness. "I don't meddle in your private life, and I don't want you meddling in mine."

The scowl on Lawrence's face eased. "Very well. Have you thought any more about the new offer for the mine? Mr. Simpkins wants an answer."

"I told you, I've already agreed to sell the mine to Palmer Chambers."

"You're throwing away a hundred thousand dollars!" Lawrence's voice rose.

Bree looked around for a place to slink away. Being in the middle of someone else's argument felt awkward. Unfortunately, Lawrence blocked her path to escape.

Lawrence glanced at Bree and lowered his voice as he continued to argue his case with his niece. "Take this offer, and you'll have enough money to leave Steve and this hick town and start fresh."

"I think you're more concerned with your share than with my happiness," Fay said. "Let's not talk about this anymore. I don't want to be mixed up with mobsters from New York, and I sure don't want them traipsing around my mine. I don't trust them, and I *do* trust Palmer."

"If you force my hand, I'll tell Steve everything."

Fay laughed, but the tinkle was gone. "What will you tell him, Uncle Lawrence? That I married him for his money and now that it's gone I'm splitting? He already knows why I married him. But in spite of your high opinion of me, I'm not leaving him. Not now. Things have changed. I've got a baby to think about." She slung her purse over one shoulder and moved away.

"You can't do this!" Lawrence shouted after her.

Fay just waved a hand over her head and kept going. Lawrence shook himself, his face a mask of bewilderment. He saw Bree staring at him and scowled then stalked off. "She's going to get me killed," he muttered.

Fay's covert exchanges were too complicated for Bree to think about. She would find Naomi and head for home. Fay could work out her own problems.

The next morning Bree woke in time to watch the sun break free of the horizon. In Bree's mind, Sunday morning should be time spent leisurely over a plate of eggs and bacon, but as she surveyed the contents of her refrigerator, she knew her kitchen couldn't produce such a repast: a near-empty tub of margarine, half a bottle of water, a plate of week-old salmon patties covered in a suspicious moldy tint that could be seen even through the pink plastic wrap. The lone apple in the produce drawer looked more like a prune.

"Nothing fit to eat here, Samson. You want to go out for breakfast?" He barked and ran to the door. "I guess that's a yes." She slipped into her jacket and hooked the leash to his collar. By the time she finished breakfast, Fay should be along for coffee.

Stepping outside into the cool morning air, she and Samson set off at an energetic clip toward Suomi Café, four blocks down Houghton Street. Two blocks in, she tugged on Samson's leash and slowed their pace to enjoy the walk. No one was stirring this early, but Bree thought everyone should see the radiant blue of the sky. The fog bell out in the harbor was tolling, and the blue that was Lake Superior glinted briefly between the houses lining the water. Another altogether glorious day in paradise.

Some would laugh at her for describing snow country as paradise, but then they likely had never smelled the cold freshness of pollution-free air or watched a white blanket of snow cloak everything in clean, pristine beauty. Bree couldn't imagine a better place on earth. A colorful autumn day like this offered a glimpse of perfection.

Rock Harbor, population twenty-five hundred if you counted Anu's chickens, couldn't be more picturesque. From the first moment Bree set foot on the volcanic soil of Michigan's western Upper Peninsula, she knew she'd come home. The Victorian storefronts looked the same as they did in century-old photographs. That fact had always been a comfort to Bree, but especially in the previous year. She'd had too many changes in her life.

Nestled at the base of Quincy Hill, Rock Harbor's three-block downtown area could have come straight from a child's storybook. The town's major businesses lined Houghton Street, which was intersected by Jack Pine Lane and Pepin Street. To stroll the village streets was to step back in time. Even the corner butcher showed a marked resemblance to Barney Fife. With the recent influx of tourists, many store owners were busy sprucing up and painting the storefronts with cheerful schemes that reminded Bree of San Francisco row houses. From her lighthouse tower, she could look down on the town and marvel at its perfection.

Suomi Café overlooked Lake Superior from its perch on the steep slope of Kitchigami Street. Named for the Finnish word for Finland, the humble café offered no exterior hint of the culinary delights inside. Just thinking of the possible menu choices made Bree's mouth water.

She quickened her step and had almost reached the café entrance when a squawk came from overhead. Bree looked up as a starling flew down at her. She ducked, suppressing a scream and barely avoiding the dive-bombing bird. The bird peeled around and came at her again.

"What's the matter with you, stupid bird?" Bree waved her arms, trying to frighten it away. She liked birds fine as long as they stayed in the trees. This one must be psychotic. It dived at her a third time, and she turned quickly for the door. Samson whined then barked at the bird before following Bree inside the restaurant.

She tousled her hair to make sure there were no feathers in it. The head waitress, Molly, a full tray in her skinny arms, nodded to her. In her forties, Molly was a whirlwind of activity every time Bree came in. It was no wonder she carried not an ounce of spare flesh on her thin frame.

Molly set the steamy plates before her customers then stopped beside Bree. "You look wild-eyed, kid. Why's your tail in a knot this morning, eh?" she quipped as she patted Samson's head. Having received his welcome, Samson went to lie down at the door.

"Some stupid bird was after my hair. It's hanging around outside your café."

Molly grinned. "Other customers have been complaining too. I think it's someone's pet. It landed on my shoulder this morning and took some crumbs right from my hand."

"Well, they ought to keep it home then!" Bree glanced around the restaurant. "The place looks packed this morning."

Every booth and table was taken. Bree looked over the pastry case. Suomi's specialty was *pulla,* a Finnish sweet roll made with sourdough bread that Bree was particularly fond of. But she didn't really want to take it back home. She'd spent too much time alone lately.

"It's usually not this busy until later. You might see if there's anyone willing to share a table," Molly said before hurrying off to the kitchen.

Bree glanced around the restaurant again. Fay sat in a corner booth with her elbows on the table. She caught Bree's eye and motioned to her. Today Fay looked like a fifteen-year-old on her way to school, her hair casually windblown and her pale complexion devoid of makeup. A backpack even lay at her feet. An ashtray holding two cigarette butts sat next to a cup of coffee between Fay's elbows.

Molly scurried by with a cup of coffee for Bree and a plate of half-eaten eggs for Samson. "For our hero," she said.

"You look a little green," Bree told Fay. "Try eating some toast or crackers."

"How long does this last?" Fay moaned. "I don't have time to be sick."

"Going climbing again today?" Bree asked, pointing toward the backpack. Though the U.P. didn't offer world-class mountains, there were some pretty good cliffs in the area.

"I might as well, if I can muster the energy. Steve is working, and I'm bored." Fay fiddled with one of the distinctive gold hoops that adorned her ears. Then she dropped her hand and sighed.

"Are you sure it's safe for you to climb?"

Fay grimaced. "I told you last night, I'm not going to change my life for this baby. I'm still me. The doctor said I could do whatever I'm used to doing."

Bree felt a twinge of guilt for the judgment in her question. No need to dig her hole any deeper. "Have you remembered anything more about the cabin and the airplane seat?"

Fay scowled. "No. Steve and I had another fight last night, and I didn't get a chance to think about it. Give me a few days. If there's anything worth remembering, it will come to me."

So the story about the woman and the airplane seat *was* just a bid for attention. Bree doubted the same could be said of Fay's encounter with Eric the night before. Bree had a feeling she should know something about Eric, something she'd read or heard. She wanted to ask Fay about him, though it was none of her business. She decided against it.

They drank their coffee and talked about last night's party, carefully skirting the arguments Bree had overheard. Fay kept glancing at her watch and fidgeting. Finally, she stubbed out her fourth cigarette and rose. "I'd better get going. I hope you find something."

Fay's diffidence made Bree second-guess whether she really did know something about Rob's plane. Her usual mode was high drama, and this understated comment seemed out of character.

Fay stepped into the aisle and right into Palmer's path. He stopped abruptly. "Just who I was looking for. I have the papers ready for you to sign. Is it okay if I drop by tomorrow night?"

Fay nodded. "I suppose so. We'll be around." Her voice seemed lackluster, and Bree wondered if it was just her morning sickness or if she wished she wasn't selling the mine. Did Fay and Steve need the money?

She moved past him. "Now, if you'll excuse me, I've got a cliff calling my name."

Palmer winked at Bree then joined two men at the back table.

"I'll come with you," Bree told Fay impulsively as she started to walk away. "We can talk while we hike." Though climbing was out of the question for Bree, they could talk on the way.

Fay shook her head. "I'm sorry, but I really need some alone time this morning."

Fay could be as immovable as a thirty-foot jack pine, and her obstinate expression warned Bree to let it go. The thought crossed Bree's mind that Fay was adamant because she was meeting someone, maybe Eric.

"Sorry to be a pest," Bree said. "I'll talk to you later."

Fay gave her a distracted smile before she hurried out the door.

Molly appeared at Bree's table. "Fay is upset, eh? She looked like she'd been crying when she came in." Molly's speech was typical of a Yooper. A blend of Finnish and Canadian cadence and an accent that Bree found charming.

Bree picked up a menu. "You know Fay. No one understands her moods."

Molly sniffed and nodded. "What will you have, eh? The *panukakkua* just came out of the oven."

Panukakkua. The thought of the custard pancake dripping with hot raspberry sauce brought a Pavlovian response from Bree. The *pulla* would wait. "You know my weakness," Bree said, nodding. "And more coffee."

"You got it." Molly tucked the order pad in a pocket of her apron and went to the kitchen.

Moments later Hilary rushed up to Bree's table with Mason in tow. Her eyes sparkled with excitement. "I knew I'd find you here. You're as predictable as an atomic clock." She dropped a newspaper onto the table. A picture of Bree and Samson stared back at Bree from the front page of the *Kitchigami Journal.* "Just the publicity my office can use!" she crowed. "It even mentions you're the mayor's sister-in-law."

Bree looked at the paper but didn't pick it up. Newspaper articles were nothing new to her and Samson. Something of a nuisance, actually.

Hilary and Mason sat down. "Where are you searching next?" Hilary asked.

"I'm starting a new sector, west of the gorge."

Mason cleared his throat. "We need to attend to the debriefing for yesterday's search as well. I thought you might come by yesterday. What can you tell me?"

She'd meant to but had forgotten all about it. Glad to get Hilary off the search topic, Bree told Mason of the clues they'd followed, the areas they'd searched, and how they had found the children. Molly brought Bree's breakfast and coffee. Mason took notes in backward looping letters simple enough for a grade-school kid to read.

Ten minutes later Hilary tapped her fingernails on the table. "Are we about done? We're going to be late for church if we don't get going." Gathering her purse, she slid from the seat and waited for her husband.

Mason shrugged. "I reckon we are now. Call me if you think of anything else, Bree, eh?" He nodded to Bree and followed his wife out of the café.

Bree lifted her cup and took a gulp. Hilary was happy with her now, but it wouldn't last long. Nothing would satisfy her but for Bree to find little Davy and Rob so they could all move on. Sometimes she felt stuck in an old black-and-white episode of *Twilight Zone*, facing a life that had been twisted by her own hands into something unrecognizable.

She shivered and looked at the *panukakkua*. It was cold.

*O*utside, the autumn sunshine lifted Bree's spirits. She'd better enjoy it while she could. Once winter hit, days of sunshine would be replaced by gray clouds. On her way to the hospital, she passed folks raking leaves and mulching flower beds. Rock Harbor Hospital, catty-corner from Siltanen Piano Repair, was an unimaginative square brick building that didn't do justice to its setting. Manicured grounds at the rear of the facility swooped down to a peaceful beach. Bree pointed to a blazing red-leafed tree close to the rear entrance and told Samson to stay. He sat obediently while she went inside.

Emily was flipping through TV channels when Bree poked her head into the room. "Hi, sweetheart. Remember me?"

Emily's face brightened. "Bree! I was just thinking about you. Where's Samson?"

"He's waiting for you in the garden." Bree turned off the TV and glanced at the other bed. Timmy's small face was turned into the pillow, and a slight snore issued from his nose. "How's your brother?"

"Okay. I get to go home when Daddy gets off work." The little girl bit her lip. "I asked Daddy to stay with us today, but he said he didn't get inventory finished yesterday because of my sen . . . sh . . . shenanigans. I think he's still mad at me."

The plaintive note in Emily's voice touched Bree's heart. "He's just glad to get you home," she said. "But I'll keep you company for a while. The nurse says it would be okay for me to take you down to the garden to visit with Samson. Would you like to do that?"

"Sure!" Emily hopped from the bed.

Bree found Emily's fuzzy raccoon slippers under the bed. "Let's hope these raccoons don't lead you into trouble like the last ones."

Emily's cheeks flushed. "I won't do that again," she said. She tiptoed to Timmy's bed and touched his head. "I'll be back in a little while, Timmy," she whispered.

Her brother just muttered in his sleep. Though his lashes fluttered on his cheeks a bit, he didn't awaken.

"Do you think we should leave him?" Emily asked. "He's my 'sponsibility."

Bree put her hand on Emily's head. "The nurses will take good care of him, sweetie. We'll only be gone a few minutes." Emily carried a heavy burden, and Bree wished she could ease it.

Emily leaned her head into Bree's hand. "That feels so good," she said. "Mommy used to braid my hair before she went away. I miss her."

Bree swallowed hard. Did Davy miss her combing his hair, or were there angels to do it for him in heaven?

Emily smiled up at Bree. "Do you think Samson will remember me?"

"I'm sure he will. He was very excited when we got to the hospital. I think he smelled your scent here." Bree took Emily's hand. "I have a wheelchair right outside the door. The nurse said you had to ride down to the garden in it."

"Cool!" Emily raced to the door and climbed into the wheelchair. Her feet stuck out in front of her, and she wiggled her raccoon slippers.

Bree wheeled her past the nurses' station and into the elevator.

"Have you ever been to Florida?" Emily asked Bree as the elevator jerked into motion.

The look on Davy's face when he saw Mickey at Disney World flashed into Bree's mind. "Yes," she said.

"Did you go to Disney World? Daddy says he's going to take us someday, and we can see our grandma."

Bree nodded slowly. "W—we took our son to Disney World for his first birthday."

"Oh, you have a little boy! I wish you could have brought him along for me to play with," Emily said. "How old is he?"

"He's in heaven now, but he would be four." She was quite proud of herself for holding her voice steady.

Emily contemplated this news. "Timmy's four."

The elevator door opened, and Bree wheeled Emily into the lobby and down a hall. Through the glass doors, Samson watched them come, and he stretched as he stood.

"What kind of dog is he? He has a curly tail."

"What we call a 'Heinz fifty-seven.' He's a mixture of several things, some German shepherd, some chow, maybe a bit of Border collie."

Bree wheeled Emily through the doors and into the sunshine of the hospital's garden area.

"Samson!" Emily cried. The dog trotted to her and licked her chin. Emily laughed and rubbed his head.

"You want to sit under the tree?" Bree asked. Emily nodded, and Bree rolled the wheelchair along the brick walk to a huge tree whose trunk was covered with ivy.

"Can I sit at the picnic table?" Emily asked.

"How about we play ball with Samson?" Bree produced a ball from her jacket pocket. Samson barked excitedly. "Samson, quiet!" Bree commanded. The dog instantly stopped barking.

"I bet you're a good mommy," Emily said. She took the ball and threw it as hard as she could into the yard.

Bree swallowed. What could she say to that? If she were a good mother, wouldn't she have thought of Davy before she called Rob? If only she hadn't upset him before he got into the plane, wouldn't they both still be here?

Samson raced across the grass, snatched up the ball, then carried it back to Emily, his tail waving proudly. He dropped it in her lap. Emily picked it up. "Oh, gross!" she said. "Dog slobber."

Bree laughed. "But it's full of love." She took off her jacket. "That sun is getting hot."

"I was cold in the woods. I didn't want to leave the cabin," Emily said.

Bree stared at her. "What cabin?"

"The witch in the woods took us to her cabin. I told you." Emily's lip trembled. "You don't believe me either!"

"You keep talking about the witch in the woods. There is no witch, Emily. You must have dreamed it." Bree was beginning to wonder if she should talk to the doctor about Emily's peculiar obsession. There was no way the story could be true. No one would have fed the children just to abandon them in the forest again, especially with Timmy so sick.

Emily's stormy expression vanished. "I like to tell stories," she said. "Maybe I'll write books someday. But I did see a lady there."

Bree sighed, but she smiled and took Emily's hand. "I think we'd better go check on your brother." Davy had had an active imagination too. Children were such a joy that way. It was better not to argue with them over their imaginary friends.

*B*y the time Bree got home, it was one o'clock, so she fixed herself a peanut butter sandwich. The day could not be more perfect. The repair on the brick wouldn't take long, if she could just convince herself to try it. This should be an easy fear to face. Little by little over the past year, she'd overcome the terrors that woke her in the night. Her fear of heights could be overcome too. But not if she didn't try, if she didn't get up and do something about it.

Bree forced herself to stand, then moved on leaden legs to the back patio where the mortar still waited. She mixed it then carried the bucket up the curving iron steps of the light tower. She fastened the leather work belt around her waist and stepped out onto the metal catwalk that circled the tower of her lighthouse home like a tiara on the head of an aging beauty queen.

The wind freshened, bringing the scent of Lake Superior to her nose. The waves along the lake made a booming sound as they struck the buoy out in the cove. Her lighthouse home had stood for over a century on a thin slice of land that thrust itself into Superior's waves with all the arrogance of a scepter extended to a penitent. But it would soon crumble around her if she didn't marshal the courage to get this job done.

Looking over the railing, a wave of dizziness swept over her, and the ground tilted. Gripping the railing with tight fingers, she whispered, "I can do this."

Fay had loaned her a rappelling harness weeks ago. Bree fastened it to the railing. Her heart raced. She knew the sturdy rope should hold her, but she couldn't help imagining spiraling down the side of the tower and slamming against the grassy knoll far below. She squeezed her eyes shut. Had there been time enough for Rob and Davy to feel this fear that dried her mouth like the Sonoran desert?

Bree swallowed and tightly gripped the catwalk post and rail. She wedged the toe of her boot against the lower rail and swung around so her back was to Superior's cold spray. Standing with one foot on the lower rail, she silently castigated herself. All she had to do was swing that other leg over the railing, and she'd be standing outside the catwalk. Why couldn't she perform such a simple action?

With blood roaring in her ears like some Superior squall, Bree gripped the railing and told herself she could do it. The bag of mortar bumped against her thigh and startled her. She closed her eyes again and shuddered. *Just get it over with.* Still straddling the railing, she tested the strength of the rope again, more to delay the inevitable than anything else.

She was going to do this. Swinging her other leg over, she stood poised on the edge of the balcony. *Now* all she had to do was step into space. The rope would hold her. The lead in her legs had turned to jelly, but she forced herself to go on. She could conquer this fear. She stepped away, and then she was walking along the vertical side of the lighthouse, rappelling down the tower. This was easier than she'd thought it would be.

Squinting against the harsh sun, she glanced up at the hook that snapped around the railing. Her eyes widened in spite of the glare. The railing was beginning to bend. Her stomach lurched. She had to get back up before it came loose.

She was going to die. Her breath came in short gasps. The railing wouldn't hold long, and she would plummet to her death. She tried to shout for help, but only a squeak slipped past her tight throat.

"What are you doing?" Naomi poked her head over the edge of the balcony. "This is not a job for you. You get back inside right now."

"I would if I could," Bree whispered.

Naomi stepped onto the metal catwalk, and it shook a bit with her steps. Bree shuddered.

"Hold on." Naomi grabbed the rope and began to wind it around her waist. In jerky movements, Bree began to rise to the balcony. She was afraid to move, afraid she would take Naomi down with her.

Naomi grunted with the exertion. "Almost there," she panted.

Then Bree was at the top, and Naomi was helping her over the railing. Both women tumbled to the shaky deck and lay gasping.

Bree's breathing began to return to normal, and she sat up. "I would have died if you hadn't come. The railing was giving way."

"I saw." Naomi's eyes were bright with tears. "Something inside, almost like a voice, told me you needed me. It had to be God," she whispered.

Irritation flared up in place of Bree's relief. Of course Naomi would give God the credit. Her gaze traveled to the misshapen railing. She felt her annoyance wane. Could it be possible Naomi was right?

Naomi touched Bree's shoulder in a comforting gesture. "You're all right. Let's get you inside."

On wobbly legs, Bree managed to walk to the door and step through into the light tower. "That wasn't pretty," she said. "Thanks." She attempted a smile. "I guess I'll have to sell this and buy one of those new tract homes going up on Cottage Avenue. Look at all the money I'd make. People would be lining up at the door to buy a dilapidated lighthouse with a crumbling tower and mold in the basement."

"Don't joke. I know what it cost you to go out there. I think you're very brave," Naomi said.

Bree looked away. If Naomi only knew. "I need a cup of coffee," she said.

Naomi nodded. "Want to join us for dinner?"

Bree didn't want to face the pity in Naomi's expression. She couldn't face her own failure again. "I'm supposed to go to Lily and Palmer's for dinner." She squeezed her friend's hand. "But thanks, Naomi."

As Bree left the lighthouse, a hint of rain freshened the air. The wind began to blow across Lake Superior, kicking up scuds of white foam and flotsam onto the beach. What had happened to her perfect day? Bree tightened her jacket around her chest and bent against the wind. The rich aroma of espresso wafted through the door of The Coffee Place. Bree followed the fragrance like it was the Pied Piper. Caffeine was what she needed.

The bell on the door jingled, and she shut the door against the wind. "I'll have a double espresso with whipped cream on top. Lots of whipped cream."

The young woman behind the counter nodded. Bree didn't recognize her. Probably new. Bree waved to her hairdresser, Sally Wilson, and nodded to Steve Asters. He got up when he saw her and moved to join her at the counter.

"I'm glad to see you," he said. A faint scratch ran across his right cheek.

"New at this shaving stuff, Steve?" Bree asked, teasing.

His hand went to his cheek and he flushed. "New razor," he said. "Can I talk to you for a minute?" He gestured to a table in the corner.

The new girl put Bree's espresso on the counter. "Sure." Bree picked up her coffee and followed Steve.

He sat in the seat opposite her. "Fay hasn't come home," he whispered, glancing around to make sure they weren't being overheard. "At first I didn't think anything about it. She went climbing this morning. But we're supposed to go to a dinner with the bank's board of directors at six-thirty, and she still isn't home." Bree glanced at her watch. Nearly three. "She promised to be home by one."

"I saw her this morning," she admitted. "About eight. She was heading out to climb."

Steve nodded. "I'm getting worried. It's not like Fay. I tried calling her cell phone, but she never answered. I'd like you to look for her."

"First things first. Have you contacted the sheriff?"

He shook his head. "That wouldn't do me any good. It hasn't been twenty-four hours yet."

"Let's call Mason. Since Fay is pregnant, he might bend the rules. I could meet him out there and take a look around."

Steve's eyes brightened and he nodded, taking his small fliptop cell phone from the inside pocket of his jacket. Bree sipped her espresso while Steve explained the situation to Mason.

"He's on his way," he said after closing the phone. "He's in Houghton. Said he'd meet you at Rock River Gorge. I think that's where she was going." Steve put away his phone. "Can you take Samson up to the ridge to look around before he gets there? Just to see if maybe

she's twisted her ankle or something? I could get you an article of clothing for the dog to scent from."

An evening at Rock River Gorge was not nearly as appealing as her
plans for dinner with the Chambers family, but she was needed. "I
have to make a call," she said. She took her own cell phone from her
pocket and dialed Lily's number. Her friend promised to keep dinner
warm for her.

"I need to get Samson," she told Steve.

Steve stood. "I'll run by my place and get something of Fay's for
the dog. Maybe a sock?"

Bree nodded. "Pick up the item with your hand inside a paper bag,
then turn the bag inside out so you don't touch the scent article," she
instructed. "Then drop that bag into another paper bag before putting
it all inside a plastic bag."

He blinked and his mouth dropped open. "Can't I just put it in a
plastic bag?"

"Nope. Do it my way so we can keep the scent uncontaminated."

Steve sighed and nodded then hurried out. Bree stayed a moment
longer to make one more call. Maybe Naomi could join her.

By the time she got home and put Samson's vest on him, the sky
had darkened to pewter. The wind shrieked through the eaves and rattled the windows of her old lighthouse. The sound always made Bree
think of Ojibwa Windigos, legendary Indian spirits who prowled for
human flesh. The delightful autumn day had morphed to early winter
without notice. Bree climbed into her insulated nylon jumpsuit and
pulled the hood over her head. She grabbed a bag of pistachios and her
ready-pack and went down the steps.

Samson followed her to the door, and they stepped outside as Steve
pulled into the drive in his new Lexus. He was dressed in a suit and tie.

Bree frowned. "Aren't you going with us?"

He shook his head. "Wish I could, but I'm expected at the dinner," he shouted above the wind. "Here's my cell phone number. Oh,

and one of Fay's socks." He handed Bree a slip of paper with his number written on it through the window, along with a plastic bag containing a sock encased in two paper bags. He began to back out.

Bree stuffed the paper in her pocket and tucked the bag under her arm. "Steve," she began.

He braked and looked at her, and she shook her head. "Nothing," she said. "I'll let you know what I find." He nodded and then sped away.

Bree couldn't believe he would go to a bank dinner rather than help search for his pregnant wife. No wonder Fay had a brittle edge about her. It also explained Eric's presence in her life.

Samson whined, and Bree waved at Naomi and Charley as they hurried across the yard toward the Jeep. Naomi wore her orange jumpsuit, and Charley had on his orange vest. Samson jumped into his kennel at the back of the Jeep then barked a welcome to Charley as Naomi steered her dog into the back also.

"Was that Steve leaving?" Naomi slid into the passenger seat and fastened her seat belt. She raked her fingers through her hair and quickly braided it. Her cheeks were pink from the wind.

"Yes. He had a fancy dinner to attend." Bree didn't bother to hide the disgust in her voice.

"He calls us out on a night like this then goes to a party?" Naomi's voice lifted with indignation.

"Yep. If I were Fay, I'd be giving him a dose of his own medicine too."

"You think that's what this is?"

"I wouldn't be surprised. She didn't seem to be her usual barracuda self this morning. I almost felt sorry for her." Bree started the Jeep and drove down Houghton Street. Leaving the town behind them, she drove out to the gorge.

Bree loved the Rock River Gorge, with its rugged falls and rapids in beautiful forests of pine and hemlock. But tonight, the thick trees deepened the gloom that had blown in with the clouds. Watching the wind whipping the trees and bending the shrubs and bushes over double brought a sense of unease to Bree's throat. Why would Fay stay out in weather like this? Maybe something really was wrong.

She drove slowly through the area looking for Fay's car and found it under the sweep of a blue spruce. Bree parked the Jeep, and she and Naomi got out. Rock River Gorge was just over the hill. It was a favorite place of Fay's; they would check there first. Naomi released the dogs while Bree fetched their gear from the backseat.

Her ears ached from the cold, and she tugged the hood of her jacket a little tighter. She heard a rustling in the thicket. Peering through the vegetation, she tried to see if anything was there. Maybe it was just the wind. She hunched her chin into her jacket then jerked her head around again. There it was again.

"Is anyone there?" For a moment she thought about Emily's witch in the woods. Then a tall figure encased in a tan uniform and a matching jacket stepped through the tangle of brush. Samson and Charley bounded to meet him. Naomi raised her hand in greeting.

"I thought that sounded like Samson and Charley." Kade scratched the dogs on the head before walking toward Bree. "What are you doing here? Weather's turning nasty."

"Fay Asters is missing," Bree said.

He processed this information in silence. "Anyone seen her today?"

Bree nodded. "I saw her this morning before she went climbing. She didn't come home. I can't imagine she's still out here, but I promised Steve I'd look around."

"Was she alone?"

The question seemed casual, but a muscle in Kade's jaw twitched, and Bree remembered his argument with Eric at Hilary's campaign party. She assumed Fay had been seeing Eric, but what was Kade's connection to him?

She forced her inquisitive thoughts away. "As far as we know."

Glancing around, she wondered where Mason was. She'd rather he got there before they started in case something really was wrong.

"Sounds like a wild-goose chase to me," Kade said. He shifted his weight from one foot to the other and pulled his coat around him. "I hear you went to see the O'Reilly youngsters today in the hospital."

"Great kids," Bree said. She opened the hatch and grabbed her backpack then slung it on. "Emily about talked my leg off."

"Mine, too. I stopped by the hospital first, but the doctor had released her so I went by the house. Have you been there?"

She shook her head. "I thought I'd stop over later in the week."

He grimaced. "It's a mess. I think young Emily has tried to be care-taker for the whole family since her mother ran off. She was trying to fix supper when I got there. Donovan invited me to eat with them. Lukewarm hot dogs and potato chips. There was a mountain of laundry on the back porch."

"I've known Donovan a long time," Naomi added. "He seems overwhelmed."

"Poor kids," Bree said. "Hey, maybe Naomi and I could stop over and get the place in order."

"I've got a day off tomorrow. Could you use some help?"

Bree's eyes widened. A man who wasn't too proud to do house-work? Now that was an unusual fellow. She took another look at Kade. Broad-shouldered with a face weathered by the sun and wind, he seemed the type to be more at home in the garage than the kitchen. There must be more to the man than met the eye.

"What time?"

"How about we meet at the house after school, say, three o'clock? I don't want to go in while Donovan is home. He seems to be as proud as Midas, though hardly as rich. I hear the hardware store is ailing. That's probably why he hasn't hired someone to help out."

"He's doing the best he can," Naomi put in.

Naomi's voice was a bit truculent, and Bree hid a grin. Her friend had it bad. She turned back to Kade. "Donovan seems pretty harried at the store." Bree felt an unexpected wave of protectiveness toward Emily come over her. Bree remembered only too well the defeat she'd felt as a child trying to keep up with the housework when her mother was gone to the bars all night, and the shame she'd felt when someone from school would stop by.

"We'll meet you at three then," she told him. "Ready to find her, boys?" she asked the dogs. Twilight was coming, and she couldn't wait any longer for Mason. Besides, Kade was here.

Samson barked at Bree as if to ask whom he was looking for. "Here, boys." She opened the sack and held it under the dogs' noses so they could sniff it. "Search!" she told them. The dogs bounded off toward a steep hill covered with vines and the small trunks of new-growth pine and birch.

Bree, Naomi, and Kade followed, trying to keep the dogs in sight. Bree loved to watch the dogs work. Samson paused in the meadow at the top of the hill and worked by zigzagging in a circle with his nose held high as he tried to catch the scent cone. He was focused and intent. Charley raced back and forth across the area in straight lines with his tail wagging, pausing occasionally to sniff out a rabbit. She could tell the moment they both caught the scent, and her heart sank.

Samson gave a little stiff-legged jump before tucking his tail between his legs. He raised his muzzle to the sky and howled, a mournful sound that raised the hair on the back of Bree's neck. Charley hung his head and whimpered then urinated on the leaves. Both dogs trotted toward the scent, but their reluctance was obvious.

Bree looked at Naomi, whose eyes were wide with shock. "They're wrong this time," Bree said. "There's always a first time."

"What's wrong?" Kade asked.

Bree didn't answer. Adrenaline surging through her body, she followed the dogs through the tangle of overgrowth and brambles, the wind driving the thorns against her legs. Eagle Rock was that direction. Even from here she could see the dark walls of the cliff jutting against the leaden sky. A creek ran through a thicket, and Bree splashed across the water. As she reached the other side, she heard Samson's whimper turn into a howl. Then Charley's howl joined Samson's, and the mournful chorus confirmed what Bree and Naomi already knew. They wouldn't find Fay Asters alive.

Stepping into the clearing at the foot of the cliff, Bree's gaze swept the scene then reluctantly came to rest on the crumpled body at the cliff base. Her head twisted at an odd angle, Fay Asters lay on the ground, her purple jacket a bright splash of color on the drab rocks.

— 6 —

Mason and his deputy arrived minutes after Fay's body was discovered, and they immediately secured the scene. Kade left to report to headquarters. Bree studied the rocky ground as high up the side of the cliff as she could see. From here there didn't seem to be any pitons in the rock face, but it was getting too dark to see. Moving closer caused bile to rise in her throat. No matter how many times she came face-to-face with death, it never failed to shock her. The strobe of the searchers' lights cast a strange glow over the tragic picture. Something about Fay's posture struck a wrong chord in Bree, but it was probably just the surreal experience of seeing Fay lying there when she'd been so alive this morning.

Bree kept her eyes downcast. What had Kade Matthews been doing out here? She told herself not to be ridiculous. This wasn't murder; Fay had just slipped. And even if there were more to it than that, Kade wouldn't have had anything to do with it. The sight of Fay's sprawled body was enough to bring gruesome thoughts to anyone's mind.

"Anything?" Naomi came up behind her. Both dogs trotted at her side.

"Not that I can see. I'm sure Mason will come back in the morning and look around when there's more light. Not that I expect him to find anything. Fay evidently just slipped. I don't see her backpack though."

"Maybe wild animals dragged it off."

Bree nodded then laid a hand on Samson's head. "We should play with the dogs for a few minutes before we go back. They seem a little depressed."

Naomi nodded. "You want to hide, or you want me to?"

"I will." Bree gave Samson a final pat and hurried away to the path that led through the woods to the road. She hadn't always played hide-and-seek with her dogs after a tragic ending to a search, but she found that Samson grew depressed if he lacked the feeling that he had succeeded. Now she or Naomi would hide a few times and let the dogs think they had found and rescued a live victim. Too bad such tricks couldn't help Bree's own growing sense of failure.

There were never guarantees at the end of any search, only hope. And too often that hope became twisted like a ship in the grip of a nor'easter until it broke apart in the waves of self-incriminating failure. But Bree determinedly clung to the hope of finding Davy's body, having the peace of knowing he was not alone in the wilderness.

Spying a clump of thick brush near the road, she hurried over to hide in it. The dogs would find her soon, but that was the point. Once they were happy again, they could go home. Maybe she could watch some TV or read a book—something to forget the failure that mentally flogged her.

She heard the dogs scramble along the path, and only a few minutes later, both dogs began to bark and lick her face. Bree laughed and threw her arms around Samson's neck.

"Good dog! You saved me." But who would save her from herself? Anu and Naomi would say God, but that was a vain hope.

Naomi reached her and held out a hand to help Bree to her feet. Bree stood and brushed away the bits of twigs and mud clinging to her pants' leg. "I'm beat. Let's head for home. The dogs seem fine, and the sheriff can take care of everything else."

Naomi nodded. "Popcorn and TV in front of the fire sound good to me. I'm freezing. You want to come over?"

Bree shook her head. "I wouldn't be fit company. Besides, Lily and Palmer are keeping dinner warm for me."

Naomi studied her face. "This isn't your fault or responsibility, Bree. God will carry Steve through this."

There it was, Naomi's answer to every problem—a too-simple answer for Bree. If He cared so much, why was there war and death and deadly disease? Why did children like Davy die?

Bree hunched her shoulders and turned away. "Let's go. I'm freezing."

"Bree—" Naomi began.

Both dogs began to howl, then they slunk toward the road. Bree's head came up, and she wheeled to look. This didn't sound good. She ran after her dog. Samson neared the pavement then veered to the right. Giving a stiff-legged jump, he began to howl then crouched in the leaves. Bree's breath came fast. The full moon illuminated the clearing a bit, and she hurried to join her dog. Charley was piddling on the leaves again too, his head down.

"What is it, boy?" Bree put a calming hand on the dog's head, but Samson continued to howl, a mournful sound in the cold air. There was a death scent here too, but Fay lay clear over by the cliffs. How was this possible? The moon glimmered around her, and she noticed the dim light reflected on a large rock. Was that something wet? Kneeling beside Samson, she touched the patch of moisture. It was sticky. Raising her fingers closer to her face, she peered at the substance clinging to her fingertips. The coppery odor told her it was blood.

"What is it?" Naomi knelt beside her.

Bree wordlessly held out her hand. Naomi stared then sucked in her breath. She stood and went to the bottom of the cliff. "Sheriff! Over here!"

Bree frowned. Opening her ready-pack, she dug out a flashlight and flicked it on. The powerful beam probed the darkness, and she focused the light on the rock. Her frown deepened. Was that hair? She started to touch it but drew back. The sheriff would have her hide if she mucked up the investigation.

"You find something?" Huffing from his run, Mason hurried toward them.

Bree pointed to the rock. "Looks like hair and blood. And both dogs gave a death response."

Mason's mouth gaped, then he shut it with a snap. "A death response? What's that mean?"

"This is Fay's hair and blood. Her dead body lay here at some time."

The sheriff's professionalism slipped into place. "Back away from the site." He turned and cupped his hand to his mouth. "Montgomery, come here. And bring Rollo with you." He shone his flashlight on the rock. "Focus your beam here too, Bree. I want to get a good look at this. We can't be going off half-cocked. Let's think about this a minute, eh?"

She aimed her flashlight beam at the rock. Naomi did the same. It sure looked like hair and blood to her. She looked away. Samson was still distressed, whining and fidgeting to get away. He had begun to eat grass as well, and Bree knew he was nauseated.

Doug Montgomery, one of Rock Harbor's deputies, came lumbering up the trail. He was a big man, though he wore his weight well, and most people stepped out of the way when he approached. Rollo Wilson, the county coroner, followed him. About forty, Rollo always wore an expression of perpetual surprise, as though life was not what he'd expected. But he was good at his job.

Rollo grunted. "Looks like hair and blood," he said.

"Bree says the dogs gave a death response here."

Rollo's eyebrows went even higher. "What's that mean?"

"The dogs say this evidence was left by Fay's dead body."

A ghost of a grin crossed Rollo's face. "I didn't know they could talk."

Bree didn't laugh. "They can talk, all right. Just look at them."

She gestured toward Samson and Charley. The muzzles of both dogs drooped nearly to the ground, and they were still whimpering with their tails tucked between their hind legs.

Rollo snorted. "I think we'll see what science has to say before we accept such nonsense." He took a plastic bag from his coat pocket and tweezed off some hair then applied the blood to glass slides. "My lab will tell the real story."

Bree gritted her teeth. Rollo was just ignorant of how sensitive these dogs were. She turned to Mason. "This makes no sense."

"Something sure doesn't smell right," Mason admitted.

The silence between them stretched out. There was only one answer, but Bree didn't want to be the first to voice it. She shuddered.

Rollo sat back then stood. "Explain this to me, Bree. Tell me how these dogs work."

Bree's gaze wandered to the dark woods. "Every human scent is different. The skin gives off dead skin cells called rafts. We each shed about forty thousand of them per minute. Every tiny raft has its own bacteria and releases its own vapor that makes up the unique scent each of us carries. When the body is dead, the scent is the same, but it has the scent of decay mixed in. That's what the dogs smell. They can't lie; they just report what they smell. Fay lay here dead at some point."

Rollo snorted again. "This hair and blood could very well be that of a deer or some other animal." He gathered up the evidence and walked toward the parking lot. "I'll have some results in a few days. In the meantime, I would suggest you don't go running around town talking about some murderer loose on the streets of Rock Harbor. We don't want a panic."

He was right about that, even if he was wrong about the hair and blood. The dogs wouldn't react like this to an animal's remains. Samson didn't know how to lie, and Bree trusted her dog's nose. He was reacting to the search scent, not a dead animal.

They all trooped single-file down the path. Fay's body had been removed, and the parking lot held only their cars—and Fay's. The sheriff's bubble-gum lights were still flashing, and Bree was glad for that bit of light. There was a murderer out there, no matter what the coroner said. *What was Kade doing out here?* Bree wondered again. He was a ranger, after all. What was so suspicious about him being in the woods? Still, it seemed too coincidental for him to appear just before they found the body.

She put her hand on Mason's arm. "Um, just so you know, Kade Matthews was here poking around in the bush when we arrived. He is a ranger and all, so that shouldn't make him an automatic suspect, but I thought you should know."

Mason's gaze grew thoughtful. "I see. I've known Kade a long time. I can't see him doing something like this. Besides, let's not jump to conclusions. It's probably a climbing accident."

Bree knew it was hard for others to trust the dogs as she did. She didn't try to argue with him. Dropping her arm, she started to get in her Jeep.

Mason stopped her. "I could use some help telling the family," he said.

Bree put up a hand and leaned against the Cherokee. "I'm no good at that, Mason. I know what it's like to be on the receiving end. Take Naomi."

"That's exactly why I'm asking you. You know what it's like."

He wasn't giving her any options. Bree pressed her lips together to stop their quivering then nodded grudgingly and tossed her car keys to Naomi. "Can you feed Samson?"

"Sure." Naomi's brown eyes were wide with sympathy.

"I still say Naomi would be a better helper. She has the words to say to comfort him. I don't have any answers."

"There are no answers for a tragedy like this," Naomi said. "Mason is right. You've been there and know what it feels like. You go ahead. I'll take care of the dogs."

Bree hunched her shoulders and followed Mason. He instructed Montgomery to finish helping Rollo with the investigation then headed toward his car. Now that Fay's body had been discovered, it struck her as even odder that Steve had refused to come with them.

"Do you know where Steve is?" the sheriff asked, opening the squad car door for Bree.

"He told me he'd be at a dinner party at his boss's. I think they live on Mulberry Drive." She slid into the car and fastened her seat belt. "Like I told you, he asked me to look for her because she was late getting home for an important party."

"Seems odd he didn't go with you to search."

"I thought the same thing. Do you suppose he could have killed her?"

"Let's not be so quick to talk about murder. Fay was pregnant, and it might have affected her balance. She could have gotten dizzy."

"That doesn't explain her blood by the road."

He sighed. "We don't know for sure it *is* her blood, Bree."

"I'm sure."

Mason just shook his head. Bree wondered how her brother-in-law really felt about Hilary's inability to conceive. Hilary's words the night of the party came on the heels of that thought. *I hate her.* No, Hilary was no murderer. She was hotheaded and self-willed, but Fay's death was not Hilary's handiwork.

No matter how hard Bree tried to convince herself, the echo of Hilary's words wouldn't fade.

"I'd better call Lily and Palmer and tell them I won't be able to stop by tonight." Bree made the call then turned to stare out the window. As they drove to town, she struggled to think of what she could say to Steve. She couldn't even remember exactly what Hilary and Mason had said to her when they had come to tell her Rob's plane was missing. It was all a blur, a merciful blur.

But the hours leading up to that moment were burned into her memory.

The phone's ring jarred Bree awake as she lay napping on the couch. Rubbing her eyes, she glanced at her watch. Rob and Davy would be heading home in a few hours.

She grabbed for the phone and punched the talk button. "Hello?"

"Bree Nicholls?" a woman's husky voice asked.

Probably a sales call, Bree thought. The voice wasn't familiar. "Yes?"

"You don't know me, but my name is Lanna March, and I'm in love with your husband."

Bree held the phone away from her ear and stared at it as though it had just grown fangs. She put it back to her ear. "What did you say?"

"I think you heard me. Rob and I are in love. If you want him to be happy, you'll let him have a divorce."

The line clicked, and Bree was left listening to a dead line, then the dial tone. Her thoughts spiraled, and she tried to make sense of what the woman had said. Rob, an affair? Impossible. But even as her heart frantically denied it, memories of late nights at work and his recent detachment flooded her mind.

Her hands shook as she dialed Rob's cell phone. After what seemed an eternity, Rob answered.

"I know, you miss us." There was a smile in his voice. "I suppose you want to talk to Davy."

"Is he close by?" Bree managed to ask.

"He's outside. I can call him."

"No, wait! I wanted to talk to you." Bree swallowed. "Who is Lanna?"

"Who?"

Rob's voice sounded strained, Bree thought. "Lanna. Lanna March. She just called here and told me the two of you are in love."

"What?" Rob's voice sharpened. "What are you talking about? Are you accusing me of having an affair?"

"Are you?"

"You seem pretty certain of it. You've found me guilty and pronounced my sentence, all without a trial." His voice was tight and clipped.

Bree ran a hand through her newly cut hair. Rob was going to have a fit when he saw how she'd hacked off her long tresses. She gave an exasperated sigh. "The woman called here, Rob. Do you hear me? She actually called here and told me if I loved you, I would give you a divorce."

"That's ludicrous! Are you making this up?"

Bree's temper flared to an even higher pitch. "You can't twist this and blame me. I'm not the one having an affair."

"I'm not having an affair!"

"Well, you can have your divorce! But I'm not going to be the one to tell Davy his father is a faithless, conniving philanderer." She slammed the phone into its cradle and burst into tears.

The phone rang, and she paced back and forth, refusing to give in to the urge to answer it. She knew it was Rob, and she couldn't listen to his lies.

The afternoon inched by at a glacial speed. The phone rang periodically, and she finally took it off the hook.

Rob was due home by six. When he still wasn't there by eight, she told herself she didn't care. He was probably with his lover. The thought made her burst into tears again. At 8:15 the doorbell rang. She went to the door and found Mason and Hilary standing there, both of them in tears. Rob's plane had gone down somewhere between Iron River and home.

C an I help you?"

Bree was jolted out of her painful memories by the harsh light spilling from the front door of the palatial home. Music echoed from the house as well. Bree recognized the blond woman who stood framed by the light from the room as Barbara McGovern, wife of the man who owned Rock Harbor Savings and Loan.

"We'd like to see Steve Asters," Mason said.

Behind Barbara, Steve Asters stood talking to a curvaceous red-head who wore a tight black dress, slit up the side practically to her waist. He glanced up, and his gaze met Bree's. His smile faded.

Barbara motioned to Steve, and he came slowly toward them. The fear in his expression heightened when he saw Mason standing behind her.

"Did you find Fay?" Steve directed his question to Bree. The color leached from his face, leaving him as pale as sand.

Bree gave an almost imperceptible nod. Suddenly, she wanted to be anywhere but in this stuffy room full of cigarette smoke and the scent of booze and perfume. The stress of the day bore down on her in an overwhelming rush of weariness.

Mason cleared his throat. "Is there somewhere we can speak in private?"

Steve glanced at Barbara with a question in his eyes. Barbara's frown deepened, but she nodded. "Follow me." She led them down the hall to a study lined with bookshelves. "I'll be with my guests if you need me." Closing the door behind her, she left them alone with Steve.

Steve ran a finger over the oak bookshelf nearest to him then thrust his hands in his pockets. "Is Fay all right?" Gazing at Mason, he seemed to be avoiding Bree's eyes.

"No, sir, I'm afraid she's not," Mason said gravely.

Steve blanched. "Is she injured?"

Mason cleared his throat. "I'm afraid she's dead, Steve. We found her at the base of Eagle Rock. Or I should say, the dogs found her."

Steve's gaze finally shifted to Bree, and she saw the shock and pain in his eyes. And something else as well. Was it guilt? She'd always heard murder was usually committed by someone close to the victim. Steve's contact with the red-headed bombshell made him more suspicious.

Steve swayed on his feet, and Bree reached out a hand to steady him. He jerked away from her grasp and walked to the window. The blinds were open, but the window reflected the light, and it was impossible to look out. Still, Steve stood staring at the window. Was he trying to gain time to think? Bree exchanged a glance with Mason. The sheriff seemed as puzzled as she felt.

Steve turned around. His eyes were dry, and he nodded to them. "I appreciate you both coming to tell me in person. Where is her body? Do I need to identify her or anything?"

Mason nodded. "The ambulance took her to the coroner's office. They'll do an autopsy."

Steve's eyes widened. "Why? You said she fell. I told her a thousand times she was going to fall and break her neck one of these days."

He was babbling. It sounded like guilt to her. She mentally shook her head. She'd watched too many episodes of *Murder, She Wrote*. This was Steve Asters, the man who had loaned her the money to buy her lighthouse, the respected manager of the bank, not some heartless murderer. Grief caused people to say and do strange things. She resolved to give him the benefit of the doubt.

"Actually, there is some question as to the cause of death. Once we get some tests back from the lab, we'll know if we're dealing with an accident . . . or something else," Mason said.

Steve's face paled even more. "I don't understand." He swiped a shaking hand through his hair.

"It's possible someone killed her and then put her body at the cliff base to make it look like an accident."

"Murder?" Steve's lips barely moved, and he swayed where he stood. He held his hands out in front of him, and Bree noticed the tremble in them. "Next you'll be saying I did it! But I've been here all evening. Ask anyone."

Mason nodded. "Shall we drive you to the morgue?"

Steve's face flushed, and he raised his voice. "I know what you're thinking! It's always the husband. Well, I loved Fay!" He paced in front of the window as his voice rose.

"Steve, no one is accusing you of anything." Mason followed him and touched his arm, but he jerked away.

Steve turned and stomped to the door. "If you want to talk to me, you can contact my attorney." He slammed the door behind him, and an oil painting of the Porcupine Mountains fell to the floor with a crash.

Bree picked it up. One corner of the frame was chipped. She felt rather battered herself. This night had brought back too many memories.

— 9 —

*N*icholls's Finnish Imports was already buzzing with the news of Fay's death by the time Bree arrived Monday morning at nine. She worked as a salesclerk in the store three days a week, and though the money supplemented the insurance Rob had left, the real reason she enjoyed her job was that it awarded her time with Anu.

The aroma of Anu's famous cardamom rolls filled the store from the bakery at the back. As well as Finnish imports, the store sold Finnish pastries and desserts. Eini Kantola, forty and as round as a snowman, rushed to greet Bree. "The radio said you found Fay's body!" She tsk-tsked, a habit that set Bree's teeth on edge. Eini's hazel eyes were bright with curiosity. Several customers turned eager faces their direction.

Bree blinked at the bombardment then nodded. "Yes, I found her."

"I thought she would come to a bad end." Sheba McDonald sniffed. Sheba made everything in town her business. With a husband who had been the county court judge for going on forty years, she knew secrets that should never be told, though she was never reticent to reveal many of them.

Sheba's hands stilled their rummaging through the sweaters, and she moved closer. "I'd seen her with that old boyfriend. If you ask me, that baby of hers probably wasn't even Steve's."

She turned to her friend Janelle Calumet, and they both began to discuss Fay's shortcomings. Bree heard mention of Steve's money troubles. So that was common knowledge as well. Surely Mason had heard the rumors too.

Eini looked at Bree. "They're saying Steve needed money in a bad way these days. I wonder if Fay had insurance."

Anu wiped her floury hands on the red chef's apron she wore. "Eini, it is unseemly to display such nosiness," she said softly. "Please return to working on the display for the Arabia china."

Eini's face fell in a comical expression of chagrin and disappointed petulance. "I'm almost done with that. Aren't you even curious about Fay's death, eh?" She turned away and went back to arranging plates on display shelves.

Bree took off her coat and went to hang it in the back room. "Thanks," she whispered as she passed Anu.

Anu followed her. "Don't thank me, *kulta*. I must admit to curiosity myself, but Hilary filled me in this morning. Did you sleep?"

"Not much," Bree admitted.

Anu nodded. "Come, have some coffee with me. Eini can handle the store for a bit." A battered table painted white with mismatched chairs sat in the middle of the break room at the back. Bree sat at the table while Anu poured them both a cup of coffee then joined her. "So, I think there is something more on your mind this morning than finding Fay's body. I'm here if you wish to talk."

"You always are," Bree said with a fond smile. "Mason told you it might be murder, right?"

Anu's blue eyes saddened. "Yes, he told me this grim news, though he tried to downplay it."

"You realize it has to be someone we know."

Anu nodded, and a shadow crossed her face. "I cannot imagine any of our friends committing such a crime."

"Everyone wears a mask, Anu. Everyone but you, that is. Sometimes I look at my friends and wonder what they really think and whether they're hiding something important from me."

"What has caused this cynicism, eh?" Anu shook her head. "It saddens me, *kulta*. Do you have suspects yet? Hilary mentioned no one."

"Several come to my mind. I haven't discussed it with Mason yet, but I couldn't sleep last night for worrying about which of my friends could have done something like this." It was after two the last time she'd looked at the clock.

"Maybe it was an outsider, someone she met while climbing."

"It's a possibility," Bree said softly. "I hope that's the case."

"You have someone in mind, I can see this." Anu wore a troubled frown.

"We ran into Kade Matthews just before we found her body. He seemed on edge." As soon as the words were out of her mouth, she wished she could snatch them back.

"Kade is like a rock. I cannot believe this of him," Anu said slowly. "He could have taken his sister to live with him in Yellowstone or on to his new post in California, but he honored his mother's request to let Lauri graduate here. A man like that does not murder."

Bree wished she could be so certain. "I'm supposed to meet him and Naomi at Donovan's house after school to help out a bit. I'll see if I can find out anything from him. I hope you're right."

"Read Psalm 112 when you can, my Bree. From the Scriptures we can learn discernment. We must pray and ask God to open our eyes to truth."

Somehow when Anu spoke of God, Bree did not bristle the way she did when Naomi mentioned him. "You are my rock," she said. "I couldn't have made it through the last year without you."

Anu leaned forward and touched Bree's cheek. "This worries me, *kulta*. Always you fear to break away from me, to face life by yourself. I see the way you hold your tongue when you wish to say what you really think to Hilary. I see how you barricade yourself in your home and fear to make new friends. If you speak your mind, you won't lose the love of your family and friends. But even if you do, loss is part of life."

"But—" Bree started to protest, but Anu shook her head gently.

"You hold so tightly because you have lost so much, but day by day I see the Bree who first came to us—the one who was not afraid to experience life—shrink into this small, driven mouse who lives only to search for a family who will never return to her. You must go on, Bree. You must let go of your fear of the future." Anu leaned forward, her voice urgent.

"How?" Bree whispered. "Hilary—"

"You must tell Hilary it is over, that you will no longer cater to her demands. I have some money to invest. I want you to start a search-and-rescue training facility. You love dogs and helping others. Reach out and take charge of your future, *kulta.* Find a reason to go forward and no longer look back. You are young, Bree, too young to sit and mourn over a life that is gone."

Something broke within her, and Bree put her hands over her face and wept. Vaguely aware of Anu kneeling beside her, she turned to her comforting arms and wept for the life that would never be. Yet when her cry was over, she felt different, less fragmented.

She pulled away from Anu and stared into her eyes. "You're right," she said. "I must let go and go on. A training facility!" A huge grin stretched across her face. "That's a dream come true, Anu. Do you know how much I love you? You're the mother I wish I'd had growing up."

Anu, tears in her eyes, stood and touched Bree's hair. "I could not love you more if you were a child born from my own body. Now this is enough emotion for one day. We have work to do. Come."

*B*ree's day rushed by. As she worked, her mind evaluated then rejected most of the suspects in Fay's death. It was a puzzle too hard for her.

Just before three, she hung up her work smock, said good-bye to Anu, and drove to the Blue Bonnet.

"Ready for some cleaning?" Bree asked as Naomi climbed into Bree's Jeep.

"Sure thing," Naomi said, setting a bucket of cleansers and rags on the floor. "You look happy today."

"It's been a good day. Busy but good." She paused then pushed on. "Anu wants me to give up the search, to start a training center for search-and-rescue dogs."

The dazed expression on Naomi's face made Bree laugh. "I'm thinking about it, but I don't know if I can yet."

"The day will have to come, Bree. I'm not trying to push you, but you have to face facts sooner or later."

"You sound like Anu. Are the two of you conspiring?"

"She's smarter than I am," Naomi said with a light laugh. "But this is something even I can see. You're still young. Someday you might want to remarry and have more children."

Bree began to shake her head, but Naomi cut her off. "I know you're not ready for that yet, but you have a future, Bree. All it takes is for you to recognize that fact and step out to meet it."

Bree didn't know what to say. "This must be the right house," she said, relieved to hear that her voice was calm and steady. "Emily and Timmy are in the front yard. Looks like Kade and his sister are here too." She swung the Jeep into the driveway behind Kade's truck and killed the engine.

Naomi sighed but said no more. They got out and opened the door for the dogs. The children bounded toward them. Timmy was pale beneath the red blotches left by the insect bites. Emily's hair looked as though it hadn't been combed yet this morning. Poor motherless lambs. Bree had been right to come today. Kade and his sister followed the kids.

Bree hugged Timmy and Emily then put her hand out to greet Kade's sister. "You must be Lauri," she said as the teenage girl came toward her with an eager smile. Bree would have known she was the ranger's sister even if she hadn't been told. Lauri was the feminine version of Kade, right down to the confident way she walked.

His tail wagging, Samson came to Lauri and sniffed her hand. "Hi," Lauri said.

Bree shook her hand. "I'm Bree Nicholls, and this is Naomi Heinonen."

Lauri glanced at Naomi but quickly turned her attention back to Bree. "I read about you in the paper." Lauri ran her fingers through Samson's curly coat. "He's beautiful. This is Samson, right? Can search dogs really follow a person's scent through the air? How long does it take to train them? Do you think I could do it?" The last was said in a breathless rush with a sidelong glance at her brother.

Bree held up her hands. "Whoa. One question at a time."

Lauri flushed. "Sorry. I've just been interested in search dogs forever."

Charley nosed against her for his share of attention, and Lauri obliged. "You boys are heroes," she crooned.

"Don't encourage them," Bree told her lightly.

"It's so cool how you found these kids," Lauri said. "I wish I could do something like that."

"Do you have a dog?"

"No. Kade is afraid a dog will chase his precious wildlife," Lauri said with a glance of resentment at her brother.

Bree smiled. "They can be trained not to chase animals."

"I like your sweatshirt," Kade said.

Bree glanced down. The sweatshirt said JUST TRY TO HIDE on the front and KITCHIGAMI K-9 SAR on the back. "Thanks." She turned. "Let me get our stuff from the Jeep. Can you kids watch the dogs while we work inside?" she asked Emily.

Emily nodded vigorously. "Our backyard is fenced. We can play there. Daddy brought us home a Frisbee to play with. Do Samson and Charley like Frisbees?"

"They'll chase you down and take it from you," Naomi told her. She reached into the car for a beat-up disk and held it out to Timmy.

"Here, use their Frisbee. Your new one would get chewed up by their teeth." Timmy grabbed it, and Samson rushed up to him and began to lick him on the face. The little boy giggled and threw his arms around the dog's neck.

"Keep them in the yard," Naomi called as Lauri, Emily, and Timmy led the dogs away. She turned and grabbed her bucket of cleaning supplies.

Bree watched them go then turned to smile at Kade. "Lauri seems to be a sweet girl."

He returned her smile, but it seemed forced. "You haven't seen her other side yet. Sometimes I think the Windigos came in the night and left this other girl in my sister's place."

Bree grimaced. "The Windigos wouldn't dare try to consume a teenage girl! Even they would find her tasteless."

Kade didn't smile. His gaze followed Lauri. "I wish I knew what to do with her."

Bree handed him the vacuum. "As another female, I can tell you there's nothing you can do but love her and be patient. What is she— sixteen or so?"

Kade nodded. "Sixteen going on thirty."

"It's a hard age," Naomi said.

"You're telling me!" Kade hefted the vacuum and followed the two women across the front yard. "When will Donovan be home?"

"About five forty-five." Bree pushed open the door and stepped inside. She blinked at the chaos. Clothes were strewn around the furniture and floor like gaily colored confetti. Her sneakers stuck to some substance on the entry linoleum. A tower of newspapers leaned precariously against the side of a recliner, and a toy train lay like a miniature wreck at the foot of the burgundy sofa. The carpet looked as if it hadn't been vacuumed in weeks.

"Holy cow," Kade whispered behind her. He set the vacuum on the floor. "Where do we start?"

"Do we even want to start?" Naomi asked.

"I've seen worse," Bree said. She set her pail of cleaners on the floor. "Raccoons had been living in the lighthouse when Rob and I bought it. Believe me, we can do this."

"Speak for yourself," Kade muttered.

Bree sent him a challenging look. "You a quitter?"

His answering scowl reminded her of a little boy who had been dared to jump from the top of the monkey bars, and she had to remind herself he was a possible suspect in Fay's murder.

"Just tell me what to do," he snapped.

"I brought some laundry baskets. Get them out of the Jeep and pile everything on the floor into them. We can sort the stuff by the rooms they go in. Then, Kade, you can dust and vacuum while I tackle the kitchen. Naomi, you take the baskets and start the laundry then try to find where the toys and other things go when you clean the bedrooms. I'd guess the bedsheets haven't been changed in weeks, so let's do that too."

Kade nodded. "This is going to take all night."

"It doesn't have to be perfect. We won't clean drawers or kitchen cupboards. You'll be surprised at how fast it goes." Naomi pulled yellow plastic gloves from her bucket.

Bree carried her supplies into the kitchen. Dishes covered every surface in the kitchen. Cheerios crunched underfoot, and ants congregated over a pile of sugar on the floor. How could Donovan allow the children to live like this?

Even as the condemnation crossed her mind, she gave a slight shake of her head. She well remembered the days and weeks she'd been sunk in despair herself. Dishes had piled in the sink, and she'd only washed them when the cupboards were empty of clean ones. It would have been an overwhelming job for a father. Two children, a business to run—no wonder Donovan hadn't been able to face it all.

Ant spray first. Rummaging in the cabinet above the sink, she pulled out a can of insecticide and sprayed the ants. Once they were dead, she cleaned them up and tossed the soiled paper towel in the trash. After loading the dishwasher, she washed the dishes that wouldn't fit. By the time she'd mopped the floor, Bree's spirits had lifted with the sheer joy of restoring calm to chaos. She tackled the bathrooms next, and the satisfaction she felt when that job was finished had nothing to do with pride in her job. And it all had taken only two hours.

She found Naomi folding clean clothes in the laundry room. "I got the bedrooms in some semblance of order," she said. "There's not a trace of Donovan's ex-wife in the bedroom."

Bree grinned at the triumph in her voice. "Don't go thinking you'll just move your stuff right in. You've got to convince him you're not like other women first. Oh—and *marry* him, of course."

"I'm working on it," Naomi said.

"Oh?"

"I said I'm working on it. When I have something to report, you'll be the first to know."

Bree laughed. "I think I'll order supper from the Suomi."

"Anything to get out of cooking," Naomi said.

Bree laughed again and went to find Kade while Naomi went upstairs for another load of laundry. She walked into the hall and found Kade holding a skateboard over his shoulder as he surveyed the closet—a jumble of boots, gloves, bent wire hangers, a skateboard with two wheels, and winter coats in disarray. Dust balls like billowing clouds stood guard over the strange assortment of items.

"What a mess," Bree said.

A wire hanger caught on Kade's jeans when he turned toward her, and he grimaced. "I figured I'd better do it, or you'd think you had to. After that bathroom, I thought you needed a break."

Bree gave a mock shudder. "Little boys don't have the best aim, do they?"

"I wouldn't know," Kade said, deadpan.

Bree laughed, the tension she felt around him easing. "What's with the skateboard? You're holding it like you want to bean someone." She wasn't entirely certain she was joking. Though she admired him for his fortitude today, she still regarded him with some suspicion. Everyone said it was impossible to suspect him, and she wanted to believe in his innocence, but the ugly picture of Fay's dead body haunted her.

He glanced at the battered skateboard in his hand. "I think someone already used it for that. Too bad Fay didn't have it with her."

Bree's merriment faded. "Sorry," Kade said. "I guess we joke about things we don't understand."

"I always thought things like that didn't happen in Rock Harbor," Bree said. Chilled, she wrapped her arms around herself. "When Rob and I were deciding where we wanted to raise our family, that was the determining factor. We wanted Davy to have what we had—the safety to play along the sidewalk with his bike and the freedom to toss a Frisbee to Samson in the front yard without one of us standing guard. How sad something like this had to happen here." She bit her lip at all she'd revealed. He had a way of getting past her suspicions.

Kade shrugged. "Maybe it's not what it seems. The blood could be a deer or something."

Was he trying to redirect her line of thinking? She shook her head. "Samson alerted on the blood. It's Fay's. He's as good as any DNA test."

"Maybe it was an accident, and the person didn't want to admit what they'd done." Kade knelt to reach the back of the closet.

Bree watched him a moment. He liked her now; did she want to run the risk of losing that by asking hard questions? Anu had said she needed to let go of that fear, that it was what kept her isolated. Be yourself, Anu had said. But Bree wasn't sure who she was anymore. She took a deep breath.

"You were there; did you see anything?" That came out wrong, full of accusation.

"You suspect me?" His eyebrows shot up.

She'd gone this far, she might as well finish. "Should I? You were there that night. I saw you. And you seemed ill at ease."

His lips compressed to a thin line, and his nostrils flared. "If you mistrust me, what am I doing here?"

"I thought you were helping out the kids." Anu was right—it felt great to speak up instead of holding back her thoughts. "Who is Eric? I saw you talking to him at Hilary's party."

His shoulders stiff, Kade turned away and grabbed the vacuum. "My cousin. Now, if you'll excuse me, I need to get back to work so I can leave. I wouldn't want you to think you were in danger."

His cousin. All the more reason to try to help him. They'd argued at the party, possibly about Fay. Did their confrontation have anything to do with her death? "Was your cousin having an affair with Fay?"

Kade turned back around, his eyes dark with anger. "I still think you're jumping to conclusions," he said coldly. "At least wait until the coroner's report comes back."

Bree shook her head. "I don't need the coroner's report to know the truth that there's a killer in our town."

"Killer. You seem set on using that term. You can't know that, Bree."

"I know it," she said firmly. "I trust Samson. Someone killed her, either deliberately or accidentally." She didn't want it to be Kade, she realized. In spite of her suspicions, she liked him.

Naomi came down the stairs, and they both turned. "I'm bushed," she said. "But Donovan will be happy when he sees the house." Pride gave a lilt to her words.

Bree grinned. "This doesn't look like the same place, does it?" Every surface shone with cleanliness. "I was going to cook dinner," she explained to Kade, "but I just ordered it from the café instead. You want to go pick it up for us?"

"I suppose."

She could tell he was still miffed. Well, he could just live with it.

Maybe it had been a small step for her today to actually question him, but it sure felt good. Anu would be proud.

"We done here?" he asked.

"I think so," Bree said.

"I'll go get the food." He grabbed his coat from the sofa, but before he opened the front door, the back door slammed, and Emily raced in with Timmy on her heels. Lauri followed with both dogs. Her face was red with exertion, and she looked happy and carefree.

"We're starved," Emily announced.

Naomi went to Emily and put her arms around her, but the little girl jerked away and went to Bree. Bree's gaze took in Naomi's agonized expression. She patted Emily and stepped away.

"Kade is going to pick up supper at the café. When your daddy gets home, you can all eat together. How about a cookie to tide you over until then?" She went to the cookie jar.

Emily's wide eyes began to turn pink at the edges, and her lower lip trembled. "I want you to be my mommy," she said.

Bree swallowed and tried to maintain her composure. She attempted to smile, but her lips just trembled. Blinking furiously, she managed a smile. "You're a sweet girl, Emily."

Kade moved between them, and Bree was grateful for the interruption. Scooping up Emily, he hugged her then perched her on his shoulders.

"You can go with me to get the food, then you can watch for your daddy. I bet he'll think you did all this work by yourself." He carried her through the door.

Timmy began to wail to go along, but Bree couldn't force herself to go to him. One step forward and two steps back.

The autumn days were lengthening. Rachel stood at the door on the moist October day and watched a ruffled grouse run through the aspens. She had trouble keeping track of the days, but she thought this was a Tuesday. Her larder proclaimed the necessity of a trip to town.

"You stay here." Rachel tousled Sam's unruly hair. Choppy from her inexpert use of the scissors, his red hair stood up like a rooster's comb. She smiled, but there was no answering grin on his pale face, just a solemn nod. Her smile faded.

Rachel knew he was used to the drill by now, though she worried every time she had to leave him. This would be the last time though. When these supplies were gone, she would take Sam to town, find out who he was. It was time. No one could blame her; after all, she'd saved his life. His limp was evidence of that. They would all applaud her for saving him.

For a moment she allowed herself to imagine the acclaim, the way the papers would laud her as a hero. A smile tugged at her lips. Maybe the news story would reach those who had accused her so unjustly. They would see how wrong they were. All her life people had said she didn't have good judgment, that she didn't think things through. She'd finally prove them wrong.

But what if this new story brought out all the hounds onto her trail again? She'd been cleared of all wrongdoing, but that hadn't stopped the nursing home from firing her and her neighbors from snubbing her. Her surfacing would be fresh fodder for the news mill.

Maybe they would bring charges against her because she hadn't returned him before now. You couldn't trust law enforcement. Look what they'd done to her. Hounding her out of a job she loved.

Her face tightened at the memories. One false story, and a career of thirty years had been swept away like tumbled debris in a flood. It wasn't fair; life had never been fair. But no, not this time. This time she would be rewarded with praise and honor. Sammy's mother would lavish attention on her son's savior.

She chewed on her lip. Maybe there was no mother to go back to. His father had been dead when she'd found the plane, and it had been a year. They'd just take him and put him in foster care, and if anyone knew the hell that could be, it was Rachel. She and her brother had been shunted from one home to another throughout their troubled childhood.

Her gaze traveled to Sam. He was always frightened. Rachel despaired of ever hearing him squeal and play like a normal child. The most animated she'd seen him had been when those children shadhowed up. She frowned. She'd had entirely too much contact with the outside world this week. First that snoopy woman climber, then those children. And that man at the mine had seen her too. What if he came looking for her?

She'd found a haven here, a place of peace and rest for her and Sammy both. But it looked like they would be driven from their safe harbor, just as she'd been driven from Detroit. What if someone came before they were ready to leave? Would they suspect her of kidnapping the boy?

"Sammy, what's my name?" she asked slowly, an idea beginning to take shape. If busybodies believed he was her son, they would be less suspicious.

His forehead wrinkled, then he shook his head, and she realized he'd had no need to call her anything before now. "It's Mother. Can you say 'Mother'?"

"Mother," Sam repeated. "Is that like mommy? I had a mommy once."

A shaft of jealousy surprised her with its intensity. She was the one who had taken care of Sam. Where was his mother? She hadn't come looking for him. "It's kind of like that," Rachel told him. "I take care of you like a mommy, don't I? I feed you and bring you treats from town."

Sam nodded.

"Can you remember to call me Mother? That's my name. Mother."

He nodded. "Mother," he repeated again.

"I'll be back by lunchtime. Don't open the door to anyone." She waited until he nodded again before she left the cabin, pulling the door tight behind her.

Dry leaves crunched underfoot, and a blue jay chattered angrily at her from the tall pine over her head. She would miss these woods. But it was time to take up her life again. Hers and Sam's. The furor had died down enough, and she could surely find another nursing job. But how did she go about finding Sam's family?

It took Rachel nearly two hours to walk to Rock Harbor. She knew she was close when she began to hear the sound of the waves and the gong of the fog bell out in Lake Superior. She quickened her step. As she entered town, she kept her floppy leather hat pulled down low over her face and avoided looking anyone in the eye.

The bell tinkled on the door as she pushed into Rock Harbor General Store. Lars Thorensen wiped his hands on his massive white apron and nodded to her. Rachel avoided his inquisitive gaze. The last thing she needed was to get into a conversation with the loquacious Lars. He could talk until her eyes glazed.

The shop had changed little since its inception in 1868 and still resembled a general store straight out of *Mayberry RFD,* Rachel's favorite show of all time. Narrow rows of basic food items stood in the center of the store. The counters and shelves that lined the walls were filled with fabric and notions, a few toiletry items such as toothpaste and deodorant, and glass jars of candy. The floor was made of wide boards of unfinished native timber. Rachel almost expected to see Sheriff Andy Taylor come strolling through the doors that led to the storeroom. Being here always made her nervous for that very reason. After her one and only brush with the law, the thought of even talking with the sheriff made her throat close up.

"I was beginning to think you lit out for other parts, ma'am," Lars said. His blond mustache quivered, and his pale blue eyes roamed over Rachel's face with an avid curiosity.

Rachel ducked her head and turned away to find what she needed. The last thing she wanted was to deal with a nosy Parker like Lars digging into her business. In a frenzy to be done with the owner's prying eyes, she hurried along, depositing items in her basket. She knocked a tin of cocoa to the floor near the checkout counter and Lars bent to retrieve it, but she snatched it up before he could touch it.

"Where'bouts in the North Woods you come from, ma'am? You don't seem to get to town much."

Rachel compressed her lips. She wasn't about to indulge in chatter. She'd learned the hard way not to trust anyone. Maybe if she refused to speak to him at all, he'd get the picture.

The bell on the door tinkled again, and two men entered the store. Rachel's eyes widened at the shiny star on the man's shirt. Blood thundered in her ears. She couldn't let the sheriff see her. She only hoped those lost kids hadn't told the authorities about her. She turned and went down an aisle then stooped to look at cake mixes.

"Howdy, Sheriff," Lars said. "I was hoping you'd stop by today— I just got in some thimbleberry jam Hilary was asking me about last week. It's from this year's berries."

"That's why I'm here. Hilary used all hers up on the campaign dinner, and she wanted to make some thimbleberry tarts for Thanksgiving. How many jars do you have?"

"Five right now, with more promised from one of my distributors by the end of the week."

"I'd better take all of it. At ten dollars a jar, I hope she appreciates it."

Her fingers tightly clamped on the basket, Rachel gauged the distance to the door. If she could just slip out unseen. But no, that wouldn't work. Lars would likely accuse her of stealing. He knew she had come in to get supplies. Maybe the sheriff would just finish his business and leave. Rachel pressed a hand against the galloping beat of her heart.

The old cash register clanged as Lars rang up the sheriff's purchase. "Any news on Fay's death? I hear tell you're thinking it might be murder."

The sheriff cleared his throat. When he spoke, his voice was sharp with dismay. "Where'd you hear that, Lars? We haven't even got autopsy results yet, let alone DNA testing. Don't go starting any rumors. I get enough of that on a daily basis."

"DNA on the blood by the road?"

"You know I can't discuss the case," the sheriff said. "And I don't know where you're getting your information, but I'd appreciate it if you zipped your lip about this until we know more."

"Is Steve a suspect?" Lars seemed undeterred by the sheriff's rebuke.

The sheriff gave a heavy sigh. "I'm not going to discuss it with you, Lars. I just remembered something else Hilary needed." His footsteps echoed against the wood floor as he approached Rachel's aisle.

She was trapped and she knew it. The best she could do was to face him and not let him see her fear. She rose with a box of devil's food cake mix in her hand.

His gaze touched her face, skittered on, then jerked back to look at her again. "Sheriff Mason Kaleva, ma'am. You look familiar. You just move to town?"

"No, no, just a summer visitor," she babbled. "I have a cabin in the woods."

"Whereabouts?"

She could see the suspicion on his face. He probably had old wanted posters plastered all over his office. Panic froze her.

"Sheriff, we got a call," the deputy said.

The sheriff's frown deepened. He gave her a final stare and turned to exit with the deputy.

Rachel let out the breath she'd been holding. Reprieved, but for how long? Now, more than ever, she had to get out of the area.

The bell on the door clanged, and she breathed a sigh of relief.

Murder. She shivered. They'd already figured out that much. How much longer before they knew all of it? She needed to get away before the trail led right to her cabin door. She had been wrong to think she could bring Sam back to a small town like this. No, she needed to stay invisible. Maybe she could turn him over to authorities in a large city like Chicago. They could track down his mother and reunite him from there. At least Rachel herself would be out of the limelight. The thought of having her face plastered on the front page again was enough to give her hives.

She finished filling her basket then carried it to the counter. The store carried an assortment of Michigan newspapers plus the *Chicago Tribune*. She grabbed one as Lars began to ring up her purchases. Lars seemed to sense her agitation, for he stared at her as he packed her supplies in the knapsack she gave him. She ducked her head so all he could see was the top of her hat. Nosy old man. Why couldn't he mind his own business? That was the trouble with a small town like Rock Harbor. People felt they had the right to pry.

Rachel knew people thought her a strange hermit of a woman, but why couldn't they see beneath her old clothes? She had the same hopes and desires they had. A place to call home, a family, peace, contentment. She thought she'd found all that here in these North Woods, but she could already feel it sliding from her grip. Seizing true peace was like trying to catch the morning mist over Lake Superior.

Her revised plans racing through her head, she nodded her thanks at Lars, took her knapsack, then rushed toward the door.

*W*hat a change to have something to look forward to. Bree sat on the couch with her legs under her and pored over a real estate book. Where could she buy land for her training center? For the first time, she saw how the publicity that came Samson's way could benefit her. An old schoolhouse was for sale about five miles out of town. It came with ten acres that ranged from meadow to forest. That might work. She'd have to call the agent and take a look.

In spite of her enthusiasm for the project, Bree couldn't seem to settle tonight. Staying home with a frozen pizza didn't sound at all appealing. Anu would be glad to have her come by for supper, or she could go to Naomi's, but neither prospect felt right. Her thoughts drifted to Fay's death. The information Fay might have had about the cabin in the woods was gone with her. But if she could track Fay's movements for the past few weeks, maybe she could get a feel for what quadrant to search. She couldn't imagine there really was a plane seat outside that cabin, but she had no other direction to look right now. At least it was a goal.

Samson needed to be fed, then she could go to town and see if she could find out anything. She fed the dog then got her coat. "Want to go out, Samson?"

His ears pricked at the word "out." He barked and ran to the back door. "No, we're going to town," she told him. She could stop by the sheriff's office to see if he'd heard anything. The blood test might be back by now. At work today, she'd hoped Mason might stop by with news, but there had been no sign of him.

The air held a hint of moisture that promised rain or snow. October was not too soon to get major snow, but they'd been lucky this year. The stars were like ship lights bouncing off the black waves of the lake. The wind had picked up, and the crash of the waves on Lake Superior was oddly soothing. Rock Harbor's streets were deserted, a pleasant state of affairs after summer's high traffic.

Visitors loved the quaintness of the town with its Victorian buildings and community activities. But for a time, the residents owned the town again. Rock Harbor had "nine months of winter and three months of company," the saying went, and that was pretty accurate. Tourists came for the fishing and hunting, for the natural beauty of this land of waterfalls, and for the festivals with their Finnish or Cornish food and fun.

Many people in the Midwest never seemed to realize the enormity of the North Woods. And it wasn't just the miles and miles of pristine forest, it was the heavy snow and frigid temperatures that hindered Bree's efforts to find her family.

Rock Harbor County Jail sat stolidly in the center of downtown, across the street from the Copper Club Tavern. Built five years ago, its white stone edifice seemed out of place amid the gracious brick buildings that lined downtown. She opened the door, and Doug Montgomery looked up from his perusal of a fishing magazine. The desk was battered with gouges made by countless deputies over the past fifty years. Montgomery eased his bulk back into the worn leather chair and gazed at her over the top of his spectacles.

His oversized head sported a great thatch of thick blond hair like some Nordic warrior of long ago, though the resemblance stopped there. The blue eyes peering at her were too dulled with apathy to ever envision sailing across the ocean in an ancient longboat. Bree had to wonder what criteria the sheriff used to hire his deputies. But maybe in a town the size of Rock Harbor, Doug was one of the best he could find.

"What can I do for you, Mrs. Nicholls?" he said.

"I don't suppose the sheriff is around?" she asked.

Doug shifted in his seat. "Nope. He left about an hour ago."

"Any news on the blood we found by the road?"

He scratched his head. "I don't know if I'm supposed to let out that information or not."

"Come on, Deputy, I'm the sheriff's sister-in-law. I found the blood." Bree took a step closer to the desk and tried to peer over the deputy's arm at the papers lying scattered under his meaty hand.

He covered the papers with an arm then slowly lifted it again. "Well, I guess that's all right then. The blood seems to be hers, all right. At least it's the same blood type. We don't have the DNA back yet."

Samson had been right. Bree's initial elation faded, and her stomach roiled. Murder in Rock Harbor, or manslaughter at the very least. "That means Fay didn't die of a climbing accident," she said slowly.

"Looks that way," the deputy said. "The sheriff called in the state police forensic experts. They're coming over tomorrow."

"What time?" She intended to tag along and see what they had to say.

"About eight."

"Thanks, Deputy." Snapping her fingers at Samson, Bree turned and went to the door. Outside, the evening winds had picked up, and she pulled the hood of her sweater up over her head. Her hunger faded in light of this more pressing news. If it hadn't been so dark, she would have been tempted to go out to the site and poke around. Instead, she settled for a pensive walk around the quiet streets.

By the time she'd crossed the courthouse square for the fifth time, her head was clearer. The neon light above the Suomi Café glared through the gathering mist along Kitchigami Street like a lighthouse guiding the ships to port. The aroma of fish stew and cabbage rolls wafted into the street, and her hunger raged to the fore again.

Across the street she saw Steve Asters exit the bank. Bree glanced at her watch. Seven o'clock. He was working late. Steve locked the door behind him then came toward her. Even from here, she could see the way his shoulders slumped.

Bree watched him for a moment before walking toward him. "Hi, Steve," she said softly.

His head jerked up as if pulled by an invisible rope. The pallor on his face deepened when he saw her, then color flooded into his skin. "What do you want?" he muttered, his gaze wandering back to the ground.

"Want to join me for a sandwich and coffee?"

"No thanks. I couldn't eat anything." He looked at the ground. "Everyone looked at me today like they think if I really loved her, I would be home grieving. Well, I can't stand the empty house. Is that so hard to understand? I don't know how I'll get through the funeral tomorrow."

"Have you talked to the sheriff?"

"He stopped in to see me about an hour ago." His gaze probed her face. "He said it looks like the blood you found by the road is Fay's. That means someone killed her, doesn't it?"

"It still could have been accidental, a hit-and-run driver maybe."

"You don't believe that," he said.

His shoulders slumped even lower, until Bree wasn't sure he wouldn't simply slide to the ground. In spite of herself, she couldn't help the niggle of sympathy she felt for him. But maybe it was all an act. She, of all people, knew how convincingly a man could lie.

She narrowed her eyes. "No, I don't believe she was hit by a car. And even if it did happen that way, it's still manslaughter, especially since whoever killed her arranged her body at the foot of the cliff." That's what had bothered her, she suddenly realized. Fay had been arranged like a mannequin. Her body had been staged, even to the arm flung out as if to try to catch herself.

"Well, it wasn't me!" Steve finally seemed to recover some life and straightened his back to stare her squarely in the face.

She'd always liked Steve, but then, whoever said she was a good judge of men? She'd laugh if it weren't such serious business.

The wind blew tendrils of hair across Bree's eyes, and she brushed them away. "Let's get out of this wind. You can at least drink some coffee."

He shrugged then followed her into the café, where she led him to a back table.

Molly came to the table. "What'll it be, Bree?" She barely looked at Steve.

"I'll have some cabbage rolls and fish stew," Bree said. "And maybe some lingonberries for dessert. Oh, and a coffee—for Steve too."

Molly wrote down the order then nodded and hurried away, returning moments later with the coffee pot. She filled their cups without comment.

"See what I mean?" Steve said. "Everyone looks at me like they think I'll pull a knife on them any second. I'll probably have to move away."

Bree dug a handful of pistachio nuts out of her pocket. "Want some?" she asked. He shook his head, and she split a shell with her thumbnail and popped the nut into her mouth. "The sheriff will find out who did it," she told him.

Steve gave a bitter laugh. "Mason's too wrapped up in the election campaign to care. As long as he has a suspect—namely, me—that's all he'll care about. I've always laughed about small-town gossip. But now the finger is pointed at me, and it's not fair! I loved Fay. We had our problems, including money. I'm not denying that. But that doesn't mean I killed her." He wrapped his fingers around his coffee cup and stared at the liquid.

Bree stared at him. Could he know something about the location of the cabin? He was her only source of information. "Do you know where she'd been hiking recently? She mentioned seeing a cabin with an old airplane seat in a ravine near it. It's probably nothing, but I'd like to check it out. I just don't have any idea of where to look."

Lost in his own thoughts, Steve didn't answer for a long moment. He finally blinked and looked up. "She never talked much about her hiking."

"Think," Bree urged.

He took a gulp of coffee. "I think maybe she mentioned hiking out near Ten Mile Peak. But she was all over the place. I can't even remember when she said something about it. Sorry."

At least it was a start. She wouldn't be searching totally blind.

Steve stared at her for a long moment, then his face grew thoughtful. "You could figure it out, Bree. Fay always said you were smarter than the rest of the town rolled together." He leaned across the table, and his voice grew excited. "Will you poke around for me?"

Committing herself to Steve—who she still wasn't convinced had nothing to do with Fay's death—was more than she was prepared to do. "I'm just a search-and-rescue worker," Bree protested. "The sheriff has called in forensic help. They'll figure it out."

Anger flashed across his face. He stood slowly, as if he wasn't sure his legs would support him. "So you won't help me either," he said dully. "I might as well have the sheriff lock me up." He turned and rushed from the restaurant.

Bree watched him go. There seemed to be a desperation about him—a desperation that could be caused by guilt.

*T*he macadam road narrowed until it was little more than a track through the thick forest. The moist scent of leaves and mold drifted to Bree's nose as she and Samson walked along the side of the road behind the state police forensic experts. She'd been surprised to find that the lead was a woman. Somehow she'd expected a thin man with spectacles and an attitude. Too much TV, she guessed.

The reality was Janna Kievari, a woman of about forty with soft brown hair styled in a becoming chin-length bob. With steel-blue eyes set above a sharp nose, her fine bone structure proclaimed Finnish heritage more loudly than did her name. Dressed in tan wool slacks and a black-and-tan wool blazer with sensible hiking shoes, her no-nonsense manner appealed to Bree. This woman emanated a fearlessness Bree intended to emulate. Janna wouldn't be afraid to ask questions, to stir the pot even if it angered someone. And neither would Bree.

Mason hadn't objected to her request to tag along, but Bree suspected it was because the sheriff was relieved to have any kind of help. Rock Harbor was not a metropolis of criminal activity, and she knew Mason felt out of his element at the nature of this crime committed under his watch.

But by the time Janna's team had collected samples and departed for Houghton, Bree knew no more than she did before they arrived. She'd hoped for some riveting piece of evidence that would indicate what had really happened. The only thing Janna said was that it didn't appear to be a hit-and-run accident. There were no impressions left by skidding tires, and the spot where they'd found the blood and hair was too far from the road.

Bree had hoped it would turn out to be just that. Someone covering up an accident would have been better than the alternative. She shivered. It was the sheriff's problem though, not hers. Her job was to trace Fay's path the last few weeks and find the woman in the cabin. Useless as it was probably going to be, it was becoming an obsession.

She glanced at her watch. If she hurried, she could get in a couple of hours of searching before the funeral. Samson nudged her hand with his nose, and she absently patted his head. "Ready to search, boy?"

He hunkered down and barked. She opened the Jeep door, and he jumped in. Bree drove out to quadrant sixteen and took Hegg Road to Rock River. Some of the most dramatic scenery in the U.P. could be found here. Volcanic rock outcroppings framed the falls and created a breathtaking 325-foot-deep gorge.

She and Rob used to come here a lot. Staring up at the last traces of fall foliage, the memories washed over her. It was so hard to reconcile the man she loved with what she knew now about his unfaithfulness. In spite of his angry denials, she'd had to face the truth. If he'd come back from the fatal trip, what other excuses would he have offered? She sometimes wondered if she would have forgiven him for Davy's sake and tried to patch up their marriage. Infidelity would be hard to live with. Besides, he might have wanted to marry that Lanna, whoever she was.

Opening the bag, she held it under Samson's nose. Davy's blue shirt, the one with the Superman emblem on the back, had been his favorite piece of apparel. Now it was merely the search article of choice. Sometimes Bree wanted to take it out of its protective bags and bury her face in it, breathe in the scent that had been her son, that aroma of mud pies, Play-Doh, and candy.

She grimaced. This was her new life now—no more dwelling on the past. Samson's great plume of a tail wagged, and he barked as if to tell her he was ready to find Davy. Though she always came out here with fresh hope, it was getting harder and harder to sustain that hope in the face of constant defeat. She would probably always search once in a while as she trained dogs in the woods, but this quadrant would be the last for a formal search. Bree closed the bag and tossed it back in the car.

"Search, Samson," she told the dog. He leaped away in a bound and raced toward the woods with his nose held high.

For a moment Bree thought he really had a scent. Her heart gave a great leap of joy, and she ran after him. Maybe today was the day. Samson seemed driven as he headed for a stand of white pine. The towering trees blocked out the sunshine, and the two raced over a thick carpet of pine needles. The softness underfoot reminded Bree of a plush carpet. Her focus was sharpened by the scent of pine.

On the other side of the pines, the forest changed to oak and hickory. Samson paused and seemed to peer through the gloom of deep woods. His tail drooped, and Bree's spirits plummeted with it. He didn't have a clue where to go next.

"Go on, boy," she urged. "Find Davy."

Samson wagged his tail and started off again, but she could tell he was wandering aimlessly, just as he'd done every time they'd searched for the past year.

She and Samson thrashed their way through thickets of brambles and vines for nearly two hours before calling it a day. In the clearing by the Jeep, Bree played fetch with the dog for a few minutes to encourage him before heading to town. She would be expected at Fay's funeral.

Would Fay's murderer be there too? She ran through the possible suspects in her mind. Eric was at the top of her list. Then Steve. And what about Fay's uncle Lawrence? It had sounded like he was involved with the mob or something sinister. Could he have been so desperate to get his hands on the mine that he killed her? Kade was still a possibility, and Hilary too, though Bree didn't want to consider either of them as candidates.

She stopped at the lighthouse to drop off Samson and change her clothes before driving to the church. Rock Harbor Community Church stood on Quincy Hill overlooking downtown. Built in 1886, it stood guard like a sentinel over Rock Harbor. The church was already filled with people when Bree walked in. Scanning the rows of pews, she saw Anu's fair hair. Bree walked over and slipped between Anu and Mason. She craned her neck to look around. Naomi and her mother sat on the left in the third pew from the front, and Bree wondered if that was their regular pew. Many of the people crowding the pews attended regularly. The last time Bree had been here was for Rob and Davy's memorial service. The need to escape made her tug at her skirt self-consciously.

Fay's casket sat at the front of the sanctuary. The lid was closed, and Bree was thankful for that. The minister droned on, and she began to fidget. She hoped something would happen that might reveal who had killed Fay, but the service progressed without incident.

Kade's cousin Eric, dressed in a T-shirt and black leather jacket, wept openly in the pew in front of Bree. His grief seemed almost too overwhelming to be real, and she wondered again if all the gossip in town was true and Fay had been having an affair with him. Maybe she should ask him.

Palmer and Lily Chambers were on the other side of the church, and Lily gave Bree a small wave. Bree smiled back, then her gaze roamed the room again. She glanced at Hilary and found her sister-in-law's gaze fastened on the back of Steve's head. The last person Bree wanted to suspect was Hilary, but the questions wouldn't go away. Did she dare ignore them?

Fay's uncle sat on the front row with Steve. Bree thought again of the argument she'd been witness to the night of Hilary's party. Fay's uncle had been afraid Fay's stubbornness would get him killed. Maybe it had gotten Fay killed instead.

Anu pressed her hand against the knee Bree jiggled. "Patience, *kulta*. Soon we will leave and have some food."

Bree stilled her knee. She wanted out of here. Mercifully, the service ended and the people began to file out. Since they were seated near the front, the church was nearly empty by the time Bree and the rest of the Nicholls family reached the door. His eyes bloodshot, Steve stood at the door, accepting condolences. Eric pushed past them and stood with his hands on his hips in front of Steve.

Steve's face twisted into a snarl when he saw Eric. "You've got some nerve coming here," he spit out.

Eric pushed his face in front of Steve's. "Look, I'm the only one here who really loved her for who she was. You make me sick, standing there pretending to mourn her. She never loved you; she just loved your money."

Eric's voice was slurred. Drunk.

Steve's face grew redder and more outraged. He grabbed Eric by his jacket lapels and shook him. Though Eric was smaller, he put his hands up and broke Steve's hold on him with ease.

"The truth is hard to take, isn't it? That was my baby, Steve. How does that make you feel? You aren't man enough to give her a baby."

Mason reached the fracas and grabbed Eric's arm. "I think it's time you left. This is no place for a fight."

Eric tried to jerk his arm out of Mason's grasp, but the burly sheriff was too strong for him. "Whacha hassling me for, Sheriff? There's your man." He pointed an unsteady finger at Steve. "He killed her when he found out she was pregnant with my baby."

"That was *my* baby," Steve shouted. "She told me about you, how you were obsessed and wouldn't leave her alone, that you wanted her to leave me. You probably killed her when she told you she was staying with me."

"I would've convinced her," Eric muttered. "She didn't mean it, and I knew she didn't."

Mason propelled Eric through the door. "Go home and sleep it off," he ordered.

Eric stumbled down the steps, and Bree watched him stagger across the street to the corner of Quincy and Jack Pine Lane. She saw Kade's truck and watched him get out. He reached out to steady Eric then took his arm and propelled him to the truck. Bree hadn't seen Kade at the funeral. She thought again of him emerging from the trees just before Samson found Fay.

She had to find out the truth about Kade, but how? The beautiful Indian summer day seemed dull even in the sunshine. She normally worked at Nicholls's on Wednesdays, but she felt a need to be outside, away from everything. Maybe Naomi would have time to look for the woman at the cabin with her.

"It's such a beautiful day, Anu. Do you mind if I slip out and do a bit of searching? Can you get along without me today?"

"I think it will be a slow day because of the funeral. Go ahead. I will see you tomorrow, *kulta.*"

Bree hugged her, then found Naomi to see if she wanted to come. She did, so they both rushed home to get the dogs. Naomi promised to bring sandwiches and meet her outside in fifteen minutes. Bree put Samson's search vest on him and grabbed her ready-pack. By 2:30 they were in the forest, heading toward Ten Mile Peak.

*O*ctober possessed a special quality of light, Rachel decided. There was a sadness to it too, a knowledge that winter was coming. The deep woods sounds had a frenzy about them, as though all nature realized time was short and it must make the best of the remaining clear, warm days.

She intended to be gone before the worst of the snow fell. The question was where to go. The only family she had in the world was her brother, Frank. He was in Chicago, and Rachel hadn't seen or heard from him in over ten years. It was unlikely he would welcome his long-lost sister, especially after what she'd done.

Rachel glanced out the cabin's kitchen window and saw Sam sitting under a tree. He held out bits of bread in his hand as he tried to coax a chipmunk to come closer. She needed to do better by him. A little boy needed playmates beyond the forest's denizens.

What was she thinking? "That's not my problem unless I keep him," she muttered aloud. Speaking the words seemed to make them take on a life of their own. Her mouth still hung open, and she shut it with a snap. She could keep him. He was young, and he'd soon forget he had any other life before the accident.

A jolt of joy quickened her pulse. Sam would be her own boy. She would finally have a real family. Did she dare do it? She squeezed her eyes shut. One month, that's all she had money for. By Thanksgiving they would have to get out. She turned and shuffled over to the scarred pine table at the other end of the kitchen.

Rachel sat at the table and opened the paper. Turning to the medical jobs section, she began to scan the possible positions. She had her RN license. It needed to be renewed every two years, so it was good for another eight months, and that's what she loved to do. Surely many retirement homes were in desperate need of help. By the time she finished, she had a list of ten possible jobs. There was no time like the present to get started.

She went to her bed and stooped, pulling out a battered manual typewriter from under the rickety cot. A grimy layer of dust coated the keys, but the old workhorse still typed like a champ. She'd done all her homework on it from the time she was in high school. Rachel plunked it on the table then went back for a box of paper. If she could find a job, they could be gone from this place within the month.

Part of her dreaded leaving. The cabin had been her haven, and the thought of facing the world's derision for a woman past her prime made her shudder. But another part of her rejoiced at the knowledge that once she faded into the obscurity of big-city Chicago, no one would ever find Sam. She could quit looking over her shoulder. He would be hers and hers alone.

Closing her eyes, she imagined watching him graduate magna cum laude from some elite college. He would tell the world how he owed everything to his mother, Rachel. Sharing his appreciation for all she'd done for him, he would let her know she'd been the best mother in the world.

She opened her eyes and smiled. Why not? She deserved a son after all she'd been through. And Sam deserved a chance in a big city. This small cabin and the heartache of the first few weeks would fade from his memory, as the pain of childbirth faded once a mother held her newborn child. She and Sam would be reborn in Chicago. And nothing would ever come between them.

After she typed the letters, she stuffed the envelopes. Tomorrow she would take them to town, buy stamps, and send them off. Setting them aside, she rose to prepare lunch for Sam. He loved peanut butter and jelly. She spread it thinly so her supply would last longer and called him in to eat.

Dirt marred his right cheek. Bits of twigs and grass stuck in his hair. "Who was the man?"

Her hand paused in midair, and her pulse fluttered in her throat. She turned to stare at him. "What man?"

"He was here just now. He talked to me."

"I've told you never to speak to strangers!" She gripped his shoulders, and he began to cry and squirm.

"I didn't—he talked to me."

"What did he say?" Her mind reeled feverishly. Was it the man at the mine? They would have to leave *now*.

"He was a hunter, he said. He asked if I'd seen any deer."

"Did you talk to him?" she whispered, though she could read the answer in the way Sam cast his gaze to the floor and shuffled his feet.

"He surprised me," he said. "I couldn't help it."

"Maybe it will be all right," she muttered. "As long as he doesn't shoot his mouth off to everyone in town." Her gaze sharpened, and she looked Sam over closely. His bright red hair would be a giveaway to someone of his true identity. But that was easily fixed. She let her breath out slowly.

"Did the chipmunk come for his supper?"

Sam shook his head. "Marcus still won't come either." He'd been trying to coax his "pet" squirrel to eat from his hand all summer.

She scooped him into her arms. "I know what's wrong, Sammy. They're afraid of your hair."

He touched his hand to his head. "What's wrong with my hair?"

"Nothing's wrong with it. But it's a bright color, and it probably scares them. If we color it, I bet they'll come right to you."

"Can we do it today?" A smile broke across his face.

"I have to go to town, so I'll get some dye for it. We'll just color it brown, and Marcus won't be afraid anymore."

A noise outside drew her attention. "Is that hunter still out there?"

Sam shrugged his small shoulders. "I guess so. He has a red-and-black hat on." She put Sam on the floor and went to the door.

Rachel grabbed her hat and sweater, a shapeless gray garment so full of pills and snags it looked as though it needed to be combed. Slinging it around her shoulders, she threw open the door and hurried into the yard.

A blue jay chattered a warning over her head, and she stared around the yard and into the shadows of the large trees that swallowed up the bright autumn sunshine. A movement caught her eyes, and she stepped hastily in that direction. A red-and-black plaid hat bobbed in the shadows as the man hurried away from the clearing. She followed at a discreet distance. Maybe she could find out who he was.

The leaves overhead blotted out the sunshine. It was colder among the trees, and she was glad she'd thought to grab her sweater. Stepping carefully through the forest, she kept the man's hat in sight. He never turned or looked to the left or the right, which struck her as strange for a hunter, but maybe he had given up for the day.

His stride was quick and confident as though he knew exactly where he was going. Finally, he paused at a large rock near the Kirin Brook. Stooping, he rinsed a handkerchief in the rushing water and mopped his face. As he turned his head to run the hanky over his neck, Rachel saw his face for the first time, and her stomach plunged to her toes.

He'd found her! Rachel didn't see how that was possible. But why else would he be here in her part of the forest? It seemed more than mere coincidence. Now more than ever, it was imperative she get out of these woods before someone else died.

*A*utumn was Kade's favorite season. Fighting black flies in summer, he always longed for the fabulous display of red and gold, the crisp, cool nights, and the rich, earthy odors. Glistening droplets of water brightened the rich hues of fall foliage.

He turned up his jacket collar against the cool dampness and settled more securely in the saddle as his gelding made his way along the path to Eagle Cliff where Fay Asters had been found. The funeral had been two days ago, but the yellow crime-scene tape still fluttered from the trees.

A hawk swooped overhead then dived. Kade heard a squeak as the bird snatched a field mouse in its talons and wheeled away with its prey. Nature could be harsh, but there was a simplicity and rightness to death in this environment.

He heard the leaves rustle ahead of him and urged his horse to break into a trot. Rounding a curve in the path, he found Bree and Samson wandering off the path in a bramble patch. "Finding anything?" he asked.

Bree shook her head and snapped her fingers at Samson. The dog came right to her. A wary look came into her face. "Nothing so far. Fay said she'd seen what looked like an airplane seat near a cabin, but Naomi and I have looked for days and haven't found anything. Fay has exaggerated things like this before, but I have to at least look. Have you seen anything in your treks around?"

Kade shook his head. "Sorry. So if you're looking for the cabin, what are you doing here?" He knew she'd scoured this area already.

"Naomi and I searched the only place Steve knew she'd been and found nothing. Her backpack was never found. I thought maybe Samson could find it. There might be something in there to lead me to the cabin and the person she talked to."

"But if it was usual for her to exaggerate things . . ."

"You never know. Maybe she really did see something."

Kade wasn't sure he wanted her poking around. She might get hurt. "Want some help?"

"I'm not sure where to start. Maybe if I begin where we found Fay's body and work backward, we could find where she was killed. Naomi and Charley are checking down the road."

"I heard forensics confirmed your initial hunches. Pretty impressive. Why were you so sure it wasn't a hit-and-run?" Kade dismounted and tied his horse's reins to a tree.

Bree picked her way through the leaves and brambles to the path where Kade waited. Samson followed. "I don't know; it was just a gut feeling. Besides, why not just leave her? Why run the risk of having someone see Fay being dragged to the cliff? What would she have been doing walking along the road when her car was in the parking lot and the cliff was the opposite direction?"

She had a point.

"Hello up there!"

They both turned to see Naomi and Charley making their way up the slope to join them. Naomi's dark braid hung over one shoulder. Her orange-and-black plaid wool jacket appeared then disappeared through the thick foliage as she scrambled up the slope. Charley gave an excited bark, and Samson scrambled toward him. Nose to nose and tails wagging, the dogs greeted each other.

"Let's check out the cliff face again," Kade suggested. "The pack could be stuck in a crevice or something." He swept aside arching bramble branches and headed that direction without waiting for an answer.

The misty fog began to lighten, and the cliff face rose from the grayness like a blue whale breaching from the sea mist. Sunshine began to filter through the rich hues of orange and gold, and the forest appeared to have gilded edges. The women tramped behind him.

Kade paused a moment to appreciate the beauty. "God sure knows how to create, doesn't he?"

Bree stopped behind him, and he heard her soft intake of breath. "Nature can be awe-inspiring."

"When you look at scenery like this, you know the creation of it had to be a conscious act. The Bible says creation was finger play for God. Did you know that? It makes me wonder what other marvels he's created in the universe."

"He destroys too," Bree said.

Kade swiveled his head at her clipped tone and caught the look of dismay on Naomi's face. So Bree blamed God for the loss of her son and husband. Who was he to judge her though? Maybe he'd react the same way if he ever faced a similar tragedy.

"I'll check out the top of the cliff," Kade said. "Why don't you and Naomi take the dogs and scour the riverbank? A wild animal might have dragged off her backpack. If she brought any food along, it could have tempted a bear or raccoon."

"You're not going to climb the cliff, are you?" Bree's voice rose with dismay.

Her concern warmed Kade. "Do I look that stupid?" He grinned to soften the words. "No, I'll go around to the backside and take the path."

Bree's stance relaxed, and she called Samson. The dog bounded toward her, then she and Naomi headed over the rocks toward the glimmering river.

Kade's breath came hard by the time he'd made his way around the hill and followed the steep but passable path to the top of Eagle Rock. From his vantage point, he could see the sweep of the river and the rounded masses of the trees like great banks of colorful mums.

Bree's suspicion of him bothered him more than he liked to admit, but maybe she had good reason. His thoughts turned to Eric, and he sighed. Things could get ugly.

*W*hy are you walking so fast?"

Naomi's plaintive voice brought Bree up short. She stopped and turned with an apologetic smile. "Sorry. There has to be some clue out here we're missing." She dug a handful of pistachios out of her backpack. "I'd offer you some, but I know you'd just turn them down." Biting reflectively into a nut, she nodded toward the forest. "Time to get back to work." She tossed the nutshells to the ground and dusted her hands on her jeans.

"You seem positively . . . driven about this, Bree." Naomi's chest heaved from exertion. "What's up with that? Mason can handle the investigation." She finally caught up with Bree. "That's his job."

Bree chewed on a nut. "I know the story about the woman and the airplane seat is probably nothing, but what if it's not? The only way to find out what Fay knew is to retrace her steps, and if that involves finding out who killed her, so be it."

"Are you sure you're not just trying to find a reason not to give up the search?"

Bree swallowed and turned away. Naomi's words had hit a little too close for comfort. "That's not it at all," she said. "I should be done with the quadrant by the new year. I'm done then if I don't find them. I told you, Anu is helping me get started with training search-and-rescue dogs. I've even started looking for a place. But I have to give it my best shot until then."

"Just so you don't go overboard," Naomi said.

Bree scanned the landscape. Both dogs began to bark then ran toward an object along the riverbank. A flash of red drew her attention, and she squinted. "What's that, Naomi?"

"I think it's her backpack!" Bree ran after the dogs. As she drew nearer, the red object came more into focus, and she smiled in triumph. Samson picked up a stick, his signal of a find, and brought it to her. She paused long enough to praise her dog then followed him to the backpack.

"Don't touch anything," Naomi warned. "Mason will want to run forensics on it."

Bree drew back her hand. Naomi was right, but she longed to open the backpack and see if it held any clues to Fay's death. "You got the cell phone with you?"

Naomi nodded. "I'll call it in."

Bree was thankful Kade waited with them for the hour it took the sheriff to arrive, though she knew she needed to get back to work. The dark shadows in the woods spooked her. Mason and his deputies arrived and Kade left to find his horse.

It was another hour before Janna and her forensics team arrived. Bree and Naomi stood out of the way and watched as they went over the backpack and combed the surrounding area for clues. Bree shifted her feet restlessly, wishing she could peer inside the pack herself. She knew Fay, and these strangers didn't.

"I think we can wrap it up now," Janna finally said. Mason stood and nodded to his officers. He joined Bree and Naomi at the edge of the action. "Good work," he told them.

His praise warmed Bree. "Any idea how the pack got down here?" she asked. "It's at least a mile from the cliff."

Mason shook his head. "No teeth marks from animals, which would have been my first assumption. My gut feeling is that the killer dumped it. But maybe the lab can come up with something."

"What was in her backpack?"

"The usual. Climbing gear like pitons, rope, a compass, that kind of thing. A bottle of water. No food, which would explain why the animals left it alone. Oh, and a notebook of some kind." He grimaced. "The backpack seems to be a dead end." His penetrating gaze lingered on her face. "This has really gotten to you, hasn't it?"

Bree nodded. "Not much I can do to fix it."

Mason shook his head at her dejected tone. "You're a crusader, Bree. If you'd been a man during the Middle Ages, you would have been the first to vie for a seat at King Arthur's Round Table. But you can't right every wrong. Sometimes bad things happen to good people." His voice held kindness, and he clasped her shoulder. "Innocent people like little Davy. You can't stop it from happening, and you can't fix it. The sooner you realize that, the easier time you'll have."

Bree didn't know what to say. "Could I take a look at the notebook when forensics is done?"

Mason released her shoulder then put his hand to his face and pinched the bridge of his nose. "We'll see," he said with heavy resignation. "Steve will want to see it first, and it will be up to him whether to let you look at it. Now I've got to get back to town." He joined his deputies and they began to wrap up.

Bree, Naomi, and the dogs went back the way they'd come, clambering over huge boulders and picking their way over slick stones along the water. Bree pulled an unopened bag of pistachios from her pocket. Before she could open them, the back of Bree's neck began to prickle. She whirled around, expecting to find someone standing behind her, but there was no one there. Samson whined, and she gave a shaky laugh. "Sorry, boy, I must be going wacko."

"What is it?" Naomi asked.

"Nothing." Bree said.

The dog didn't seem to sense anything, but then he often ignored scents he hadn't been told to search for. Bree started off toward the Jeep again. The tingling feeling returned in a rush, and she glanced around uneasily as her breath became sharp in her chest. Another panic attack? She fought the encroaching terror.

Her gaze scanned the shrubs around her, but she saw nothing. Still, the feeling of being watched persisted. If she told Naomi, she'd likely say it was God pursuing her. She shook her head nervously. More likely it was her imagination; Samson and Charley remained unconcerned. But all her self-reassurances failed to quell her panic.

Her pace quickened, and the bag of nuts slipped from her hand. She and Naomi were practically running by the time they got to her Jeep. She opened the back door and let Samson in then slid quickly into the driver's seat. Starting the Jeep, she slammed it into reverse and floored the accelerator. Bits of gravel spit from under her tires, and the vehicle roared toward town.

*H*er breath fogged in front of her in plumes. Rachel rushed from tree to tree and watched until the red Jeep disappeared from view. She bent over at the waist, panting with exertion. A bag of nuts lay at her feet. Sam loved nuts. She picked up the bag and stuffed it into her pack.

Her breathing finally relaxed. She wasn't as young as she used to be. There had once been a time when crowds cheered as her long legs ate up the fifty yards to the finish line. Now those same legs were layered with more fat than muscle, and the last crowds she'd heard had been howling for her conviction.

People were too quick to judge others. Just because she lived alone and worked with old folks, the public had been quick to believe she would kill to put them out of their misery. They didn't understand that the love of her work came from the friendships she'd formed with these elderly folks. She'd been innocent.

Rachel worried her lower lip between her teeth. Those women and their dogs had been too close. Could the one woman be Sam's mother? Same red hair. Rachel set her jaw. No. It was ridiculous. Besides, he belonged to her now. With his hair dyed brown, he didn't even look like the same boy. She had to find some way to get that red-haired woman's focus away from here. At least until Rachel found a job somewhere. Maybe she would hear soon from the applications she'd mailed out yesterday.

She could feel the blood pumping through her veins as she walked toward the cabin. Sam would want his lunch. "Such a good boy, so obedient, a boy any mother would be proud of." She said it aloud now, and the pride she felt calmed her anxiousness.

*N*early an hour and a half later, Rachel located the path she'd marked in such subtle ways only an expert would be able to follow it. Her gaze scanned the clearing. Sam had stacked the wood she'd chopped before heading to town. Some of it had fallen over, but for such a young child, his efforts were praiseworthy. Her lips curved in approval.

She cocked her head and listened, but the only sound in the clearing was the rasp of her own breathing. Sam must be inside, where she'd told him to stay once he finished his chores. Rachel pushed up the sleeve of her wool jacket and glanced at the watch on her wrist. Nearly two. Sam was probably starved. Though she always fixed him a peanut butter sandwich before she went on her excursions, he rarely ate it until she walked in the door.

She didn't know whether that was because he didn't like to eat alone or because his fear of being abandoned killed his appetite. Her own stomach rumbled like an avalanche coming down Squaw Peak, and her pace quickened.

Sam was sitting on a chair at the table. His peanut butter sandwich lay before him, unwrapped and drying. Jerking his head around at her entrance, he stared at her through frightened green eyes. A tremulous smile touched his lips as Rachel went quickly toward him.

"You still haven't eaten, son. Were you waiting for Mother?"

Sam nodded. "My tummy's hungry."

"You don't always have to wait for me, darling. That's why Mother fixed you a sandwich before I went to town. I don't want your tummy to complain. You go ahead and eat, and I'll fix me something and join you."

Sam looked down at his sandwich with obvious reluctance then picked it up and bit into it. He chewed slowly, his gaze fixed on Rachel. She hurriedly tossed her knapsack on the floor and went to the old table that served as her counter. She slathered peanut butter on bread then mixed Carnation milk powder into a glass of water and gave it to Sam.

"Drink up, son. Milk gives you strong bones." She eased herself onto the other chair.

Sam drank it down with gusto, his upper lip coated with white by the time he set the glass back on the table. "Can we have reading lessons after we eat?"

"Maybe. I saw you got the wood stacked."

He nodded, his face bright from the approval in her tone. "And I made my bed. Yours too." His small chest swelled with pride as he said the last.

"What a good boy you are! I brought you a surprise."

"You did? Can I have it now?" He gulped the last bite of his sandwich. "I'm all done with lunch."

"Bring me my knapsack." Rachel's heart felt as though it might burst with love for the boy—her son, she reminded herself—as he jumped to his feet and limped across the floor to her discarded bag. It was too heavy for him to pick up, but that didn't stop Sam. He grabbed it by one strap and tugged it across the rough floor until it lay at Rachel's feet.

"Can I look inside?" he asked.

"I'll get it. I might have another surprise for later," she said with a wink. She'd picked up a surprise for him after she mailed her letters. She drew the knapsack onto her lap and opened the flap. Sam's eyes widened when he saw the bag of nuts in her hand. "'Stachios," he squealed. He clapped his hands together. "Can I shell them?"

"If you think you're big enough."

"I'm big now. See how big my hands are now?" He held out his small hands for her inspection.

"I had no idea," she said solemnly. "Okay, you are now the official sheller of nuts. Do you need the nutcracker?"

"Oh yes, *please*," he breathed.

Rachel kept the nutcracker in a chest beside the supply cabinet. She didn't need the nutcracker for pistachios, but it helped Sam manage the task, and he got such pleasure out of using it. "You can get it out," she told him.

He raced to the chest and threw open the lid. His small face shone when he pulled out the nutcracker soldier. Running his fingers lovingly over the chipped and worn paint, he brought it back to the table and climbed back onto his chair.

"It might be easier for you to use it on the rug," Rachel suggested. She helped him get started shelling the nuts then settled back on her chair and watched him.

His lower lip was caught between small white teeth, a frown of concentration furrowing the spot between his eyes. An aching wave of love washed over her as she watched the boy. Her son. Hers alone. And no one would ever take him from her.

u

*T*he puppies tumbled over one another in the large metal cage and barked in high yips. Rock Harbor's Humane Society reeked of animals, but the doggie smell was as fine as the most expensive Paris perfume to Bree. Between fruitless searches on her days off and a busy sale going on at the store since Monday, she'd looked forward to this ever since Lauri called on Wednesday and asked her to help her pick out a puppy. Bree had called Palmer and coaxed him into meeting them here. Saturday wasn't a busy day at his fitness center, and he'd finally agreed.

Now Lauri sat on the floor surrounded by puppies, and the sound of her laughter warmed Bree's heart. Lily and Palmer had brought the twins as well, and their squeals of delight brightened the scene even more.

"I want this one," Lauri announced. She picked up a black-and-white puppy and rubbed his fat belly. "His name is Zorro."

"You've made a good choice," Bree said, nodding in approval. "His eyes are clear and intelligent, and from his coloring, I'd say he has some Border collie in him. Borders are good search dogs." She scratched the pup's head, and he wiggled all over with joy. "You realize your brother is going to kill me? He didn't want a dog. Did you even tell him you asked me to help you today?"

Lauri dropped her gaze guiltily and shook her head. "But he'll get over it when he sees how darling Zorro is," Lauri said.

Bree wasn't so sure. She'd noticed the tension between Lauri and

Kade at the O'Reilly house and could sense the rebellion in Lauri. She hated to make things worse.

"I'll be your training center's first customer." Lauri nestled the dog against her, and Zorro nibbled on her chin. Bree laughed and patted the puppy's head.

"And we'll be the second," Palmer said. "What about this pup, Bree?" He held a yellow Lab in his cupped hands.

"Oh, he's darling," Bree said. "He's a good choice too. He'll make a loving, loyal pet. Are you getting one for each of the girls?"

"I think we'd better start off with just one," Palmer said.

"He's afraid he'll be the one stuck taking the dog for walks until the girls are old enough to do it," Lily said.

"I already *know* that will be my job." The playful whine in Palmer's voice made them all laugh.

"Now these pups have all had their shots," Mathilda Worrell said. The older woman shuffled across the floor to her desk.

For as long as Bree could remember, Mathilda had run the animal shelter, though she must be nearly seventy by now. With hair as white and springy as fresh baby's-breath, her faded blue eyes peered through gold spectacles with such genuine love and interest that no one ever took offense at her meddling. Everyone from the mayor to the children called her Aunt Mathilda. She'd always seemed indomitable, but today Bree noticed a bit of grayness in her normally pink skin as the woman lowered herself into a desk chair and gave an uncharacteristic sigh.

"Are you all right, Aunt Mathilda?" Bree hurried to the desk when the older woman put a hand to her forehead.

"Fine, fine." Aunt Mathilda waved a hand in Bree's direction. "This dratted murder has just been wearing on my mind. I've spoken to the Lord about it nearly every night, but he is silent on the subject. For the life of me, I can't imagine who would want to hurt that sweet child."

"Sweet child" was not how Bree would have described Fay. Self-centered forest sprite maybe. But Aunt Mathilda never saw bad in anyone.

"Folks are saying it was her husband. You don't think Steve would do something like that, do you? You know I don't like to gossip, but folks are scared. With Fay dead, we have to watch out for one another. It worries me so to wonder who in town could be capable of such an act," Aunt Mathilda said.

"It could have been anyone." Bree was barely listening as her thoughts drifted back to Fay's death. It did seem odd that Steve had asked her to look for Fay but refused to go along. Fay had often complained about his obsession with his work, but maybe he used work as an excuse to stay away from a wife he didn't love. The line between love and hate could be blurry.

Aunt Mathilda finished writing the receipt for Lauri's dog. "He'll make you a good pet, dear."

Lauri threw her arms around Bree. "Thanks so much for helping me get a puppy," she said, her face shining. "When can we start training him?"

"First, we'll just work on obedience and establishing yourself as the alpha dog."

Lauri grinned. "I'm the alpha dog? What's that?"

"Sounds like science fiction," Palmer said.

"There's a pecking order in a household, and puppies need to discover the place doesn't revolve around them. Since they're so young, it shouldn't be too hard for them to figure that out. You're the boss of his pack, the alpha dog." Bree scratched Zorro's ears, and the dog squirmed with delight then peed on Lauri.

"Oh no!" Lauri held him away from her wet sweatshirt. "Bad Zorro!"

She started to swat him, but Bree stopped her. "You only want to punish him for disobedience. He's just a puppy. He'll learn to control his bladder just like children learn to use the toilet." She smiled to soften the sting. "Give him some time."

Lauri nodded and, still holding the puppy away from her shirt, started toward the door.

"We'll run Lauri home," Lily said.

"Thanks," Bree said. "Work on bonding with your dogs for the next few days. This weekend, concentrate on calling him to you then rewarding him when he comes. He has to learn he's *your* dog. And when he comes to greet you after school or work, walk in and don't make a fuss over him. If you make a huge fuss, he'll think he's the alpha dog. That will cause him stress when you leave and he can't protect you. Start off right, and it will make things a lot easier. Palmer, you figure out a name for yours yet?"

"Jasper," Lily offered.

"He looks like a Jasper." Bree scratched the dog's ears.

Palmer shrugged acquiescence. He and Lily managed to corral the girls and the dog and get them all into the van for the drive home.

"Hey, why don't you come to church with us tomorrow?" Lily asked.

"The roof would fall in if I ever came to a church service." Bree tried to deflect her refusal with a laugh, but a part of her wanted to accept.

Aunt Mathilda turned her penetrating blue eyes on Bree. "That's no laughing matter, Bree. The Hound of Heaven is searching for you. Can't you hear his baying, Bree? Don't ignore him, child."

"The Hound of Heaven? Sounds ominous." Bree would indulge her. Besides, she was curious.

Aunt Mathilda smiled. "Jesus, child. Jesus is looking for you, searching for you. He'll follow you wherever you go. You can't run from him or hide where he can't find you. All this searching for your boy and your husband is just another way of running from his call and blocking out his voice. If you want to run, run *to* him, not away."

Bree raised her eyebrows. She didn't like where this conversation was headed. Hound of Heaven, indeed. Her mind flitted to Naomi's showing up just when she was about to fall to her death. She pushed the thought away. "I didn't know you thought I was such a sinner, Aunt Mathilda."

"We're all sinners, child. Every last one of us. I've seen you this past year, trying to atone for yourself with good deeds, turning all meek and mild, afraid to make a peep that Hilary doesn't approve of. It won't work, Bree. You've got courage, child. Use it to do yourself some eternal good. Take a good, hard look into your heart. Turn to God for forgiveness, then forgive yourself too."

Bree hadn't come in here for a sermon. "See you later, Aunt Mathilda. Call me if you hear anything important." Shivering in the wind, she tried to put the image that Aunt Mathilda's words had conjured out of her mind. Visions of some slathering dog howling as he chased her was too scary to think about. Though everyone told her God was a God of love, all she'd seen was his hand of judgment. If he'd judged Rob's sin, he'd taken innocent Davy as well. She wanted nothing to do with a God like that.

Rock Harbor Savings and Loan was across the street and two doors down from the animal shelter. The bank windows glinted in the late October sunshine. Bree glanced at her watch. Eleven. The bank was open on Saturday mornings; maybe Steve would be working. She pushed open the ornate door and stepped onto the tile floor. Steve was walking toward his office. Bree hurried to catch up with him.

"Steve, you got a minute?"

"I guess." He held the door open for her.

She followed him into the office with Samson close on their heels. The dark mahogany desk gleamed, and the plush chairs matched the desk and the bookcases that lined one wall.

Bree sat in one of the guest chairs. "How are you doing?" she asked.

"Why do you care? You're so suspicious of me you won't even help me try to find Fay's real killer."

"I . . . I want to help. But I don't know exactly what I can do."

He leaned forward eagerly. "You'll help? I just want you to take the dog and poke around, see if you turn up any clues, maybe trace where she was the last few days before she was killed."

Which was precisely what Bree had been doing. She suppressed a sigh. "All right. Now, how are you doing?"

He looked away. "I'm getting by. The house is sure quiet. You know how Fay was, always yammering about something. You know, I'm the first to admit we had our troubles. I knew her old boyfriend had been calling her, but to find out the baby might . . ." His voice trailed off.

"You don't know that for sure," Bree said. "Eric might have just wanted to hurt you."

"He did a good job of it. I guess I could have the baby's DNA tested to see for sure, but I don't think I want to know. Sometimes ignorance is easier to take."

And sometimes it plays you for a fool. Bree had been the ostrich type too often in her marriage. If she'd been more in tune with things, maybe Rob wouldn't have strayed. She had chalked up his distraction to work. Now she knew better.

Steve swiveled his chair around to the coffeepot on the credenza behind him. "You take your coffee with cream?"

"And a little sugar," she said. He stirred the coffee and handed it to her. Smiling her thanks, she wrapped her cold hands around the warm cup.

Steve took a gulp of his black coffee. "I'm sure you didn't come by just to see how I'm doing."

"I just thought we ought to team up . . . see what we can find out. I need to find out where that cabin she mentioned is too. I'm not having much luck finding it," Bree explained.

"You know how Fay was—she always had to be center stage. I wouldn't put too much stock in what she said about the cabin and the airplane seat. It sounds pretty far-out."

Bree nodded. "That's what I thought too, but since she died, I can't seem to get it out of my head. I just want to find it and make sure."

"Sorry I can't help you more there." Steve picked up a pen and twirled it around in his fingers. "I just hope the sheriff is checking out Eric thoroughly. His temper has gotten him into trouble before."

"Could I poke around in her things at home, see if she wrote down anything, left any clues about this?"

"I guess, but I don't think you'll find anything. Give me a few days though. The house is a mess, and I've got a maid coming to clean it up in a couple of days. Give me a call next week."

Bree didn't doubt it was a mess. She remembered her own state of confusion and disarray, and the memory stirred her sympathy. "Another thing . . . Mason has a notebook that was in Fay's backpack. You mind if I take a look and see if it mentions the cabin?"

"Sure, that's fine. He showed it to me. I don't think there was much in there except for ramblings about different trails."

Which might be exactly what she needed.

He eased back against his seat again. "Please don't stop believing in me, Bree," he said softly. "I loved Fay. Keep poking around, and you'll discover I didn't kill her."

She nodded, although she couldn't shake her doubts. "I'll call you next week." Bree moved past him to leave, and he shut the door behind her. Glancing at her watch, she saw she only had fifteen minutes before she'd promised to be at Nicholls's. Saturday wasn't her usual day to work, but Anu had an appointment and needed her help.

Nicholls's Finnish Imports was bustling with shoppers sorting through the new treasures. Anu had just stocked the new merchandise she'd brought back from Finland two weeks ago. Bree paused to glance through a stack of wool sweaters and grabbed one for herself, a bright green one with navy trim. She stashed it behind the cash register then went to find her mother-in-law.

"There you are," Anu said. "I was beginning to wonder if you would make it."

"Looks like you need all the help you can get. This place is packed!" Indeed, even more shoppers had crammed into the small store until there was barely room to walk around.

Anu smiled. "They could smell the *pulla* from down the street. I made a fresh batch, and every shopper must get one." She untied her apron. "My thanks for taking over for me, *kulta.*"

When Anu was gone, Bree wandered through the store, answering questions as best she could and chatting with the customers about everything from children's homework to the latest news. Being part of the woof and weave of Rock Harbor never failed to bring a sense of grateful joy to her life. This was her home, and these folks were her family in all the ways that really mattered.

Just after five, she escorted the last of the customers out and shut the door. Folding sweaters at the table by the front window, she glanced out into the street and saw Fay's uncle Lawrence talking to Steve. Lawrence had his fists clenched and his face thrust into Steve's. Both men were red-faced, and their shouts carried indistinctly through the window. Bree opened the door and stepped out to the sidewalk.

"It's stupid to go through with that sale now!" Lawrence was yelling. "We can get twice that from my contact in New York."

"It's my copper mine," Steve said tightly. "You might have browbeaten my wife, but don't try it with me. I'm a man of my word. The matter is closed."

The man doubled up his fist as though he might punch Steve in the nose, but instead he wheeled and rushed away. Bree knew they had to have been talking about the old Copper Queen.

Lawrence Kukkari had been a bit eccentric and difficult ever since he'd returned from Vietnam. If he could cause a problem, it seemed to make him happy. His letters to the editor of the newspaper were legendary in Rock Harbor. It seemed every time Bree saw him, he was angry. Could he have been angry enough to kill Fay over the mine, believing he could get Steve to see things his way about backing out on the sale to Palmer and taking the higher offer instead?

His hands clenched at his sides, Steve watched Lawrence walk away, then his gaze settled on Bree. "There's another suspect for you, Bree," he called. "Why don't you investigate why he practically forced Fay to agree to sell that useless copper mine? I've half a mind to cancel the sale altogether just to spite him. I'd do it too if I didn't like Palmer so much." He gave a disgusted snort and turned to walk away.

Bree ran down the sidewalk. "Wait, Steve." She ran to catch up with him. "Did Fay ever say anything about that other buyer of Lawrence's being with the mob? I overheard an argument she had with him. She told her uncle she wanted nothing to do with his buyers, that they were mobsters."

Steve frowned. "We didn't talk about the mine much. It belonged to her and Lawrence, and I tried not to get involved."

He turned and walked away. Bree stared after him thoughtfully. Maybe she'd just make a visit out to the mine next week and see if anything was stirring around the old place.

Rachel smoothed the three letters flat against the table. A future. She and Sam might have a future. The first two letters were the standard "Thank you for applying, but we've already filled the position" type, but the last one had brought a smile to her face. She'd read it over and over, and the words were still the same after two days.

The director of a facility called Golden Years Nursing Home, a Mary Bristol, had invited her to come for a job interview. Rachel hadn't thought that far ahead. What could she do with Sam? She would have to take the bus to Chicago, and her funds would barely cover the cost for herself. There was no way she could take Sam. Besides, she'd have to spend the night on a park bench, and she couldn't endanger her son that way.

She glanced at him, playing with his toys by the stove. Surely he could stay overnight by himself. Though she figured he couldn't be more than four years old, he was smart and resourceful. And even more important, he was obedient. If she told him to stay inside and not to go out for any reason, he would do just that.

Frowning, she decided to worry about it later. In the letter, the director had asked her to call and schedule an appointment, which meant she'd have to go back to town. She'd tried to call before she left town two days ago when she first received the letter, but the woman had been out of the office. According to her secretary, Rachel was supposed to call her today, Friday.

She hurriedly dressed and put on her boots. "I have to go to town,

Sam," she told him. "I'll get the wood chopped before I head out."

Sam stared at her for a moment then pushed his bowl of cereal away. "Can I go?" he asked.

From the hopelessness in his voice, she knew he already expected the answer. She hesitated. Why not allow it this once? He could stay in the trees while she used the pay phone. No one would see him. And even if someone did, the color on his hair was fresh. No one would ever recognize him.

The thought of the red-haired woman and her dog flashed through her mind. She lived in Rock Harbor. But Rachel couldn't stand the helpless, lost look on Sam's face any longer. It was unlikely that the woman would be anywhere near the pay phones. They wouldn't be in town more than five minutes.

"Okay," she said finally.

An expression of disbelief crossed Sam's face, followed by incredulous joy. He bounded to his feet. "I'll help you chop wood," he said eagerly.

"I'll do it. You need to rest for the trip to town."

Rachel chopped wood all morning. After lunch she told Sam it was time to go. They would get to town about three. Taking his wool jacket from the hook by the door, she held it out for him to slip into. "We'd better get going."

For nearly two hours they walked through brambles and over hills, past streams and thick forest. At times Rachel carried Sam when his small legs got too tired.

When they crossed the road, he cried out, "It's Pooky!" He limped to the ditch where the koala bear lay partially covered by leaves. "Didn't Timmy and Emily want him?" he asked. He cradled the stuffed bear in his arms.

"I bet they dropped it by accident," Rachel said.

"I need to find them to give it back," he said.

"Come along," she told him. No use in upsetting him by telling him he'd never see those kids again. They trudged toward town. The sounds of vehicles and people reached her ears as they paused on a hill overlooking Rock Harbor.

Curls of smoke rose from the houses and cottages below them. Rachel scanned the streets close to the line of phone booths that was her destination. No sign of the red Jeep. Sam gripped her hand and started to walk forward with her, but she gently disentangled his small fingers.

"You have to stay here," she told him.

"You said I could come!" He sat on the ground and began to sob, his wails growing louder and more pronounced.

Rachel hardly knew what to do. Never had she heard him cry like that. His usual reaction of disappointment was a silent tear or two. But he must be very tired—they'd never traveled such a long distance before. She knelt beside him and pulled him onto her lap.

"Hush, Sammy. I won't be gone five minutes."

"But I wanted to see Emily and Timmy," he sobbed. "They need Pooky."

"Timmy and Emily are home with their mommy and daddy," she said. "We don't even know where they live."

"But I want to see them!" He wailed louder, and Rachel looked around nervously. If someone heard his cries and came to investigate, they might be in big trouble.

"Tell you what," she said. "You stay here real quiet like a mouse, and when I get back, we'll walk around the perimeter of town and see if we can find Timmy and Emily. If they're outside by themselves, we'll stop and say hello. Will that do?"

Sam's tears dried, and he nodded.

Rachel stood with him in her arms then set him on the ground. "Now remember, be very quiet."

Sam nodded. "I 'member."

Clutching her letter with the woman's phone number, Rachel took off at a dead run down the hill. Her legs wobbled, and her head spun with fatigue. Entering the phone booth, she pulled the bifold door shut behind her and opened the letter with shaking hands.

Her palms slick with sweat, she dialed the phone and waited.

A woman's voice answered. "Mary Bristol."

"Hi, Ms. Bristol, this is Rachel Marks. I received your letter about setting up an interview?" Rachel hoped her voice didn't betray her nervousness. Confidence, that's what sold an employer.

"Ah, yes, Rachel."

She heard the woman shuffle pages, then her voice came back over the line. "Can you come Monday at nine?"

"Um, that's a bit soon. Would next Wednesday work for you?"

In a voice heavy with disappointment, Mary Bristol told her they were in desperate need of someone but finally agreed that Wednesday would be acceptable. As she hung up the phone, Rachel wondered what she could wear. Somehow she had to overcome the bad impression she'd made by not agreeing to come when the woman wanted. It needed to be something professional and attractive, both traits that Rachel wondered if she even possessed anymore. Maybe if she stopped at Goodwill, she could find something she could afford.

She yanked open the phone booth door and trudged up the hill to where she'd left Sam. She didn't see him. "Sam," she called softly.

The only answer was the call of a gull from overhead. "Sam!" She raised her voice and turned to stare around her at the thick phalanx of forest crowding close.

The trees seemed to press in on her. She couldn't lose him, not now. He couldn't have gone far. Rachel began to run from tree to tree. Perspiration poured down her face and clung to her back. "Sam!" Tree branches reached for her, and she fought her way through them.

Think, Rachel. Where could he have gone? An instant later, she heard children laughing and whirled to see where the sound had come from. Leaning against a massive oak tree for support, she stared down the hill into a yard enclosed with a white picket fence. Three children were swinging on a swing set.

Her frantic gaze raced from face to face. Emily, Timmy—and Sam. Relief flooded through her in a rush of sweetness that left her nearly sinking to her knees. No one had taken him. He was still hers and hers alone.

The children turned at her approach. Emily's eyes grew wide with fear, and Timmy's feet thumped on the hard dirt, stopping the movement of his swing. He looked at his sister uncertainly.

"Hi," Emily said. Her voice trembled, but she raised her gaze to meet Rachel's hard stare.

Rachel was too distraught to care if she frightened the children. She opened the gate and rushed into the yard. Sam hadn't seen her yet. His eyes were closed as he swung his legs and pumped the swing higher into the air.

Watching him for a moment, Rachel felt a shaft of pain so strong she wondered if she might be having a heart attack. His carefree abandonment was a new sight to her. A child was supposed to be like this, wasn't he? Had she deprived the child she loved from the happy existence he deserved?

Squeezing her eyes shut, Rachel rubbed them with her fists. When she opened her eyes, Sam's gaze was boring into hers. His features froze in a blanket of guilt. One toe dug into the dirt until the swing was merely rocking side to side.

His frantic gaze jittered to his friends. "I found Emily and Timmy. Timmy missed Pooky."

Struggling to control herself, Rachel rushed forward to grab him by the arm. She'd never mishandled him before, but now she found herself shaking him by the shoulders.

"You know better than to wander off," she hissed. Her breath came in ragged gasps. "What if someone had seen you?"

Sam whimpered, and his face went white. Too late, Rachel remembered his injuries. Stupid, that's what her brother always said.

"Don't hurt him," Emily said in a small voice. "It was my fault. Mine and Timmy's. We saw him on the hill and called to him."

Rachel whirled to face them. "Leave him alone from now on, do you hear me? You could have lost him to me." Aware she was babbling but unable to control herself, she whipped back around to Sam and turned him to face the hillside. "Go, Sam. Run to the top of the hill. I'll follow you."

Sam took off like a deer with a dog at his heels, though with his limp his progress was slower than she would have liked. As Rachel followed, she could feel the stares of the children boring into her back. All she could do was hope they had enough sense to keep their mouths shut.

She stopped at the gate and turned to face them again. "You tell anyone about us, and I'll come to you in the middle of the night and take you away. You hear me?" She saw the stuffed bear clutched in Timmy's hand. "And don't tell anyone about the bear. Not anyone, do you understand?"

Timmy's face screwed up with tears and he nodded. Emily gulped but held her head high. "We won't tell anyone," she said.

"You'd better not," Rachel warned. As she ran through the gate, she passed the kitchen window and saw a teenager talking on the phone. The girl's mouth dropped open and she came closer to the window. She just prayed the girl hadn't seen Sam. Her lungs burning in her chest and her eyes hot with unshed tears, she raced up the hill.

What had she become that she would frighten children? And even her own Sam had looked at her through terror-filled eyes. Rachel felt such self-loathing, she wished she could die. But all she could do was get them both home and out of these woods before those children finally told someone about her.

*N*oiselessly, Naomi pulled the door shut behind her then breathed a sigh of relief that her mother hadn't awakened from her afternoon nap.

The last thing she wanted was to be peppered with questions about what she was doing. Naomi wasn't even sure herself what she was doing.

She'd hung out at the hardware store for two weeks, and while Donovan seemed to enjoy her company, he had yet to extend an invitation to dinner or a movie or otherwise indicate he saw her as anything more than a friend. Naomi grimaced. Maybe she was fooling herself. What made her think an attractive man like Donovan O'Reilly would be interested in her? He could have his pick of women in Rock Harbor.

Naomi shifted the offering she held in her hands, and the aroma of cheesy potatoes baked with thick chunks of ham drifted to her nose. The warmth of the dish contrasted sharply with the cold thud of her heart. What would he think when she showed up at the door? She gulped and headed toward her Honda CR-V.

Charley pressed his nose against the living room window and stared after her with a mournful expression. Naomi opened the truck door and set the casserole inside then wiggled her fingers at her dog. Charley disappeared from the window, and she knew he would ignore her as punishment when she returned. He hated to be left behind.

Maybe she should have brought him. Charley might have helped break the ice with the children, especially Emily. The little girl made no effort to hide her disdain of Naomi. Naomi didn't understand it. At church the children flocked around her, and she was the baby-sitter of choice for half the town.

Naomi glanced at her reflection in the rearview mirror. Her own anxious brown eyes peered back at her, and she nearly groaned aloud. Add a pinafore and she'd look like a little girl. Her cheeks were too round, and those ridiculous curls just added to the immature effect. Maybe she should have straightened her hair and worn something besides jeans, but she'd wanted her arrival to appear casual.

Keeping an eye on the traffic, which in Rock Harbor was no chore, she dug through the paraphernalia in her purse and pulled out a red lipstick. Maybe that would add a sheen of sophistication. But the slash of red across her lips merely made her look like a little girl playing dress up. She blotted it with a tissue and sighed. You'd think a woman of nearly thirty-two wouldn't look like such an ingénue.

She parked in front of the house, taking a deep breath before she climbed out with the casserole in hand. Donovan's car, a blue Ford sedan, sprawled across the driveway like he'd been in too much of a hurry to park in a straight line.

Naomi's legs wobbled as she walked to the door. She pinned what she hoped was an impersonal smile on her face as she pressed the doorbell firmly. When Donovan opened the door and she found herself staring into his dark blue eyes, she lost the carefully rehearsed speech.

"Oh, um, hi, Donovan. I had some . . . some casserole. I mean, I made too much casserole for supper and thought of . . . um, have you eaten yet?" Heat rose up her neck and settled in her cheeks, and she knew she looked like a rosy-cheeked child. Donovan, bless his heart, didn't seem to notice her agitation, and Naomi felt a wave of gratitude come over her.

"Naomi, hello. Come on in. You're a godsend. I was just staring in the refrigerator, wondering what I could fix. The kids are nattering about that witch of the woods again and her little boy. I swear, I don't know where they get their imaginations." He stepped aside to allow her entry then followed her to the kitchen.

The children were seated at the kitchen table. Emily's eyes darkened with hostility when she saw Naomi, but Timmy ran to her and threw his arms around her legs. Naomi's grip on the casserole dish loosened, but she managed to hang on to it. Setting it on the table, she scooped Timmy into her arms. He wrapped himself around her like a monkey, and she enjoyed the feel of his small body nestled against her.

"I'll get the plates out," Donovan said. "You'll join us, won't you?" The earnestness of his expression warmed Naomi like soup on a snowy afternoon.

"I'd like that." She ignored Emily's glare and settled onto a chair with Timmy still on her lap. Glancing around, she noticed smears of mud on the kitchen floor and piles of dirty dishes in the sink. Their top-to-bottom housecleaning hadn't lasted long, but then it wouldn't with two children around.

Timmy wound one of Naomi's curls around his finger and gazed into her face with rapt attention. Naomi smoothed the hair back from his face. "How about we get you washed up for supper?" she told him. "Come on, Emily, you could use a wash too."

Emily put her small hands on her hips and scowled. "I can do it myself. I don't need *your* help."

"Emily, mind your manners," her father said sharply. "Go along with Naomi."

Emily's scowl deepened, and she stomped after Naomi and Timmy. In the bathroom she refused to look at Naomi. Naomi put Timmy down, and he went to the sink.

Naomi glanced around the cluttered bathroom. Towels lay on the floor in crumpled heaps. Two boats lay upside down in the bathtub, and a rubber duck sat motionless in a shallow puddle of water on the floor. She picked up the towels and hung them on the side of the tub to dry, taking time to mop up the standing water as well.

"Are you a maid or something?" Emily's upper lip curled.

"No, but there's nothing wrong with doing housework. Don't you like an orderly home? I always find it soothes me to have everything in its place."

"I like my house just fine," Emily proclaimed. She flounced to the sink and washed her hands with gusto, flinging water onto the already spotted wall and floor.

Naomi bit her lip. How could she reach this little girl? She cleared her throat. "You have such pretty hair, Emily. Is your mother's hair that color?"

Emily's noisy splashing grew still. "Don't talk about my mother," she said in a muffled voice. "I don't need another one."

What a stupid comment! She'd forgotten Donovan's ex-wife hadn't been back to see the kids since she left. Town rumor had it that she'd moved to California and was modeling. The woman was beautiful, but Naomi couldn't see how any fame or fortune could replace her two darling children.

"Is that why you don't like me? You think I'd try to take her place?" Naomi touched Emily's shoulder, and the little girl flinched away.

Lifting her chin, Emily glared at Naomi. "You want to be my friend so Daddy will like you. But I don't want you for a friend. I want Bree to be my friend and for Daddy to like her."

Naomi gulped. Were her feelings for Donovan so apparent? Looking into Emily's sneering face, she saw a loneliness there that broke her heart. "Bree is my friend too," she said quietly. "Can you and I just be friends without involving your daddy?"

Emily stared at her suspiciously. "I'll have to think about it." But the set of her chin told Naomi her mind was made up and she wanted nothing to do with any grown woman except Bree.

Naomi stood. "We'd better eat before our supper gets cold." It had been a mistake to come. Donovan probably saw right through her as well. Her face burned as she dried her hands and followed the children back to the kitchen.

Donovan had made an attempt to clear some of the clutter while they were gone. He turned a tired but eager smile toward them that soothed Naomi's bruised ego.

They sat at the table, and Timmy said grace. Naomi spooned the casserole onto plates while Donovan poured milk for the children.

"I'm afraid all I have is milk or water," he said.

"Water is fine," she told him.

He poured water for both of them and sat beside her. Naomi caught a whiff of his cologne, a warm, spicy scent. His warmth radiated into her arm, and her throat grew so tight she wasn't sure she could eat.

She cleared her throat. "What was this about the witch of the woods?" she asked.

"Ask the kids," Donovan said with a heavy sigh.

Naomi lifted an eyebrow as she looked at Emily. "Is this the same person you saw in the woods when you were lost?"

"Yes, but she didn't have her hat on today," Timmy put in eagerly. "Sam came to play, and she was mad."

"Sam?"

"Her son, I guess. He's not supposed to go anywhere unless she says it's okay," Emily said with a warning look at her brother. "We're not supposed to talk about it. She said she'd get us in the middle of the night if we told. But it's okay to tell you, Daddy, right? We can tell you without getting into trouble?"

"You can tell me anything," Donovan said. "But there is no witch of the woods, Emily. You know that."

She thrust out a chin that looked like a small version of Donovan's own. "There *is*, Daddy. We saw her, right, Timmy? We were swinging after school, and there she was."

Her brother nodded. "And Sam."

"That's enough, kids," Donovan said. "Lauri was here with you, and she didn't say a word about a woman and her son. Imagination is fine, but lying is not, and you both know it."

"Lauri was in the house talking to her boyfriend," Emily said. "Sam was only here a few minutes."

"Just like William, the talking tiger who came for a visit last summer, right?"

Emily flushed. "That was just pretend, Daddy; this is real."

"Emily, that's enough. I won't tolerate lying, and you know it. Now eat your supper and don't say another word about it."

Emily evidently recognized her father's warning tone, for she picked up her fork and lapsed into a sullen silence. "They were here," she muttered under her breath, too softly for anyone except Naomi to hear. Emily flashed a glare at Naomi, as if daring her to tattle.

Naomi gave her a tiny smile of sympathy. Emily must be very lonely to hold to her story that way. "After supper, I'll push you in the swing," she offered.

A tiny flicker of interest lit Emily's eyes but quickly died. She picked at her food listlessly. Timmy began cramming the food into his mouth until he looked like a chipmunk.

Naomi smiled in amusement then turned to catch Donovan's gaze. Was it her imagination, or was there an awareness in Donovan's eyes she'd never seen before? Her cheeks grew hot, and she looked down at her plate.

"Um, I'm glad you stopped by," Donovan said. "I'd been meaning to call you."

Naomi was afraid to breathe. "Oh?"

He cleared his throat. "Yes, I wondered if you'd be willing to go shopping with me and the kids Sunday after church. They need some new clothes, and I'm hopeless at stuff like that."

Her warm glow faded. Was he interested only in free help? She risked a glance at him and found him still staring at her. Her gaze probed his, and what she found there eased her worries. There was something between them. It might not lead anywhere, but she had to find out what their relationship could be.

"I'd like that," she said softly.

Donovan's gaze held Naomi's for a long moment. Emily threw her fork to the table and pushed her chair across the tile with a screech, breaking their exchange. Naomi winced. The little girl flung her napkin to the floor and ran from the room. The back door slammed.

Donovan rose. "I don't want her outside alone. Bears were raiding the restaurant's garbage last week, and though they should be in their winter dens by now, I don't want to take any chances."

Naomi touched his forearm. "Let me go," she said.

He hesitated but then nodded and sank back onto his seat. "Don't take her attitude personally. She's been difficult since Marika left."

"I remember how I felt when my dad died. She's just lost and afraid of the future." Naomi stood. "Have you tried to contact Marika—see if she could come visit them? That would help."

"She didn't leave a forwarding address. All correspondence was through her lawyer, and once the divorce was final, even that stopped. I don't even know where she is."

Naomi gave him a sympathetic smile then went to find Emily. Glancing out the window of the back door, Naomi saw her sitting in a swing, her elbows on her knees and her chin cupped in her hands.

The remembered pain of loss brought tears to Naomi's eyes. She had been about Emily's age when her father had died, and some days she still missed him with a fresh intensity that resurrected the horrible day in vivid Technicolor. She hurried to join Emily.

November had arrived this week. Snow was late this year, but it couldn't be far off. A cutting wind blew from the woods, and Naomi wrapped her sweater more tightly around her chest. Emily wasn't wearing a jacket either.

"Hi," Naomi said softly.

Emily swiveled in the swing and stared at her with eyes so miserable Naomi wanted to cry with her.

"I'm in trouble, aren't I?" she said. "I always get in trouble. I bet Daddy wishes you and Bree never found me in the woods."

"Oh, sweetheart, your daddy loves you so much. He would never wish that." Naomi stepped closer. "Here, put my sweater on, and I'll push you."

Naomi shrugged her arms out of the sweater and helped Emily into it. The cold wind punched through her thin turtleneck and chilled her whole body. Emily settled back onto the swing, and Naomi grabbed the cold steel of the chain and gave a gentle push.

"My daddy died when I was about your age," Naomi said after a long minute.

"He did?" Emily said. "Was he killed in a climbing accident like Mrs. Asters or did he get cancer like Anika's mommy?"

Naomi hid a smile. Children related everything to their own experiences. But then, she guessed everyone did the same. "No, he was the captain of a ship that sank in Lake Superior."

"That's sad," Emily said. "I would go to Bree's lighthouse and watch for him to come back."

"He's in heaven though. I wouldn't want him to leave a nice place where he's happy."

"I want Mommy to come back." Emily thrust out her chin. She turned, gave an uncertain look in Naomi's direction, and asked in a small voice, "Are you going to be my new mommy?"

"I'd like to be your friend," Naomi said. "Can we start there?"

Emily dug the toe of her sneaker into the ground and stopped the swing. "Okay," she said, getting out of the swing. "I'm cold. Can we go inside now?"

"Sure." Naomi was glad to. Her bones hurt with the cold.

"Oh look!" Emily ran forward and stooped in front of the sandbox. "See, I told you Sam was here." She held up a small glove. "This is Sam's."

Naomi frowned and took the glove. Something inside her stomach twisted, and she was glad Bree wasn't here. The glove looked similar to ones Davy had once worn.

She handed it back to Emily. "We'll have to give it back to Timmy."

"It's Sam's," Emily insisted. "Timmy doesn't have gloves like this."

She certainly was sticking to her story. Naomi wanted to chuckle, but she knew the child would be offended. As a child, Naomi had had an imaginary friend, Wendy, and she'd been highly offended when her mother refused to believe Wendy existed. Emily would grow out of it soon enough. At least Sam was there for Emily when her mommy wasn't.

She ruffled the top of Emily's hair. "If you beat me inside, I'll make some fudge and we can play a game."

"You don't believe me." Emily pouted. "Call Lauri and ask her. Maybe she saw Sam and the witch."

Looking into the child's confident eyes, Naomi couldn't bear to shatter her trust. "All right, let's do that."

Emily's huge smile was Naomi's reward. She followed the little girl back inside. Donovan had stacked the dishes around the sink, and Naomi made a mental note to wash them after calling Lauri. She left Donovan in the kitchen and went to the living room. Emily showed her Lauri's number in the back of the phone book.

Lauri answered in a breathless voice rife with expectation. She probably hoped it was her boyfriend.

"It's Naomi Heinonen, Lauri. I have a question about this afternoon. Did you see a woman in the backyard with the O'Reilly children?"

Lauri's answer flipped Naomi's heart right over. Her hand shook as she hung up the phone. "Let me see that glove again," she told Emily. She took the glove and turned back the cuff. Her eyes grew wide at the initials she saw there.

She rushed to the kitchen. "I have to go see Bree," she told Donovan.

Some Friday nights at the store were boring, and this was one of them. No one had entered for the past hour, and Bree was ready to close the place down and head for home.

"Bree?"

The door to Nicholls's slammed, and Bree heard Naomi rushing through the aisles.

"Bree, come quick!"

Naomi sounded . . . well, Bree wasn't sure she'd ever heard the note of incredulity resonating in her friend's voice, a kind of breathless hope and wonder. She came from behind the counter at the back of the store.

"Back here. Don't have a coronary. What's wrong?"

Naomi rushed to her and grabbed her by the arms. "You're not going to believe this!" She took Bree by the hand and pulled her toward the break room. "Where's Anu? She should hear this too."

Anu poked her head out from the break room. "What has happened? Perhaps the clock on the courthouse has begun to chime again after fifty years of silence? Or the Coast Guard has spotted the Loch Ness monster?"

"Better. Sit down, both of you."

Her eyes sparkling, Naomi waited. Bree and Anu looked at each other.

"Perhaps we'd better humor her," Anu said. She pulled out a chair and sat down, folding her hands in her lap.

Bree did the same. "Tell us now, or you'll never get another of Anu's sweet rolls," she threatened.

"Okay, here's the story: I took a casserole over to Donovan's." She frowned at Bree. "Don't look so surprised. I told you I was going to see if there could be anything between us. Anyway, the kids were talking about the woman they saw the day they were lost in the woods. The witch in the woods, remember?"

"I'd forgotten."

"It's not a fantasy. I called Lauri, and she saw her too—today. And look here." With a flourish, Naomi pulled a glove from her pocket. "Doesn't this look like Davy's?"

Beside her, Bree heard Anu's soft inhalation. Her own lungs seemed to constrict. She reached out and took the glove in her hand. "Yes," she whispered. "He had a pair just like this."

"Look at the tag." Naomi's brown eyes sparkled with tears.

Her hand shaking, Bree rolled the cuff. On the label, printed in black marker, were the letters DRN. David Robert Nicholls. Her fingers went numb, and her vision blurred. "It's his; it's Davy's," she whispered. "Why would she have Davy's glove?"

"She must have found it," Naomi said. "This woman must know where the downed plane is. If we can find her, she can tell us where the plane is. You'll finally have closure."

Just when she was ready to move on, the door she was about to shut had swung wide open again. Bree clutched the glove in her fist and brought it to her nose. "It doesn't smell like him anymore."

"The woman's son was probably wearing it. This has to be the woman Fay was talking about—the one with an airplane seat in a ravine near the cabin."

"The backpack!" Bree said.

"What is this?" Anu asked.

"In Fay's backpack there was a book, a log or notebook of some kind. Mason said I could look at it when he was done, but he hasn't called to tell me to come get it." Bree stood.

Anu caught her hand. "Please, *kulta*, do not let this drag you back to the past. I've seen your efforts to move forward. While I want to bury our loved ones, you must not find a new obsession in locating this woman. You still have no idea where to look."

Bree's exhilaration ebbed. "Just until the first of the year," she promised. "But surely you agree that we should follow this lead."

Anu nodded. "But if it dead-ends, you must let it go, Bree. If God ordains the forest must keep Rob and Davy, we must accept his decision."

Everything in Bree's heart shouted that she would not, could not let it go. For the first time, the realization of her quest seemed possible. Anu couldn't ask her to turn her back on this. Her free hand curled around Davy's glove so tightly that her nails cut into her palm.

Anu sighed. "Go see Mason. I'll close the store," Anu said as she released her hand.

Bree bent to kiss her mother-in-law's forehead. "I love you, Anu," she whispered. "I'll call you."

Anu patted her cheek, and Bree grabbed her coat from the rack against the wall. "Let's go," she told Naomi. Now more than ever, it was imperative that she trace Fay's whereabouts. The key to finding her family rested in her ability to find out what had happened to Fay.

Bree and Naomi ran down the street toward the Rock Harbor County Jail. A cold rain drizzled, stinging Bree's face as she loped along just ahead of Naomi. She burst through the doors to find Mason behind his desk, a roast-beef sandwich halfway to his mouth.

"Mason, I need to see Fay's notebook—the one in her backpack." Bree shook the cold water from her hair.

Mason put down his sandwich. "What's this all about?"

Bree hadn't let loose of Davy's glove for a moment. The texture of the wool kept her from thinking it had all been a dream. She held it out wordlessly.

Mason's eyebrows shot up as he took the glove from her. "Davy's?"

The door crashed open, and Hilary rushed into the room. "I stopped by the store and Mother told me the news." She hurried to her husband's side and snatched the glove from his hand. "It *is* Davy's."

"Would someone please tell me what's going on?" Mason demanded.

Naomi quickly explained. Hilary danced around the room, waving the glove like a trophy, then spun around to Bree and hugged her. Bree clung to her tightly. Apparently Hilary had forgiven her for their tiff the night of the campaign party.

Mason stroked his chin. "I reckon we could take a look at that notebook. It doesn't say much though. I didn't see anything about a woman and a cabin." He went to the back room.

"You have to find this woman, Bree," Hilary commanded. "Drop everything you're doing and find her."

Hilary usually ordered her around, so why did this particular command cause something within her to rise up and rebel at the demand? She had intended to drop everything anyway, but all at once she'd had enough of meekly obeying to keep the peace. She wasn't an extension of Hilary's brother; she was Bree Nicholls, a woman in her own right with hopes, dreams, and desires. Somehow she had to make sure her efforts to resurrect the old Bree didn't fizzle like green wood in a fire.

She lifted her chin, but the words of independence died on her tongue when she stared into Hilary's face. "I will," she said. "I'll do everything in my power to find the woman."

Mason came in with the notebook in his hand. "Here it is, but like I said, I don't think you'll find anything in it." He held it out to Bree, but Hilary made a grab for it.

"Let me see. I'm a fast reader. I'll take it home and read it tonight." Hilary held the book to her chest. "I'll call you in the morning, and we'll decide what to do next."

Bree's hand dropped. She saw the look of censure on Naomi's face and hunched her shoulders. "Let's go, Naomi," she said.

Back outside, the cold wind stung her cheeks. Naomi walked silently at her side toward the lighthouse.

"Why do you let her do that to you?" Naomi burst out when they finally reached the gate to Bree's home. "I thought you were developing some backbone lately. You curl up like a pill bug when it comes to Hilary."

"You don't understand," Bree said.

"You're right, I don't understand. I remember what you were like when you first came here. Bright, interested in everything, open about your feelings. Now you never talk about how you feel. It's 'Yes, Hilary,' and 'I'll take care of that right away, Hilary.' You never say no to her. You poke fun at her and laugh when I call her the poodle, but the minute she arrives on the scene, you crumple. What gives?"

Bree wasn't sure she could explain it. "I never had a sister before," she began. "When we moved here, I was desperate for Hilary to like me, for everyone to accept me. I don't know how it happened, but little by little, as I tried to fit into the Nicholls family, I left pieces of myself strewn along the way. I'd always felt like a misfit. My mom is an alcoholic, and I never knew my dad. What did I know about how a real family acted? So I tried to emulate Hilary, to become someone she would approve of."

The wind teased tendrils from Naomi's long braid and blew them out around her head in a halo. Her eyes softened. "Bree, that must have been awful. But God loves you just as you are. His opinion is the only one that matters. We all have things we wish we could change about ourselves. You admire Hilary's self-assurance, the way she fits in. But she's not perfect, and you know it."

Bree nodded.

"So be yourself, speak your mind, be your own person. God created you for a purpose."

"You sound like Anu," Bree said softly.

"Anu is a wise lady. Listen to her." Naomi gave her a little shove. "Now go feed your dog. Tomorrow we'll figure out what to do next."

"I'm going to Palmer and Lily's for a late supper. We've been trying to get together for nearly two weeks. Can you and Charley get away tomorrow? We'll take the dogs to Donovan's and see if they can pick up the scent."

"Sure. What time?"

"Early. Maybe seven-thirty? I'd like to start tonight, but it's already dark. Daylight would be better."

"See you then." Naomi squeezed her hand then jogged toward the Blue Bonnet.

Bree hurried inside and fed Samson, then she and the dog climbed into the Jeep. It was already later than she'd planned. The Chamberses would be wondering what had happened to her.

When Bree arrived, after the warm greetings and the cries of delight from the twins at Samson's appearance, they went right to the dining room table. Lily had fixed a big pot of vegetable soup with warm, crusty rolls made from her grandmother's recipe.

After supper, Palmer lit a fire. Paige and Penelope giggled and climbed on Samson's back as if he were a pony while he panted on a rug in front of the great stone fireplace. Their new puppy yipped and tugged on Samson's fur with a ferocity the adults found comical.

Lily brought Bree a mug of hot spiced cider. Wrapping her cold fingers around the hot cup, Bree settled back against the plump sofa cushions. "I love this room," she told her host and hostess. "It reminds me of a ski lodge, with the exposed wooden beams and that wonderful fireplace."

"That's why we bought it," Lily said. She sat beside Bree and offered her a cookie. "It reminded us of the ski lodge in Lake Tahoe we go to so often. Palmer did such a great job on the fireplace, but I thought we might end up in divorce court before it was over. You know how anal he is about his tools, and when he couldn't find that one screwdriver, he accused me of using it."

Palmer gave her a wounded look. "I never loan my tools, so I thought you or the twins had taken it."

"Where was it?"

Lily shrugged. "He never did find it."

Bree chuckled at the sight of another family's minor tiffs. She missed that camaraderie. She took the plate of cookies and passed them to Palmer. "Those look great, but I'm stuffed. I haven't had a meal like that since the last time you had me to supper. My meals usually consist of peanut butter sandwiches or a cup of soup."

"No wonder you're so slim," Lily scolded. "I'll have to invite you over more often and fatten you up."

"I hope that's not the only reason you invite me over," Bree said with a laugh. She felt a real kinship with Lily and Palmer. Lily had rushed to be with her the minute she heard about Rob's plane going down. For months, Palmer had blamed himself. Rob had asked him to give the plane a once-over before the trip, but Palmer had gotten held up on a business trip to Milwaukee. Palmer had cried with Bree the minute he got back to town. Their support and encouragement had been vital to her. They still were.

"You know better," Lily said.

"How's the investigation going?" Palmer asked. He sat in a brown leather armchair with his feet propped on a matching ottoman. "Sad business."

"It's not going anywhere fast," Bree told him. "There are no real leads I know of. Samson and I found Fay's backpack, but Mason said there wasn't much of anything extraordinary in it. Hilary took Fay's notebook home tonight to see if there are any clues in it."

"You should let Mason handle it. Why are you getting involved? It might be dangerous," Lily said.

"You're not going to believe this," Bree said. She told them of the woman and the discovery of Davy's glove. "So you see, this woman could be my link to the plane."

Lily clapped her hands. "Oh, Bree, how wonderful! I know finding them means everything to you. You've kept so much of yourself bottled up this past year. I do pray for closure for you."

Bree took a sip of her hot cider. "You had some business dealings with Fay, didn't you, Palmer? Had you finalized the deal to buy that old mine?"

He nodded. "Pretty much. The papers were ready to be signed. Steve is dragging his feet now, but I think we've got all the kinks ironed out and are ready to close the deal."

"I still don't understand what you want with that old place," Lily sighed.

"Our town will die if we don't get some tourism," Palmer said. "That old mine will make a great living museum. I could buy another mine, but I'm glad this deal is going through. It might help Steve out a bit. Besides, I'm doing my part to save a slice of Yooper history."

Bree leaned forward. "Did Fay ever mention the plane crash to you?"

Palmer's brow furrowed. "Not that I recall. Oh, she was sorry about it when it happened, of course. Why?"

"I need a clue for where to look for that cabin. Fay was all over the U.P., and it's as hard to know where to look for the woman's cabin as it is to know where to look for the plane. I'm going to Donovan's tomorrow to see if the dogs can pick up her scent, but if that fails, I'll have to figure out where to look next."

"You don't suspect a link between Fay's death and the plane crash, do you?" Palmer asked.

Bree considered his question then slowly shook her head. "Not really a link. How could there be? The crash was nearly a year ago, and it was an accident. But maybe retracing her steps could lead me to the woman. Besides, Steve has asked me to help."

Lily moved the fire screen back into place and returned to sit beside Bree. "You do what you have to do," she told her. "Though Palmer wants to help Steve by taking this mine off his hands, I'm still not convinced he didn't kill her himself. He had plenty of motive."

Palmer frowned. "Steve is too strait-laced for murder. He's not dangerous, but the real murderer sure is. I don't want you to get hurt, Bree. Whoever killed Fay is dangerous. He may not want to hurt you, but if you keep poking around, he may have no choice."

"I'll be careful," Bree said. "I have Samson, after all."

At the sound of his name, Samson pricked his ears forward and got up. The girls protested and called to him when he came to stand at Bree's knees. He pressed his cold nose against her hand, and she rubbed his thick fur. "You'll protect me, boy, won't you?" He whined, his dark eyes full of love, and she petted his back.

Palmer snorted. "Samson is a great dog, but I'm afraid the only danger a prowler would face would be getting licked to death."

Samson seemed to understand this slur on his integrity, for the fur on his neck stood up, and he gave Palmer a long stare. They all laughed.

"Better watch out, Palmer, or Samson will show you just how protective he can be," Bree said.

Palmer leaned forward and patted the dog's back. "He doesn't scare me any."

Samson gave him another long stare then turned back to Bree.

"I think you've offended him," Lily laughed. "Maybe a doggie treat will sweeten his mood."

"I happen to have one in my backpack." Bree dug into her pack and pulled out a box of doggie treats. Palmer took one and offered it to Samson. The dog sniffed it but turned away and laid his head on Bree's knee.

"He's never done that before." Bree rubbed her hands over her dog. "I wonder if he's getting sick."

She grasped Samson's chin and raised his head so she could look into his eyes. The dog's dark and alert gaze reassured her. He pressed his nose against her hand again. Frowning, she rubbed his head. "He seems to be all right. I don't know what's up with him. Maybe he's tired. I'm beat myself."

"Let me put some of these cookies in a plastic bag for you to take home," Lily said hastily when Bree rose to say her good-byes.

"I wouldn't turn them down." Bree scooped up Paige and hugged her. The feel of the little girl's warm body, round and innocent, brought back so many memories, both good and painful. She set her down and grabbed up Penelope.

"How much do you love me?" she asked the child.

Penelope wrapped her arms around Bree's neck and squeezed.

"Wow, that much?" Bree hugged her close and kissed the petal-soft cheek.

The little girl nodded, and Bree kissed her again before setting her down. "I'd better get going. Samson and I are going to get back on the search trail again tomorrow."

"Good luck," Lily said. "I'll be praying."

"Thanks." She wanted to say it wouldn't do any good, but maybe her heart was changing about that. Someone seemed to be watching out for her.

"And watch your back," Palmer advised.

"I'll be careful," Bree promised. "Nothing is going to happen to me." Lightning didn't strike twice in the same place. Fate had tapped Rob and Davy on the shoulder and left her alone. She had a feeling that state of affairs wasn't going to change.

She drove home and parked the Jeep. Walking to the door in the cold night air, she heard wolves howling in the distance. Samson growled low in answer and sounded much like a wolf himself. The sound brought back Aunt Mathilda's words about the Hound of Heaven, and Bree shivered. Such nonsense was just that—nonsense. Wasn't it? Bree didn't know anymore.

— *14* —

*S*aturday dawned with more cold rain drizzling from a glowering sky. Everything was gray, from the sky to the wind-whipped waves on Lake Superior. Not a good day for a search, but Bree didn't have time to wait for good weather. With a yellow rain slicker and hat covering her orange jumpsuit, Bree would stay mostly dry, but the dogs would be wet and muddy by the time the morning was done.

Hilary had called first thing in the morning to report she'd found nothing in the notebook. She agreed to meet for coffee at two and give Bree the notebook then. Bree loaded the gear in the Jeep then drove to Naomi's and honked the horn. Naomi dashed through the rain and hopped into the car.

Shaking the water from her hair, she slammed the door. "Wouldn't you think it'd be snowing by now? I'd rather have snow than this heavy rain."

"Me too. Though the dogs should have no trouble getting the scent. The problem is the glove has been handled so much."

Naomi seemed lost in thought as they drove to Donovan's. Bree thought about asking her what was happening with her quest to get closer to Donovan, but she held her tongue. There was nothing more annoying than being questioned about your love life when nothing was going on.

The O'Reilly house was dark when Bree parked the Jeep. A dim blue glow brightened one window. "The kids must be watching cartoons," she said.

The women got the dogs out of the vehicle, then Bree let them sniff Davy's glove. She wasn't too hopeful for the day's search. Too many people had handled the glove. The scent they needed would be overlaid with the entire O'Reilly household, her own scent, Hilary's, Mason's, and Naomi's.

Sure enough, the dogs nosed aimlessly through the brush and grew more dispirited as the rain continued to pelt them. They found no clear scent cone to follow. "This is getting us nowhere," Bree said after an hour. "It's nine o'clock. I'm ready to pack it in and head home. It was a long shot anyway."

"You go ahead. I'll walk back. I'm going shopping for clothes for the kids with Donovan today." Her color high, Naomi winked at Bree and took Charley toward the front door of the O'Reilly house. "I bet there are two kids ready for some breakfast."

"Good hunting," Bree called with a chuckle. She put Samson in the Jeep and drove home.

Her lighthouse seemed warm and welcoming. The rain had finally stopped, and the clouds were breaking up. A fire would be welcome after the wet search. She toweled off Samson then lit the gas log in the fireplace. After a hot shower, she'd feel almost human again. A half-hour later, dressed in jeans and a warm fleece top, she took the wool throw from the back of the couch and curled up in front of the fire.

Though the morning's search had been fruitless, Bree felt a sense of hope and purpose. At least she had a clue now.

Rob's Bible still sat on the end table by the window. Bree's gaze lingered on it. How could it hurt? She reached for it hesitantly. Anu had said to read Psalm 112 for words of wisdom on discerning true motives. She held the Bible to her nose and smelled the aroma of leather and print. Rob had read this book every morning, yet he'd still betrayed her. She almost put it aside, but she bit her lip and flipped open the cover to the table of contents. She found the page number for

Psalms and flipped through the thin pages almost to the middle of the book. She turned to number 112.

> *Praise the LORD.*
> *Blessed is the man who fears the LORD,*
> *who finds great delight in his commands.*
> *His children will be mighty in the land;*
> *the generation of the upright will be blessed.*

These verses reminded Bree of Anu. Hilary was respected and had married well, and even Rob had been someone the town looked to for leadership as fire chief.

> *Wealth and riches are in his house,*
> *and his righteousness endures forever.*
> *Even in darkness light dawns for the upright,*
> *for the gracious and compassionate and righteous man.*
> *Good will come to him who is generous and lends freely,*
> *who conducts his affairs with justice.*

She frowned as she thought of Steve. He loaned money generously, though it wasn't his own money. Did that apply? This was harder than it looked.

> *Surely he will never be shaken;*
> *a righteous man will be remembered forever.*
> *He will have no fear of bad news;*
> *his heart is steadfast, trusting in the LORD.*
> *His heart is secure, he will have no fear;*
> *in the end he will look in triumph on his foes.*
> *He has scattered abroad his gifts to the poor;*
> *his righteousness endures forever;*
> *his horn will be lifted high in honor.*

The wicked man will see and be vexed,
he will gnash his teeth and waste away;
the longings of the wicked will come to nothing.

The wicked man was the one she was after. But she still didn't know how to pick him out. She ran through the suspects. Steve, Eric, Lawrence, Kade. And Hilary, though Bree didn't even want to think about that. But she couldn't rule her out yet.

Her gaze wandered back to the verses. *Wealth and riches are in his house.* Did that mean every person as rich and respected as Hilary was righteous? Surely not. She would have to ask Anu.

The words she'd read were strangely comforting. She'd been taught religion was a crutch for weak people, and she'd been appalled when Rob began to attend church and take Davy with him. They'd fought long and hard about it, but he'd refused to budge. If a Christian could do what Rob had done to her, what good was being a Christian? She wished she could talk to Anu about it, but she'd never told Rob's family of his infidelity. Let them keep the perfect image they had of him.

Samson put his cold nose against her bare ankle, and the wet sensation jolted her out of her reverie. She put the Bible aside. The sun had finally come out, and she could get her chores done, though the mud outside wouldn't make it easy. "Ready to get going, Samson?" Those flower beds wouldn't get mulched by themselves.

The dog woofed, practically dancing with excitement. What she should do was get that brick repointed, but there was no way she would ever climb out on the tower again. Handyman work had never been her forte. Before Rob's death, her expertise had started and stopped with wallpaper and paint, but little by little she was learning. She would have to pay someone to do it, though her bank balance might complain. After she mulched, she would make some calls. Snow would arrive any day, and the tower would never make it through another Upper Peninsula winter.

Samson followed her as she went downstairs and out the kitchen door to the backyard. She grabbed the pitchfork and began to layer straw onto her strawberry beds. The straw was soggy and heavy, and soon she was perspiring. After a few minutes, Samson turned his head and barked.

"What is it, boy?" Probably something as simple as the black squirrels raiding the bird feeders. As far as Samson was concerned, the neighborhood answered to him.

"I heard there was a tower around here somewhere about to fall down." Kade's deep voice startled her.

Bree jerked at the sound, and the straw on her pitchfork flipped onto Samson's head. He gave her a wounded look and shook himself. She laughed, and Kade's deep chuckle joined hers. Dressed in jeans and work boots with a rope slung over his shoulder, he grinned at the dog's outrage. A Chicago Cubs cap, marred with flecks of paint and dirt, was pulled low over his eyes. A leather apron hung from his right hand.

She set down the pitchfork and wiped her fingers on her jeans. "You look like you're ready for work." A surprising warmth spread through her belly at the sight of him. Anxiousness too. Was he angry about the puppy? Maybe he'd been too mad to call her on the phone and wanted to confront her in person.

He opened the gate and stepped inside the backyard. Samson rushed to him and rubbed his head against Kade's hand. Kade grabbed the dog's head in both hands and worried it back and forth. Samson growled playfully, pleasure in every line of his posture.

Kade released the dog and turned to Bree. "I bet you didn't know brickwork was the way I put myself through college."

Bree's eyes widened as the reason for his attire penetrated. "How did you know it needed doing?"

"I ran into Naomi and Donovan at the coffee shop this morning, and she mentioned it. I wasn't sure I should even help after the way you sandbagged me with that pup." His eyes narrowed. "You knew I didn't want her to have a dog."

Uh-oh, she'd known it was coming. "She needed one, Kade."

His mouth twisted. "If you could hear that puppy cry at night." He shook his head. "But the worst of it is she isn't taking responsibility for him."

Now Bree did feel guilty. "She's only had him a week. Give them time to adjust."

"I don't have much choice." He grinned, but it was feeble. He moved forward and grabbed her bucket. "Okay if I use this?"

"Sure. Naomi was with Donovan? Were the kids with them?"

"Yep. Looked like one big happy family."

Bree couldn't help the delighted grin that spread across her face. "She must be making headway."

"Looked that way to me, if by making headway you mean her and Donovan becoming an item." He took the hose and sprayed water in the bucket then began adding dry mortar mix from a bag.

Bree watched until she realized she was admiring the muscles in his back as they rippled under his shirt. Her cheeks heated and she looked away.

Kade gave the mortar a final stir. "It looks about ready. Show me how to get to the tower, and we'll have this job done in no time." He stood and hefted the bucket in one hand.

Much as she hated to accept charity, right now Bree felt like hugging him in gratitude. "This way," she told him. He followed her as she led him through the kitchen and up the steps to the second floor.

"I like your house," he told her. "You've done a great job on the floors. Naomi told me you and Rob did most of this yourselves."

High praise indeed, since he seemed to know something about house restoration. Bree's spirits lifted. "I'll just be glad when it's all done." His compliment gave her an inordinate amount of pleasure.

She paused outside the door to the catwalk. Her mouth went dry as her hand reached for the door handle. She didn't want to go back out there, but with Kade's attention on her, she had no choice. The handle resisted her, but she managed to thrust open the door and step outside. Thankfully, there was little wind, but the metal walkway shuddered under their weight. Her stomach plummeting, Bree gripped the railing tightly.

Kade moved past her and set down the bucket. He strapped on the leather apron and pulled a trowel from its pocket. Unwinding the rope from his shoulder, he tied it to the bucket, which he tied to the railing. He then opened a window and attached a harness to a post inside the tower. Within two minutes he was rappelling down the side of the tower.

Bree watched him and wished she could be so nonchalant about dangling forty feet from the ground. Gingerly moving to the railing, she peered over the edge and watched as he began to repair the mortar.

"It's not as bad as I was expecting," he called up to her. "The way Naomi talked, I thought the tower was about to crumble away. It just needs a little shoring up. I should be done in about an hour. There's no sense in you keeping a death grip on that railing. Go back inside, and I'll tell you about my fee when I'm done."

His fee? Her bank balance left much to be desired. Still, at least she hadn't had to do the job, and if she had to, she could borrow some funds from Anu. Her gratitude overwhelmed her disgruntlement at having to pay Kade for the job. He surely wouldn't charge her as much as a brick mason would.

He didn't seem to notice her surprise. He paused to swipe a hand across his forehead as a bird squawked from the power lines in front of the house.

Kade lifted his head. "Mazzy!"

A starling lifted from the lines and came swooping toward him.

"Watch out!" Bree shouted. She ducked as the bird tried to land on her head. Picking up a trowel, she tried to swipe at it.

"Don't hurt her, Bree! Mazzy, come," Kade called. The bird squawked again then flew down and perched on Kade's shoulder.

"You know this bird?" Bree blinked. How had he trained a wild bird to come when he called? Though he had a compelling personality, she found it hard to believe his charisma extended to wild animals.

"She thinks I'm her mother," Kade said, shooting an impudent grin up at her.

Bree covered her mouth and chuckled. "I can't imagine anyone less like a mother."

Kade's grin faded. "Or a father, according to Lauri." When he reached around and held out his hand, Mazzy stepped onto it. "I found this one on the ground, barely hatched and without feathers. I fed her until she was ready to scavenge for food then turned her loose in June, but she's hung around all this time."

"I didn't think it was possible to feed baby birds. Did you chew up the worms and regurgitate them for her?" Bree laughed again at the incongruous thought.

"She liked cat food mixed with water just fine, didn't you, girl?" He leaned back in the harness and stroked the bird's head. "I would get some on my finger then poke it down her beak. She gobbled it right up."

"You're a man of many talents," Bree said.

"Yeah, well, don't think you're getting something for nothing," he warned. "You'll have to pay for it with your time." Her smile faded as she realized his fee did not likely involve monetary payment. If he asked her out, what could she say? Her heart told her she wasn't ready for any new relationship. Not now, maybe never.

"I'll make some coffee," she said abruptly. "Come inside when you're done."

He nodded. "I'll rappel on down to the ground and come in the back door."

As Bree backed away from the rail, Mazzy came squawking toward her. Bree ducked inside and shut the door, barely avoiding the bird's demented attempt to perch on her head.

She found a tin of chicken downstairs in the pantry and decided to make chicken salad. It felt strange to be preparing a meal for a man again. Strange but good. She hummed as she chopped celery and walnuts then stirred in mayonnaise.

By the time she'd prepared lunch, she heard Kade in the backyard cleaning up his tools. Bree's palms prickled. How stupid to react like that. She'd been out of contact with everyone but family for too long.

One of the verses she'd read in the psalm came to her. *His heart is secure, he will have no fear.* That certainly applied to Kade. Giving of himself and dangling fearlessly from the tower to help a friend. Did that mean she could cross him off the suspect list? She wished she knew for sure.

A few minutes later, Kade opened the back door and stepped into the kitchen. He took off his cap and apron and hung them on a peg by the door. "The coffee smells good."

"You don't even have any mortar on you." She was usually covered from head to toe with paint or any other material she worked with.

He winked at her. "What can I say—I'm neat. I take my coffee black."

Bree poured him a cup of coffee then made the chicken salad sandwiches and placed them on plates. She set them on the table and pulled out her checkbook.

"How much do I owe you?" she asked.

"Whoa, I never said you would have to pay in money." He took the checkbook out of her hand and tossed it on the table.

Here it comes. She crossed her arms over her chest. The last thing she wanted to do was offend him, but anything more than friendship between them was impossible. She couldn't deny the thought brought her a mixture of elation and terror; however, it was a dizzying proposition she'd rather not face.

When she didn't respond or even laugh, Kade frowned. "You didn't really think I would charge a friend for something like this, did you?"

"Are we friends? I thought we were just acquaintances."

His frown turned to a scowl. "You sure keep that wall high around yourself, don't you? I don't have any designs on you. The good Lord knows I already have my hands full with Lauri. I don't need another difficult relationship." He pointed a finger at her. "You owe me. Thanks to you, I'm saddled with a pup I expressly told Lauri she couldn't have. Now you have to fix it."

"What's he doing?"

He sighed and took a bite of his sandwich then broke off a piece and tossed it to Samson. "Lauri's dog is driving us both crazy. He doesn't do anything he's supposed to do. Could you come out and give us some more pointers? You owe me."

"I'm sorry, Kade, I'd forgotten all about the puppy." How could she have been so self-centered? She'd promised Lauri to get started on the training right away, but the days had slipped past too quickly. Some trainer she was. "I'll be glad to do that. I have about an hour and a half before I have to meet Hilary for coffee. How about I come out now?"

A grin of relief spread across his face. "Great. If Lauri concentrates on something else, maybe those moods of hers will get better." He spread his hands. "What am I doing wrong with her?" he asked.

"You're asking the wrong person," she said. "I'm no good at sibling relationships. I'm an only child, and I don't even know where my mother is. I waffle like a kite without a tail when it comes to standing up to Hilary, and when it comes to speaking my mind I'm a sphinx."

"Sounds to me like you just did pretty good with speaking your mind." His gaze caught and held hers. His grin broke the tension between them. "What you're describing is exactly how I feel with Lauri. I can't seem to talk to her. I used to be the perfect older brother.

She would brag about me to her friends, and she never missed calling me every Saturday night. When I moved in, everything changed."

"Could it be because you've quit being her brother and are trying to parent her?" Bree offered the advice tentatively, aware she didn't have the right to judge anyone else's actions. Not when her own had been so faulty.

Kade didn't seem to take offense at her criticism. "I've wondered about that. But she's as wild as the porcupine under my front porch and just as prickly. She needs *some* guidance. If I didn't parent her, she'd be out every night with only God knows what kind of riffraff."

"Are you sure?" Bree asked quietly. "Maybe if her brother was there to run around with and show off to her friends, she'd want to stay home more."

"You don't understand, Bree." Kade rose and grabbed his hat from the peg. "I'd better get going. I need to pick up some dog food on the way."

She was an idiot. Advice had a tendency to turn into a rabid dog and bite the one who offered it. She followed Kade and Samson out the door.

They were both silent as Kade drove out past the city limit sign. He stopped at Konkala Service Station and ran in to buy dog food while the women waited in the truck. Once he was back in the vehicle, he turned onto Whisper Pike and entered the forest.

When the silence threatened to grow uncomfortable, Bree cleared her throat. "I'm sorry," she said. "You know your sister better than I do."

Kade made a noncommittal sound. Bree tried again to break the silence. "I haven't seen Naomi all morning. Did she say what she was going to do after lunch with the O'Reillys?"

"Something about going shopping with them."

Bree raised an eyebrow. "Sounds like she's making definite progress. She's meeting me this afternoon to see what we can find out about . . ." She let her voice trail off. Maybe she shouldn't talk about it with him. There was still the issue of his being at the scene the night Fay died.

"Find out about what?"

He might know something about the woman. She didn't have to tell him everything she knew. "Have you seen a woman around in the woods? Shapeless clothes, old fedora on her head, maybe a little kid with her?"

Kade frowned. "Not that I can remember. Who is she?"

"I guess that woman the O'Reilly kids saw was real. I thought she might have seen the plane's wreckage."

"Why would she feed the kids then abandon them in the forest?" Kade's voice rose. "If Timmy had died when she could have helped him—" He broke off and shook his head. "I'll keep an eye out for her, but it sounds like a slim chance, if you don't mind my saying so."

She *did* mind. Terribly. But once again, she swallowed how she really felt and settled back against the seat with a shrug. He didn't know the full story, and it was just as well.

A woodpecker, no doubt after beetles and other insects, pounded on the wall of the old cabin. Rachel had tried to shoo him away on numerous occasions, but he always came back, and now she was too distraught to care.

Sam's disobedience in town yesterday had given her pause over what to do with him while she went to Chicago. What if he disobeyed again and wandered off into the woods? With travel time, she'd be gone two days. Maybe she should take him with her. But even as the thought crossed her mind, she rejected it. Sam was too fragile to sleep on a park bench. Thanksgiving wasn't far off, and the autumn nights dropped to freezing and sometimes even lower.

There was no help for it. She would have to leave him home alone. Her gaze lingered lovingly on the boy. He sat coloring quietly on the rug in front of the wood stove. The wood stove! She gave a small gasp. Sam had never put wood in the fire. This was a different wrinkle in the problem. Rachel rubbed her forehead.

Could she find some discreet person in town to watch him? But she knew no one. She'd been careful to keep her distance, to meld into the background like a neutral wall color. People talked in small towns, and she knew a few people had noticed her on her infrequent excursions, but the rumor mill would rev up if she brought a small boy to town. That was out of the question.

Her gaze sought the wood stove again. "Sam, you're a big boy. Would you like to learn to help Mother by putting wood in the stove?" No one knew the danger of fire better than Rachel. But surely he was big enough to do a simple task like keeping the fire going.

Sam's head jerked up, and his green eyes widened. He scrambled to his feet. "I can do it!"

Rachel joined him in front of the stove. "This is very important, Sam. If you make a mistake, you could burn the house down. I want you to pay close attention."

He nodded, anticipation gleaming in his small face as if she'd offered him candy.

"Okay. First, you open the damper. See this thing? You move it so it's straight up and down. Can you reach it?"

Sam came around to the side of the stove and reached up. "Like that?"

"Exactly right," she said. "Then open the door to the stove. Take the poker and move the logs around until they are lying tightly against the coals."

Gingerly, Sam took the poker in both hands and managed to prod the logs a bit. It wasn't perfect, but it would have to do. Rachel nodded. "Good. Now grab a log and put it on top of the others, laying it the same way. Do three of them that way."

Sam laid down the poker and grabbed the first log. Puffing, he shoved it into the stove. He wasn't strong enough to push it where it needed to go, and it rolled out onto the floor along with hot coals. Rachel grabbed the bucket of water she kept near the stove for that purpose and doused the coals.

"Sorry." Sam looked as though he might cry.

"It's okay, Sam. It's my fault. You're not quite big enough yet." Rachel felt near tears herself as she finished loading the stove. Chewing on her lip, she knew she had no choice. She'd leave plenty of blankets. Sam would be warmer inside the cabin with blankets than he would be sleeping out in the open air with only his coat. And during the day, the temperature shouldn't be too bad.

"I have to leave in the morning, Sam. I'll be gone two days. I want you to stay in the cabin except to use the privy."

Sam's lips trembled. "Two whole days? Why can't I come?"

"I have to find us a new place to live, a better place. You can come with me next time. But I don't want you to bother the stove. I know it's a little chilly, but just stay bundled in the bed with the blankets. I got you a new book to read too." Sam liked nothing better than a new book, which was a good thing, for she knew he would need good reading skills to make it through med school. He would make her proud someday.

But her bribe did little to calm his agitation. "Who will take care of me?" He thrust out his lower lip, and tears pooled in his eyes.

"You're a big boy, Sam. You can help Mother by feeding yourself, can't you? I'll leave you some nice boiled eggs, a few peanut butter sandwiches, and cereal. I even got you some cookies. See?" She opened the cookie jar and was gratified to see his eyes go round. Cookies were a rare treat.

Then his lips trembled again, and tears spilled down his small face. "I'm scared. I don't like to be alone. What if the wolves come back?"

"They can't get inside the cabin," she said. "Besides, they won't bother you. Winter hasn't come yet, and they have plenty to eat."

"A bear could get in."

Rachel hid a smile. "You'll be fine, Sam. When was the last time we saw a bear?"

His forehead wrinkled, and he bit his lip. "I don't know."

"Exactly. The bears will leave you alone. You can practice printing your letters all you want. There's plenty of paper. I know it will be lonely, but I have to go, son."

"Take me with you." He began to cry in earnest, and Rachel wavered. She'd worry about him every minute anyway. If he were with her, at least she wouldn't have that anxiety.

Then she shook her head. "I have to talk to a lady about a job, and you would just be in the way. It might make me lose the job, and I must have it."

Sam threw himself against her and began to wail. Rachel gathered him against her and sat in the rocker with him in her lap. "Hush, Sam. I thought you were a big boy. These two days will fly by, you'll see. Now be Mother's big boy. We only have each other to depend on. I'm counting on you to be strong for me."

He hiccuped and buried his face against her chest. Rachel began to sing all the nursery rhymes she could think of, from "Farmer in the Dell" to "Three Blind Mice." Her gravelly voice would win no awards, but Sam seemed to like it. Soon his sobs changed to deep breathing. As he slept nestled against her, Rachel knew there was nothing like motherhood. Her life was so different with this little person in it. She cuddled him closer and dozed off herself.

Shadows darkened the room when she awoke. Though the fire had gone out, the warmth of Sam's small body kept the chill away. She laid him on his cot then began to prepare the food he would need while she was away. If only there were some other way. But there was no use wailing over what couldn't be changed.

Soon things would be different. It was only two days, she told herself. Two short days. She deserved to be happy after everything that had happened. And Sam too. Though he never talked about it, the nightmares in the beginning had been horrific. He'd hung in the seat belt beside his dead father for at least an hour before she rescued him. But those days were over, and the memories had already faded. His nightmare came less and less, and soon he'd have no memories of any life but the one he shared with her.

*B*ree's enthusiasm was subdued when she entered The Coffee Place. Playing with Zorro had been a real treat, though Kade hadn't said much as she gave him tips on training the puppy, and she knew he was still annoyed with her observations of how he was treating his sister.

Hilary was already seated in a booth by the window overlooking the water. She'd ordered two mochas and pushed one toward Bree. "I've talked to Mason," Hilary said without preliminaries as soon as Bree sat down. "He saw that woman."

"What? Where?" Bree half rose from her chair.

"At Lars's store. She was getting groceries. He said she looked vaguely familiar, but he got busy and didn't follow up on it until this morning. She was on a wanted poster."

"She's a criminal?"

"The police were looking for her in connection with the murders of twelve nursing home residents in Detroit. But when Mason called, the Detroit police said she'd been exonerated. The poster was an old one. Mason is over at Lars's to see if she mentioned in what direction her cabin was located."

That must be why she'd abandoned Emily and Timmy by the road. She wanted to avoid being seen. "So at least we know Rock Harbor is the closest town to the cabin," Bree said slowly. "That narrows the search down some."

"Not necessarily. Mason has no idea how she got here. She could be driving considerably out of her way just to stay hidden."

Bree's elation died, and she nodded. "Then we wait to hear what Mason has to say."

"There he is now," Hilary said.

Mason's face was grim. He sat next to Hilary and nodded to Bree.

"Well?" Hilary demanded.

"Lars has seen her several times. She comes in with a knapsack and hiking shoes, so he thinks she walks in. But he has no idea where she comes from. She just shows up at the store, gets her provisions, and hurries out. He says he's tried to engage her in conversation, but she never responds much. She comes in every couple of weeks, though she's been in a little more frequently lately. She might be due to come in next week. We could stake out the store and watch for her."

"I don't want to wait that long." Bree gave a heavy sigh. "She could be anywhere then—north, south, east."

Mason nodded. "That about sums it up."

"Then we're back to Fay. I need to go through her things at her home and see if there are any clues there. Any new leads in your office?" Bree asked.

"We're looking into the boyfriend, Eric Matthews."

"Matthews?" Hilary questioned.

"He's Kade's cousin. Been in jail for three years for assault and battery and just got out on work release. As an interesting note, Fay was the one who pressed charges. He beat her up pretty badly. I'm surprised she had anything to do with him once he got out."

"I saw them quarrel the night before Fay died," Bree said.

Mason frowned. "And you're just now telling me this?"

Bree hunched her shoulders. "It didn't amount to much. I knew you'd be looking into him."

"Good grief, Bree, you know better than to keep information like that to yourself." Mason's voice rose, and his glare grew more pronounced.

"Sorry, Mason; you're right. He was just ticked she didn't show up when she was supposed to. She told him she'd be along and to go back and wait. That's it."

His frown faded. "Not much, like you said, but with his history, it's likely he's our killer."

"He was angry that night. I gathered he thought she was stringing him along. He said something about not letting her call the shots this time."

"You holding any other tidbits to yourself?" he asked.

Bree glanced at Hilary from the corner of her eye. There was no way she was going to tell Mason she suspected Hilary. "What about Steve and her uncle?"

"We're looking at both of them. Lawrence had an argument with her over selling the mine, we know that much. And Steve could have killed her in a jealous rage when he found out the baby might not be his."

"He didn't seem to think the baby could be Eric's," Hilary put in.

"Yes, well, he'd say that now, wouldn't he?" Mason said.

Was it her imagination, or was there some tension between Mason and Hilary? Bree studied them covertly. Hilary would barely look at her husband, and Mason didn't have his arm around her as he usually did. Could Mason suspect his own wife?

"And Kade?" she asked in a small voice.

"He was out there on a call about poaching. I confirmed it with his office. The call came in about an hour before you saw him. That's not to say he couldn't have done it. He is Eric's cousin, and there could be some connection. I'm checking into it."

"I think I'll stop by the bank and ask Steve if I can look through the house today," Bree said, rising to her feet.

"Oh, I almost forgot . . ." Hilary dug in her briefcase. "Here's the notebook. Not much in it though."

Bree nodded her thanks and headed out to see Steve. He was in his office, and after some reluctance he gave Bree permission to check out the house. Within minutes she was on her way out of town.

The Asters home was about two miles out of town down Lamppa Lane. After parking at the end of the long driveway, she and Samson walked to the front door of the gracious two-story brick home. Steve had told her the door was unlocked, and the knob turned easily. She stepped inside onto a ceramic tile floor. The entry opened into the dining room to the left. Steve had spared no expense to turn his home into a showplace, according to Fay, and the Aubusson rug under the mahogany dining room table was ample testament to that. All the furnishings had the feel of elegant simplicity that costs the earth.

Where to start? "Let me know if you hear anything," she told Samson. "Stay." She left the dog in the dining room and went past a china cupboard filled with charming crystal figurines of every animal imaginable. Peeking into the kitchen, she saw cherry cabinets and a tumbled marble countertop. A kitchen desk ended the row of cabinets.

She froze. Was that a sound? The sound of her heart pounded in her ears, and she couldn't tell. Then it came again, and her breath eased out. It was just Samson coughing. Why was she so on edge? Steve knew she was here.

She went to the desk and opened it. A hanging file folder held bills; another file held things like insurance policies. She opened the one marked "Life Insurance" and scanned it. Bree blinked at the figure, not sure if she was seeing all the zeros correctly. One million dollars. Steve would have a very good reason to kill Fay. She put the policy back in its folder and continued to look. Rent receipts on several properties they owned in town, old correspondence, Christmas cards.

Bree flipped through the contents of another folder. A letter from a firm called Brannon, Metz & Associates caught her eye. It threatened legal action if the past-due amount of two hundred fifty thousand dollars wasn't repaid within thirty days. Fay had said Steve was out of money, and this proved it. But was that motive enough to kill his wife?

Besides, maybe selling the mine would have eased their financial woes. The money might be a good enough reason if he hated her for having an affair as well.

She closed the desk drawers and made sure everything looked in order before going down the hall to the bedrooms. The master bedroom was at the end of the corridor. It looked like something out of *Arabian Nights*. Opulent silk bed coverings in gold and purple and ornately carved furnishings dazzled Bree. She blinked then moved toward the walnut dresser. She opened a drawer.

Running her hands over Fay's things made her ashamed. She should have waited for Steve; then she wouldn't feel so intrusive. She started to close the drawer, but it wedged in the track. She yanked at it and heard a clunk as something fell out the back. Frowning, she knelt and reached a hand under the dresser. A leather-bound book lay on the floor. Bree took it and sat on her heels. The leather cover was embossed in gold: Fay Asters. She laid it on the bed and continued her search. An hour later, the leather diary was the only possible clue she'd uncovered. That and the insurance policy. She'd have to mention it to Mason, though he probably already knew.

She started toward the front of the house. Samson whined then growled low in his throat.

"Someone's coming, boy?" She heard a noise from the front yard, the muffled sound of a car door slamming. Bree stepped out of the bedroom and glanced out the entry windows. A white van bearing the words MERRY MAIDS on the side sat in the driveway.

She was done here anyway. Taking the diary with her, she opened the door and told Samson to go to the Jeep. Waving at the maids, she got in the Jeep and drove toward town.

The red light on the answering machine was blinking when she walked in the door. Dropping her coat on the chair, she punched the play button and heard Steve's voice: "Bree, this is Steve Asters. I got the autopsy report. Could you meet me at the Suomi at four? I'll be there. I hope you get this message and can join me."

The message ended. Bree glanced at her watch. Nearly 3:30. She would have to get moving if she was going to meet him. She looked at Fay's diary longingly then perched on the edge of a chair in the hall and opened the book.

Fay's distinctive writing slashed across the first page. *January 1.* Nearly eleven months ago. Bree flipped through the pages. They were all diary entries. It would take her awhile to read all of it. Fay's writing was tiny and difficult to decipher. Bree closed the book and went to the living room, where she slipped the diary into the top drawer of the desk. She locked the drawer, something she never did, then pocketed the key.

"Come along, Samson," she told the dog. He obediently followed at her heels.

Suomi Café bustled with customers, and Bree saw no spare tables when she stepped through the door.

"Bree!"

She turned at the sound of her name and saw Steve waving to her from a booth along the right side of the room. Jostling past Molly with a quick greeting, she slid into the seat opposite Steve.

"I wasn't sure if you'd be home to check messages," he said. "I'm buying today. What would you like?"

"Just coffee," she said. "I've eaten lunch." She folded her hands together in front of her and stared at him. "You said you had something to tell me."

He motioned to Molly. "Let me get our order in, then we'll talk."

While he gave Molly their order, Bree studied him. He seemed to have aged since Fay's death. He needed a haircut, his tie was askew, and there was dust on his suit jacket. This was not the put-together man she was used to seeing.

Finished with the waitress, Steve turned back to Bree with a smile she thought was supposed to be ingratiating, but she found it merely sad. Something was missing in Steve now, a vital something that had abandoned him. Maybe Fay had been the spark that gave his life meaning.

Molly brought their coffee. Bree thanked her and took a sip while she waited for Steve to gather his thoughts. His hands shook as he poured sugar from the dispenser into his coffee and stirred it.

"How are things going for you?" she asked.

"Terrible." He stared into his coffee cup then sighed. "The official autopsy report came back late yesterday. The coroner says the injuries aren't consistent with a fall from the cliff. A blow to the back of the head killed her. The other abrasions were postmortem. She was likely arranged at the cliff bottom, not killed there."

Barely daring to breathe, Bree sat back in the booth. Though the news didn't surprise her, she shuddered.

"None of her injuries is consistent with being struck by a car." He stirred his coffee absently. "I'm glad you're helping me, because I'm scared—scared the sheriff will think I murdered her. I wasn't the perfect husband, but I always intended to stay married to her."

For some reason, Bree believed him. Maybe she was gullible, but his grief seemed genuine. She didn't know what to think. This could all be a ploy to get her on his side. Steve might want her to argue his case with Mason. She would agree to help him only so she could find out what Fay might have known about Rob's plane crash.

"I found a diary in the bedroom," she said.

Steve blinked as though awakening from a trance, and Bree realized he'd been lost in his own thoughts. He shook his head. "Fay was always writing things down in her leather diary or that notebook she carried. I hadn't found her diary. Where was it?"

Bree told him. "I took it with me. I hope that's all right."

He nodded. "I'd like it back when you're done though."

"Of course."

Steve shifted restlessly and ran a hand through his hair. "On second thought, my lawyer says the authorities will try to pin this on me. I don't want to give them any more opportunity to do that than they have already. Maybe I'd better take a look at that diary first." A wall seemed to go up around him, and he pushed away his coffee.

"I'm only interested in seeing what she might have said about that woman. I won't pass along anything to Mason."

He stared at her doubtfully then nodded. "Can I trust you, Bree? I don't seem to know who my friends are anymore."

Bree nodded slowly. "I won't tell Mason anything incriminating. I'm only looking for something to lead me to the cabin in the woods."

"I'd still like to see it first. Please bring it to me tomorrow."

"I will." She'd just take a quick peek tonight.

Molly brought Steve's food. The aroma of the chicken pasty made Bree's mouth water, even though she wasn't hungry. "I haven't had a pasty in ages," she said. "These are the best in town. They have rutabaga in them," she added in an attempt to diffuse the tension.

"Those old Welsh miners knew what was good stuff," Steve said, taking a bite.

He ate in silence for a few minutes then cleared his throat.

"She left me with a zillion things to clear up," he said. "The sale of the mine should be done by next week, and I'm dealing with her uncle and all his demands as well as the final details."

"You're still selling it to Palmer then?"

"It's what Fay wanted, and I just don't have the energy to renegotiate with anyone else, so yeah, that's what I'm doing."

Bree had to wonder if that million-dollar insurance policy had anything to do with his decision not to pursue another buyer. It would also account for his desperation to find out who killed Fay. The insurance company would be unlikely to pay until they were sure Steve had nothing to do with it.

Everything about Fay's death seemed to go back to the mine. The mine was only about five miles from Eagle Rock. Could the mine have been where Fay's murder took place? Bree shuddered. Maybe she was clutching at straws, but it wouldn't hurt to check it out. Soon there would be a lot of activity going on out there. Palmer's grand plans to turn it into a mining museum called for quite a bit of construction and massive cleanup efforts. If there were any clues to be found, she'd have to find them right away. Maybe she could get out there tomorrow.

Steve pushed away his half-eaten pasty. "I have some things I want to clear off my desk before I go home. I'd better go. Thanks for believing me, Bree."

Bree watched him leave and wished she could give him the trust he needed.

What about Eric? Fay had been just a girl when she fell for his lines the first time. She'd thought Fay was too savvy to fall for him a second time, but Bree knew there was no guarantee of that. Some mistakes were easy to repeat. She thought of her marriage to Rob, which led to thoughts of Kade Matthews. She longed to put the past behind her and move into a relationship with someone like him, but she didn't know how. Her marriage had lasted eight years. The last time she'd dated, she had been a freshman in college, and she and Rob had married the following summer. Here she was, with her thirtieth birthday looming in four months. What did one do on a date these days? The thought of finding out left her as frightened as hanging from the side of the light tower.

Kade groaned and threw his arm over his eyes. That dratted puppy of Lauri's had cried all night. He'd lost count of how many times he'd climbed out of bed and reheated the water in the water bottle. Even the ticking of the alarm clock failed to soothe Zorro, and the pup clearly wanted others to share his pain.

Kade's eyes felt gritty. What really sounded good was pulling the shades and going back to sleep, but he'd be late for church if he didn't get moving. Skipping altogether seemed an attractive option, but he knew he couldn't do that. He was the morning's worship leader, plus he'd promised to take over Mike Farrell's Sunday school class while Mike visited family in Boston. He had to get up.

He tossed back the covers and swung his legs over the edge of the bed. Zorro heard him stirring and promptly began to whine and cry in his box by the outside door. Kade sighed and shuffled out of his bedroom to check on the puppy. Why was he doing this? Lauri had promised to care for the puppy herself, yet last night she'd wheedled him into taking over that job yet again while she went to a slumber party at a friend's house.

When she came home today, Kade intended to remind her that Zorro was *her* dog. No more shirking of her motherly duties. If she didn't want to care for the puppy herself, he would take the dog back to the pound, though the thought pained him. Still, he had to be firm. Lauri needed to grow up and face her responsibilities. He'd give it a few more days.

Kade picked up Zorro and grimaced at the mess in the box. He started to clean it up then stopped. No, this was a job Lauri needed to do. He took the puppy outside and tried to get him to potty, but Zorro hadn't figured out what to do yet. He attached a long rope to the puppy's collar and left him outside. There was no snow forecast for today, though the air was nippy. Still, the pup's coat was thick, and he'd be fine.

*K*ade's fatigue dropped away once he was among his church family. He kept watching for Lauri—she was supposed to bring her friend to church today—but by the time service was over, she still hadn't shown up. His initial anger escalated when he got home; she wasn't there either.

He fed the puppy then stalked to his truck and took off toward town. Lauri's friend Tracie Mitchell lived in a house on the outskirts of Rock Harbor. Kade pulled up in front. He stared at the house but saw no movement. The siding used to be red, but the color had worn away in most places. Most of the shutters had blown off, and the ones still attached tilted at an angle as they clung to the sides of the windows with only one screw. An assortment of tricycles and toys littered the porch, which was missing a few boards.

He got out of the truck and strode to the steps. Careful to avoid the missing tread, he went to the front door and knocked. There was no answer, so he pounded harder.

"I'm coming. I'm coming. Keep your pants on." The irritated voice coming through the door sounded female.

The door swung open, and Kade faced a woman with wispy blond hair scraped back from her forehead into a clip at the back of her head. She shuffled the baby on her hip and stared at him.

Her pale blue eyes regarded him with suspicion. "Mrs. Mitchell? I'm Lauri's brother, Kade. I wonder if I might have a word with my sister?"

"She ain't here. I ain't seen her since Tracie moved in with her dad in Marquette a month ago."

Kade digested the news in silence. His anger grew, but he managed to keep his voice calm. "I need to find my sister. Do you have any idea where I could look?" Whatever Lauri had been up to, it wasn't good.

Mrs. Mitchell gnawed on her bottom lip. "I 'spect you could check their hangout by the river. You go past Wilson's barn and turn at that dirt track that leads back to Rock River. Park at the river and take the path to the right. Go 'bout a mile, and you'll come to a fork in the path. Turn left, and it will take you to a lean-to by the river the kids all use." A child behind her began to whine, and she slammed the door in Kade's face.

He stood on the porch for a moment then gave a heavy sigh and went to his truck. He made a mental note to call the pastor's wife and suggest that some women call on Mrs. Mitchell and offer the church's help with the house. Then he started the truck and pulled away. It would be like Lauri to assume Kade would wait for her to show up. But Lauri was in for a big surprise. He was done giving her the benefit of the doubt. He should have cracked down harder, sooner. His stomach churned at the thought of what she'd been doing all night. And with whom.

He drove through town to the other side, past Wilson's barn. He almost missed the dirt track. No wonder he'd never noticed it before; it was nearly overgrown with brambles. Kade heard the thorns screech over the paint on his truck as he squeezed down the lane.

After a short time the track widened a bit, though heavy vegetation and tall trees nearly blotted out the sun. Potholes made the going slow, and once he almost hit a tree stump poking up through the fallen leaves. Rounding a curve, he nearly hit a woman in a heavy navy sweater. She wore an old leather fedora on her head and looked vaguely familiar. Kade had a feeling he should know her, but he couldn't make the connection. He assumed he'd seen her around town a time or two.

Her eyes startled and went wide. For a moment she looked as though she might run, then she straightened her shoulders and watched him pass before turning toward town again. He wondered briefly what she was doing back here. He'd seen no houses or anything that hinted of permanent residences.

He finally reached the river and parked. The river was barely more than a stream after the dry summer they'd just had, though he knew in the spring it would boast some beautiful waterfalls. He got out of the truck and took the path Mrs. Mitchell had told him about. Walking along the narrow dirt walkway, he found plenty of evidence that teenagers frequented this area: gum wrappers, soda cans, the remains of a Snickers candy bar, and the ubiquitous cigarette butts. Looking closely, he noticed some of those butts had been hand-rolled.

His lips tightened. Lauri had better not be dabbling in drugs. He'd send her away to military school or something if he had to. He walked as quickly as he dared along the uneven path and finally came to the fork Tracie's mother had mentioned. He turned left and minutes later heard the sound of young voices.

The scent of wood smoke drifted to his nostrils, and he quickened his steps. Pushing his way through a brier patch, he saw a group of four teenagers seated around an open fire. His gaze went to his sister. She sat on a blanket on the ground, leaning back against the legs of a boy who was sitting on a log. She was smoking like the rest, but he was relieved to see it wasn't marijuana.

"Hey, what time is it?" The red-headed girl tossed another log on the fire as she asked. Kade recognized her as Mindy Sturgeon, the high-school principal's daughter.

"Two o'clock," the boy behind Lauri said.

"Holy cow," Lauri said. "I'd better get going. I've missed church, and Kade will be spitting bullets." She started to her feet, but the boy grabbed her by the ponytail and pulled her back against him.

"Relax. He'll get over it. We've got all day yet."

Kade stepped out from the trees. "Wrong," he said. "Party's over."

Lauri screeched and jumped to her feet. The rest of the kids stood hastily and tossed away their cigarettes. Shock rippled over his sister's face, but Kade could see the anger underneath the way he could see a rock at the bottom of a riverbed.

"What are you doing here?" she demanded.

"I might ask the same question of you," he said dryly. "I understood you to be at Tracie Mitchell's, but her mother tells me she hasn't seen you in weeks. Weeks, Lauri." He pressed his lips together. The rest could wait until they were at home. "Get your things."

"Hey, man, we weren't doing anything wrong—" the boy began.

"Stow it," Kade said. Obviously ill at ease, the rest of the kids stood with their hands thrust in their pockets. "Do your parents know where you are?" he asked.

The boy glared at him defiantly while the other two looked at the ground. This kid was bad news waiting to make the front page. "I didn't think so," Kade said. "What are your names? And don't try to lie your way out of this."

"Chip Elliott," one of the boys said. His brown hair was tousled, and he wouldn't meet Kade's gaze.

Mindy opened her mouth, but Kade cut her off. "I recognized you, Mindy." He turned his glare to the boy. "Who's Mr. Smartmouth?"

The boy's defiance was only a veneer. Kade saw panic flicker in his eyes. The teenager mumbled something.

"What was that? Speak up," Kade said sharply.

"Brian Parker," the boy said a little louder.

Brian Parker. Kade's gaze narrowed. "You Max Parker's boy?" Max would have a coronary. The town doctor was proud of his social standing and kept his family in order.

Brian's brave front dissolved. "You're not going to tell my dad, are you?"

"I haven't decided yet," Kade said. He didn't like meddling in other people's business, and it wasn't his job to police Rock Harbor's teenage population. Maybe he'd better stick to his own responsibilities. But he'd let the kids sweat it out a bit. Maybe next time they'd think twice about being so foolish.

He saw Lauri hadn't moved. "Get your things," he told her. "Unless you want your friends to hear what I have to say."

Lauri dropped her gaze. He waited while she went to the lean-to. The silence was long and uncomfortable for the kids, who shuffled their feet and looked everywhere except at Kade.

When she reappeared with a backpack over her shoulder, he addressed the group. "I suggest you all head for home as well. It might be good to confess before I find time to talk to your parents myself."

The kids scattered, and Kade took Lauri's stiff arm. Lauri jerked out of his grasp. "I don't need your help," she snarled. They walked back to the truck in tense silence. He knew she wouldn't hold her anger for long.

Lauri threw herself into the seat and slammed the door. His mouth tight, Kade slid beneath the steering wheel and jabbed the key into the ignition. The engine roared when he floored the accelerator, and it felt almost as satisfying as if he had been able to let loose the roar of rage building in his own chest.

The tires spun in the soft dirt, then the truck moved away from the river. Kade eased his foot off the pedal. The sandy track was too treacherous to go fast, much as he might want to expel his frustration by driving recklessly. He glanced at his sister. She stared out the window, her jaw tight. Then rage burst from her in a flood of bitterness.

"You've ruined my life; I hope you know that!" The gaze she turned on him would have burned him if his own anger hadn't been just as hot.

"Let's not discuss this until we get home," he said tightly.

"Everything always has to be your way, doesn't it? Well, not today.

Let me out of this truck." She struggled with the truck door and managed to open it.

Kade hit the brakes as Lauri hurled herself out of the truck. He threw the transmission into park and jumped out, leaving his door open. Lauri had landed in a patch of raspberry brambles. The harder she tried to extricate herself, the more deeply the thorns pierced her.

"Oh, ow!" She began to cry. Blood marred her forehead, and droplets appeared on her arms.

"Stop thrashing. Let me help you." Kade took out his pocketknife to cut her loose. Laurie kept still, her only movement coming from her chest as she sobbed.

"You don't care about me," she wailed. "I'm just a nuisance to you and everyone else. I wish I'd died with Mom. I hate my life. I hate this town, and I hate you!" Freed from the briers, she sat up and buried her face in her hands.

Her words stung. Could she really hate him? Kade knelt beside her. "That's not true, Lauri. You're the most important thing in my life. You're the reason I'm here in Rock Harbor. I want to do what's best for you." He swallowed and dabbed at the blood on her forehead. She stood.

"You don't even know me anymore, so how can you know what's best?" Spent from her rampage, she let her hands fall to her sides. "Just leave me alone." She brushed past him and got back in the truck.

Kade wished he knew the magic words to reach his sister. She was getting sucked away from him in a whirlpool of rebellion that would ruin her life. He couldn't let that happen. Somehow, there had to be a way to reach her.

At six o'clock, darkness still cloaked Rock Harbor. Snow had finally come to the U.P. Nearly six inches of it blanketed the ground this early Monday morning. Naomi had thrown a coat over her exercise shorts and T-shirt and stood shaking with cold on the lighthouse porch. She rang the doorbell then waited to hear the patter of Samson's feet and his soft woof before letting herself in. Bree had lit every candle in the place, and their apple-cinnamon fragrance welcomed Naomi.

She shut the door behind her and rubbed Samson's head. He whined and wiggled all over with pleasure. "Where's Bree, boy?"

He woofed softly again and turned to look up the stairs. Shrugging out of her coat, Naomi tossed it over the mourner's bench in the entry then went up the steps.

"Bree?" she called. She followed the sound of a rhythmic thudding down the hall to the door on the left. Through the open door, she saw Bree running on the treadmill in her exercise room. She wore a head-set, and her face was a mask of concentration.

Her jerk of surprise was almost comical, and Naomi grinned. Bree slipped the headset down to her neck and turned off the machine.

"Is it that time already?" She grabbed a small towel and mopped her face. "Get the aerobics video ready while I get some water."

"You trying to show me up? I'd have rubber legs if I tried to run before aerobics." Naomi took the Denise Austin aerobics disc out of its case and popped it in the DVD player. She knew Bree trained hard.

They both had to in order to manage the grueling ordeal of tramping over rough terrain on searches.

Bree went to the small refrigerator in the corner and took out a bottle of water. "Want some?"

"Not yet."

Bree took a long swig, and Naomi studied her friend's face. Had she been crying again, or was the redness merely from exercise?

Bree saw her staring. "I'm fine, so don't fuss."

"You've been crying."

Bree took another swallow of water. "It snowed last night."

"I know." Naomi knew Bree was obsessed with the snow and cold. She wished Bree could understand her son wasn't beneath that cold blanket of snow. But it did no good to harp on it. Maybe she'd feel the same way if it were her son lying out there somewhere, his bones naked and uncovered. This world seemed so real, sometimes it was hard even for her to imagine what heaven must be like.

"Let's work up a sweat. I'm not ready for this cold yet. And turn on the sauna," Naomi added.

"I already did," Bree said. She picked up the remote and pressed the play button.

It was better not to talk about some things. They did their aerobics routine then went to the sauna. Naomi stretched out on the slatted cedar bench closest to the ceiling where the air was hottest. She had a book with her but laid it aside. Bree lay on the high bench along the other wall.

Bree rolled over on her stomach. "You haven't told me about your date." Her tone was mildly reproachful.

"It wasn't a date. The kids were there."

"Then why are you blushing?"

"I'm not blushing! It's the heat." Naomi couldn't help the stupid grin that took control of her face.

"It's a sad state of affairs when I have to hear about my best friend's love life through town scuttlebutt." Bree rolled back over and crossed her arms under her head.

"I don't really have a love life, so there's not much to tell." Naomi didn't know why she was so reluctant to talk about it. Maybe she was afraid talking about it would break the special connection that seemed to be developing between her and Donovan.

Bree sat up and stared at her. "Is this serious or something? We've always talked about your men friends, but right now you look the way Samson does when he's rolled in something dead: defensive and ashamed all at the same time. Give me the scoop, or I'll have to treat you like Samson and send you outside."

Naomi managed to laugh at Bree's feeble attempt at humor. "I don't know how he feels yet. I'm afraid to know."

"You know how you feel so soon?"

"It's not soon. I've always liked Donovan," Naomi protested. "And now that he's free . . ."

"You don't intend to let him get away again, is that it?"

Bree said the words mildly, but they stung. "Is that so wrong?" Naomi whispered.

"No, sweetie. I just don't want to see you get hurt. A man in Donovan's position might grab hold of the first available female. I want you to be loved for yourself, not because the guy needs a caretaker for his kids. You're too special to settle for that."

Naomi squeezed her eyes shut. "I'm thirty-two, Bree. I want a home, a family," she said huskily. She didn't want to face Bree's doubts—the same ones that kept her tossing in bed at night. Donovan *did* seem desperate. Who wouldn't be? But in spite of that, she clung to the hope he could love her for herself.

"There are worse things than being unmarried," Bree said.

Naomi knew that was true, but being with Donovan and his children felt right. She felt like a puzzle piece that fit perfectly into an empty spot. She'd prayed and prayed about it, and she really believed the Lord approved of this match.

The women left the hot, cedar-lined room and jumped under the cold shower spray before going back to the sauna. Questions roiled through Naomi's mind. What if this didn't happen for her? What if Donovan was merely using her because he needed someone for the kids? She wished Bree hadn't brought it up.

"You still haven't said what you did Saturday," Bree said.

"We went shopping for school clothes for the kids. Emily had outgrown all her jeans, and Timmy needed new shoes. Then we all went to lunch at the Suomi." Naomi smiled at the memory of their day.

"How did that go?" Bree asked as she led the way back to the sauna.

"Emily is still on her guard with me. She wants you to marry her dad." Naomi attempted a smile. Bree frowned.

"Is that why you didn't want to tell me about it? I told you I wasn't interested in Donovan."

"I know she's just a child." Naomi chuckled, but it had a hollow quality to it. She yawned. "This heat is making me sleepy. I suppose it's about time to get out."

"I have some breakfast burritos in the freezer. You want to stay for breakfast?" Bree stood and clicked off the sauna heater.

"No thanks. I need to get home. But you and I are supposed to go to Anu's for supper tonight. She's fixing spinach lasagna." Naomi followed Bree to the cold shower spray for the final time. "I'll drive tonight. Pick you up about five-thirty, eh?"

"Now that's an offer I can't refuse," Bree said with a smile. "Hey, don't forget your book."

Naomi shook her head. "I lose more books." She took it and followed Bree out of the sauna. Naomi could see the worry in Bree's eyes and wanted to reassure her, but how could she now that the same worry had rooted in her own heart? She might be setting herself up for a world of hurt. If she wasn't willing to take a risk though, she might as well be dead. Without risk, she had no hope of gain. She pushed away the doubts and decided to concentrate on her day. They had supper with Anu to look forward to. She just had to deal with a million details at the bed-and-breakfast first.

Anu greeted them at the door with a hug then put them to work chopping vegetables for salad. The aroma of the lasagna, pungent with garlic and spices, filled the house. Bree loved Anu's house. Furnished with clean-lined Finnish furniture in a light wood, it was homey and welcoming. The three women had often gathered in the kitchen for heart-to-heart talks. Arabia china in a warm yellow color accented the blue-and-white decor.

"Sit down, girls." Swathed in a bright blue apron, Anu came into the dining room with the lasagna. "Supper's ready."

When they were seated, Anu said grace and Bree found herself listening to the words. Was Anu really thankful for every morsel of food she ate, every blessing God brought to her?

Anu lifted her head and began to ladle the food onto their plates. "Bree, what are you finding out about poor Fay?"

"Not much," Bree admitted. She was getting tired of that question. Everyone seemed to think she had an inside track on the investigation just because she'd found Fay's body. There were no answers in sight. Fay's murder seemed just as random and senseless today as it had the night Samson and Charley discovered her body.

"Mason seems overwhelmed by it all," Naomi said.

"Fay's old boyfriend is back in town," Anu interjected.

"He's been here since the funeral," Naomi said. "I think Mason considers him a suspect."

"Yes." Anu nodded. "I told Mason to look at him."

"Do you know him?" Bree asked in surprise.

"He used to be my gardener. Hot-tempered, though a fine worker.

One day he threw the pickax through the shed door when it got stuck shut. Two weeks later, he ripped out my prize roses when his sleeve got tangled in the thorns. I had to ask him to leave."

"Wow," Bree said. "I had no idea. What did he do? Did he leave?"

"He pounded on the door and smeared mud on the windows." Anu raised her eyebrows for effect. "Mason had to come. This was before Eric went to prison."

"So Eric's temper is nothing new to Mason," Bree said.

"Oh no. But you must stay away from him, *kulta*. He is a danger-ous man. I can see from your expression you want to know more, but you cannot get involved with that man."

"I read that psalm you told me to read," Bree said. She paused to study their expressions. "You should see your faces. Don't look so surprised!"

Anu collected herself. "And what did you see there? Did it help you?"

"It made me wonder about Rob," she admitted.

Anu's hand stopped partway to her mouth with a forkful of lasagna. "What about Rob?"

Though she'd been steeling herself to bring up this subject with Anu, her courage nearly failed. "He claimed to be a Christian, yet he did things that were wrong."

"I won't ask you what sins my son committed, as I'm sure they were many and varied," Anu said. "No one is perfect, my Bree, only forgiven in Christ. I must confess to my own besetting sins of pride and jealousy. God helps us to overcome our sins, but we often slip and fall. What part of the psalm made you think of Rob?"

"The part about a righteous man being remembered forever. People still talk about him and mention things he did."

Joy radiated from Anu's face. "How lovely to hear that, *kulta*. Did you find anything else in the Scripture?"

"I saw you in there," she said.

"Me?"

"'Blessed is the man who fears the LORD, who finds great delight in his commands,'" Bree quoted.

Color flooded Anu's face.

"I think I can rule out Kade as a suspect too, now that I've gotten to know him better," Bree said. "That psalm says a righteous man will never be shaken. Kade is like a rock. And he's fearless. You should have seen him dangling from the tower."

"'His heart is secure, he will have no fear,'" Anu recited.

"I didn't know you suspected him!" Naomi said. "He would never do something like that."

"Well, he was at the scene just before we found Fay, remember? And he *is* Eric's cousin, so for a while I wondered if he helped Eric get rid of her—if Eric killed her, of course."

"You have too much time on your hands," Naomi said. "It's caused your imagination to run wild."

"So who do you still suspect?" Anu said.

Bree wanted to tell her what Hilary had said the night of the party but kept her mouth shut. There were just some things a mother didn't need to know. "Steve, Eric, and Lawrence," she said. "I want to talk to Eric. He spent a lot of time with Fay, if we believe town gossip. Maybe he saw the woman in the hat. I don't know where he's staying though."

"Sheba McDonald might know where he is," Anu said. "Mason should ask her. But let Mason handle this, *kulta*."

Bree didn't ask how Sheba would know. Sheba knew everything. She didn't say anything more. Mason would know where Eric was, and Bree didn't want Anu to know she was going to poke around.

Anu carried the leftover lasagna to the kitchen, and Bree and Naomi collected the supper dishes.

"Have you told your mother about Donovan?" Bree asked Naomi as they worked.

Naomi shook her head. "I'm not sure how to approach it. If she's in favor of the idea, I'll have to suffer through her advice and meddling. If she's against it, she'll likely snub Donovan on the street and begin to question my every movement."

"She'll be livid if she finds out from someone else." Bree understood what it was to fear a parent, but Naomi had no real reason to be afraid of Martha.

Naomi sighed. "I know. I'll do it soon."

Bree suspected that if Naomi would just once take charge of her life, Martha would back off. But she knew it wasn't in her friend's nature to be aggressive. Naomi was one of those dear souls who watched to see what she could do for others, someone who would rather serve in silence.

Whoever got Naomi for a wife would be a lucky man, though Rob's opinion had been different. He'd always said a wife like Naomi would bore a man silly. But then Rob's tastes had run to bungee jumping and skydiving.

Bree wondered about the other woman in his life, Lanna March. How had he met her? How long had he been seeing her? She would probably never know, and maybe that was best.

While Anu was starting the dishwasher, Bree slipped into the living room and made a quick call to Mason. He told her Eric was at a deer camp near Big Piney Creek, but he cautioned her not to go alone. He would go with her as soon as he took care of other business. Bree didn't answer. She hung up and asked Naomi if she would mind going with her. "If you're sure you can take the time away from Donovan," she added with a grin.

"Of course," Naomi said. "You shouldn't go alone."

"I don't want to wait for Mason. He can't go for a couple of days. If we go at midmorning, we won't disturb the hunting."

"Give me a call when you're ready to go."

More snow fell Monday night. Tuesday morning, Bree figured there was close to eight inches of snow on the ground. She was running late and rushed to shower. Toweling off, she heard the trill of her cell phone. As she wrapped the towel around herself, she quickly checked the display and saw Kade's name on the caller ID.

She finished dressing before calling him back. "What's up, Kade?"

"Some fool hunter has gotten himself lost in the woods." Kade's voice was rough and gravelly, as though he hadn't slept. "Can you grab Naomi and get out here? The guy's been missing since yesterday at three."

"They just now reported it?" Bree was already beginning to gather her things.

Kade gave a weary sigh. "They were too drunk to notice, I guess. And the guy left his coat behind. All he's wearing is a flannel shirt with a vest. It got down below twenty last night." He told her how to get to the location.

"You call Naomi while I finish getting ready." She clicked off the phone. "We've got a search, Samson," she told her dog.

By the time she picked up Naomi and made it out to the scene, nearly an hour had passed. The sun felt good on her face, and she hoped the missing hunter was someplace where the sun could warm him. But the North Woods were so thick that in some places the sun never hit the ground.

The command center was still being set up when she arrived at

Loon Falls, about two miles off Beaver Road. A truck was backing the familiar trailer into position in the snowy clearing. Kade saw Bree and Naomi and waved from the tree line. Bree parked, then she and Naomi let the dogs out and went to meet him.

His tired eyes blinked above dark circles that almost looked like bruises. Bree had a hunch that something more than the missing hunter had robbed him of sleep. Something in his eyes—pain?—made her want to fix whatever it was. Maybe she would have a chance to talk with him about it later. The realization that she was glad to see him unsettled her.

"What've we got?" she asked him.

"Bubba Martin, age twenty-three. His friends are still very unconcerned." Kade shook his head. "If they're the best he can do, he's hurting."

"I don't know him," Bree said. Even the name Martin didn't sound familiar.

"He's from down around Ironwood. His mother is on her way."

"We have any articles of clothing?" Bree turned and stared into the woods. With that much time elapsed, the young man could be anywhere. It didn't sound like his circle of friends was the type to have any real wilderness survival savvy. He probably didn't even know enough to stay put and wait for the searchers.

Kade moved closer and held out a paper bag with something white inside. "He wore this T-shirt yesterday."

"I'll give the dogs the scent," Naomi said, taking the bag. The dogs each thrust a nose into the bag then began to strain at their leashes.

Bree and Kade both turned and began to walk toward the woods. Bree knew she needed to keep things on a professional level with Kade, but being near him was like standing on the lighthouse tower during a storm—scary and exhilarating at the same time. She hadn't reacted to any man like this since Rob. The feelings were unfamiliar and terrifying.

She wanted to step closer, to nestle her head against his shoulder, to turn her cares and worries over to someone bigger and stronger than herself. It was a feeling she needed to guard against. No one could solve her problems.

"How's Zorro?" she asked. Better to keep things distant.

He sighed. "Chewing everything. And Lauri's no help. She's gone more than she's home."

She glanced at him. "I could come over for another lesson." As soon as the words were past her lips, she wanted to snatch them back. The last thing she needed was to be around him more. He likely felt nothing for her but friendship anyway. But all the rationalizing in the world didn't change her longing to get to know him better.

"That would be great! When can you come?"

His eagerness heartened her. "Maybe this evening, if it's not too late by the time we find our missing hunter." She was committed now. His gaze caught and held hers. The awareness in his eyes dried her mouth, and she finally looked away.

They reached the edge of the woods. "Want me to let the dogs go?" Naomi had a leash around each wrist, and the dogs practically dragged her forward in their eagerness.

Bree grabbed Samson's leash. She took his head between her hands. "You ready, boy?" The dog panted with excitement and whined. She unclipped his leash and let him go. "Search, Samson. Go find him."

The dog raced off into the woods with Charley close on his tail. Naomi, Bree, and Kade ran after them. A sense of déjà vu came over Bree. Their search for the O'Reilly children seemed eons ago. So much had happened in the two weeks since.

Funny how life could twist on you like an unfamiliar road until you weren't sure which way you were pointed anymore. That was just how Bree felt. She'd started out to find Rob and Davy, yet how long had it been since she'd really searched for them? Little by little, life was beginning to creep back in. She didn't know if she was happy or sad. Maybe she'd turned a corner.

The dogs were on a hot trail. Their posture told Bree the hunter couldn't be far.

Sure enough, thirty minutes later the dogs began to bark, then Samson came bounding to her with a stick in his mouth.

"Show me, Samson," Bree commanded. The dog led her over fallen trees dusted with white snow then around a stand of pine to a small clearing. A young man huddled against the side of a jack pine.

"Bubba Martin?" she asked.

He blinked slowly, and she realized he was suffering from hypothermia. She opened her ready-pack and pulled out a blanket. "Pour him some hot coffee from the thermos," she called over her shoulder to Kade and Naomi. Naomi moved first.

Bubba shivered. "So cold," he whispered.

"We'll get you warmed up," she promised. Naomi handed the coffee to Bree, and she lifted it to Bubba's lips. A sense of accomplishment washed over her in a warm tide. Another successful search. But her euphoria quickly collapsed. What did it all matter if the most important search of her life ended in failure?

When they got back to the command center, Bubba's mother was there, a bleached blond in her early forties with angry brown eyes. She rushed to her son and began to harangue him in a voice that caught Bree's attention. Frowning, she stood and listened. She'd heard that voice before.

Then it came to her. Lanna March.

Bree approached the pair. Bubba's head was down as his mother berated him.

"Yes?" she snapped when she realized Bree was staring at her.

"I think the paramedics need to check Bubba. He's suffering from exposure and hypothermia."

"Who are you?" the woman growled. Her scowl deepened.

Bree called herself a fool for thinking Rob would have anything to do with a woman like this. "I'm Bree Nicholls."

The woman's face sagged, and she backed away. Her gaze darted away from Bree's. "Fine, you take him to the ambulance. I'll meet him at the hospital."

"Wait, you never told me your name," Bree called.

The woman ran to her car, a mid-eighties Ford with rust eating the wheel wells. She slammed the car door and sped away.

Bree had always possessed a knack for voice recognition, and she was sure that woman was the one who had called her, the one who wanted her to let Rob go. But why would she be afraid of Bree? Shaking with the revelation, she stumbled back to the trailer and filled out the necessary paperwork, then she and Naomi drove to the deer camp where Eric Matthews was supposed to be holed up.

Big Piney Creek was only five miles away. After Bree parked the Jeep, they got out with the dogs and began to walk back to where Mason said the deer camp was located.

Naomi was uncharacteristically quiet. She kept stealing glances at Bree, and it was making Bree uncomfortable. "Spit it out, girlfriend. What's on your mind?"

Naomi bit her lip. "You really like Kade, don't you?" she said finally.

Bree gulped, and heat rushed to her cheeks. "Is it that obvious?"

"Only to me. Weren't you just yelling at me about not telling you everything?" Naomi said in a teasing tone.

"I just recognized it myself," Bree said. "I didn't realize it until he walked toward me this morning. Isn't that stupid? It's like there's this connection between us. I can't explain it."

"I know just what you mean. Like you can almost tell what he's thinking by looking at him."

Bree nodded. "I don't know where it will lead, if anywhere. I'm not sure I want it to lead anywhere. My life is such a mess, and I don't want to involve Kade in the fallout."

"Kade's a Christian, you know," Naomi said softly.

The comment came like a slap of cold water in Bree's face. A real wake-up call. It was something she didn't want to deal with. All the more reason to keep him at a distance.

"Rob was a Christian, but—" She broke off.

"But what? So he let you down or hurt you in some way. Are you sure you're not just angry with him for dying, for leaving you here?"

"I wish it were that simple." She'd held her guilt so close for the past year, she didn't know if she could reveal it even to Naomi. But the more she had tried to hide it, the more fearful she'd become of opening herself up to the future.

"Then what is it? I've seen you change this year, Bree. You never used to have all this insecurity. Tell me."

"Rob was having an affair!" Bree waited for Naomi's reaction.

Naomi put her hands to her face then lowered them and stared at Bree. "Not Rob. Are you sure?" She brushed the snow from a log then lowered herself onto it. "Sit down. I have to chew on this a minute."

Bree sat beside Naomi and laced her fingers together in her lap. The snow muffled the sounds of the forest, and she listened to the silence. "A woman called the day his plane went down. She said they were in love and if I wanted him to be happy, I'd let him go."

"Did she identify herself?"

Bree nodded. "Lanna March. Her number was unlisted. I called Rob on his cell phone. He denied it, but his anger was so out of proportion, I knew it was true. That was just minutes before he got in the plane to fly home. Don't you see, Naomi? I killed him and Davy! If I had waited, discussed it calmly when he got home, my family would still be alive."

"So that's why you're afraid to speak your mind anymore," Naomi said.

"What if I hurt someone like that again and never have the chance to make it right? I wanted him to feel the same hurt I did. Rob was a good pilot. I wrecked his concentration."

"You can't know that, Bree. There could have been something wrong with the plane, a wind shear; any number of things could have caused the crash. It wasn't you though, and you can't change who you are because of some misplaced sense of guilt."

"That woman at the search, Bubba's mother. Her voice reminded me of Lanna's. For a minute I thought—" Bree broke off in thought, then she set her jaw. She knew she was right. She never forgot a voice. "In fact, I'm just sure it was her voice. But she's much older than Rob." She ran a hand through her hair. "Oh, nothing makes any sense."

"If you're sure she's the one who called you, we should check her out," Naomi said thoughtfully.

Bree didn't want to think about Lanna anymore. She glanced at Naomi. "What do you think of Rob's Christianity now?" Bree asked.

"I'm disappointed in him, but he was human, Bree. Being a Christian doesn't change the human nature we all still deal with. God doesn't recognize degrees of sin. Rob's sin was no worse than telling a little white lie or gossiping or losing your temper. God forgives it all. His love is unconditional."

Unconditional love. Bree had never thought of it that way before. Her heart longed for that kind of acceptance. Anu accepted her in that way, but Bree worried how her mother-in-law would react if she knew Bree's heart fully. For the first time, she understood the appeal of accepting God's love. The God of Bree's experience was a mischievous cat who played with his creation like a ball of twine until it was a hopeless mess. But God hadn't stepped in to save her family—didn't that prove his disinterest? She wished she could believe in this unconditional love idea.

The women let the dogs roam a bit before starting off for the creek. Bree rehearsed what she would say to Eric. Tramping through the woods, they made plenty of noise to alert any hunters to their presence.

Their bright orange gear should show through the foliage, but just to be sure, they sang for a while then talked loudly and shouted to the dogs.

Bree hated deer season. Michigan had allowed a short extra gun season this year, and as she and Naomi walked through the pristine winter wonderland, Bree saw the evidence of the hunts: Hunters' tree stands, spent shells, broken arrows, and patches of blood littered the white snow. Though she understood the need to keep the deer population under control, she hated the violence of the method.

It was nearly three o'clock by the time they arrived at the camp. Bree stepped over a line of beer cans that encircled the site like an aluminum fortress. Four men lay snoring on top of their sleeping bags while a fifth lay on the hood of a battered green Ford pickup. The fire in the center of the camp had gone out, but the men were either too drunk or too tired to care.

Bree glanced at each face. She recognized a few, but she didn't see Eric.

"There are eight sleeping bags," Naomi pointed out. "Three men are gone. Let's look around. We'll find them quicker if we split up. You check the creek, and I'll wander through the woods a bit."

"Don't forget to make noise," Bree warned her.

Naomi nodded and took Charley with her. Bree whistled for Samson, and they went down a rocky path to the creek bed. The snow had made the slick rocks treacherous. Standing on a boulder, Bree glanced across the Big Piney. Only a trickle of water passed over the rocky surface of the creek.

Singing "Jailhouse Rock" at the top of her lungs, Bree wandered along the edge of the creek for several minutes then turned to go back. Samson pricked his ears and whined. "What is it, boy?" She paused and listened. The faint echo of voices reached her ears.

She pushed through a thicket of brush and found three men sitting along the bank of the creek. They stopped talking when they saw her. The Larson brothers and Eric Matthews.

Blue eyes as cold as a glacier looked her over. "You're that dog woman," he said. "Fay's friend. I suppose the cops got you following me too? What'd I tell you, Mitch? That idiot husband of Fay's has turned the whole town against me."

"You seem to have done that on your own," Bree said. A low growl escaped Samson's throat, so she kept a hand on his head.

"What's that supposed to mean? I had nothing to do with Fay's death," Eric said.

"I didn't say you did." She moved closer and stared into his face. There was a coiled tension in him that made her wary.

"No, but you and everyone else looks at me like they think I'm the Boston strangler."

"Calm down, Eric." Mitchell Larson, a heavyset man of about forty, leaned over and handed Eric a beer. "Let's see what the lady wants."

Eric took the beer and popped the top. Taking a big swig, he wiped his mouth on his sleeve. "Okay, dog lady, what do you want? It can't be an accident you're here."

Bree had to tread warily with Eric's temper already on edge. "No, I was looking for you. I hear you're out in the woods a lot, and you spent some time with Fay. I'm looking for a cabin Fay said she came across. A woman lives there. She wears an old leather fedora. Have you seen a place like that?"

Eric frowned. "What makes you think I'd tell you, even if I did, eh?"

"What harm could there be in telling the truth?"

"You want the truth? How about this—I didn't kill Fay. Why isn't the sheriff checking out her husband? He's the one with something to gain. The fine, upstanding bank manager needed the insurance to avoid bankruptcy."

Bree had seen the letter at the house threatening legal action if Steve didn't pay a bill of two hundred fifty thousand dollars. How much more did Steve owe? "How do you know this?"

"Fay told me."

"You went to jail for hurting her."

His face darkened, and he got up. Bree took an involuntary step back, and Samson lunged at Eric. She grabbed his collar when Eric pointed a gun at the dog's head.

"Get out of here, you and that mangy mutt of yours. I loved Fay. This town is bent on making sure I never forget what I did. That was a long time ago, and I was young. I loved Fay." His face contorted. "She forgave me, even if no one else did."

Against her will, Bree found herself believing him. "She was a married woman with a baby on the way."

"That marriage was a mistake, and she knew it." He waved his gun in the air. "Steve doesn't want to believe it, but that was my baby."

"How do you know?"

Misery filled his face. "I just know. She would have gone away with me."

"Even if you had to force her?" Bree knew she was skating near the edge of his temper, but she had to goad him once more.

He pointed the gun at her head. Samson snarled and struggled to free himself from Bree's grip. "I should shoot you now, you and that dog," Eric snarled. "You do-gooders are all alike. You think you know what's best for the world, and the rest of us just need to shut up and follow your rules. No rules would have kept Fay and me apart. She knew it, and I knew it." He gestured with the gun. "Now get out of here before I live up to everyone's expectations."

Bree knew she'd reached his limit, so she turned to go. Samson didn't want to leave. He kept growling and lunging toward Eric.

"Hey, Eric, that dog would make good target practice. We could say we thought he was a deer." Marvin Larson jeered and threw a rock.

It hit Samson on the rear, and the dog whirled with a snarl. It was all Bree could do to hang on. Tugging at his collar, she managed to drag him away. It wasn't until she found Naomi and made it back to the Jeep that she realized she was shaking. That could have gotten ugly. She should have had a man with her. Someone strong like Kade.

She told Naomi about the encounter as they drove back to town.

"Do you believe him?" Naomi asked.

"I didn't want to," Bree admitted. "But I think he might be telling the truth. I saw some papers at Steve's house that indicated he was in financial trouble. I have to tell Mason."

No clear plan came to either of them. They stopped at Mason's office and told him what Bree had found and what Eric had said. He growled at her for not waiting for him then promised to look into it. After letting Naomi out at the Blue Bonnet, Bree turned back up Houghton Street and drove out toward Kade's cabin. Her palms felt sweaty where they gripped the steering wheel. Telling herself she was a mature woman of twenty-nine instead of a giddy teenager on her first date did not help them dry out.

Kade's truck was parked outside the cabin when she stopped. He was in the yard with Zorro and Lauri. Lauri waved an excited greeting. "I've been working on what you told me," she said proudly as Bree climbed out of the Jeep. Zorro ran to Samson. The older dog sniffed the puppy then pointedly ignored him.

"See how Samson is treating him? That's because he's the alpha dog," Bree pointed out. "That's what you have to do with Zorro. I'm not paying any attention to him yet either. You wait until he's not begging for attention, then call him so he knows to come on your terms, not his."

"It seems so mean," Lauri said. "He's just a baby."

"He's a canine baby. He'll be more secure once he knows what to expect." After the puppy wandered off a bit, Bree snapped her fingers. "Zorro, come."

At the sound of his name, the puppy raised his head. Bree knelt and patted the ground. "Come, Zorro."

The puppy raced toward her, his black ears laid back with his efforts to move quickly on short legs. "Good Zorro," Bree said, scratching his ears. "Now you call him, Lauri."

While Lauri practiced the tips, Bree found her gaze straying to Kade. Was that admiration in his eyes? Her chest felt tight.

"Want to see what I do here?" he asked.

"What do you mean? You live here, right?" She walked toward him.

He grinned and took her arm. "Among other things. I'll show you the important stuff." He took her out back to a series of pens.

The gentle touch of his hand on her arm sent a warm glow through her. What was wrong with her? She wanted to stop right here in the middle of the path and burrow into his arms, which was stupid because she didn't want to get involved, especially with a Christian.

The sight of the animals made a good excuse to pull away. "Oh, you have deer!" She reached out to grab a handful of corn in a box near the pens.

"Orphaned wildlife," he corrected. "I'll let them go once hunting season is past." He pointed out a raccoon and a porcupine as well. "Sometimes I have birds—you've met Mazzy—as well as a bear cub or two. I just released two small black bears last summer."

"Kade Matthews, modern-day Dr. Doolittle," Bree said, smiling.

He grinned. "I wish I could talk to them too. It might make my job easier."

"How did you get started doing this?" She tossed a handful of corn to the deer and laughed when the smallest one came right up to her and ate out of her hand.

"When I was ten, my dad brought home a baby raccoon whose mother had been killed by dogs. I named him Mask—not very original, but I sure loved him. Dad insisted I release him when he could fend for himself, and I was devastated. But as I grew older and helped return other animals to the wild, I realized how wise Dad was. It's my way of tending the garden."

Bree frowned, not sure what he meant, and he saw her puzzlement.

"As in tending the garden like God assigned Adam to do. In Genesis, God told Adam to name the creatures and tend the garden. I take that to mean we should care for his creatures and not deplete the resources. The earth is ours to use but not to squander. I try to do my small part."

How rare, Bree thought—a middle-of-the-road approach to environmentalism. A small raccoon reached out to Kade with tiny hands, and he picked it up. It patted his face then crawled to his shoulder and perched there comfortably. Bree laughed and decided she was glad she'd taken the chance to learn more about Kade.

Anu was right. Scriptures did reveal things about a man. Kade was one of the gracious, compassionate, and righteous ones. She'd thought she could rule him out of the murder, but now she was certain.

— *19* —

Rachel kissed the sleeping boy on the forehead as she tucked the covers around his chin. She loaded the wood stove with as much fuel as she dared then damped it down so it would burn long and slow. The cabin might not be as warm as it could be, but the fire would last longer this way. No amount of wood would make it last two days though.

She stood on the threshold of the cabin and glanced back toward Sam. She wished she didn't have to leave him alone, but she had no other option. Sam would be fine as long as he stayed inside and under the covers.

Sighing, she shouldered her backpack and eased the door shut behind her. When she heard the latch click into place, she turned and made her way across the clearing, dimly lit by the first rays of sunrise.

Her breath plumed in front of her as she walked toward Ontonagon. There was no bus or taxi service from Rock Harbor, and she had no money for a ride to Ontonagon even if one had been available.

It was nearly 9:30 by the time she reached the bus station. She jostled her way aboard amid a crowd of passengers and found a seat at the back. She'd barely slept the past two nights for worrying about Sam; now she fell asleep before the bus had finished loading.

She awakened as the bus neared Chicago nearly thirteen hours later. When the bus finally stopped, she disembarked and stood in the middle of the crush of passengers as they pushed and shoved their way to the next bus. What should she do now, and where should she go? The cold wind off Lake Michigan sliced down her back, and she zipped her jacket to her chin, jammed her hat down low on her head, and pulled on her gloves.

She turned and plodded through the crowd. Once clear of the masses, she glanced around at the Chicago skyline, twinkling with light from the skyscrapers. Rachel had forgotten what it was like to be in a big city. She felt more alone here than in her little cabin in the woods.

She had one shot at not having to stay out in the cold all night. She made her way to a phone booth and perched her backpack on the cold steel ledge near the phone. Fumbling in the pack, she found a slip of paper with a number written on it. There was no guarantee the number was still good. It had been nearly ten years since she'd last spoken to her brother.

Her hands shook as she dropped two quarters into the pay phone. Once the phone began ringing, she almost hung up. What would she say to him after what she'd done? But the thought of huddling in the cold all night was a strong goad.

"Hello."

The voice was gruff but familiar. She wet her lips. "Frank? It's Rachel."

The pause was long, then Frank finally responded, "What do you want? I figured you was dead by now."

"I need a place to stay tonight. Just for one night. I leave tomorrow." Hating the pleading tone in her voice, she drummed her fingers on the cold metal shelf in the booth.

"Don't you think you've done enough to me and my family?"

"Please, Frank. I have nowhere else to go. I'll just sleep on the floor and be gone tomorrow."

Frank snorted. "I guess you can't do any more damage. Where are you?"

Relief as sweet as a summer rain washed over Rachel. She gave him her location and hung up. What had swayed Frank to allow her to stay? He still sounded just as bitter. She found a spot in a doorway sheltered from the wind and settled down to wait. The nervousness she felt made her jittery, and she wished she had a cigarette. She hadn't had any money for smokes in over a year though.

About half an hour later she saw a car cruising slowly down the street. Maybe that was Frank. She stepped out of the doorway and into the beam of a streetlight so he could see her. The car pulled to the curb. The window went down and she stepped to the door, her heart in her mouth.

"I don't have all day. Get in if you're coming," Frank said.

She got in the car. The blast of warm air from the vents made her eyes water, but the heat felt heavenly. After fastening her seat belt, she turned to look at her brother. He was staring at her through bushy gray eyebrows.

"You ain't changed much," he said. "Hair's grayer, like mine." He snorted a laugh as he pulled back onto the road, but his eyes were still suspicious. "What you doing here?"

"Job interview," she said. "You don't look different either."

He patted his stomach. "Hannah's fattened me up some."

"It looks good on you. You were always too thin."

He grunted. "Don't think you can get around me with flattery. I still hate your guts. You burned down my house!"

Rachel gulped. "I was just trying to help, Frank. I thought if you had the insurance money, you could keep Paulie out of jail."

"And instead, you nearly put me in there with him! You always were stupid, Rachel."

"Then why'd you come get me?" she snapped, annoyed with him for bringing up all the old baggage. But then what had she expected? All her life she'd heard she didn't have any common sense, and while what she'd done to his house might prove that to some people, Rachel had known it was the only way to save her nephew. Was it her fault the plan had taken such a bad turn?

"Because of you my daughter has never married. What man would have her with all those burn scars on her face?" Frank slammed the steering wheel with his hands.

Rachel hunched over against the door. "I didn't know Hannah was still in the house," she said. "You know that, Frank. I never would have done anything to hurt her."

Frank's antipathy was so strong that Rachel struggled to breathe. This had been a mistake. There was no forgiveness in the man. Several miles later, Frank sighed and his animosity seemed to leak away. "Yeah, well, you never did have no sense, Rachel. But you always had a good heart." He stopped at a small, one-story house. Built in the forties, it couldn't be more than eight hundred square feet. "Here we are. Hannah's working tonight."

"What's she do?"

Frank snorted. "She's a nurse like you."

Frank parked then slid his bulk out of the car and plodded up the walkway. He twisted the key in the lock and opened the door. "Home sweet home," he said.

The air smelled of stale cigarettes and beer, just like the house she'd burned down. Rachel followed him inside.

"Leftover casserole's in the fridge if you want some," he told her.

By the time she finished eating, Rachel and Frank had settled back into their old relationship. He was as hungry for companionship as she, hungry enough to grudgingly forgive her. By the time she left the next morning, he had agreed to let her and Sam move in until they found a place of their own.

Life in Chicago suddenly became more attractive. She and Sam could move right away, even if she didn't get this job. If she lived in the city, she could find employment in no time.

In a way, the whole scene felt familiar. She slipped back into city life as if slipping into a comfortable sweater she hadn't worn in years. The sights, sounds, and smells of the city gave her a sense of place, something she'd missed in the woods.

Frank dropped her off for her interview the next morning. Dressed in wool slacks and a nice sweater left over from her days as a nurse, she felt like her old self, confident and put together.

When she walked out an hour later, she had a job. Her heart sang as she changed her clothes and headed for the bus station. She and Sam would be so happy here.

*T*he fire had gone out hours ago. Sam huddled under the blankets, but he still wasn't warm. When would she be back? He hated to be alone. When he was alone like this, too many thoughts whirled in his head. Sometimes strange memories tried to poke their way through. Sometimes he could almost catch them.

Some of them were good. He remembered his mommy, his daddy, his dog. Whenever he tried to talk about these thoughts to *her*, her mouth pinched up like she'd eaten a lemon. She told him not to think about them. Sometimes he remembered his daddy yelling. Then the plane crashing in the trees. He hurt all over and he'd tried to wake Daddy up, but he wouldn't wake up.

If he thought hard enough, he remembered that he had another name once, but he couldn't think what it was. Every day it got harder for him to catch the memories—as hard as it was for him to catch the chipmunks. They didn't like his new hair color any better than the old one.

Sam clasped his arms around himself. Maybe he could light the fire. She had said not to try, but she'd been gone a long time. She was gone when he woke yesterday, and then the fire had gone out when it got dark. He'd shivered all through the night, and he was still cold.

It would be even colder soon. The sun was going down, and the wind had started to blow hard.

The wind blew snow under the door and around the windows. Biting his lip, he slipped out of bed. He already had on his slippers, but even they hadn't helped his feet stay warm. He dragged a blanket with him and wrapped it around his shoulders. First he should use the privy. She had left a potty inside, but it was smelly and nasty. Sam's lip curled. He'd go outside.

Opening the back door, he stepped into the yard. The snow came nearly to his knees, and he struggled to get to the little shed behind the house. Sam moved quickly. He left the privy door open a little so he wouldn't be in the dark.

It was spooky to be out here alone. She always came with him and talked to him outside the door. What if a bear came and ate him? Or wolves. He'd heard the wolves howling last night, and he'd cried. She would be disappointed in him. Only babies cried, she said.

He finished and hurried back to the house. He breathed more easily when the door was shut and latched. He rewrapped the blanket around his shoulders then walked toward the stove. If he could use the privy by himself, he could do something as easy as lighting a fire.

He touched the stove. It was cold, as cold as he was, maybe colder. The lever turned easily in his hand, and he looked inside. The ashes were white, and wind whistled over him with the stove open.

He glanced at the pipe thing. What had she called it? He stood on his tiptoes and managed to turn the thing straight up and down, as she had shown him. He'd watched her start a fire a hundred times. He couldn't count to a hundred yet, but he knew it was a lot. The kindling was in a box by the door. Trailing the blanket behind him, he took a handful of the kindling with his free hand and tossed the pieces into the stove.

No, wait, that wasn't right. He had to put newspaper under it. He pulled out the kindling, piece by piece, and laid it on the floor in front of the stove. There was a box of newspaper by the bed. He took a piece, wadded it up the way she always did, and laid it in the stove. Then he piled the kindling on it. Taking a deep breath, he picked up the box of matches beside the stove.

She said never to play with matches, but this wasn't playing. If he didn't do something, he would freeze like the dead fox he'd seen last winter. He bit his lip while he opened the box of matches and took one out. Holding the box as he'd seen her do, he ran the match across that rough strip on the box. The match burst into flames, and it startled him so much he dropped it. It fell to the stone in front of the wood stove and quickly went out.

Sam took out another match. He held the box and the match at arm's length and squinted his eyes. Striking the match, he barely flinched this time when it flared. He held it to the paper in the stove. The paper flamed, and Sam grinned. He'd soon be warm, and she would be so proud of him. Crouching in front of the stove, he basked in the bit of heat radiating from the burning paper.

The dry kindling caught and began to crackle. Sam watched for a few minutes, mesmerized by the dancing flames. He held his hands in front of the fire to warm them. The fire popped and snapped, a wonderful sound to Sam. He longed for the fire to really start heating up the room.

Slowly, he fed the flames with more kindling. As long as he stayed right in front of the stove with the blanket wrapped around him, he felt warm. He knew he needed to throw some of the larger logs on the fire, but he was afraid. What if he put them in wrong and they rolled out again? All his work would be wasted.

Soon the kindling box was almost empty. Sam took the last handful and put it on the fire. He might as well try to do something now. The fire would soon be out anyway. Struggling with the weight of it, he picked up a split log. He leaned into the stove and pushed the log onto the flames with all his might.

The log seemed to turn in his hands before it hit right in the middle of the fire. The kindling scattered, and several pieces flew out the stove door. One landed on Sam's blanket. It smoldered then flared into flame. Sam screamed and turned to run.

$\mathcal{B}$ree curled up on the sofa and sipped her tea. Warm and content, she almost didn't answer the door when the bell rang. Samson padded to the door and waited expectantly. The bell rang again. She tossed the fleece throw off her legs and reluctantly went to the entry.

Hilary stood on the porch, huddled in a sheepskin coat. "It's freezing out here." She brushed past Bree and came inside, stomping the snow from her boots. "Mason is working late tonight, and I was bored. Want to order a pizza?"

"I just warmed up some leftover chicken enchilada casserole Martha sent over. There's plenty left. You want some?" Bree took Hilary's coat and hung it in the closet under the stairs. She ordered Samson into the living room. No sense in riling Hilary with his presence.

"Sounds good. I wouldn't turn down a cup of hot coffee either." Hilary followed her into the kitchen.

As Bree heated Hilary's meal, she wondered how she could bring up Hilary's outburst at the party. Her suspicions would nag her until she laid them to rest.

Hilary sat at the small dinette in the corner. "Mother wants to know if you'll bring some of your cranberry salad and the sweet potato casserole to Thanksgiving this year."

"I think I've still got the recipes here someplace," Bree said. Had Hilary really come by because she was bored? Under normal circumstances, Hilary would have just called to ask about Thanksgiving arrangements. Bree set the casserole in front of her sister-in-law along with a cup of coffee then sat across the table from her.

"Smells good." Hilary chased several forkfuls of food around the plate before she set her fork aside. "Mother told me you're giving up the search," she said.

Ah, the real reason for the visit. Bree steeled herself for Hilary's cajoling. "I'll search until the first of the year, then I'm going to get busy with a training school. I've found a couple of possible sites." Hilary was blinking rapidly, and Bree looked away. Tears might make her lose her resolve.

"I just came by to tell you I agree with your decision," Hilary said.

Bree wasn't sure she'd heard correctly. Wide-eyed, she stared at Hilary. "You . . . you agree?"

"Mother told me I was being selfish, and I guess I was. I've been pretty hard on you this past year. I know we've had our differences, but you'll always be my little sister."

This was a softer, more vulnerable Hilary than Bree had ever seen. "I've only ever wanted your approval," Bree said in a low voice.

"You've driven yourself to find Rob's plane, and I haven't been very appreciative. I'm sorry." Hilary smiled ruefully. "I'm not easy to live with; just ask Mason. I blow my top and say things I don't mean when I should keep my mouth shut."

The perfect opening. "Don't we all. Just like what you said about Fay the night of the party. I knew you didn't mean it."

Hilary frowned. "What did I say about Fay?"

"That you hated her, and her baby should have been yours."

Hilary waved a hand. "I was just upset about the doctor's news. You never really forget your first love, but Steve and I would have been divorced before a year was out. I need someone stable and patient like Mason. I wouldn't trade him for a dozen Steves." Her eyes darkened with pain and she looked at her casserole. "We're doing what we can to get Mason's sperm count up. We haven't given up hope yet. For a while I'd forgotten God is in control."

Bree wanted to know this Hilary better. She thought of Psalm 112. There was something in there about a righteous man being steadfast and trusting in the Lord. Hilary hadn't killed Fay. Relief washed over Bree until she felt almost giddy.

By the time Hilary left, Bree sensed a new friendship building between her and her sister-in-law, a new understanding. This family would survive the tragedy and go on. It was time to put the past away.

Davy was gone. The first step to accepting that fact would be hard. She looked toward the stairway. There was no time like the present. Leaning forward, she caressed Samson's ears. "I think maybe it's time, boy. You want to help me?"

The dog whined and got up. Stretching, he nosed her hand.

"Let's do it," she told him. Together they walked up the steps. Bree stopped at the closet at the top of the stairs and took out the empty boxes stacked inside. Her heart began to slam against her ribs. It had to be done, she told herself.

Tears pooled in her eyes, and through a blur she walked to Davy's room and pushed open the door. She would start with the toys. Kneeling beside the toy box, she packed the blocks first. Davy had loved his blocks. Together they would build towers, then he would chortle with glee and knock the blocks in all directions. She had bought him a box of Lincoln Logs for his third birthday, and he was fascinated with the various ways he could make them fit together.

Sobs spilled from her throat as the memories washed over her. She hugged a teddy bear to her chest and rocked back and forth. She couldn't do this. Maybe she should ask Naomi to do it for her. The bear still smelled faintly of baby powder and bubble-gum toothpaste.

She slowly pulled the stuffed animal away from her chest and placed it to one side. Davy's favorite stuffed animal, a koala bear he'd called Pooky, had gone down with him in the plane. She would keep this one instead. She drew in a deep breath, then another. The rest of Davy's stuffed animals went into the box. She forced herself to move forward.

Step by step, she could get this done. She opened the closet and began to pack Davy's clothing. The little suit he'd worn to Hilary's first campaign party, the sweats that matched his daddy's, the bib overalls he'd worn when they'd made mud pies.

She allowed herself to dwell on each memory. The process would be a cauterization of sorts. If she could get through this, she could get through the rest of her life.

The dresser was next. His small underclothes, socks, and T-shirts went into the box. She pulled out his Barney swim trunks and remembered the way he turned as brown as a squirrel over the course of the summer. Shouting with laughter, he would scream, "Watch me, Mommy," then plunge into the icy waves that splashed Superior's shoreline.

The cold water never seemed to bother him. Even when his lips would turn blue, he would beg to stay in the lake. Rob had called him their baby salmon, all slippery and glistening from the water. Shaking, she sat in the rocker until she could go on. The memories crashed over her with the force of a Lake Superior nor'easter. For a few moments she thought she might sink beneath those crushing waves just as the *Edmund Fitzgerald* had done.

She left the chair and went to the bed. Davy's Superman bedspread, sheets, and curtains were as he had left them. Four quick flips and the bedspread was folded and in the box. Then she stripped the sheets and tossed them into the box as well. She dragged the toy chest under the window and closed the lid. Standing on top of it, she could just reach the curtain rods. The hooks didn't want to let go any more than she did, but she finally managed to release them, and the curtains dropped to the floor.

Four boxes. Davy's young life had been reduced to four boxes. Bree stood and looked around the stripped room. Her heart felt equally stripped, and raw as well. She would ask Kade to help her move the bed to the attic. Maybe she could find a queen-size bed at the second-hand furniture shop. The room was large enough for one, and then her cousin and his wife could have a decent night's sleep when they came to visit, though that wouldn't be for some time. They were working in Saudi Arabia for the next two years.

Somehow, taking the boxes of Davy's things to the attic seemed wrong. One by one, she carried them downstairs to the kitchen. She wished she'd thought of it sooner, but she knew what to do now. She would just have to work harder to accomplish it. Her Carhartt overalls hung on a peg by the back door. She started to put them on then realized it was too dark to pick the right spot. Tomorrow she would dress warmly and dig a hole under the apple tree that held Davy's tree house. There she would bury Davy's things.

She would finally have a grave site of sorts where she could place flowers and remember her son—something better than an empty grave at the cemetery. The search was over. She would let it go now. Life wouldn't be the same without her boy, but she couldn't live in the past anymore. The future beckoned, and she was ready to face it. She would help Steve find who killed Fay. If that led to the woman in the cabin, fine. But if it didn't, she was okay with that too.

*T*he snow slowed her progress. Rachel plodded through the drifts with the sun shining weakly through the trees. Sam would be so glad to see her, and even more glad when he heard the news. No more cold cabins for them. By this time next week, they'd be far away from here, somewhere no one could trace them. Somewhere no one could separate them.

She stopped to catch her breath and checked her watch. Nearly two o'clock. Her inner compulsion to see Sam, to make sure he was all right, drove her on. He was such a little boy, and she knew she should not have left him home alone for two days. It had turned colder than she'd expected while she was gone. Ten inches of snow covered the ground, and she wished she had her snowshoes.

Frank would declare her predicament more evidence of her poor judgment, but then he had never given her credit for anything. Necessity was a hard taskmaster. He had just intended to let Paulie go to prison. Even when she'd provided the way out, Frank still hadn't intervened for Paulie. Her nephew deserved better from his own father. Maybe when Paulie got out of prison, he would come to visit her. Surely he knew what she'd done for him.

She would even let him stay with her, once she and Sam got their own place. Or maybe they'd get a place big enough for the whole family. Smiling, she started off toward the cabin again. She made it the rest of the way in just over fifteen minutes, and the sight of the cabin warmed her. A light shone through the window, and she frowned. Sam shouldn't be wasting the kerosene that way. But maybe the lad was frightened.

She sometimes forgot just how young Sam was. He often seemed so much older than four. Those eyes of his had seen horrors no child should witness. He never spoke of his dead father, but she saw his memory in the boy's eyes. As she pushed the lever to raise the inside latch, the scent of smoke, strong and acrid, burned her nose, and her heart raced.

"Sam?" Alarm made her speak louder than she'd intended. A charred blanket lay by the wood stove. The stove door stood open and wind whistled through the cabin like through a wind tunnel.

Frantic now, she rushed forward. She heard a groan. "Sam?"

"It hurts." Sam raised his head from where he lay on the floor near the back door.

Soot covered his face and hands, and his pajamas were black with it. One sleeve had been burned, and even from here, she could see the blisters on his arm.

She rushed to kneel at his side. "Sam, what happened?" His body was chilled. She examined his arm. Second-degree burns, nothing worse. And only in one small area. There seemed to be no other damage.

She scooped him into her arms, carried him to the bed and bundled him beneath the covers, then rushed to build a fire. The kindling box was empty. Confusion churned her mind. This was the second time he'd disobeyed her in the past few days. What had happened to her sweet, obedient son? His disobedience had hurt him. She pushed away the guilt she felt for leaving him alone. He would have been fine if only he'd obeyed her. Necessity was a hard taskmaster.

She grabbed the ax by the door and quickly shaved some kindling from a split log. Within minutes she had a fire blazing, and its pleasant warmth began to creep into the room. Ignoring his pain-filled eyes on her, she washed his burns and applied a salve.

"This is what happens when you don't mind your mother," she told him.

"I tried to do it like you showed me," he murmured.

"Don't try to blame me for your misbehavior," she said. "I told you to leave the fire alone."

"I was so cold."

Rachel bristled. He didn't know what cold was. She was the one who had traipsed through the cold Chicago wind all night, and for what? To give a nice home to an ungrateful child. She trembled with the urge to punish him then reminded herself he'd already reaped the consequence of his disobedience.

"The fire jumped on me. Mommy always said to 'drop and roll,' so that's what I did."

His mommy. He hadn't mentioned her in months. "I'm your mother now," Rachel said sharply. She tossed the water out the back door then busied herself with cleaning up the mess. She could not pack with the cabin in this mess. They would be on the bus for Chicago in two days. Frank had promised to pick them up at the station.

She would give him a stern lecture about obedience tomorrow. Frank would toss them out if she couldn't keep the boy under control. If Sam didn't do what he was told, she didn't know what she would do. He had severely disappointed her. She would have to make him understand that.

When Rachel finished cleaning, she pulled on a flannel nightgown and crawled beneath the covers next to her sleeping son. There was so much to do over the next couple of days. But she would breathe easier once they were gone from this place. No one would ever find her and Sam once they reached Chicago.

A distant hum woke her. From the brilliance of the morning light, she knew it had snowed overnight. She ran to the window and surveyed the blinding landscape. There was at least eighteen inches of snow on the ground. The racket increased, and she caught a glimpse of a snowmobile moving fast through the trees. The rider must be an idiot to travel so fast over this terrain, especially under such conditions.

The sound trailed away in the direction of the old copper mine. Rachel frowned. Could that have been the man she'd seen carrying the woman's body? What was he doing snooping around here? Sam was still in a deep sleep. She quietly pulled on her clothes then let herself out of the cabin.

Her snowshoes hung on a nail outside the door, along with her binoculars. She slipped the binoculars over her head then put on her snowshoes and started toward the mine. She loved the woods after a deep snow. The peace and serenity soothed her. All she could hear was the sound of her own breath whistling through her teeth as she tramped through the winter wonderland.

The sound of the snowmobile died suddenly, and she guessed from the sound that it had stopped at the mine. Hurrying as fast as she dared, she struggled through the snow until she came to the edge of a clearing. The old Copper Queen, its wooden shaft and outbuildings weathered and dilapidated, sat at the far end of the clearing. The snow had stopped falling, except for the occasional flake, and she had a good view from where she crouched.

Over the past fifty years, the forest had reclaimed much of the area, but the Copper Queen still stood tall and proud. Last summer Rachel had come here and poked around, hoping to find some relic of the grand old lady's heyday. But all she had ever picked up were old bottles and a few quartz rocks.

The rider had parked the snowmobile near the entrance of the main offices. She didn't dare leave the cover of the trees. He had to come out sooner or later. She scanned the surrounding area and detected nothing that concerned her.

Crouching on her haunches, she settled back to wait, though she knew she would have to head back if he didn't come out soon. Her stomach growled with hunger, and Sam would want breakfast when he awakened.

Rachel took a deep breath. She loved the air's sharp, cold freshness. She would miss this in Chicago. But the cabin would always be here. Maybe she and Sam could come up for an occasional visit. No, that wouldn't be a good idea. Once they were gone from here, they needed to stay gone. She and Sam would have to disappear—without a trace.

A movement caught her eye. She tried to bring the binoculars to her eyes, but the brim of her leather fedora blocked her view. She took it off and laid it beside her then focused the binoculars. A man carrying a duffle bag came out of the building. His face was turned away, and Rachel cursed.

"Turn this way," she whispered.

As if he heard her soft words, the man turned fully toward her. Through the binoculars, Rachel saw his face clearly. It was the same man, just as she had suspected. His cheeks were red with cold, and the concentration lining his face told her that whatever he carried was important. He secured the bag onto the back of the snowmobile and hopped onto the seat. The roar of the engine cut through the cold air. Then he pointed the snowmobile directly at Rachel.

Panicked, Rachel scuttled back farther into the brush. She didn't come out until the sound of the engine faded, then she scrambled to her feet and rushed toward home. She'd had no business even coming out here other than to satisfy her curiosity. It was stupid to put herself in danger like that. If he'd seen her, he might have killed her just like he killed that woman.

Hurrying into the cabin, she latched the door behind her with a relieved sigh. The sooner they were gone from here the better.

"I'm hungry." Sam's plaintive voice broke into her thoughts. "It's cold in here."

He was right. The fire had gone out while she was gone, and the chilly wind had quickly stolen the remaining warmth.

"I'll have it going again in a jiffy," she said cheerfully.

"Are you still mad at me?" Sam's woebegone face peeked over the edge of the covers.

"I'm not angry, but I'm very disappointed in you, Sam." When his face crumpled in tears, she softened her tone. "You must learn to always obey me, son. Always. I only want what's best for you."

He began to sob, and Rachel went to take him in her arms. "There, there," she soothed. "We're going to leave here in a few days, Sammy. You'll have other children to play with, and a nice house with heat that comes out of registers instead of a stove. You won't ever again have to worry about being cold."

"Never?" He hiccuped and rubbed his nose on the back of his pajama sleeve.

"Never. I promise. Won't that be fun? We'll be in a big city with lots of other people."

"What about my squirrel?"

"Well, we'll have to leave Marcus here. He wouldn't like it in the city. He wouldn't have as many trees to play in, and it would be hard for him to find nuts."

Sam screwed up his face as he thought about it, then he nodded. "Can I come back to see him sometimes?"

"We'll see if we can find you a new squirrel in Chicago. And we can walk along the lakeshore and feed the ducks. That will be fun." She kissed him on the forehead. "Now let's take a look at your burns this morning. How are you feeling?"

"My arm stings. Can I have Captain Crunch?"

"We're all out of Captain Crunch, but I have Cheerios." She ran her finger over Sam's burns, and he flinched. Pressing her lips together, she went to fix his breakfast.

After breakfast she tackled the laundry. She heated water on the stove and dumped it in the washtub. She propped up the washboard in the tub and rubbed the clothes against it vigorously. As she worked, Rachel imagined the life they would have in Chicago. Never again would she be alone; she would always have Sam, and he would always love her. No one had ever really loved her, not even Frank. But someday Sam would thank her for saving his life, for putting him through school. He would show his gratitude by taking care of her when she got too old to take care of herself.

School. She would have to get a forged birth certificate and immunization records. Then she could get Sam to a doctor for the shots he needed to go to kindergarten. It would all work out.

Draping the wet clothes on a retractable line across the cabin, she finished the laundry as quickly as possible. They needed more wood. She went to the door and took down her coat. Where was her hat? Her heart dipped. She'd lost it, probably at the mine. She had to have her hat.

She got Sam dressed. "How would you like to play a game, Sammy?"

His head bobbed up and down. "What kind of game?"

"A spy game."

"What's a spy?" His tongue poked out as he worked at tying his shoes.

"Someone who watches what is going on and reports back to headquarters. You be the spy, and you can report to me."

"That sounds fun!" He jumped to his feet.

"Get your snowshoes on," she told him.

He stopped at the door. "I don't like the snowshoes. I want to play in the snow without them."

More disobedience? This was getting to be a habit, and one she intended to break. "Don't argue with me. Get your snowshoes on."

Sam's lower lip thrust out, and he shook his head. "I don't want to."

Rage boiled over, and Rachel grabbed him roughly by the arm. Too late she realized it was his injured arm, and he cried out. "It's your own fault," she said. "Now get outside and get your snowshoes on like I told you."

Sobbing and holding his arm, Sam did as she said. She didn't know what had gotten into him. If he kept causing her this much trouble, what would she do? This must be what all the magazines meant when they talked about children becoming rebellious. What would it take to break Sam of that streak?

Sam slowly strapped on his snowshoes then stood and waited while she put hers on.

"Let's go," she said curtly.

It was slow going with Sam. Rachel was beginning to wish she'd left him home, but she needed him to keep watch for her. They finally reached the mine. She paused and listened but heard nothing.

"Follow me," she told Sam. She led the way across the clearing to the building where she'd seen the man. "I want you to stand guard here. Your job as a spy is to listen for any people or snowmobiles," she said. "If you hear anything, just yell for me, okay?"

He nodded. "Okay. But hurry. I'm scared."

He was always scared. When she got him to Chicago, she'd have a doctor look at him. She patted him on the head, turned on her flashlight, and went down into the shaft building. An hour later she was dirty and tired but no wiser. It was going to take someone smarter than she was to figure out what that man had been doing there.

When she exited the mine, she saw a man standing with Sam. The boy was crying and trying to get away from him. Did Sam know him? There seemed to be a frightened recognition on his face. She looked around for a weapon and grabbed a chair leg from a pile of rubble. Creeping forward, the snow crunched beneath Rachel's boots and the man turned to face her. The breath left her lungs when she saw the gun in his hand.

"I'd put that down if I were you," he said casually. A sock hat covered his hair, and the rest of his form was buried in a thick coat. He held up her fedora. "You were here before, weren't you? What did you see?"

She let the chair leg drop from her fingers. "Nothing. You with a duffel bag, that's all. Let go of my boy." She hadn't heard his snowmobile.

"I want you to keep your mouth shut about what you saw."

"I don't know who you are anyway."

"You could point me out. But now that I've seen the boy, I know you don't want to draw attention to yourself."

"What do you mean? Please, let go of my son," she whispered.

The man grinned and released Sam. "Go to your *mother*, boy."

He knew she wasn't Sam's mother. Her fear ratcheted up a notch. Sam limped toward her, and she grabbed his good arm and dragged him close to her side. "I'm not saying anything." Sam clung to her tightly.

"Good. Because I know someone who would be very interested in finding the boy. Someone who has been looking for him. You obviously know where the plane is. You're going to take me there. Let's get going."

She balked. She had to come up with a plan. "It's too far in the snow."

"My snowmobile is over there." He motioned to a dip in the terrain in a stand of aspen. "Move."

"The boy is tired," she protested. "Come tomorrow, and we can go while he's having his nap."

"I've been looking for it for a year. I don't intend to wait."

She had no choice but to follow him across the snowy ground. He got on the snowmobile and motioned for her and Sam to get on behind him. There would be room for the three of them; the man was slim and Sam was small. Sam began to whimper.

"Hush," Rachel said sternly. She had to think.

The man turned the key to start the snowmobile, but all it did was click. He muttered an oath under his breath and tried again, but the engine still refused to start.

"Get off," he growled. "I'll have to walk back. I'll be over to see you tomorrow. You'd better be there, or you'll be sorry."

Her tongue wanted to form words of defiance, but all Rachel managed to do was nod. She wished she had his gun. She wouldn't hesitate to use it. No one was going to take her boy. It was only after she was home again that she realized her fedora was still at the mine.

This time it could stay there.

*B*ree checked her watch. Nearly one. The heavy snow prevented her from burying Davy's belongings, and she had nothing else pressing to do today. She had been meaning to get out to the mine, and there was no time like the present. With her snowshoes, the snow cover was no problem. She put Samson in his search vest then gathered her ready-pack. She stuffed Fay's diary into the backpack and headed out. Though she'd been reading the diary carefully from back to front, Fay's minuscule writing made for slow reading, and so far she'd found nothing but Fay's selfish musings about her empty life. Steve wanted it back today.

Bree drove up Houghton Street and saw Naomi walking down the street with Charley. Bree stopped the Jeep and rolled down the window. "Hey, I'm heading out to take a look at that old mine. You want to come?" Charley barked, and Bree grinned. "I think he answered for you. You're not busy, are you?"

"Not unless you count avoiding my mother's questions," Naomi said. She put Charley in the back with Samson and climbed in.

Bree stopped at the bank and grabbed the diary out of her backpack. "I'll be right back," she told Naomi. She walked back to Steve's office and handed it to him. "I'd like to look at it again as soon as possible, Steve."

He nodded. "I'll glance through it as quick as I can. I just have to protect myself. I hope you understand."

She nodded. "I'd better go. Naomi and I are going out to check the mine."

His head jerked up. "I might join you after I finish here."

"I can use all the help I can get." It was about time Steve started taking a more active role. She left him and hurried outside.

"What's your mom have to say about you seeing Donovan?" Bree asked Naomi when she got back into the Jeep.

"I may have to move out." Naomi grinned to show she wasn't serious.

"That bad?"

"Terrible. I never should have told her I was interested in Donovan." Naomi put her head in her hands and rocked it from side to side in a mock expression of pain then leaned her head back against the seat. "She wants to invite Donovan and the kids over for supper. Now I ask you, Bree, doesn't she get it that things haven't gone that far? We're just friends exploring where it might lead."

"Has Donovan said that?"

"Well, sort of. He asked me if I'd ever wondered what might have happened if we'd dated in high school."

"You deserve someone really wonderful, Naomi. I hope Donovan is the one." And though she didn't say it, Bree hoped Naomi's marriage—if it got that far—would turn out better than Bree's own. But that wasn't fair. The early days had been happy, and maybe they would have been again. She would never know.

"What are you thinking about? You have a strange look on your face," Naomi said. "You've been different lately. Even Mom remarked on it."

"Different how?"

"I don't know exactly. Maybe more at peace with yourself—or maybe it's just resignation. I can't tell."

At peace with herself. That sounded good if she could make it a reality. "I'm trying, Naomi. I think one day soon I'll be able to go forward and not be stuck in the reruns of my life. The memories will still be there, but they won't consume me like they used to." She gave a self-conscious laugh. "I packed up Davy's things last night. I thought I'd make a guest room."

"Oh, Bree, that's wonderful!"

Bree blinked and glanced at her friend before turning her attention back to the road. "You approve? I thought you'd be horrified and wonder what kind of mother I am."

"I've worried about you turning Davy's room into a shrine. You'll always love Davy. We both know you'll always mourn him. But it's time, Bree."

Bree parked the Jeep by the highway. The road back to the mine was too snow-covered to see the dangerous potholes and tree stumps, so it would be safest to walk in.

"What are we looking for?" Naomi asked as they got out and allowed the dogs to race on ahead. They could wander until it was time to go home.

"I'm not really sure. A lot of details about Fay's death seem to lead back to this mine. Maybe it's coincidence, but I want to be sure."

"You mean you wonder if someone killed her for money?"

"It's possible." Bree ticked the suspects off on her glove-covered fingers. "Her uncle wanted her to sell to the New York conglomerate so he could get more money than what Palmer was willing to pay. He might have killed her to stop the sale. Of course, Steve nixed that idea, but Lawrence couldn't have known that ahead of time."

Naomi wrinkled her nose. "This is getting too scary for me, Bree. You need to let Mason handle it. New York conglomerates, big insurance policies, huge debts, and a boyfriend just out of jail. It's all too horrible."

They reached the mine, and Bree pointed to the ground. "Looks like someone's been here recently. I wonder if it's all related to the sale?"

Numerous footprints had tamped down the snow all across the clearing. Bree walked toward the main building. "Let's check the main shaft."

"Talk about stumbling around in the dark," Naomi grumbled. "We have no idea what we're looking for."

"Something worth killing for," Bree said. Darkness yawned through the mine shaft building's open door, which was attached by only one rusted hinge.

Bree didn't really want to go in, but she was done with fear. Fear had kept her silent when she should have talked to Rob about where their marriage was headed from the moment he grew distant; fear kept her from speaking her mind and being herself; fear of the future trapped her in the past. In all the ways that really mattered, she'd been a coward, and it shamed her. But no more.

She fumbled in her backpack for glow sticks and handed one to Naomi. Together they broke the sticks, and an eerie green light forced back the blanket of darkness. Bree immediately felt better. Naomi followed as they pushed deeper into the shaft building.

A giant steam hoist rose in front of them like some ravenous prehistoric beast. Bree had heard the hoist could lift eight tons of copper ore. Naomi uttered a tiny scream then gave a shaky laugh. "It looks like it wants to eat someone," she said in a hushed whisper.

"We could offer it Eric Matthews," Bree said. When they both laughed, she felt better. This wasn't so bad. She could do this.

Stepping over paper, discarded crates, and piles of rock, they walked farther into the shaft. They came to a split in the hall. Bree looked down each branch as far as she could see.

"You go left, and I'll go right," she told Naomi.

"I think we should stay together," Naomi said. "What if part of this old mine falls on one of us?"

"It seems sturdy enough. It will take us forever to search if we don't split up." The sooner they finished this job, the sooner they could get out of this dank place. The stale air in here made her think of tombs and graveyards, a macabre thought that brought a surge of panic. She swallowed her fear and turned to the right.

"I don't like this," Naomi called as she headed down the other hall.

It might not be the smartest thing to go alone without the dogs, but it would take too long to round them up. Besides, the walkway only went down. A damp chill radiated from the yawning hole, and she didn't want to enter it, but Bree forced herself to go on. She would never find the answer to Fay's murder if she didn't find some courage.

Down, down she went, the dim light of the glow stick lighting the way. The darkness seemed a living thing that teased her beyond the reach of her stick's feeble light. When she couldn't stand it anymore, she grabbed her flashlight and flipped it on. The bright white light pushed back the shadows, and she caught her breath again.

Several kerosene lanterns lined the shelves along the way. Maybe there was fuel in one of them. She looked closer and saw they were all full of kerosene. Evidently the fuel wasn't worth hauling out of here—lucky for her. Fumbling in her pack, she pulled out a box of matches and lit one of the lanterns. Holding the lantern high, she resumed her descent.

She came to a split. So much for there being no way to get lost. She'd just have to remember which way she chose. Chewing her lip, Bree saw a track running along the ground to the left. She'd follow it. If she didn't find anything in fifteen minutes, she would go back. She set the stopwatch function on her watch. She walked for what seemed like forever, but when she checked the time, only five minutes had passed. She looked up. A barrier stood in her way, and she stopped. It was a huge door that stood partway open to a room carved out of stone. Maybe it was an office or something.

She walked inside and stumbled over the rock that held the door open. The rock shifted, and the door slammed shut. With a cry, she flew to the door and grabbed at the handle. It wouldn't budge. Placing the lantern on the floor, she twisted the knob with both hands, but it didn't turn at all. She began pounding on the door.

Bree shouted until she was hoarse then looked at her watch just as the fifteen-minute alarm went off. Full-blown panic loomed at the edge of her mind, but she fought it. She reminded herself she was a professional. The key was not to panic. Naomi would get the dogs, and Samson would find her.

The darkness pressed in on her, and she grabbed the lantern and held it high. The room seemed to be a makeshift office of some kind. An old desk sat in one corner, its metal drawer rusting from the damp. Several equally rusty filing cabinets stood against the other wall. Several filthy blankets were heaped on the floor in one corner, evidently the haven of some homeless person in the dim past.

The touches of humanity in the room calmed Bree's rising terror. Sucking in several deep breaths, she found her cell phone and tried to dial. No signal. She put it away slowly. All she could do was be calm and wait. Easier said than done.

Setting the lamp on the desk, she pulled out the office chair and grabbed an old rag to wipe it down. After examining it for bugs and spiders, she eased into it. Though her heart still throbbed with trepidation, she no longer felt as though she might begin to scream uncontrollably. What could she do to keep her mind off her predicament?

The desk beside her held six drawers. The metal shrieked when she opened the first. She poked gingerly at the contents: rusty paper clips, pencils, a chalkboard eraser, an assortment of yellowed labels. The next drawer held papers, and she pulled them into the light. The crabbed handwriting was hard to read, but Bree soon got the hang of it.

Ledger sheets documented measurements of ore and sales to smelting companies. A letter dated May 1965 to a person named Wilson Cutter in Detroit caught her eye. According to the letter, a new vein of ore had been discovered at the Copper Queen. Gold. But the mine closed in July of 1965. Bree frowned. Had it been a false alarm, or had this letter never been sent? Maybe someone had found out about the gold in the mine.

Another paper, folded in half, fluttered to the floor. She grabbed it, but before she could open it, a clank sounded outside the door. Stuffing the paper into her pocket, she sprang forward and began pounding. "I'm in here!" she shouted.

Moments later she heard Samson's whine. He began to bark, then the deeper tones of a man's voice reverberated through the door.

"We're here, Bree; I'll get you out," Kade shouted through the door. "The door's locked, but I have a crowbar. Naomi, over here! I've found her."

Metal screeched against metal as Kade pried the hinges loose. "Stand back," he called.

Bree stood away from the door, and it crashed inward. Dust flew into her face, and she coughed as she stumbled into Kade's arms. Samson barked joyously then leaped onto her leg. She patted his head then leaned against Kade's chest.

He hugged her tightly, and she burrowed into his strong embrace, just as she'd longed to do before. It was just as she'd imagined. With his arms tight around her, she felt safe and protected.

He spoke into her hair. "What were you thinking, prowling around down here all alone?"

She finally pulled away and slanted a grin into his face. "A good investigator goes where the clues are."

He grinned back. "A good investigator doesn't get lost."

"Bree!" Naomi's shout echoed down the cavernous hall, and the dim glow of her light stick grew brighter. Charley raced ahead of his owner and jumped on Bree in an ecstatic show of relief. Moments later Naomi rushed out of the darkness and grabbed Bree in a tight clutch.

Both women burst into tears.

Kade looked at Samson and sighed. "Don't try to understand it, boy."

The women giggled and wiped their tears before trooping out of the dark mine into the clearing. Bree stepped into the open air and stretched her arms to the sky. "I wasn't sure I'd ever see the sun again." It had started snowing, and the fresh cold air smelled wonderful after the staleness of the mine.

Kade rubbed Samson's curly coat. "With this dog, I don't think you'd ever have to worry about being lost. He would always find you."

Bree knelt and threw her arms around Samson's neck. "And I never even thanked you, Samson." He whined eagerly and licked her on the chin. She buried her face in his fur and hugged him again, then stood. Laughing, they struggled through the snow and toward their vehicles. Samson moseyed off into the woods. After a few minutes, he began to bark.

"What is it, boy?" Bree called. She left Kade's side and hurried to where the dog stood in a stand of white pine. Samson poked his head out of a thicket. He had something in his mouth. Bree bent over and took it from him.

"Find anything?" Naomi called.

Bree turned and held up something brown. "It's a hat," she said.

Naomi frowned. "Let me see." She joined Bree and took the hat. "A floppy brown leather hat," she murmured.

"What's so special about that?" Kade asked.

"Remember the O'Reilly kids and their witch? They said she wore a floppy brown leather hat. And Mason said the same thing."

Kade slapped his head. "I've been so caught up with the way Lauri—I forgot until just now! I saw her!"

"Where?" Bree grabbed his arm.

"Out by Rock River on Sunday."

"Let's see what Samson can find out." She held the hat under Samson's nose. "Samson, search!"

The dog sniffed the hat then turned and ran off into the woods. Naomi had Charley sniff it as well and sent him out. The threesome followed, but it became clear after a few minutes that the dogs didn't have a scent. Bree and Naomi called them back and headed toward the car with Kade. Bree managed to hide her disappointment. She didn't want Kade to feel worse than he already did.

"Are we done here?" he asked.

"I guess so. Hey, you never told me what you were doing here."

"I was answering a call about a deer hit by a car out this way and saw your Jeep," he said. "I thought I'd see what was going on. When I got to the mine, I heard Naomi shouting your name, and I knew something was wrong. We called the dogs and started looking for you. I was afraid you'd gotten stuck somewhere—or worse."

She turned to check on the dogs and found Samson at the edge of the forest. He was whining and his tail was tucked between his legs. "What's wrong, boy?" She walked over to where he sat. Kade followed.

The dog seemed distressed, his brown eyes almost speaking to them in misery. Kade patted his head. "What's wrong with him?"

"He's acting like he does when he gets a death scent," Bree said. She glanced around. "I don't see anything though."

The wind had blown the snow off a pile of rocks nearby, and Kade caught a flash of red-black. "What's that?" He knelt and brushed more snow away. A reddish stain covered one of the rocks, and spatters of the same substance dotted several others. "It looks like blood."

"Blood?"

"You tell me. Would Samson give a death alert on an animal's blood?"

Bree shook her head and stared at him. "What if it's Fay's blood?"

"That can't be right," Naomi said. "Unless . . ."

"Unless she was killed here and moved to the other site. He got her out of the car by the road, laid her on the ground for a minute, then hauled her to the cliff bottom," Bree said.

"Let's get Mason," Naomi said.

Bree called Mason on her cell phone. "He's on his way," she told them. Bree and Naomi let the dogs continue to search while they waited for the sheriff.

*M*ason and Deputy Montgomery finally showed up and had barely had time to take samples of the bloodstains when they got a call about a hunting accident. Mason promised to call when he had news.

"Let's go to your place," Naomi said when the sheriff pulled away. "The snow is really coming down, and we don't want to get stuck out here."

Bree drove slowly back to town, with Kade following in his truck. The wind blew the snow in gusts across the road, and she strained to see through the whiteout. When they got to her lighthouse, she made some coffee then paced the kitchen, wishing Mason would call.

"Quit pacing," Kade ordered. "Let's think of something to do to keep us occupied."

All three were silent for a moment.

"We could get that light going in the tower," Kade offered.

"She's been working on it," Naomi said. "She won't ask for help."

"What needs to be done? I'm pretty handy with a hammer." He flexed his muscles and the women laughed.

"A Fresnel lens needs to be installed. It's bulky and heavy though. Rob sent the original one out for repair. It came back about a week before he died and has been in the garage ever since."

"What are we waiting for? I'm going to get it." Naomi headed for the back door.

Bree found the expression on Kade's face unsettling. A softness eased around his mouth and eyes that made her mouth go dry. "Do I have dirt on my nose?" she asked him.

"Sorry. I was staring, wasn't I?" He stood. "Let's get that light installed."

Bree took Kade to the garage and pointed out the Fresnel lens tucked in the corner under the wooden worktable. He dragged it out.

"Don't you need permission to light these towers over the harbor?" he asked as the three of them maneuvered it into the house.

"Rob applied for a permit as soon as the lens arrived," Bree explained. "It's been sitting on my desk for months."

Kade nodded. They paused in the kitchen for a rest.

"I hope you're planning to feed us after this," he said, wiping his forehead. He eyed the stairs warily.

"Um, you don't know what you're asking," Naomi said, laughing. "Unless you like frozen pizza or popcorn."

"I've eaten my share of frozen pizza," Kade said.

Bree's cheeks grew hot. "I can cook more than frozen pizza." She grinned weakly. "But I think that might be all that's in the freezer." She really had to do something about eating better.

"I knew it," Naomi said, gloating.

"Now let's hook this baby up." Kade patted the lens.

They had to stop and rest several times, but they finally managed to get the lens to the light tower. The women left Kade to do his job and went to the living room.

Naomi dug her book out of her backpack. "I think I'll read awhile and unwind. I'm at a really exciting part."

Naomi's comment reminded Bree of the paper she'd found at the mine office. She stuck her hand into her pocket and pulled it out. Unfolding it, she read the top: "'The Hound of Heaven,' by Francis Thompson." Mathilda had said something about a hound of heaven the day they'd been at the animal shelter. Curious, Bree began to read.

The language was hard to follow at first, but then the literature studies she'd done in college kicked in and she read on more smoothly. As the poem talked about the "Hound of Heaven" stripping away all to leave nothing but God, something tugged at Bree's heart. Was that what he'd been doing to her?

"Look at this, Naomi," she said, holding out the yellowed paper.
"What is it?" Naomi took the paper. "Where did you get this?"
"At the mine."

Naomi frowned. "How strange. Of course it *is* a poem from the eighteen hundreds. Maybe someone else felt God's pursuit."

"You sound like you believe he does that—pursue. Did you understand the poem?" Bree looked down at the words again.

"It's an allegory about how God pursues us to bring us to himself. He is who you need, Bree. Can't you see how he's been chasing you, caring for you? Samson and Charley are driven to find lost hunters and kids; God is driven to pursue you. He saved you from the fall from the tower. Kade *just happened* to be out by the mine today, and I never could have gotten that door open without him."

"A coincidence," Bree said, turning away, though a part of her longed to know it as something else.

Naomi gently persisted. "Anu says coincidence is a nonbeliever's way of explaining God's hand at work. Can't you see God's providential hand in your life?"

God's hand in your life. The words penetrated Bree's heart, and she saw the truth. *I am He Whom thou seekest,* the poem said. It was God she needed. A heavenly Father who truly loved her and cared for her soul.

She put her hands to her cheeks. "You're right, Naomi. I'm tired of running. I want what you have, what Anu has."

Naomi prayed with her, and when Bree raised her head, the colors of the world had shifted as though she'd stepped out of a black-and-white TV into a cinematic event. There were no clanging bells, no singing birds, but she felt the whisper of another presence. Her Hound of Heaven had found her, and she was his. "Thank you, God," she whispered. "Thank you."

*T*he next morning Bree hummed as she rummaged through the cabinets for something edible. Even the sight of Davy's boxes failed to dampen her spirits. There would be time enough to bury them. She felt certain she would see Davy again someday, and that joy eased her sadness.

Too excited to eat cold cereal for breakfast, she decided to go to Nicholls's for coffee and cinnamon rolls. She wanted to see Anu's face when she heard the good news. Kade had been overjoyed last night and had insisted on making a fancy dinner to celebrate her decision. He'd gone to the store and brought back enough supplies to feed an army. He'd made beef stroganoff fit for a king.

She grabbed her coat and the book Naomi had left behind. She could drop the book off on her way home from the store. Though it was only seven, she knew Anu would be there by now. Bree and Samson trudged down Negaunee and onto Houghton Street through the snowdrifts. She used her key to let herself in. The aroma of yeast and cinnamon was enticing.

"I hope you have enough for me," she called out as she walked toward the back of the store.

"Bree, I wasn't expecting you. You're up early." Anu hugged her, leaving a smudge of flour on Bree's jeans. "Oh, dear, I'm sorry."

Bree brushed at the flour. "It's coming off, don't worry. Those smell wonderful. Can I have one?"

"Of course. Coffee is on too." Anu's gaze was sharp as she took in the smile on Bree's face. "You look different this morning, *kulta*. Has something happened? You've found a place for your new business perhaps?"

"Better." Bree poured a cup of coffee and took a cinnamon bun from the pan. Licking the icing, the grin spread on her face, and she giggled.

"You look positively giddy," Anu said. "What is it?"

"I'm a Christian," Bree said simply. "I'll see Davy again, and Rob." The burden of her pain and disillusionment over Rob's betrayal was gone now too, she realized. It no longer crushed the life from her.

Anu cried out and rushed to hug her. Bree set her breakfast on the table and embraced her mother-in-law. Anu held her at arm's length. "Now you are truly my daughter in all ways," she said. "Remember this moment, *kulta,* this first love for God. Holding to it will see you through the storms life brings."

"There are more?" Bree asked with a smile.

Anu wanted to hear all about Bree's journey toward God, so they sat at the table and drank their coffee while Bree explained the events of the past few weeks.

"Have you talked to Mason or Hilary?" Bree asked finally. "Did you hear what I found at the mine yesterday?"

Anu shook her head. "I had a church meeting last night, so I didn't get home until after ten."

Bree told her about the blood.

"The mine is so familiar." Anu pursed her lips. "So familiar. My husband Abe worked at the mine the year before it closed down. As the accountant, he was good friends with Matthew Kukkan, Fay's grand-father. There was some talk of looking for gold at the mine. Silly, eh? My Abe told them even if there was gold, it would be too expensive to extract from the copper ore."

Bree gave a frustrated sigh. "But we still don't know if the murder had anything to do with the mine or if Fay was killed in a jealous rage by one of the three men."

"And what of the woman who might know where my Rob's plane crashed? Any news of her?"

"We found her hat out by the mine yesterday, but the dogs couldn't pick up her scent." Bree was still thinking of the gold. "I wonder if it would be more feasible to extract the gold now?"

"You must ask Mason. Not that it matters now," Anu said. "I don't know why I even mentioned they'd thought to look. Nothing ever came of it."

"I think I'll stop by his office now." Bree rose and bent to kiss Anu's cheek. "Thank you for being such a good example for me to follow," she whispered.

Anu touched her cheek. "Now you must carry the light, my Bree. Remember the psalm: 'Even in darkness, light dawns for the upright.' That is you now. Let your light shine here in Rock Harbor."

"I'll try." Buoyant, Bree called Samson, and they went out into the snow again. Mason wasn't at the office, but Montgomery said he'd be back around 8:30. She had time to drop off Naomi's book.

Bree rang the doorbell at the Blue Bonnet then tried the door. Martha or Naomi had already unlocked it, so she stepped inside. "It's just me," she called.

Martha bustled down the hall, a voluminous chef's apron tied around her rose-colored dress. "Bree, dear, you're just in time for breakfast."

"That's what I was hoping for," she said. "I had a *pulla* and coffee with Anu, but I'm still hungry."

Martha laughed, and her cheeks turned pink. "You can join Naomi in the dining room. We don't have any guests until tomorrow, so it's just us."

"Even better." Bree went through the parlor to the dining room. "Hey, girlfriend, you left your book at my house last night. Again."

"I knew I did when I tried to find it last night." Naomi took the book with a shamefaced laugh.

"You need to carry your books on a string around your neck." Bree smiled and sat beside her friend.

Martha wanted to hear all about Bree's newfound faith. When they were done, Bree went to call Mason, but the phone rang before she could dial.

"I'll get it," she called. "Blue Bonnet," she answered.

"Naomi?" a deep voice asked.

Bree recognized Donovan. "Hello, Donovan. This is Bree."

"I wonder if you could ask Naomi to come over right away?" Donovan sounded distraught.

"What's wrong?" she asked sharply.

"A contractor has a bad water leak and needs supplies right away. I need to hurry in and open the store. I was hoping Naomi could watch the kids for a few minutes until the bus comes."

"We'll be right there," she assured him. She rushed to the kitchen to get Naomi.

Five minutes later they were running up the walk to the O'Reilly house. Donovan met them at the door. He thanked them quickly as he ran out. Just as Bree and Naomi went to find the kids, a wail came from the end of the hallway.

"Timmy's locked in the bathroom!" Emily threw herself into Naomi's arms. Bree was glad to see a bond seemed to be developing there.

"We'll get him out quickly," Naomi said, running a hand over Emily's hair. "Does your daddy have a screwdriver somewhere?"

She nodded and ran to get one.

Bree took the screwdriver and stuck it in the lock. "Call Kade in case I can't get this open," she told Naomi.

Naomi carried Emily with her and went to the living room, where Bree heard her call Kade and ask him to come over. Bree spoke soothingly to Timmy on the other side of the door as she worked on the lock. Jiggling and twisting the screwdriver, she finally heard a click.

"I think I've got it!" She turned the knob, and the door opened. Timmy fell into her arms. She picked him up, and he wrapped his legs around her. The feel of his small body brought a lump to her throat.

She and Naomi soothed the children then began to help them get ready for school. Ten minutes later the front door banged, and Kade's voice called from the entryway, "Everything okay?"

Still carrying Timmy, Bree went to join Kade. "Got him. He's okay, just shook up." She smoothed the hair back from his face and pressed her lips to his forehead. "Ready to get down?"

He nodded, and she put him down. "I want Pooky," he said.

Bree froze. Her chest felt so tight she could barely breathe. "Pooky?" she finally choked out.

Timmy went to the couch and rummaged under a blanket. He turned triumphantly and held out a small, brown koala bear. "Pooky," he said.

Time rolled backward like a riptide. Bree swallowed hard.

"Timmy, *no!*" Emily said. "You're not supposed to tell. The witch of the woods will come back and hurt us. Remember how mad she got at Sam?"

The witch of the woods again, but who was Sam? Bree held out her hand. "Can . . . can I see Pooky a minute?" she asked. She was dimly aware of Naomi joining them in the living room. Keeping her eyes on the bear, she managed to walk forward on legs that felt no stronger than spaghetti. Davy's bear was like a part of him. She'd longed to find it.

Her hands shook as she reached out to take the stuffed animal. There must be hundreds of these little bears around, she told herself. But a tingle went up her arm when she touched the bear and saw the Barney swim trunks it wore. There was a raspberry stain on the right leg over Barney's face from when Davy had helped her pick enough berries to make a cobbler. Closing her eyes, she clutched Pooky to her chest.

"Oh, dear God, help us," Naomi prayed in a hoarse whisper. "I've been here several times and never seen it."

"We hided it," Emily whispered. "We didn't want her to get mad."

Slowly, so slowly, Bree eased down onto the couch. She heard her voice as if from a great distance. "Timmy, where did you get this?"

"Sam gave it to me."

"Who's Sam?"

"We told you!" Emily said impatiently. "He belongs to the witch of the woods. He's her little boy. He gave it to Timmy when he was sick, but then Timmy dropped it. When Sam visited us last week, he said he'd found it and still wanted Timmy to have it. We weren't supposed to tell anyone."

Bree was trembling as if she were weak from the flu. She was afraid to breathe, afraid she would wake up. A little boy in the woods with a woman who seemed bent on avoiding people. And now Davy's favorite toy. What did it all mean? Logic said the woman had found the plane and given Davy's things to her little boy, which was what she'd assumed about the glove. But what if it was more than that? Was it possible? She was afraid to breathe, afraid to really look at it clearly.

She pulled Emily to her. "This is very important, Emily. What did he look like?"

"Don't jump to conclusions, Bree," Naomi said. "The woman gave it to her son."

"What's going on?" Kade asked.

Bree blinked and stared up at him. "This belonged to Davy," she whispered. "It's his favorite toy. I'm sure he had it with him when the plane went down."

Kade's eyes widened. He knelt beside the children. "We need to find this witch of the woods, kids. Can you remember anything about where her cabin was?"

The urgency got through to the kids, for they grew sober with eyes as round as sand dollars. Emily looked as though she might cry. "It was dark, and we were lost," she said.

"I know; I know," Kade said, patting her on the shoulder.

Bree suddenly remembered the hat. "Kade, would you get my ready-pack out of the Jeep?"

Recognition at what she wanted with the pack came into his eyes, and he nodded as he went quickly to the door. He returned moments later with the pack in his hand. Bree took the pack and unzipped it. She pulled out the hat.

"Hey, that's her hat!" Timmy said.

So the witch and the woman Fay saw were one and the same. "What did Sam look like?" she whispered.

"He was little like Timmy," Emily said. "And he had dark brown hair."

Brown hair. Her stomach plummeted. Davy's was red like hers.

"What about his eyes?" Naomi asked.

"Green!" Timmy announced triumphantly. "Like my marble."

"Like Bree's?" Naomi asked.

Emily tipped her head to one side and stared at Bree. "Yes, just like yours," she said. "And he had freckles like yours too."

"And he limped," Emily added.

Bree stared at Naomi. "Is it possible?" she whispered.

"I'm afraid to hope," Naomi said quietly.

He couldn't be alive, could he? This was surely just some other child who'd been given things from the wreckage of the plane. Bree's heart warmed from the tiny hope that flickered there.

"We're going to be late for school," Emily said in a small voice. "We missed the bus."

"Show me where you saw the woman," Bree said to Kade, jumping to her feet. "We'll drop the kids off at school then go out to where you saw the woman." She wasn't sure she could drive, she was shaking so hard. "Can you drive?" she asked Naomi. She nodded and took the keys.

Naomi got the kids into their coats. On wobbly legs, Bree walked to the Jeep and got in on the passenger side. Naomi buckled the children into the backseat then got behind the wheel. Kade put the dogs in the rear compartment before he climbed into the backseat.

"Pray hard," Naomi said, slipping the Jeep into gear.

Bree nodded. She'd started pleading with God as soon as she realized this might not be a dream. Thankfulness welled up in her. The sense of God's presence was a comfort she'd never expected.

*T*he discard pile by the door had grown larger. Rachel knew she could only take what she and Sam could carry. She had no time or money to make another trip out here. They would buy what they needed in Chicago once she started earning some money. They had to get out of here before that man came back. He frightened her, and Sam had cried for hours when they'd gotten back to the cabin. He'd clearly recognized the man.

The pitiful stack of things they would take lay on the bare mattress. "You ready to get packed up, Sammy?"

He nodded. "Why can't I take my books?"

"They're too heavy, son. You've read them all anyway. I'll buy new ones you haven't read yet when we get to our new home."

"Can I take *The Little Engine That Could*? It's not heavy."

He'd read that book so many times the copy was dog-eared and grimy. But he was right; it was light. "I suppose. If there's room."

"There's room." He scampered to the bed and began to pack his small backpack.

He owned little. Just the bare necessities she'd managed to buy.

Three pairs of pants and shirts, four sets of underwear and socks, and the coat he would wear out of here. Rachel resolved once again to do better by him once they were in Chicago. She joined him at the bed and packed her own meager possessions.

She was frantic to get away. The cabin seemed almost claustrophobic to her today. What if the man came back before they were gone? What did he want with Sam's plane? Outside, the sun shone brightly on the snow and nearly blinded her. Inside, it was dark and confining. They would leave this place behind and never look back.

The past was just that—the past. The future beckoned as brightly as the snow. Maybe she should change her name. And once she got some money stashed away, they could leave Chicago and go where there was no chance of ever running into that man.

She and Sam would be new creatures, born this day into a world of possibilities. The dreams she held for Sam were grand; she knew that. But possible. Anything was possible today. They just had to get out of here.

Sam finished packing his backpack. "I'm ready," he said. "Are we going to eat first?"

"Are you hungry already? It's only nine o'clock."

"A little." He looked shamefaced.

"How about some beef jerky to gnaw on?"

He nodded eagerly.

She got him some jerky. "Think you can eat it while we walk? It will take several hours to walk to Ontonagon."

Sam nodded. "I can walk."

"Okay." She opened the door and grabbed their snowshoes from the hook outside. "Let's get these on."

Once they were ready, she shut the door behind them and left it unlocked. Let some other needy person find a haven here as she and Sam had done. It had served them well, but it was time to move on.

"Wait, I forgot my yo-yo!" Sam struggled through the snow back to the house and disappeared inside. He reappeared moments later with his yo-yo clutched in his hand. "Emily gave it to me."

"Well, put it in your pocket, and let's get going. Say good-bye, Sam. We're off to a new life."

"Bye, Marcus," Sam called to his squirrel. Marcus chattered from his tree and watched as they walked across the clearing.

Rachel turned for one last look. It was done. No one would ever find them now.

$\mathcal{B}$ree's chest was tight with a mixture of hope and disbelief as they neared town. Her goal was so close. Naomi turned off on Summit and stopped in front of the school. Kade helped Emily and Timmy out of the Jeep and walked them through the school doors. The preschool teacher took charge of Timmy, and Emily went on to her class. When Kade returned, they drove down Houghton Street, intent on getting to the forest. As they passed the bank, a figure stepped into the snow-covered street to flag them down. Steve's face was red with the cold, but he wore an excited grin. He waved Fay's diary in his hand. Naomi stopped, the Jeep's back end fishtailing a bit. Steve ran to Bree's door, and she lowered her window.

"You won't believe it!" he panted. He flipped open the diary. "Look." He pushed the open diary under Bree's nose.

Impatient with the delay, she glanced at the words: *The assayer says there's gold in the mine. Gold. I can hardly believe it. Does he know? This changes everything.* "Who's 'he'?" Bree asked.

"I don't know. But this has to have something to do with her death. We need to talk. Where are you headed?" Steve asked.

"We might have a lead to my family," Bree said. She didn't want to take the time to explain it.

Steve's eyes widened. "I'll come with you. We'll talk on the way." He didn't wait for an answer but got in the backseat with Kade.

"I carry an extra pair of snowshoes; you can use those," Bree said. "But you're going to get cold in those pants." Steve was dressed for the office, not for hiking through heavy snow. The temperature today hovered near zero, and a cold wind blew out of the north. Steve didn't seem to care.

Naomi drove out along the access road to Lake Superior. The waves tossed foam onto the beach, and the wind whistled through the Jeep's grille.

"I'm having a hard time staying on the road," she muttered. Her knuckles were white as she fought with the wheel.

"Want me to take over?" Kade asked.

Naomi nodded and pulled over, then she and Kade exchanged places. The delay made Bree want to scream with frustration. Half an hour later they stopped at the track where Kade had seen the woman.

"This is it," Kade said. "There's too much snow to risk taking the Jeep in. We'll have to go on foot."

Bree let the dogs out. Then she pulled out Pooky, the hat, and the paper bag with Davy's shirt she'd been using as a scent article. She pushed back her hair impatiently as the wind teased it from under her parka hood and blew the curls into her eyes. She knelt beside her dog.

Samson whined as though to ask what was wrong. She put her arms around him. "I'm depending on you, boy. I can't do this alone. Please, please, find them." Samson whined and licked her face. Tears leaked from her eyes and soaked the fur at his neck. Holding the stuffed bear and the hat under his nose, she let Samson sniff them. Then she had him sniff Davy's scent article. His tail began to wag when he smelled Davy's scent.

"Find Davy, Samson." Bree let go of Samson and started after him with her heart in her throat as he bounded away. "Please, God, let it be Davy," she whispered. The cold wind stung her face, but she barely noticed. Intent on keeping up with Samson, she plodded over the snow-covered ground in her snowshoes, not caring whether the rest of the team was managing to keep up. The dogs seemed to know right where they were going. Samson bounded over and through snowdrifts with his nose high in the air. His tail waved grandly, and exhilaration seemed to pour off him in waves.

Bree had never seen Samson so excited. But no, she was setting herself up for a crushing disappointment. At the end of this search, all she was likely to find were dead bodies, not her Davy alive and well. Naomi was probably right: The woman had found the wreckage and had taken Davy's things home to her own child.

But wasn't the wreckage exactly what she'd spent the past year looking for—her husband's and son's dead bodies? With that goal finally in sight, it seemed a poor trophy. Their souls were what mattered. And for the first time in her life, she was at peace knowing they really weren't out there under this thick blanket of snow. Heaven was where they were residing. And as she'd told Anu, she would see them again.

They came to an old road that crisscrossed through the forest, and Bree paused to rest. Steve panted beside her as he hurried to keep up. "This borders Asters land," he gasped, out of breath. His dress slacks were wet with snow. "Another old mine is down that way. That one was abandoned back in the eighteen hundreds and has never been the producer the Copper Queen was."

Kade sat on a stump poking up through the snow and pushed his hat back from his forehead. "I think they've lost the scent."

The dogs nosed around the clearing for several minutes, but it was clear Kade was right. The rising frustration in Bree's heart brought tears to her eyes. They'd been so close.

"Did you see anything else in the diary?" she asked Steve. She'd only briefly skimmed it, but Fay's handwriting was hard to read. It was the only lead they had.

"Truthfully, I just started looking at it this morning. I was almost afraid of what Fay might say about the baby." Steve pulled it out of his jacket. He brushed the snow from a downed tree then settled down on it. Bree pulled out a handful of pistachios. Kade took a few, but Steve, and of course Naomi, refused them. Bree sat beside Steve as he flipped through the pages, skimming quickly. He was used to Fay's poor penmanship and seemed to have no trouble reading it.

About five pages from the end, Steve made a sound. Bree leaned over to see.

Steve read it aloud. "'The most peculiar thing happened today. I was hiking in the woods and ran across a cabin near Big White Rock. I knocked on the door, and a woman I'd met earlier came to the door. I hadn't realized there were any cabins in that area. She seemed scared when I showed up and asked for a glass of water. It might be my imagination, but I thought that old seat in the ravine beside the cabin looked like an airplane seat. I think I might investigate a little more and find out who she is." Bree jumped to her feet. "Big White Rock. You know where that is? It doesn't ring a bell with me."

"I know it!" Naomi put in excitedly. "We're in the wrong spot. It would be quicker to drive to Lake Richmond and go from there. Come on!"

"I know it too," Steve said. "It's near some of my land."

They raced back to the car. Since she knew where they were going, Naomi drove. They headed along snow-covered dirt and gravel roads to Lake Richmond, a small haven for loons deep in the North Woods. Naomi drove the narrow road until it petered out near a stand of jack pine.

"Big White Rock is about two miles west of here," she said.

"Fay didn't say which direction from the rock," Bree said.

"The dogs will know," Kade said. He opened the back hatch and let the dogs out, and they all put on their gear again.

Bree had the dogs sniff the items again, and within seconds Samson had the scent. He raced off with his tail held high. Her heart surged, and she hurried after him, the sound of her snowshoes *whoosh-whooshing* in the cold air. Samson ran as though he knew right where to go. He kept pausing and looking back impatiently as if to ask why she couldn't keep up.

All Bree could do was focus on putting one foot in front of the other. Over wind-swept hills and valleys filled with snowdrifts, they followed the dogs. The minutes ticked by as the sun rose higher in the sky.

They finally reached a creek bed and crossed it, their boots crunching through the top layer of ice to the cold water trickling beneath it. Chilled through and through, Bree willed herself to the crest of the hill on the far side.

Below them in a clearing sat a small log cabin.

"That's got to be it!" Steve shouted.

Excitement ran through Bree like an electric current, and she saw the same thrill on her friends' faces. Bree ran full tilt down the hill to the front door of the cabin. She knocked on the door. "Hello!"

When no one answered, she cautiously pushed the door open and peered inside. Her stomach twisted when she saw the single empty room inside. She saw a box of old clothes beside the door. Samson raced past her and grabbed a toy fire engine in his mouth. His tail beat a furious dance in the air as he licked the toy and whined.

A child had been here, but was it her child? Bree could only watch Samson's reaction and thrill to the possibility. "Where is he, Samson? Search!"

The dog barked then dashed from the room. He dropped the fire engine as he ran toward the backyard and vanished into the woods.

"Wait for me!" Bree ran after him, plunging into the deep shadows of the forest.

Bree could sense Samson's excitement, and it fueled her own. They had to be very close. Kade, Steve, and Naomi thrashed through the brush behind her, but she didn't wait on them. She could conceive of nothing beyond this moment of pushing past brambles, struggling over rough terrain on her snowshoes, and keeping her gaze on her dog. Samson paused at the top of a hill and began to bark excitedly. He disappeared, and Bree struggled on to the top of the slope.

Below her in a clearing sat a woman on a log. Beside her was a small figure. The woman rose and put her hands out as if to ward off the dog's attack, but Samson paid no attention to her. He ran straight to the small figure. Even from here, Bree could see the little boy's fearlessness. He jumped up and ran toward the dog.

"Sam!" the woman cried.

"Sam!" the little boy shouted. He threw his arms around Samson's neck, and the dog licked his face in a frenzied display of joy.

Bree knew her legs were moving, but the scene seemed to freeze as a still life, the air around her a vacuum. Laboring against the atmosphere that kept her from the child, she pushed on, and finally the little boy's face grew closer. He was laughing, and she'd seen that dimpled grin thousands of times. Her gaze traced the contours of his cheeks, his pointed chin, the wide forehead so like her own.

The hair beneath the knit cap was darker than Davy's, but nothing could hide the fact that her son stood before her, alive and well. He looked up, and his green eyes widened. His arms fell away from Samson's neck, and the dog stood still as if he sensed this was Bree's turn.

Bree had almost reached him. "Davy?" she whispered. She wanted to touch him, but what if he disappeared as he always did in her dreams? His face blurred as tears stung her eyes.

"Mommy?" he asked.

The strength drained from her legs and she collapsed to her knees in front of him, her fall cushioned by the snow. His small fingers touched her face with a tentative touch as though he was as unsure of her as she was of him. Bree folded him in an embrace, and he snuggled against her as if there was no place he'd rather be. "Davy, Davy," was all she could say. His hair smelled of wood smoke and little boy. She buried her face in his neck and breathed in the scent of him, an aroma better than any *pulla* or *panukakkua.*

He wrapped his arms around her and burrowed closer. If it was a dream, she wanted never to awaken. He felt whole, but was he really all right? She ran her hands over his back and legs as he clung to her and refused to let go. He didn't wince at her probing fingers but sighed in contentment to be in her care.

Davy finally pulled away. He cupped her face in both his hands, a mannerism she'd almost forgotten. "Where were you, Mommy? I couldn't find you."

"I've been looking and looking for you, sweetheart. Samson and I have never stopped looking for you." Bree was sobbing so hard she could barely get the words out. She'd almost given up, she realized with a sense of shame. How good God was that he had brought this incredible blessing to her.

"I knew you'd find me," he said. "You and Sam." He reached out and caressed the dog. Samson wiggled all over with pleasure and pushed his nose between Davy and Bree. Bree threw an arm around the dog and drew him into the circle. Her family. The three of them.

Kade, Steve, and Naomi reached them. Naomi was sobbing and clinging to Kade's arm for support. Steve stumbled along with a dazed look on his face.

There were tears in Kade's eyes as well, and Bree's heart was touched by his compassion and empathy.

"This must be Davy," he said.

Bree was so full of emotion, she could barely whisper, "Davy, this is Kade Matthews. He's been helping me look for you. Naomi and Steve too."

Naomi knelt in front of them and held out her arms. "Remember Aunt Naomi?"

Davy nodded and limped over for a hug. His forehead wrinkled as he thought. "Where's Charley?" He released her then went back to Bree's arms.

"He's out looking for you. His nose isn't quite as good as Samson's," Naomi said.

There was a bark from the top of the hill, then a reddish shape came streaking toward them, and soon Charley was all over Davy in a dance of joy.

Gradually, Bree became aware of the woman standing at the edge of the group. Her arms hung slackly at her sides, and her face was a mask of misery. Bree stood with Davy in her arms. She faced the woman and wondered what she could say. At least the woman had kept him alive. But why hadn't she brought him to town and reunited him with his family the minute he was found?

"Who's your friend, Davy?"

Her son's small face grew solemn. "Her name is Mother. She takes care of me," he said.

From his short explanation, Bree gleaned a wealth of information. No one else had ever taken her place with Davy. He had never accepted this woman in Bree's place. Her heart was too full to speak. She tried, but nothing came out.

Swallowing, she tried again. "Who are you?" she whispered.

The woman raised pale blue eyes shadowed with sorrow. "Rachel Marks, ma'am."

"I want to know everything," Bree said. "How you found him and why you kept him and where the plane is."

Rachel nodded. "I know."

"Let's take you home, little guy," Kade said.

The woman's gaze darted left then right as though she might bolt, then she slowly reached out a hand and grasped Bree's. "I'm sorry," she said. "I loved him so much, you see." Tears slid down her windburned cheeks. She dropped Bree's hand and followed them up the hill.

Bree carried Davy slowly while the rest of the group hurried ahead.

This was her time with him. She would remember the feel of his small arms clinging to her neck forever. His breath warmed her cheek as she recited everyone who would be glad to see him. "Grammy Anu, Aunt Hilary, Uncle Mason—they've all missed you so much. And remember the twins, Paige and Penelope? You won't believe how much they've grown."

Davy made a little sound of contentment. "Is Daddy coming too?"

Bree caught her breath. She wondered how much he remembered of that terrible day of the crash. "You and Daddy went fishing," she said. "Wasn't it fun for just you and Daddy to go fishing—just the boys?"

"I didn't like it when Daddy yelled."

"Daddy yelled?" Bree asked. Rob had been a loving and caring father. He'd rarely raised his voice to Davy. "Why did he yell at you?"

Davy stiffened, and his voice came out offended. "No, Mommy! At Uncle Palmer."

Confusion made her pause to catch her breath. "Uncle Palmer went fishing with you?"

"I guess so." Then he shook his head. "No, I 'member. He came to visit us at the lake."

"Why would Daddy yell at Uncle Palmer? We don't yell at friends, remember?"

"I know. But Daddy didn't want Uncle Palmer to do some things. Like hurt people. We don't hurt people."

"Who did Uncle Palmer want to hurt?" Bree was growing more confused. Palmer had never mentioned he'd seen Rob and Davy. In fact, he'd mourned the fact he hadn't been able to check Rob's plane before the crash.

"I guess Daddy, 'cause he hit him."

"Uncle Palmer hit Daddy? Where?"

"In the nose. There was blood, and I cried." He said the words matter-of-factly.

"Do you know why he hit Daddy?"

"I don't know," Davy whispered. "But Uncle Palmer found gold."

Gold. The only place he could have found gold would have been at Fay's mine. And Fay was dead. *And so was Rob.* In her diary Fay had written that she wondered if "he" knew. Could the "he" she referred to be Palmer? Bree's mouth was dry with an unnamed dread. Palmer wouldn't hurt anyone. Would he?

Another thought slipped through her mind like a Windigo wraith. *Palmer worked on airplanes in the military.* Bree didn't want to entertain such a thought, but the suspicions were multiplying.

Davy put his palms against her cheeks and pulled her face in front of his. "Don't look scared, Mommy. We got away from Uncle Palmer."

Bree didn't know what he meant, but she decided not to ask him any more questions now. She didn't want him to see her agitation, and he'd been through enough. There would be time to sort it all out later.

"Put your head against my shoulder and take a nap," she told him. "Everything is fine, sweetheart. You're with Mommy now, and we're going to be okay." But even as her son's breathing deepened and his weight sagged in her arms, her thoughts tumbled over one another like rabbits running from hunters. She couldn't believe it, could she? There had to be some other explanation.

"The plane is just over there." Rachel's soft voice startled her so near to her right side.

Bree looked to where Rachel pointed. A deep ravine ran along here. Bree swallowed hard. Rob's body lay there under a blanket of snow.

Naomi came up beside her. "Let me take Davy," she said softly. "Go on. This is what you've been searching for."

In a daze, Bree carefully handed her sleeping son to Naomi. Steve and Kade flanked her as Rachel led the way to the ravine.

"I hope you don't mind, but I didn't want the animals to get the man, er, your husband, so I buried him."

Relief flooded her. "Thank you," Bree whispered. She stood on the edge of the ravine and looked down at the plane. The Bonanza Beechcraft was level with the top of the ravine, and the wind had swept it clear of snow. One wing was shattered and bent, the windshield was missing, and most of the top appeared to have been sheared off.

Bree closed her eyes. She'd searched eleven months for this moment. The crushed plane was mute evidence of the horror Davy had gone through, of Rob's last moments on this earth. Why had it gone down? He and Palmer had kept it in perfect shape. Palmer. Could Palmer have actually hurt Rob? She was afraid to think it through.

She'd come this far. Opening her eyes, she gripped Kade's hand, thankful for his steadiness and concern, then she slid down the ravine to the plane. Steve followed while Rachel turned away and rejoined Naomi and Davy. Bree fumbled at the door, but it refused to open. Kade wrenched it open for her. Though it was hard, she needed to do this—see if there was anything in the plane's cabin that might reveal the truth about what had happened.

She'd expected bloodstains, but the brown seats and effects of the weather hid most traces. Many of the gauges were shattered. Davy's blanket was in the back. It had brown stains on it, which probably accounted for Rachel's decision to leave it behind.

"What are we looking for?" Steve's face was pinched with cold.

"Davy said something strange. He told me Palmer fought with Rob, that he'd found gold, and was planning to hurt someone."

Steve took half a step back. "Are you saying you think *Palmer* might have killed Fay?"

All Bree's doubts coalesced into deep suspicion. "More than that. I think he might have had something to do with the crash. He's an airplane mechanic. He never told me he stopped to see Rob and Davy at the fishing cabin. All he's ever said is how much he regretted being gone so he couldn't check out the plane for Rob. He blamed himself. What if he really is guilty?"

They all fell silent. Bree's gaze met Kade's, and she saw the anguish in his eyes, pain for her. It gave her strength to know his soul was so tuned to hers.

"I'll help you," he said. "Any idea where to begin?" He entered the plane and stooped to look around.

"No. We need to see if we can figure out what caused it to crash." It seemed a hopeless task amid the jumble of debris. "Not that I know a thing about the mechanics of this plane."

Kade knelt and began to go through the rubble. Rob's tool chest lay upended against the rear seats. Tools were scattered beside it. At a loss, Bree knelt and began to pick up the tools with her gloved hand and put them back in the toolbox.

She remembered when Rob had bought these tools. He'd bought a complete set of Stanley screwdrivers because he liked the black-and-white handles. Seeing them here on the floor of the crashed plane pained her. Maybe Davy would like to have them someday.

"Hey, come out here!" Steve called.

Bree scrambled over the wreckage, and Kade followed her. They found Steve crouched under a wing.

"Look."

The jumble of wires he showed them meant nothing to Bree. "What's wrong?"

"Someone has shorted out this fuel transmitter. See this wire? It's been jumpered across the contacts."

"What does that mean?" Bree asked.

Steve sighed. "It would make the gauge read full when it wasn't."

Bree leaned in closer to look and saw something glint back inside the wing. She reached in and touched it. A screwdriver. She pulled it out. It was red, blue, and clear, not white and black.

"Something wrong?" Kade asked.

"This isn't Rob's. He always bought Stanley. This is a Craftsman." She turned it over and caught her breath.

"What is it?" Kade moved closer.

She held it out. The letters PLC were engraved on the handle. "Palmer's initials. He always marks his tools like this."

"Maybe Rob borrowed it," Kade said.

"Palmer never loans his tools."

The silence was almost palpable. "I like Palmer," Steve said. "I always have. Why would he kill Rob? Fay I can understand, if she found out about the gold and wasn't going to go through with the sale. The diary makes it sound like she'd hired an assayer to look at things."

"That might be why she wouldn't let me join her the morning she died," Bree said. "I assumed she was meeting—" She broke off with an apologetic look at Steve.

"You assumed she was meeting Eric," he finished. "It's okay."

"So Palmer must have met her at the mine," Bree continued, "killed her there, and taken her to the cliff to make it look like an accident."

"Maybe," Steve said. "But how do we prove it?"

"We need to get Mason out here for fingerprints," Kade said. "The National Transportation Safety Board too, to investigate the cause."

"Are you guys about done?" Naomi spoke from the top of the embankment. "I'm freezing, and Davy has grown since the last time I lugged him around."

The discovery of Palmer's screwdriver had left Bree shell-shocked. This couldn't be happening. An incident about tools tickled the edge of her memory, but she couldn't seem to grasp it, no matter how hard she tried. It did no good to try to force it.

"We're coming," Bree finally called back.

A few minutes later, they gained the shelter of the cabin. They shucked their snowshoes at the door, then Naomi went to the stove and began to build a fire while Kade went out to split more wood.

Davy opened his eyes when Bree laid him on a cot. She took his coat off and ran her hands over his arms and legs. He winced when she touched his arms. Frowning, she eased him out of his shirt. There were red marks on his arms that looked like burns. She bit her lip. He needed to be seen by a doctor. Continuing her examination, she noticed his leg was still a bit crooked, obviously from a break. But at least he was alive.

He lay quietly under her gentle touch, his eyes drooping as he became warmer. She started to stand.

"Don't go, Mommy," he murmured.

Leaning down to kiss him, Bree caressed his hair. "I'll never leave you," she whispered against his ear. He gave a contented sigh and closed his eyes again. She kissed his forehead and backed away.

Kade came in with an armload of wood. He dropped it by the stove then went to Bree. He touched her shoulder and whispered, "Steve and I have been talking. My cell phone is dead. I'm not sure if the battery needs to be charged or if the service is down, so we can't call for help. Why don't we go for a couple of snowmobiles? It would be easier on Davy if he didn't have to walk, and it's a long way for you to carry him. I'd be glad to carry him, but he doesn't know me. A snowmobile would have you all out of here in no time."

"That's a great idea," Bree said. "Rachel seems harmless. Naomi and I will find out what we can from her while you're gone."

Kade nodded. "I feel sorry for her. She obviously loved Davy very much." He paused to regroup his thoughts. "We'll be back in an hour or so. There's plenty of wood for the fire." He put his palm against her cheek and smiled down into her eyes. "God gave us an incredible miracle, didn't he?"

The touch of his hand added to the crazy sensations swirling inside her. "I can't believe it's real and not a dream."

"Believe it. You've got a little boy to take care of again."

Steve closed the door to the stove and joined them. "Louis Farmer has snowmobiles, and he's only five miles away. We'll get to the Jeep and be back in no time."

Bree nodded. "Just hurry. I can't wait to see Anu's and Hilary's faces."

Kade let the dogs out, then he and Steve left. Naomi followed them out to make sure the dogs didn't trail after them.

Bree's gaze found Rachel standing awkwardly in the corner as if she wanted to escape notice. "Have a seat, Rachel."

Rachel regarded her silently before going to the rocker by the window. She looked out anxiously before easing down into the seat. They sat in silence for a long time.

"Tell me how you found Davy," Bree finally began. "Why didn't you bring him to town to find me?" She struggled to keep the anger from her voice. "Didn't you realize he had a family who mourned him? I thought he was dead."

Tears overflowed as Rachel squeezed her eyes shut. "I—I didn't mean to do anybody any harm. I moved out here to have some peace and quiet." She gulped. "M—my picture had been in the papers for weeks, and I was tired of it. Everyone thought I was responsible when some of my patients died in the nursing home where I worked, and even after the jury said I was innocent, reporters camped outside my house and called at all hours. Everyone saw the accusations, but no one seemed to care when the truth came out." She pressed her lips together.

"What about Davy?"

Her lips trembled. "When the plane went down near my cabin, I rushed to see if I could help. The man was dead, but the little boy was still alive. He kept muttering, 'Sam, Sam.' So I just started calling him that." She looked out the window again.

"He's always called our dog Sam," Bree murmured.

Rachel nodded. "Anyway, he was real bad off. Both legs were broken, and he had a concussion. I didn't dare leave him, and besides, I'm a nurse. No one could take better care of him than me." Tears trickled down both cheeks.

"What about the burns?" Bree wanted to know.

Rachel dropped her gaze. "He tried to start a fire when I wasn't around."

Horror moved in a freezing wave over Bree. "He could have been killed!"

"But he wasn't," Rachel said with a touch of defiance.

Bree thought there was more to the story than the woman was telling, but she'd find it all out later. At least they were minor burns. She would call the doctor right away. "Go on with the rest of the story," she told Rachel.

Rachel nodded. "By the time he was well enough for me to take him into town, I couldn't do it. I never had any kids of my own, you see. Sam—Davy, I mean—he and I took to one another right off."

"Did he ever ask for me?" Bree asked. Jealousy scalded her with red-hot fury. Davy was *her* son. Though she should just be thankful this woman cared for him, she couldn't help the burning resentment.

Rachel nodded again. "In the beginning. As time went on, he seemed content here." She clutched her hands together in her lap. "You have to understand . . . I loved him so much."

Rachel's obvious sincerity softened Bree's anger.

"When the man said people were looking for him, I knew I had to get away."

"What man?" Bree asked.

"I don't know his name, but he's buying the old mine." She nervously looked out the window again, as if searching for something. "He killed the bank manager's wife, and I knew he'd kill me too. I saw him put her body in his trunk."

So it was all true. But why had Palmer killed Rob? Could Rob have threatened to blow the whistle on his plans? Could that have been his motive? She had to find out the truth.

"He knew you had Davy?" That hurt too. Palmer had witnessed her grief all these months, and for the last few weeks, he'd known Davy was alive.

Rachel nodded. "He said if I didn't tell what I saw, then he wouldn't tell that I had Davy."

Bree heard Samson's welcoming bark and went to the door. Before she could open it, Mason burst in with Naomi on his tail. His gaze centered on Bree's face, and he went to her and enveloped her in a huge hug.

"Kade called me on his way to get the snowmobiles. He said his cell phone must have been in a dead spot because he got a signal once he was on the road. Where's Davy?" He spotted the little boy lying on the bed. Tears came to his eyes. "Wait until Hilary and Anu hear. I haven't called them yet. I thought you'd want to surprise them."

"I do," she said, a smile curving her lips at the thought of their wonder. "But there's more, Mason." She quickly filled him in on what she suspected about Palmer.

Rachel stood and turned to the window. Bree watched her as she spoke to Mason. She was wringing her hands.

Mason seemed to absorb it all quietly. "We've got Rachel to testify that she saw him carrying Fay's body, but we need proof he killed Rob."

The distant whine of a snowmobile reached Bree's ears. "Are they back already?" she said, glancing at her watch. "It's too soon."

"It's him," Rachel cried, clearly agitated. "He told me I had to take him to the plane today. I was hoping we'd be gone before he got back. You have to get away; he'll kill you!"

Naomi and Mason stared at her, but Bree ran to Davy and scooped him up. He awoke and smiled sleepily at her. She popped him into his coat. "I've got an idea," she said. She handed Davy to Naomi. "Go with Aunt Naomi, sweetheart. She'll take you out to play with Samson and Charley."

Davy frowned and reached for his mother. It hurt Bree not to be able to take him in her arms.

"What are you going to do?" Naomi asked.

The roar of the snowmobile grew louder. "Mason, grab our snow-shoes from out front. And the dogs—get them in here." Bree snatched up some of the discarded clothes by the door and hurried to the bed. She stuffed them under the blanket to make it look like Davy's small body still lay there.

"Rachel, act like nothing is wrong. Take him to the plane. Mason and I will be hiding nearby. We'll surprise him, see if we can get him to confess. Naomi, keep Davy out of harm's way."

"I don't like this," Naomi said, putting on her snowshoes. The dogs whimpered, sensing something was wrong.

"I don't either," Mason said. "But it's the best shot we've got." He and Bree put on their snowshoes as well.

The whine of the snowmobile stopped abruptly by the front door. "Go, go," Bree hissed. She hurried to the back door and shooed Naomi through with Davy and the dogs, then she and Mason followed. She could only hope and pray Rachel would be able to carry off her part of the plan.

She sent Naomi, Davy, and the dogs off to the west while she and Mason headed east to the plane. "Let's get inside," she told Mason. He nodded, and they climbed inside and crouched down out of sight.

The minutes ticked by as the cold seeped into Bree's bones. Then she heard voices approach.

"Down there," Rachel said.

"At last." Palmer's voice was exultant.

Bree's stomach flipped, and she clutched his screwdriver in her hand.

"I think you should let me confront him," Mason whispered.

"You're backup," she whispered. "He'll think he can overpower me. He won't know you're here, and he'll reveal more to me." Mason sighed, and she knew she'd won.

"Wait here," Palmer told Rachel. "I need to retrieve something from the plane, then I'll be out of your life." The *whoosh* of his snow-shoes came closer.

Bree's chest hurt with tension. Glancing at the screwdriver in her hand, she remembered the incident she'd been trying to think of. When she'd eaten dinner with the Chambers family, Lily had mentioned a tiff they'd had when Palmer couldn't find a missing screwdriver. Evidently, he'd figured out where it was.

Bree rose from her hiding place and held up the screwdriver. "Looking for this, Palmer?"

He stopped in his tracks. Shock slackened his mouth, then his eyes went flat and hard as he recognized the screwdriver in her hand.

"You were our friend, Palmer. How could you kill Rob? Was it because he was going to stop you from getting your hands on that mine?"

"We were buddies," Palmer said. "He should have been excited to be a part of it."

"You never counted on his faith interfering, did you? He told you it was wrong, and you couldn't let him tell Fay about the gold."

"Looks like you've got it all figured out."

"Enough to know you killed my husband. Why don't you tell me the rest?"

Palmer gave her the smile she'd once found charming. "I wanted him as a partner for the new venture. We could have extracted the gold with new technology and made a fortune. He thought we should tell Fay and Steve about the gold and let them decide whether to sell with full disclosure. I couldn't believe it! He wanted to turn down a chance to make millions. Millions! What kind of man would do that?"

"A righteous one," Bree said. This sounded more like the Rob she knew.

Palmer made a face. "I knew he would blab everything when he got back."

"My call didn't help his distraction," Bree murmured.

Palmer grinned. "I thought you'd tell everyone about that."

For a minute what he said failed to register. Then her eyes widened, and she wanted to hit him. "*You* had someone call. There was no other woman, was there? Rob was never unfaithful," she whispered.

"People would think he downed the plane out of guilt."

Bree just managed to keep her shock in check. "Her real name is Lanna Martin, not March, isn't it?"

"You figured that out too, huh? You're smarter than I gave you credit for."

Bree struggled to reconcile this cold stranger with the man who'd been such a good friend. "I met her," she said. The familiarity of the woman's voice hadn't been her imagination. "You went to the lake to make sure Rob hadn't told anyone about the gold."

"I went to try one more time to convince him. I didn't want to kill him, but the creditors were hounding me. I would have lost everything."

"But he still wouldn't listen, so you sabotaged the plane and made sure he wouldn't spoil your plans. You didn't care about killing Davy with him." It was almost too much to take in. "And Fay found out about the gold anyway, so you had to kill her too. I would imagine you called her on her cell phone and had her meet you at the mine."

Palmer shrugged. "Very good."

"The assayer had told her about the gold, and she was going to cancel the sale. So you killed her and put her body at the foot of the cliff." She moved from the plane cabin to the ground and approached him, even though Mason had warned her to keep her distance. She wanted to look in the eyes of the man who'd befriended her, the man she'd turned to when she grieved. Bree wanted to strike him, to put her hands around his neck and choke the life out of him. She stared at this man she'd known and loved as a brother.

In one smooth movement, Palmer's hand dipped into his jacket and came out with a gun. "You wanted to find Rob. Now I'll just have to send you where he is." He cocked the hammer on the gun.

Bree stared into the barrel of the gun. She couldn't let Davy be orphaned. Why hadn't she listened to Mason's warning? At all costs she had to stay out of Mason's line of fire. He would know how to handle Palmer.

Mason popped up with a gun aimed at Palmer. "Throw down your gun," he ordered.

Palmer didn't even blink. His arm snaked out and pulled Bree against him. He pressed the gun against her head. "Drop it, Mason," he ordered.

"You drop it," Mason said.

Bree trembled, but it was more from anger than from fear. Palmer couldn't be allowed to get away with it. "Don't listen to him, Mason," she said.

"You have no choice, Sheriff," Palmer said. "Shoot me, and my gun goes off."

For a long moment, Bree thought Mason would refuse to drop his gun, then a hiss of frustration came from his throat, and he tossed the gun to the ground, where it disappeared into the snow.

"Come along, Sheriff. It's cold out here. I think we can conclude our business back at the cabin." Holding Bree in front of him, he marched his prisoners back up the hill. They met Rachel at the top, too terrified to have considered running for help, Bree imagined.

If only Samson were here. If only she had a weapon. Palmer meant to kill them; she could see it in his darkened eyes, blank as a reptile's.

Inside the cabin, he grabbed a rope hanging on a nail by the door and tossed it to Rachel. "Tie them up. Be quick about it."

Rachel slowly took the rope and tied Mason to a chair, then tied Bree's hands behind her back.

"Make it tight," Palmer said.

Rachel cinched the rope. The rough hemp bit into Bree's wrists, and she winced.

"Now tie her to the chair by the bed." Palmer moved closer and watched as Rachel pushed Bree into the chair and looped the rope around the back.

Bree flexed her muscles, thankful she'd been working out and had muscles to flex. Maybe she could create enough slack to work her way free. She prayed for God to send help. Her mind raced for a way out. The gun pointed straight at her heart. If she could keep Palmer talking until Kade and Steve got back, maybe they could overpower him.

Her heart leaped when she heard a familiar sound at the door. Samson. His low growl told her he knew something was wrong. "How much does Lily know?" she asked, desperate to distract him.

"None of it. She would have talked to Fay. She's way too honest. We always said we balanced each other out." He laughed uproariously at his joke. He motioned with his gun toward Rachel. "Sit down." When she obeyed, he lashed her to the rocker.

Bree had to keep him talking. "So why move Fay to the cliff? Mason would likely have assumed she fell and hit her head at the mine."

"Authorities investigating her death might have found something. I couldn't run the risk. She was already dressed for climbing, and I thought no one would be the wiser."

This was like something out of *Invasion of the Body Snatchers.* The Palmer she thought she knew would recoil at the thought of murder. Who was this man?

"Enough chatter. I'm afraid the time has come to say good-bye, and I have to admit it makes me sad. Lily will be devastated, and I so hate to make her unhappy." His eyes held a sheen of moisture as though he really did regret what he had to do.

"What are you going to do with us?" Rachel asked in a small voice.

"I thought about locking you in the mine and caving it in, but your bodies would eventually be found. I should shoot you, but it needs to look like an accident." His gaze wandered to the stove. "A fire. There will be no evidence left to determine cause of death."

"Our skeletons will be lashed to chairs," Bree said desperately. "And you think that won't look like foul play?" Think, think. What could she use as a weapon?

"I'll have to take that chance," Palmer said. "With a little luck, the rope will burn up too."

How long had it been since Kade and Steve left, maybe an hour? They should be back by now.

Palmer approached the stove and picked up the packet of matches lying there. Samson was growling and whining even louder outside the door. Bree had one chance. She shrieked at the top of her lungs. "Samson, help!"

Palmer brought the gun around in alarm as seventy pounds of brown, black, and white fury crashed through the window. Glass shattered inward with a shower of shards. Snarling, Samson leaped onto Palmer and seized his hand in his jaws. Both man and dog crashed to the floor, Palmer kicking and shouting as Samson pinned him down with his teeth on his arm.

Wriggling her arms in the ropes, Bree felt the strands loosen.

Screaming in anger, Palmer tried to bring the gun up to shoot Samson, but the dog whipped his head back and forth, and the gun flew from Palmer's fingers. With his front paws on Palmer's chest, Samson pushed his muzzle against Palmer's throat.

At the feel of the dog's teeth, Palmer screamed and thrashed. "Get him off me!"

"Lie still, Palmer, or he'll tear your throat out," Bree warned.

Bree finally felt the rope give. Twisting her wrists, she managed to get one free, then the other. She jumped to her feet and dived for the gun.

Bree pointed the pistol at Palmer and moved to untie Mason. "Samson, release," she commanded.

With a final growl, the dog stepped back, his eyes still following Palmer's every move. Palmer shook himself and got slowly to his feet. His wide-eyed stare fastened on the gun in Bree's hand.

"You know you won't use that," he said easily. He started toward her, but Samson immediately moved to block him. The dog's low growl stopped Palmer in his tracks.

"I will shoot you if I have to," Bree said. "I won't let you hurt anyone else." She'd never shot a gun, but she'd empty every bullet in this gun into Palmer if he forced her.

"Sit in that chair," she ordered.

Palmer must have seen the intent in her face, for his smile faded and he moved slowly to the chair. Keeping an eye on him, Bree finally got Mason free and gave him the gun. She picked up the rope and tied Palmer to the chair.

An ironic smile touched the corners of his mouth. "You've surprised me, Bree. I didn't know you could be so ruthless. Have you thought about what this will do to Lily and the girls? You could just let me go. I'll get Lily and the twins and leave town."

"You killed two people, Palmer," Mason said. "Even if she wanted to, I couldn't let you go."

Bree called Samson to her. She saw the bloody tracks he left on the floor. "You're hurt," she said softly. She knelt to check on the dog's wounds. Once she made sure the blood was from superficial cuts, she put her arms around him and buried her face in his fur. He'd risked his life for her. "Thanks, Samson," she whispered as he licked her face. Then she rose to go to her son.

Kade and Steve parked the snowmobiles outside Louis Farmer's barn and thanked him. Bree carried her son through the snow to the Jeep. She knew she could put him down and let him walk, but she couldn't bear to let go of him. If God hadn't sent Samson at the right time, they would all be dead. There was no doubt in her mind that once Palmer realized Davy was missing, he would have tracked down Davy and Naomi and killed them too.

Steve and Kade both offered to carry Davy for her, but she refused. She wanted to get him home and pore over every inch of him to make sure he was all right. His good arm clung tightly to her neck, and she breathed in his little boy scent with a joy so overpowering she thought her heart would burst.

He was several pounds heavier and a bit taller; otherwise, he hadn't really changed in the year they'd been separated. But Bree knew he had undergone psychological changes after the ordeal he'd been through. She would ask the pastor at Rock Harbor Community Church if he could recommend a good counselor.

She couldn't seem to shut off the tap of tears. The rest of the family would be overjoyed. Bree could only imagine Anu's and Hilary's reactions. The whole town had mourned with her; now they would all share her joy. Her happiness was tinged with sorrow for what Rob and Fay had gone through. And what Lily and the girls would go through in the years to come.

They reached the Jeep, and she buckled Davy in with the seat belt beside her in the back. Kade drove, with Naomi in the passenger seat and Rachel in the back with Bree and Davy. Steve had offered to help Mason transport Palmer.

Davy leaned his head against Bree and fell asleep before they reached the main access road. Bree curled her arm around him and pulled him close. She'd nearly lost him a second time. Anu and Naomi said coincidence was how a nonbeliever explained God's hand in the world. Now she knew there was no such thing as coincidence. God moved in the world as he saw fit.

They reached the edge of town, and Bree asked Kade to drive straight to Anu's store. Hilary should be there today too. "Lay on the horn and drive slow," she told him.

Kade grinned and obliged. Bree felt like a queen as they rode toward Nicholls's. She lowered the window and shouted into the air, "He's alive! He's alive!" The horn blared in cadence to her shouts.

Davy woke up at the commotion, and she pulled him onto her lap. "Wave, Davy, wave," she whispered.

Folks came to their doors to see what the disturbance was about. "Davy's alive!" she yelled again.

Davy peeked over the side of the window and waved. "Do I know them?" he asked.

"They know you," she assured him. Some ran after the car when they recognized Davy, and by the time the Jeep reached the store, the crowd had grown to the status of a parade.

The Jeep rolled to a stop outside Nicholls's Finnish Imports. Bree threw open the door and scrambled out with Davy in her arms as Anu and Hilary came to the door.

"What is going on?" Anu said.

"I've found him. It's Davy! He's alive!" Bree said through sobs.

Disbelief and shock rippled over Anu's face. Tears began to stream over her cheeks as her expression registered recognition. "Davy?" She closed her eyes then opened them again.

Hilary dropped the white vase she held, and it shattered on the sidewalk. She put her hands to her cheeks and began to weep. Stumbling over the broken pottery, she and Anu ran toward the Jeep.

Bree rushed to meet them. "Remember Grammy, sweetheart? And Aunt Hilary?"

Shyly, Davy nodded. "Grammy gave me Pooky," he said.

The color washed out of Anu's cheeks until she was as pale as the pieces of pottery littering the sidewalk. "It is my Davy," she whispered. She held out her arms, and her grandson looked at Bree then stepped into them.

Anu hugged him for several long moments before she gently passed him to Hilary. Around them, the townspeople murmured, and Bree saw many wiping tears from their cheeks.

Hilary kissed Davy. "Remember me and Uncle Mason?" she asked.

Davy regarded her for several seconds then nodded. "You have a train in the garage," he said. "I saw Uncle Mason. He arrested Uncle Palmer."

Hilary gasped and looked to Bree. Bree nodded and made a shushing motion.

"That's right," Hilary said. "You and Uncle Mason put the train together."

Davy twisted in Hilary's arms, and he looked through the crowd until his gaze found his mother. "Mommy," he called.

Bree knew she would never tire of hearing that word. She went to him, and he reached for her. She pulled him close, and he wrapped his legs around her and put his head on her shoulder.

"I'm tired, Mommy," he said.

"We'll go home soon," she promised. Home. Their lighthouse would be a real home again. The thought brought tears flooding back to Bree's eyes. Though she hated to let go of Davy, she passed him to Naomi and asked her to take him into the store to see if he needed to potty. Quickly she told Hilary and Anu how she'd found Davy.

"Mason has taken Palmer into custody. He killed Fay." She paused. "And Rob."

Hilary gasped and put her hand to her mouth. Her wide eyes filled with horror. "What are you saying?" she whispered. Beside her, Anu swayed, and Hilary put an arm around her mother.

"Palmer found gold in the mine." Bree quickly explained Palmer's schemes.

"Poor Lily," Anu murmured.

The women fell silent. The past months of wrestling with Rob's infidelity had given Bree a taste of what Lily would go through, except Bree had been fortunate to discover her husband really was the honorable man she'd married. Lily would have no such comfort.

Naomi brought Davy back outside, and the family and townspeople milled around, talking and rejoicing with them.

The crowd finally began to disperse, and Bree was ready to head back to the house when Mason showed up. He got out of the vehicle the grimness around his mouth easing when he saw Bree with Davy in her arms. "This makes everything worthwhile." He took Davy in his arms, and the little boy patted his face. Mason's eyes welled up with tears.

"What about Palmer?"

Mason handed Davy back to Bree. "In jail and in shock. I hate to have to tell Lily," he said in a low voice. "I need to find out what this woman knows," he nodded toward Rachel.

"I was just heading home. You can question her there."

While the happy reunions were going on, Rachel Marks had sat motionless in the backseat of the Jeep. Her stony face stared straight ahead, but Bree was sure the woman wasn't as stoic as she seemed. She'd seen the emotion in Rachel's face when she proclaimed her love for Davy.

Kade moved to Bree's side. "Davy's tired, and you're exhausted," he said. "Let's get you home."

"Come with me?" she whispered. He nodded and pressed her hand. She felt the promise in it. The future seemed as bright as the sun bouncing off Lake Superior.

Naomi kissed Bree on the cheek. "Just drop me by my place. I want to tell Mother and then call Donovan and the kids. Emily and Timmy will be so excited to know they can play with Davy anytime."

They piled into the Jeep, and Mason followed in his SUV. Bree dropped Naomi off at the Blue Bonnet then parked in front of the lighthouse. Exhausted from the day, Davy had fallen asleep again, so Bree carried him, eagerly guarded by Samson, up the stairs to his room.

"I'm making coffee," Kade called up after her.

She was so glad he'd come with her. She needed him here, and he'd sensed it. Standing at the door to Davy's room, she realized the room was stripped of his possessions, so she carried him to her bed. She would restore his room before he awakened.

Rachel and Mason were in the parlor when she went downstairs. Rachel stood against one wall with her hands behind her. She pressed herself against the plaster as though she wished she could sink right into it, and Bree felt a twinge of pity for the woman.

"The coffee will be ready in a few minutes," Kade said. He came to stand behind her and put his arms around her waist. She leaned back against him, thankful for his strength.

"Do you want to press charges?" Mason asked Bree.

What could Bree say to that? While she hated that the woman had kept her son from her, Bree was grateful she had saved Davy's life.

Mason waited, and fear replaced the stoicism on Rachel's face.

Bree shook her head. "I'm not going to press charges, Mason. Davy is alive. I can thank her for that. God must have sent her to him."

Tears welled in Rachel's eyes, and she dropped her head. "Thank you," she whispered.

Mason nodded then questioned the woman about what she'd seen, scribbling notes. "I'm going to need an address where I can reach you when Palmer's case comes to trial."

Rachel gave him her brother's address in Chicago. "Can I go now?" she asked.

Mason nodded. She walked to the foyer and looked longingly up the steps. "Could I see Sa—Davy, one more time?"

Bree hesitated and turned to look up into Kade's eyes. "What could it hurt?" he said softly.

Davy was sleeping anyway. She reluctantly left the warmth of Kade's arms to lead the way to her bedroom. Samson lay on the floor beside the bed, and Bree knew it would be many days before the dog let the little boy out of his sight.

Davy lay on her Ohio star quilt with one arm flung out to the side. It was a pose he'd adopted as an infant, and tears clogged Bree's throat to see it again.

Rachel clutched the doorjamb as she watched the sleeping child for a few moments. "Thank you, ma'am," she said. "If he ever asks about me, would you tell him I love him very much? I wouldn't want him to think I deserted him."

Bree nodded. She touched Rachel's arm. "Before you go—I want to thank you for burying my husband." Her grieving for him would begin again, as it must. He hadn't betrayed her, after all. It was going to be hard to forgive herself for the way she'd screamed at him, the accusations she'd flung.

"I knew the boy would want his father buried."

"Thank you then from both of us," Bree said. "And thank you for caring for my son."

"You won't forget to tell him what I said?" Rachel's faded blue eyes swam with tears and a resignation that tugged at Bree's sympathy.

"I'll tell him," Bree said. She escorted Rachel down the steps. "Mason, could you run her to the bus stop? It's a long walk to Ontonagon."

Mason nodded. "Let me get my coat." He motioned for Bree to follow him to the living room.

Bree followed him. "What's wrong?"

"You sure that was wise?" Mason asked.

"I couldn't put the woman who saved Davy's life in jail," she said softly. "And I feel so bad for Lily and the girls. They'll be devastated. I need to go to her."

He pressed her arm. "You've got a little boy to enjoy right now. Give Lily a chance to absorb the blow. She might blame you at first."

He rejoined Rachel in the entryway, and they left.

"It's been quite a day," Kade said. "Ready for some coffee?"

Bree followed him to the kitchen. The coffee aroma made her stomach rumble. "We haven't eaten all day," she said.

"I thought I'd whip us up something. You're all done in." He handed her a cup of coffee. She took a gulp, and the hot liquid began to warm the places that were still chilled.

"First, I need to make up Davy's bed," she said. "Unpack his things. I'd packed them all away."

"I'll help you," Kade said. He carried the boxes to Davy's room.

Bree took great joy in making Davy's bed and putting away his toys while Kade hung the curtains back on the windows.

"I have something else I want to do," Kade said. "Come with me." He led her up the stairs to the light tower. The Fresnel lens glittered in the bright moonlight. "I came by with my electrical kit this morning, but you'd already left. The door was unlocked, so I went ahead and hooked up the electricity to the light." He reached over and flipped a switch.

Light flooded the tower then began to strobe out over the water. Bree let out a cry of delight. She turned to Kade and stepped into his arms.

"You light up everything around you just like this tower," he whispered into her hair. "I'm thankful God brought you into my life." His lips brushed hers in a feathery kiss full of promise.

Then his cell phone trilled.

He sighed and dug it out. "Hello." He listened without interruption. "I'll be right there," he said. He clicked off the cell phone. "It's Lauri. Her car died over by the high school. I'd better go get her."

"Come by in the morning for breakfast."

He smiled and brushed the back of his hand across her cheek. "You're really something, Bree Nicholls."

"So are you, Ranger Matthews." She pressed her cheek against his hand. "See you tomorrow."

"I'll let myself out. The rest of the family will be descending any minute, so take advantage of your time with Davy." He hugged her and quickly walked toward the steps. She followed him as far as the second-floor landing, then waved as he went on down to the front door.

Back in Davy's room, Bree had just placed the last of his books on a shelf when she heard the patter of his feet down the hall. The click of Samson's nails on the hardwood floor accompanied him.

"Mommy?" He stood in the doorway, rubbing his eyes. As his gaze wandered around the room, his eyes widened. "I forgot about my room."

She held out her arms, and he ran to her. "I kind of forgot you too, Mommy. Why did I forget?"

"You'd been hurt, sweetie." She smoothed the hair back from his forehead. "We have lots of time for you to remember everything."

"I'm glad to be home, Mommy." His small face sobered. "Can we go get Daddy and bring him home too?"

Bree's exhilaration faded. "Do you remember the crash, sweetheart? The plane crash."

Davy's eyes grew wide, and he nodded slowly. His green eyes filled with tears. "The plane hit the trees. Daddy yelled."

Bree struggled with the tears that burned in her eyes. "Daddy was hurt really bad. He can't be with us anymore. He would if he could."

Davy buried his head in her lap and wept. "I miss Daddy. She said he was in heaven. Can we go to heaven to see him?"

The floodgates of Bree's tears opened, and she wrapped her arms around her son. Their tears mingled as she cried for her lost husband in a way she'd never been able to before. Her stomach knotted with pain as she wept for the years they could have spent together watching Davy grow up, and for the male role model Davy would never have. Soon she would bring Rob home too, to rest in the Rock Harbor Cemetery with his grandparents.

Davy's tears finally stopped, and Bree's as well. She gathered him into her arms. "We'll see Daddy again someday, but not for a long time. Daddy wants you to grow up to be a fine man, one with integrity and the same kind of strength and honor he had. Someday I'll tell you all about what kind of man your daddy was. All that matters now is that God brought you home, where you belong. Let's thank him for that."

"We have to thank Sam too." Davy reached out and patted the dog. Samson's tail swished eagerly at the attention.

Bree petted the dog. Her own personal "hound" had followed a bit of heavenly intervention and found Davy. He would always be her earthly reminder of how God had searched for her and found her, even as she wandered in her own wilderness.

Beyond a Doubt

For my parents, Peggy and George Rhoads

And my "other parents" and in-laws,
Lena and Carroll Coble

Your love and belief in me gave me wings.

Acknowledgments

For reading my manuscript in the early stages and offering advice: my husband, David Coble; Kristin Billerbeck; Denise Hunter; Diann Hunt; and Rhonda Gibson. It would be impossible to write without your encouragement and support!

Special thanks to:

The wonderful writing group Chilibris. No one else can understand the writer's life except other writers, and you are the best!

My prayer partners: Kristin Billerbeck, Lori Copeland, Diann Hunt, Denise Hunter, Crystal Miller, and Deborah Raney, who listen when I wail and commiserate until it doesn't hurt anymore. Thanks, girlfriends!

My fabulous agent: Karen Solem of Spencerhill Associates. Hand holder, encourager, as well as deliverer of a swift kick in the seat when needed. A mover and a shaker who gets things done. Thanks for all you do! You've been a real blessing in my life.

My extraordinary, wonderful editors: Ami McConnell at Thomas Nelson Fiction and Erin Healy. It's amazing the way you both hone and sculpt a manuscript! I'm so thankful for both of you. You make the editing process a joy. I've become a revision junkie!

The wonderful crew of copyeditors, cover geniuses, and marketing geniuses at Thomas Nelson Fiction. The polish you give my manuscript is amazing!

My family and church family: How could I get through the busy days of writing without the support and encouragement of my wonderful family and my caring church, New Life Baptist Church? Love you all!

Please visit my Web site at *www.colleencoble.com.* I love hearing from my readers!

Prologue

*B*itterness tore at Quentin Siller with the same ferocity as the cold wind that ripped at his jacket. Bree and Anu Nicholls stood on the front porch, barring his way to the door. Quentin scowled as he waded through the snow on the front lawn. Meddlesome busybodies. They'd interfered the last time he had to discipline his wife.

Bree Nicholls was a looker with that red hair and eyes as green as his old truck, but she needed a man to make her toe the line. She and her mother-in-law both. That's what happened when women dried up—they turned into witches who poked their long noses into a man's business. If not for the Nicholls women, his happy home would still be just that—happy. Until they began to tell his wife she didn't have to submit to his authority, things had been just fine. A little slap or two never hurt anyone. A few bruises would teach his wife to listen to what he said. Didn't the Bible say that a man was to keep his house in order and have an obedient wife and children? That's all he was doing. Now Karen actually questioned him. She would have to be taught to keep her mouth shut.

His anger, trapped in his chest, nearly choked him. He stopped at the base of the steps and glared at these women who dared to bar his entry to his own house. "Get out of my way!"

Anu Nicholls stretched out an entreating hand. "Quentin, this time you broke her nose." Her voice broke. "You may not come inside today. You must get help for your anger."

Rage in a red tide as hot as a July day made him dizzy. These women would pay for their interference. He started up the steps.

Bree's dog, Samson, a German shepherd/chow mix, growled softly and took a step toward him. Quentin stopped, clenching and unclenching his hands. Bree stepped in front of her mother-in-law. "Don't try anything, Quentin. The sheriff is on his way over. You're breaking a restraining order." She pointed at a suitcase. "Karen packed some of your things. I'm sorry, but you'll have to find another place to live."

"Just for now," Anu added. "Your pastor is waiting to talk with you. Please, Quentin, you must get help before you kill Karen. We wish to save your marriage, but first you must get control of yourself." Her voice softened. "I know you love your family, Quentin. And they love you. But you can't keep hurting your wife."

He sputtered, anger leaving him incoherent. "You have no right," he said tightly. "That's my house and my wife." He put a foot onto the step and continued to mount the stairs.

The dog's growl grew menacing, but in Quentin's state of mind he imagined he could tear the mongrel limb from limb. His anger consumed him, and his vision narrowed to a pinpoint. Suddenly, a heavy hand yanked him back.

"You're already facing assault and battery," Sheriff Mason Kaleva said. "Don't add another charge to it."

A burly man in his thirties, the sheriff wasn't someone most people wanted to tangle with, but Quentin was past all fear. He struggled to no avail against the officer's grip. The sheriff dragged him to his car and shoved him into the back. After being read his rights, Quentin found himself booked and jailed for breaking the restraining order.

When he finally posted bail several hours later, he knew what he had to do.

The North Woods crowded in around her, cutting off all possibility of escape. The brambles tore at her skin and left trickles of blood where they touched. Davy was calling for her, crying out for her to find him. Perspiration matted her hair to her forehead, and she pressed on through the thorns. She had to find him. He was depending on her.

They said he was dead, but she knew it wasn't so. He was out here somewhere. Samson barked, an urgent sound that propelled her past the thicket. A cabin lay in the valley before her. He was down there. Her son was waiting for her. Samson barked again and rushed forward.

Bree Nicholls awoke with a start. She forced herself to take deep breaths. In and out, in and out. She and Samson had found Davy in a cabin very much like the one in her dream. He was just fine. But the terror of the nightmare didn't leave her. Had Samson really barked? Maybe something was wrong.

She slipped out of bed and tiptoed down the hallway to her son's bedroom. Moonlight filtered through the Superman curtains at his window. Her bare feet whispered across the smooth oak floor until she reached the bed. She touched a small hump in the covers, and her hand sank to the mattress. She gasped, and her hands roamed the tousled blankets and sheets.

She stepped to the wall and flicked on the light. "Davy?"

The doctor had said to make sure she didn't startle him when he was having one of his night terrors. She went to the closet and looked on the floor. Only a jumble of baseballs, his father's mitt, and some Playmobil pirates lay on the floor. She looked under the bed. Not there. Panic rose in her chest in a rush of cold dread.

She ran to the door and called for her dog as she rushed down the hallway. "Samson!" The dog could lead her to her boy. At the top of the stairs, she touched the light switch and a welcome brightness lit the way.

She reached the bottom of the steps. "Samson, come!"

She heard the click of his nails on the hardwood floor of the entry. He came through the door into the living room, his tail down, a sure sign of distress. He pressed his cold nose against her leg, bare below her knee-length nightgown.

Bree rubbed his ears. "Where's Davy, boy? Find Davy."

The dog whined and padded down the entry hall toward the back of the house. Four years old now, he had the stamina of a German shepherd mixed with the heart of the true mutt he was. She followed him. He pushed through the swinging door to the kitchen. A musty scent wafted up from the open basement door. Surely Davy wasn't down there. What if he'd fallen? Frantic now, Bree flipped on the basement light, grabbed the flashlight on a shelf at the top of the landing, and rushed past Samson down the stairs.

There was no sign of Davy at the foot of the stairs, and she felt the tension in her shoulders ease a bit. At least he hadn't fallen. "Davy?" she called, still careful to keep her voice soft and as unconcerned as she was able.

A whimper answered her, but in the cavernous shadows of the basement, she couldn't tell where it came from. Samson pushed past her and padded toward a shadowy recess. The dog lay on his paws and stared under a bulky table laden with Rob's tools. He looked back toward Bree as if to ask what was taking her so long.

She went to the table and dropped to her knees. "Davy, I'm here. It's okay. You're safe."

The flashlight's beam revealed her son's small form. Wedged

under the table in a small hole where the concrete had broken away from the wall, Davy lay curled in a fetal position, his thumb in his mouth. His favorite book, *The Tale of Three Trees* by Angela Hunt, was clutched against his chest. Right now he looked even younger than his four years. Bree reached out and touched his face. "Hey, pumpkin, found you. You ready to quit playing hide-and-seek and get back to bed?" It was all she could do to keep her voice light.

Davy blinked slowly and pulled his hand away from his mouth. "Mommy," he said. "I'm thirsty."

"Well, come on out from there and I'll get you a drink of juice." She shoved the table out of the way then scooped him into her arms and held him tightly. She could feel his heart beating as rapidly as hers.

He buried his face against her neck. "I was trying to find you, Mommy. But she wouldn't let me go."

Davy never called the woman who found him after the plane crash by her real name, Rachel. It was always "her" or "she." Bree stroked his damp hair. "You're safe now, pumpkin."

The doctor said it was very important not to let him know how his night wanderings upset her. They more than upset her. They took her back to the terrible year she and Samson had spent searching for the plane wreckage and his body.

Instead, a wonderful miracle had awaited her, but the trauma of separation had scarred them both. She clutched her son more tightly until he stirred restlessly. "Let's get you upstairs," she said with a cheeriness she didn't feel.

She snapped her fingers at Samson, but the dog was busy scratching at the hole Davy had burrowed into. "Come on, Samson. It's late."

She started toward the steps, but still the dog didn't follow. Frowning, she watched Samson. As one of the best search-and-rescue dogs in the country, he could find a flea in a haystack. Right now he was acting as if he was on a mission. He whined and scratched at the wall again.

Bree flicked on the flashlight and shone it on the open hole. The beam revealed a bigger space than she had originally perceived. What was back there that had Samson so upset? He growled and dug tenaciously.

The flashlight's beam flickered, and she turned it off. "Come on, Samson. We'll see what's back there tomorrow." Still holding Davy in one arm, she reached down and tugged at the dog's collar. He ceased digging reluctantly, then followed her up the stairs. She made a mental note to call Kade tomorrow and have him help her take a look.

*J*ulia Child's gravelly voice was enough to compete with fingernails on a chalkboard, but Bree didn't notice, so intent was she on the woman's instructions. His night terror of just hours before forgotten, Davy sat on the bar stool, his thin legs swinging and his gaze on his mother as she watched Julia on a small kitchen television mounted under the cabinets. Floury hand prints marked Bree's jeans, but she would change into a clean pair of slacks before dinner.

Samson lay on the floor in a patch of sunshine streaming through the kitchen window. The Snow King had tightened his grip on Michigan's Upper Peninsula. Outside the Nichollses' lighthouse home, thick floes of ice floated in Lake Superior like great white whales stretching in the morning sun. Spring's gentle touch would wrest the U.P. from winter's clutches in a few more weeks.

Bree kept stealing glances outside as she worked. She loved Rock Harbor, Michigan. Small but quaint, it perched along Lake Superior with the water to its west and massive stretches of North Woods surrounding the rest of the small town. Good people lived here, many from Finnish stock, hardy and sometimes painfully honest. She couldn't imagine living anywhere else now.

Her tongue poking the side of her mouth, Bree measured the cinnamon and dumped it in the bowl with the apples. She would turn out a great pie if it killed her. Her mother-in-law, Anu, had told her not to bother, that she could make the pies for Easter. But with the store's twentieth anniversary bash going on, Bree didn't want Anu to have to do it all. Besides, now that Davy was home, Bree needed to learn to cook better. It was fine for her to live on peanut-butter sandwiches and canned soup, but it wasn't good enough for her son. She'd been working on her culinary skills for several months now, but cooking wasn't something that came naturally.

She took a moment to glance at her son. He'd only been home a little over three months, and she still didn't get enough of looking at him. His heart-shaped face was a miniature version of Bree's own, though his nose was his father's, as were his ears. The best of them both, Rob had always said. The thought of her late husband was both a pain and a pleasure. But slowly she was getting on with her life. At least that's what she told herself.

"Can I have some 'stachios?" Davy asked.

He coughed, a hacking sound that brought a frown to her face. "You doing okay?" she asked, wiping her hands on her jeans again.

He sneezed. "My tummy feels funny."

Was he getting sick? Last night's excursion to the basement might have given him more than bleary morning eyes. She put down the wooden spoon and went to him, putting her hand on his forehead. It was cool and dry. He sneezed again. "Are you getting a cold?" she asked anxiously.

"I want to eat."

Surely that meant he was fine. But she wouldn't take any chances. She reached for the phone and dialed Dr. Parker. He promised to come by, and she hung up feeling guilty. She hated to take advantage of an old family friend, but Davy was still weak from his ordeal, and she wanted to make sure he got well as quickly as possible.

She pulled the bag of pistachios to her and dug out a handful for him. "You want me to help you open them?"

"I can do it." He worked his mouth as he struggled with the nut then smiled in triumph as he succeeded in cracking it.

She turned back to her pie. Maybe she could get it in the oven before the doctor got here. Julia was droning on about aluminum foil on the edges of the crust, but Bree didn't have any foil. She listened with half an ear and finished the pie, then flipped the channel to the Cartoon Network for Davy.

The doorbell rang just as she slid the pie into the oven. She wiped her hands on her abused jeans and went to the door. Dr. Max Parker stood smiling benignly on her front porch. Tall with regal bearing, he'd always reminded her of an aging lion with his head of white hair and eyes that seemed to see right through her.

"I'm being silly, aren't I?" she laughed, stepping aside for him to enter. Her spirits always perked up when he was around.

"We can't be too careful with our star boy." His deep voice was as calming as rhythmic waves along the lakeshore.

"You are always so gracious, even when I call at inconvenient times."

"You know I never mind checking in on this little guy. I brought him into the world, but he'd be special even if I didn't."

Her anxiety decreased a notch just looking into his imperturbable face. "He's coughing and says his tummy feels funny." She led the way to the kitchen where Davy was still watching television and eating pistachios.

Bree watched as Dr. Parker listened to her son's chest. His "uh-huhs" and "hmms" took her anxiety back up again. Surely it was just a cold.

Dr. Parker straightened. "I think you'll live, young man," he said.

Davy was paying no attention to the doctor. His focus was on *Scooby Doo, Where Are You?* Bree, however, felt almost giddy at the prognosis.

Dr. Parker put a hand on her shoulder. "You worry too much. He's fine—maybe just a slight cold or allergy from the furnace heat. It looks like he's even gained some weight. My colleague says his counseling sessions are going well."

"I guess." Bree moved restlessly. The topic was not one she enjoyed.

"You don't sound too sure." The doctor put his stethoscope in his bag and closed the clasp. "What's wrong?"

She glanced at Davy, then led the doctor out of the kitchen into the entry. "I almost think the counseling is making things worse. Davy goes wandering several times a week."

"Give him time. He's been through a lot. You both have. I'll talk to Dr. Walton about it next week." He turned toward the door, but his attention was caught by the newspaper on the table. "Good picture of Anu." He picked it up. "She's quite a lady."

The admiration in his voice made Bree hide a smile. "I don't know what Davy and I would do without her. She's really excited about the store's twentieth anniversary. Big sale. She's in Helsinki buying for spring. You'll have to stop over when she gets back."

"I will," he agreed, heading toward the door.

Bree followed him. "Thanks for coming over like this. I really appreciate it."

"It's what friends do," he said, smiling. He squeezed her shoulder as he exited. "Davy is recovering nicely. Spend plenty of time with him, and he'll soon be himself again."

As he went down the walk, Kade Matthews's pickup pulled into the drive. She waited with the door open, flinching at the cold wind that blew down her back. Across the road, puffs of snow nestled in the nooks of tree branches as if they'd been left behind in a snow-ball fight.

Kade came toward her, and just looking at him gave her pleasure. He was all male, from his wide shoulders to his strong, capable hands; Bree felt safe in his presence. That was something she'd never felt with another man, not even Rob.

He kissed her, a lingering touch that left her breathless. He brought feelings to the surface she'd thought were dead and buried. She broke off the kiss with a smile of apology and stepped back.

He grinned then flexed the muscles in his arm. "Me Tarzan. I bring big sledgehammer. Lead me to concrete wall."

Bree grinned and poked him in the solar plexus. He grunted and acted as though he was hurt. She laughed. "We might not have to take it down, you know."

He flashed her a cocky grin. "Maybe we could just take it down for fun," he said. "I was ready to get out of the house, and I can use the workout. Besides, exercise is good for what ails you."

"Lauri?"

Kade shrugged and rolled his eyes then strode toward the kitchen. "Hey, Davy," he said.

Davy looked up from watching his cartoon. "Hi, Kade," he said, his attention quickly shifting back to the cartoon.

Kade turned back toward Bree. "Spurned for a cartoon," he said. "I'm crushed. But I should be used to getting the cold shoulder." His tone was wry but held affection.

"He's still missing his daddy." Bree patted Kade's arm.

"Is he still wandering around in the night?" Kade asked, star-ing into her face.

Bree nodded. "Several times a week. I'm taking him to see Dr. Walton again on Monday."

"It will just take time. He was cooped up in that cabin with Rachel for nearly a year. Who knows what makes someone like her tick, or how long what she did will affect him? A normal person would have notified his family right away. Have you heard anything from her?"

"No. Davy mentioned her last night though, when I found him in the basement. And the other day he asked where she was. I just told him she'd gone to start her new job. He asked if she was living where she didn't have to carry wood for the fire." Suddenly cold, Bree clasped her arms around her. She didn't like to think of those dark days. At least Rachel had taken care of her son, even if she'd tried to steal him.

Kade slipped his arm around her. "He's safe now," he whispered.

Tears pooling, she nodded against his chest. "Yes, and I thank God for that every day." The strength of his warm arms was a haven she didn't want to leave. She stepped away reluctantly. "You ready to get to work?"

"Lead me to it."

She grabbed a flashlight and went to the basement door, pausing to flip on the light.

"Davy," she called, "we'll be downstairs." Stepping carefully, she led the way down the narrow steps to the basement and across the damp concrete floor. The back corner was lit with a bare bulb attached to a joist.

"Right here." She shoved the table. "Let's move this out of the way."

Once the table was out of the way, Kade inspected the concrete wall, running his hands over the smooth surface. Bree loved his hands. They reminded her of bear paws. He was a good man. She picked at the loose concrete around the hole. "Samson seemed almost driven to get back here." She aimed her flashlight beam inside but couldn't see anything.

Kade squatted beside the wall. "Wonder why they even put it up? It's newer than the other walls. Look at the concrete—it's a different color." He flashed a slanted grin at her. "Maybe someone buried a treasure here."

The wall was about six feet wide and went from the concrete floor to the floor joists of the first floor above them. The other walls were stained and dark, and this concrete was much lighter in color. Bree had never noticed the discrepancy before. Some investigator she was.

She grinned. "I'm never that lucky."

"It shouldn't take much to knock it down and find out."

"You promise my home's not going to cave in when you do?"

"Nah," Kade said. "This is no support wall."

"Let's get it down then."

"You got it." Kade hefted the sledgehammer to his broad shoulder and took a wide-legged stance. "Stand back. I don't want you to get hit by flying concrete."

Bree stepped back, stifling a giggle. Was there anything a man enjoyed more than power tools and demolition? Kade brought the heavy tool down in a wide arc. It struck the concrete with a sound that made her wince. The sledgehammer barely chipped the surface of the wall. Kade cleared his throat and stood a bit taller and uttered a hoarse cry, the equivalent of his Tarzan yell. Gripping the sledgehammer more tightly, he swung at the wall again and then continued to pound at it. The ringing in her ears increased, and she clapped her hands over them.

A second hole appeared then widened. Kade paused long enough to shine his flashlight into the space to gauge how deep it was. He picked up the sledgehammer again and began to pound the wall once more. Concrete dust flew into the air; then the wall began to crumble.

He kicked the debris out of the way and stepped forward to peer into the small cavern his work had revealed. "Where's the flashlight?" he asked.

"Right here." Bree flicked it on and handed it to him.

The beam probed the darkness. The dim light illuminated something heaped in the back corner.

Bree stepped forward to see what it was. Kade put his arm out to stop her. "Call Mason," he said. "We've got a body here."

The final bell echoed in the hallway. Lauri Matthews slammed her books into her locker and grabbed her jacket. If she never saw these beige walls again, she would dance through the streets. Two more years of this agony—how could she stand it? She looked at her classmates and felt ancient in comparison. No one else had to deal with an older brother who acted like Hitler.

Several of her friends stood giggling by the water fountain as they watched the track team walk by. Morons, all of them. Lauri headed down another hall so she wouldn't have to deal with their juvenile laughter. None of them really cared about her anyway. They were just her friends because she was going out with Brian Parker, the school hottie. Until Brian had noticed her, she was just a face in the crowd.

She'd had a few friends, but they'd dropped her when the "in" crowd had picked her up. Sometimes she saw her former best friends, Dinah and Ruth, staring at her as though she held the answer to all their problems, and she had to turn her head. They wouldn't fit in any better than she did. If she could, she'd turn the clock back to last year when she was just Lauri Matthews, living with her mother and giggling on her bed with Dinah and Ruth talking about how ridiculous Andi Boone looked in that short cheerleader skirt with her meaty thighs, and trading secrets about which boy had spoken to one of them in the lunchroom.

She gnawed on her thumbnail as she walked toward Brian, who

waited for her in his shiny car. He gave her that familiar smile, and it occurred to her that she should bolt like a deer from a hunter, run to her mother's safe arms, smell the scent that was particularly her mom: musk cologne mingled with the fresh scent of Downy fabric softener. But she couldn't.

Brian kept smiling, and she forced her face to respond though misery dogged her footsteps. Reaching the car, she threw her backpack into the backseat and climbed in. He leaned over and kissed her, and she turned her head so that all he caught was the side of her cheek.

He grimaced. "What's with the mood? I've had it, Lauri." He turned the key and gunned the engine. Several boys turned to stare and grin. Brian dropped the car into gear and roared out of the school parking lot.

Lauri stayed quiet. What was there to say? Life was impossible and refused to get better. The future stretched ahead of her without a glimmer of light.

Brian glanced at her. "I've got soda in the back. Want to check out some of the cabins?"

She knew what he really wanted. What else was there anyway? She was trapped in this pit she'd chosen of her own free will. "I guess. Are the other guys going to be there? Is there another delivery?"

"Nope, just the two of us." His lecherous smile turned her stomach. "How did your algebra test go?"

At least he was showing some interest in her as a person. Her chilly feelings toward him warmed a few degrees. "Okay. I think I passed anyway. You do okay on your English test?"

He let out an exasperated sigh. "I think I bombed it. That's okay though. Old man Pynonnen wouldn't dare flunk me. Dad gives his drama department too much money."

Lauri felt sorry for Brian's dad. He worked hard at the clinic and gave a lot of money away to good causes. Brian was always there with his hand out, and he didn't really give his dad any respect. Brian didn't know how lucky he was to even have a dad. But who was she to judge? She knew she'd never given her own mom the respect she deserved.

"Do you hate coming home to an empty house? That's what I miss the most—Mom being there, asking how my day went."

Brian shrugged and looked away. "Yeah, well, my mom never much cared what I did and where I went. Good riddance, I say. I miss Gramps more than her."

"I don't get to see my grandparents much." Lauri chewed a sliver of nail off her thumb.

"Gramps was great! He was in pain a lot though, ever since World War II. He got shot and the doctors couldn't get out all the shrapnel. He was doped up on painkillers most of the time. But when the demons weren't on his back, he was a lot of fun. He taught me how to sail one summer." Keeping one hand on the steering wheel, he slipped his arm around her with a sly smile. "But who cares about old people? We've got the whole evening ahead of us."

Lauri didn't answer. Her mother had mattered, and she'd taken her for granted. Was she even now doing the same thing with Kade? Kade had given up a lot to come back to Rock Harbor. He had hoped never to come back here, and she knew it.

When they were growing up, he was butting heads with Dad all the time. Lauri had forgotten that, mostly because she'd never understood it. She remembered her father as a great giant who tossed her in the air and tickled her tummy. But her brother spoke only of a hard, inflexible father who said Kade would never measure up. He had wanted to prove that he could make it on his own in someplace new, and now, thanks to her, he was stuck back here in Rock Harbor.

Lauri frowned and looked out the window at the passing forest. In science they'd studied metamorphosis. Kade had metamorphosed into the father he despised. Maybe she should point that out to him.

Brian drove for what seemed forever then turned on a muddy track that followed Lake Superior's shoreline. He parked at a cabin she'd never seen before and jumped out of the car. He surprised her still more by opening her door. "Hey, I'm sorry for the way things have been lately," he said. "Let's kiss and make up, okay?"

She forced a smile, suspicious of his sudden friendliness. "Whose truck is that?" she asked, pointing to a blue Dodge crew cab parked across the road. The surprise on Brian's face was obviously fake. She narrowed her eyes. "I thought you said it was just the two of us."

He grabbed her backpack. "Maybe you can do your homework while I talk to them for a few minutes."

She jerked her backpack out of his hands. "If I'd known you were going to meet those jerks here, I would have had you take me home!"

He spread his hands. "Hey, it's just a little business to take care of."

"I already know what kind of business it is, and I don't want to be a part of it!" Flipping her backpack over her shoulder, she stalked to the house. The lock was already jimmied, so she went on in.

Looking around, her breathing quickened. She knew it was wrong to break into cabins like this, but the pull of the forbidden had become almost an addiction for her. Poking through other people's private belongings, she imagined their lives, perfect lives that made her long to have grown up as someone else.

She went to the bedroom. It was the room that usually held the most secrets. Her heart did a little dance when she saw the cedar chest at the foot of the bed. Chests like this always held treasure. Dropping her jacket and backpack on the floor, she knelt and lifted the lid.

The aroma of cedar overwhelmed her with memories. Her grandmother in Grand Rapids had a cedar chest full of old memorabilia that Lauri used to sort through every summer. Jackpot. The chest was filled with boxes, scrapbooks, and photograph albums. Brian could spend the rest of the day with his friends as far as she was concerned.

Reverently, she lifted the first box and opened the lid. It held a jumble of loose color photos. Her smile froze when she recognized the smiling lady on the top photo. With a little girl on one side and a boy on the other, a much younger Anu Nicholls smiled at the camera.

Lauri's gaze darted around the room. Who would have photos of Anu and her family? Lauri sorted through the box. Every picture in it was of Anu, by herself or with the children. Someone was . . . obsessed.

Fear soured Lauri's stomach. Was Anu in danger? She couldn't find out without broadcasting to all of Rock Harbor that she'd broken the law by breaking in to someone's cabin. In spite of the way things were at home, she wasn't keen on being sent to an institution for juvenile delinquents.

Lauri had never felt such conflicting emotions. Anu Nicholls was one of her favorite people in the whole world. Lauri often stopped by the store and bought *pulla* on her way to babysit Donovan's kids. Lately, Anu had taken to showing her how to make the Finnish delicacies she carried in the shop.

How could Lauri protect her without getting in trouble?

Lauri's eyes widened, and she began to smile. Maybe she could solve the mystery herself. If she prevented someone from hurting Anu, surely no one would ask how she came by the information. Maybe she could actually redeem herself, prove to Kade that she was not the troublemaker he believed her to be.

In a fever of excitement, she began to go through the cedar chest.

One box contained military medals and another, children's drawings. The childish signatures at the bottom made her blink in astonishment. Hilary and Rob, Anu's children. Of course.

She searched further and stopped when her hand touched cold metal. Two guns lay on the bottom of the chest. Lauri checked them. They were loaded.

Snatching her hand away, she scooted back on her heels away from the cedar chest. Her heart felt as cold as the metal on the firearms. Biting her lip, she forced herself to continue looking. There had to be some clue to the identity of the cabin's owner.

She sorted through a jumble of old coins—some from other countries—and several boxes of baseball cards. Her hands went still as she realized she was leaving her fingerprints all over the stuff. But it was too late now. She laid each box aside as she finished with it. One side of the chest was empty now, and she continued to pry.

In one box she found handcuffs, duct tape, and rope. She felt sick as she wondered if someone intended to kidnap Anu. But why? She'd never hurt anyone. Money maybe. Everyone said Nicholls' Finnish Imports had been a Cinderella kind of success story.

Flipping through a newer photo album, Lauri came across a recent picture of Bree and Davy. A large red circle was drawn around Davy, and Lauri felt her heart flip. Maybe Davy would be used to get at Anu. Was that possible? Nausea rose in her at the thought that this little boy might be put through even more than he'd already endured. She had to find a way to keep that from happening.

*T*he naked bulb seven feet above the cracked concrete floor of the basement cast an anemic glow over the small room. Bree stood with her arms clasped around her amid boxes and bags prepared for Goodwill. She felt shaky and struggled to maintain a composed expression, even though Davy wasn't around to require her calming influence. Her best friend and next-door neighbor, Naomi Heinonen, had come the minute Bree called and carried Davy off to safety at her house. She'd taken Samson too.

The acrid odor of blackened apple pie burned her nose. Maybe she could try again later. Easter was still four days away. She shuffled, arousing the dust. The cold concrete made her feet ache. Bree didn't want to see what lay beyond the demolished wall, but she couldn't keep her gaze away from the small area illuminated by Kade's flashlight. Goose bumps pricked her arms, and she rubbed them away.

Her brother-in-law and town sheriff, Mason Kaleva, and one of his deputies, Doug Montgomery, poked cautiously through the contents behind the wall. Deputy Montgomery had always reminded her of a Saint Bernard, big and clumsy but full of heart. The Michigan State police forensics experts from Houghton would arrive any minute, and the deputy would have to let them take over—a circumstance he wouldn't be happy about.

"We need more light," Mason said. "Bree, any chance you have some kind of floodlight?"

"In the garage," she responded. "I've got a halogen light that clamps on." She tried to force her frozen muscles to move, but she was still in shock. A body in her basement? And she'd lived here four years, all this time over a graveyard. She shivered.

"I'll get it," Kade said. He handed the flashlight to Mason, then squeezed her arm as he went past her to the basement stairs.

His touch gave Bree courage, and she stepped over an open box of baby toys to the spot where Mason crouched. "Can you tell anything about the body?"

Mason's bulky figure swung toward her, and he shook his head. "Forensics will have to tell us more. The skull is crushed. And it's obviously from a long time ago. No telling how long this wall has been here."

Kade quickly returned with the halogen work light. He plugged it in, and Bree blinked at the brightness. Its stark brilliance revealed the age and shabbiness of the basement. It also exposed the skull inside the cavity. She turned away, bile burning the back of her throat.

Though she wanted to turn and rush up the steps, this was her house, her responsibility. Swallowing, she forced herself forward, though it felt as though she moved against a stiff wind.

She crouched beside Mason. "Anything else in here?" Amazed at how calm her voice was, she leaned forward to get a better look.

A deep crack ran along the left side of the cranium, and just above the ear was a sunken spot. Rotted dungarees and a red shirt covered most of the skeleton, and the body lay curled in a heap. A brass lantern was on its side just past the body's left arm. There were also a leather-bound book and a small metal box.

She reached out to take it then drew her hand back.

"What is that?" Mason asked.

"It looks familiar, but I can't place it. Let me think about it.

I did a lot of research when we bought the lighthouse; it will come back to me."

"We'll know more once forensics gets done with this." He stood and backed away from the cavity. "Everyone away from the site."

Bree was only too glad to obey. She went to Kade, wishing she could lean against his broad chest. He switched off the bright light, and the sudden dimness made the nooks and crannies of the basement take on sinister shadows. Her uneasiness deepened.

She hastily turned and went up the stairs, telling herself not to be ridiculous. This death had no power to hurt her or her son. But the safe haven of her home had been tainted with the corruption below. An impulse to make sure Davy was all right overwhelmed her. She grabbed her coat and went to the door.

"I'm going to get Davy," she called.

She heard Kade's deep voice behind her but didn't pause. Outside, the icy wind nearly took her breath away. Lake Superior was covered in drifts, as was her backyard, some nearly as high as her kitchen window. The cold stung her skin and made her nose run. She plodded through the snowdrifts and got to her Jeep. A yellow ball with a smiley face painted on it perched on her antenna. It helped warn other drivers of her presence when driving in deep snowdrifts.

Her lighthouse home sat alone on a finger of land jutting into Lake Superior's cold spray. At the beginning of the narrow road out to her lighthouse were her nearest neighbors, the Heinonens. Navigating the drifts with practiced ease, she drove down Negaunee Road to the Blue Bonnet Bed and Breakfast Naomi ran with her mother.

A light shone from the windows, and its cheer lifted the gloom of the overcast day. Festive icicles hung from the gutters, and colored lights winked through the snow on the shrubs. The three-story

Victorian and all the other houses in town would not shed their Christmas garb until April, still two weeks away.

Bree parked in front then hurried up the walk, which was quickly disappearing in spite of the morning's shoveling. Residents of Rock Harbor didn't bother plowing their driveways in the winter. They merely shoveled the area in front of the garages. Most garages had been built just a few feet from the road instead of being attached to the house. It was impossible to keep on top of plowing the snow.

Bree pushed the door open and stepped into the hall. "Naomi? Davy?" she called. Charley, Naomi's golden retriever, came to greet her, and she scratched his head. Samson rushed to greet her as well. She ran her fingers over his thick fur, taking comfort in his eagerness to see her.

"We're in the parlor, dear," Naomi's mother, Martha, called.

Bree went through the door into the parlor with the dogs trotting after her. Davy and Naomi were bent over a game of Chutes and Ladders at the table in front of the fireplace. Martha sat in the rocking chair on the other side of the room with her knitting in her hands. Martha was dressed impeccably in a pink dress with matching shoes, not a hair on her head out of place.

"There's my boy," Bree said.

Davy smiled but his attention stayed on his game. "Mommy, can I stay here? I don't want to go home yet."

Bree swallowed her disappointment. Maybe she was expecting too much from him. While she wanted to spend every second with him, he was beginning to relax and get back to normal. And that was good. At least she tried to tell herself it was.

She ruffled his hair then settled onto the sofa. Apple candles spiced the air with a warm and homey fragrance.

"You beat me, you little twerp," Naomi said, getting up from her chair.

Davy giggled. "Let's play again," he begged.

"No way. You cheat," Naomi said, winking. "Besides, I need to go for the final fitting of my wedding dress in an hour. Want some coffee, Bree?" Her gaze signaled for Bree to follow her to the kitchen.

Bree got up reluctantly. The last thing she wanted was to rehash the events that had transpired in her basement, but she trailed behind her friend.

The kitchen was decorated with every conceivable kind of chicken, from chicken wallpaper to chicken stencils on the cabinets to a collection of chicken cookie jars. The black-and-white checkerboard floor was a nice foil for all the colorful ceramic figurines and containers loaded atop the cabinets. Bree had always wondered how Martha became so obsessed with the fowl assortment. Some of the things in her collection had been bought over forty years ago. Maybe she should come up with some kind of motif for her kitchen. It might be something Davy would enjoy. Cows maybe?

With the kitchen door shut behind her, Naomi lifted the coffee carafe and faced Bree. "Do you know who it is?"

Bree shook her head while Naomi poured. "Not yet. When I get a chance, maybe after Easter, I'm going to go to the library and do some research on the town history. I think it's murder though."

"Murder?" Naomi said the word like it was the furthest thing from her mind. "Why murder?"

"Mason's not calling it that yet, but the skull was caved in. And why else would it be entombed behind that wall? I don't like to think something like that happened in my house." She gave a shaky laugh. "Maybe that explains the strange noises I sometimes hear. It's a ghost."

"You know there's no such thing," Naomi said.

"Rob used to say we had gremlins." She smiled to show Naomi she was joking. Bree took the cup Naomi offered and lowered herself into a chair. Would she be able to take Davy and spend the night in that house? What other unpleasant surprises might she find there? Maybe it was time to sell the old lighthouse. But as quickly as the thought came, she rejected it. Davy needed the stability of familiar surroundings. She would have to get over her squeamishness.

"What noises are you talking about?" Naomi shut off the coffee-pot warmer.

"I was kidding. Old houses make noises. It just took some getting used to when we first moved in.

"It's more likely bats."

Bree shuddered. "I'd rather face gremlins. But enough about this or I'll be too spooked to sleep there tonight. I can't believe you're getting married in a week! A winter wedding seemed a little crazy at first, but you were right all along. It's perfect."

Naomi's face softened and took on a dreamy expression. "You know, Bree, I never thought I'd ever be this happy. I keep waiting for the other shoe to drop. My life can't continue to be this perfect."

"God knows you deserve this happiness. What is it the Bible says? Something about God giving us our desires?"

"Delight yourself in the Lord, and he will give you the desires of your heart." Naomi pirouetted around the kitchen floor. "Donovan is everything I've ever dreamed of. And two lovely children as well."

"You so deserve this. He'd better treat you right, or he'll answer to me." Bree watched the glow on her friend's face and felt a trace of envy. Her own halcyon days as a wife grew dimmer with each passing day. She should have rejoiced that the pain was fading as well, but she fought tears instead.

Bree felt Naomi's gaze and looked up to find her friend studying her. "What?" she asked. "Do I have concrete dust on my face?"

"You've been strange lately, almost sad. I was getting used to seeing you just giddy with joy after Davy came home. What's wrong?"

Bree grimaced, which was better than crying. "I wish I knew.

It's almost like the postpartum depression I went through after Davy was born. Sometimes I wake in the middle of the night sobbing out loud. I think it's probably . . . guilt." She whispered the last word and dropped her gaze to her lap. She plucked at the threads on her jeans, still blotched with flour.

"What do you have to feel guilty about?"

"I keep remembering my hateful words to Rob." Her voice broke. "I let him go to his death thinking I believed him to be the kind of man who would break his marriage vows." Bree stared into the murky depths of her coffee and wished she could see how to do what she knew she must.

"It's my fault he's dead and that Davy endured all that turmoil. My fault he's going to grow up without his father." She felt Naomi slip a comforting hand onto her shoulder. Bree reached up to take it.

"God is going to redeem all that, remember? Besides, you didn't sabotage his plane—Palmer did."

"My head knows, but my heart is another matter."

She clung to the promises she was reading for the first time in the Bible, but how did she get rid of feeling like she'd failed?

Naomi sat beside Bree and put her coffee cup on the table. "Any woman would have reacted the way you did. You didn't know it was all a lie, a ploy to cover his murder."

"Davy had another night terror last night. What if he's scarred for life?"

"Stop it!" Naomi leaned forward and took Bree's hands in hers. "He's been through a horrible trauma, Bree. Give it time. Dr. Walton will help him adjust."

"That's what Dr. Parker says. But every time Davy wanders off I have to relive that year of searching for him. I can't stand it."

"Just give him time," Naomi said soothingly. "And give yourself time. God has forgiven you; you should forgive yourself too."

"I wish it were that easy."

The phone jangled on the wall by the door, and Bree jumped. Naomi went to answer it. She started writing on a notepad attached to the wall and asking questions like, "How long has she been gone?" and "Where was she last seen?"

Bree tensed when it became obvious it was a search-and-rescue call. Anu had helped her open Kitchigami Search-and-Rescue Training Center, and with spring approaching, she was expecting frequent calls. The last few months had been a remarkably light time for her team, but that wouldn't last, though she'd been glad of it through the winter. It had allowed her to devote her time to Davy.

Naomi hung up the phone. "Gretchen Siller is missing. Karen thinks she's been kidnapped."

"Oh no! Quentin?" Bree's heart constricted with terror for the little girl. The man might do anything. He reminded her of a rabid dog she'd seen once. It looked perfectly normal until she looked it square in the face, and then it became all snarling teeth and wild eyes.

Naomi nodded.

"They should never have let him out of jail!"

"They can't do anything unless he does something first."

"Let's hope today isn't that day," Bree said grimly.

$$- \mathcal{G} -$$

The winter storm had finally blown itself out, and the afternoon rays peeked through the clouds. Sheer sunbeams touched roads unaccustomed to the extravagant warmth. The top melting layer with heavy snow underneath made for treacherous driving conditions. Snowdrifts several feet high hemmed in the highway so that it was barely wide enough for Kade's truck. One wrong move and he'd be in the ditch.

Kade drove into the parking lot that served the park headquarters of the National Kitchigami Wilderness Tract. Most of the snowmobilers had gone home for the season, and the parking lot held only two SUVs. In another few weeks, motor homes, campers, and vans would rumble along the narrow gravel tracks and fill every available parking space.

He turned, and a smile lifted his lips. His baby-wildlife refuge center was almost finished. The brick building matched the main building, except it had large windows for people to peer through to watch the wild babies. Kade stepped inside and glanced around at the cages. Some had branches awaiting bald eagles and northern spotted owls. Others would house black-footed ferrets, gray wolves, and Canada lynxes. A mesh-covered aviary behind the building was underway, and a fenced-in area for bighorn sheep would be the last thing constructed.

A new interactive educational room held displays of endangered species. Kade looked with pride at the elaborate displays for mountain beaver, eastern puma, and pygmy owl. He itched to be able to throw open the doors and allow the public inside.

The front door opened and his boss, Gary Landorf, stepped in.

Head Ranger Gary Landorf was a slight man in his early fifties. His quick movements and keen dark eyes had always reminded Kade of a ferret. He ran the park with an iron fist that seemed out of keeping with his small stature.

"I need to see you a minute, Kade." His boss strolled into the center. "Everything looks ready to roll."

"We're ready, sir."

"Got the coffee going?" Ranger Landorf's shrewd gaze skittered over Kade's face. "You look harried. Something wrong?"

Kade went to the small refreshment table by the door and poured two cups of coffee. He wasn't sure if he should say anything about the body at the lighthouse, then decided it wouldn't matter. The news would hit the paper by tomorrow anyway.

"Bree Nicholls and I discovered a skeleton in her basement this morning."

Landorf's eyes widened as he accepted the coffee. "You seem to have a remarkable propensity for sniffing out crime. A skeleton, eh? Well, I hope it's nothing that will distract you from your real job." His voice held a note of warning.

"No, sir," Kade said.

"We've got a situation I'm putting you in charge of. I'm getting more and more reports of break-ins at the cabins on National Forest property. Seems to be many more than usual. I've gotten five reports just this morning, most from folks who have showed up to rent them."

"Anything missing, or just vandalism?"

"Neither really. Just evidence of someone having been there. Almost as if they're either living there or looking for something. I want you to find out what's going on and who's behind it."

Landorf dug some papers out of his pocket and extended them to Kade. "Most are in the White Lake area near the Superior beach. It's remote, so maybe we're just dealing with kids who think they can get away with it."

From his boss's tone, Kade could tell he had no choice. He took the reports. "This will eat up quite a bit of time I meant to spend on the rehabilitation center. We're due to announce its opening in a few weeks."

"That's insignificant compared to this other problem. It will wait if it has to."

Kade wasn't about to give up his pet project. He'd been trying to get this accomplished for more than eight months. "We'll be getting calls for orphaned baby wildlife any time. I'm not nearly ready to take care of them yet." Last year he'd received at least fifty calls from people wanting help caring for orphaned wildlife. He'd taken some in at his own home, but the need was more than he could handle on his own. "I'd like your permission to construct a few pens to house any baby wildlife that are brought in. I want to do more than aid the endangered animals."

Landorf frowned. "I've given you some leeway on this project against my better judgment. It's one thing to help endangered species or those indigenous to this area, quite another to take in nuisance animals like starlings or squirrels. They proliferate and overrun endangered species' habitats. I want to give some more thought to what we allow to come into the center. We'll reevaluate it next year and maybe expand it then. Let's not get ahead of ourselves."

Kade gritted his teeth and opened his mouth to object.

The head ranger held up his hand. "That is all I'm prepared to say right now, Ranger Matthews." He turned to go then paused. "There's one more thing. The horses we bought for patrol have arrived. I've assigned you a bay gelding by the name of Moses. Once the snow melts, you can take him out. You might stop in at the new stable and make his acquaintance."

Kade pressed his lips together. His boss slapped him with one hand and threw him a bone with the other.

He stuffed the papers from Landorf in his pocket. "I'll see what I can find out." It was all he could do to hold his tongue as Landorf smiled with satisfaction and exited the center. As soon as the door was shut, Kade dropped onto a chair and raked a hand through his hair. Now what? Kade had always tried to be a team player, but standing aside now was more than he could do. The wildlife orphan center was too important.

Landorf was an area homegrown boy. He'd gone away for ten years and come back a year ago. His familiarity with the area gave him the belief that he knew all there was to know about the Kitchigami Wilderness and how it should be run. All that talk about giving it some more thought was just evidence of Landorf's plan to bury it. He knew perfectly well Kade wouldn't spend all the center's resources on nonindigenous animals.

Kade reached for the phone then drew back his hand. The last thing he wanted was to come off as a disgruntled employee. He would think about what he wanted to say before he called.

He dug out the papers Landorf had given him and read through the reports. The tract of campsites and small cabins near White Lake overlooked a stretch of beach that saw few visitors, even in the summer. It was going to be tough to find the culprits, though his boss was probably right about the teenagers.

He frowned. The only items that seemed to be missing were things like bottled water and beef jerky. Other than jimmied locks, nothing had been damaged, except for snow damage to one cabin after its door had been left open. He got up. No time like the present to see what he could find out.

Kade fired up his snowmobile and rode out to White Lake. On his way he passed four men, also on snowmobiles. They didn't wave when he passed, which was unusual, and Kade looked them over as he went by. They seemed careful to keep their faces averted. Kade thought about stopping to see what they were up to but then gunned his machine and kept on going. There was no law against wanting privacy.

It took him nearly an hour to navigate the winding snowmobile paths. White Lake was small, only a mile in diameter. It was a favorite haunt of trout fishermen and wildlife enthusiasts, in part because it was so remote that only the truly dedicated came. Nestled in massive groves of oak and aspen, the lake was only a two-mile hike from a beautiful Superior beach.

Kade glanced at the first spot on his list. The cabin was on a ridge that had panoramic views of both Superior and White lakes. It also had suffered the most vandalism. He stopped the snow-mobile in front of the small cabin. The door had been so badly damaged that it hung at an angle from the doorframe. Ice coated the linoleum floor. The moisture had caused the floor to buckle and Kade felt as though he was rolling over hills as he walked across it. Small animals, mistaking the open door for a welcome, had been busy at work as well. He saw piles of raccoon droppings as well as teeth marks on the table legs. Foam had been pulled from the couch and easy chair by the fireplace. Some damage had come from humans. Tossed pillows, scattered food items, and ripped draperies told of a deliberate vandalism animals couldn't match.

Kade kicked aside a pillow someone had dragged from the bed-room and went to the kitchen, a small area hardly bigger than a closet and just as dingy. Cabinet doors hung open, a feat small ani-mals would be unlikely to be able to perform. Several packages of beef jerky had been ripped open, and the empty wrappers lay on the wooden counter.

Kade felt the back of his neck prickle and whirled around, but no one was there. He was getting spooked and wasn't quite sure why. Shaking off the uneasiness, he went through a doorway into the bedroom. Cigarette butts and empty soda cans littered the floor, but he couldn't tell if they were from the upended trash can in the corner or from the intruder—or intruders. There was no way of knowing if the break-ins had been caused by one person or several, though if the cigarette butts and soda cans were any indication, it might be as many as four or five.

He took a plastic bag out of his pocket and picked up some butts with gloved fingers. Several different brands of cigarettes had been smoked, another indication that a group was responsible.

One brand looked familiar, and his hand froze in midair. This was the type of cigarette he'd found in Lauri's car. He'd confronted her about them, but she claimed she wasn't smoking. They belonged to a friend, she'd said. But the shade of lipstick on the butt in his hand looked suspiciously like his sister's.

He pressed his lips together then dropped the bag in his pocket and went to the door. When he got outside, he saw a glint in the trees. Shading his eyes with his hand, he stared at the spot. Moments later he saw a movement, then the sound of a snowmobile engine roared to life. He saw a flash of red as the snowmobile sped away, too fast to tell what make or model.

Someone had been watching him. He slogged through the snowdrifts to where he'd seen the movement. There were footprints in the snow, size twelve just like Kade wore, by the looks of them. Several cigarette butts lay on the ground, and he picked them up. Maybe they would match some from the cabin.

This was getting stranger by the minute. There was nothing in the cabin. But someone watching it implied something more sinister than kids out on a lark.

He mounted his snowmobile and drove to the next report. This one was even more curious. It was closer to Superior than to White Lake. A small trailer, it showed signs of having been properly closed up for winter, with pipes drained and everything sealed. But the toilet held water, though nothing came from the taps in the bathroom and the kitchen. Very strange. Someone must have poured water from a bucket into the toilet in order to use it.

Outside, Kade found another cigarette butt that looked like the brand he'd found in the woods. He went to the next report and the next. They were all similar. Small signs of winter visitors, and always the cigarette butts. Either it was a very popular brand of cigarette or the same person had been at each of these locations.

Feeling grim, Kade walked back to the snowmobile. He resolved to question Lauri the minute he got home.

*B*ree parked the Jeep behind the sheriff's car. The Siller house was an aging two-story with asbestos siding and crumbling green shingles. The once-galvanized roof was more rust than shine, but the fence surrounding the property was in good shape, and the shutters were painted, as was the porch, evidence that the Sillers cared about aesthetics. Rather, Karen cared. Quentin only cared about his beer and his hunting.

The people swarming the yard had packed down the snow underfoot. Karen Siller was on the porch, the skin around her dark eyes blotchy from crying. Her dog, Patch, pressed against her leg as though he didn't know what to make of all the people invading his territory. Mason stood beside Karen, jotting down notes in his small leather notebook.

"He's taken Gretchen," Karen said after Bree embraced her. Her slim shoulders shook with the intensity of her weeping; then she pulled away and fumbled in the pocket of her ratty sweater for a tissue.

"What happened?" Bree wanted to cry with her.

Karen nodded. "I heard a noise and came out to the front yard. Gretchen had been on the porch writing in her diary. She got it for her eighth birthday and loves to scribble in it. When I got there, I saw Quentin's car speeding away. Gretchen was in the passenger seat." She clenched her hands into fists. "I had a feeling he was going to do something like this. I should never have pressed charges in the first place. Who knows where he's taking her!"

Though there was no trace of accusation in Karen's voice, Bree wanted to look away. She'd urged Karen to put a stop to the abuse. Maybe this was her fault. But what choice did they have?

"At least she's with her father and not some maniac who wants to hurt her," Bree pointed out. But her words failed to ease the torment in Karen's eyes, and Bree couldn't blame her. Who knew what Quentin would do? So far he hadn't harmed his daughter, but if he got frustrated enough, he was liable to do anything. They had to find the little girl.

"I don't suppose the window was down?" Bree asked without much hope.

Karen brightened. "No, but the back passenger window is broken. Quentin put his fist through it one day, and he never had it fixed. That helps, doesn't it?"

"Sure does!" This was more than Bree could have hoped for. The scent drafts would drift out the window and leave a trace the dogs could follow. "We have a chance to pick up the scent. Let's get the dogs on it. Do you have a scent article?"

Karen nodded and held out a plastic bag. Bree opened it then also opened the two paper bags inside to reveal some socks. Though Karen had been a search-and-rescue student of Bree's for only two months, she'd obviously remembered the training about how to collect scent articles.

"She wore those last night," Karen said. "I wish Patch was up to speed. I would have gotten him right on the trail. But she doesn't have Samson's nose." Karen's SAR dog, a ten-month-old Great Dane, looked up at the sound of her name.

"Not many dogs do," Naomi said. "Charley is good, but Samson is in a league by himself."

Samson whined as if to ask why they were talking about him.

He pressed his cold nose against Bree's hand. Dressed in his orange vest, he moved restlessly. Samson loved nothing more than searching—except Davy and Bree.

Bree forced her attention back to the job at hand. Kneeling beside Samson and Charley, she held the bags open under their noses. The dogs sniffed eagerly then strained at their leashes.

She tossed the Jeep's keys to Mason. "You want to follow us in the Jeep?"

He nodded and headed to her old red Cherokee.

Bree and Naomi led the dogs to the street. "Search!" Bree commanded. Holding on to their leashes, the women let the dogs drag them along the pavement until they deduced the direction of Quentin's car. Then they piled in the Jeep and went to the next crossroad. They got out of the vehicle again and let the dogs determine whether Quentin had turned at this street or not. The dogs led them due east out of town.

Mason gunned the Jeep out past the city limits. It was a search in fits and starts, as they had to stop and check the direction at every crossroad. Out of Kitchigami County, he turned south on Highway 26, which led to Mass City. Evidently Quentin's tactic was to stay on the highway and drive straight out of the U.P. as fast as his wheels could roll. By dusk they were in Rockland. The dogs indicated Quentin and Gretchen had gone on toward the small town, and Bree wondered if they were stopping for supper or gas.

"I doubt he would take time to go in a café to eat," she told Mason. "I bet he'll just grab snacks at the convenience store. Let's check there."

Moments later Mason pulled into a gas station, a small Standard station with aging pumps. The dogs started whining and trying to get out of the Jeep as soon as Mason stopped the vehicle behind a beat-up brown Chevy Cavalier. Rust sprouted on the trunk lid like brown bulbs trying to come up through hard Michigan shale.

"That's his car," Naomi whispered to Bree. "I saw him come by once when I dropped Karen home."

"Stay here," Mason said. He got out of the driver's seat and walked to the car.

Bree couldn't see any small head in the passenger seat. Maybe Gretchen was in the store with her dad. Too bad. It would be easier to handle this if the little girl was separated from Quentin. It would be traumatic for her to see her father being taken into custody.

Ignoring Mason's admonition to stay in the vehicle, Bree opened her door and got out. Mason frowned at her then shrugged and jerked his head to signal her to go ahead of him.

"Get Gretchen outside," he mouthed.

She nodded and stepped into the convenience store. Only one small room, it held an assortment of candy and snack offerings, a few bottles of oil and transmission fluid, and a rack of outdated magazines. Gretchen was perusing the candy aisle, but Bree saw no sign of Quentin Siller. She watched the little girl a minute. Dressed in faded jeans, Gretchen wore her brown hair in two braids tied with red ribbon, and a small frown crouched between her eyes. She probably didn't know what to make of her dad taking her off like that.

Bree needed to get the little girl out of here. Stepping quickly to Gretchen's side, she put a hand on the child's shoulder. "You never know who you'll run into in the strangest places," she said in a cheery voice.

Gretchen's face brightened when she saw Bree, and she hugged her. "Where's Samson?" she asked. "Are you on a search-and-rescue mission?"

"Sure am. Hey, why don't you come out and say hello to Samson and Charley? They'd love to see you." They'd probably lick her to death. The dogs loved Gretchen.

"Okay." She followed Bree to the door. With one hand on the doorknob and the other on Gretchen, she heard a door squeak on its hinges, and her stomach tightened. From the corner of her eye, she saw Quentin Siller emerging from the men's room.

He wore a gray T-shirt that said BORN TO FISH. The scruffy beard made him look as though he'd been fishing for the past week. His gaze darted around the room, and when he saw her, his mouth opened like a bass with a hook in its jaw.

"Hey there. What are you doing with my daughter?"

Bree quickly pushed Gretchen through the door and pulled it shut behind her. Propelling the little girl past Mason, she got her in the Jeep as the sheriff blocked Quentin's charge through the door.

"Is Dad mad? Maybe I should go back."

"No, he's fine. Your mom sent me to find you."

Naomi immediately positioned herself so Gretchen couldn't see what was going on and began to talk loudly. Bree left the child in Naomi's competent care and went back to see if Mason needed her.

"You're under arrest on kidnapping charges," Mason said calmly, slapping a set of handcuffs on Quentin. "Plus you violated the restraining order. Man, you're in a lot of trouble. Why didn't you think about your daughter before you pulled a stunt like this?"

Quentin failed to look repentant. "You can't lock me up. She's my own daughter."

"I can and I will. There's a federal law prohibiting parents from taking their children without permission from the custodial parent." Mason's tone was rough and impatient.

"You want me to wait until your deputy gets here?" Bree asked.

Mason motioned with his head. "There he is now."

Bree turned to see Doug Montgomery ease his bulk from the

sheriff's car. His massive head reminded her of a Rottweiler, and today he looked just as pugnacious. His holster slung low on his hips, he lumbered toward them.

"The cavalry has arrived," Mason said. "Get on out of here, Bree. I don't want to run the risk of Gretchen seeing us putting her dad in the car."

"Don't I get to say goodbye to her?" Quentin whined.

"You've caused her enough trauma for one day," Mason said.

Bree went back to the Jeep and hopped in. In the rearview mirror she saw Mason and Doug putting Quentin in the back of the squad car.

She smiled at Gretchen. "Ready to go?"

"Hey, where's my dad?" Gretchen turned with an anxious glance.

"I told him I would take you back to your mom's," Bree told her. She braced herself for tears or entreaties, but the little girl smiled with obvious relief and wrapped her arms around Samson's neck. "I told him I didn't really want to go today," she said. "I have homework to do." She scratched Samson's ears. "Someday Patch will be able to search like Samson and Charley. Mom says I can learn search-and-rescue when I get older, like Lauri."

Lauri. Right now the teenager wasn't a person Bree would want Gretchen to emulate. The thought hurt. Kade had been trying so hard to reach her, but the girl had a wall up as thick as Superior's ice floes. Maybe Bree could take her shopping with Anu when she returned from Helsinki. The girl really warmed to the older woman. Anu said she'd been hanging out in the store all winter.

She glanced at Naomi beside her in the passenger seat. "Nervous about the wedding? At least I kept you busy today."

Naomi turned back from Gretchen. "Did you have to remind me?" She laughed. "I'm only kidding. I can't wait!"

"Emily called me yesterday and about talked my ear off. I think she's as excited as you. I'm not looking forward to wearing that dress though. I look like death in pink. The least you could have done was pick out a flattering color for your matron of honor."

Naomi groaned. "You know I had nothing to do with it. Pink is Mom's favorite color, and after arguing over *my* dress, I had no energy left to battle for yours."

"I'll forgive you this one time." Bree said. "You're going to be a beautiful bride. No one will be looking at me anyway."

"Kade will," Naomi said slyly.

Bree turned her head a bit to hide the sudden heat in her cheeks. Naomi was probably right. She told herself to stay focused on Davy's needs. Once he was on an even keel, she could consider what the future might hold for her and Kade.

Several cars were parked along the street at the Siller residence. She stopped behind a police car and turned off the engine.

"Let's go see your mom, Gretchen," she said. She got out and opened the door for the little girl.

Karen rushed out before they reached the porch. Half-crying and half-laughing, she scooped Gretchen into her arms and smothered her face with kisses.

She cupped her daughter's face in her hands. "Why did you go with your dad? You knew it wasn't his weekend with you."

Gretchen wiggled in her mother's grasp. "He said he changed with you." Her tone was bewildered.

Bree could see she had no idea what the fuss was all about. "Why don't you discuss this later?" she said under her breath to Karen.

Karen ignored her. "You are not to go off with him like that," she scolded. "You didn't even have your clothes. Your father—"

Bree grabbed Karen's arm and shook her head. Gretchen gave her mother a somber glance then walked slowly toward the house. "At least she has a father," Bree whispered, "even if he wasn't thinking clearly today."

Karen blinked and swallowed. "I'm scared, Bree," she whispered. "What if he comes back?"

"He's in custody and in a lot of trouble. Maybe now he'll listen enough to seek help for his temper."

"He hates me now. And you." Karen bit her lip. "I never wanted my marriage to be like this. I still want to love him, but I'm too afraid of him. I'm scared for you too, Bree. You and Anu. He blames you two for all our troubles. He's too blind to see it's his own fault."

"We can handle ourselves," Bree assured her. "I'm not afraid of Quentin."

A siren screamed by, and Bree turned to look. It was heading out of town. Another police car followed that one, and then a third. A car screeched to a halt in front of the Siller residence. Then Bree's cell phone rang.

Mason's voice came over the line. "Quentin has escaped. I've called in reinforcements to try to find him, but be careful. He may come looking for you."

— 6 —

School was such a bore. Sitting in algebra class, Lauri found her thoughts drifting to the stuff she'd found in the chest. It bugged her, but how could she go about finding who owned it and what his intentions were? She wasn't the investigator Bree and Naomi were, and Zorro didn't have the skills of the other dogs either. But she had to try.

The last bell rang. She tossed her books in her locker and went to find Brian. He was shooting hoops with two other boys in the gym. He saw her and waved but continued to toss the ball with the other guys. Lauri motioned for him to come. He frowned but threw the ball to a friend and walked toward her.

"What's up? I'm kind of busy."

"Aren't we going out to the cabin today?"

"You usually aren't too eager to do that. What's up with you?"

"Nothing. I'm just bored. Can we go now?" Lauri tapped her foot on the gym floor.

"I guess. Sheesh, you change like the wind."

"I'm a girl. We're allowed." Lauri smiled to show him there were no hard feelings. She just wanted to get out of here. She watched Brian jog to his friends and explain. He grabbed his other shoes and sat beside her on the bleacher.

"The guys said they'd be there at four. I can't stay long. The old man wants me to shovel the driveway before the party tonight. I don't get it. He can hire someone for that. Why do I have to do it?"

"I hate it when you whine. You've got it better than anyone here, and you complain when your dad wants to teach you a little responsibility."

He shot her a dark look. "I don't see you swallowing it when your brother wants you to stay home and do the laundry. You're the one complaining then."

"Kade doesn't give me everything the way your dad does," she snapped. "And he doesn't nag you to death either. You're lucky to have a dad at all." There. That was the real reason Brian's attitude bugged her. At least he had a dad.

Neither spoke as they drove out into the forest. Several times Lauri started to apologize, then pressed her lips together and stared out the window at the thick trees.

"Are we going to the same cabin?" she asked finally.

"Yeah." He glanced at his watch.

"Why are you mixed up in this anyway? It's not like you need the money. What if you get caught?"

"You don't understand, and I can't explain it to you," he said. "There's more to it than you know."

"So tell me!"

"I can't. My dad—" he broke off and gripped the steering wheel.

"Don't try to blame this one on your dad. You're the one who got mixed up in it. I understand trying to be independent, but this is just stupid. Your dad would be really disappointed in you if he knew."

"A lot you know," he muttered resentfully.

She blew her breath out through her mouth. "Okay, let's just drop it. Whose cabin is it anyway?"

"It belongs to the forest department."

"I know that! Who's renting it?"

He shrugged. "Just a guy I know."

"Klepto?"

"Nah, he's just a hack like me. One of the big boys is in town right now."

"Big boys?" Lauri snickered to cover her worry. What would one of Brian's cohorts be doing with a chest full of memorabilia of the Nicholls family? She had thought it might be a local kid, maybe someone obsessed with Bree. "Is he from around here?"

"Why are you asking all these questions? You usually don't care as long as they stay out of your way and keep you supplied with your smokes."

Lauri shrugged. "Just making conversation."

"Well, don't. You'll get in trouble if Neville hears you."

"Neville?"

Brian clamped his lips shut. "Just shut up, okay? I don't want you messing this up for me today. It's important."

"And I'm not?"

"I didn't say that!" He swore and pounded his palm against the steering wheel. "You make me so mad sometimes, Lauri. Why can't you be like other girls?"

"If I was like everyone else, you wouldn't be with me," she said. She'd better quit goading him.

"Sometimes I wonder why I am." He turned the car into the lot at the end of the rough, rutted track that led to Lake Superior and killed the engine. "Wait here. I don't want him to see you."

Lauri didn't answer. Brian got out of the car and jogged to a small outbuilding at the edge of the forest. He disappeared inside. She waited a few minutes to make sure he wasn't returning right away, then opened the door and eased it shut as quietly as she could.

Damp leaves rustled beneath her sneakers in spite of her stealth, and she winced. She'd intended to creep to the building and try to listen, but that wasn't going to work. They'd hear her for sure. She retraced her steps and moved toward the cabin.

Maybe there was something inside she'd missed. She'd had no time to look things over well. With any luck, Brian and the others would be tied up awhile.

The cabin door was unlocked. She stepped inside and glanced around. Nothing much had changed. She walked quickly to the bedroom and looked inside. The chest was still there. Glancing out the window, she could see the shed from here. The door was still closed. She breathed a sigh of relief and went back to the bedroom door. There was a back door on the other side of the kitchen.

She stepped back to the chest and flung open the top. Everything was in a jumble, just as she'd left it. Maybe he hadn't seen it yet. She quickly pulled everything out and tried to remember how it had been the first day. She went through every item, piece by piece, but found nothing new, no clues to the identity of the hoarder and the reason he'd collected these things.

Layering things neatly, she put everything back as well as she could remember. Disappointment made her frown. This visit had been pointless. She heard a noise and jumped up, rushing to the window. The shed door was open and Brian stood in the doorway with other guys behind him. He was pointing toward the cabin.

She whirled and raced toward the back door. The voices grew louder as she pulled the door behind her. She slunk along the back wall and crouched under the window. The wall shook a bit as the front door slammed.

"Can you get the stuff to me by the day after tomorrow?"

Lauri didn't recognize the voice, but it sounded older, more like Brian's dad's age. She had to see who it was. Gripping the edge of the windowsill, she peeked in the window. The man's back was to her. Since he was dressed in a thick coat and hat, she couldn't tell anything about his appearance.

Brian saw her, and his eyes widened. She shook her head and put her finger to her lips. He narrowed his eyes and frowned at her, then turned his back. Whew. He wasn't going to give her away. Maybe this was the Neville he had warned her about.

Moving as silently as she could, she hurried back to his car.

Kade pulled in the driveway and blinked in surprise. Lauri was actually home. What were the chances of her being home at seven o'clock? About as likely as the ice on Superior being solid in April. Zorro, his ears laid back in the wind, raced to greet him as Kade walked across the yard. The dog was wet with snow, and he threw himself against Kade's leg.

Kade knelt and scratched the pup's head. Nearly four months old, Zorro was turning into a fine young dog, standing above Kade's knees. His black and white markings made him look like a bandit. At least he was glad to see Kade.

Zorro followed him to the door, but Kade stopped the dog when he would have followed along inside. "You need to get cleaned up first, Zorro." The dog whined as Kade shut the door behind him.

The sweet aroma of cookies permeated the three-room cabin. "Smells like chocolate-chip cookies," Kade said, sniffing in appreciation. His mouth watered in anticipation. When was the last time Lauri had baked him something?

The cabin's kitchen and living areas were combined, and two bedrooms stood off the large middle room. His gaze went to his sister as she slid cookies onto wax paper. Sixteen and full of the power of her young beauty, she drew eyes wherever she went. Silky brown hair fell nearly to her waist when it wasn't pulled up in a ponytail as it was today, and her blue eyes seemed so guileless. Kade knew better though. She possessed the selfishness of youth in fatal doses.

Lauri sniffed but didn't look at him. "They're not for you. I have a party to go to tonight. I just got home half an hour ago, and I don't have much time to get them done."

Kade barely refrained from rolling his eyes. He should have known. "Am I allowed one?"

"One and that's all," she said.

Kade tried not to mind the disdain in her voice and stepped to the counter. He picked up a warm cookie and bit into it. The sweet chocolate failed to tame the sour taste in his mouth at what he had to do. He would ease into it.

"Hey, want to take in a movie with me Friday night? We can go eat at a nice restaurant first. I'll even buy you a new . . . uh, pair of jeans." He'd been about to offer her a new dress, but that would have been a mistake. The last time he'd seen her in a dress was their mom's funeral.

Her hand poised over the pan of cookies, Lauri turned her head slowly to look at him. "What are you talking about? You know I have a date with Brian."

Kade wanted to tell her she could do better than Brian Parker. Though he was Dr. Max Parker's son, the boy was as wild as a moose and just as dangerous.

He deliberately kept his voice soft. "Then you say when. I'd like to spend some time with you."

Her eyes widened. "Since when?"

"Since always. You're my sister, and it seems like I never get a chance to see you. I want to change that."

Lauri's ponytail swung against her back as she shrugged. "You could have fooled me. Most of the time you're glad to see me leave."

"That's not true, Lauri. I think you know that. I've gone looking for you often enough." And found her in situations she knew better than to be in, he added silently. He just prayed this fiasco involving the cabins wasn't one of them.

"Only because it's your job," she said with a resentful glance.

"If I've made you feel that way, I'm sorry," he said softly.

Her eyes narrowed at his soft tone, and she sniffed. "So you say today." She pulled a container from a cabinet and began to load the cookies into it.

Kade tried to keep a light tone. "So when can we go?"

She turned a calculating gaze on him. "No reneging on your offer for new jeans?"

"Nope."

"Can I have a new top too?"

"You drive a hard bargain, but sure, no problem."

Her gaze studied him. "What's this all about, really?"

"I'm your brother, not your jailer," he said. "We seem to have lost track of that, and I want to find it again."

"And keep me in line along with it, right?" She turned back to the cookies.

Kade wondered if she didn't want him to see that his offer had touched her. He believed the sister he loved still resided somewhere inside the tough shell Lauri presented to the world. He'd keep chipping away until he found it. What did he have to lose?

"How about one day next week after school?" Lauri said, her tone a bit subdued. "After I get home from sitting for the O'Reilly kids."

Kade grinned wryly. If only God would get hold of her heart. Lauri had a lot to offer. Other kids looked up to her. She could have a tremendous impact for good on her school if she would try.

"Friday maybe?"

"Whatever."

"We're on then," he said. Now he needed to tread carefully. "You been out to White Lake lately?" Was it his imagination or did she pale at his question?

She didn't answer.

"Well?"

"What's with the third degree?" she asked, her voice full of resentment.

"All I asked was a simple question."

"There's accusation in it. What have I done now?"

There was no help for it. Kade pulled the plastic bag from his pocket and fished out the cigarette he thought was hers. "Recognize this?"

Her eyes widened. "That's not mine!"

"It looks like your lipstick. And it looks like the kind of cigarette I found in your car."

"I'm not the only one who smokes that brand!"

"Then you admit you've been smoking?"

She clamped her lips shut and glared at him. "I thought you said you weren't my jailer!" She scooped up the container of cookies and bolted for the door.

Kade thought about letting her go, but after second thought he went after her. "Lauri, wait." The roar of her car engine covered his call, and she sped away before he could reach her.

*L*auri hated this old red Plymouth. Why couldn't she have been born into a family with money like Brian? He drove a hot black Mustang while she had to make do with this piece of junk. She drove along the snow-covered road toward town. How much did Kade know? All she had to do was keep her mouth shut. That was stupid of her to let it slip that she was smoking.

If only Mom were still alive. She'd make Kade ease up on her. Couldn't he see she was an adult now? She was sixteen years old, for Pete's sake! She was old enough to make her own decisions. It was all his fault she was stuck in this backwater town. If not for his misguided sense of responsibility, they could be in California right now.

Pulling the car into Brian's driveway, she sat back and stared at the house backlit by the setting sun. Would she and Brian have a house like this someday? The Swiss chalet–style house faced Lake Superior and had its own beach. A long pier reached out into the water where their large yacht, *Kitchigami Belle,* was anchored in the summer. Today, of course, there was no sign of water, just ice and snow as far as she could see.

Lauri fully intended to learn to sail that boat this summer. And she knew Dr. Parker would teach her. He liked her, even if Kade couldn't stand Brian. She liked Dr. Parker almost better than she did Brian. He was easy to talk to and not judgmental. He said that when he retired he'd take her and Brian on a long boat trip clear to the Atlantic.

She could be on a boat right now in California if not for Kade. She could be doing a lot of things, maybe even acting. A movie director might have seen her and signed her up if she'd just had the chance. But not here in Rock Harbor. The only thing she could do here was go crazy.

She swung her long legs out of the car, liking the way her tight jeans showed off their shape. Holding herself erect in a way that showed her figure to its best advantage, she carried the cookies to the house. She'd almost reached the door when a wave of sadness swept over her. Why couldn't someone love her for herself and not for her looks?

She longed to have her friends look up to her, to be a hero like Bree. Zorro had a long way to go though. An instant image of Anu's kind blue eyes swept through her mind. If she could help save Anu, it would be a start, even if it was only a start for her to respect herself.

She shook off her melancholy mood and pressed the doorbell

button firmly. A few moments later the door swung open, and Brian smiled at her with a look of pride. The possessive way he took her arm irritated her, and she pulled away.

"What?" he said.

"Don't jerk me around like some Barbie doll," she said. She stepped inside and pulled the door shut behind her.

He held up his hands defensively. "Well, excu-u-se me!" He stalked toward the family room.

Lauri, feeling oddly disconsolate, trailed after him. Brian plopped on the tan leather sofa in front of the TV. He pointedly ignored her, and Lauri knew he would stay that way until she apologized. As far as she was concerned, he could sulk awhile. She put the cookies on the counter then went to the small refrigerator behind the wet bar in one corner and got a beer.

Kade would have a cow if he knew she was drinking. But she liked the buzz it gave her. It had taken awhile to get past the taste though. She grimaced at the first swig then wiped her mouth with the back of her hand.

"Get me one too," Brian called.

Lauri obliged and sat beside him. She studied the curve of his jaw and the way his mustache was trying to grow in fits and starts of peach fuzz. "Brian, do you love me?" she asked softly.

"Sure I do, babe. I've told you plenty of times." He leaned over and leered at her. "And I could prove it once again. The old man is gone until at least eleven, and the sauna is just waiting for us."

Her eyes stinging with tears, Lauri looked away. She was the one who'd been asked to prove she loved him. If he really loved her, wouldn't he have wanted to wait until marriage? Wouldn't he have thought of her instead of what he wanted?

Brian huffed in exasperation when she failed to respond to his teasing. "What is with you lately, Lauri?"

"Sex is not all there is to love," she said in a muffled voice. She wouldn't look at him.

"I thought we'd have a fun time tonight, and you're acting like a prude. Has your brother been hammering at you to go to church again?" He sounded hurt, his little-boy act that usually brought her around to what he wanted. Tonight it left her cold.

Lauri didn't answer him. She got up and put her unfinished beer on the coffee table. "I think I'll go," she said.

Brian jumped to his feet and ran his finger down her cheek. "Hey, don't go. Everyone's going to be here in a half hour. I even got some champagne. Have you forgotten it's our six-month anniversary? We started going out six months ago today."

Lauri had forgotten, but it didn't matter. All she wanted was to be by herself. She shook off Brian's hand and rushed to the door then hurried down the driveway to her car.

Driving away from the house, she swallowed the lump that had formed in her throat. What was wrong with her? Brian loved her, and she was acting like an idiot. If she wasn't careful, Sarah Cappo would be only too glad to move right in.

She resisted the impulse to return to Brian's house and apologize. His attentions held no antidote for her pain. Anu would welcome her, but in spite of looking up to the older woman, she wasn't who Lauri wanted. She wanted her mother, and she wanted someone to love her. Weeping softly, she drove out to the cemetery.

Snowdrifts covered most of the headstones and should have made it difficult to find the one she wanted, but Lauri had been here so often she could have found it in the dark. She battled her way through the drifts to her parents' stone. Dropping to her knees, she brushed away the snow. She didn't want her parents to be the way she was, so cold and alone.

She looked at the graves. THEODORE JAMES MATTHEWS. LUCILLE MARIE MATTHEWS. When she had a baby, she was going to name it after one of her parents. No one had ever loved her like her mother and father.

She threw herself on top of the snow that mounded her mother's grave. "Mom, why did you leave me?" she wailed. "I'm so alone without you."

7he sheriff and his men were out in force the next few days looking for Quentin Siller, but he'd gone into hiding. Bree didn't care about Quentin. He was likely out of the state by now. She had much more important things on her mind, like seeing Anu now that she was back from Finland and preparing for Davy's first Easter back home with his family.

This was Bree's first Easter as a Christian, and though she'd been a part of the traditional dinner at Anu's ever since marrying Rob, this year the religious holiday held special meaning for her. Jesus had come up out of the grave, and he'd done so for *her*. She still couldn't fathom that kind of selfless love, especially when she thought of the way she'd treated Rob.

With Davy on her lap, and Kade and Lauri on either side of her, Bree couldn't imagine being any happier. The family deliberately avoided all mention of Quentin Siller and the body in the basement and concentrated on enjoying the day and one another.

Bree had attempted another apple pie. It was lopsided and a bit scorched on one side, though everyone assured her it was good. One bite of it herself and she got up and dumped it in the trash.

"It's not fit to eat," she said. "Next year it will be perfect. I'll listen to Julia more carefully next year. I was out of foil and didn't cover the edges."

She saw the grin Kade tried to hide and burst into laughter herself. "Just wait and see," she promised.

"Can I help you with the dishes?" Bree got up to follow Anu.

"I was about to challenge Davy to a game of Fish, so we'll pass," Kade said.

"Yeah!" Davy said, jumping up to run to the table where Anu kept his games.

"I'll help." Lauri followed them to the kitchen.

"I have the dishwasher," Anu said. "But I always want your company."

Bree began to scrape scraps onto a paper plate for Samson. "Does missing your husband at holidays get easier with time?"

Anu paused with a dish in her hand. "Abraham never enjoyed family meals. Sometimes I look back and wonder how we ever got together. We were so different. And after I became a Christian, our differences grew even more."

"I thought you'd always been a Christian," Lauri said, handing a plate to Bree. Her grin showed she wasn't serious.

Anu smiled. "Ah, I was a wild thing in my youth, though I know it is hard to imagine now when you see me as an old woman."

"You're not old!" Bree and Lauri said at the same time.

"You see through the eyes of love," Anu said, touching Lauri's nose. "But I wanted many things when I was young—pretty clothes, a nice house, perfect children. Things that should not have mattered. And Abraham liked having other men admire me, so he let me buy whatever I wanted. One day I went to church with a friend and saw for the first time how shallow my life was. My desires began to change when I met Christ a few weeks later. I often wonder if that is what really drove Abraham away. He knew the old wife was gone forever."

"A better one replaced the old," Bree said.

Anu smiled and began to load the dishwasher. "Not better, just redeemed."

Lauri didn't feel like staying home. Kade was parked in front of the television, and she aimlessly wandered through the kitchen. Though the day had gone well at Anu's Easter celebration, Lauri felt as if she'd been cooped up all day. She could bake cookies or make popcorn, but neither idea held any appeal.

"I'm going for a drive," she told Kade. She grabbed her keys and coat and went toward the door.

"Now?" Kade glanced at his watch. "It's nearly eight."

"I won't be gone long. I'll just run by the convenience store and get a soda and a candy bar. Want something?"

"Nah, I'll make popcorn if I get hungry. Want me to come with you?"

That was the last thing Lauri wanted. Being around him all day had been enough of a chore. She managed to bite back the retort hovering on her lips and merely shook her head. "See you later."

Lauri's thoughts turned back to the cedar chest as she made her way along the dimly lit streets. She needed to find out about those pictures, but who could she trust? Bree? She rejected that idea at once. Bree's first loyalty would be to Kade. Maybe Naomi would help her. Or Anu. But she hated to worry Anu until she knew what was going on. Naomi would be her best ally. Maybe she could find a time to talk to her when Bree wasn't around.

The gas pumps of Honkala Service Station were in sight when she saw Brian's car go whizzing by in the other direction. He was talking with obvious animation to Klepto, and neither one noticed her tentative wave. She pulled to the side of the road and turned around, intending to catch up with them and join in whatever plans they had for the evening. As she turned the car around, she saw Brian's taillights wink then go out. He was either driving with no lights or he'd stopped the car.

Curious now, Lauri put out her own lights and let the car inch forward along the side of Whisper Road, turning onto Echo Canyon Road. She had little trouble seeing in the bright moonlight. This road led to a dilapidated boat ramp no one used anymore. Lauri couldn't remember the last time she'd been down this way.

She thought the boat ramp was only a few more yards, so she killed the engine and got out quietly. What were the boys up to? Spying on them gave her the same rush as looking through other people's belongings. Brian would wig out if he knew what she was doing. She'd have to be careful.

She veered into the muddy grass where her footsteps would be muffled. The shape of Brian's car loomed in the darkness, and she slowed. She didn't see or hear either of the boys. Maybe they were still in the car.

But as she slid down a hill that led to the dock and Lake Superior, she heard voices. Angry voices. Her heart pounded in her ears. She dropped to her knees and crept to a thicket where the vegetation stopped and the sand began. Brian stood with hunched shoulders while another man berated him.

The sound of the waves hitting the beach muffled the inflection, but the words carried to where Lauri lay.

"This is the biggest haul of your career. I could have gotten any number of guys to help, but you swore I could trust you." He said something else, but the surf obscured the words.

Lauri couldn't make out the speaker's face in the darkness. Swathed in a heavy coat, he stood with his back to her hiding place. Maybe it was that Neville Brian had been talking about.

"It won't happen again," Brian mumbled.

"If it does, you're going to be feeding the fish in the lake. You just cost me nearly twenty thousand dollars."

"I ran out of gas."

The man slapped his palm against his forehead. "What was I thinking? That I expected you to be old enough to check stupid details like whether you had enough gas? I must have been crazy."

Lauri winced. Poor Brian. What had he missed by running out of gas?

"I'm sorry," Brian said. "I can go out now."

The man pushed Brian, and he fell to the ground. "It's too late now." The man swore and kicked Brian where he lay.

Lauri curled her fingers into her palms. She couldn't help him. Should she get back to her car and call for help on her cell phone? Was Brian in real danger?

Before she could decide what to do, the man swore again and grabbed Brian by the arm, hauling him to his feet. "I'll try to set it up again for Saturday. Don't disappoint me again."

"I won't, I swear." Brian was practically stammering.

"Saturday night. Nine o'clock. If you're late, you'd better turn tail and run."

Which was exactly what Lauri decided she'd better do. She shuddered to think what they'd do if they caught her here. She knew about part of Brian's "business," but this sounded more serious. She grabbed a root and tried to pull herself up the hill then lost her balance and tumbled into a bush. The vegetation rustled loudly.

"What's that?"

Galvanized by the alarm in the man's voice, Lauri shot to her feet and launched herself up the hill, all thought of maintaining secrecy lost. She heard feet pound after her, but she had a head start and reached her car in time to speed away as two figures crested the hill. Hopefully, they were too far away to identify her or her car.

Her throat tight with fear, she slammed her foot to the accelerator and pointed the Plymouth toward home.

*T*he strobe of the Fresnel lens in the lighthouse guided Bree home. The holiday had been as perfect as Anu knew how to make it. Bree thought of the way Anu shone Jesus' light to everyone she met. If Bree could be a light that led others to Jesus, her life would have meaning and purpose. It was all very well and good to rescue lost people—how much more lasting to rescue their souls. Stopping the car in front of the lighthouse, she resolved to do better at emulating Anu.

Samson began growling softly when Bree opened the car door. "What's wrong, boy?" she asked. The hair on the back of her neck prickled, and she stared into the darkness. Was it Quentin? She'd never been afraid here in Rock Harbor.

Bree looked around for something she could use as a weapon, but all she found was a flashlight. It would have to do. She ran the window down and listened in the darkness. The last two days had brought spring temperatures, and Lake Superior was beginning to thaw. The sound of the ice cracking in the lake mingled with the howling of wolves in the forest, a familiar but spine-chilling sound.

She was getting spooked for no reason, though Samson continued to growl. Maybe she should let him out. She leaned across the seat and opened the passenger door. Barking, the dog leaped out and ran off into the darkness.

"Hey!" A man's voice came from the bushes across the street.

Should she get out? She glanced into the backseat where Davy lay sleeping. She heard Samson yelp, and that settled her dilemma. She jumped out of the car and pressed the remote to lock the Jeep. With the flashlight held high, she rushed to help her dog.

"Samson!" Her dog's barking grew to a frenzied pitch; then he yelped again. A man's deep voice swore viciously, then the bushes parted, and she saw Samson tackle a dark form. Samson had his feet planted as he tugged at the man's jacket. The dog skidded on the melting snow, and the man pulled free. He raced toward the woods and disappeared into the trees.

Bree called Samson to her when he would have chased the man. Samson barked and pranced back to Bree with his head and tail in an obvious victory stance. "Good boy." She knelt and ran her hands over him. There was no sign of any injury, and she was thankful for that. He'd probably been kicked, but he was burly and hard with muscle. Glancing around into the dark night, she shivered. It had been too dark to tell for sure, but she thought it might have been Quentin. Something about the man's outline seemed familiar.

Her hands shook as she unfastened Davy's car seat and carried him inside. He'd somehow managed to sleep through all the commotion. She placed Davy in bed and pulled off his new cowboy boots. He murmured but didn't awaken as she undressed him and slipped him into his pajamas.

Leaving Samson on guard, she went downstairs to call Mason. But first she turned on every light in the house. Maybe it wasn't the smart thing to do, but it made her feel safer. Mason promised to be right over. His worried tone made her own uneasiness grew.

She started to go out to unload the Easter baskets and leftovers she'd brought home from Anu's, then hesitated in the entry hall. Her neck still prickled, and she tried to tell herself not to be silly. She glanced out the door window, but there was no sign of movement. She might as well wait for Mason. No sense in taking any chances.

The phone rang, and her pulse kicked into overdrive at the sudden sound. She put a hand to her stomach and laughed hollowly at the way the ring had spooked her. She grabbed the receiver. "Hello," she said. There was only silence on the other end. "Hello?" Bree said.

"You're gonna pay," a man's voice growled. "You're gonna wish you'd kept your pretty nose out of my business. Thanks to you I've lost everything. I'm going to see you do the same, starting with that dog of yours."

Her heart slammed against her ribs with the force of a ship hitting the rocky Superior shore. "Quentin? Listen, there's no need to go trying to scare me. We all just want you to get some help and get back home with your family."

He gave a harsh laugh. "Scared now, aren't you? You're going to be even more scared by the time I'm through with you."

She heard the phone slam down on the other end, and Bree gripped the receiver with white knuckles as the dial tone echoed in her ear. She clicked off the phone and put it down on the table. That must have been him outside. She saw headlights through the window and grabbed her coat and went outside.

Mason got out of his car. "Where was he?"

"There." Bree showed him where the man had tussled with Samson, and while he probed she unloaded her Jeep. The cracking of the ice had intensified and sounded ominous in the warm spring air.

"Found a few cigarette butts, nothing much," Mason reported a few minutes later. "I'll have a deputy keep an eye out. Sounds like he's wanting to scare you more than anything."

"He's doing a good job of it," she said. She told Mason about the call.

He scowled. "I'll have a tap put on your phone. We'll find him. Try not to worry."

She nodded. Focusing on Quentin Siller was something she was determined not to do. She wouldn't let fear take control of her. God was in charge, not Quentin. God would watch over her and Davy. She had to cling to that knowledge.

"Any news about the skeleton?"

"I took a look at the leather book. It's a lighthouse keeper's jour-nal. A man named Peter Thorrington. I'm trying to see what I can find about Thorrington now."

"Did you read all of it?"

"Yeah, but it's no help. It just documents details about the run-ning of the lighthouse."

"You think the skeleton is Thorrington?"

"Maybe. It makes sense. We'll see." He pressed her shoulder. "I'll have a man watch the house tonight. I'll mosey around out-side until you lock up."

Bree went inside and locked the house then waved to Mason from the window to let him know everything was all right. She closed the blinds and put on a Twila Paris CD that Anu had given her for Christmas. Just this morning she'd read in the Bible, in the book of Philippians, that she should focus on things that are true and good and praiseworthy. She'd give it a try.

The weather had broken, and melted snow ran like new creeks from the roads and heaped snowdrifts. The town paper's article about the discovery of the remains in Bree's basement was picked up by the state papers on Tuesday. Both motels in Rock Harbor were filled with reporters.

On Wednesday, Kade stopped over at the Kitchigami SAR Training Center to check on Bree. She was outside with Naomi and four students with their dogs. Bree's new training center was a pole building about thirty by thirty feet that sat in a tract of land surrounded by woods. The lake behind the building was perfect for water-search training. It had been open only since the first of the year, but Bree already had some good students. Kade ran his window down and watched for a while.

"Take your dogs around back where they can't see," Bree instructed. "Cassie, you stay here. You can be the victim today."

Kade had never seen the woman Bree called Cassie. She stood off by herself as though she didn't want anyone to talk to her. Dressed in army boots and fatigues, she wore her blond hair short and curly like Bree's.

The rest of the students took the dogs around the building. Cassie got in what Kade had been told was a scratch box, a rough wooden box with a guillotine-type door. Bree dropped the door into position. Carrying a bag with the scent article, she went around the corner.

Kade grinned and stretched out his legs. He never got tired of watching the dogs work. He couldn't make out what Bree was saying, but he'd watched often enough to get the gist of it. The dogs were smelling the scent article, and the students would release each dog individually and see how long it took them to find Cassie in the box.

He heard a bark, then Charley, Naomi's golden retriever, came racing around the corner. He drove straight for the scratch box, jumping up on it and barking. He grabbed a stick on the ground then carried it to Naomi with his tail held high in triumph. Naomi praised him, rubbing his ears.

Each of the dogs got a chance. Zorro took the longest, nosing around the meadow nearly five minutes before catching the air scent. All the dogs eventually found Cassie. Kade got out of the car and strolled toward the group.

"Good dog," Naomi said, rubbing Zorro's head. "One of these days Lauri and Zorro will be as famous as Bree and Samson."

Kade didn't miss the expression of gratitude on his sister's face at Naomi's praise for Zorro. Naomi slung her arm around the girl's shoulders, and they walked over to await Bree's final instructions.

While Bree was talking, Samson ambled over to meet Kade, and he ruffled the dog's ears. Too bad Davy didn't show this much excitement when Kade came over. He wondered if the little boy was napping inside the building. When Bree finished giving the class instructions for the underwater cadaver search that would be done on the weekend, she dismissed everyone. Naomi and Lauri walked off together. Kade tried not to be hurt by the way his sister ignored him.

Bree smiled when she saw him. "I noticed your truck."

"I like to watch you work," he said. "Where's Davy?"

"Hilary took him out for lunch." She nodded toward a television van parked across the road with a camera trained on her.

"These reporters are driving me crazy. Who would have thought old bones would generate so much attention?"

Kade linked arms with her, and they turned toward the building. "It's because of the lighthouse connection. It brings to mind spooky old buildings, pirates, and buried treasure. Unsolved murders are always interesting. I'm fascinated myself."

"So they're saying it's murder now? Has Mason announced that officially? I haven't talked to him today."

Kade shrugged. "Mason just says it's suspicious, though the forensics team hasn't reported back yet. He told me there was a report that the last lighthouse keeper disappeared. That's when the light was shut down. No one ever learned what happened to him."

"Peter Thorrington," Bree said.

"How do you know?"

"Remember that leather book? It was Thorrington's lighthouse journal. Nothing of interest in it, Mason says."

Kade took her arm and they went toward the SAR center. Inside the building, Bree moved over by the window and settled cross-legged on the floor beside Samson. Samson yawned, then moved over to plop his head on her lap. She absently played with his ears, and the dog gave a sigh of contentment. Kade could understand it; he'd like to be in Samson's place. She picked up a brush and began to work it through the burrs in his coat.

Bree sighed heavily. "I'm exhausted."

Bree *looked* beat. Dark circles bloomed under her eyes, and the flesh around them looked puffy. "Did you get any sleep last night?"

"Not much. Davy had another nightmare. Easter was so busy, and I think he's remembering more and more of his daddy."

Kade winced inwardly. Bree was dealing with so much, though he knew she didn't begrudge her son one minute of the attention he needed. "Want to go to the movies with me and Lauri Friday?"

She finally looked up and met his gaze. "You're taking her out?"

"Yep. She wasn't what I'd call overly excited, but at least she agreed to go. I had to bribe her with shopping, though." He laughed, but the fact hurt. Two years ago she was pestering him to take her to the movies all the time.

"I'd better stay out of the picture. You need this time alone together. Besides, I hardly think she'd like to see the new Disney film Davy wants to see."

She probably was right. Lauri would probably take Bree's presence as another sign she wasn't important to him. He glanced at his watch. "I guess I'd better get going."

She pushed Samson off her lap and stood, brushing the hair from her jeans. "Let me know how it goes, okay?"

A well of deep longing took him by surprise. He reached out and tucked a red-gold curl behind her ear then traced his fingers along her jaw line. Her green eyes darkened at his touch, and he leaned forward and embraced her. The light scent she wore, something woodsy and enticing, slipped up his nose in a heady rush. Her head nestled against his chest at just the right height.

He kissed the top of her head. Times like these were too few and far between. "I've missed you," he whispered. "Seems like lately we haven't had time to say two words to each other. Can we plan a date soon, just the two of us?"

Her head nodded against his chest. "I'd like that."

He pulled away, then touched his fingers to her chin, tilting her lips up to meet his. The kiss was warm and undemanding, and he kept his love for her tightly in check, though it was getting more difficult all the time. Kade knew in his heart that they belonged together. They were just waiting on timing.

Releasing her, he turned toward the door still holding her hand. "Pray for us."

"Always," she said.

*K*ade spent the next two days working on the baby-wildlife center. It was ready to receive its first occupants. Landorf drifted by on Friday morning to look it over.

"Remember what I said," he warned. "No animals other than endangered species." Kade stopped forking hay into pens and pushed his hat back from his face. "I'd like to talk to you about that some more," he said.

"I've said all I'm going to say about it," Landorf barked, stalking away.

Watching him go, Kade realized he was going to have to make that phone call to Landorf's superiors. Something had to be done. The wildlife-center project had been approved by Washington, and Landorf was set on squashing the plan.

Kade worked all day, then went home to meet his sister. Lauri was waiting when he got to the cabin. Dressed in jeans with holes in the knees and a red sweatshirt, she looked about twelve. Love tightened Kade's throat. She had no idea how important she was to him, but he could try to show her even if she refused to accept it.

"You mean I get to take out the prettiest girl in Rock Harbor all by myself?" He grinned and handed her a tiny bouquet of flowers he'd bought at the florist on the way through town.

Lauri looked at them as though they were some alien species. "What are you up to?" she asked, her eyebrows lifted in suspicion.

Kade sighed. "Nothing, Lauri. I just wanted you to know how happy I am that you're going to come with me today."

"You think I'm a thief and a juvenile delinquent who breaks into cabins," she reminded him.

"Can we just forget our fight and have a good time today?" He held on to his temper by a thread. She tossed her head and grabbed her coat, a fake fur thing that swathed her in fuzz and made her look even more like a little girl, though Kade knew better than to tell her so.

"This is going to be a long night," she muttered.

Trying not to feel hurt was like rolling a snowball uphill: It could be done, but he had to be careful or the effort would overwhelm him. He buttoned his curt response and just smiled. "Where do you want to eat?" He held the door open for her.

She shrugged. "I don't care. I'm dieting."

He opened his mouth to tell her she was too thin then closed it again. She wouldn't listen to him anyway. His throat tight, he followed her to the truck, and they drove to the Suomi Café in silence broken only by the radio blaring some music that was too mumbled to make out the words.

His nerves were thrumming like drums by the time they reached town. Lauri ordered a chicken pasty, and he got a beef one. "We're as predictable as heavy snow in January," he remarked as Molly turned to go to the kitchen with their order.

Lauri made a face and took a sip of her drink. Across from her in the booth, he watched the expressions on her face: boredom, disdain, maybe even a little fear. What could they talk about? He didn't know how to reach her anymore. This was harder than he'd expected.

"How was school this week?"

"Fine." She fiddled with her straw and looked out the window.

"Where did you and Brian go last week?"

She turned her head to glare at him. "What is this, twenty questions? If I'd known I was going to get the third degree, I wouldn't have come."

He held up his hands. "Sorry. What would you like to talk about?

I was just trying to make conversation." Her wary expression soft-ened, and he knew she'd been expecting him to come back at her with angry words.

She shrugged. "Why don't you like Brian?"

Kade hesitated. He wanted peace with Laurie, but what good was that without honesty? "He's not good enough for you." What a cliché that sounded. But it was totally true. Brian Parker was trouble.

"You think no boy is good enough. What's wrong with him?"

"He's wild, he has too much money to blow, Dr. Parker doesn't keep tabs on him at all, and he's too old for you."

"He's only eighteen!"

"There's a world of difference between sixteen and eighteen. I worry he'll pressure you . . ." His voice trailed away. He wasn't about to bring up sex with her.

"To what? Sleep with him?" She blew her bangs out of her eyes with an exasperated huff. "So what?"

His heart froze. "Are you saying you have?"

"I'm not saying anything. You're impossible!"

Kade swallowed. "Talk to me, Lauri. Tell me how you're feeling. Is Brian pushing you?" He longed to have the boy's scrawny neck beneath his fingers. He'd teach him to leave Lauri alone.

Lauri looked away, and Kade saw the indecision on her face, the longing to talk to him. Molly brought their food just as Lauri opened her mouth. She shut it again and looked down at her plate, her hands in her lap. The moment was lost. Kade stared at his plate, his appetite gone.

He picked up his pasty and took a bite. It was as tasteless as clay. Lauri picked up hers as well, but before she bit into it, two young men stopped at their booth. In their early twenties, they had a hard look that made Kade wary.

"Hey, Lauri, could you give Brian a message for me?" The oldest, a young man with sleepy eyes, thrust an envelope in her hand. "Here."

"Sure." Lauri stuck it in her purse in such haste she nearly knocked over her soda.

She avoided Kade's gaze, and his uneasiness increased. "Aren't you going to introduce me to your friends?" Kade stood and held out his hand. "I'm Kade Matthews, Lauri's brother."

"The ranger man?" The three exchanged handshakes. "How's it goin'?" The pair backed away and turned toward the door without waiting for a reply. "See you around, Lauri."

What were they trying to hide? Kade's thoughts turned again to the break-ins at the cabins. "What's the note?"

"Search me."

"I don't want you in the middle of it, Lauri. I think you should let me see the note."

"No way!" Her blue eyes glittered with rage. "Stay out of my business, Kade!"

"I can't. I'm your brother and I love you."

"Then leave me alone." She burst into tears.

Her sobs unnerved Kade, and he finished his meal in silence.

The wheezy call of a phoebe came from the maple tree above Lauri's head. Spring was her favorite time of year. The bleak hopelessness of winter usually melted away with the heavy snow cover, swelling the Kitchigami River to near flood levels. Green tips of wildflowers pushed through the brown carpet of matted, dead leaves. A trout splashed in the river as if in joyous wonder at the warm sun.

Lauri sat on a large rock with Zorro at her feet. Everyone was here for training today: Eva Nardi, Lauri, Ryan Erickson, Cassie Hecko, Karen Siller, and Naomi.

Zorro lay panting on the ground. Most of the dogs were off chasing rabbits. Bree had worked them hard today. Zorro was even too tired to chase the sparrow scrabbling in the leaves five feet away from his nose. Davy played with Samson, though the dog was too tired to do more than walk after the Frisbee the little boy tossed.

"I have an extra candy bar if anyone wants one." Lauri dug into her pocket and pulled out two Snickers bars.

"I've got my pistachios," Bree said. Shells lay around her like confetti.

"I'll take it," Eva said. She grabbed the candy bar. She settled back against the tree trunk and munched her candy in silence as usual.

"You're lucky you haven't turned green, Bree," Eva said. Blond and blue-eyed, Eva reminded Lauri of a Nordic goddess. Twenty-five and nearly six feet tall, she towered over Bree and Lauri. She stretched like a lazy cougar in the warmth, obviously relishing paramedic Ryan Erickson's gaze on her.

Eva had fascinated Lauri from the moment they met. She seemed so self-assured, so . . . *everything* Lauri would like to be. Lauri had been digging for information about her private life but so far had been unsuccessful. When anyone asked Eva about her family, she changed the subject.

"She is green. She's just covered it up with makeup," Naomi said.

Bree grinned, then dusted the pistachio shells from her hands and stood. "You bunch of wimps ready to get back to work yet?"

"Please, anything but that," Lauri moaned. "First you dragged me out of bed at seven o'clock on a Saturday, and now you're cracking the whip before I even get my candy bar eaten. What a slave driver!"

Bree twirled an imaginary mustache. "And zat is only ze beginning, my little chickadee! Soon you vill be begging for someone to save you."

Lauri giggled. "I'm already begging. You want me on my knees?" She slipped off the rock onto her knees in the mud and clasped her hands together. "Oh please, please, let's quit. Zorro is begging too. He's ready to hide in the brambles."

Bree tipped her head to one side and looked at the girls. "Come on, one more search. You're not tired, are you, Eva?"

Eva gave a shamefaced grin. "I admit I'm bushed as well. I was up a little late last night."

Her guilty expression made Lauri bite the inside of her mouth to keep from laughing out loud. "New boyfriend?"

"No, the same one. I wanted him to stay over last night, but he gave me some excuse about having to get up early for work. He didn't leave until three, and I got up at six for the training."

Bree frowned. "Eva, you want someone who will love you for

yourself, not just hang around for sex."

Lauri looked away but watched Eva and Bree out of the corner of her eye. It shocked her to hear Bree echo the very thoughts she'd had about Brian. She rubbed the grass beneath her hand and tried to be invisible.

Eva waved a hand in the air as if she didn't care, but her face grew pink and she looked away. "Bree, this isn't the Victorian era. You don't have to marry a man to sleep with him. I just want to be happy."

"And are you?" Bree's voice was hushed, and she glanced at Lauri.

"Hey, I'm not eight," Lauri said. "This is a discussion I'm interested in. Did you sleep with your husband before you were married, Bree?"

Bree bit her lip, and her eyes darkened. "No, but not because of any morals of my own, I'm sorry to say. Rob was a Christian, and he always treated me like I was special. I didn't understand at the time, but after we were married, I was glad we'd waited. It made it something special. I'm ashamed to admit Rob wasn't the first though." Her voice was low, and she didn't look at any of them.

Karen laughed shakily. "We all make mistakes. Look at the mess my life is in." She tugged a handful of grass loose and let it drift through her fingers.

Cassie looked away as if the intense emotion in the group was getting to her. Ryan cleared his throat and bent over to tie his shoe, clearly wishing he were somewhere else.

Lauri kept her gaze on the efforts of an ant on a log by her hand. The ant was struggling with a burden many times larger than it was, a feeling Lauri knew only too well. That was how her relationship with Brian made her feel—weighed down. But she didn't know how to change. Her friends would make fun of her if she ditched a hottie like Brian. The trouble was, he *knew* he was all that.

She glanced at Naomi. Maybe this was something she could discuss with her.

"Well, religion is fine for you, but leave me out of your little fantasy," Eva said. She smiled, but the strain didn't leave her eyes. "My dad tried to beat religion into me, and it never took then, so don't expect it to take now."

Bree smiled. "A very wise woman once told me it's not about religion, it's about a relationship with God. I thought she was crazy at the time, but she was so right."

"I love being right," Naomi said with a smug grin.

"Come on, let's do one more search." Bree held out her hand to Eva. "Call your dogs." She waited until the dogs were all at their owners' feet. "I've hidden some of Donovan's dirty socks in various places."

Naomi grinned. "Do you promise to wash them when we're done?"

"I thought you'd want to train Donovan to do that."

"Ha! He's looking forward to turning that job over to me."

Lauri grinned. Being around Naomi always lifted her spirits. The dogs sniffed the scent article, another sock.

"Search, Zorro," Lauri said. She wanted him to shine today. He was young and high-spirited with potential, but so far he'd meandered aimlessly while the rest of the dogs raced right to the quarry. If she could be like Naomi and Bree, maybe her life would be worth something. The first chance she got, she would tell Naomi about what she had found at the cabin. She'd vacillated long enough.

Zorro ran back and forth across the clearing, his nose in the air. The next minute he raced toward a heap of rocks on the west side of the Kitchigami Search and Rescue headquarters. He began to bark.

Bree smiled. "Looks like he's getting the hang of it."

By the time each of the other dogs had found a scent article, it was nearly three o'clock. Even though all she wanted to do was go home and take a nap, Lauri knew she couldn't put off talking to Naomi. She followed Bree and Naomi into the pole barn that served as search headquarters.

The facility was plain and serviceable with concrete floors and bins for storing vests, scent articles, and gear. Bree's office was at the back. Glassed in, it held a battered gray desk and an old filing cabinet for their case files.

Bree headed that direction now. "Davy, Samson needs a bath. You want to do the honors?"

"Yeah!" Davy scampered forward.

The dog perked up his ears at the mention of "bath." He stood and yawned, then padded expectantly toward the doggy wash area.

Bree laughed. "Before long we'll need to start checking for ticks too. I'll get the water started."

"Charley needs a bath too." Naomi tugged at her dog's collar, and he whined. He didn't enjoy a bath nearly as much as Samson did.

"Want to clean Zorro up?" Bree asked Lauri.

"He needs it. But I was wanting to talk to Naomi about something."

Bree's eyebrows raised. "Davy and I will take care of the dogs then. Feel free to use my office. Stay as long as you like. I need to run over to the library."

Naomi dropped her ready-pack off her back. "Just a minute, Lauri. Let me put my equipment away."

Great. More time to think. Just what she didn't want. Lauri sank onto the brown sofa at the back of the office. Bree's open Bible lay on the coffee table, and Lauri picked it up. A passage in 1 Peter was underlined in red.

Your beauty should not come from outward adornment, such as braided hair and the wearing of gold jewelry and fine clothes. Instead, it should be that of your inner self, the unfading beauty of a gentle and quiet spirit, which is of great worth in God's sight.

Lauri put down the Bible as if it were hot. What kind of attention could a girl get by following that advice?

Naomi stepped back into the office. "Want a soda? Bree usually has Pepsi and Dr. Pepper."

"I'd love a Dr. Pepper."

Naomi got them both a soda from the small refrigerator. "I baked some oatmeal cookies last night. Have one?"

Lauri took a cookie and bit into it. "These are good."

Naomi took a cookie too. "What's up?"

Laurie set the cookie on the edge of Bree's desk. "It's kind of hard to talk about. I don't want to worry you, but I think you should know. Will you promise me to keep this to yourself?"

Naomi looked at her sharply. "I'll try. But I care about you, Lauri. If Kade needs to know something in order to help you, I might have to tell him. I can't promise."

Lauri bit her lip and took a deep breath. "Okay, I guess that will have to do. Um, my friends and I, well, we like to hang out at the cabins along the Lake. I know we're not supposed to break in, but at least we don't have grownups watching every move we make. We don't hurt anything."

Naomi was frowning. "Breaking and entering? You could get arrested, Lauri."

"Now you sound like Kade."

"Kade knows you're doing this? I thought you said he couldn't be told."

Lauri shrugged. "He suspects. We're done now though. Everyone will be coming back for the season, so don't stress. That's not what I needed to tell you."

"Oh, sorry. Go on."

"I found something at the last cabin we were in. Something that kind of scared me."

Naomi's eyes widened. "Okay, I'm listening."

Gaining confidence now that Naomi wasn't grabbing the phone to call Mason or Kade, Lauri continued. "I found a chest there with pictures in it. Pictures of Anu and even Hilary and Bree's husband when they were kids. There was a picture of Bree and Davy too. And scary stuff like handcuffs and loaded guns."

"A picture of Davy? Where is this cabin? Maybe Mason can catch him there."

"You know who it is?"

Naomi nodded. "I bet it's Quentin Siller. Maybe that's where he's hiding out."

"I don't know, Naomi," Lauri said, frowning. "It was a lot of stuff. There's even school drawings with Bree's husband's name on them."

But Naomi wasn't listening. "Look, you've got to take me out there. We need to check this out."

"You're not telling Mason, are you?"

Naomi hesitated. "I guess not," she said. "I don't want to get you in trouble. Let's see what it is first." She glanced at her watch. "We have about three hours before I have to be at a bridal shower."

two-story stone structure, the Rock Harbor Carnegie Library was on Jack Pine Lane in the block behind Nicholls' Finnish Imports. The children's library was on the first-floor walk-out basement level. It sported a bank of computers, donated by Dr. Max Parker three years ago, and bright, colorful posters. The wood shelves were low enough for children to reach with ease.

Thankfully, the library was deserted. Bree didn't have time for any chats today. She frowned at the microfiche machine. It had been ages since she used one of these. Who knew when Rock Harbor would be able to afford new technology? It was nearly an hour before she found what she was looking for.

She printed out the article on the former lighthouse keeper, Peter Thorrington, and stuffed it in her purse. Glancing at her watch, she rushed toward the door. If she was late to Naomi's shower, she was dead meat.

*T*he cabin looked innocuous enough. Naomi parked the car down the road and got out. "It looks deserted," she whispered to Lauri.

Zorro whined in the back, and Lauri let him out. "Quiet," she told him.

Naomi grabbed the binoculars from the front seat and trained the lenses on the cabin. "Nothing's stirring there," she told Lauri.

Lauri didn't know if she was relieved or disappointed. "Come on." Lauri led the way through the bare trees, quickly covering the muddy ground.

The door to the cabin was firmly closed. "You think it's locked?"

"It wasn't last time I was here."

"We can't break in," Naomi said. "This is park property. I'll look through the window to the bedroom. If it's like you said, I'll call Mason in. Which way?"

Lauri pointed out the bedroom window. "You can boost me. I'll look." She led the way to the window. Naomi interlaced her fingers, and Lauri hoisted herself aloft to peer in the window. The grimy window made it hard to see into the dark interior. She waited a minute until her eyes adjusted. "Oh no!" she gasped.

"What is it?" Naomi huffed breathlessly.

"It's gone!" Lauri frantically rubbed at the window, but the view didn't change. "The bedroom is totally empty. Looks like whoever was living here moved everything out."

*T*he man shifted from his hiding place long enough to startle a rabbit, then melted back into the shadows. He couldn't be seen. Not yet. His gaze never wavered from the neat white house across the street. It could have been sitting on a hillside in Finland.

They may have taken Anu Nicholls out of Finland, but they would never succeed in taking Finland out of her. He was eager for today's first sight of her. He gave a bark of laughter. He brought the binoculars to his eyes and focused on the house's picture window. A slim figure came into view, and his fingers tightened on the binoculars. It wasn't time to move yet. But soon.

*T*hanks for helping me, you guys." Bree walked with Naomi and Lauri as the dogs ran ahead. "I've been jumping at every shadow and second-guessing every sound since Naomi told me about the cedar chest at her shower yesterday. You're a good friend to let us know about this, Lauri. If Davy or Anu is in danger, we need to stop this guy."

Lauri followed silently. She cast a glare of resentment Naomi's way. She'd thought she could trust her. If this got back to Kade, Lauri was in big trouble. "You think the dogs can help?" she asked Bree. She tossed a stick to Zorro, and he raced to grab it and bring it back to her.

"Can't hurt," Naomi said. "If the dogs can pick up on the last people to be on the porch, maybe they can track him to his lair."

She stepped onto the porch and went to the door. "Samson, come." Her dog ran to her, his tail wagging. "Come here, boy." The others followed with their dogs.

"Take a sniff, Samson." She pointed at the doorknob. He thrust his nose against the door then whined. The other dogs sniffed around the porch too; then Bree rubbed Samson's ears. "Search, boy!"

He whined again, then ran through the door and out into the meadow. His tail held high, he ran back and forth across the meadow trying to get a scent. At one point it looked as though he might have picked up something, but he stopped at the end of the road with a despondent air.

"This car must have had its windows up," Naomi said.

Bree nodded. "At least it was worth a try. I've got to find Quentin. And soon."

*T*he afternoon sunshine pouring through the windows onto the light maple floor felt like a blessing from God, something Bree needed this Saturday morning. She was about to lose her best friend. Maybe that was a bit melodramatic, but things changed when a friend got married. Naomi would no longer have the freedom to just pick up and go with Bree whenever she wanted. But that was okay. Naomi deserved this happiness.

She stretched and looked around. Anu's shop made her feel safe. Even Davy seemed most content when he was playing at his grandmother's feet here. The scent of new clothes on the racks and *pulla* from the bakery mingled into an aroma of well-being that warmed her. Bree glanced across the display table to where her son crouched on the floor with his crayons and Superman coloring book. Samson lounged nearby.

Anu caught her gaze and smiled, and the peace in it brought an answering smile to Bree's face. She and her mother-in-law were soul mates, and there was nowhere Bree would rather be than right here with Anu and Davy. But there was a lot to do this afternoon. Thankfully, the store was nearly empty of customers.

Anu must have seen her fidgeting. "You must not fret. Everything will be done. It does not all fall on you, *kulta*. Eini has already gone over to help." Anu's employee was also the church wedding coordinator.

"I know, but Naomi is depending on me." Bree had never stood up with anyone before, and the thought made her stomach flutter. It seemed somehow appropriate since her best friend was about to start a new life.

"Yoo-hoo!" Hilary's voice echoed from the entry.

Bree's sister-in-law came through the door. "Wonderful day, isn't it?" Hilary hugged her mother, then dropped a kiss on her nephew's head. There was a hidden excitement in her manner that made Bree study her face. She even gave Bree a hug.

"Any news on my skeleton or Quentin Siller?" Bree asked.

Hilary sat beside Bree and poured a cup of coffee from the carafe on the counter. "Forensics is checking the dental records. Apparently a skeleton that old doesn't rate any speed when there are current crimes to be working on. We'll know something soon. Nothing on Quentin though. Mason is pursuing the Peter Thorrington angle while he waits to hear the autopsy results."

"Peter Thorrington. For many years his name was always on Abraham's lips," Anu said.

Bree sat up in surprise. "What do you remember about him?" she asked, glancing surreptitiously at her watch. Naomi would be expecting her, but this was important too.

Anu continued to unpack boxes. "He and Abraham were good friends. The four of them—my husband, Peter Thorrington, Gary Landorf, and Max Parker—did everything together. They ran a charter business for a time and also did some ship salvage. They fished together, and we wives spent much time together as well. I miss those days." Her smile was sad. "I have been thinking about the old days ever since Mason suggested that your skeleton might be Peter." She held out her hand, adorned with a green ring, to Hilary. "I found this a few weeks ago and have been wearing it ever since. It's an emerald."

Hilary took her mother's hand for a closer look.

"Your father gave it to me just before he left us. He said something about it tiding me over through rainy days. As if I would sell it! Though I must admit there were times I considered it. It has been in my cedar chest for years."

"It will look perfect with your dress," Hilary said. "It's probably not worth much though; the color isn't very good. Typical of my father." Her voice was full of disgust.

"When did Peter disappear?" Bree asked.

Anu twisted the ring on her finger. "The last day I saw Abraham was the day after Peter disappeared. So it would have been June 12, 1976," she said decisively. "Beulah—Peter's wife—she was never the same after that. Many in town wondered if she had drowned Peter. He was not the most faithful of husbands. But she would be incapable of something like that." She glanced at Bree. "His widow has the landscaping business on the edge of town, Beulah's Bounty."

"I know that nursery." Bree nodded. "Did you ever suspect foul play?" Bree began to wonder about the timing. Could Abraham have had anything to do with Thorrington's death? She rejected the idea at once. Anu would never have married someone capable of murder. Still, people change.

"Not at first. The authorities questioned Beulah but never accused her, though as I said, many wondered."

Hilary nodded. "Mason intends to investigate thoroughly. If he can get his mind on it after our news this morning."

She smiled with a radiance Bree had never seen in her before. Something was up. Hilary seemed about to burst with suppressed excitement. "Spill it," Bree commanded.

Hilary needed no more encouragement. "I'm pregnant!" She clapped her hands together, and her pale complexion held a blush that brightened her eyes.

"Oh, my *kulta!*" Anu cried out. She held out her arms, and Hilary stood and rushed into them.

Both women began to weep, and Bree found tears in her own eyes.

"What's going on, Mommy?" Davy asked, his green eyes wide.

"You're going to have a new baby cousin," Bree said, scooping him up and holding him close.

He wiggled to get away, and Bree tried not to show the hurt. She put him down. Was she smothering him, or was there really something that was causing Davy to pull away from her? Give him time, everyone said. She worried that time would just make him too grown up to want her hugs, and then she would have missed everything.

She managed a smile and went to embrace her sister-in-law. "I'm so happy for you, Hilary," she said. "You've been trying for so long. God is good, isn't he?"

Hilary nodded, her eyes misty. "Mason is just giddy. I ran a home test two days ago, then visited the doctor this morning."

Davy went up to his aunt. "Where's my baby cousin? I want a boy cousin."

Hilary picked him up. "I'll see what I can do. The baby is in my tummy right now, and it will be a long time before it's ready to come play with you."

Davy smiled and patted Hilary's face. He seemed to have no trouble with his aunt's affection. Bree swallowed the lump in her throat. She just had to be patient. God had miraculously saved Davy. She could only trust he would work things out in this area too.

Looking at her watch, Bree gasped at the time. "I've got to go! The wedding is in two hours."

"Can I stay with Grammy?" Davy asked. Hilary put him down and he went to stand by Anu.

Bree's gaze went to Anu, and her mother-in-law nodded. "Go along, *kulta*," Anu said. "I will bring him to the church at the proper time."

"His clothes are in the Jeep. I'll get them."

Her son preened. "I have a new suit," he confided to his grandmother.

"And I'm sure you will look very handsome today," Anu said. "Give your mommy a kiss before she goes."

Bree knelt. He kissed her quickly, and she managed to keep from pulling him into her arms. She had to give him space.

Rock Harbor Community Church overlooked the town from its perch on Quincy Street. Festive streamers flew from the portico, and the sign out front announced the upcoming nuptials. What could be seen of the sign above the still-melting snowdrifts, that is. Inside the church, chaos reigned. Men were bringing in extra chairs to line the aisles for overflow seating, the florist was arranging altar and pew flowers, and the caterer was bringing in equipment for the final food preparation.

Bree walked through the church back to the nursery where Naomi said she would be getting ready. It was the handiest place since it had a rest room with mirrors as well. She entered the room and found just as much activity in the nursery. Clad only in her slip and pantyhose, Naomi sat in a chair while hairdresser Sally Wilson worked on her. Sally was trying to pile the brown tresses on Naomi's head, but the straight, fine locks refused to cooperate and strands hung in Naomi's eyes.

Martha Heinonen was going through a box of corsages and boutonnieres at a child's table. She and her best friend, Sheila McDonald, looked ridiculous perched on stools meant for three-year-olds.

"Bree, there you are!" Martha said. "Naomi was fretting that you'd been called away."

"I would have to be tied up or knocked out to miss this wedding," Bree said.

"My hair is just not working." Naomi sounded near tears. "Maybe I should just wear it down like I always do."

"I like your hair down," Bree said. "Besides, if you don't even look like yourself, you may hate your wedding pictures."

Naomi brightened. "Oh, you're right."

"All brides wear their hair up," Martha said.

"I didn't," Bree said.

"You have short hair," Martha said.

"I didn't then." It was going to be hard to keep from thinking about her own wedding day.

"Bree's right, Mom," Naomi said. "I want to look like myself." She raked her fingers through her hair, and hairpins flew like confetti.

Sally put her hands on her hips. "I just spent an hour putting those in!"

"Why don't you see what you can do with Martha, and I'll help Naomi," Bree suggested.

Sally huffed but went to poke her fingers in Martha's smooth hair.

Naomi gave her a grateful smile. "What about my makeup? My hands are shaking too much to do it myself."

"Makeup's not my forte, but I think I can make you look presentable." Bree put her handbag down.

"Just presentable, huh? Maybe I should do it myself anyway." Naomi smiled then got up from her chair and swept her hair back from her face. "I brought some pretty hair things too in case we needed them."

She was sounding more cheerful, and Bree knew she'd arrived just in time. Her friend could face down any danger except her own mother.

Bree moved to take the hairdresser's place. She hugged Naomi tightly, and her friend clung to her for a long moment. "You nervous?" she whispered against Naomi's hair. An almost imperceptible nod confirmed Bree's suspicions.

"It's going to be fine." She pulled away and took Naomi by the shoulders. "Donovan and the kids are lucky to have you. Relax and enjoy today."

Naomi managed a smile. "It's a deal. Now can you do something about this hair?" She sat back on the chair.

Bree grabbed a brush and began to arrange Naomi's hair. As she worked, Bree told her what she'd learned about Peter Thorrington.

"His wife murdered him, you mark my words," Sheila McDonald said, sticking a pin in a corsage as if she wanted to stick it in Beulah Thorrington. "I've always believed that. She acted like butter wouldn't melt in her mouth, but I could see straight through her. I told Sheriff Mackey to check into her, but he eventually swallowed her sweet act like everyone else. You'll see—they're going to find out she killed him and buried him in the wall."

"But why would she do that?" Bree didn't want to accept the obvious. She'd already learned that rarely led to the truth. Besides, Sheila was the town gossip. Married to Judge McDonald, she claimed to know when anyone in the town so much as sneezed.

Sheila sniffed. "He ran with anything in a skirt." She turned to Martha. "Wasn't it just the week before he disappeared that Beulah caught him out at Shady Lanes Motel with a waitress from the Copper Club? Or maybe it was two. Anyway, the time doesn't matter. My cousin's wife heard Beulah say she wished he was dead and that she'd like to be the one to rid the world of his presence."

"Lots of people say things they don't mean when they're mad," Martha said.

Bree had never been able to figure out why Martha and Sheila were such good friends. Martha hated gossip, and Sheila freely dispensed it to all who would listen.

She put down the brush. "You look beautiful. Now for some makeup." She applied blush to Naomi's cheeks. "What happened to the waitress?"

Sheila waved her plump, bejeweled fingers in the air. "I'm not sure."

"I heard she got married," Sally put in.

"What was her name?"

Sheila thought for a moment. "Odetta something," she said. "Her brother still lives out on Veda Street, I think. He works at the paper mill in town. I heard she moved over toward Houghton."

"Syers," Sally said. "Odetta Syers. I used to cut her hair."

Bree's mind continued to whirl as she finished Naomi's makeup. "Any other family?"

"Peter has a stepbrother," Martha said. "Ted Kemppa, but he didn't get along with Peter much."

"He was one of the ones most vocal about Beulah's guilt!" Sheila said in an indignant voice.

"Is he still around?" Bree asked.

Sheila nodded. "He's a supervisor at the paper mill."

The mill was the main place of employment in Rock Harbor. There were several leads there. She'd have to follow up.

Bree smiled. "Hey, you guys, this is Naomi's *wedding*, not a courtroom. Let's forget stuff like murder and mayhem and concentrate on love, sweet love." She put her hands together in a pious attitude and segued into a *Princess Bride* persona. "Mawwiage . . . mawwiage is what bwings us togevah today . . . mawwiage and twue wuv."

The two women looked at one another and burst into laughter. Then in unison they quoted one of their favorite lines from the movie. "Then wuv, twue wuv, will follow you fowever. . . ."

"This is your perfect day," Bree said, hugging Naomi.

Naomi's smile faded. "I'm freaking out!"

Her mother hurried to her side. "Now, Naomi, take some deep breaths. It's going to be fine."

"It's nearly time," came a muffled voice from the other side of the door. Eini Kantola stuck her head in the room. "It's almost time," she chirped.

Naomi moaned and buried her face in her hands.

"Stop it—you'll ruin your makeup," Bree commanded. She grabbed Naomi's arm and pulled her to her feet. "We've got to get you in your dress." She carefully freed the beautiful white dress from the hanger, then slipped it over her friend's head. Once the zipper was up and the buttons were fastened, she arranged the veil and stepped back. Naomi's shoulders were bare, and the dress clung in all the right places, then flared out into a long train.

Bree tried to speak, but the words lodged in her throat. "You . . . you look beautiful." Behind the veil, Naomi's eyes were blue pools.

Bree swallowed, then turned away to change into her dress. She held up the offending garment with disdain. Pink was the worst color a redhead could wear, and she was getting stuck in it all day. The satin dress slipped over her head, and Naomi zipped her up.

"Do I look as hideous as I feel?" Bree muttered.

Naomi hugged her. "You look lovely as always."

Bree wrinkled her nose, then turned Naomi toward the door. "Let's get you married."

Martha dabbed at her eyes. "My baby girl is getting married," she whispered. She hugged her daughter and didn't seem to want to let go.

Bree let Martha have a moment with her daughter, then cleared her throat. "We'd better go. Donovan may think you're backing out."

"Never," Naomi said. "I've waited for this moment my whole life."

Bree picked up Naomi's train, and they went out the door. The music was already echoing in the hallway. Canon in D. The last wedding Bree had attended had been her own, and the familiar tune brought a wave of memories washing over her.

To keep them at bay, she gazed into the church to see who was in attendance, but there were so many people it was a blur. Then she saw Hilary, Mason, and Anu. They were smiling. Davy was craning his neck and waving to his best friend, Donovan's son, Timmy, as he stood at the back of the church with the rings on a pillow.

Bree took a deep breath and began to walk down the aisle behind Emily, who was scattering rose petals, and Timmy, who was bearing the rings as though they were the most precious thing in the world. Bree's gaze met Kade's where he waited as Donovan's best man. The love she saw in his eyes made her steps falter; then she raised her head and smiled back at him. Somehow she and the children found themselves at the front of the church. Emily slipped her hand into Bree's.

The stirring sound of the Wedding March pounded out, and

the guests stood to watch Naomi come down the aisle. Everyone gasped and stared. There was never a lovelier bride than Naomi. The beauty of her soul just enhanced her outward loveliness. Tears sprang to Bree's eyes. Her gaze met Steve Asters's, and she knew he was thinking about his own lost bride just as Bree was remembering her lost groom.

The ceremony passed in a blur, but the rock Bree found herself clinging to was Kade's steady gaze as the bride and groom exchanged vows. Would she and Kade ever say those vows to each other? She knew she wasn't ready for that yet, but her heart yearned to belong to someone again, yearned for that camaraderie that is found only when two people are joined like Donovan and Naomi. And Bree found herself wanting that with a desperation that surprised her.

The church parking lot was packed with people. Darkness was fast approaching, and the festivities had been going on for hours. Quentin Siller sat shivering in his car. Even with the heater going full blast, the broken window let the cold wind in to blow down his back. If it weren't for the Nicholls women, he'd be in the fellowship hall with his wife and daughter. The rest of the town was welcome, but if he dared show his face, the sheriff would throw him in jail.

The injustice of it twisted in his gut, and he clenched his fists. At least he had a new job waiting for him, a new life in Florida. But first there was unfinished business here. The Nicholls women would pay for what they had done. Then he'd take his daughter—and keep her this time—and disappear. He had a week to accomplish his goals—plenty of time for what he planned. This town wouldn't soon forget Quentin Siller.

Glancing across the street, he saw someone else watching the festivities. An older man with stark black hair combed straight back from a high forehead had arrived in a nondescript blue Plymouth, a rental from the look of it. Some out-of-towner likely rubbernecking.

He directed his gaze back to the church. Anu Nicholls moved in front of the window. She was laughing, her head thrown back. She wouldn't be laughing when he got done with her. He thought he still had the rifle in the trunk. Maybe he should give the new-lyweds a send-off they wouldn't soon forget.

Lauri wandered around the reception with a glass of punch in her hand. She felt invisible, a ghost that flitted through people's lives without being noticed. No one smiled or said hello. The attention was focused on Naomi and Donovan. As it should be, she knew. She saw some empty seats in the corner and made her way there.

She caught a glimpse of Ruth and Dinah, her best friends since kindergarten. At least they used to be. They were talking and laughing together, and Lauri looked away. That part of her life was over, Brian had told her. She was part of his group now, the cheerleaders and jocks. But she'd seen the hurt on her friends' faces when she started eating with other friends at lunch.

"Whew, I need a breather." Naomi fanned her flushed face and collapsed on a chair beside Lauri. "Where'd you get that punch? I'm dying of thirst."

"Here, you can have mine if you want. I haven't touched it."

Naomi took the cup and drained it with a long gulp. "I needed that," she said.

"You have cake in your hair."

Naomi laughed. "I wonder how it got there? I warned Donovan to be careful when he fed me the cake. He was a good boy and didn't smash it in my face."

"I saw. That was no fun!"

"It was a lot more fun than having to wash it out of my hair tonight." Naomi's gaze lingered on Lauri's face. "Is something wrong, sweetie? You don't seem to be enjoying yourself. Where's Brian?"

"He's around here somewhere." Probably chasing after Sarah Cappo. Lauri was beginning to wonder if it might be good riddance.

"There he is. Looks like he's heading this way." Naomi squeezed Lauri's hand. "Before he gets here, I just want to offer a little advice. I know it's none of my business, but I hate to see you tie yourself down to a boy at your age. You've got lots of time to get serious. Look at me. I'm thirty-two and just now getting married. The world won't end if you don't have a boy's class ring on your hand every minute. Get some other interests; keep up with the search-and-rescue training. There's so much good you could do."

She stood. "Just think about it."

"Sure." Lauri quit listening. What did Naomi know about the need for approval that drove her? She barely noticed the new bride wander off to mingle with other guests. Her gaze was too intent on Brian. She wondered fleetingly how much trouble he was really in.

"Hey, this is boring. Want to get out of here for a while?" Brian grabbed her hand and pulled her to her feet.

"Kade will kill me if I leave."

"With all these people, who's to know? Come on." He tugged her toward the door.

As they exited the church and stood on the steps, Brian stopped. "Hey, wonder what Neville is doing here?"

"Who?" Lauri squinted through the twilight but could make out nothing beyond a shape in a car.

"Neville. Remember, Miss Snoop, at the cabin? He's in that car across the street. Looks like he's watching us." Brian started down the steps. "You wait here. I'll go see what he wants."

*T*he reception hall boomed with laughter and celebratory music. Bree held a glass of punch in one hand and Davy's hand in the other. With so much racket and so many people, he was perfectly content to stay close to his mother.

Martha and her friends had been cooking for days, and appetizing aromas piqued Bree's appetite. Bree had attempted to make some meatballs from Julia Child's recipe book, but they hadn't turned out very well, so she'd left the cooking to Martha.

There were many people she didn't know here. Were any of them responsible for Peter Thorrington's death? Naomi had said most of the town would be here, probably even Peter's brother and wife. Maybe she could find Ted Kemppa and find out what he remembered.

She reined in her thoughts. This was a wedding, not a time to be eying people with suspicion. Naomi's laugh rang out above the hubbub, and Bree glanced over at the cake table.

"Hi, Bree!" Gretchen Siller grabbed Bree's hand. Her mother was right behind her, a slight frown between her eyes.

Bree squeezed Gretchen's fingers. "I wondered if the two of you were here."

"We were a little late," Karen said. "Quentin called just as we were walking out the door." She turned to her daughter. "Why don't you go get us some punch and cake? Take Davy with you." As soon as the children bounced away, she turned back to Bree. "I don't know what I'm going to do, Bree. He says if I don't lift the restraining order, he's going to take Gretchen and disappear. I'm scared."

She looked as if she hadn't slept in days.

"Have you told Mason?"

Karen nodded. "But what can he do? He can't seem to find Quentin. Maybe I should take him back."

"Not until he agrees to get some help! You know what will happen, Karen. What if you're not around and he decides it's Gretchen's turn to feel his wrath? Neither one of you should be in that position. You want to come stay with me?" Bree wasn't sure that would help much since Quentin was likely already watching her place, but at least they'd be together.

Karen hesitated then shook her head. "He'll find us no matter where we go."

"What about going to stay with family or friends away from Rock Harbor?"

"I guess I could go to my mother's in Wisconsin, but it would be the first place Quentin would look."

She was probably right. Bree tried to think of where else she could send Karen, but nothing came to mind. "I'll talk to Mason," she said finally.

Gretchen and Davy came back with punch and cake, and the two women turned as the bride and groom joined them.

"Whew, I'm pooped already." Naomi's cheeks were pink.

Bree smiled and handed her a cup of punch. "Thirsty?"

Her friend was radiant, and Donovan's harried look had been replaced with a contented expression that warmed Bree's heart. Naomi deserved this happiness. Emily and Timmy hovered close as though they wanted to make sure she didn't get away.

"Time to throw the garter and bouquet," Anu said at her elbow. "I will take charge of my grandson while you go up."

Bree laughed and turned to look for Kade. Would they be the next couple to tie the knot? The thought was both exhilarating and terrifying. She went into the front of the room. The photographer hurried to take a picture of Donovan removing Naomi's garter.

Donovan sat on a chair and rubbed his hands together. "I've been waiting for this," he said. He reached down and grasped Naomi's ankle. Naomi put on a horrified expression, though Bree could tell it was all she could do not to giggle. Donovan held the garter in the air triumphantly, then turned his back on the crowd and sent it sailing through the air.

It flew so high it nearly got caught on the light fixture before it came tumbling down, straight into Kade's hands. The stupefied expression on Kade's face made Bree laugh.

"I get to be best man," Donovan said with a grin.

"You threw it at me on purpose," Kade accused.

His gaze caught Bree's, and she saw a warm promise in his eyes. She gulped.

Naomi turned her back to the crowd. "Now my bouquet." She hefted the flowers in front of her, then flipped them over her head. The bouquet turned end over end, then dropped into Bree's waiting hands. She lifted the flowers to her nose and breathed in the sweet aroma. Her gaze was drawn to Kade's again. He smiled his crooked smile again, then started toward her.

Naomi held a fist in the air in triumph. "Gotcha!" she called.

Bree dragged her fascinated stare from Kade's face. "I'll get you for this," she whispered. She felt an incredible sense of happiness. The love in Kade's eyes made her heart turn over. At least she thought it was love—he'd never said the words. Sometimes she wondered if he ever would.

Kade reached her and took her hand. "Want some punch?"

"That would be nice." Nice. How stupid she sounded. She felt as if she was shaking.

They started toward the refreshment table; then a door slammed. A car backfired, and Bree felt something pass by her cheek.

"Get down!" Kade shouted.

Bree looked at him in bewilderment, then he shoved her to the ground as people began to scream. His weight knocked the breath out of her. She tried to push him off, but his hands pressed her back against the hard floor.

"Someone's shooting." Kade's breath whispered across her cheek.

"Anu's been hit!" Mason yelled.

"Davy!" Bree screamed. "Where's my son?"

Kade paced like an agitated tiger around the perimeter of the room. The bedlam had finally subsided. Davy was safely ensconced in Bree's arms, and Mason had corralled everyone out of harm's way. Everyone but the bride and groom. He'd allowed them to slip away with Emily and Timmy. The Smoky Mountains during spring break awaited them, and they wanted to get as far as Milwaukee before it got too late.

Dr. Parker had rushed to Anu's side, and Kade saw him hovering over her like a protective knight. The bullet had grazed Anu's arm, barely breaking the skin, and she'd waved away their concern. Had the shot been aimed at Anu, or was it just fate she'd been struck? Mason and his men were crawling over the yard for clues to the shooter's identity, but darkness hampered their efforts.

Lauri was missing. Once Kade had ensured Bree's safety and found Davy, he'd gone looking for his sister only to be told she'd last been seen getting into Brian Parker's car. And though the fact would have sent him into a furor any other day, today he was relieved. At least she hadn't here when the shot was fired.

Mason stepped back inside the room. He motioned to Kade, and Kade wound his way through the throng to his side.

"Find anything?" Kade asked.

"Got an eyewitness who recognized Quentin Siller's car earlier." Mason said grimly.

"You think he was targeting Anu?"

"We know he hates her and Bree both. We're going to have to put a guard on them until he's found. I'm going to try to talk them into staying with us."

"Good luck."

"I'd better get people out of here." Mason stepped into the crowd.

Kade went in search of Bree. He found her sitting on a chair beside Anu and Hilary. Davy was in Bree's arms, asleep, and she and Hilary were fussing over Anu. Dr. Parker had bandaged Anu's arm. Poor Bree, after all she'd been through. Kade wished she'd let him help her carry her burdens, though part of her attraction was in her chin-up, face-the-worst attitude.

The doctor patted Anu's shoulder and straightened up, taking her hand. "You'll be fine, Anu, not even a scar most likely. I've cleaned it. Just put vitamin E on it several times a day until it heals."

"Thanks, Dr. Parker." Bree said. "Should someone stay with her tonight?"

Dr. Parker grinned. "She's fine, Bree. Really. It's just a scratch." He glanced at Anu's hand. "Pretty ring. I've never seen you wear it before. New beau? Should I be jealous?" The twinkle in his eye made them all laugh. Anu blushed.

Mason made his way to the head of the room. His face was drawn with fatigue. He put his hands on his hips and raised his voice above the excited chatter. "You can all go home now, but one of my deputies or I will be coming around to ask questions. If you think of anything that might aid our investigation, please call the office."

The crowd immediately began to thin. Kade couldn't blame them. Who knew when another shot might be fired? The next time it might be deadly. The shot had whizzed right by Bree's head.

A deputy hurried in to confer with Mason. Kade watched their body language. It looked as though they might have found something. Mason clapped the other man on the shoulder, then came toward the rest of the family.

"Anything?" Kade asked quietly when Mason stopped beside him.

Mason nodded. "We found the slug, a two-twenty-two."

A high-range rifle. "No idea what he was aiming at?" Kade asked.

Mason's gaze went to Anu.

Bree's eyes widened, and she shifted her son from one arm to the other, then settled the sleeping boy against her shoulder. "No one could possibly want to hurt her," Bree said. Her firm tone dared anyone to contradict her words. She moved closer to Anu, and the older woman patted her hand. Dr. Parker began to frown.

"I wish we could be sure of that," Mason said. "Quentin Siller has told several people he would make the two of you 'pay.' I thought he was just spouting off, but he seems to be more dangerous than that."

"That's ridiculous! Bree and Mother did nothing but help get Karen out of danger." Hilary said. "You have to find him, Mason."

"You are all overreacting," Anu said firmly. "I am certain it was someone trying to disrupt the wedding."

"Why would anyone want to disrupt the wedding?" Mason asked. "I'm afraid we have to take this very seriously. It might have just been a fluke, but I'm not going to take any chances. I think you should stay with us until I figure out what's going on, Anu."

Anu was shaking her blond head before Mason even finished. "I will not be driven from my home. God has cared for me all these years, and I believe he will watch out for me now. Besides, you two need this time to plan for the baby."

"There's plenty of time for that." Hilary moved restlessly. "If you won't stay with me, we'll move in with you." Her hand strayed to her still-flat belly in a protective posture.

"You are always welcome, my *kulta*, but I will not be coddled. You will stay in your own home." Anu thrust out her chin.

"Mother, you have to listen to reason!"

Anu lifted her hand. "You are the ones who must listen. I will be fine. I have lived on my own for many years. I have your father's shotgun, and I know how to use it if necessary."

"That won't do you much good if it's a sniper like today," Bree said, her voice gentle.

Kade knew she was worried, and he moved closer to her. He took her hand and pressed it, and she gave him a grateful smile. To his surprise, she left her hand in his.

"I could stay tonight," Dr. Parker said.

"You all worry too much," Anu said gently. "I must get home. Alone. I'll be fine. I don't want anyone to stay."

"We all need to be going," Mason said. "I want everyone out of here while my men go over the place with a fine-tooth comb."

"What about Siller?" Kade asked. "Could he have been targeting Bree?"

"There's no way of knowing for sure who he was aiming at." Mason's voice was grim.

Kade didn't want to talk about it anymore. He didn't want to think of the possibility that something might happen to Bree. "I'll see Anu and Bree home," he said.

"That's not necessary," Bree said. "I've got my Jeep."

"Then I'll follow you," Kade said firmly. Sometimes she was just too independent. She shrugged but gave him no more argument.

He took Davy from her and nestled the small, warm boy against his shoulder. Davy opened his eyes sleepily and saw it was Kade. He stiffened, but Kade soothed him with a pat, and he sat up a bit in Kade's arms and looked around the room.

"Where we going?" he asked. "I want some ice cream."

"Home. Maybe we can play a game. If you want to. And I'll go get you some ice cream."

Davy's green eyes brightened, and he nodded. "Okay." He wiggled. "I want to walk."

Kade put him down and watched Davy reach for his mother's hand. She smiled down at her son with expansive love. Kade felt like such an outsider at times like this. It seemed impossible that he would ever be a part of charge to this family circle. But Kade wasn't a quitter.

As they came out of the church, sirens screamed out of the darkness. A fire truck came tearing by, followed by another one. Kade turned and looked in the direction they were heading, but it was too dark to see smoke. The only buildings that direction were the lighthouse and the Blue Bonnet. The fire trucks passed the Blue Bonnet.

Bree seized his arm in a tight grip. "My house!" she gasped. "Samson is in there!"

Kade scooped up the boy and handed him off to Hilary. "Take Davy!" He grabbed Bree's hand, and they ran toward his truck. He slung himself under the steering wheel. Bree was already in the passenger seat. With the truck's tires slipping on the wet road, he stomped on the accelerator and sped toward the lighthouse.

He could smell smoke but saw no flames. Maybe the smoke had alerted the fire department soon enough that they would be able to save the structure. Bree gripped the armrest on the door as though it was all she could do to stay in the vehicle. Her dog was like her second child.

Kade wanted to reassure her but couldn't find the right words. Typical of him. They had to save the dog they all loved. They raced down Quincy Hill and tore down Cottage Avenue. He took the corner onto Harbor Road, the truck's rear tires sliding sideways on the wet pavement. Bree was crying now, her lips moving as she prayed.

Kade swallowed the hard rock in his throat. "Dear God," he prayed aloud, "please let Samson be safe. Send an angel to guard him right now. He's important to all of us."

"Amen," Bree whispered. She managed a tremulous smile of gratitude and passed the back of her hand over her wet cheeks.

They reached the lighthouse, and Kade slid to a stop. Killing the engine, he jumped out, but Bree was already racing up the walk. A fireman stopped her at the fence gate, and she struggled to get past him.

"My dog!" she cried. She tore her arm loose from the fireman's grip and screamed out his name. "Samson!"

Kade heard a bark; then Samson came racing around from the back of the house. He streaked right for Bree and leaped up onto her. She sank to her knees and buried her face in his fur.

"You smell like smoke," she whispered when she raised her head. She looked up at the fireman. "How did you get him out?"

"He was waiting for us by the front door when I broke in. The fire is contained. As near as we can tell, it started in the basement."

*B*ree couldn't seem to slow the tap of tears. Samson licked her face, and she smoothed the curly fur around his face. "Good boy," she said. "You knew to get out, didn't you?"

She looked up at the fireman. "Do you think I should get him checked out? How much smoke did he inhale?"

"I think he's fine." The fireman knelt and roughed the dog's ears, an action Samson welcomed with a happy smile. "He's a good dog."

"I don't think I've met you," Bree said. She knew most of the firemen, because Rob had been fire chief for two years before he died. The man's face was covered with soot, but the admiration in his blue eyes was hard to miss.

He took off his helmet and gloves, then wiped his forehead, but he just made the soot streaks worse. "Nick Fletcher," he said. "I've only been in town a couple of weeks."

Bree held out her hand. "Bree Nicholls," she said.

He shook her hand, holding it just a bit longer than necessary. "Are you married, Bree Nicholls?"

She laughed and dropped her gaze from his admiring one. "I'm widowed," she said.

"And taken," Kade said, stepping forward. He held out his hand to help her up.

Bree suppressed a smile. Kade never seemed to say how he felt, but his proprietary manner told her he cared.

Nick glanced at Kade. "Sorry. I didn't mean to be out of line." But he continued to stare at her with admiration.

Bree looked away, unsure how to handle this. She curled her fingers through Samson's collar and decided to change the subject.

"How much damage is there?"

"Hard to say. It's mostly smoke damage," Nick said. "There's a couple of charred floor joists in the basement, but nothing too troubling. I recommend you find another place to stay until you get a company in here experienced in removing smoke. Your insurance company will know who to send over."

Bree nodded. "My husband was a fireman," she said.

"Oh yeah?" Nick looked pleased. "You must like firemen."

Kade let out an exasperated sigh, and Bree suppressed a grin. Nick was just trying to impress her, a tactic she decided to forgive. She rather liked his self-confidence.

"Well, I certainly loved my husband," she said.

"What do you need from inside? I'll go get it," Kade said.

"I'll go with you," Bree said. "Stay," she told Samson. The dog obediently lay down on one of the few patches of snow left and stretched out with a look of exultation on his doggy face. Bree laughed, then went toward the front door.

Nick trailed behind her. "We've got the windows open to air out the smoke, but it will probably be pretty bad still."

Bree could see Kade struggling to control his temper. She put her hand on his arm, and he flinched. Nick still followed them, and Bree wished he would leave them alone for a few minutes, engaging though he was. She couldn't talk properly to Kade with Nick overhearing.

"Hey, Fletcher! Come here and give me a hand." Another fireman struggling with a coil of hose waved from the street. Nick shrugged apologetically then jogged over to the fire truck.

"Finally," Kade muttered.

At his tone, all thoughts of placating him left her. Pressing her lips together, Bree marched ahead of him into the house. She needed some clothing for her and Davy, as well as his favorite books. The stench of smoke struck her almost like a physical blow, and she wrinkled her nose. The acrid, penetrating odor reached deep into her nasal tissues and lungs. She went up the stairs and down the hall to the bedrooms.

"If you'll collect some things for Davy, I'll get my clothes." She refused to look at Kade.

He took her arm and pulled her around to face him. "What's eating you?"

She glared at him. "You are what's eating me. Nick was just being pleasant."

He dropped her arm and took a step back. "He was putting the make on you. But maybe that's what you want. I guess I was mistaken about what kind of relationship we have. My apologies." He ground out the words through tight lips, then turned and went down the hall to Davy's room.

If he'd ever once say he loved her, maybe they could move forward. Bree was beginning to think he'd never say it.

Anu moved around the house like a hummingbird, joyous over having Bree and Davy with her. Bree's tension eased, and she hurried to help Anu make up the spare beds. Davy was chattering excitedly about being able to stay with Grammy, and Samson followed them all around as though he wasn't sure what was happening.

It was ten o'clock by the time they got Davy settled down enough to sleep. Samson lay on the rug beside the bed and kept guard over his boy. Bree gave him a loving pat, then followed Anu down the hall to the living room.

"I will make us some chamomile tea," Anu said. "It will help you sleep."

While Anu made the tea, Bree picked up a photo album she'd never seen before. She flipped through the pages and saw a tall man with blond hair and Rob's smile playing catch with a small boy, probably Rob, since he looked so much like Davy. The unexpected encounter with Rob's image made her heart hurt.

Anu came back into the room carrying a tray with tea and cookies. Her smile widened when she saw the album in Bree's hands. "I see you have found my treasure. I put it away when Abraham left. It seemed time to bring it out again."

"Does it still hurt?"

Anu cocked her head to one side as she considered the question. "Yes and no. I grieve for the years he lost with his children, but the personal pain God has healed. I know his desertion accounts for much of Hilary's overbearing manner. She seeks to prove she is worthy of love. As she grows more secure in God's love, she can relax."

Bree remembered their earlier conversation. "You said Peter and Abe disappeared about the same time. Do you think there could be a connection between Peter's death and Abraham's disappearance? I mean, is it possible whoever killed Thorrington killed your husband as well? That he didn't desert you?"

Anu's smile faded, and her hands slowed as she stirred the sugar in her tea. "I must admit the thought has troubled me. It is possible. But then I remember the ring he left me, almost as if he knew he was going away."

Bree nodded, turning the possibilities over in her mind. Another idea occurred to her, but this one she wouldn't mention to Anu.

"I see the wheels rolling, *kulta*," Anu said with a smile flitting over her face. "You let Mason handle it."

"I'm just going to poke around a little. Maybe talk to Peter's family. Anyone else who might be worth talking to?"

"The waitress, if you could find her. Maybe Mason would know how to track her down." Anu wrinkled her nose in a wry gesture. "I should not be encouraging you. Still, it would be amazing to know the truth of what happened to Abraham."

Bree knew how important closure was. She resolved to do all she could to give that to her mother-in-law. Anu was the mother she'd always longed for, the exact opposite of Bree's real mother. Bree bit her lip. Someday she knew she was going to have to forgive her mother. Track her down in whatever rat hole she was living in and face the demons of her own past. But not today.

"What do you think was really going on with that shot at Naomi's wedding?"

"Probably young men having a good time."

"Really, Anu. You don't think anyone would be targeting you?" Though Bree desperately wanted to believe the shooting was a prank, it seemed ridiculous.

"Pooh. You sound like Mason. You both worry too much."

"But Quentin?"

"He is angry at us both," Anu admitted.

"I hope Mason finds him soon."

"Enough of problems," Anu said, lifting her teacup to her lips. "We shall focus on God's goodness. Nothing good or bad happens to us but what it first passes through the Father's hand."

"Amen," Bree said with a smile.

She and Anu finished their tea and she went to bed. The unfamiliar mattress kept her twisting restlessly in the bed. She tossed and turned as images of the wedding, the fire, and Kade's hurt expression ran through her mind.

Just as she thought she might doze off, the sound of a car door and several men's voices raised in anger put all her senses on alert. Her heart thumping, she eased out of bed and pulled back the edge of the curtains. The street lights looked blurry and distant through the fog that had rolled in off Lake Superior. A man's voice swore viciously; then several car doors slammed and an engine roared off toward town.

Bree strained to see through the fog, but whoever was out there seemed to be gone now.

It was a long time before she slept.

*I*n her dreams, she heard Rob calling to her. His boat was sinking amid choppy whitecaps in the middle of Lake Superior. His hand reached above the heavy waves. She tried to catch it and pull him to safety, but his fingers kept sliding off hers until finally there was nothing left but the boat's debris.

Bree sat up and rubbed tears from her eyes. She reached for her Bible, the source of comfort she'd come to rely on.

She opened to the last passage she'd read last night before bed, Micah 7:19.

You will again have compassion on us; you will tread our sins underfoot and hurl all our iniquities into the depths of the sea.

Did that really mean all her sins were all gone? How could God not look at her and see all that she'd done wrong in her life? Was this turmoil in her life punishment from God for her sins? When she'd turned to him she thought her worries would be over. Instead, new problems seemed to slam into her with the force of a Superior nor'easter. Wasn't life for a Christian supposed to be different? She brooded about it. It seemed a hard thing to accept. Why would God allow such terrible things to happen, not just to her but to everyone? To good people like Anu, like Davy? She had no answers.

Sighing, she got dressed, then got Davy up and bathed. He was in a good mood, chattering about his new toy and his new fireman friend. She took his hand and went down the hall to the kitchen. She could smell the *pulla*, and her stomach rumbled.

Anu had already made coffee, and they sat down at the breakfast table. Anu kept stealing glances at Bree's somber face, and Bree knew it was only a matter of time before her mother-in-law asked what was wrong.

Anu held her tongue until Davy went to play in the other room. She fixed a fresh pot of coffee and poured Bree a cup. "I think it is time you told me what is wrong, eh, *kulta?*"

Bree took the cup and tried to smile, but faltered.

"Is it the fire? You must not worry. You and Davy are welcome here as long as you need to stay. The insurance company will soon have your home habitable again."

The coffee was hot, and Bree sipped it carefully, then set it on the table beside her.

"You are not speaking," Anu observed. "It will not go away to keep it inside."

"It won't go away if I talk about it either," Bree said.

"Fears shared are fears halved," Anu said.

"Words of wisdom, I'm sure. But don't you get tired of me always crying on your shoulder?"

"Never, my *kulta*. You know I am always here for you."

"I know." Bree paused. "I'm just struggling to understand why God let the fire happen, why he allowed Naomi's wedding to be marred. I thought he would care about us as his children. Who has served him better than Naomi? Or you? I love him so much, and I want to serve him. But I still wonder how he works. I could never stand back and let bad things happen to Davy. So how can God? Maybe he's punishing me."

Anu sat down beside her. She sighed, and a smile tugged at her lips. "Ah, you ask the perennial question: Why do bad things happen to good people? Sometimes it even seems as though those who have no knowledge of God fare better than his children do."

"Exactly!" Bree shifted in her seat. "I don't understand."

"I'm not sure we can truly understand," Anu said. "God's ways are sometimes mysterious. But I've always thought of it like this: Who disciplines Davy when he is wrong? His mother or the neighbor?"

"I do, of course."

"Why?"

"He's my child, my responsibility. I love him and want him to turn out right."

"Ah, there you have it. And we are God's responsibility. Not all our trials are discipline for sin, but he sometimes allows trials so that our faith might be strengthened, and so that we might come nearer to his side."

Bree thought about it a minute. "But sometimes they make us turn on God."

"Then they reveal the true state of our hearts. Jeremiah 17:9 says, '*The heart is deceitful above all things and beyond cure. Who can understand it?*' We can even deceive ourselves into thinking we are Christian or that we are following God. But when adversity comes, the true believer will still weather it standing, though he may go through a fire of doubt. This is God's mercy to us, to strengthen our faith and our hearts. Allow this adversity to bow your knee to God and accept his will."

Bree pondered the words. "Just as I must sometimes punish Davy because I love him and want him to grow into the right kind of man, God wants me to grow into the right kind of Christian."

"You can choose how you respond to this adversity, my *kulta*. God allows us to choose."

"I want it to draw me nearer to God," Bree said, relieved to discover her words were true. She never wanted to go back to the days of wandering without God. She realized that even in her anxiety over Davy, the body, the shooting, and the fire, she'd always been aware of God's presence. He held her hand.

Anu patted her arm. "Then that's what will happen." She stood and began to clear the breakfast dishes.

Bree stood and stretched. A weight had been lifted from her shoulders. She thanked God for caring enough about her to make her stronger. What was a little fire compared to that knowledge?

She went to the window and looked out. A glint caught her eye, and she squinted. A dark shape near a fir tree moved, and she realized it was a man. A man with binoculars trained on Anu's house.

Bree gasped and shrank back behind the curtain. Samson heard the sound of her dismay. He quickly trotted to her side and thrust his nose against her hand. Growling softly, he laid back his ears.

"It's okay, boy," she whispered, curling her fingers in his soft fur. Who could be out there? She glanced around for the phone. It was on the stand by the sofa. Could he see her grab it? Maybe it would be better to go to the hall and dig her cell phone out of her purse. She moved quickly along the wall and went through the door into the entry, shadowed by Samson.

Dialing Mason, she sat on the small bench against the wall, her hands icy. She prayed for him and not Hilary to answer the phone. The phone rang and rang. Bree tried his cell number but got his voice mail. She had to have some help. Biting her lip, she shakily dialed Kade's number. After last night, he might not want to hear from her, but she had no choice.

"Hello." Kade's deep voice immediately calmed the jitters in her stomach.

"Kade, it's me. There's someone watching the house with binoculars. I'm scared."

"Are you still at Anu's?" His voice was sharp with concern.

"Yes."

"I'll be right there. Call the sheriff's office." He clicked off his phone.

The office. Of course. She dialed 9-1-1 and explained the problem. The dispatcher promised to send someone without a siren or lights. Bree wanted to catch whoever was out there.

She slipped her phone into her pants pocket and went to the door sidelight. She couldn't see the man from this angle, so she slunk along the wall back to the living room. Standing behind the curtain, she stared at the spot where she'd seen him. No one was there.

Panic fluttered at the edges of her thoughts. Maybe he had moved closer. And Anu never locked her doors. She raced to the front door and shot the deadbolt home. The back door! She hurried through the dining room to the kitchen.

Anu was sitting at the kitchen table looking through a stack of cookbooks. "I cannot remember which book my recipe for *Tiikerikakku* is in."

"Tiger cake is the least of our worries," Bree said. She rushed to the door and quickly locked it.

"Whatever is wrong?" Anu half rose, then sank back into her chair.

"Someone is watching the house through binoculars. But I can't see him now."

Anu's eyes widened. "Quentin?"

"Probably." Bree bit her lip. "But I don't know. He was too far away to tell." Something about the man nagged at her. This man seemed older, bigger. But if not Quentin, then who? Her unease deepened.

A thunderous knock sounded on the front door, and Bree and Anu stared at one another. Bree took a step toward the door to the dining room, but Anu stopped her with a finger to her lips. Bree swallowed.

Then the knock came again. "Sheriff's office!" a gruff voice called.

Bree sagged with relief, then hurried to fling the door open. Anu followed her. Kade was running up the walk behind the two deputies who stood on the doorstep. He pushed past them and swept her into his arms. She leaned into his embrace and buried her face against his chest. The scent of his aftershave comforted her, and she clung to him.

He kissed the top of her head, then put his hands on her shoulders and pulled her away to stare into her face. "Are you all right?"

"We're fine. It just scared the daylights out of me."

"You want to show us where you saw the man?" one of the deputies asked.

Bree nodded. Still holding Kade's hand, she stepped outside and pointed. "He was by that fir tree."

"Could you tell what he was wearing?"

"A black jacket with a yellow shirt underneath. And dark pants. He had a hat on that hid his face." The deputies nodded, then began to walk toward where she'd seen the man.

"I'm going with them." Kade kissed her, then jogged across the street behind the officers.

Mason's car turned the corner and stopped in front of the house. He jumped out and hurried to Bree, wearing a ferocious frown. "I just heard you spotted someone watching the house. What's going on?"

Bree explained it all to him, and he went to join Kade and the deputies. Bree and Anu watched them searching through the snow. They found something and put it in a plastic bag. Bree grew chilled and grabbed her coat from the entry closet. She saw Davy watching from the window.

She would try to distract him. He didn't need to be worrying. "You about ready for church?" she asked him.

"What's going on, Mommy? Why is Uncle Mason outside?"

"He's just looking for someone."

"The bad person who hurt Grammy?"

"Maybe. But we're okay," she hastened to add. "Go get your Bible and jacket from your room."

He didn't argue but got up and went to his room. She slipped to the window.

Mason and Kade were heading toward the house while the deputies got in their car and left. They stopped to talk to Anu, then they all came to the house. Bree went to meet them.

Mason's face was grim, and Kade put his arm around Bree as though to brace her for more bad news.

"Find anything?" Bree asked.

"Some cigarettes."

"They're a weird brand," Kade said. "I think they're Canadian.

But I found a bunch of butts just like these at the site of some cabin break-ins. Something is going on, but I'm not sure what."

"That's not as important as the other thing I found out this morning," Mason said. "Your fire was arson."

The news confirmed Bree's worst fear.

"Someone threw some kerosene-soaked rags in the basement right in that alcove where you found the body. Looks like he broke a window in the basement. He probably hoped it wouldn't be discovered until too late, with everyone at the wedding. As it is, we got lucky. Whatever he was hoping to cover up, he didn't succeed."

Samson could have died. And what if she and Davy had been home? She had to find out what was going on. That chest of photos Lauri had found just proved Quentin's instability. "I thought you'd gone through everything there," Bree said. She resolved to go through the basement inch by inch and see what she could find. If Quentin Siller had left a clue, she would find it.

"I do not like this." Anu crossed her arms over her chest protectively. "It is good you are staying with me."

"But I don't want to put you in danger," Bree said. And what about Davy? Her fingers tightened into fists. She had to get to the bottom of this before the culprit hurt someone she loved.

— 4 —

On Monday morning around eleven, Bree drove her Jeep to Rock Harbor's downtown and parked behind Mason's car at the sheriff's office. She felt the need to do something. Yesterday's scare had hardened her resolve.

Before she could get out of the Jeep, Mason exited his office. He saw her and came straight over. "Got time for a piece of pie and coffee? I was just coming to see you."

"How about lunch instead?" She let Samson out, then fell into step beside Mason. "I'm hungry."

"Fine by me."

The Suomi Café was bustling as usual. Bree and Mason stood by the door until Molly could seat them.

"Where's Davy?" Mason asked.

"With Anu. I told her I needed to talk to you."

Before Mason could answer her, Molly, her frizzy hair pulled back at the nape of her neck, came up to them. "You're here for fresh pasties, eh?" Her Yooper accent was a combination of Canadian and Finnish inflections.

"You got it, Molly," Mason said.

"I thought you might be by. I saved some leftovers for Samson." Molly led them to a booth with a window, then quickly brought coffee. "Beef for both of you, eh?"

"Sure." Bree laced her fingers together and glanced at the door to make sure Samson was behaving himself. He lay stretched on the floor like a sultan while Molly and the other waitress brought him homage—and food.

"That box by the body in the basement," Bree said, turning back to Mason. "I figured out what it is. It's a lighthouse keeper's service box. It held polishing cloths on the side and was used to keep the lights and equipment clean."

"I know. I showed it to Wanda at the antique shop and she told me."

"With his journal there as well, the skeleton has to be Peter Thorrington."

"Forensics says the same thing, according to the dental records."

"So what's next?"

They halted the conversation as Molly brought their hot pasties. Bree dug into hers with gusto. Beef, potatoes, carrots, and rutabagas stuffed into a folded-over pie crust—a Yooper favorite.

Mason grinned when Bree wiped a bit of gravy from her chin. "Maybe we need to get you a bib."

"You're going to be buying lots of those pretty soon. With everything going on, I haven't had a chance to congratulate you. I'm thrilled for you! Davy can't wait."

"We're pretty excited," Mason admitted. "I'd been talking to Hilary about adoption, but you can guess how well that went over."

"You hoping for a boy?"

"I really don't care, as long as the baby is healthy." Mason's smile couldn't get any wider. He took a bite of his pasty. "But back to the body in your basement."

"Do you know for sure yet if it's murder?"

He nodded. "Autopsy came back this morning. The skull was crushed in three places. Blunt-force trauma."

A familiar voice interrupted. "Hey, you two mind if I join you?" Steve Asters, his tie askew, stood beside their booth.

"Hey, Steve. Where've you been?" Bree moved over, and Steve

slid into the seat. "I didn't get a chance to do more than say hi at the wedding, but I haven't seen you around in weeks."

"Bank seminar in Boston. I heard what's been happening here. You can never seem to stay out of trouble, Bree. Though I guess I can't complain."

Steve's eyes darkened at the allusion to his wife's murder. Bree patted his hand. "I see you have your house up for sale."

"Yep. It was always more what Fay wanted. I'm content with a smaller place over by the Lake. I think I have a buyer already."

"Anyone we know?" Mason asked.

Steve nodded. "Cassie Hecko. I haven't met her yet, but it sounds like it's a go."

"Cassie!" Bree exclaimed. "I had no idea. She just showed up to train her dog a couple weeks ago."

"You know her?" Steve picked up his coffee cup.

"Just from a few days of training. She doesn't say much."

"She's some kind of scientist. I guess she does research wherever she wants to."

Bree made a mental note to get to know Cassie better, though so far the woman had been resistant to Bree's prying.

The trio conversed while Bree and Mason finished eating. Mason took a last swig of coffee. "I guess I'd better be going. Bree. I'm heading out to check on some leads. You want to come along?"

"Sure." Bree laid a tip for Molly on the table while Steve stood to let her out. "Let's get together for coffee soon," she told him.

"You got it. See you guys later."

Mason held the door open for Bree. "You want to ride with me, or should we take your Jeep?"

"I'll drive. I've got Samson." She snapped her fingers at Samson, and he got up from his post by the door and followed them to the car. "Where to?"

"Beulah Thorrington's. This isn't something I'm looking forward to," Mason said as he got in the passenger side of the Jeep.

"Surely she won't be shocked. The newspapers have speculated for days that the remains might be her husband's."

"She'll still be upset at the confirmation."

Bree nodded. "So where we heading?"

"Beulah lives just past Konkola Service Station." Mason's voice turned grim. "I've been through the old files when he was first reported missing. The previous sheriff was pretty lackadaisical about it. The final note was that Peter had likely run off with his mistress."

"You don't suppose she's buried in my basement too, do you?" Bree shuddered.

"I'm going to look around a little more. Did you hear from the insurance company this morning?"

Bree nodded. "They said they'd have it cleaned up next week. I should be able to go home by next Monday or Tuesday. What about Quentin Siller?"

Mason shrugged. "Nothing yet. He seems to have disappeared into the woodwork like the cockroach he is."

"Cockroach?"

"Any man who would kidnap his own child and put her through that trauma should be stomped into the ground." Mason scowled and turned off the radio.

"Spoken like a soon-to-be father. But of course I agree with you." Bree glanced at him and grinned. "Hilary have the nursery ready yet?" she quipped.

Mason pressed his lips together and looked away. "Almost. She hauled out the Penney's catalog last night and ordered a bunch of stuff online."

Bree's smile died. "I hope . . . I hope things turn out all right."

"I wish she'd waited too. We've had our hopes crushed before. Of course, this time she's really pregnant. But things can happen."

"We'll pray she has a perfect pregnancy." Bree passed the service station. "Which house?"

Mason pointed. "The small yellow one."

A gold Chrysler PT Cruiser that nearly matched the house color sat in the driveway. Bree pulled in behind it and killed the engine. "Thanks for letting me come with you," she told Mason.

"I knew it would be next to impossible to keep you out," Mason said. "Besides, I need all the help I can get if I'm going to solve this one."

"Stay," Bree told Samson. He whined, then lay back down on the seat, his dark eyes morose.

She walked ahead of Mason to the front door. Painted a bright red, the door made for a cheerful welcome. A red porch swing moved lazily in the cool breeze. Beulah Thorrington had a good eye for color and balance. The lot to the side was filled with plants and shrubs for her landscaping business, Beulah's Bounty.

Bree had been past here many times but had never stopped. Beulah seemed to have done okay by herself, like Anu.

Mason rang the doorbell. A TV blared from inside the house. The sound was suddenly cut off, and heavy footsteps echoed through the door. Bree's stomach tightened.

The door swung open, and a woman stood blinking at the bright sun that flooded her face. In her sixties, she'd obviously used the color bottle to hold back the gray hair, but nothing could stop the ravages of wind and sun from etching her face. Her dark hair was cut in a bob that just touched the curve of her sagging chin, but the effect was somehow softening and youthful. She wore black and white sweats that did nothing to flatter her round figure.

Her smile faded as her gaze traveled from Bree to Mason's uniformed figure. She paled. "Sheriff, you have news?"

"Beulah Thorrington?" Mason asked.

"Yes." Her gaze switched to Bree. "You're the dog woman, aren't you?"

"May we come in a moment?" Bree said. "We need to talk to you about your husband."

Beulah nodded and stood back to allow their entrance. She shut the door and led them to the living room. Folding her hands over her ample bosom, she glared at them. "I've said all I'm saying about Peter. I didn't have anything to do with his death. Those bones are his, aren't they? Now you're back here wanting to know if I killed him. Well, I didn't!"

"Why don't we all have a seat?" Mason said.

With obvious reluctance, Beulah sat in an overstuffed wing-back chair near the window. Mason and Bree both sat on the sofa.

"Just quit pussyfooting around and tell me the truth." Her tone was truculent.

"I've received confirmation that the remains are those of your husband."

Beulah looked away, but not before Bree saw a sheen of tears in her eyes. Her shoulders slumped as the defiance leached out of her face. "I knew it," she said softly. "What happened?"

"That's what we're trying to find out. It's obviously murder. His skull was crushed."

Beulah twisted her plump hands in her lap. "Well, I didn't have anything to do with it. I haven't seen him since 1976."

"Apparently no one else has either."

Mason's tone was deceptively casual, but Bree knew he was missing nothing of Beulah's reaction. Bree stayed silent and watched too.

Beulah held a hand to her chest. "The jerk ran off and left me." Beulah's face sagged. Several tears ran down her face, and she wiped them away with the back of her hand. "I don't know why I'm crying. I got over him long ago."

"What can you tell us about your husband?" Mason took out a pen and paper.

Beulah's stunned expression began to fade, and she blinked rapidly. "You already know he was the lighthouse keeper. When we were first married, things were good. He was always laughing, playing jokes. A good man. Then about six months before he disappeared, he changed." She looked at Mason. "You want to hear all this?"

"Yes. It might be important."

"He started staying out late, sometimes even all night. And he had money I know he didn't get from his job. Once he brought me a diamond necklace. I took it to the jeweler, and he told me it was worth a thousand bucks. That was a lot of money back then."

It was a lot of money now. Bree leaned forward. Beulah seemed to be telling the truth, but nothing was making any sense.

"You have no idea where he got that kind of money?" Mason asked.

"I asked him. He said his ship had come in. Well, the only ship I knew he'd had anything to do with was when he rescued the captain of the *Seawind.*"

"When was that?" Bree asked. She pulled out a notepad and made a note.

"About the time he started acting so weird. Maybe six months before he disappeared."

"What was the rescue about?" Bree hadn't heard anything about the *Seawind.* She needed to get back to the library.

"The *Seawind* was a cargo ship that went down in the same storm that sank the *Edmund Fitzgerald.* All the crew died except for the captain, Argie Hamel. But I can't see how it could be related," Beulah said.

Bree remembered the old Gordon Lightfoot song. The *Edmund Fitzgerald* went down in November 1975. That would have been about six months before Peter started acting strangely, as Beulah said.

"At this point, we don't know what's related and what isn't," Mason said. "Go on."

Beulah looked away. "Not much more to say. His drinking buddies were more important than me and the kids. One night he just didn't come home."

"Is Susan Hamel, the photographer, related to Argie?" Bree asked.

Beulah nodded. "She's his sister."

"When did you find out about Peter's girlfriend?" Mason asked as tactfully as possible.

Beulah shot him a look of disgust. "I didn't find out about that until after he went missing. The sheriff asked if I'd killed him because I'd found out about *her*. I got a little upset."

"I have witnesses who remember you saying you would like to see him dead—before he disappeared."

Beulah blanched. "No, that was after. And I was just spouting off. I wouldn't have hurt him, though I might have scratched *her* eyes out if I had the chance."

So she said. Bree thought Beulah was hiding something. But what?

What do you think?" Bree's hands gripped the steering wheel. Samson was asleep on the backseat, his fluffy tail curled around him. Bree couldn't gauge Mason's reaction. He stared out the Jeep window, his gaze distant and contemplative.

"I think she knows more than she's saying."

"You ever heard of *Seawind*?" Bree knew there were many wrecks from the deadly nor'easters in Lake Superior. And the old song about the lake never giving up her dead was quite true. The cold water preserved the bodies, and they never floated to the top.

Mason shook his head. "I need to go to Marquette on business this afternoon. Could you head over to the library and see what you can find out?"

"Sure. I was planning on taking Davy anyway. Story hour is this afternoon." Bree smiled at the thought of her son's delight in story hour. His books were his most prized possessions. Maybe someday he'd be an author himself.

Bree dropped Mason at the office, then parked outside The Coffee Place. She got out and let Samson out. He licked her hand as though he sensed the disquiet she felt after talking with Beulah. She snapped her fingers, and they both set off toward Nicholls'. Davy was helping his grandmother with a display of Finnish Earthreads, a new import earring. Bree had bought her first pair last week and loved them. A gossamer-light gold chain threaded through her lobe and hung down at the back of the ear. The weight of the chain kept the earring in place without a back that pinched. She knew Anu would sell dozens once women tried them.

Davy looped the chain of one earring around his wrist and held it up for Anu to see. "Look, Grammy, it makes a bracelet. Maybe Mommy would like one."

Bree stopped in her tracks with Samson's cold nose nudging her leg. A smile tugged at her lips. So he did think of her when she was gone. She felt like skipping, but she moved forward at a more sedate pace.

Davy saw her. "Me and Grammy are having fun. I don't want to leave yet."

"You have a doctor appointment, and I thought we'd go to the library early. We could get you some new books before story hour starts."

His smile returned. "Can you come too, Grammy?" He tugged on Anu's red smock. Samson left Bree and went to Davy. Davy knelt, then threw an arm around the dog and leaned his head against Samson's flank.

"I must stay and work at the store, *pojanpoika*. But you and your *äiti* will enjoy your day together." Anu caressed his red curls.

Bree never got tired of looking at Davy. The awful dark brown hair coloring had grown out, but his sleepwalking was taking its toll. Dark circles rimmed his eyes, and he was pale.

He finally gave up his pleas and stood, his fingers still touching Samson's head. The dog walked with him as Davy came toward Bree. She held out a hand and smiled at him. His small hand fit into hers, and she squeezed his fingers gently.

She reminded herself that God would see them through this. Bree had to trust in that. He'd already wrought miracles in her life. She just had to hold on and wait for him to work it out, something that was easier to think about than to do. She wanted Davy whole and free of the past *now*, but she knew that wasn't realistic—not after what he'd been through.

She squeezed her son's hand and felt an answering pressure. "After we go to the library, would you like to stop and get ice cream?"

His eyes widened. "With nuts?"

"Sure." They reached the Jeep, and she buckled him in his seat in the back. "Speaking of nuts, do you want some pistachios?"

His smile brightened. "Thanks, Mommy! I was getting hungry." She dug in the glove box and pulled out a bag of pistachios. It was hard to say which of them loved pistachios more.

He sucked the salt from a nut, then struggled to split it with his thumb. Bree smiled at the concentration on his face and climbed into the Jeep. Samson yawned and then hung his head over the seat to rest his chin on Bree's shoulder. She patted his nose and started the car.

Today was turning out to be a good day after all. Davy was smiling, and the sullenness that had so darkened her spirits had lifted from his face. At least for now. Humming the Elvis tune "Hound Dog," she drove to the doctor's office at the corner of Ingot Street and Rock River Road.

She took Davy's hand and went inside. The brick building held a small surgical room as well, and the office still smelled of new carpet and fresh paint. She checked in with the receptionist; then she and Davy settled in to wait. As usual, her son went straight for the books. His lips moved as he sounded out the words to *Harold and the Purple Crayon: Dinosaur Days.*

The words were too big for him, but he was trying. Although he was only four, he could already read most first-grade primers, a fact that had Bree curling her fingers into her palms. Before the accident he was already learning to read easy words, but Rachel Marks had taught him even more. Bree had missed that time, and it would never come again.

She glanced at him from the corner of her eye. But what was she complaining about? There was so much to look forward to that she could forget what lay behind. School days, his permanent teeth coming in, his first baseball game, learning to whistle . . . the list went on and on. Just a few months ago, this bright future did not exist.

She flipped through a copy of *Dog Fancy*, but her mind wasn't on the photos or articles. Puzzling over the death of the lighthouse keeper, she wondered again what Beulah was hiding. Nothing criminal, she was sure. Bree's gut told her the woman was innocent of Peter Thorrington's murder. But why not tell Mason everything?

A nurse called Davy's name. Bree put down her magazine, but Davy took the book with him down the hall to the first examining door on the left. It had been decorated especially for children with Winnie the Pooh wallpaper and brightly colored leather chairs that matched the examining table.

The nurse left them in the room, and Bree looked at Davy's file still sitting on the desk. She always had to resist the urge to look through a medical file. Today the desire to open that manila folder was even stronger than usual, but before she could decide whether to risk the doctor's reprimand, she heard his footsteps outside the door.

Dr. Max Parker's booming voice filled the room as he stepped inside. "How's my favorite boy today?"

"I'm okay." Davy kept his nose stuck in the book.

Dr. Parker grinned. "Let me be the judge of that." He listened to Davy's lungs and heart, then sat on the stool and rolled over to the desk, where he jotted down some notes in the record.

Bree leaned forward, lowering her voice. "Could I talk to you a minute?"

He looked up, his brows drawing together. "Something wrong?"

"Yes . . . no. I don't know." She bit her lip and looked over at her son.

Dr. Parker stood and went to the door. "Sally, we have a young man ready for his new pack of crayons and coloring book." He helped Davy down. "In fact, I think we've got one with dinosaurs."

"Really?" Davy's eyes were wide.

"I believe so." The doctor handed him off to the nurse, then shut the door behind them and settled back on his stool. "What's up?"

Bree twisted her hands in her lap. "His night terrors are no better, Dr. Parker. What can I do to help stop them? At least two or three times a week I have to go looking for him. Is there something I should be doing to give him more security? I feel so helpless."

"Are you spending enough time with him? Search-and-rescue is a demanding job. Maybe you should give it up for a while."

Bree's chest thumped in an uneasy rhythm. "I have a new business to run. We have to eat."

"I hardly think Anu would let you two starve. You know I don't hold with mothers working before their children go to school."

Bree stared at him. Did she hear him right? "You can't be serious," she said uneasily. "I'm a single mother. I take him to the training center with me every day. The only time he's away from me is when I'm on an actual search." Was the doctor trying to make her feel *more* guilty? Her stomach roiled, and she swallowed.

"That's all very well and good, but I hardly think you're giving him your undivided attention when you're at the center."

Bree clenched her fists together, and her nails bit into the palms of her hands. Dr. Parker was a bit old-fashioned, but he meant well, she told herself. "Most mothers don't have undivided attention to give. When they're home, they have housework and other things to attend to," she pointed out. "I hate to sound argumentative, but I think you're hardly being fair. I'm doing the best I can." Her voice shook with anger.

He shrugged. "You asked my opinion, so I'm giving it. You need to spend more time with him." He stood, then went to the door and turned. "His next counseling session is next week, isn't it? I'll ask Dr. Walton to try to push him just a bit more and see if we can get to the bottom of it. Just think about what I said."

As if she would do anything else. Bree followed him into the hallway. She had to provide for her son, and she didn't want to take charity from Anu. Her mother-in-law had already done more than enough in providing the funding for the search-and-rescue center as well as the job at Nicholls'. Rob had left her a small life insurance policy, but she'd put that aside for Davy's education. It was possible to use it, but she would only do that as a last resort. Besides, she couldn't just stay home and cater to him, could she? Was that even the right thing to do?

She'd always believed children needed to know they were loved, but they needed responsibility too, and to know they had a place in the larger scheme of things. Kids today sometimes seemed to be so privileged that when they grew up they expected life to treat them with kid gloves. Her grandparents' generation had grown up working on the farm and helping out around the house; they had grown up with the ethics of hard work and responsibility. She and Rob had always wanted to instill the same in Davy.

Driving toward the library, she explored all possible ways to spend more time with Davy. They could collect rocks and quartz along the shore every Saturday, weather permitting. Sundays they always went to Anu's for dinner with the family, and it was important to continue that tradition. Evenings they always spent together. Maybe she should get him a puppy of his own to train. That might help him be more a part of the training center.

Lost in thought, Bree almost didn't see the blue car until it swerved across the yellow line on Cottage Avenue and came straight at her. The sight of Quentin Siller's maniacal grin behind the wheel nearly made her scream. She jerked the steering wheel to the right. The Jeep's tires shrieked, and she fought to keep the vehicle on the street. A glint of blue reminded her that Lake Superior was just over the embankment. She turned the wheel with the skid. The Jeep fishtailed, then finally came to rest in the gravel just inches from the guardrail.

She turned to check on her son, thanking God he was buckled into his car seat. "You okay?" she croaked.

He nodded, and she checked Samson, then turned to look for Quentin. She half expected to see him out of the car and coming toward her. He was gone, leaving only the fading glare of his brake lights as he slowed at the stop sign on Jack Pine Lane, then sped out of town.

— *16* —

*M*ud sucked at his feet, and he tugged them loose impatiently. The last thing he had time for today was traipsing all over the North Woods. The kid had been a nuisance for too long. Today he intended to end it. One way or another.

Moisture ran in rivulets through the woods with the melting snowbanks. He hated this time of year. Once the flowers were up, it wasn't too bad, but he hated being dirty. Bacteria and disease bred in the wet dankness of the woods. Some days he wondered why he stayed around these parts. He should have left here long ago.

The path ended abruptly at an old mine shaft, one of many that catacombed the worn mountains and hills around Rock Harbor. He'd found this one by accident the summer he turned thirteen. It had become his hideaway, his sanctuary. It galled him to no end that he had to share it today, but he could think of no other good place to meet when the kid had called.

"You're late, Hippo man." The kid stepped from the shadows.

"I couldn't get away." He hated it when the kid called him that. He hid his irritation, then dropped his backpack and wiped the perspiration from his face. "What was so important you had to see me today?" It always surprised him to see the kid. He looked just like his father, and resembled him in more than just looks. They were both too intense for his taste.

The kid had a half smile on his face that he didn't trust. He seemed almost . . . euphoric.

"Let's get it over with," he snapped, suddenly impatient with the whole mess. "I have a million things to do back in town. Did you pick up that new shipment last night?"

"No."

"What? I told you if you missed it, we wouldn't get it at all." He curled his hands into fists and took a step toward the kid.

"Do you ever think about what you're doing?" the kid asked. "I mean, do you ever wake up in the night and worry that the cops are going to catch up with you—or even worse—that God is frowning at what you're doing? And that he's angry?"

"What's this, a church service? The earful on Sunday mornings is quite enough, thank you very much! Besides, we're not hurting anyone. We're just catering to the marketplace."

"I used to try to tell myself that too." The kid nodded sagely as if he held the answer to all the world's problems.

"Oh, for Pete's sake!" The man pulled out a cigar and lit it. The smoke scent curled and mingled with that of pine and moss.

"My mother says there are angels looking out for us all the time, that I have a guardian angel." The kid gave a slight smile. "I used to think that was stupid, but not anymore."

"I suppose you're going to start talking about demons next. Or flying saucers." The man waved his cigar in the air. "The only demons I believe in are the ones on a man's back when he's in pain. We drive those demons far away. This is a good deed we're doing."

"I wish I could believe that."

Incredibly, the kid's eyes filled with tears, and his disgust for the boy increased. "Grow up! I'm proud of what we do. You should be too."

The kid gave a bark of laughter. "Proud? I think my mom would disagree with you."

"What's your mother got to do with this? She was no saint in her younger days." If the kid only knew. But looking into the face that seemed suddenly older than its years, he wondered if maybe the kid *did* know.

"I wasn't raised to do this kind of thing. I've brought my mom a lot of grief. It's time I turned over a new leaf."

"You've already done that. I've heard about your visits to the schools, and how you've been telling kids to stay off drugs. I thought maybe it was just a cover."

The kid shook his head. "A cover? I wish it were that simple." He pulled out a key and tossed it to him.

His fingers closed around the cold metal. "You can't quit."

"I just did."

"You need me!"

"Not anymore. I have Jesus."

The realization of what the punk was saying stopped him cold. "And I suppose next you think you have to confess."

"I'm thinking about it."

The kid turned to walk away, and a rage rose inside him that he could not suppress. He yelled in anger and tackled the boy from behind. He gripped the kid's head between his hands and began to pound it against the ground. The earth was too soft to do much damage, but he continued to thump the punk's head against the grass until he managed to wriggle loose.

"Stop it!" the kid panted. He heaved the man off his chest and got up. "You're too old for this. I don't want to hurt you."

Shaking, the man clenched and unclenched his fists. "You're not going to destroy what I've worked nearly thirty years to build. I won't let you."

"I'll try to leave you out of it. But you'd better lay low for a while."

The kid's look of compassion made the man's rage spike again. "Don't do this. I'll make you sorry you were ever born."

"Most days I already was. I had to do something with the guilt that was eating me alive. For the first time in my life, I feel really clean. I'm making a new start with Jesus. You should give him a try yourself." The boy turned and walked toward the path.

He wouldn't give that comment the dignity of an answer. Through narrowed eyes, he watched until the forest swallowed up the kid's slim form. The punk would get to see his Jesus sooner than he ever imagined.

*B*ree was still shaking by the time she reached Anu's store. Before she got out of the Jeep, she looked both ways down the street. She unbuckled Davy from his car seat and took his hand. Samson followed them into the store.

Anu's smile of welcome faded when she saw Bree's face. "*Kulta*, what has happened?"

Davy ran forward. "A car almost crashed into us!" he announced with great drama.

To her son it had been an adventure. To Bree it had been a terrifying close call.

Anu opened her mouth, but Bree shook her head and nodded toward Davy. "Davy, Grammy bought you a Dr. Seuss book. It's in the break room. Why don't you run and get it? You can turn on the TV in there if you want too."

"Cool!" Davy, with Samson in close attendance, went eagerly toward the break room.

"You must have coffee." Anu went to the coffeepot and poured two cups. She pulled out a chair near the bakery display for Bree. "Tell me what happened."

Bree told her about Siller almost running her off the road. Anu clucked her tongue and grew more sober. "I shall call Mason."

"I suppose we'd better." Bree sipped her coffee while Anu talked to Mason.

"He's coming right over," Anu announced.

Barely two minutes later Mason came hurrying in the door. He joined the women at the table and took down all the information Bree gave him, then put his notepad away. "I have to find that guy. He keeps slipping through the cracks."

"I—I think I might know where he's hiding," Bree said. "I should have told you sooner, but things have been so crazy with the wedding and all, and I wasn't sure it was related."

"What?"

"A friend told me she saw a trunk in one of the cabins the Kitchigami Wilderness Tract owns. The trunk held all kinds of stuff about the Nicholls family, pictures of Anu and me, even some old ones of Rob and Hilary. I think it might be a sign of Quentin's obsession."

"Who told you this?"

"I'd rather not say. I don't want to get them in trouble. They shouldn't have been in the cabin either."

Mason frowned. "I need to know, Bree. They might remember more under questioning."

"I questioned them pretty thoroughly. And I went out to the cabin. The chest is gone now anyway. But it still tells us where he's hanging out. That's why I told you, just so you could check the cabins. Please, don't make me break a confidence."

Mason's scowl deepened. "I don't like being kept in the dark about anything."

"If I thought this person could help, you know I'd tell you in a minute. But I know she can't." Too late Bree realized the telltale *she.*

"It's Lauri, isn't it?" Mason took out his notepad.

"Don't say anything to her, Mason. Please, I'm begging you. She already isn't sure she can trust me. This would be proof."

"I would add my pleas to Bree's," Anu said. "I've been trying to reach out to Lauri myself. She's been coming by to learn the old Finnish recipes and seems to be slowly opening up. Don't ruin it, Mason."

"I guess I'm outnumbered," he said, putting away his notepad. "Okay, for now. But the first sign I get that she might know something to help me nab Sillers, I'll have to talk to her."

"I won't try to stop you if there's a chance she can help," Bree said.

"I guess that will have to do." Mason was obviously disgruntled. "Anything else you're hiding from me? You seem pretty stressed. Is it just Sillers?"

Bree glanced at Anu. "I took Davy to see Dr. Parker."

"He is all right, isn't he?" Anu asked immediately.

"Yes, he's fine. But Dr. Parker thinks I'm not spending enough time with him. He thinks I should quit my search-and-rescue work and be with him all the time."

"You're doing an important job, Bree; don't ever doubt that," Mason said. "I know it's hard after what you and Davy have gone through. But you'll find your way through it all."

"Davy knows he's loved," Anu said. "You must not let Max's words rattle you. I will have a talk with Max."

"Don't do that. I don't want him to think he has to handle me with kid gloves."

"Davy will be all right. Just give him some time," Anu said.

Bree noticed her mother-in-law made no promises about not talking to Dr. Parker, and she sighed. The last thing she wanted was for the doctor to think she had enlisted Anu to fight her own battles. Maybe she should call him back and talk to him herself. She was probably making too much of this. It was just his opinion. He was of a different generation, and he had never faced the realities of being a single mom.

If it weren't for Rob's family, she often wondered how she would have managed. Some women didn't have that support. At least they would never go hungry, and Davy would never go without the essentials of clothing and shoes. She wanted to provide those things for him herself though, and with the training center beginning to take off, she had high hopes of even being able to pay back Anu for her initial investment.

Not for the first time, she wondered how her life would have been different if Rob had come home from that fishing trip. She feared she still might be in this situation as a single parent, though perhaps Rob would still be alive. Would she have listened to his pleas of innocence, or would she have believed that phone call? It was so hard for her to forgive, to put suspicion aside. She'd inherited that tendency from her mother. But she vowed things would be different for her son. He would be able to trust her word and count on her.

— 19 —

The whine of the ATV's engine echoed off the snow-covered slopes of the mountain range to Kade's left. Yesterday, Wednesday, a report had come in that a series of shots had been fired in the Rock River basin area. As remote as it was, Kade wondered who had even been around to hear the shots. He had to wonder if it was a hoax. Such things were not unheard of. Some people got a malicious pleasure out of sending a park ranger on a wild-goose chase into rough terrain. Some days he wished he'd taken that promotion in California instead of being in charge of park security.

In another few weeks, he could get onto the trail with his new horse instead of riding this noisy ATV. But right now the machine plowed through the spring mud with little effort. Spring had come nearly a month early this year, a fact no one was complaining about. The day's mild temperatures held a touch of welcome warmth.

He paused and shut off the engine. Silence descended in a blanket of calm. Being in the forest was like walking with God. He drew in a deep breath of pure sunshine and fresh air. Life felt good this morning, better than usual. Lauri had actually been acting more herself lately, and that had Kade's heart singing like the finches in the trees above him. If only it would last. He spotted a flash of yellow and paused to enjoy the sight of a yellow warbler ruffling its feathers. Smiling, he marked the sighting in his logbook and continued on his way. The songbirds' return officially marked the return of spring, though patches of snow might not be gone for several weeks.

Restlessness had plagued him for several months now. At first he'd put it down to cabin fever, but now that spring was here, he was forced to admit it might be something more. Did God want to move him on? If he could take Bree with him, he wouldn't think twice about packing his things and hightailing it out of Rock Harbor. He'd never intended to settle here. Rock Harbor held too many painful memories.

Every time he thought of his father, his stomach tightened and the old rage rose like bile in his throat. The Holy Spirit had been pricking him lately about his refusal to forgive his father, but he couldn't seem to let go of it. He had even spoken the words "I forgive you, Dad," aloud, hoping that voicing them would cause him to really be able to do it. But in the end, the anger refused to die.

He took a swig from the canteen on his belt, then started the machine again and drove toward a stand of white pine. The basin lay just over the next rise. It was already nearly ten, and the filtered sunlight reached the forest floor in patterns of shadow and light. Steam rose in places where the sun shone the hottest, though it would be many days before the ensuing mud dried. Black flies would be out in droves soon, a situation Kade was none too eager to see approach.

Trudging to the top of the hill, he looked down into the basin area. Rock River tumbled in glorious abandon, tossing white-tipped waves onto the rocky shoreline and rushing headlong toward Whetstone Falls. The sound of the falls was a soothing roar in the distance, but Kade knew that closer up the sound could be almost deafening this time of year. The spring runoff caused the waterways to swell and filled the waterfalls that merely trickled much of the rest of the year.

Kade accelerated the ATV down the slope to the riverside. A

huge smile stretched across his face from the exhilaration of the wind. He shut off the engine and dismounted, then walked along the bank, studying the ground and looking for signs of any poaching. This time of year there was no legal hunting of any kind. This was the season when the wild raised its babies, and Kade intended to enforce that law.

Around the bend and nearer the falls, he came upon a pile of rags. On closer inspection, he realized it was a man's shirt and pants. Black-and-red-checkered flannel and heavy duck trousers. He frowned and touched the pile. Dry and fresh, not left over from last autumn's hunting season. Odd.

He lifted the clothing and inspected it, but there was no name on either tag and nothing under the clothes except more mud. The shirt and trousers didn't even have dew on them. Frowning, he dropped the clothes and continued toward the falls. Kade pushed through the tangle of blackberry shrubs and stood at the crest, where the water plunged into Lake Superior nearly two hundred feet below. The lake was more water than ice now.

The roar of the falls overwhelmed all thought and sensation. He stared into the whirlpool at the bottom of the falls, then lifted his eyes. Out in Lake Superior he could see an ore freighter plying the shipping lanes on its way to Sault Ste. Marie.

The scene was picture-perfect until Kade's gaze settled on something caught in the rocks at the top of the falls. He peered closer then gasped. Clothed only in underwear, a body had been snagged by a low-hanging tree branch. Even now the rushing water tugged at it, attempting to nudge it over the cliff and into the waiting lake below.

Kade wasn't sure if he could reach the body without tumbling over the falls himself, but he had to try, though even from here he could tell the man had to be dead. He quickly pulled a rope from his backpack and lashed it to a tree. Tying it around his waist, he secured his footing and began to inch his way along the slippery rocks toward the man.

He gasped at the cold clutch of the water, and his ankles and feet quickly grew numb. The rushing water made for slow going, and several times Kade teetered and nearly fell into the raging river, a fatal error if it happened. If he didn't drown, hypothermia would kill him in minutes. The water swirling around his ankles nearly toppled him again, and he knew it was no use to try to wade farther out. He needed to call in help.

Backing out of the water the way he'd come, he soon gained the safety of the shoreline. He radioed headquarters, and the ranger who responded promised to send backup and call Sheriff Kaleva. Kade went back to the edge of the river and eyed the body again. He needed to do something to keep it from going over the falls.

Untying the other end of his rope from the tree, he made a loop. He began to twirl the rope above his head. It had been years since he played cowboys and Indians. The last time, his father took his rope away from him and lashed Kade with it until welts formed on his legs, all the while screaming that life wasn't about play.

Trying to remember the feel of the rope twirling in his hand when he could rope any tree stump in his yard, he closed his eyes and prayed for God to help him. He opened his eyes and concentrated. He let the loop go and nearly let out a whoop of exultation when it settled over the man's arm.

He tightened the rope in tiny increments to make sure it didn't slide off, then secured it to a tree until help arrived. Once it was secure, he decided to see if he could find any clues as to who the man was and what he'd been doing in the river half-naked.

It was likely a suicide. Why people wanted to kill themselves by going over the falls was a mystery to him, but every year there was at least one numskull who decided to get his name in the paper that way. Kade had too much fight in him to understand how someone could just give up like that. His own life hadn't been easy, but whose was? The thought of tossing God's gift of life back in his face that way made him shudder. He wouldn't want to stand before God and whine about how hard it had been to simply put one foot in front of the other.

The glimmer from something shiny caught his eye, and he stooped to inspect the ground. A silver money clip lay among the quartz and tumbled rocks. It was empty. The sun had heated the metal, and it felt warm in his hand. He turned it over and saw the initials BLM. He tried to think who it could be, though from here the man didn't look familiar. And there was no guarantee it hadn't been lost last summer by a hiker.

The roar of an ATV, muffled by the sound of the falls, came from behind him. He turned around and squinted. Mason surely wouldn't be here already. Two ATVs raced toward him. Kade's eyes widened when he saw the guns in their hands. From here he could see the man's shock when he saw Kade staring at him. The man on the right shouted something at the man next to him. The machines slowed, then the big man on the right raised his gun and fired. A shot came zinging past Kade's ear.

Kade dived for cover behind a massive rock. He was a sitting duck if they surrounded him. Though he was armed, he'd never had occasion to even take his gun out. There was no time like the present though. He unsnapped his holster and pulled out his weapon. Though he often practiced, it felt heavy in his hand knowing he might have to use it to defend himself.

He peered around the rock, then ducked back as more shots came whizzing his way. This was awkward. It was impossible to shoot without being able to see what he was aiming at. Slithering on his belly, he scooted through the melting snow and mud to a group of three rocks about ten feet away. Bullets slammed into the snow bank by his head, but he gained the shelter of the outcropping.

The rocks angled around him in a fence of protection. The ATVs sat abandoned by a cluster of trees. The men must have gone into the trees for cover, or maybe they were even now creeping toward him, circling around from the other side. He turned. Nothing. Then another shot zipped by his shoulder, nearly creasing the fabric of his jacket. This time Kade saw the flare from the end of the rifle. He took aim and managed to get off a shot that ricocheted off a tree.

The shooter ducked away. Kade smiled grimly. The man probably hadn't realized Kade was armed. Moments later the engines roared to life, and the men raced away. Kade hadn't been aware he was holding his breath until he realized his chest hurt. He exhaled and stood. What was that all about? Had the men been coming to retrieve the body from the river? If so, then it surely wasn't suicide. He watched the distant machines until they faded from view and only the sound of their racing engines still echoed. Then that too was gone.

This made no sense. He went back to the river's edge. The man's body was still trapped by the tree limb and anchored by the rope. With new resolve, Kade studied the ground and the surrounding area. In a brush pile twenty feet into the forest he found a backpack partially hidden under a bramble patch. He started to grab it, then realized he shouldn't touch it. Mason would want to check it for clues.

Kade heard the rumble of an ATV approaching. Maybe that was his backup now. He noted the location of the backpack and went to meet them. Mason and one of his deputies rode two ATVs. Kade waved to them and went to stand near the river.

Deputy Doug Montgomery swung his bulk off the machine and followed Mason to the river's edge.

"What we got here?" Mason asked.

"More than meets the eye," Kade said. "Two guys on ATVs

took some shots at me, then left when I returned fire. I had assumed it was a suicide, but I'd say something happened here the men didn't want to get out."

Mason's eyebrows arched, and he straightened. "They shot at you? You get any bullet fragments?"

Kade hadn't even thought of that. He'd just been looking for other evidence. "Check by the boulders." He gestured to the trees. "There's a backpack over there."

Mason followed him to the backpack and pulled on gloves before he knelt to examine the contents. Unzipping it, he riffled through the contents: clothing, a small radio, packages of dehydrated food, gum, and at the very bottom, a wallet. "Maybe this will at least tell us who he is." He flipped open the wallet, and Kade peered over his shoulder. A driver's license showed a young man with a wide smile and red hair. Benjamin Lee Mallory. The same initials as the money clip. The wallet held no money either, which was strange. Robbery didn't seem to be a motive for the men on the ATVs, but then they might have been the clean-up crew.

Mason stuffed everything back in the backpack, then put it in a plastic bag he pulled from his pocket. He instructed Deputy Montgomery to search for bullets while he followed Kade to where the rope tethered the body.

"Good roping," Mason noted. "Let's see if we can get him to shore. I brought a body hook." He turned. "Hey, Montgomery, get the hook off my machine."

The deputy nodded and went to the four-wheeler. The hook looked small in his meaty hands. Mason took it and unwound the wire then handed the end to his deputy.

"Fasten that to the undercarriage of my ATV."

After nearly half an hour of exertion and failed attempts, they succeeded in hauling the body to shore. The man lay stretched on the rocks faceup. He looked barely old enough to shave, though his driver's license said he was born in 1976, making him almost thirty. Kade wished he was anywhere but here.

"Ever seen him before?" he asked.

Mason shook his head. "Nope." He knelt over the body. "Looks like he was shot." He pointed to a neat hole in the man's chest.

"This makes no sense!" Kade burst out. "Did you notice where he was from?"

Mason shook his head and pulled the wallet out of the bag. "Says Houghton," he said after perusing it for a minute. "Wonder what he was doing down here? And this is pretty remote. Anything strange going on here lately?"

Kade started to say no then stopped. "Now that you mention it, we've had some break-ins at cabins along Superior just north of here. I thought it was probably just kids trying to find some secluded places to meet."

"Mind if I take a look at them?"

"Nope. As long as I can tag along."

"Not a problem. When can we go?"

"Anytime you say."

Mason looked back at the dead man. "Let's get him to town and see what we can find out about this first."

*T*he good smells from the kitchen made Bree's mouth water. Davy was curled in the crook of her arm reading a new book Anu had brought him. She knew they looked the perfect picture of mother and child, and with Dr. Parker's criticism still fresh in her mind, she felt almost smug; the good doctor himself sat across from her in the easy chair by the window.

"Anu is quite a cook," Dr. Parker remarked. "I can't tell you how long it's been since I had a home-cooked meal. I was delighted Anu invited me to stay."

"Well, you didn't have to come by to apologize. It's only right we feed you for your trouble."

"You're a good mom, and I know I was suggesting otherwise at the office. Sometimes I forget the world isn't like it used to be any-more."

"Did your mother never work?"

"Actually, yes, she did. When my father came home from World War II, he couldn't work. When the money ran out, she had to go to work in the copper mine office. She hated it. I hated it. I'm afraid that experience colored my view on women working for all eternity."

Bree had always heard the Parker family was filthy rich and practically built the town. This was a new side. She didn't know what to say.

Dr. Parker smiled. "I can see you're shocked. Sometimes we do what we have to do though. My mom did. You do." His face hardened, but there was sadness in his eyes. "And so do I."

Anu called them to dinner, and there was no opportunity to ask what he meant. He seemed to have it all, but who did, really? Bree wondered if he was lonely. He'd made no secret of his admiration for Anu.

After he left, Bree helped Anu clean the kitchen. "You've known Dr. Parker a long time," she said, putting the milk away.

"Max has not had the easy life it seems on the surface," Anu said, nodding. "His father expected much from him. When his father came home crippled with pain, nothing was ever the same at his house again. He often talked of how his mother never had time for him once his father arrived. He was an only child, and her attention had been solely devoted to him until that time. When he talked with Abraham, he often said he intended to make enough money that his wife could stay home and raise their children, even if it meant working two jobs."

"They only had Brian though."

Anu nodded. "His wife, Becky, never wanted kids at all. She tried to talk Max into giving her an abortion, but he wouldn't do it. When she drowned, I think it was almost a relief to Max; she treated Brian so badly."

"No wonder that kid is so messed up. I hate it that Lauri is mixed up with him. I like Dr. Parker, but his son needs to grow up."

"Max has spoiled him," Anu admitted. "But providing the best of everything for his family is very important to Max. Too important, really. But he's never understood that."

"We never really know what shapes us into the people we become," Bree said.

*B*ree caught her lip between her teeth and glanced down at the recipe book. She'd been sure this would take her mind off Quentin

Siller, but it was impossible to focus on cooking when he was out there somewhere.

"You need some help?" Kade sat on a bar stool at the kitchen counter watching her. Davy was reading his book for the umpteenth time. At the rate he was going, he'd need another copy of *The Three Trees* for his birthday.

They'd been running in different directions all week, and it was good to hang out with Kade, even if it was in the kitchen. She smiled at him and turned back to her recipe book. "No, I can do this." She put the sauce on to boil and began to stir, as the directions said. "This will be the best fettuccine you've ever had." She hoped. The white sauce sounded tricky. Maybe she should have tried something easier, but she'd wanted to impress Kade.

"I'm sure it will be. You're a fine cook."

Bree nearly giggled at the bravery in his voice. She raised her wooden spoon and waved it at him. "Don't ever tell a woman she's a good cook in that tone of voice."

The smile vanished from his face, and he nodded soberly. "Got it. Dare I say I look forward to this with all the anticipation of a man who has to eat his own cooking?"

"That's about all it's going to be. Something you haven't cooked." Her giggle escaped, and he grinned with her.

The sauce began to bubble, and Bree stirred it furiously. Anu would be home from the store soon, and Bree wanted to surprise her with a meal all ready. The salad waited in the refrigerator, and the dessert, a New York–style cheesecake she'd bought, was ready to go. This sauce was the real test.

It boiled away then began to thicken. Almost instantly it congealed into thick lumps. "Oh no!" she wailed. She grabbed the handle and dragged it from the heat. "What's happening?"

Kade leaned over her to take a look. "Uh-oh. What kind of cream did you use?"

"Whipping cream." She nodded to the empty carton and

continued to stir. She'd followed the directions perfectly. She felt like sitting in the middle of the floor and wailing.

Kade picked up the carton. "This is the ultrapasteurized kind. It doesn't always work right."

"Now you tell me." Bree picked up the pan and dumped its contents down the garbage disposal. "Now what do I do?" It was more an exasperated remark than a question. She gave him a winning smile. "You want to run to the grocery for some canned sauce?"

The corners of his lips lifted. "Sure. Do I need to go right now?"

She shook her head. "You can wait half an hour or so." She went to the refrigerator. "Want a Pepsi?"

"Sounds good."

She grabbed two sodas and handed one to him, then plopped onto the stool beside him. So much for her grand scheme. She suddenly realized she was frowning as she stared at her son. The doctor's words still preyed on her mind.

Kade popped the top on his soda and took a swig. "You've been quiet tonight."

"Do you think I'm gone from Davy too much?"

His eyebrows shot up. "You spend every spare minute with him and take him to work with you. How could you possibly spend more time with him than you already do?"

"Dr. Parker thinks I'm not giving him enough time," she said softly. The doctor's words had haunted her all week, in spite of his apology.

"Is he trying to lay a guilt trip on you? Davy is lucky to have you as a mother and lucky you have a job you can share with him. He loves going to the dog-training stuff. What more does the doctor think you should do?"

"Quit working at my business and let Anu support us. I actually considered it, but this afternoon Anu mentioned how slow business has been and that she's going to have to cut back on some of her workers' hours." Bree bit her lip and leaned forward to take a handful of pistachios. "I couldn't ask her for help. She's done so much already. I'm not about to put her in a position to support us."

Bree had a big training day coming up in a few weeks that would bring in several thousand dollars. It seemed somehow wrong to be thinking about money when it came to her son's emotional health though. She had to do what was best for him regardless of money issues. But she had to support him too.

"We had a scare on Monday too," she said. "Quentin Siller nearly ran us off the road. I called Mason and he sent a deputy out, but he was long gone, of course."

"Did he stop?"

She shook her head. "He just kept on trucking. I half expected him to come at me with a tire iron." She shuddered. What would she have done?

A frown furrowed his forehead. "I don't like this," he muttered.

She was sorry she'd brought it up. "You've been quiet too," she observed.

"I got a call about possible poaching out near Whetstone Falls. I didn't find any poachers, but I found a dead man. And some guys on four-wheelers took some shots at me when I did." He said the words in a matter-of-fact way.

Bree blinked. "They *shot at you*?" She sat up straight on the sofa and turned to stare at him. *No more, Lord. I can't take any more.*

He nodded grimly. "They left when I returned fire. Mason helped me get the body to shore and back to town. The autopsy is being done tonight."

"Who was it?"

He shook his head. "Benjamin Mallory from Houghton. Late twenties and dressed only in his skivvies. If the men on the ATVs hadn't come after me, I would have guessed it was suicide."

"What's Mason say?"

"He's stumped too. The guy worked at a cannery in Hancock. He's got some juvenile delinquency–type stuff on his record, but his mother has no idea why he'd be at Rock River or what he'd been up to."

Hancock was just over the river from Houghton, and basically the two were one town. A fish-packaging plant. "Maybe he was scouting for a spot for a fish farm?" That was a stretch, and they both knew it. The lakes near Rock River would be inaccessible even if the area wasn't in a national forest protected from harvest.

"Mason is investigating. He'll figure it out."

"This is all getting out of hand," she said. "Skeletons in my basement, arson, someone taking shots at the wedding, and again at you. Can all this be connected somehow? It all seemed to start with finding Thorrington's remains in my basement."

"If there's a connection between Mallory's death and that, I'm missing it somewhere. Hey, speaking of the wedding, when are the newlyweds coming home?"

She knew he had changed the subject to ease her worry. He was so thoughtful of her, so kind. She was lucky to have him. "Tomorrow. I can't wait to see Naomi. She's going to flip out over everything that's going on."

"Maybe we could have dinner with them when they get back."

"With the kids too! We could have it here or at Naomi's new home."

"Or at my cabin, though it's pretty small."

Kade's cabin was beyond small; it was minuscule. But it suited him and Lauri. "How have things been with Lauri?"

Kade shrugged. "Still blowing hot and cold. But she's been strange. Sleeping a lot and kind of lethargic. I've been thinking about taking her to see Dr. Parker."

"That doesn't sound good. Could she be depressed?" Bree knew all about depression. When Rob's plane went down with him and Davy in it, she'd wanted to die herself. She smiled as she looked at her son and thanked God again that he'd brought them through the pain.

Kade sighed and ran his hand through his thick thatch of hair. It was a bit longer than usual and curled at the nape of his neck. Bree couldn't resist the temptation. She leaned over and ran her fingers through it. He looked up and smiled the slow smile that always made her heart beat a little faster.

"She might be depressed," Kade said, taking her hand and pressing his lips against her palm. "I've been worried about that. You think I should make her go to the doctor?"

Bree found it hard to think with him so close. "It couldn't hurt."

"How's the house coming? I love Anu, but I miss our evenings together."

His breath whispered across her face, and she leaned into his embrace. "Pretty good. I should be able to move back home soon, maybe two or three days."

"Good."

He tipped her chin up, and his lips came down to meet hers. All thoughts of her ruined dinner fled, and she snuggled into his embrace. Kade would keep her and Davy safe.

$\mathcal{B}$ree awoke in the dark. She lay blinking in the dim light from the streetlamp. It was raining. The nudge came again, and she turned. Samson bumped her arm again then licked her face and whined. Davy. She glanced to the bed beside her, but her son was missing. Panic surged, and she rolled out of bed.

"Davy?" she called softly. Where could he be hiding? Samson whined and went to the closet. At least this time he hadn't wandered far. She stepped to the closet door and opened it.

Rob had grown up in this room. It held two twin-size beds and all the little-boy things Rob had collected. His baseball bat, mitts, and balls were clustered on a rack in the corner. The dressers and beds were painted in red, white, and blue and held several collections of Star Wars figurines.

The closet was full of boxes of Rob's old memorabilia that Anu was keeping for Davy, and he often sought this place when he was missing his daddy in an especially poignant way. Bree pushed the baseball and Boy Scout uniforms out of the way. A bulge under Rob's Michigan State fuzzy throw moved.

"Sweetie, are you awake?" Bree pulled the throw away from her son's face. Sweat matted his hair to his forehead, but he was asleep. She gathered him into her arms, pressing her lips against his damp forehead. He muttered and flailed restlessly, but his eyes stayed closed. Bree breathed in his little-boy scent, then sat on the edge of the bed rocking him back and forth and praying until his restless stirring ceased. When he was finally serene, she laid him back in bed.

She should be exhausted. In fact, she *was* exhausted. She just wasn't sleepy. Samson settled on the foot of Davy's bed and looked at her. "It's okay, boy," she whispered. He whined and got down from Davy's bed. Thrusting his cold nose into her hand, he nudged her until she petted him. His thick fur had a couple of burrs in it, and she worked them loose.

He licked her hand then started to go back to Davy's bed. Just under the window, he stopped and stiffened. The ruff on his neck stood up, and a low growl emanated from his throat.

Bree's ches tightened. She slipped out of bed and peeked out the window to see what had disturbed the dog. Her hand sought his head, and she patted him. "Shhh." If Davy woke up, the whole house would be in an uproar the rest of the night.

It was probably someone walking by. The rain fell harder. *Why would someone be walking in the rain?* She pulled back the curtain a bit and peeked out. A car was parked across the street, but she couldn't tell if the dark form she saw was someone in the car or merely a shadow.

She could feel every thud of her heart, and she shivered. Should she call someone? There was no law against parking across the street. She spied the glowing red tip of a cigarette; then the car began to move. It turned the corner and was gone. Only after the street was empty did she realize the car lights had never come on. Swallowing hard, she tiptoed back to bed and crawled under the covers. Her feet and hands were frozen, and not just from the cold floor. She fought back the fear. Whoever it was, he was gone now. She'd tell Mason about it tomorrow. There was no use disturbing him now. Besides, the car had actually been parked in front of the neighbors'. So many scary things had happened lately, she was beginning to assume everything was connected to her and Anu, when it could have been something totally innocent.

Anu smiled when she saw Bree. "Good morning, my *kulta*. How did you sleep?"

"Not very well," Bree admitted, tightening the belt around her terry robe. She stood yawning in the sunlight, wondering if she'd imagined the events of the night before. In the light of the day, her night terror seemed distant and ridiculous. She would say nothing to Anu, she decided. She likely had a case of jumping to conclusions, and she didn't want to worry Anu.

"A cup of coffee will perk you up," Anu said. "Help yourself while I prepare the *nisu*."

The Finnish sweet bread was a favorite of Bree's. She poured a cup of coffee, then sat at the kitchen table and watched her mother-in-law. Still slim and lovely, Anu was everything Bree wanted to be. But it wasn't Anu's appearance Bree so admired; it was her calm acceptance of life, her optimism as she faced the future in spite of difficult circumstances, the wisdom and love she poured out on her family and friends. Bree knew Anu's faith had a lot to do with her attitude. She was a role model for Bree. Her own fragile faith cracked in the face of small obstacles, and she longed to be a rock like Anu.

"Why the long face?" Anu asked. "Something more than fatigue?"

For a moment Bree was tempted to tell Anu how incapable she felt, how sometimes she wanted to give up the struggle with her guilt, to forget what God expected of her. In some ways it might be easier. But she also knew she couldn't; she'd made an eternal choice. Anu would understand and try to comfort her, but this was a struggle Bree had to face on her own. And she *would* face it.

"Just tired," she said. "Did you hear anything in the night?"

"Other than the rain? No. I slept like those old heart-pine logs still on the bottom of Lake Superior," Anu said. "I have been so tired lately." A shadow passed over her features. "Though he has been gone for thirty years, I have thought much of Abraham lately. Next month would have been our thirty-eighth wedding anniversary."

"Do you think he's dead?" Bree hated to ask the question, but in her mind Abraham must have died. Otherwise, surely he would have sent some word to Anu and his children.

"Sometimes I think yes and sometimes no." Anu shrugged. "The pain of his desertion is gone, but I still pray for his soul and wonder what became of him. Max was always convinced something happened to him. He never believed Abraham would leave me and the children. But no trace was ever found, though Max helped me look."

"I've been meaning to ask you about something you said the other day. You said he was friends with Peter and some others. Who were the others again? Max was one, right?"

Anu nodded. "Yes. They called themselves the 'Do-Wrongs,' though I hated the name. Gary Landorf, Peter Thorrington, Max Parker, and Abraham. They were always together, from bowling in a league together to fishing on their charter boat." She twisted the emerald ring on her hand.

"Gary Landorf—that's Kade's boss. I don't know much about him. Did he help you look too?" Bree knew Kade didn't think much of his boss, but that might be racked up to personal differences.

Anu shook her head. "He transferred out of Rock Harbor a few weeks after Abraham disappeared. It is only recently he has come home. He stopped by to see me when he first arrived and asked if I'd ever heard from Abraham." She gave a sad smile and touched Bree's cheek with gentle fingers. "It was a long time ago, *kulta*. And a complete mystery."

"I intend to figure it out."

"I do not wish to see you get hurt," Anu said.

"I'll be fine." The aroma of *nisu* grew stronger. "Yum, that smells good. I think I'll get a shower while that's baking."

Anu's expression was troubled. "I do not like the thought of you poking around in this, my Bree. Let Mason handle it."

"Mason has all he can do trying to figure out that fresh murder along Rock River," Bree said.

"He knows for sure that was murder?"

"The guy died of a gunshot wound. And why else would those men shoot at Kade? It's clearly no accident." Bree took a sip of her coffee, then put down the cup and went down the hall to the bathroom.

As the hot spray from the shower head hit her, she planned her day. First she would go to the paper mill here in town and talk to Peter Thorrington's stepbrother, Ted Kemppa. It was Tuesday, so he should be there. After that she would talk to Captain Argie Hamel's sister, Susan. Though Susan had never been on the *Seawind*, she might remember something about Peter's involvement in Argie's rescue.

And with this new information about the shipwreck, another trip to the library might be in order. In fact, maybe she'd do that first. Davy could come along and get some books. Susan's photography shop was just across the street from the library. Maybe she could pop in there a minute too.

She combed some gel through her hair and scrunched the short red curls then climbed into jeans and a sweatshirt. By the time she was dressed, Davy was stirring. Bree sat on the edge of his bed and tousled his hair. He smiled at her sleepily, and she pulled him into her lap when Samson moved out of the way with obvious reluctance. She lived for mornings. The feel of Davy's warm, small body snuggled close to hers would carry her to tomorrow. She rested her chin atop his silky red hair.

"Mommy, can we go see Daddy?"

This was a common question. Bree had tried to explain to him that his daddy was in heaven, but then he asked to go see him there. How did a mother explain death when she didn't really understand it herself?

She rocked him back and forth in her arms a bit. "Okay," she said. "I'll show you where Daddy is sleeping." Was she making a mistake to take him to the grave? Was he ready for that? She didn't know what else to do.

She bathed him and had him put on his jeans and a long-sleeve shirt; then they ate breakfast with Anu. At the refrigerator she poured her son a glass of orange juice and told Anu what she planned. Bree was relieved to see Anu agreed.

"It is time, *kulta*," her mother-in-law whispered.

Half an hour later, Bree pulled into the small cemetery behind Rock Harbor Community Church. They'd moved Rob's body from the woodland grave Rachel had laid him in right after Thanksgiving, before the heavy snows began.

She hadn't been here herself since the funeral. Yards of snow and drifts as high as the house eaves had buried the site since early December. Her stomach felt as though a giant fist clenched it in a tight hold that nearly made her sick. Samson whined in the back-seat then pressed his nose against her neck.

"It's okay, boy," she said softly. She parked, then let Samson out of the back. Bree gripped Davy's hand as they skirted patches of thick mud, treading on stones scattered through the cemetery. She knew the grave was in front of the gazebo and slightly to the right. The obsidian stone was etched with a mountain scene and the words from Psalm 16: *I said to the LORD, 'You are my Lord.'*

"Mommy, you're hurting my hand."

Davy's complaint broke the rigidity of Bree's body. "Sorry, sweetie." She loosened her hold on his hand and scooped him into her arms. "This is where Daddy's body is sleeping. But it's just his body. The real Daddy is with Jesus. Remember the way he smiled and the little crinkles at his eyes? And the way he used to read to you and pretend to be all the characters? That's the real Daddy."

Davy nodded, his eyes wide. He looked down at the tombstone. "Why doesn't he wake up?"

"Because Jesus needed him more than we did." Even as Bree said the words, she wondered how that could be. Was Rob dead because of an evil man's actions and because evil was more powerful than God? Or had God really allowed his murder for a reason? She didn't understand why there was evil in the world that overcame good. Rob had died because he refused to condone evil. She and Davy could be proud of his integrity, but it didn't make up for the fact that he was no longer in their lives. Or that she'd never had the chance to make amends and ask for his forgiveness. He would have offered it too—she knew that was so. Then why couldn't she forgive herself?

A chill wind blew from the forest to her left, and she shivered. *Where are you, Rob? Can you look down and see us here? Does God allow you to watch over us?* She wished that was true. Rob would never let anything bad happen to them. But Jesus was even more trustworthy, she reminded herself. Rob was just a man. A good man, but a man nonetheless. Jesus was God.

Davy squirmed. "I want down."

Bree set him down, and he walked slowly to the mound of mud. The grave had not yet been seeded, and the melting snow had left the ground a quagmire.

He knelt beside the mound. "Hi, Daddy. I'm mad at you. You should have told God no, that you couldn't come. It's not fair. You should tell Jesus to let you come home."

Bree squeezed her eyes shut. She wanted to stop him, to tell him his father couldn't hear him, and that even if he could, there was no way he would ever come back. But Davy needed to vent. Her heart throbbed painfully.

When Bree opened her eyes, she found Samson curled against the boy. Davy had wrapped his arms around the dog and buried his face in Samson's fur. She moved forward to join them. When she touched Davy, he flinched.

"Why didn't you come find us, Mommy? If you'd found us, Daddy wouldn't have gone away to heaven."

"Yes, he would have, Davy," Bree said, kneeling in the wet grass. "No one can say no when Jesus says to come with him."

"Daddy could have. He's strong. You just didn't get there in time. The doctor could have fixed him. Why didn't you get there in time?"

Bree was weeping openly. "I tried, pumpkin. Samson and I tried as hard as we could to find you. Are you mad at Samson too?"

Davy's face was screwed up as though he wanted to cry but was fiercely trying not to. "I'm mad at you, Mommy. I don't love you anymore." He jumped to his feet and rushed to the Jeep.

Samson whined and started after the boy, then turned back to lick Bree's wet cheeks. Bree could tell he didn't know who to comfort first. "I'm okay, Samson. Go to Davy," she whispered. The dog licked her again, then turned and ran after Davy. He jumped into the backseat with her boy.

At least Davy was expressing his feelings now, and that was a good thing. So why did it hurt so much?

*W*hat a rotten morning. Crawling to the sink, Lauri grasped the edge and pulled herself to her feet. She leaned over and splashed cold water on her face, gasping at the relief it brought. She stared at her face in the mirror. White as the sand on Rock Harbor Beach. She looked bad. Really bad. How could she go to school like this? But she had to go. Today was the big algebra test, and she'd studied hard for it. If she stayed home, Kade would think she was trying to skip the test.

Gritting her teeth, she grabbed her toothbrush and squeezed some Crest onto it. The minty taste pushed back the nausea even more. She'd make it. With a flick of the brush through her hair and a touch of makeup, she looked better. Not great, but better. Her stomach rebelled at the thought of breakfast, though she knew she should try to eat something. Maybe a few crackers. Eggs or frozen waffles would make her sick again. Luckily, Kade had left early— some big meeting at work he'd been anxious about. She hadn't listened too well last night as he'd rambled on, but it had something to do with what a jerk his boss was being. Served Kade right though. Let him see how lousy it was to have to deal with unreasonable demands.

Lauri went to the kitchen and found a sleeve of saltine crackers. Munching a few of them, she went back to her room and packed her backpack. Rummaging through its contents for her favorite barrette, her hand touched the plastic wrapper of the sanitary napkins she always carried.

The blood drained from her face as she pulled one out. When was the last time she'd had her period? Her hands shook as she grabbed her school calendar out of her backpack. It had been over a month, hadn't it? She counted back. She was more than two weeks late.

Her legs refused to support her, and she slowly sank to the edge of the bed. Could it be? Everything in her rebelled at the thought. There was no way she could be pregnant, was there? She felt the need to throw up again, but this time from sheer fright.

Kade would kill her. She'd have to drop out of school in her sophomore year. There was no way she'd face the sly smiles and hurtful remarks of the catty girls at school. She wasn't a whore—she wasn't. Brian was the only boy she'd ever done it with. But everyone would call her that. For the first time, Lauri was glad her mother wasn't alive.

But maybe she was jumping to conclusions. There could be some other reason for her nausea and late period. She could have cancer or something. In fact, cancer would be preferable. For a moment, Lauri imagined herself wasting away in the hospital. Dressed in a gorgeous peignoir, she would watch as classmates filed in to see her, expressing their grief at the thought of losing her.

She shook herself out of her reverie. There was only one way to find out. If she hurried, she could stop at the drugstore on the way to school. Cramming the rest of her things into her backpack, she grabbed her jacket and ran to her car.

There was a free parking space right in front of the drugstore. She pulled into it and killed the engine. Glancing around, she was relieved to see the streets were fairly empty. She grabbed her wallet out of her backpack and went inside.

Where did she find what she needed? Other girls had giggled about scares like this, but Lauri had never imagined the trauma of it. She hurried to the feminine-hygiene aisle and found what she was looking for. But which test was best? She wanted something accurate. She finally settled on one that promised to turn pink with a positive test. If she *was* pregnant, she wanted a girl.

Walking toward the counter, she stopped in the aisle. What if someone saw her buying this? They would know. Maybe she should wait and go out of town after school. She started to put it back, then turned with sudden resolve back toward the counter. No way could she go through the whole day worrying about this. She had to know.

The clerk was new, a complete stranger, so she was thankful for that. She forked over her money, then carried the test to the car, putting it in her backpack. At first break, she would go to the rest room and take it.

Lauri's fingers felt numb as she pulled out the pregnancy test and opened the package, her hands shaking so badly it took several tries to tear it open. After reading the instructions, she went to the toilet stall and followed them.

She would have to wait five minutes. She stared at her watch. Her thoughts whirled in a kaleidoscope of confusion.

The seconds ticked by in an agony of delay. Lauri dared not look at the test strip until the time was up. She wanted to know, yet she didn't. Chewing on her thumbnail, she waited. Finally, she took a deep breath and held up the test strip. The pink line was in the test results window. For a moment she stared at it, certain she was looking in the wrong place. Maybe it was the collection line that showed it was working properly. But a closer look showed the other pink line that showed the test was correct.

She was going to have a baby.

Closing her eyes, she swayed on the toilet seat. *Stay calm*, she told herself. A girl today had options. She could abort it. But even as the thought crossed her mind, she knew she could never do that. What would her mother think? She believed her mother was in heaven looking down on her. Her mother would be horribly disappointed in her if she ever did something like that. No, abortion wasn't an option.

The future stretched before her: a series of scenes like a movie. Late nights changing diapers, a baby crying constantly, dances she wouldn't be able to go to, parties she'd never attend, students who would turn their backs on her.

On shaky legs, she exited the stall and went to the bench. She'd just settled on it when the swinging door to the gym opened and her old friend Ruth came in. Her sweet round face invited people to tell her their troubles.

"Hi," Ruth said. "You okay? Have you been crying?"

There was such a wealth of caring and genuine love in Ruth's voice that the hold Lauri had on her emotions broke, and she burst into tears.

"Nothing's okay," she sobbed.

Ruth rushed to her side and put her arms around her. "What's wrong, Lauri? Can I help?"

That was something Lauri had forgotten about Ruth—her giving, helpful nature. She was a Christian too, which had been something that once attracted Lauri to her, but as her path went in another direction, it had made her pull away from Ruth. Now Lauri knew she needed something bigger than herself to turn to.

"I don't know what to do." She buried her face against Ruth's shoulder and cried. When the tears were spent, she pulled away and wiped her eyes shakily.

"You want to talk about it?" Tears stood in Ruth's eyes as well.

"I'm pregnant," Lauri said with stark simplicity.

Ruth's brown eyes widened. She swallowed, and her Adam's apple bobbed. "Are you sure?"

Her friend's careful tone nearly brought the tears to the surface again, but Lauri managed to swallow them down. "Yes, I'm sure. I just took a test."

Ruth gripped her hand. "Yikes! What are you going to do? Have you told Brian?"

Bless her friend for knowing Lauri well enough to know that only one boy could be the father. "I just now found out. I don't know what I'm going to do."

"Maybe he'll marry you."

"No, I don't want to marry him." Stating it so baldly shocked Lauri to her core. She didn't love Brian. She didn't want to marry him. She didn't even want to be his girlfriend anymore. The price was too high. Too bad she hadn't realized that a few months ago.

If Ruth was surprised, she managed to keep it to herself, for she just squeezed Lauri's hand. "How can I help? I'll do whatever you need me to do."

"I'm sorry," Lauri said with heartfelt humility.

"For what?"

"For not being your friend. For forgetting how important our friendship was."

Ruth absorbed the apology for a few moments. "That's okay. I knew you were just star-struck."

Good term. But the stars had sure taken a hike now. For the first time in months Lauri looked at her life and realized what a mess she was in. But at least she had a friend. That was more than she'd had this morning.

"What should I do, Ruthie?" she whispered.

"I don't know." Ruth returned the pressure on her hand.

"What would you do?" Lauri knew that was a ridiculous question. Ruth would never find herself in this situation because she planned to stay a virgin until she married. If only Lauri had been that smart.

"What about . . . adoption?"

To give away her own flesh and blood? "I don't know," she said doubtfully. A vision of Naomi's smiling face flashed into her head. She cared enough that she'd taken time out from her own wedding to counsel Lauri, not that Lauri had been ready to listen at the time. But if she could make sure her baby had a mother like Naomi, maybe she could do it.

"You don't have to decide now," Ruth pointed out. "You'll need to talk to your brother. He'll help you."

"He'll kill me," Lauri said, her shoulders drooping.

"No, he won't. Dinah and I always wished we had a brother like yours. You've been pretty mean to him lately, like you've . . ." She broke off and looked away.

Lauri winced. She *had* been mean to everyone, even her two best friends since grade school. Had the problems with Kade been mostly her fault? She closed her eyes and sighed. Lately it seemed everything was her fault. And she didn't know how to fix any of it.

"Maybe you're right," she said, opening her eyes. "I don't want to tell him. I'm not sure I can."

"Want me to come with you when you do?" Ruth was still holding her hand.

Lauri sighed again heavily. "Don't I wish! But this is something I'd better do myself. You don't want to witness a murder."

"He's not going to touch you."

"I might wish he would. It might hurt less than his words."

Both girls fell silent at this bit of truth. "You going to tell him tonight?" Ruth chewed on her lip.

"I don't know. Maybe. I have to work up the nerve."

"It's just going to bug you until you do. Might as well get it over with."

"Maybe." The bell signaling the end of break sounded. Lauri stood. "Want to sit together for lunch?"

Ruth's eyes widened, and for a minute Lauri thought she might cry. Shame overwhelmed her at what she'd put her friend through.

"Sure. Dinah too?"

"Yeah. I want to tell her what a bonehead I've been."

Lauri wiped away the last trace of tears from her face. Her stomach heaved at the thought of telling Kade. He wouldn't take it nearly as well as Ruth had.

*I*t was all Bree could do to stack sweaters on the display table. Naomi should be home anytime. It seemed her best friend had been gone for years instead of days. So much had happened.

She glanced at her watch again. Nearly eleven o'clock on this Saturday morning. Her cell phone buzzed at her waist. She grabbed it up. "This is Bree."

"Bree, it's me. What's going on?"

"Mrs. O'Reilly, you're home! When did you get in?"

"Just now. I called your house and got the answering machine saying to call you at Anu's. Why are you staying there?" she demanded.

"Well . . ."

"Spill it!"

"Someone set a fire in the basement of my lighthouse. You'd just left town after the wedding, and we were cleaning up the church."

"Oh, Bree, no! Who would try to destroy that wonderful old lighthouse?"

"We don't know. Luckily, the blaze was caught before it did more than minor smoke damage. The cleanup is almost finished, and I'm about ready to move back in."

"Praise God! But arson, Bree—that's so scary." Naomi sounded near tears.

"Tell me about it! I have lots more to tell you too. Some strange things have been happening. When we get together, I'll tell you all about it. I've sure missed you."

"I'd say I missed you too, but we were almost too busy to even realize how long we'd been gone. The kids loved the mountains, and we looked through all the tacky souvenir shops and watched for bears, all the fun stuff. But it's good to be home. When can you come over?"

"Can I come today?" Anu would let her slip away.

"Don't be silly! Of course. Come for lunch?" Naomi suggested.

"It's a date. Davy will be thrilled to see Timmy. You mentioned bears, and it reminded me I need to pick up some bear spray for my ready-pack. Want me to get you some too? The bears are out of their dens by now. We're going to do a deep-woods training session next week."

"Yeah, I'm out too. When can you come over?"

Bree glanced at the stack of sweaters she needed to finish. "Give me an hour."

*D*avy bounced with excitement on Naomi's walk. Rushing ahead of Bree, he pressed the doorbell then turned the doorknob.

"Wait a minute, Davy. This isn't like when Naomi lived next door. You can't just go rushing in. Other people live here too." Bree caught up with her son and took his hand.

The door flew open and Naomi enveloped Bree in a hug. "Gosh, I've missed you! Why on earth didn't you just come in?"

"I wasn't sure if Donovan was here or not. I felt funny just barging in." Bree looked around, trying not to focus on how much things were going to change now between her and Naomi.

"You don't have to knock," Naomi said.

From the trepidation in her voice, Bree knew the difference

in their circumstances was just now hitting her friend. She dug in her pocket. "Here's your bear spray. Got any bears hanging around?"

"Only Donovan when he hasn't had his coffee," Naomi said with a grin.

Bree smiled. "You look marvelous! I've never seen you so relaxed and happy. Marriage must agree with you."

"You might say that," Naomi agreed smugly.

"'Wuv, twue wuv,'" Bree deadpanned.

Naomi made a face at her, then knelt to hug Davy, who allowed it, then raced past her with Samson on his heels to find Timmy.

Bree followed Naomi into the kitchen. She sniffed the pot of soup and smiled. "Where's Donovan?"

"At the hardware store. I think he might be gone awhile." The front door banged, and Naomi smiled. "I guess I was wrong. There he is now."

Donovan came through the kitchen door and went straight to Naomi. Bree watched him kiss her. "Hey, you two, no PDA."

"We can have all the public demonstrations of affection we want," Naomi said smugly. "I'm a married woman now."

Donovan grinned and kissed her again. "I'll check on the kids," he told them. "I know you two have a lot to catch up on."

"Coward," Bree called after him. "You're just afraid we'll set you to washing carrots."

"Guilty as charged," he said with a laugh.

Bree turned back to Naomi. "I'm so happy for you, I could cry," she said.

"Looks like you're on the verge already. Now tell me everything that's going on."

Bree sighed. "You won't believe it. Quentin is still lurking around Anu's; at least I think it's been him I've seen."

"Have they proved he set fire to your house?"

"No, but who else would want to torch my place? He tried to run me off the road, and that proves how enraged he is at me and Anu."

Naomi nodded. "I'm not arguing with you. Did you find out for sure whose body was in your basement?"

Bree nodded. "The lighthouse keeper, Peter Thorrington."

"He's the guy who rescued Argie Hamel, right? My mother is good friends with Argie's sister. She's told me some of the old stories."

"You won't believe this, but it turns out Peter was also friends with Abe, Parker, and Landorf, and he and Abe disappeared about the same time. I've even wondered if Abe Nicholls' disappearance is connected. I just feel it's all tied in somehow, if I can just figure it out."

"Maybe we're just not seeing the connection yet."

"I'll figure it out. I have to," Bree said grimly.

"Stalkers, arson—this is scary stuff, Bree. I'm not sure you should get any more involved. Let Mason handle it."

"He has his hands full with another murder out at Whetstone Falls."

"Another murder?" Naomi grasped the edge of the counter. "Turn my back for a week, and you're up to your pretty neck in intrigue."

Bree told her about Bejamin Mallory. Just being able to talk about it helped. What would she do without Naomi? "I have to figure it out," Bree said.

Naomi sighed. "You're like a pit bull when you get your teeth into something. I'll have to help you then. The kids are back to school next week. We'll see what we can find out."

"Oh, I *have* missed you!" Bree exclaimed. "Talking to you helps me focus my thoughts. What would I do without you?"

Naomi grabbed a spoon and went to stir the soup. "Luckily, you don't have to find out," she said.

*M*ason's office was humming with activity when Kade walked in. The fax oozed out several pages, then paused and oozed out three more with great exertion. One woman sat waiting on a chair. Dressed in fatigue pants and army boots, she was doing something with her Palm Pilot as she asked a deputy some questions about the town. Kade recognized her as Cassie Hecko, Bree's new student. She was new to town, and Kade knew little about her. Cassie had started bringing her sheltie to search-and-rescue training and was close-mouthed about her past.

She ignored Kade as he walked past her and down the hall to Mason's office. Mason's door was open, and he sat in his chair looking out the window.

"Doesn't look like you're swamped with work," Kade said, shutting the door behind him.

Mason grinned. "I've got plenty to keep me busy, just don't have the ambition to start. Hilary had me up half the night talking baby names."

Kade smiled. "Then I assume you're ready to talk shop for a while?"

"You're here to see what I found out about Benjamin Mallory, eh?" He rummaged through the stack of papers on his desk. He pulled out a piece of paper and read it aloud. "Benjamin Mallory, age twenty-nine, dropped out of high school when he was sixteen, picked up for possession of an unregistered firearm at age eighteen, possession of marijuana at nineteen. He was even suspected by the Canadian government of being involved in smuggling, though nothing was ever proved." He cleared his throat. "Here's where it gets interesting. According to the Houghton department, he got a job at the fish cannery and was a model employee. I talked with his parents, and he apparently became a Christian and changed. He went to schools and talked to kids about staying off drugs and staying in school. A guy like that doesn't seem the type to be killed in the woods and be involved in men with guns."

"No, he doesn't." Kade thought quickly. "Unless he crossed wires with someone supplying drugs to high-school kids. You have cause of death back yet?"

Mason nodded. "Gunshot wound, just as we thought."

Kade winced. "Man."

"Forensics is still going over the clothing and backpack you found. No news so far."

"Any word on the shooters who came after me?"

Mason shook his head. "I ran a check on ATVs in the area, but of course that was pretty much a dead end. There are hundreds of them here, just in our county. I just hope forensics can come up with some clue. Houghton is going to pursue some leads on their end at the schools and the mill."

Kade stood. "Thanks for the info. Can I remove the yellow tape from the area, or are you still going through everything?"

"Leave it up another couple of days. I want forensics to have a chance to get all they need."

"Will do." Kade left and hurried out to his truck. Glancing at his watch, he saw he was running late for the press conference to announce the opening of the new baby-wildlife center. He called headquarters and told the secretary to tell Landorf he'd be a little late.

He drove along dirt roads now thick with mud from the melting snow. More than once his truck slued in the curves. Finally arriving outside the new wildlife center, he sighed when he saw the media vans. There were more than usual. He stepped inside the building, and a barrage of flashes began to go off in his face as photographers took pictures. The room was full to bursting with men and women who turned eager faces to him.

Blinded by the lights, he stood and gaped at the crowd. What was going on? A new wildlife center wouldn't generate this kind of frenzy.

A blond woman he recognized as Dawn Anderson, anchor for KPTV, thrust a mike in his face. "We understand you discovered the murdered body of Benjamin Mallory. Where was the body when you found it?"

"I—"

Another reporter interrupted, a man in his midtwenties who wore a button that said CHICAGO'S FAVORITE NEWS. "Is it true, Ranger Matthews, that someone took some shots at you? Do you believe the murder is mob related?"

Kade felt surrounded by a pack of coyotes. He held up his hands. "I have no idea how you all heard about this, but please address Sheriff Mason Kaleva with your questions. I have nothing to say on the matter. I'm prepared to talk about our new center, but that's all."

Gary Landorf held up a hand. "Please, folks, I'm sure Ranger Matthews will be happy to answer your questions in a few moments. If you'll all wait in the media room while I have a word with him, we'll join you there."

His smile never dimmed as the reporters filed past, and his nods reminded Kade of those animals with the bobbing heads that sit on a car dash. When the reporters were safely stowed away, Landorf's smile went out as if it had been switched off.

"I expect you to cast this park in a positive light." Landorf set his jaw in a pugnacious way that made Kade want to punch him. "This is a prime opportunity to garner some free publicity and to show how a professional ranger handles problems in the park."

"Did you tell the press about the murder before or after they showed up?" Kade didn't care that his question was belligerent. He should have guessed his boss would blow this up. "I simply found the guy. I have no knowledge to pass along. They would be better off talking to Mason. He's got the cause of death back and knows more than I do."

Landorf's expression turned greedy. "Tell them what he told you."

"Absolutely not. Mason told me in confidence. I have no idea what is safe to tell the media."

"You'll do what you're told, Kade! I won't have the park accused of withholding information from the press."

"Then you shouldn't have called them, should you?" Kade knew he was getting in deeper and deeper, and that Landorf wouldn't soon forget his insubordination. But Kade was sick of the man's politics.

Landorf's mouth tightened. "Kade, I've overlooked your hot-dogging in the past, but no more. Get in there and answer their questions."

Hot-dogging! His boss was the one who tried to grab every bit of publicity. Kade hated being in the limelight. Gritting his teeth, Kade turned and stomped to the media room. He would not tell them anything. He'd try to steer the questions to the new baby-wildlife center. That's what they were supposed to be here for anyway. If Landorf didn't like it, he could jump in and answer for him.

The reporters stared at him as though he was road kill and they were vultures waiting for him to quit moving. He pressed his lips together and stood in the aisle a minute. His boss slipped into the back row and crossed his hands over his chest as if daring him to disobey his orders. Kade moved down the steps to stand in front of a podium with a mike.

"Let me start by telling you what I found yesterday." He could simply tell the truth without jeopardizing Mason's investigation. "About two o'clock yesterday afternoon, I found a man clad only in his underwear in Rock River. His body had been snagged by a tree limb; otherwise he would have gone over Whetstone Falls. I called headquarters and the sheriff's office for assistance. While trying to recover the body, I was fired on by two men on four-wheelers. They left when I returned fire. With the aid of the sheriff, we recovered the body of Benjamin Mallory from the falls. He was a Houghton resident. If you have any other questions, you can see Sheriff Kaleva."

"He's not talking," a reporter said from the front row. "What has he told you?"

"I'm not at liberty to say. Now on to the news here at the park, which is what this meeting was scheduled for. We're about to unfold this new baby-wildlife center. I have pictures to show you on the screen, and then I'll be glad to take you on a tour of the facility." Out of the corner of his eye, he saw Landorf's scowl deepen.

"About the murder," the reporter began again.

"I've said all I'm prepared to say," Kade said shortly. Ignoring the disgruntled murmurs, he turned back to his notes and began to drone on about the new center. They could put that in their pipes and smoke it. He wasn't going to betray Mason's confidence, no matter what his boss had to say.

The grumbling settled down after the slides began to flash across the screen, and he even heard some laughter when he showed the slide with a baby raccoon washing its face in a stream. The tension eased from his shoulders as he began to share his passion for helping orphaned wildlife, but before he knew it, he was treading on dangerous ground.

"It's not just endangered species that need our help," he said. "Residents take these creatures in and do more harm than good in the end. We want them to call us. We can spare some compassion for small orphans when we have the resources to save them."

"What percentage of orphaned wildlife will be endangered species?" one man in the back row asked.

Kade hesitated and saw Landorf's warning scowl, but he felt reckless today. "Right now, 100 percent of them. But my dream is to see a facility that is open to any wildlife in need of aid and support. I hope to see our department come to that decision as well."

"How can concerned citizens help get that done?" the reporter who had pressed for information about the murder wanted to know.

"They can write park headquarters, speak about it in the media, and donate money for the center," Kade said. "I can use all the help I can get."

There was a smattering of laughter at his words, and several turned to stare at the head ranger's tight-lipped face. The snickers died, and after a few more questions the reporters began to file out of the room for the tour of the facility. Kade knew he was in for it.

"I want to talk to you when you're through," Landorf said in a clipped voice. He turned on his heel and stalked out of the room.

Kade gathered up his notes and stuffed them into a folder. He led the reporters through a tour of the building, showing them the cages for the smaller wildlife, then took them out back to the aviary and pens for larger animals.

The reporters asked more questions and took pictures, and he thought the tour went very well. When the last of them had gone, he cut across the parking lot and went inside park headquarters. On the way through the lobby he snagged a cup of coffee, then went down the hall to Landorf's office. He stood with his shoulders squared and his hands behind his back.

"You were way out of line, Ranger," Landorf said.

"Yes, sir."

"That's all you have to say? No explanation for your insubordination?"

"You know how I feel about the center, sir. It just came out."

"I'm afraid I'm going to have to write you up, Matthews. This will go in your record. If you had any dreams of moving on to bigger and better parks, you have just killed them with your own hand." Landorf pulled a paper toward himself. "Get out of here before I throw something at you. You wasted a perfect opportunity to garner goodwill for the park. Instead you let them see there was a conflict about the center and made it look like you were just a civilian who happened onto a dead body, just a good ol' boy with no ambition. Make no mistake, if I could fire you over this incident, I would. In the future, I'll handle the media myself."

Which was what his boss had wanted all along. Landorf was always looking for ways to put himself and his department in the limelight. Kade suddenly felt sorry for his boss. From scuttlebutt he'd heard around the office, he knew Landorf was single and had returned to Rock Harbor to care for an overbearing mother. This office was probably the only place he felt he had any power.

"What are you staring at?" Landorf snapped. "I said get out of here."

"Yes, sir." Kade escaped to the hallway and went to his office. Shutting the door, he leaned against it and took a deep breath. That hadn't gone well. He'd never been written up for anything. His job was something he took seriously, something he sought to excel in. But there had been nothing else he could do. Landorf's railings reminded Kade of the constant belittling he'd heard from his father.

You'll never amount to anything, Kade. When you're sixty-five, you'll still be in Rock Harbor working in some dead-end job and wishing you'd listened to me. You could be a vet or a doctor, but you're throwing your life away to work for the park service. What kind of job is that for a man? You'll never make the money you could make as a vet. You can help animals that way too.

Kade put his palms over his ears. "Shut up, shut up," he whispered. Though he knew the words should have no power over him, he ached with a fierceness that surprised him.

His father was gone now, buried for over ten years. His words should have lost the power they once held. Kade bowed his head and prayed for his heavenly Father to remove the last vestiges of the little boy who was afraid to run and climb into his daddy's lap.

The boats rocked in the water as the waves lapped against the sides. "Okay, now watch your dogs," Bree said. "The difference between a mediocre dog team and an exemplary one is in learning to read your dog's body language. Somewhere out here, I've dropped the cadaver scent. When your dog recognizes the scent, he may do one of several things. His tail may go down and then he may leap into the water. He might defecate or urinate. Don't scold him if he does. He's just reacting to the stress of the scent."

"What does Samson do in a water search?" Cassie Hecko asked. She sat with her hands folded in her lap.

"He leaps overboard and bites at the water where he detects the scent. I'll let him go first to demonstrate." She leaned forward and took Samson's head in her hands. "Search, Samson. Go, boy!"

She began to putter the boat along. Samson leaned his head to the left and whined. Bree turned the boat in that direction. "Notice how Samson let me know which way to turn? You have to read your dog's body language."

Samson broke into a volley of barks, then leaped over the side of the boat and began to bite at the water by a large boulder just offshore. "He's found it," Lauri said. "I don't know if Zorro will ever be able to do that."

"Sure he will. All the dogs will. It just takes practice." A glint of metal caught her eye, and she turned to look. A man in khakis stood along the shore with binoculars to his eyes. Quentin Siller.

"I'm sick of this," she muttered. She veered the boat to the boulder. "Take over, Naomi," she said. She stepped onto the boulder. "Come with me, Samson." The dog clambered out of the water onto the rock and shook himself, then raced after her.

Bree stumbled over the rocks. "Quentin, I want to talk to you," she called.

He dropped the binoculars and reached down toward the ground. Too late Bree recognized the item lying on the grass at his feet—a rifle. He casually grabbed hold of the stock and brought the barrel up to point at Bree.

Bree dived for the ground as a bullet zinged over her head. Quentin could have shot her if he had wanted to. He was just warning her to stay away. Samson growled and launched himself at Quentin. "No, Samson!" she cried, reaching out toward him.

Foolish, that's what she was. Bree raised her head as her dog closed the distance between himself and Quentin Siller. If Samson was injured because of her impetuousness, she'd never forgive herself. "Samson, come!" she cried.

Quentin brought the gun around as Samson leaped for his chest. Another shot went off, and Bree heard her dog's ferocious growl. She scrambled to her feet and looked around for something to use as a weapon. Nothing, not even a branch.

Samson lunged and sank his teeth into Quentin's wrist. He howled and dropped the gun. Swearing, he turned and ran off into the woods. The thrashing of branches was followed by the slam of a vehicle door.

Dragging the gun toward her like a trophy stick, Samson came proudly to Bree. "Good dog," she crooned past the dryness in her mouth. "That scared me half to death."

Her students came running from the boats. Bree called Mason and told him to find Anu before Quentin found her.

*T*he man waited beside the abandoned warehouse ten miles out of town. He glanced at his watch and huffed impatiently. Kids today didn't have the work ethic they once had. He remembered when the young men he hired always showed up on time and did what they were told without arguing. At least these guys had done the job well. The sheriff didn't have a clue who had made his little problem go away. Permanently.

Finally he heard the blat from the old jalopy the men drove as it roared along the dirt road. He went to his car and got out his briefcase. He laid it on the hood of his car and opened it. Forty-five hundred dollars was a small price to pay for a job well done.

The car stopped and two men got out. They came toward him, and he mentally shook his head at their leader's belligerence. Lempi would end up dead or in jail one day. He had a chip on his shoulder the size of the Ontonagon Copper Boulder.

"Let's get this over with so I can get home," he said. "I promised you each fifteen hundred. Here's your money." He held out envelopes with the money in them.

Lempi put his hands in his pockets. "The rules have changed. We hadn't counted on things going this far. We want five each."

"Five thousand! Are you nuts? I don't have that kind of money."

"Oh, come on! You make so much money off us, you could move on anytime. It beats me why you're still here."

"I'll move on when I'm ready," the man snapped. "I'm not paying any more money. You agreed on fifteen hundred, and that's what you're getting."

"The sheriff might be interested in talking to you if he knew about your little operation."

"He'd be more interested in talking to you. You pulled the trigger."

"I could cop an easy plea."

"You could." He regarded the insolent pup through narrowed eyes. "But you'd still go to jail for a lot of years. No one gets off scot free when the rap is murder."

Lempi paled. He grabbed the manila envelope the man still held out. "Okay, fine. But you're going to have to start coughing up more money, or you can find some other lackey."

That was the last thing the man wanted to do. There wasn't time right now. His biggest shipment of the year was about to take place.

"I'll double what you're making. But you're going to have to do another little job for me."

Lempi's budding smile faded. "Another shooting?"

The man hesitated then slowly shook his head. "Not yet, though I'm not ruling it out. I want you to search Anu Nicholls' house." He told them what he was looking for. "The man who finds it gets a bonus of twenty-five hundred dollars."

Lempi snorted. "Peanuts! Make it five grand."

"Four, and that's it. I'll do it myself before I pay more."

"I'll do it," Vern spoke up. "Quit fighting like a pack of dogs. We're supposed to be a team."

"I'm glad someone realizes that," the man said. "I need it done soon. Like tonight or tomorrow. Are you both in?"

They nodded. Time to mend fences. He put his hand on Lempi's shoulder. "You have a prosperous future ahead of you, son. Just reel in your impatience and trust me."

"You're about as trustworthy as a barracuda," Lempi said, his face expressionless. "You proved that with Ben."

The man's smile faded. "He was going to blow the whistle. It was all of our necks on the line."

"Cut the friendship bit and tell us what we have to do. You want the old broad dead?" Lempi asked.

"Not yet. Just find it for me."

"What if she shows up while we're working?"

The man hesitated then shrugged. "It shouldn't be too difficult to search the place while she's gone."

Lempi nodded. "But if she shows up, she's toast."

He shrugged. "Whatever."

The library was full to overflowing with children. Excitement shone from Davy's green eyes. He tugged his hand out of Bree's and ran forward to join his friends in the circle of children waiting to hear today's story. Samson followed and was greeted with excitement by the children. Thank goodness the whole town had adopted the dog. He'd be frantic if he had to leave Davy.

"I thought I might find you here." Hilary poked her head in the room. "I brought my secretary's little girl down for story hour. Nothing was going on at the office, and Lynette had an appointment in Houghton." She turned to the little girl at her side. "Join the other kids, Meredith."

Bree brightened. "Hey, would you mind watching Davy for me then? I'd like to check the old papers upstairs, then maybe run across to Susan Hamel's shop if I have time."

"Just make sure you're back in an hour. I promised Mother I'd come by for coffee."

Bree nodded then went up the steps to the main library. The reference librarian helped her search for information about the *Seawind*.

All she knew was that it had gone down in the same November storm that had carried the *Edmund Fitzgerald* to the bottom of Lake Superior as well. The pair scrolled through old microfiche until Bree found what she was looking for. Argie Hamel, the captain of the ship, had been the only crew member to survive the storm, but he died of his injuries a few days later. Not much new information there. What role did Peter play in Argie's rescue? Was there any connection between Argie's death and Peter's?

"Hey, I had no idea I'd find a pretty lady at the library."

Bree swiveled in her chair and stared into the face of Nick Fletcher, the new fireman. He wore a grin that brought an answering smile to her face. The admiration in his gaze warmed her.

"What are you doing here?" she asked.

"What's the matter, didn't you know firemen like to read too?"

Rob never had. He'd rather take a beating than read a book. "I thought you guys were too macho to read." She looked him over and liked what she saw. Slim but muscular, he leaned against the bookshelf and stared down at her with a lazy smile.

"I'm the studious kind." He thumbed in the direction of the exit. "I feel a chocolate craving coming on. Want some homemade fudge from the Suomi?" he asked with a smile that brought a light to his eyes.

He must have had a lot of experience with women. He seemed the type. She opened her mouth to turn him down as politely as she could when Davy came running up the steps with Samson on his heels. He skidded to a stop and his eyes widened when he saw Nick.

"Daddy?" he quavered. He ran full tilt at Nick, and the fireman scooped him up a bit awkwardly.

Daddy? Why had Davy said something like that? She studied Nick again. Though he had Rob's coloring, Rob's shoulders had been wider, and he had deep dimples. She didn't see any obvious resemblance.

Bree managed a smile. "This is Mr. Fletcher, Davy. It's not Daddy. Daddy's in heaven, remember? Where's your Aunt Hilary?"

Davy was paying no attention to her. He was staring up at the fireman with a fascinated expression. Samson broke the no-barking rule in a volley of excited yips.

The librarian scowled. Bree hastily grabbed Nick's arm. "Let's go for now." Trying to hide her anger and discomfiture, she hurried out the front door into the spring sunshine.

She snapped her fingers at Samson and he trotted at her heels, glancing back at Davy and Nick with obvious longing. With Davy on his shoulder, Nick hurried down the street after her. Her son's giggles were music to her ears and a torture as well. She sensed Nick had no thought for what grief his actions might cause. And even if he did, she thought it wouldn't matter to him. He seemed to know what he wanted, and right now, she seemed to be it. She had to admit his pursuit gave her a heady feeling.

She reached the Suomi Café and held open the door for Nick, still carrying her son. Davy couldn't take his eyes off Nick as they browsed the confectionary display. Samson flopped at Davy's feet and lay his head on the floor.

Molly hurried to the counter. "Hey, Bree, got a sweet tooth today, eh?"

"Always, Molly. I'll have a cashew pasty." All the Suomi chocolates were called some kind of pasty.

"Give me the same," Nick said. "I think this young man looks like he needs one of the peanut-butter pasties."

Davy was staring at Nick. "I 'member now. You're not my daddy," he told Nick.

"Nope, but I'd like to be your friend. Is that okay?"

"Can we go fishing?"

Bree's gut twisted. Rob and Davy had fished together. It was their special time. "Kade said he'd take you too," she blurted out before she could help herself.

"I want to go with Mr. Fletcher," Davy said, his chin thrust out.

"Hey, pardner, I don't fish, but we could go to the zoo sometime.

If your mom says she'll come along too." Nick glanced at her with a smile that reached his eyes.

Bree had to smile back. He really was smooth. "We'll see," she said.

"Mommy! Say yes," Davy commanded.

"Say yes, Mommy," Nick mocked softly.

The gleam in his eye told her he knew he had her over a barrel. "I'll have to check our schedule," she said firmly.

Kade had been there for her when no one else was around. He'd rushed to her side and protected her for months, giving her space when she needed it but remaining steadfast. He was no flash in the pan, no good-time Charlie. But maybe Nick wasn't either. She didn't know him well enough to say. But watching him with her son, she realized Nick possessed something very important nonetheless: the ability to make Davy forget the dark days behind him. That was something she couldn't discount easily. His well-being was more important than her own. Even if Nick wasn't what she needed, he just might be what Davy needed.

The door to the café opened, and Hilary rushed in. "There you are, Davy. My goodness, you scared me. I took Meredith to the door to meet her mother, and when I got back, he was gone." Her smile faltered as her gaze traveled to Nick.

Guilt made Bree glance down; then she told herself she was being silly. She was free to see whomever she wanted. It had taken weeks for Hilary to accept the fact that Bree was seeing Kade.

"When I couldn't find you at the library, I started combing the stores. Your Jeep was still parked outside, so I knew you couldn't be far." Her smile seemed forced as she eyed Nick from the corner of her eye.

Bree cleared her throat. "I'm sorry I didn't come find you before we left. Hilary, this is Nick Fletcher. He's a new fireman here in town, and he helped save the lighthouse. Nick, our mayor, Hilary Kaleva."

Hilary shook Nick's hand but asked no questions, which was quite unlike her. After a tight nod, she turned her attention to Davy. "You know better than to run off, young man! You scared me half to death."

Davy's mouth was rimmed in chocolate. "I wanted Mommy."

Hilary tousled his hair, then turned to Bree. "Can we talk a minute?" she asked in a low voice with a glance toward Davy.

"Sure." Bree put down her spoon and got up. "Stay here with Mr. Fletcher a minute, Davy. Mommy will be right back." Bree followed Hilary to the door. Stepping into the sunshine, she linked arms with her sister-in-law. "You're looking wonderful, Hilary. Pregnancy must agree with you."

The smile that lit Hilary's face blazed with joy. "I've only had a little morning sickness, and it's gone by ten. I never realized what fun it was to pick out baby things. I think poor Mason is quite bewildered by the way his high-powered wife has been replaced by a little housewife with a Penney's catalog."

Bree burst out laughing. "He'll think he's been transplanted to Stepford." She hummed the tune to *The Twilight Zone.*

Hilary's chuckle was a bit shamefaced. "I'm so happy I can hardly stand it. I keep thinking life can't stay this wonderful."

Bree hugged her. "I pray for only the best for you."

"Thanks." Hilary released her and stepped back. "Mason wants to know if it's all right to poke around in your basement some more. He'd like your permission to take out a wall he noticed the other day too."

"I'm fine with that. When?"

Hilary glanced at her watch. "In about an hour."

"Fine. Hey, would you want to take Davy with you to your mom's? I'd like to go see Susan Hamel."

484 Colleen Coble

"Sure. I'm heading over to the store now."

"You're sure you don't mind?"

"Are you kidding? I love to be around my nephew." Her smile faltered. "What about that fireman?" She hesitated. "He sort of reminds me of . . . Rob."

Hilary too? Bree just didn't see it. "Davy too." Bree told her about Davy calling Nick "Daddy" and running into his arms.

Hilary's face went white. "No one can take Rob's place," she snapped, very much the old Hilary.

"No one is trying to," Bree assured her. "He's nothing like Rob really. He's much more devil-may-care." She laughed to show Hilary she had nothing to worry about in regard to the fireman.

Hilary's rigid posture eased. "That's fine then," she said finally. "I'll leave Davy and Samson with Mother. When do you get to move back to the lighthouse?"

"Now they're saying this weekend. Anu is gracious, but it has to be stressful having a houseful when she's used to time alone."

Hilary smiled. "She's reveling in it. You know how Mother is." She went toward the door. "I'll give the overeager fireman your regrets," she said with obvious relish.

Bree bit the inside of her mouth to keep from laughing. Hilary would take great delight in squashing Nick's enthusiasm. She glanced at her watch. There was just enough time to finish checking out the library microfiche.

"I'd better say my goodbyes myself," she said.

*S*omeone was sitting at the microfiche machine when she entered, and Bree rolled her eyes in frustration. She browsed through the bookcases until the woman left, then hurried to take her place. She popped the proper film back in the machine, then began to scroll through it to see if she could find anything else about the shipwreck.

There it was, dated two weeks after the storm. She scanned the article hurriedly. It spoke of the severity of the storm and how several other ships were lost that night. The cargo was mentioned as being copper ore, which was what Bree had heard before. Still nothing surprising that she could see, but she would read the article more closely when she had time. She printed a copy.

She scanned ahead a few days and found the obituary for Argie Hamel. The article was stark with the barest of information. No help there. It was getting late. She printed that too, then stuffed it into her backpack and exited the library. She hurried across the street. Susan Hamel was first on her list. She grabbed a mocha, then cut across the yard behind the jail to Jack Pine Lane. Now to ask Susan a few questions.

Ducks in a Row was a small shop tucked between Rock Harbor Decor & Picture Framing and Maronen Women's Apparel. The name had been coined from a picture of baby ducks Susan Hamel had taken at sunset. Numbered prints of the famous photo now graced hundreds of homes across the country.

Bree thought Susan took her duck fetish to new heights of the ridiculous. Bree never saw her around town but that she was wearing some kind of clothing with ducks on it. But the promotion had paid off, and her photos of pampered pets, wildlife habitats, and landscapes had gained wide renown in the U.P. and beyond.

Her shop boasted a wild extravaganza of the duck theme. The sign itself was shaped like a duck, and various duck decoys, plush ducks, and duck figurines filled the display windows. As Bree pushed open the door to the shop, a duck sound emanated from somewhere above her head, startling her so badly that she nearly dropped the iced mocha.

"Welcome!" Susan was arranging landscape photos on a display wall of dark-blue cloth on the east side of the shop. Tall and rangy, she wore her dusty-blond hair in an array of careless curls. Today she sported a lime-green pantsuit with a black duck trim.

Bree was thankful to see the shop was empty except for Susan and a salesclerk. Bree walked toward her. "Hi, Susan. I don't know if you remember me, but we met at one of Hilary Kaleva's campaign dinners. I'm Bree Nicholls."

"Of course, the search-and-rescue wonder woman." Susan's smile was genuine, and she held out her hand in a lady-of-the-manor way.

Bree wasn't sure if she should curtsy or genuflect. She settled for a firm handshake. "I wonder if I might ask you some questions?"

"Me?" Susan's laugh was light. "What have I done now?"

"Nothing," Bree assured her. "It's about your brother."

"Argie?" Susan's smile twisted in a wry line. "No one has been interested in him for years now. I saw in the paper that they found the body of that lighthouse keeper who rescued him after the storm though. The body was found in your basement, wasn't it?"

"Yes. About your brother—can you tell me what you know about the shipwreck and subsequent events?" Bree took a small notebook from her backpack and rummaged for a pen, then waited to hear the story. She looked for a place to set her mocha.

"You've got one of those fancy espresso drinks. I never did understand why anyone would pay four dollars for one of them when they could have a cup of java for fifty cents." She gestured to two chairs clustered around a small table in the back corner. "Come sit down and I'll have a cup of coffee with you. Only I'll have the real thing."

Bree followed her to the table. "Your brother died just a few weeks before Peter Thorrington disappeared. What can you tell me about the shipwreck?"

Susan poured herself a cup of coffee. "The ship owners blamed Argie and kept saying they needed the cargo from the ship, whatever that was."

"Let's go back to the beginning. Tell me what you heard."

"Why are you so interested?"

"I want to make sure the danger to my son is past. Some strange things have been happening lately." The next thing Bree knew, she was relating the stalker at the house, the gunshots, all of it. "I think it might be Quentin Siller, but maybe this old murder is connected to him somehow. I need to pursue all avenues."

"All right, let's see. I heard about the shipwreck on TV. I was living in Milwaukee at the time and came right away, but Argie was dead by the time I got here. No one could really say what happened to him. He'd been found onshore alive but with a broken leg and seemed to be recovering nicely. He was out of the hospital and in high spirits from what I've heard. Then a couple of days after the wreck, he was found dead on the beach. He hadn't drowned, but no one could say what had killed him other than maybe internal bleeding from the trauma of the shipwreck. After the funeral the ship owners seemed suspicious of Argie. They began to say he'd scuttled his own ship to take the cargo for himself. Like he could steal copper ore! I got mad. I went back to Milwaukee, packed up my belongings, and moved here to find the truth. Thirty years later I'm no closer to solving the mystery of what happened to my brother than we are to having a world free of war."

"You don't think he really died from injuries he sustained in the shipwreck?"

"Nope." Susan took a sip of coffee. "Several things don't add up for me. For one thing, wouldn't the doctors have been able to tell he was bleeding internally by blood tests or something? And the fact that there seemed to be a cargo the owners were concerned about just sent off flags in my head. I talked to Argie briefly on the phone right after the shipwreck, and he seemed almost euphoric. He was normally quiet and almost morose. There was something going on, but I've never been able to figure out what it was."

Bree considered Susan's position. What if Argie Hamel had been killed just like Peter Thorrington? She sipped on her iced mocha and tried to make sense of this new possibility.

"Any idea at all why the owners were so worried about the ore?"

Susan shrugged. "No, but they were so insistent that I wondered for a time whether they were really after something else. Something smaller. Maybe something Argie could have carried on his person."

Bree pondered this. "Drugs?"

"Never in a million years," Susan said. "Argie and drugs were light-years apart. Maybe some illegal import."

"Documents maybe?" Bree brainstormed. "Money? Jewels?"

Susan shrugged again. "Whatever it was, we're right back to where we started. I know of no reason why anyone would want to hurt him."

The web of mysterious disappearances just kept getting stranger and stranger. Since they were so long ago, they shouldn't matter, but Bree had the distinct feeling that they *did* matter, that things were heating up and beginning to spin out of control.

You Bree Nicholls?" Ted Kemppa's scowl matched his voice.

The reception room at the paper mill was crowded with men and women walking through on their way home. Bree stood and held out her hand. "Yes. Thanks for seeing me, Mr. Kemppa. I'd like to ask you a few questions about Peter Thorrington."

He snorted. "Figured that's what it was about. Saw the newspaper report. We can talk on the way to my truck; then I'm out of here. What do you want to know?" He turned and stalked to the door.

The paper mill had been in business over a hundred years. It had grown in fits and spurts over the years and was the largest industry in Rock Harbor, employing eight hundred workers and stretching its tentacles of influence as far away as Copper Harbor and Marquette. Ted walked as though he wanted to get as far away from the mill as he could.

Bree hurried to keep up with him. "Were you shocked when

your stepbrother's body was discovered? What had you thought happened to him?"

"I can't say I'm too surprised. Peter was a couple of fries short of a Happy Meal. I could see where he might get sideways with someone and be disposed of. He was an annoying S.O.B. too. Always trying some new scheme and wanting everyone else to jump on the bandwagon with him."

"You sound as though you didn't much like him," she observed.

"I didn't. He and me were like oil and water." He stopped and Bree almost barreled into him. "I can see the wheels turning in that pretty head of yours. And the answer is no. I didn't have anything to do with his murder."

"His body was found in my basement. Where did you think he was all these years?"

"Off with another woman. I'd run as fast as I could if I was saddled with someone like Beulah."

"Did Peter have any enemies you know of?"

"Every person he scammed out of money was after his head."

"What kinds of scams did he run?"

They'd reached Ted's truck, and he slung his lunch box inside and turned to her. "You name it, Peter tried it. One time he sold land in Arizona that turned out to be tied up in litigation from the 1800s. Another time he took donations for new firefighting equipment that never made it to the fire department."

Bree tried to hide her shock. "Why didn't the Coast Guard fire him?"

"They never knew. Peter was always good at hiding his true nature. Most people saw his friendly face and never guessed what was behind it."

"You sound bitter. What did Peter ever do to you?"

"What didn't he do? He made my life miserable. He could smile and make you believe the moon was made of solid diamonds.

My own mother took his part over mine time and time again. One look in Peter's innocent face and she believed every lie he ever told about me."

He slung himself under the wheel and slammed the door then rolled down the window. "You're right, I'm bitter. I can't say I'm sorry to hear that he got his."

He turned on the engine and gunned it. Then the truck moved away from her in a cloud of blue exhaust. She stared after him.

She'd gotten more than she bargained for out of Ted. No one else, other than Beulah, had indicated Peter might not be the fine, upstanding lighthouse keeper he appeared to be. It would take more digging to find out. If only Ted had given her some names. Finding people Peter had scammed thirty years ago would be nigh to impossible without some leads.

She started toward her Jeep and found a man standing near the front bumper. He wore a backwards ball cap that made his round face look Moon-Pie shaped.

"You're Bree Nicholls, eh?" He put a toothpick in his mouth and chewed on it.

"Yes, who are you?"

"Jeff Syers." He spat a piece of the toothpick onto the ground.

Syers. Where had she heard that name? Then it came to her. Peter Thorrington's girlfriend was a Syers. She stared at him warily. "Odetta's brother?"

"Yep." He jerked his head. "Saw you talking to Kemppa. I'm sure he weren't no help."

She took a step nearer. "I've been wanting to talk to your sister. Could you tell me where I might find her?"

"I'll do you one better than that. Follow me and I'll take you to her. She'll tell you some stuff that will make your hair curl."

"Has she spoken to Mason?"

"She doesn't like cops. You coming or not?"

Bree glanced at her watch. "I'll follow you in my Jeep." Anu wouldn't be expecting her for another hour. "How far are we going?" She hurried to the door of her Jeep.

"Halfway between here and Houghton. Not far."

"No one seemed to know what had happened to her. She's been here all along?"

Jeff shook his head. "She moved away, got tired of all them old biddies talking about her. But she's living with me now, and I won't let none of them hurt her. I told her they'd forgotten all about her by now."

"She won't be upset that I'm dropping in on her?"

He tossed the toothpick to the ground. "Nope." He walked past her and got into a light-green pickup. His taillights flashed, and she followed him out of the parking lot. She had to keep her foot to the accelerator to keep his truck in sight.

Twenty minutes later he stopped in front of an aging two-story edged with metal flashing on the roof to keep ice dams under control. Jeff went directly to the front door. Bree hurried after him and stepped onto the porch beside a pot of plastic flowers that drooped listlessly beside the door.

Jeff twisted the doorknob and went inside. He held the door open behind him for Bree to step into the darkened interior that smelled of cooked cabbage mingled with cinnamon candle.

"I'm in the living room," a breezy voice called. The speaker sounded young, at least as young as Bree.

"I got her, Odetta." Jeff grabbed Bree's arm and thrust her through the doorway into a small living room crammed with ceramic angels in every nook and cranny. Angels filled three display cabinets and covered every table surface. Angel pictures hung on the walls, and a wreath decorated with an angel figurine hung above the television.

Bree became aware that her mouth was hanging open. She closed it and managed a smile as she tore her gaze from the angelic assortment and focused it on the woman seated in the overstuffed chair.

Odetta Syers looked like a cherub herself. Her blond hair clustered about her small head like a halo, and her peaches-and-cream complexion would have made a seraphim proud. Her bright-blue eyes held a childish wonder that made Bree smile.

"Hello, I'm Bree Nicholls." She held out her hand.

Odetta's eyes widened, and a delighted smile lifted her mouth. "I've been wanting to meet you. Excuse the mess." She stood and began to clear the magazines from the sofa. "Have a seat." She turned a grateful smile on her brother. "You're a dear to bring her to me, Jeff. Why don't you fix some coffee and bring it in while Bree and I have a chat?"

Jeff nodded and left the room. Bree sat gingerly on the sofa. "Your brother said you might have some information about Peter Thorrington's death."

Odetta nodded sagely and leaned forward in a confiding manner. "Would you care for some candy?" She held out a crystal angel dish with hard candy so old it had begun to turn white.

"No, thanks, Miss Syers."

"It's Mrs. Mallory, now. But call me Odetta, dear."

The name Mallory sounded familiar, but Bree didn't stop to ponder it. "What can you tell me about Peter's disappearance?"

"My Peter was quite a man," Odetta said, taking a piece of candy. "He could sing like an angel. I still miss him, you know. But he found something on that ship that went down. Something worth selling his soul for, was what Peter told me. I told him the angels said it wasn't good to chase money that way, but he had such dreams. He was going to give Beulah enough money to keep her happy, then marry me." She dabbed at her eyes.

Bree shifted uneasily. The woman definitely seemed a little off. "You and Peter were . . . involved?"

Odetta acted as though she hadn't heard. "He was so excited, said he was going to be rich, filthy rich. Then things changed." She scowled, then her smile came out again and she held out the candy dish again. "Candy, dear?"

"No thanks. What changed?"

Odetta seemed to collect her thoughts. "Something scared him. The night before he disappeared, he came to see me. He said he was in terrible trouble and that Abe was fit to be tied. I think Peter was afraid of him." Her smile dimmed. "I never saw him again."

Bree swallowed. "Are you saying you think Abe Nicholls killed him?"

Odetta gave a delicate shrug. "It's what I've always thought."

Bree's mouth felt as dry as Rock River in summer. She'd wondered but hadn't allowed herself to seriously consider the thought. *Please, God, don't let Abe be guilty of such a thing.* It would break Anu's heart.

"Why would Abe kill Peter? And why didn't you mention this to the police?"

Odetta seemed not to hear. She turned and opened a brass box ornamented with a delicate angel. "Peter gave me this to take care of the baby." She held out a velvet pouch.

Bree took it and opened it. A shimmer of small diamonds fell into her palm.

"I've sold some of them over the years, just enough to take care of the baby."

"What baby?"

Odetta ignored her again. "I hear you talked to Beulah too. Did she tell you how she got her start for her landscaping business?" Odetta's guileless blue eyes glinted.

Bree remembered Beulah's reference to Peter's inexplicable income. "Not exactly."

Jeff entered with coffee. "Did she ask you about Benjamin?"

"Benjamin?" Bree asked.

"Her son. Benjamin Mallory. I say his death is connected to this all somehow."

Benjamin Mallory. Of course. The man Kade had found shot in the woods. She stared at Odetta. For a grieving mother, she seemed serene.

"I'm sorry," Bree said. "I had no idea."

Odetta waved her hand. "Ben is here with us now. I see more of him now than I did before he passed on."

Bree's neck prickled. Did this woman know more than seemed possible? "Do you have any idea who might have killed your son?"

Odetta leaned forward. "The hippo. He ordered it."

"Hippo?"

Odetta nodded. "That's what Ben called him."

"Did the hippo kill Peter too?"

Odetta's deaf ear had returned. "Just before you got here, Ben told me to tell you to be careful. You're in danger, dear. You and your family."

Mason's car was parked in front of the lighthouse. Bree killed the engine and went inside. Picking her way through the scaffolding and work crew, she inspected the work that had been accomplished so far. Most of the soot had been cleaned from the walls, with the exception of the dining room. Black still marred the plaster there, and the worn wool rug under the table looked beyond hope. She'd wanted to replace it anyway. She wandered into the kitchen. The cleaning had begun in here since much of the heavy smoke had poured up the basement steps. Bree sniffed. A hint of smoke remained, but the cleaners had assured her it would soon air out. They were cleaning the soot first, then sealing everything with a coat of paint.

Clattering and banging noises were coming from the basement, and she heard a heavy tread on the steps. Mason, his face tired and dirty, stepped into the kitchen. "I need a glass of water," he said. He stopped when he saw her face. "What's up?"

She told him. His face paled beneath the dirt. "Let me get this straight. Odetta Syers says she thinks Abe Nicholls murdered Peter and left town before he could be found out? I sure hope she's wrong." His voice was shaky.

"She had a bunch of diamonds, Mason. She's wacky, but there might be something to her story. And get this: Benjamin Mallory is her son. Peter's son."

Mason's frown deepened. "I talked to her then, when I was investigating Mallory's death. I didn't make the connection. Don't tell Anu," he commanded. "Hilary either. Not in her condition." He paused. "No, no one must know, not until we get to the bottom of this."

Bree nodded. "What's going on in the basement?" Before he could answer, she heard a loud banging, then a crash as something fell over.

Then Deputy Montgomery's voice. "Mason, I think we've found something."

Lauri was getting tired of these cheap thrills. Sooner or later they were going to get caught breaking and entering. But the boys had to show their contempt for authority by knocking out windows and vandalizing cabins. The only reason she was here was because she wanted to find who was watching Bree and Anu. She pretended to take a sip of the beer Brian handed her. She didn't want to hurt the baby.

"Like it?" Brian asked.

She gave him a small smile. "It's fine." The smell nauseated her.

"Fine? It's the best in Canada. People are clamoring for it. We're going to make a fortune." He stared at her, a frown creasing his wide forehead. "What's wrong with you lately?"

If by "wrong" he meant that she'd quit laughing at everything he said and doting on his every word, she hoped he'd never see that simpering fool again. The trouble she was in had shown her what a fool she'd been. She shrugged off his hands caressing her back and stood. Crossing her arms, she went to stand by a stack of firewood outside the tiny cabin that was their retreat for today. This was one of the cuter ones they'd used. It had a neat porch that looked out on the water.

Brian's arms dropped to his side, and he started whining. "Why'd you even come out here if you're going to act like that?" He huffed and kicked a stick out of the way. Lauri rolled her eyes. "Women!" he said.

"When are *they* leaving?" she asked, jerking her head toward the other boys who stood talking by the fence.

He looked sly. "Is that what this tantrum is all about? You wanted to be alone with me?" Brian stepped closer and rubbed her arm. "There's a sauna out back here."

She forced herself not to flinch. "That has nothing to do with it! I just wondered when we could get out of here. They—" she broke off as the three guys approached.

It occurred to her suddenly that Kade had every reason to be suspicious when he'd met them at the Suomi. All in their early twenties, Butch had blond hair with black roots and a cocky manner that made Lauri want to insult him. Fuzz had a nondescript goatee the color of dirty straw and was so skinny he looked like someone from a refugee camp. The other one, Klepto, seemed the most dangerous to Lauri. She didn't like the way his pale-blue eyes looked right through her. It was eerie, almost like he walked on another plane. She figured he might be on drugs or something. Maybe they all were.

"Got the shipment stowed," Fuzz said, a cheerful edge to his voice.

Klepto shot him a menacing look. "Shut it, Fuzz," he said, his pale eyes settling on Lauri.

Lauri shivered and pretended not to hear. Nothing was happening here. "I'm getting hungry," she announced to Brian. "Let's go back to town."

"See what you can find inside," Klepto commanded Lauri.

Everything in her rebelled at his condescending tone, and she wanted to spit in his face. Fear kept her silent though. Once he'd pulled a knife on Fuzz, and she wasn't sure Brian could—or would—protect her. She stood rooted to the spot until he glowered at her, then she took a hesitant step toward the cabin door.

"She's not your slave." Brian's protest was weak.

"She said she was hungry. We all are. Women know how to cook; that's why you invited her along, right?" Klepto turned to face the trail.

The other guys turned to look, and Lauri heard the sound of the brush rustling. Then an older man popped through the opening.

This was Lauri's first good look at him, and he was older than she'd thought when she first saw the black hair. He was at least in his fifties. His dark hair was balding on top and seemed stark against his skin, almost like he'd dyed it Elvira-black, but that was unlikely. Men didn't dye their hair, did they?

His smile was almost cherubic and contrasted with his eyes, which seemed tired and cynical. Dressed in tan chinos and a red shirt, he carried a satchel in his right hand.

The smile dimmed when he saw Lauri and Brian. He stopped in the path. "Who are these folks?"

"Just some friends of ours."

She noticed that Klepto was uneasy, and Lauri almost laughed at the way he hurried to justify their being here.

"You can talk in front of them," Klepto said. "This is Brian Parker."

The lines between the man's eyes smoothed. "I'll take your word for it, Klepto, if you're vouching for them."

"You bring it?" Klepto's gaze went to the satchel in the man's hand.

"Of course I have it." The man tossed the bag at Klepto's chest, and the young man caught it.

Klepto unzipped the bag and eyed the contents. "Is it all here? The amount we agreed on?"

The older man jerked his head toward the cabin. "We need to talk." He began to walk in that direction.

"Hey, Neville," Butch began.

Neville whirled with a scowl. "Don't use my name!"

Butch went white. "Sorry," he said. "Never mind."

"I'm not sure why I bother working with you. You're all such amateurs." He nodded to Klepto. "Come with me. I'll show you where to load my stuff."

The five men headed toward the car, far enough away that Lauri couldn't hear what was said. She watched the man Butch had called Neville. The stillness in his shoulders and the occasional stab of his finger toward Klepto's chest said he was firmly in control. Lauri told herself she wasn't afraid, but the sour taste in her mouth whispered another story. This was a man to steer clear of. She watched for a while; then Brian glanced her way. He said something and jerked his head in her direction, then came toward her.

"You'd better go inside and see if you can find us something to eat," he said.

"Who is that guy?" she whispered.

"You don't want to know," Brian said in an undertone. "I don't think Neville is his real name, but anyone who can make Klepto as timid as a hound pup isn't someone you want to mess with. I've heard the others talk about how he can grab you by the throat before you know he's moving, and how he once lopped the ear off a man and ate it."

"You're kidding, right?" Lauri tried to laugh, but the mental image of the ear kept the chuckle from reaching her lips.

Brian shrugged. "Who knows? I think the ear thing might be made up, but I've seen the way he moves quicker than a cougar after a deer. He scares me."

Lauri wrapped her arms around herself. She felt caught in a whirlpool as big as the one at the foot of Whetstone Falls, and she was no closer to finding out who owned that chest. She went to the house.

Riffling through the kitchen, she couldn't find anything to eat. Maybe she could look around inside while the men were out there.

She went to the bedroom. Several boxes were on the floor of the open closet. Lauri pushed them and gasped. The cedar chest was crammed behind the boxes. Did it belong to that Neville guy?

She stepped to the window and unlatched it. Luckily, it was a new window and slid up a few inches with no noise. She listened.

She didn't know the guys well enough to determine who was speaking other than Brian and Fuzz. Fuzz's whiny, nasal voice was easy to pick out, but the other two had low growls too similar for her to differentiate.

"It sounds like you've got this all thought out." Brian's voice was clear.

Was it her imagination, or did she detect a trace of worry in his voice?

"I always have it thought out." Klepto maybe. "And we'll all stand to make five grand each."

That meant whatever they planned was going to net them twenty thousand dollars. Lauri gulped. That was a lot of pistachio nuts, as Bree would say. A big batch of cigarettes and booze? She narrowed her eyes to slits and continued to listen.

A low growl came again. "We don't have much time. The boss wants it done before the shipment comes in next month."

"It will be. Now let's get out of here. Brian, don't bring your girl here again."

"She's inside?" There was a long pause, and Lauri could only imagine Brian's guilty expression. She heard someone swear, then the sound of feet pelting toward the door.

Frantically, Lauri threw herself on the bed and closed her eyes, aware her chest was rising and falling too fast as adrenaline coursed through her body. She willed herself to breathe deeply. She curled up on her side and tucked her head into the pillow, musty though it was.

The front door banged, but she lay inert as though she were

deeply asleep. Moments later Brian called her name; then she felt him standing in the doorway watching her.

"She's asleep," he whispered. "She's been sick a lot lately."

"Count your lucky stars." Neville's gruff voice sounded nearly at the foot of the bed. "I don't want her prying through my things."

Lauri's heart fluttered like a bird trying to escape her fist. *His things?* Was he the one watching Anu and Bree? A slight shudder wracked her body, and she felt a rising nausea. She fought it, forcing herself to draw in deep breaths.

Would he kill her if he knew she'd seen the photos? She had a sinking feeling he planned something bad for Anu and Bree. It was up to her to stop him, but she had no idea how to accomplish that feat. With a sudden clenching of her stomach, she knew she was going to throw up. She rolled over and bolted to her feet. Rushing past the men, she barely made it to the yard before she bent over, and her stomach gave a violent heave.

Shuddering, she crouched in the yard and vomited until her stomach was empty.

"Oh gross," she heard Fuzz say behind her.

The door to the cabin slammed, and she could hear only muffled voices from inside the cabin. At least she was alone. She felt better after vomiting. A hand pump stood on a small concrete pad near the front door. She went to it and pumped until cold water splashed into her hands. After splashing some on her face, she gulped a mouthful of fresh water and rinsed her mouth out.

Somehow she had to stop that man from whatever it was he'd planned. But how? She had no illusions of her own brains or ability in that arena. He looked like he could chew her up and spit her out. *Think, think*, she told herself. But no answer came.

The cabin door opened, and Brian stepped onto the porch. "You okay?" He sounded genuinely worried.

"I'm fine now. Must have been something I ate." She smiled and walked toward him. Information would help. She still had no idea what this was all about. "Sorry I didn't find anything to eat. I was feeling so lousy, I thought I'd take a nap."

He put his arm around her as soon as she stepped onto the porch. "I think we're about done here anyway."

Rats! She'd wanted to see what else she could find out. But she knew where this place was, so she would bring Bree and Naomi here later.

*B*ree hurried down the steps to the basement, nearly tripping as her body tried to beat her feet there. Maybe Deputy Montgomery had found the *Seawind*'s treasure, but likely it was just rubble from some previous owner.

Halogen lights were still strung up around the basement, and their stark glare revealed every corner of the room. Montgomery crouched in the hole that Bree and Kade had knocked down. Another deputy held a flashlight that illuminated the rubble from the second wall the sheriff's department had demolished.

"What did you find?" Bree stepped over the rubble of the other wall the men had torn down.

"Wait, let me in there." Mason pushed past her and the men conferred. After several long minutes, Mason turned back to her. "Look at this, Bree."

Bree pushed forward and knelt beside him. A small green satchel, protected in the hidden cavity, lay among the rubble. The initials A. N. had faded but were still distinguishable. "Abe Nicholls?"

"That would be my guess." Mason unzipped the satchel and glanced inside without touching the contents. "Tools. Looks like bricklaying stuff. Abe was a brick mason." He pulled on a pair of rubber gloves and poked through the satchel. His movements stilled, and he inhaled.

"What is it?"

"A wrecking tool. It looks like it has hair on the end of it."

"After all these years?"

"Hair doesn't decompose," Mason said. His gaze caught hers. "Maybe Abe walled the evidence in here figuring no one would ever find the murder weapon."

"But why would he leave such incriminating evidence behind?" Bree squeezed her eyes shut. She would do anything to protect Anu from further pain. This news would be devastating.

"Maybe he didn't think anyone would ever find it. Better buried here than found on him." Mason took her arm. "Back on out of here. I don't want the site contaminated any more than it already is by my men crawling around in here. Lucky for us the second wall protected this cavity from the fire."

"I need to go check on Davy anyway," Bree said. She wanted nothing more than to bury her face in Davy's neck and smell his warm little-boy aroma. Maybe then she could forget the fear that left her feeling vulnerable. She just wanted all this to be over.

"I assume this means I can't move back in this weekend?" She had been hoping that a good sleep in her own bed would help her forget the danger that seemed to be lurking around every corner.

"Shouldn't matter as long as you stay out of the basement," Mason said.

"No worries then." Bree gave a shaky laugh. "The last thing I want to do now is poke around down here. It's like disturbing a graveyard. Do you think there's anything else down here?"

"There are no other walls that aren't part of the original basement, as far as we can tell."

That was good news, if she could just forget the fact that a man had been buried here. Thank goodness she didn't believe in ghosts, or she'd be jumping at every sound in the night.

"I'll be at Anu's if you need me."

Mason only grunted in return as he went back to work. Bree hurried to her Jeep. She longed for her son. All the day's events left her wanting to make sure he was okay.

Sometimes she felt like a piece of thistledown, blown about by the eddies of unseen forces in her life. Especially lately, she had no control over anything. But maybe control was an illusion. God was really the one in control, though it was easy to forget that. She wanted to be in her own home, tending her little boy and forging a future.

Sighing, she parked outside Anu's house and went in. An unfamiliar voice carried down the hall. A male voice. She peeked around the door into the living room and froze when she saw Davy sitting on Nick's lap. Her little boy looked completely at home, his arm wrapped around Nick's neck and one foot swinging lazily. Davy and Rob used to sit together like this.

Bree squeezed her eyes shut and sank back against the wall, her heart rebounding against the walls of her chest. She didn't want Davy hurt, and he was forming an attachment to Nick way too fast. In her mother's heart, she recognized it wasn't healthy. What should she do?

Samson must have smelled her, for he gave a welcoming *woof* and came to meet her. She wrapped her fingers in his fur and squared her shoulders. No one would fix this problem for her. Pinning a smile to her face, she walked into the living room.

She returned Nick's smile. Davy's contentment was wonderful to see. Pushing away the voice of caution, she grabbed a handful of pistachio nuts from the bowl on the table and sat in the chair opposite the sofa.

"Where's Anu?" she asked.

"In the kitchen fixing dinner. I'm invited to stay."

Bree almost laughed aloud at the absurdly pleased expression on Nick's face. "I see. I'd planned to pack things up tonight so I can move back home tomorrow. I'm afraid Anu and Davy will have to entertain you after dinner."

His face fell, and she chuckled. "Davy loves checkers," she said.

He poked Davy in the ribs, and the little boy giggled. "You up for a mean game of checkers, my man?"

"Will you let me win?" Davy looked up at him with calculating charm.

"No way! You have to let me win. It's my turn."

"We haven't had turns yet, and I'm the littlest."

"I'm the biggest, so I should go first."

Davy giggled again, and Bree's heart warmed toward the fireman. Maybe she shouldn't make snap judgments of Nick. Maybe he was more responsible than he seemed. "I'll help Anu with supper," she said, rising and going to the hall.

Nick kept them all laughing through dinner, even Anu, who initially seemed reserved around him. Before Bree realized it, they'd spent an hour around the table.

She pushed back her chair. "I'd better get to packing up."

"How about some pie for dessert first? I'll buy." Nick's expression was bland.

He had to know he had her boxed in. What little boy would want to turn down pie? She bit her lip. "I really need to pack," she began. "Besides, he's had plenty of sweets today."

"Mommy, please!"

Feeling trapped and not just a little cross about it, Bree gave in with ill grace. "We can't be gone long," she said. "And you have to share it with me. You don't need all that sugar."

Anu tried to get out of it too, but Nick cajoled her until she gave in as well, and the four of them walked downtown to the Suomi.

Originally opened when Joki Luepke immigrated from Finland, the Suomi's specialty was hot lingonberry pie, but it was now made by Joki's grandson, also a Joki. The pie made tonight's trek worth it.

Bree savored the taste as long as she dared, then glanced surreptitiously at her watch. Another hour, gone. Too long on a night when she had so much to do. She swallowed the last of her pie and glanced at her son. He was yawning.

"We'd better head back." Davy gave her no argument, so she knew he was tired. "Want me to carry you?"

He shook his head and leaned against Nick. "I want Mr. Fireman to carry me."

"Mommy will carry you," she said firmly. Davy didn't put up a fuss but wrapped his arms around her neck and buried his face against her chest. He'd gained weight, and the heavy sag of his body in her arms quickly began to tire her as they walked home, but she persevered.

She should talk to Dr. Parker about this latest wrinkle, see what he said. Was it good or bad to spend time with Nick? Bree didn't like it. Samson trotted at her heels. Bree was panting by the time they neared the house.

"Shall I take Davy?" Anu asked softly.

"We're almost there now," Bree reassured her. "I'll just pop him in bed." She hefted him to her other arm. Samson growled as they neared the porch. "What is it, boy?"

Anu patted the dog's head, then stepped past him and opened the front door. Bree stepped into the hall.

And stopped dead in the middle of it.

Items were strewn across the floor—ripped cushions, pillows, broken candle containers, books, magazines, and knickknacks. Someone had upended every drawer in the house and left the drawers among the debris.

Bree stood gaping at the destruction. It seemed almost wanton, as though the person hadn't found what he wanted and was determined to show his rage. She backed away from the littered floor.

"Call Mason," she told Anu. "Wait! Let's get out of here in case someone is still around. My cell phone's in my Jeep."

Anu followed her to the Jeep, but Nick stayed behind. Bree could see his shadow moving through the house. His cautious posture revealed his uncertainty. She laid Davy on the backseat of the Jeep, then opened the front door for Samson. He jumped inside.

"Guard," she told Samson. The ruff on his neck stood up, and he began to prowl back and forth. The man who tried anything with his boy would live to regret it.

She fumbled around on the front seat and finally located the cell phone. Punching in Mason's number, she got the answering machine. Exhaling in frustration, she dialed the sheriff's office. The dispatcher told her the sheriff was at the hospital with Hilary and couldn't be reached.

"Please send someone to his mother-in-law's. The house has been broken into." Bree disconnected the call, then dialed Naomi to tell her what had happened. No one answered at Naomi's, so she left a message telling her friend what had happened, then stood next to Anu to wait.

Minutes later a siren shrieked in the night, and she could see the pulsing red light come toward them. Her tension began to ease with the arrival of help. Nick was still moving around inside, so whoever had broken in was long gone.

She suddenly wanted Kade, his strength and calming presence, his take-charge attitude that got things done. Even as her hand started to dial his number, she changed her mind. Nick was here, and that would raise questions she wasn't ready to answer. She would just have to make do. Nick was a fireman, after all, and perfectly competent.

Then why didn't she feel as safe in his presence as she did in

Kade's? Maybe it was just that she knew Kade so well, knew the stubborn bent to his mind, the tenacious way he worked until he solved a problem. But for all she knew, Nick could have those qualities as well.

Bree embraced Anu. The trembling in her mother-in-law's shoulders strengthened her resolve to find and punish the person who had done this. "You okay?"

"I am fine."

The smile she gave Bree did little to reassure her. "You don't look fine. Why don't you sit in the Jeep? That wind is cold."

Anu allowed Bree to tuck her into the passenger seat. "Who would wish to break into my home?" Her voice was bewildered. "I have nothing of value."

"I don't know. But we aren't staying here. As soon as the deputies are sure no one is in the house, I'll get a few things and we'll go to the lighthouse. The bedrooms are all cleaned up."

"I would like that." Anu sounded close to tears.

Bree put a protective hand on her mother-in-law's shoulder. No one was going to hurt Anu. She was too precious to them all.

Kade was later than usual tonight. It was already dark when he rode his horse, Moses, into the corral at headquarters and dismounted. He frowned. Lauri was here somewhere. Her battered red car was parked near the wildlife center. He curried and fed Moses, then headed toward the center. Half-afraid to see what kind of mood his sister was in, he approached with some trepidation.

"Lauri?" His footsteps echoed in the silent building. The fluorescent lights hummed. "Are you here?" He went down the hall to the nursery area and poked his head in. Lauri was sound asleep with her head on his desk. He glanced around at the cages. Two baby raccoons, their eyes still closed, lay curled together in a bed of wood shavings. Lauri must have brought them in.

He watched his sister sleep for a few moments. Relaxed in sleep, her face held none of the usual petulance. She looked like the carefree baby sister he still loved. He dropped into the chair opposite the desk and stretched his legs in front of him.

Lauri stirred then opened her eyes. "Hey," she said, sitting up and rubbing her eyes. "I must have fallen asleep." Her gaze went to the cage. "I found their mother dead in a trap outside the den. Can you keep them alive?"

"I'll do my best. Did you feed them?" Best not to tell her he'd likely get in trouble for anything but an endangered animal in the cage. Not that he cared.

"No one was here and I didn't know what to feed them. I tried to call Bree, but she wasn't home."

The tiny raccoons rustled in the wood shavings. "They're probably hungry. I'll feed them now. You can go on home if you want."

"I want to help. Besides, I need to talk to you."

That sounded ominous. Kade checked the chart to see how much formula to prepare, then went to the refrigerator and got out some esbilac powder, a milk substitute that was safe for many small animals. He warmed it in the small microwave on the counter.

He handed one of the bottles to Lauri. "You can feed one. Here, hold it like this." He flipped the raccoon on its tummy, then put the bottle in its mouth. "Clamp your hand over its muzzle until it figures out how to suck on it." He smiled as the raccoon began to suck eagerly at the bottle.

A sense of camaraderie descended on the room as they each cradled an orphaned raccoon.

"My bottle's empty, and it's still hungry," Lauri said.

"They'll die if we overfeed them. They don't know when to stop. It's had enough." He went to the sink and rinsed out a washcloth. "Now wash its face. If you leave the milk on it, they can lose their fur."

Lauri washed the little animal's face gently. "Gosh, you know a lot about baby wildlife."

Kade laughed. "You said you wanted to talk to me?"

"I knew you'd have to stay here late tonight with the baby raccoons, so I brought you supper. You hungry?" She went to a cooler in the corner that Kade hadn't noticed.

"For me?" Kade tried to hide the surprise from his voice but knew he failed miserably when she flushed and nodded.

"Isn't cornbread and beans one of your favorite meals? I found Mom's recipe book and used it for the cornbread, but I didn't have time to cook the beans properly, so I bought them. I hope they're okay. I'll just warm them in the microwave."

She actually sounded as though she cared whether or not the beans were what he wanted. Hiding his amazement, he smiled. "I buy them all the time. I've never had enough patience to cook them. They're pretty good in the jar."

"Oh good," she said.

Lauri wiped her hands against her jeans in a gesture that touched his heart. Why was she so nervous? Something must have brought this about, but Kade had no idea what it could be. Had she flunked out of school, or maybe gotten suspended?

He was none too eager to find out what it was this time.

"Anything I can do to help?"

Lauri shook her head. "It's all ready. You wash up."

The bathroom was down the hall on the right. As Kade lathered his hands, he decided he wouldn't ask any questions. They might turn her good mood into a black storm of tears. He would enjoy it while he could.

When he stepped back into the nursery, he found bowls of steaming bean soup on his desk. There were even napkins. This must be serious.

"Looks good," he said, glancing quickly into her face, then looking away. Her eyes looked red. He wondered if it was from the heat or if she'd been crying. He swallowed past the constriction in his throat and sat down. Grabbing a piece of cornbread, he crumbled it up in his soup and picked up his spoon.

The soup was hot and savory. "It's good," he told her. "Thanks." They ate in silence for a while. Kade kept stealing glances at her face. She avoided his gaze and chewed as if it was something that had to be done.

"I've got cookies for dessert," she said with a forced cheerfulness. She offered him a small baggie of chocolate-chip cookies. He took two and got up to go to the refrigerator.

"I've got milk. You want some?" he asked.

She shook her head then hesitated. "I guess that would be good for me," she said in almost a whisper.

Since when did she care about what was good for her? He grabbed two cartons of milk and went back to the desk. The tension between them was taut. This was ridiculous to tiptoe around his own sister like she was some kind of maniac who might attack him. Why couldn't she say what was on her mind and get it over with?

He bit into the cookie and swallowed. "How was your day?"

Her hand froze in midair. The color drained from her cheeks, and she put her cookie down and folded her hands in her lap. She took an audible breath. "Okay," she whispered. "Um, there's something I need to talk to you about."

"Oh?" he prompted.

"I . . . I . . ." She broke off and gulped.

"What's wrong? I'm not an ogre, Lauri. I'm your brother. I love you. You can tell me."

"You'll hate me," she whispered.

"I could never hate you," he said.

"I know I've been giving you a hard time," she said. "I'm sorry."

An apology? Kade eyed her with rising apprehension. "What's this all about, Lauri?"

"I'm pregnant." She blurted out the words like they might gag her.

Kade's head snapped back as though from a blow. The air grew close, and he swallowed hard. Pregnant. His mind refused to wrap itself around her words.

Kade gritted his teeth. "How did this happen?" he snapped.

Lauri shoved back from the table so hard she almost toppled it. "How do you think it happened? I'm not a little girl anymore. I'm not a virgin either. Does that answer your question?"

Kade blinked at the onslaught. He stretched out his hand to

Lauri, but she ignored it. Her arms crossed, she turned her back to him and went to stare out the window, dimly illuminated by the light of dusk. Kade's tongue felt thick, and his anger leached away like groundwater draining to the creek.

He pushed his chair away from the table and stood. Taking a hesitant step, he went to her side and put his hand on her shoulder.

She shrugged it off. "Don't touch me!"

"I'm sorry, Lauri. I'm just surprised. I didn't mean to yell at you. I'm not as good with words as you are. But I do love you. I'll be here for you. Whatever you need, I'll try to supply it. Wh . . . when is the baby due?"

"I don't know how you figure it. Maybe November." Her words were nearly inaudible, and she sounded as though she might cry any minute.

"We'll have to add on to the cabin," he said, almost under his breath.

She whirled and shook a finger in his face. "There you go again, assuming you know what's best for me! I haven't decided what I'm going to do yet."

Kade's anger resurfaced. "If you're thinking about an abortion, you can just put that right out of your head!"

"I'm sixteen. I don't need anyone's permission to do what I want!" She flounced away and ran to the door. Moments later the door to the center slammed.

Kade followed her. He stormed to the parking lot. "This is too important for you to run away. That's what you always do—refuse to face facts. I will not allow you to have an abortion if I have to confine you to your room. What do you think Mom would say if you murdered your baby?"

"Kade, don't you think I've thought of that? But if I have this baby, I'll have to drop out of school! I'll never have any life." Lauri opened her car door and got in, fumbling with her keys.

"You should have thought of that before you let that slime ball touch you," Kade snapped.

Lauri threw a schoolbook at him, then followed it with an empty can of soda. He dodged the book and caught the can.

"Stop it!" he commanded.

"I should have known you'd just throw your weight around. I should have just run away."

His anger fizzled at the frantic tone of her voice, and his shoulders slumped.

He leaned against the car and ran his hand through his hair. "Let's start this conversation again, okay? Can we discuss what you want to do, Lauri?"

His soft words defused his sister's anger. He could see it evaporate the way the mist over Lake Superior vanished in the morning sun.

She sniffed, and her eyes flooded with tears. "I don't know," she whimpered. "I don't know what to do."

"You don't have many choices," he said. "I can't believe you would seriously consider abortion though."

A tiny flare of anger in her eyes was quickly extinguished. "No, I wouldn't do that," she admitted. "But I don't want you telling me what to do."

"Okay," he said after a long pause. "Do you want to marry this kid?"

Lauri slung her legs out of the car, then pulled them up to her chest and clasped them in her arms. She shook her head. "The thought of having to put up with him for the rest of my life makes me sick."

His relief was overwhelming. "We can find a good sitter after the baby is born, and you can go back to school."

Lauri was silent for several moments, her gaze distant. She bit her lip and looked away. "What about adoption?"

It hurt his heart to think about giving away a part of Lauri. He kept silent as long as he could stand it, then shook his head. "I don't know, Lauri. Could you stand to do that?"

"I don't know. I don't know what to do." The last was a wail, and she rubbed her eyes with her fists.

"Would you let me pray for us all?" He asked the words with humility, certain she'd turn up her nose at the idea. She'd refused to come to church with him for weeks.

"I guess it would be okay," she said.

He took her hand and bowed his head. There was no guarantee Lauri was doing the same, but he didn't peek. At least she was allowing him to pray for her. He asked God for wisdom, for direction, and for his will to be done. All the time he prayed, he was conscious of her tight grip on his hand.

He finished but kept possession of her hand. "Are you scared?"

She lifted her chin and her eyes flashed. "That's a stupid question! Wouldn't you be scared?"

"Yes." He didn't voice it, but he'd wondered if she had enough sense to be frightened. If the thought of a baby scared her, why had she let that jerk touch her?

She was looking at him with wide eyes, and he knew he needed to give her some direction. "We'd better make an appointment for you to see Dr. Parker," he said. When the words were out of his mouth, she winced, and he realized the impossibility of that. "Sorry, I wasn't thinking. I'll ask around and see who might be good in Houghton. I'll take you there."

"You'll go with me?"

The joy in her voice broke something in him, a hard shell he'd erected to stave off the hurt he felt every time she turned away from him. "I want to be there," he said softly. "I wouldn't let you go through this alone." He smiled. "Hey, maybe you're not even pregnant. You took a drugstore test, right?"

Her jaw flexed, and anger replaced the joy. "I'm not a child, Kade! I'm not stupid. I got the most accurate test and did exactly what it said. Besides, I've had morning sickness. That's why I even thought about it."

He nearly groaned aloud. Trying to talk to her was like walking through hot lava. He held up his hands. "Okay, okay. So you know what you're doing."

His appeasing words failed to quench the storm clouds gathering on her face.

"You always do that! I hate how you treat me like a child. Just leave me alone."

His tentative smile just made her look away and begin gathering up the dinner items. Their truce was over. He sighed. Morning sickness. Somehow that made it more real. His sister was really going to have a baby. He was going to be an uncle. That was a curious thought. Then he remembered she might give the baby away and told himself not to get too attached to the thought of a baby. Much as he loved children, he loved his sister more. She needed to do what was best for her—and the baby.

His cell phone rang, and he pulled it out of his pocket. He listened to Naomi's frantic voice, and his throat tightened. "I'll be right there," he said. He turned to Lauri. "That was Naomi. Anu's house was broken into and trashed. Bree took Anu to her lighthouse. Will you come with me?"

$\mathscr{B}$ree felt jumpy, like she really wasn't safe even in her own home. It seemed as though all the people she loved were depending on her, and she was frightened she would let them down. She put Davy to bed, then went downstairs to the living room.

Nick and Anu were seated on the sofa. The television was on, but the volume was turned down. Anu seemed her usual imperturbable self even though nearly everything she owned had been tossed around her house like flotsam after a storm. Bree wasn't so sure she could face trouble like that with such equanimity.

"I fixed us some drinks," Anu said, indicating a tray with glasses of iced tea and cookies she'd scrounged from Bree's cupboards.

They were probably stale by now. Bree took one and bit it. Fresher than she thought. She felt as jittery as Samson just starting a search. She was missing something, but she couldn't put her finger on what it was. Somehow all these events had to intersect. But nothing made any sense.

She paced the floor and went to stare out the window. Nick came to stand beside her.

"Is there anything I can do?" Nick asked. "I'd like to help."

Samson looked up from where he lay in front of the TV and moved restlessly. He got up and padded to Bree, inserting himself between her and Nick. She laughed and rubbed his head.

"I appreciate that," she told Nick. "But I'm fine. We're fine.

You don't have to stick around all evening. Anu and I will just watch some television until Mason gets here."

"I wonder if we should call the hospital," Anu said. "I am surprised Mason has not called. Why would they go to the hospital in the evening?"

"Tests are scheduled in the evenings sometimes," Bree said. Still, Anu was right. Something felt wrong. Normally, Mason would have dropped everything for Anu—Hilary too.

"I could call and check," Nick offered.

He could probably get more information than either of them could. The fire and sheriff's departments worked closely together. Bree nodded. "Would you, please?"

He winked, and she felt herself blushing. She handed him the phone and he punched in the number. Listening with half an ear, she wandered to the fireplace and knelt to start a fire. The logs were all laid out with kindling and paper, and all she had to do was put a match to it. The paper blazed, and the kindling lit.

She heard Nick asking questions, but it appeared even he wasn't getting anywhere. The fire was blazing by the time he gave up and punched the phone off.

"No luck?"

"Even my offer of chocolate failed to sway her. All I found out was that Hilary had been in the emergency room but had gone home."

Anu's frown deepened. "Something is not right," she muttered.

"Nick could take you to Hilary's," Bree offered. "Davy is already asleep, or I would take you."

Anu nodded, but the doorbell rang before they could talk about it any more. With Samson on her heels, Bree hurried to open the door. Kade and Lauri stepped inside.

A wave of relief choked Bree, and she stumbled into Kade's arms. She hadn't even realized she needed to cry until the tears soaked his shirt. She felt safe in his arms. Samson nuzzled her leg anxiously, and she gave a final sniffle, then pulled away. Lauri had left them, and Bree could hear her talking to Anu in the living room.

"Sorry," Bree said. Samson whined and bumped her hand. She patted his head. "I'm okay, boy."

Kade put his hands on her shoulders and stared down into her face. "Naomi called and told us about the break-in. Is everyone okay? What happened?"

He listened intently as Bree explained, then pulled her into his arms again. His tenderness was a healing balm. He put his arm around her shoulder, and they went to the living room.

Nick was laughing at something Lauri said. Kade stopped abruptly at the door to the living room when he saw Nick. The concern on his face morphed to confusion; then a stern wall replaced the warmth on his face.

"What's *he* doing here?" His frown deepened as he stared at Bree.

Bree felt a need to make excuses, then caught herself. Nick had been a big help today. There was no reason for Kade to be so prickly.

"He's a friend checking to make sure we're all right. Just like you," she said stiffly.

Kade flushed. "I see."

His fists remained clenched at his sides, and his jaw was thrust out. Bree expected him to start circling Nick any minute like a dog looking for a weakness he could attack. She supposed she should feel flattered, but she didn't. Nick was standing now too, his shoulders slightly forward as though he would relish a chance to fight. Bree wanted to throw them both out on their ears. She was too tired to deal with this tonight.

"We were out for pie and came back to the break-in," Bree said.

"With him?" Kade jerked his head toward Nick.

"I don't see a ring on her finger." Nick faced Kade down.

"Oh, stop it, both of you! I have more important things to deal with tonight than your machismo. I think you should both leave."

The hurt in Kade's blue eyes made her regret her words, but she refused to be made to feel like a possession. She was free to choose her own friends. She didn't want to be put in the position of being told whom she could speak to.

"Enough of this foolishness," Anu said. "I must go to Hilary. Kade, would you mind running me over to her house?"

"Is something wrong?" For the first time Kade seemed to realize something was going on here.

"Hilary has been at the emergency room. It's probably nothing." Bree's gaze focused on Lauri. The girl seemed different tonight, more solemn and grown-up. "Actually, I'd like to go too, but Davy is sleeping. Lauri, do you suppose I could get you to stay here while we check on Hilary?"

"Sure. I'll just watch TV."

"I'll take you over," Nick said to Bree.

Bree didn't like the sidelong glance at Kade any more than she'd liked Kade's reaction. "I'll just go with Kade and Anu. But thanks." The look of triumph Kade shot in Nick's direction made her regret her words. She should have just taken the Jeep.

She turned to Anu. "You ready?"

"Yes, let us go."

Bree nodded and picked up her handbag. "We shouldn't be long," she told Lauri.

"No problem. I'm fine."

Bree itched to talk with the girl and see what was going on with her. Something was up. "There's soda in the fridge and frozen pizza in the freezer."

"I already ate, but thanks." Lauri sank onto the sofa and picked up the remote control. "Go ahead; everything's cool."

"Okay." Bree led the way to the door. Outside on the porch she pulled Nick off to one side while Kade and Anu went toward Kade's truck.

Nick's eyes were as warm as a caress, but their expression made her uncomfortable. Just because she'd defended him didn't mean she wanted a relationship with him.

She held out her hand. "I just wanted to thank you for being here for us tonight. I appreciate all you've done."

"I'm here for you. Just remember that." He ignored her hand and leaned forward, putting his fingers on her chin. He leaned down as though he intended to kiss her.

Bree drew back. "Good night." She pulled her hand away and hurried down the steps. Kade was scowling, and she wanted to sigh. It was no fun being the rope in a tug of war. She climbed into the truck. She sat in the middle and let Anu take the spot by the door.

Kade got in beside her and slammed the door harder than necessary. She pressed her lips together and resolved not to talk to him. His shoulder pressed against hers as they rocketed through the streets toward Hilary and Mason's home. Bree could smell the spicy cologne he wore, and she wished things were different tonight. It had been a horrendous day, and under different circumstances she would have welcomed his comforting arm around her as they drove toward Hilary's.

The truck stopped in front of the Kalevases' house, nestled in a woods beside Lake Superior. Mason called it their "mausoleum." Nearly six thousand square feet, it was an imposing place that had always seemed cold to Bree. It was a showplace, not a home.

"Want me to come in with you?"

Kade was cutting her no slack with his cold tone and manner. "Suit yourself," she snapped.

His face was shadowed in the darkness, and she couldn't see if her words hurt him, but she almost didn't care. His shrug was almost imperceptible, but he got out of the truck. She ignored the door he held open for her and slipped out the passenger side after Anu.

Anu didn't wait for her or Kade but rushed to the door and walked on in. "Hilary!" Bree and Kade stepped into the entry hall behind her.

They finally heard footsteps coming down the hall; then the door opened. Mason looked haggard with dark circles under his eyes. His eyes were red and watery.

"I just tried to call you," he told Anu.

"What's happened?" Anu took his hands in hers.

"Hilary started spotting and we were afraid she'd lose the baby. She's confined to bed rest right now."

"Oh, my *poika*, I am here." Anu whispered. "We will take much care of her now. And pray. Where is my Hilary?"

"In the bedroom. She's supposed to rest, but I don't think she's asleep."

Anu and Bree went up the sweeping staircase and down the hall to the master bedroom. On the way Bree saw the completed nursery, and tears surged to her eyes again. *Please, God, don't let her lose this baby. She wants it so much.* As they neared the bedroom, they heard the muffled sobs beyond the door.

Anu pushed open the door and hurried into the bedroom with Bree close on her heels. "My *kulta*, I am here."

"Mama!" Hilary sat up in the bed with her arms outstretched, and her sobs grew louder.

Anu rushed to take her daughter in her embrace. Hilary burrowed against her mother's chest. "Pray, Mama. I can't lose this baby!"

Anu eased her daughter back against the pillows. Hilary's eyes were red from weeping, and Anu shook her head as she looked down at her daughter.

"We will pray, Hilary. Never fear. God is with us in this trial. I will take care of you until the danger is past."

Hilary nodded, and her eyes closed. "I think I can sleep now," she murmured. Her breathing evened out as she snuggled into the pillow.

Anu leaned down and kissed her sleeping daughter's forehead. "Come, Bree, let us go downstairs and help Mason. He is just as worried as Hilary."

Bree followed her down the stairs where they found the men having coffee in the kitchen. Kade's calm, reassuring voice seemed to have calmed Mason. Bree's earlier anger with him faded.

Kade was telling Mason about the break-in at Anu's house. Mason's brusque, competent manner had resurrected itself as he scribbled in his small notebook. When he saw his mother-in-law, he went to her and put his arm around her. "How are you?"

"Fine, fine." Anu waved away his concern. "My home is only things, Mason. The important thing is Hilary and the baby."

"I'll find out who did it," he promised.

Bree knew he needed a distraction, something to temper the fear in his heart. She poured herself a cup of coffee. "Coffee, Anu?" she asked.

Anu shook her head. "I must go back to Hilary. She might awaken."

The phone rang, and Mason turned to answer it. He listened intently, then hung up and turned to Bree. "We need you and Samson and the team. Quentin Siller has taken Gretchen again. This time at gunpoint."

The moon hid behind clouds, and the night was as fathomless as Superior's deep waters. Bree's earlier exhaustion had fallen away with the call, and she was eager to get to the search. Maybe they would finally take Quentin Siller into custody and this whole scary stalking business would be over. She was certain Quentin was the one who had been watching them, and the break-in at Anu's made a perfect distraction while he took Gretchen.

The dogs were ready to search. Kade had taken Davy to Anu at Hilary's so Lauri and Zorro could join the search. Eva Nardi and Ryan Erickson arrived together, though Eva's golden retriever, Riley, outran Ryan's dog, Mickey, and leaped up on Bree, nearly dancing with joy. Though only Samson and Charley were fully trained, it couldn't hurt to have the other dogs and trainers along.

Mason and his deputies tramped through the mud at the Siller residence. They would conduct a grid search while the dogs and their handlers fanned out into the forest behind the Siller backyard.

Karen Siller paced the dark yard, her strides jerky. Her face was as pale as the moon. "I should never have pushed him," she gasped. "I knew what he was capable of. This is all my fault."

Naomi put her arms around her. "You had to stop his abuse. It wasn't good for Gretchen either."

Karen wiped her nose. "At least she was home where I could keep her safe."

Bree thought she detected censure in Karen's voice, and she bit her lip. "Why did he run into the forest, does anyone know?" He couldn't elude them on foot, not with the entire force out tightening the noose.

"His car wouldn't start and he couldn't find the keys to my car. I wouldn't tell him where they were." Karen's words were spoken with self-recrimination. "I had no idea he'd run into the woods. He . . . he threatened to shoot me, but I knew he wouldn't do it. Not in front of Gretchen. He has a cell phone. You've got to find him before he calls for a buddy to come get him!"

Bree believed the man would do anything. She looked around at her group of students. "Let the dogs smell the search article," Bree said. Karen got out the bag containing some of Gretchen's socks, and the dogs sniffed the clothing. Bree could almost feel their eagerness to get started.

The handlers all gave their dogs the command to search, and the dogs raced around the clearing. Samson picked up the scent immediately. His tail went up, and he rushed toward the forest. Bree followed.

She didn't like night searches. It was hard to keep up with Samson, and the darkness hid all kinds of peril that she could clearly see in daylight, like potholes, downed limbs, and tree trunks. Naomi was to her left, Ryan and Eva to her right, as they all followed their dogs.

Bree smiled to see that all her canine students had caught the scent. Even young Bubbles, Cassie's sheltie, seemed to be following something. Bree shone her flashlight in front of her as she hurried to try to keep up with Samson. Charley and Naomi had gone off in another direction, and she felt alone out here in the dark.

They'd been told not to approach Quentin but to let Mason and his men know when they'd located him. They had to be close by the way Samson was acting. His ruff was on end, and she realized he was agitated. Was it because he knew Quentin was dangerous? She slowed and began to look around cautiously.

Samson crashed through a thick area of brush, and she heard a man's voice swearing at him. Quentin. Bree fumbled at her belt and grabbed her cell phone. She called Mason. "We've got him," she whispered. She told him the coordinates, then hung up. The rest of the team should be here shortly.

The man thrashed in the thicket some more, and Bree heard Gretchen crying. Clenching her jaw, she wondered if she should try to rescue the little girl by herself. Mason would be furious, but it was hard to listen to those heartbreaking sobs and the way her father yelled at her to shut up.

Samson snarled softly, and Bree knew she'd have to do something or Quentin might shoot her dog. She whistled softly, a bird imitation she'd been trying to get Samson to answer to. Samson failed to come, and she knew she'd have to call him even if it revealed her presence to Quentin.

"Samson, come!" she called as quietly as she could. Maybe Quentin wouldn't hear her but her dog would. She heard Samson yelp, and all thought of safety flew from her mind. She clicked off her flashlight, then plunged into the thicket, fighting the thorns that pierced through her heavy denim jeans. Struggling, she managed to get the thicket to release her and tumbled to the ground on the other side.

She found her cheek resting on a boot. A man's boot. Her gaze traveled upward to rest on Quentin Siller's triumphant face.

He shoved her face with his boot. "Get up," he said.

Bree looked around for Samson as she got to her feet. "What did you do to my dog?" she demanded.

"You'll join him soon enough," Quentin snarled. "Why couldn't you leave me alone? Gretchen is my daughter. She wants to come with me."

"Is that why she's crying?" Bree hoped to throw him off balance. Her hand sought her flashlight hanging on her vest. Closing her fingers around it, she tried to decide if it would be more effective to hit him with it or to shine it in his eyes and make a run for it.

"No one is going to keep her from me," Quentin said again. His agitation was evident in his voice, and he rocked back and forth on his heels.

"Where is she? I want to make sure she's all right." Bree tried to put a note of command in her voice, but it was hard when her throat was so tight with fear. Where was Samson? She began to pray for God's help, something she wished she'd done before she ever started out.

She heard a small whimper and looked to her left, straining to see through the darkness. "Samson?"

The whimper came again, and she could barely make out a dark shape on the ground. "Samson!" She started to rush to him, but Quentin grabbed her arm.

"No, you don't! You and me have a score to settle." He roughly marched her in front of him toward the sound of the river. Bree struggled to get away. She was not leaving her dog. But the tight vise of his grip on her arm made her wince, and she was helpless to pull her arm from his grasp. He propelled her toward the water, and in the glow of his flashlight, she saw Gretchen.

The little girl slouched on a large boulder by the river. She jerked her head up at their approach. "Bree?"

"I'm here, honey. Everything is going to be okay."

Quentin shoved her toward Gretchen, and Bree stumbled and fell to her knees on the rocky ground. A sharp stone cut through her jeans and stabbed into her leg. A warm trickle told her she'd been cut, but Bree felt no pain. Her adrenaline was too high.

Gretchen slipped from the stone and ran to Bree. "Leave her

alone, Daddy!" She put her small hand on Bree's shoulder. "Are you okay?" she whispered.

"I'm fine, sweetheart. Don't worry." Bree said the words with far more assurance than she felt. How long would it take for Mason to get here? How would he know where to look for sure?

An urgency thrummed through her veins. Everything was depending on her. She heard a dog barking in the distance and thought it sounded like Bubbles. He wouldn't be much help, but maybe Charley and Naomi would be along any minute. Naomi would know what to do.

She felt along in the dark, and her hand touched a smooth, round rock. Perfect for throwing. Though it was too small to hurt him much, she might be able to create a diversion. He had a gun though. A rock wouldn't be much defense against a gun. But if she could knock out his flashlight, she might be able to get Gretchen away in the dark.

Hefting the rock in her hand, she waited. Quentin was fussing with a cell phone, trying to get a signal and failing. He cursed and threw the phone in the water. As he did, he moved so his flashlight aimed toward the rocky bank where Bree crouched with Gretchen. Without stopping to think, she let the rock fly through the air, praying as it arced. To her amazement, it smashed into the flashlight in his hand. Darkness accompanied the sound of breaking glass. Quentin began to yell and swear in a way that brought the adrenaline surging through Bree's body.

She seized Gretchen's hand and pulled her with her as she ran for a line of trees to her right. "Crouch low," she whispered to the little girl.

Gretchen's frightened whimper spurred Bree on. If they could slip into the trees, he'd never find them in the pitch-black night. Quentin was shouting and swearing for them to come back. Two more steps and they would be in the trees. Bree scooped Gretchen into her arms and plunged into the cool recesses of the forest. Bree couldn't see her hand in front of her face. She didn't dare flick on her flashlight.

"I'm scared," Gretchen moaned. "I want my mom."

"Just hang on," Bree said in her ear. "I'll get you out of here." Which direction was the camp? And where would she find Samson? She'd become disoriented in her dash for safety. She thought the thicket she'd come through was to her left, but she wasn't sure.

"Bree?"

The whisper sounded like Lauri; then Zorro bounded through the brush and licked Bree's hand. More rustling came; then a breathless Lauri stumbled against Bree.

"Shhh," Bree whispered. "Quentin will hear us. I've got to throw him off our tail."

She set Gretchen on the forest floor, and the little girl threw herself against Bree's legs.

"Don't leave me!" she wailed.

"I'm not going anywhere without you. And Lauri is here with us too." Bree put Gretchen's hand into Lauri's. "See, here's Lauri. You hang on to her hand and follow me." She began to feel her way through the trees to her right. If she wasn't able to use her flashlight, they'd be in trouble. She could use her GPS, but in the dark they might fall down a cliff or break a leg in a hole. The rest of the dogs would have to find them. Worry about Samson gnawed at her. She had to find him.

Quentin was still much too close to use the light. She could hear him just yards away. Muttering to himself, he thrashed through the underbrush with as much finesse as an angry bear. Bree angled away from him cautiously. As soon as the sounds of Quentin's anger faded, she felt for her flashlight. She had to take the chance. They couldn't get out of here without light.

She switched it on, and the bright beam pushed back the edges of darkness. Gretchen's sigh of relief was echoed in Bree's own heart. She left it on long enough to get her bearings and check her GPS, then flipped it off again when she heard Quentin's renewed noises and knew he'd seen the light.

She led the way as quietly as possible. Pausing at a downed tree, she listened. Nothing. Then she heard Quentin stumbling through leaves and over the rough ground. He knew she'd be searching for Samson. It was up to her. She tucked her flashlight into her belt. Her fingers closed around a thick branch.

"Be with me, Jesus," she whispered. "Stay with Lauri," she told Gretchen. She gripped the branch with both hands and swung it to her shoulder, then went as quietly as she could in the direction of the noise.

"Stupid dog-woman, I should have killed her right off." Quentin stumbled through a thicket.

Bree swung the branch in the direction of his voice. She felt the stick hit and heard him groan; then the bushes rustled. She grabbed for her flashlight and flipped it on. Quentin lay in a bed of last autumn's wet leaves, a trickle of blood oozing from his forehead.

He held a hand to his head and sat up. "You'll pay for that," he snarled. He got up on all fours and shook his head as though to clear it. Bree took a step back and stopped. Running away would accomplish nothing. She had to end this now.

Planting her feet, she hefted the branch. As he started to rise, Bree whacked him across the back of the head with the branch again. The heavy contact shuddered through the branch with sickening reality. He fell face first, and this time he stayed down.

Bree dropped the branch and shuddered. She knew she should tie him up, but she couldn't bring herself to approach him. What if she'd killed him?

"Bree!" Gretchen called from behind her.

Bree turned to go to Lauri and the little girl. The brush rustled and her light shone on Kade just as he burst through the thicket.

Relief coursed through her at the sight of his bulk. "Kade, thank God! I have to find Samson. He's hurt. And Quentin is right there." She shone her light on the man's prone form.

"Are you all right?" Kade started to take her in his arms, but she broke away. "Samson!"

Samson whined just off to her left. "Samson?" she called more softly. "Come here, boy." She heard him get up and shake himself.

"You take Quentin," she told Kade. She rushed toward her dog. He was moving much too slowly, and he staggered a bit. Moments later his cold nose thrust into her hand. She dropped to her knees and buried her face in his fur. "Thank you, God," she murmured. Running her hands over him, she used her flashlight to search for any sign of injury, but he seemed to be fine. It was likely that Quentin had clubbed him and knocked him out, but Samson was a trooper. He licked her face, and she laughed softly.

Mason and his deputies burst onto the scene, their floodlights lighting the area and revealing Quentin beginning to rouse from his stupor. He threw his hand up over his eyes. Mason soon had the man handcuffed.

His eyes on Bree, Kade patted Samson. "Are you okay? You weren't supposed to go in. You could have been killed!"

In spite of his words, his tone was tender, and the next thing Bree knew she was in his arms. He was shaking, and she knew she'd scared him. He patted the top of her head, then bent to kiss her. She clung to him for a long moment, then realized she needed to attend to Gretchen. She ran her hand over Kade's cheek. "Thanks for finding me," she whispered.

The little girl was sobbing softly. Bree took Gretchen and cuddled the little girl. "It's okay. It's all over," Bree crooned. "Want to go find your mom?"

Gretchen hiccuped and nodded. Bree put her down. "We'll go right now. Come, Samson," she said. She wouldn't rest easy until she checked out her dog in a good light. It might not hurt to have the vet take a look too. The old town vet, Carson Meeks, loved Samson as if he were his own dog.

She glanced at Kade, and their gazes locked. He looked away first. With a last lingering glance toward Kade, she took Gretchen's hand and led her from the forest.

At ten minutes to midnight Mason stepped back through the door into the sheriff's department waiting area. Only Kade and one diehard reporter remained. Mason's face was drawn with fatigue, and dark circles bloomed under his eyes. He stopped when he saw the two waiting men.

The reporter immediately began to hammer the sheriff with questions about Quentin Siller. What was his motive for taking his daughter? Had the girl been traumatized? Was Mr. Siller a danger to society? Would he be allowed to post bail? Mason's face was a mask of impassive weariness as he answered the reporter in clipped tones. The newsman recorded Mason's answers, then disappeared into the cool, dark night.

"Coffee?" Kade went to the coffeepot along the wall and poured Mason a cup. He handed it to the sheriff, who gave a sigh of gratitude before sinking onto a wooden chair.

"I won't keep you long," Kade said with an apology in his voice. "I just wondered if Quentin said why he's been stalking Bree, and why he set fire to her house and broke into Anu's."

Mason gave a heavy sigh. "He's not talking about that. Claims he didn't set fire to the lighthouse. All he's admitting to is shooting at the wedding reception and stalking Bree and Anu. Once he demanded his lawyer, he zipped his lips and just glared at us. He's going to be a tough nut to crack. But at least he's off the streets. We'll all rest easier tonight."

The way Mason spoke made Kade think there was something that was going to keep the sheriff up. "What aren't you telling me?" he demanded.

Mason raised his brows at Kade's tone. "It's personal, Kade. Nothing to do with the investigation." An unutterable weariness and sorrow seemed to permeate the sheriff's words.

"I'm a good listener," Kade said, pulling up a chair beside Mason.

Mason looked away and blinked rapidly. Kade put his hand on the sheriff's shoulder. "What's wrong, Mason?"

"You know Hilary might lose the baby," the sheriff said, his shoulders slumping. "I'm afraid if she does, she'll leave me. All the difficulty we've had getting this far—it's my fault, not hers. If she'd married someone else, she'd have those kids she longs for."

Kade didn't know what to say. His fingers tightened on the sheriff's shoulder. "I'm sorry," he said huskily. "I'm sure Hilary doesn't blame you. This is in God's hands, not yours."

Mason rubbed his eyes. "Thanks. God's intervention is the only thing that will help. I just worry about Hilary and her mental health. She's been so happy since we heard the news. That baby means everything to her—to me too, but I'm not sure Hilary is ready to accept God's sovereignty when it comes to this. I may lose everything."

At times like this, Kade wished he had the wisdom of Solomon. Though he knew the Scriptures, no pat recitation of verses could help. "Let me pray with you, Mason, right now. We'll ask God to keep that baby safe."

A tired smile of gratitude lifted Mason's face.

They bowed their heads, and Kade prayed for God to be very close to Mason and Hilary, asking him to protect the life that was growing in Hilary's body.

Mason's eyes held a sheen of moisture when he lifted his head and gripped Kade's hand. "Thanks, my friend. I'd better get home to her. I'm sure Anu is hovering over her, but I should be there too."

Kade stood and yawned. "Bed sounds mighty good to me too."

Mason flipped off the lights. His bulk was outlined in the window from the streetlight. Even in the dark, Kade could see his dejection. If only there was some way to fix it. He slapped Mason on the back, and the two of them went out into the darkness.

*B*ree knocked on the door of the O'Reilly home. She was still exhausted from the events of the night before. Samson whined behind her through the open window of the Jeep. "I won't be but a minute, Samson," she told him.

Naomi opened the door. "Hey, girlfriend. What's up?" Donovan stood behind her, his jacket on as if he'd just arrived or was just leaving.

"Lauri called and wanted to talk to us both. She sounded pretty upset, so I told her I'd track you down and see if you had time to go out with me. She's not expecting us for an hour, but I thought maybe we could get out there sooner and get back so Anu doesn't have to keep Davy very long. She's going to pick him up from his counseling session when he's done and take him with her to Hilary's, but I want to get back as soon as I can."

Naomi glanced up at Donovan with an appeal in her eyes. "You mind?"

"You go ahead. I'm on my way to the store anyway." He kissed her on her nose and winked. "Later, sweetheart," he said in his Humphrey Bogart imitation.

Naomi grinned and kissed him quickly. "I'll call you later," she promised.

She followed Bree to the Jeep. "Hey, Samson," she said. She petted the dog, who thrust his head into the front seat, then settled back against the seat. "How's Davy's counseling going?"

"Better. Ever since we went to the cemetery last week and he admitted he's mad at me, he's been almost his old self. I think he just had to get it out. We've talked about it some more at bedtime, and Anu has been talking to him about how Rob's death wasn't his fault either. I guess that's been part of it. He's been transferring his anger about being helpless to save his dad to me. That's what Dr. Walton says too."

"That's understandable. Kind of like when kids go through their parents' divorce—they feel it's somehow their fault. I know Emily does."

"How's it going at home? You liking married life in spite of the blended-family challenges?"

"I *love* it! Donovan is wonderful, and the kids are beginning to accept me."

Naomi smiled, but Bree thought it didn't seem quite genuine. "So what's wrong?"

"Wrong? Nothing's wrong."

"Come on, I know you. You're worried about something."

"Oh, it's nothing. It's just silly." Naomi shrugged. "Donovan got a letter from Marika today. She wants to see the kids."

"That's good, isn't it? Emily especially has been feeling abandoned by her mother. Where's she been all this time?"

"She didn't say. But that's not what I'm worried about." She looked down at her hands in her lap. "What if Donovan still has feelings for her?"

"You've got to be kidding! I saw the way he looked at you just now. That's a man in love if I ever saw one."

Naomi's smile was feeble. "I'm being stupid, aren't I? It just feels too good to be true, like I'm just waiting for the other shoe to drop."

"You listen to me, Naomi Hen—er—O'Reilly! Donovan isn't stupid. You're a dream come true for him. Any idiot can see he adores you too. Don't go stressing about things that aren't there."

Naomi leaned over and squeezed Bree's arm. "You're really smart, you know that? I don't know what I'd do without you."

"Good. Now that we have that settled, hand me some pistachios out of the glove box."

*N*o one answered the door at the Matthews cabin, but Lauri's car was out front. Bree let Samson out, and he ran to sniff noses with Zorro. The place had a stillness about it that was usually restricted to empty houses. The only sound was the chattering of a squirrel on the roof. The squirrel peeked over the edge of the porch, then jumped to a low-hanging tree limb. The corrals for orphaned wildlife were empty, any inhabitants transferred to the new center.

Bree tried the doorknob. It turned easily in her hand, and she opened the door. "Lauri, it's Bree." Stepping inside the cabin, she listened for the teenager.

"You're sure she said to come here?" Naomi followed her inside. She wandered toward the kitchen and looked out the back window.

"Positive."

Zorro barked, and Bree turned to see Lauri trudging down the slope from Lake Superior. Her face was tear-streaked. When she caught sight of Bree and Naomi, her face crumpled even more. She sat on the grass and wailed like a child.

Naomi rushed to put her arms around her. "Lauri, what's wrong?"

"I'm pregnant," Lauri burst out.

Bree knew her face registered her shock. "Oh, Lauri," she said. "Does Kade know?"

"He hates me." Lauri's face crumpled. "I'm tired of hurting," she whispered. "And I can't deal with the guilt anymore. He's trying to be nice, but I can see the disappointment in his eyes. When I woke up this morning, it all came crashing in on me. I'm just glad my mom isn't here to see what I've done with my life."

"Sweetheart, God can take that guilt away," Bree began.

Lauri pulled away with an angry jerk. "You sound like Kade!" Her rebellious expression faded. "I can't tell God I'm sorry. This is too big."

Even as Bree comforted the girl and tried to tell her God would forgive anything, she realized she'd been having the same struggle. It was easy to see how God would forgive Lauri, but hard to believe he would forget her own mistakes. Did God shake his head at her obstinacy the way she mentally shook her head at Lauri's?

Bree mused it over. She'd been clinging to her guilt the way a chocolate addict hoarded truffles, feeding on it in her secret heart of hearts. It was a sin to doubt what God had done in her life. She had to let it go, for her sake and for Davy's. From now on when the old shame raised its head, she would remind herself that those sins were gone, beyond a doubt.

The dogs scampering around their feet, they went back to the cabin. Bree prayed for guidance as she thought of how to reach Lauri. Leaving the dogs outside, they went into the living room. Lauri, her face white with exhaustion, collapsed on the couch. Her posture of dejection broke Bree's heart.

"What can we do to help?" Bree asked.

"Nothing. Kade says I have to face the consequences. I told him I would." Lauri closed her eyes, and tears slid down her pale cheeks.

"We all do," Naomi said. "It's never fun. The best thing is to just own up to God and to those we've hurt and ask for forgiveness. Then take it when it's given."

But what if the one you hurt wasn't around anymore? Bree's heart constricted.

"Own up about everything?" Lauri looked away. "There's a lot. Besides, every time I think I've done that, I still feel guilty."

"Sometimes asking for forgiveness can be a daily thing," Naomi said. "We know we don't deserve it, and we still try to whack ourselves on the head for our stupidity. So we keep turning our guilt over to God until we can finally believe he means what he says about it—that it's gone."

Bree had never heard anyone admit it was sometimes hard to forgive yourself. She had thought she was the only one who struggled with that.

Lauri thrust out her chin. "Well, I didn't mean to dump on you. That's not why I called."

"What else is wrong?"

"I found the cabin where the stuff is now. I can take you there."

*T*he small cabin was on a bluff overlooking Lake Superior. It appeared deserted.

"I hope he's not around." Lauri gnawed on a thumbnail.

"Who?" Bree asked.

"The guys call him Neville, but I don't think that's his real name. Come on." She shoved her door open and got out.

Bree and Naomi followed her with Samson close on their heels. Lauri approached the front door and twisted the doorknob.

"It's locked," she said. She slammed her palm against the door. "We have to find a way in." Lauri darted around the side of the house.

Bree followed her and found her struggling to push up a window. "Lauri, don't! Let's call Mason. I should have done that right from the beginning." Lauri was already halfway through the window. Bree made a grab for her ankle to haul her back outside but missed.

Lauri landed on the other side with a muffled groan. "I'll meet you at the front door."

"We have to get her out of there," Bree told Naomi. "This is all wrong." They went to the porch. Bree glanced around uneasily. The door opened, and Lauri grabbed her hand.

"Hurry! He could come back anytime!" Lauri dragged her inside and Naomi followed.

"Guard, Samson!" Bree commanded. Her dog began to prowl back and forth across the porch.

"It's in here," Lauri called impatiently.

The cabin was empty, but Bree was still nervous. The sooner they found what Lauri had to show them, the sooner they could get out of here.

Bree entered the bedroom to find Lauri tossing items from a cedar chest. Her questions died in her throat as she glanced down at the picture Lauri thrust into her hands. A picture of Bree, Anu, and Davy. Davy's face was circled in red. She put a hand to her throat.

"There's more. Look." Lauri pulled out old pictures of Rob, Anu, and Hilary.

"Who is this Neville? What does he look like?" Naomi demanded.

"This is him." Lauri put another picture in Bree's hand. "But he looks older now."

Bree stared down into a face she'd seen before. She swallowed past the constriction in her throat. There had to be some mistake. "You're sure this is Neville?"

"Yes, he's got that funny widow's-peak hairline," Lauri said.

"Who is it?" Naomi asked. "I can tell you recognize him."

Bree couldn't breathe. "It's Abraham, Rob's father," she whispered.

"You're kidding!" Naomi leaned over her shoulder and stared at the picture.

"What can you tell me about this man? How do your friends know him? What's he doing here?"

Lauri bit her lip and looked away.

"Spill it, Lauri. We have to know all of it."

Lauri sighed. "Brian's friends have been smuggling some stuff from Canada. Nothing that bad," she added hastily when the two women gasped. "Just cigarettes and beer. It's stupid, really. Just small stuff for the thrill of it and to have a little spending money. But they seem to be planning something bigger, something they didn't want me to know about."

"And this Neville is involved in the smuggling?"

Lauri nodded. "The guys are afraid of him." She gulped. "Sheesh, I'm afraid of him. He's a scary sort of guy."

Looking down into the smiling face of the young man in the photograph, Bree found it hard to believe he could be a criminal. He had a baby face with a cherubic smile that reminded her so much of Rob. She didn't want to believe this man could be capable of anything criminal. This was worse than finding out he was dead. Lauri looked out the window. "We need to get out of here. He could come back anytime." She began to put things back into the chest.

Two minutes later they were back in the Jeep heading out of the forest. "I need to talk to Mason about this," Bree said. "And Kade."

"Not Kade! He'll kill me." Lauri leaned forward from the backseat. "You have to leave me out of this."

Bree gave a loud exhale. "Kade isn't the ogre you make him out to be, Lauri. He won't kill you."

"No, he'll wear that disapproving look, just like my dad used to with him. It will be worse than being dead."

"He loves you, Lauri. You can talk to him."

Lauri sat back against her seat. "No way! You don't know how he gets."

"You're going to have to tell him about this, Lauri. You said you would face your consequences. That's part of it."

"That's just great," Lauri muttered. "He'll be overjoyed."

*N*aomi glanced at her watch. "I hope this doesn't take long. Donovan was picking the kids up from school, and I don't want them driving him crazy for too long."

"They're his own kids, girlfriend," Bree said. She regretted her words when she saw the pain flash across Naomi's face. "Not that you don't love them too," she added hastily. She rapped on Beulah Thorrington's red front door.

Beulah opened the door, and her smile of welcome faded to suspicion. "What do you want? I told you everything I know."

Bree put a foot in the doorway. "I just had a couple of other questions to ask. Nothing too taxing." She smiled with all the warmth she could muster, and Beulah reluctantly stepped aside to allow her and Naomi to enter. Bree left Samson on the front porch.

"I don't have much time. A client is coming by for some shrubs." She led the way to the living room. "Have a seat. I've got iced tea if you want some." The offer was made with diffidence, but Bree accepted. She wanted a chance to look around. While the woman went to the kitchen, Bree stood and walked around the room. Potted orchids and hanging spider plants filled the small sitting room.

"Look at this," Naomi whispered, holding out an old photograph. "This was on the mantel. That's Dr. Parker, and that must be Abe Nicholls, but who are the other two?"

Bree studied the photo. "Anu mentioned this group to me a

few days ago. I think that one might be Kade's boss, Gary Landorf. I can't tell for sure though."

The clank and clatter of kitchen utensils fell silent in the kitchen, and the women sat down hastily just before Beulah came back in with a tray of iced tea.

"This is sun tea I brewed myself," she said gruffly.

Bree and Naomi each took a glass. "Delicious," Bree said, putting the glass on a coaster. "Thanks for your time."

Beulah's eyes were secretive. "Like I said, I really don't know much more than I've already told you."

Bree picked up the photograph. "Who are these men?"

"Oh, that's the Do-Wrong Gang." Her gruffness fell away for a moment and she smiled at the memory. "Peter always said if there was trouble to be gotten into, they would find it." She leaned forward. "That's Peter there. The guy in the Chicago Cubs hat is Gary Landorf. This was the early days when there were four of them. When Max went off to med school, he didn't have much time for their shenanigans."

She hadn't talked to Gary, Bree realized. Or Dr. Parker, for that matter. "What kind of trouble did they get into?"

Beulah looked away. "Oh, just kicking-up-your-heels kind of stuff. Drinking too much, playing poker, shooting out windows, mudding in their trucks on the courthouse lawn . . ." She broke off.

"And?" Bree prodded.

Beulah shrugged. "A bit of smuggling from Canada, cigarettes, beer, liquor. They just liked to ride the edge, Peter used to say."

Bree and Naomi exchanged a look. Smuggling. Kids' stuff, from the sound of it, but what if there was more to it? Abe was apparently still involved. Either there was a lot of money in Canadian liquor and cigarettes, or something else brought in enough money to kill for.

The whole thing unsettled Bree. She had to figure this out. She didn't want Abe showing up and upsetting Anu and Hilary, especially since Hilary was so vulnerable right now. She had to figure out what he was planning.

"There must have been some money in smuggling," she remarked.

Beulah shrugged. "Peter was always looking for some way to make money."

"You said he had a lot of money to throw around in the months before he died. From smuggling?"

"I don't know." Beulah thrust out her chin.

Bree went another direction. "What about the rest of them?"

Beulah took a sip of her iced tea. "Max was first to go. Med school. He'd come back now and then. Peter and Abe stayed here. After those two disappeared Gary went off to college and then to train for the park. They were always looking for ways to turn a buck. Nothing ever amounted to much though. A few hundred dollars here and there. Their big score—" She broke off.

Bree could tell she wished she hadn't said anything. "Their big score? What was that?"

Beulah bit her lip. "They had high hopes for scavenging the wrecks, especially *Seawind*, but when Peter went missing, I knew that was just a pie-in-the-sky too."

The shipwreck again. What had been on that ship? "Do you have any idea what they were looking for?"

Beulah didn't answer. "Want some more tea?"

"Maybe they found something. Is that where you got the capital to start your business?"

Beulah looked as if she'd been slapped. "I was never messed up in their stuff," she snapped.

"Then how did you get started? I heard you sold something Peter left you."

"Who told you that?"

Bree decided to tell her. Maybe jealousy would loosen the woman's tongue. "Odetta Syers."

Beulah froze. "Where did you find her? That tart would say anything to hurt me. It's not enough that she tried to steal my husband. Besides, this is none of your business."

Bree leaned forward. "Strange things have been happening to me and my family, so I would say that it is. Think of Anu Nicholls, Beulah. She said the two of you were good friends."

Beulah's eyes softened. "Anu is a special lady," she said.

"Then won't you help me for her sake?"

Beulah looked down at her hands. "I have nothing to say."

"Odetta showed Bree some jewels. Diamonds," Naomi put in.

Beulah's mouth tightened. "I have nothing to say," she repeated.

"She said I should ask how you started your nursery business." Bree touched the petal of an orchid standing next to the sofa.

"I think it's time you left." Beulah got up and went to the door.

Diamonds, that had to be it. Those might be worth enough for someone to kill for.

Lauri drove along the rutted track, her car going airborne when she hit the potholes the spring thaw had left. What was she going to do? She glanced down and became aware of her fingers splayed over her abdomen in a protective gesture. She snatched her hand away. What was she thinking? She wasn't ready to become a mother.

Her thoughts drifted to Naomi, and with a sudden decisive movement she turned the car and headed to the O'Reilly house. Just looking at the house gave her warm, fuzzy feelings. Her baby could be happy growing up here with Timmy and Emily for brothers and sisters.

Nausea rose in her as if she'd just gone two rounds on the Demon Drop at Cedar Point Amusement Park. She rang the doorbell anyway. She rubbed slick palms against her jeans.

"Lauri, what a nice surprise! You just missed Bree." Naomi stood back from the door to allow Lauri in. "I've been baking some turtle bars. They're still hot. You want some?"

Lauri followed Naomi into the kitchen. The room was warm and fragrant with the smell of chocolate and caramel. She sniffed appreciatively. "Yum, that smells great. I could eat a horse. I don't know what's wrong with me, but I have to have something all the time."

"You're eating for two." Naomi slid a paper plate with three turtle bars on it across the table to her. "One for you and two for the baby."

Lauri grinned. "This kid will weigh a ton."

"I've got soda. It's even your favorite: Dr. Pepper." Naomi went to the refrigerator.

Lauri ran a finger in the gooey mixture of chocolate and caramel that had oozed from the turtle bar. "I suppose you're wondering why I'm here."

"No, should I? I thought you just stopped by to see me." Naomi put the soda in front of Lauri and slid into a chair across the table from her. "So much for my ego." She smiled.

Lauri managed a laugh, then blurted, "I was wondering what your plans are for the future." Gosh, that sounded terrible. How did she go about asking if Naomi was too old to have a baby?

Naomi raised an eyebrow. "Well, I'm going to be the best wife and mother I can be. Charley and I are going to continue to improve in our training. I'm going to be a friend to you and Bree. Have I left out anything?"

"Mother to Timmy and Emily? What about kids of your own?"

Naomi smiled. "It's a little early for that."

"Can you, I mean, are you planning to have some of your own?" Lauri nibbled on her turtle bar.

Naomi looked at Lauri with compassion in her eyes. "What's this all about, Lauri?"

"I want you to take my baby." There. She'd done it.

Naomi blinked and audibly exhaled. "I see. Have you talked to Kade about this?"

"Not really. He isn't sure about adoption. I think he wants me to keep it. But I'm not ready to be a mother!"

"Well, this isn't something to decide in a hurry," Naomi said. "I hadn't really thought about adopting a baby. But I'm not opposed to the idea. I could talk to Donovan and Kade if you're sure about this."

"I'm sure." She hoped she sounded stronger than she felt.

"Then we'll pray about it," Naomi said. "I don't want to do anything unless this is God's will for all of us."

"I'm sure it's God's will," Lauri said, her confidence rising. Who was she to be saying what the Lord's will was? On the other hand, the idea was too perfect not to be just that.

— *30* —

*T*he men were waiting for him. He parked under an old maple tree and walked toward the picnic area. This clearing was so remote, most people never stumbled across it, which was just fine with him. He dreaded what he had to do today, but she hadn't left him any choice. Sad, really. The future could have been so different.

"I have a rush job for you," he said, laying his briefcase on the table. "But it has to be done right. No screwups."

Lempi scowled. "Are you saying we screwed up the last job? We did just what you told us. I think your information is wrong."

"Look, I have to retrieve my possession. I'd hoped no one else would be hurt, but I'm taking off the kid gloves now. I want you to force Anu to tell where it is. If you have to use her daughter-in-law or her grandson to scare her into telling the truth, then do it."

"Count me out." Vern said. "I ain't going to jail for you. Getting rid of Ben turned my stomach. No more hurting people."

The man didn't try to argue. "Fine. If you don't have the guts for it, I don't want you. How about you?" he asked Lempi. "Are you in?"

"For a price." Lempi stretched out his legs and patted his pocket for his cigarettes.

"Five thousand dollars."

"A hundred," Lempi countered.

The man gasped. "Are you nuts? I'm not paying that kind of money!"

Lempi shrugged. "Suit yourself."

"Never mind. I'll take care of it myself." The man picked up his suitcase and walked toward his car. Anu would tell him the truth. She'd do anything to protect Bree and Davy. He allowed himself a pang of regret for what he'd have to do.

*T*he morning sun danced on the sprigs of green breaking through the mulch of dead leaves. Bree dropped the Jeep into gear. "Now we tackle Gary Landorf. I hope Mason can find out something about this Neville person today. He was really upset to hear that Abe might be hanging around here. We're not sure how long we can keep this from Anu."

"You still think it's diamonds the Do-Wrongs were after?"

Bree nodded. "If they're from the smuggling operation, Beulah might be afraid she'll have to return the money."

"What do you think Gary Landorf will tell us? It was a long time ago."

"Maybe more about the smuggling ring."

"You think he'll actually admit to it?"

Naomi had a point. Considering recent events, he had all the reason in the world to lie. "Maybe I can trick him into telling the truth," she said slowly.

"How?"

"I don't know. Let me think about it. Hand me some pistachios. I always think better with something to eat."

Naomi sighed. "They'd give me indigestion." She pulled a small bag of nuts from the glove box and gave them to Bree.

Bree split a nut and popped it into her mouth. She settled against the back of the seat for the drive out to the rangers' station.

The CD played softly in the background. Elvis was singing "All Shook Up." Bree chewed on another nut. What if she shook up Gary—made him think she knew more than she really did? It was worth a try.

"You thinking about Kade?" Naomi asked. "You've got a funny look on your face."

"Elvis," Bree said. They both laughed.

Then Naomi chewed on her lip. "Lauri wants me and Donovan to adopt her baby."

"You're kidding! What did you say?"

"That I'd talk to Donovan and Kade and pray about it."

"What was Donovan's reaction?"

"He's not opposed to the idea. I'm just not sure yet. I might want to try for a baby of our own. Not that there wouldn't be room for Lauri's baby too, if that's what God wanted. But it's hard to know what to do."

"Well, we already know you're a great mother! Has Lauri said anything to Kade yet?"

"Not yet. And now that we have the subject back to Kade, we can talk about how you're about to blow it. Have you explained about the fireman guy?"

Bree shot Naomi her best withering look. "There's nothing to explain. I haven't really talked with Kade since we found Gretchen." She sighed. "He's probably still mad at me after meeting Nick Fletcher at the house." Naomi was quiet, and Bree glanced at her. "Your disapproval speaks louder than words," she said.

"You're going to mess up a good thing with Kade. The fireman is cute, but he's not right for you. Kade is."

"Davy really likes Nick." Bree couldn't help the defensive note in her voice.

"Davy isn't the one who would have to live with him forever. Don't ever pick out a husband because of someone else's opinion. If I'd listened to my mom, she would have had me marry Sam Carter around the corner, and I would have been bored in six months."

"I don't understand why Davy has never bonded with Kade. Kade tries so hard with him too. Nick doesn't even have to try—it's just there."

"You are the mother, Bree. Don't make the mistake of letting Davy run your home."

"He isn't." Bree's defensiveness moved up a notch. "But he's been through a lot, and I don't want to rock the boat too much."

"Taking charge of your home is not the same as rocking the boat," Naomi pointed out. "Kids find security in having someone in control."

"Since when did you become such an expert?" Bree laughed, mostly to hide her irritation.

"You need to decide what *you* want. If Kade were mean to Davy or something like that, it would be different. But you know he loves your boy. And he loves you. Most importantly, he loves God."

"He's never really said he loves me," Bree said after a moment. "Maybe that's the problem."

Bree parked the Jeep at the national park headquarters and blinked rapidly at the sting in her eyes. "I suppose you're right. I don't want to lose him." She *had* hurt Kade. Hurt was all over his face when he'd come in and seen Nick with her and Davy.

Still, Davy liked the fireman. Naomi didn't understand what it was like to watch her son blossom in a man's company. She didn't know Bree's need to see his smile glow. It was hard to know what to do.

"Just pray about it."

Bree smiled gratefully and pulled the key from the ignition. "You're a good friend, Naomi."

"I know," Naomi said smugly. "But I expect a swift kick from you when I need it too."

"Stay," Bree told Samson. The women got out of the Jeep and

walked inside the park headquarters. Bree's gaze wandered around the large room. Bree stopped to admire an intricate bark basket in the Ojibwa Native American display. There was no sign of Kade, and Bree was surprised by the degree of disappointment she felt. This might have been a good opportunity to mend fences. She also needed to talk to him about Lauri.

A uniformed woman was behind the information counter. Bree approached and asked to speak with Gary Landorf. The woman pointed out his office, and Bree and Naomi walked down the hall. The door was open.

Bree could see why the man reminded Kade of a ferret. He had the same long, sinewy muscle structure. She rapped her knuckles against the open door.

He looked up from his perusal of the papers on his desk. "Yes?"

"You're Gary Landorf?"

"Last time I checked. Are you reporters?" His gaze glided over Bree's face, then slid to her left hand as if checking out her marital status. His grin widened.

"Um, no. I'm Bree Nicholls, and this is Naomi O'Reilly. We'd like to ask you some questions."

"Come in, ladies. What can I help you with?" He smiled in what Bree assumed he thought was a winning manner, but it left her cold.

Bree and Naomi sat in the chairs across from his desk. "We want to talk to you about the Do-Wrongs."

He raised an eyebrow. "Now there's a blast from the past. I haven't heard that term in thirty years. Most of those friends I hung around with are dead or gone from the area. Why are you asking questions?" He snapped his fingers. "Wait a minute—Bree Nicholls. You're the dog woman, the one in the lighthouse where Peter's body was found, right?"

"Yes, and I'm trying to find out what I can about Peter

Thorrington." She smiled and warned herself to go easy. There was plenty of time to spring her big question.

"Peter and I were great friends. I never did understand it when he just up and disappeared."

"Did you ever try to find out what happened to him?"

Gary shook his head. "I left that up to the authorities. I went off to college shortly afterward."

"You were a bit older than the usual college student." Bree indicated the graduation picture on his desk. He'd already begun to lose his hair.

"It took awhile to save enough money. My mom raised me by herself, and she couldn't afford to send me."

Another windfall from somewhere? That meant at least two of the group seemed to have acquired money from out of nowhere. "I assume you got the money from the sale of the gems?"

Gary drew a deep breath, and his eyes widened. "Gems?"

She'd rattled him. "Beulah told me about the gems and how you'd split them. She said that's how you got the money for school."

"Peter swore he never told her!" He snapped his mouth shut and shot her an angry look. "If you're lying—"

Bree ignored him. "Did you smuggle the gems in with Peter's help?"

He got up and looked down the hall then shut the door. "Look, I don't know what you're fishing for, but you've got it all wrong. We didn't smuggle any gems in."

"Just cigarettes and liquor?"

He stared at her, and his left eye twitched. "My, you have been doing some digging, haven't you? That was kid stuff. We were teenagers."

"Was it only you and Peter who found the gems?"

"Once again, I don't know about these gems you keep bringing up."

"Were the gems onboard the *Seawind*? The four of you had a legitimate salvage boat. There was no need to hide what you found." Her eyes widened. "Unless you intended to keep the owner's share as well."

Gary stood and went to the door. "I think I've said all I'm going to say."

She tried again. "What about Abe and Dr. Parker? Did they know what you'd found?"

"Either leave or I'll have to ask the security ranger to show you out." Gary's lips were pressed together, and his nostrils flared like a bull about to charge.

Bree sighed and stood. "Thank you for your time, Ranger Landorf," she said. "I'll be in touch."

He slammed the door behind them.

"Wow, you handled that great!" Naomi said. "I was impressed. Did Mason teach you that trick of getting a suspect all shook up so they spill the beans?"

"Elvis," Bree said with a cheeky grin. "Let's go see Dr. Parker."

*B*ree studied Dr. Parker's certificates on the wall of his office. Graduated from Michigan State, then on to medical school. Next to it, a copy of the Hippocratic oath. Another wall held pictures of his parents. Dr. Wilbur Parker had served Rock Harbor for twenty years before the war. One wing of the hospital had been named for the Parkers, and the family had funded nearly every worthwhile cause in the county.

"Just the sight I need after a long day's work," Dr. Parker said, shutting the door behind him. "Two beautiful ladies and one handsome dog." He reached out to touch Samson, but the dog jerked his head away and moved to the window to stare longingly at a squirrel perched on the low-lying limb.

"Spurned for a bushy-tailed friend," the doctor said with a laugh. "Coffee, ladies?" He went to the coffeepot on the credenza by the door.

"I could use one," Bree said.

"Same here," Naomi said. "If you've got milk."

"Milk builds strong bones and teeth. Of course I have milk. But you didn't come here to discuss milk. What can I do for you? Davy still sleepwalking?" He handed them their coffee and went to sit at his desk.

"He seems to be getting better. But that's not why we're here. I recently found out you used to be close to Abe Nicholls and Peter Thorrington."

"My, yes, we were great friends in our younger days. Perhaps that's why I feel such a fondness for Anu."

"You called yourself the Do-Wrong Gang," Naomi put in.

Dr. Parker smiled. "Indeed. The three of us plus Gary Landorf. Juvenile name of course, but then we were scarcely more than children ourselves. We liked to get out and howl at the moon occasionally."

"I hear Peter and Gary found some jewels. What do you know about that?" Bree asked.

"Jewels? You mean like rings and stuff?"

"I think it was more loose stones." Bree sipped her coffee, suppressing a grimace at the stale, bitter flavor.

"I have no idea. They never shared them with me if they did. Is that how Gary could afford to go off to school? I always wondered. My father offered to send him, but he was too proud to accept charity. Then the next thing I knew, he was leaving. That explains a lot."

"And Peter gave Beulah some stones as well. She started her landscaping business with them. We're trying to figure out where they came from. Did you have any idea where they might have found them?"

Dr. Parker shook his head. "Not a clue. But by the time Peter disappeared, we'd drifted apart anyway." He glanced at his watch. "I have an appointment tonight, so I'm going to have to leave you. Sorry I wasn't more help. But you've answered some questions for me, at least."

He came around the desk and opened the door for them. "Give Anu my best."

Bree wanted to pound her head against the wall in frustration. Elvis's methods weren't working very well with Dr. Parker. Maybe there was nothing for him to tell. Could she be wrong about the stones? If so, she hoped the kindly doctor wouldn't hold it against her the next time she brought Davy in to see him.

Kade rode his horse along the trail. His saddle leather creaked, and he settled himself more squarely on his mount. It felt good to have the sun shining on his face. Spring was finally here full force, though even now winter could come back for a quick blast of snow. He knew Moses was as glad to be out of the stable as Kade was to be away from headquarters. A phoebe trilled over his head, and he reined in his horse and noted the bird's location in his logbook. Gulls swooped over the cliff to his right, and he could see the clear blue of Superior. Days like this made him glad he was in Rock Harbor.

Moses's hooves clopped against random stones, and Kade leaned in the saddle as he rounded a curve to the cabins he was checking today. The break-ins had started up again, and he was at a loss to figure them out. The cabins in question today stood in a row along a bluff that had steps carved in the rock right down to the water.

He heard the sound of voices as he neared the first cabin. Sliding to the ground, he tied his horse to a tree and made his way through the underbrush. The mud was thicker here, viscous and hard to walk in. He got through the worst of it and onto rockier ground. Pulling his binoculars from their case at his waist, he focused them on the cabin. A group of boys stood near the well. Laughing and talking, they didn't seem to be in any hurry.

One of the boys turned around, and Kade caught his breath. Brian Parker! These boys were up to no good. They were not going to be happy to see him. He hesitated, then put his binoculars away. Even though Lauri now claimed to dislike the little scumbag, he didn't want to get her defensive tendencies going. She might think he was picking on the kid because of what he'd done to her.

Even so, he did not relish getting the boy in trouble. He liked Dr. Parker, and this was sure to bring him grief. Besides, what kind of Christian did this make him? Had he made even one attempt to get to know Brian, to tell him about Jesus? No, he hadn't. The truth of the matter was, he didn't want the boy around, Christian or not. If he'd made more of an attempt, maybe his sister wouldn't be in trouble now.

He narrowed his eyes. Was Lauri involved? Acid burned his stomach.

He called headquarters for backup, then adjusted his hat and walked forward, keeping his gaze on the boys. Kade recognized them from his night out with Lauri at the café. What were they up to with all those boxes? At least a dozen large boxes were stacked near the steps to the water. The boys were so intent on one another that they didn't notice his approach.

Brian was the first to see Kade. His mouth went slack, and he took a step back. "K—Kade. What are you doing here?" His gaze darted past Kade as if to see whether he was alone.

"I might ask you the same thing," Kade said dryly.

"Uh . . . I mean, we're just talking."

Kade's gaze went to the cabin. "You left the door open."

Brian bit his lip. "I—"

"You're all under arrest for breaking and entering." He nodded toward the boxes. "Open one of those for me, please."

The boys looked at one another. Brian shuffled slowly forward. "We found it," he said.

"Right."

Brian popped open a box and stepped back. It was full of Canadian cigarettes, and Kade recognized them as the type Lauri had been smoking, though she claimed she wasn't smoking anymore. "How about that bigger one there?" He pointed at a box near the porch.

Brian sighed and did as he was told. That box contained Canadian beer. "Okay, anyone want to explain? Someone dropped this off earlier, right? And you're loading it up to distribute it. How much you make on this haul? A thousand? Two?"

The boys said nothing. "You might as well spill it. You've been caught red-handed with the goods."

"Don't say anything," an older boy with a petulant expression warned. He folded his hands across his chest and glared at Kade. "We got nothing to say to pigs."

"Oink, oink," Kade said. "I'm proud to be on the side of law and order, tough guy. We'll see how you feel after a night behind bars."

"We're not going to jail, are we?" a younger boy whined.

The rumble of a truck engine echoed through the trees, and one of the boys turned to flee. Kade grabbed his arm and slung him to the ground. He landed in a swamp of mud and grimaced, then put his head in his hands.

"My dad's going to kill me," Brian moaned.

"Mine too," the boy on the ground said.

"Can't you let us go if we promise not to do it anymore?" Brian asked. "Besides, if you arrest us, you'll have to arrest Lauri. She's involved too."

Kade had a feeling it would come to this. What a slime ball, to try to involve his own girlfriend. "She's not here now, is she? But you are. And I'd say you're in a peck of trouble."

Brian swore, and for a minute Kade thought the boy might tackle him. Brian clenched his fists and took a step closer.

"Come on. You want a piece of me?" Kade asked. He would welcome the chance to pummel the boy. Stupid punk. But then Kade's backup arrived and Brian backed off.

The boys were put in the truck, and Kade called ahead to tell Mason he was bringing them in. When he clicked off his cell phone, he remembered the boy he'd found in the river.

"Any of you boys know Benjamin Mallory?"

The shock and consternation on the boys' faces was all the answer he needed.

*G*lancing at her watch, Bree decided she had time to run over to the jail and tell Mason about her talks with Landorf and Dr. Parker. Maybe he had heard something on his inquiry about Neville. She was supposed to pick up Davy at Nicholls' in an hour. She hurried down Jack Pine Lane to Houghton Street. As she turned onto Houghton, she saw Kade's truck pulling away from the sheriff's office. Her pulse quickened, and she lifted her hand in greeting. Maybe they could talk this morning.

His truck kept on going, and she knew he hadn't seen her. Bree stared after him. A stinging behind her eyes made her blink. She brushed the moisture from her eyes. They were going to have to talk. She missed him and was only beginning to realize how much.

Bedlam reigned inside the jail. Bree saw several young men and recognized Lauri's boyfriend, Brian. The deputies marched them out of the lobby. Mason stood scribbling on a form. He stuck his pen in his pocket, then looked up and saw her.

"What's all that about?" she asked, approaching him.

"The boys were caught smuggling as well as breaking and entering. They're implicating Lauri as well, so Kade is hurting pretty bad. Did you see him on your way in?"

No wonder Kade hadn't been looking around. Bree felt sick. A storm was about to break over Lauri's head.

"Then Abe must be the ringleader of these boys. You think you can get them to talk?" She fumbled in her purse. "Here's an old picture of him. Can you ask if this is the leader they called Neville?"

Mason took it and nodded. He turned to a deputy. "Put Brian Parker in an interrogation room." He waited a few minutes, then followed with Bree.

Brian's face was white, and he fidgeted with the hem of his shirt. He shot Bree a pleading look. "Hi, Mrs. Nicholls."

"Hello, Brian. We have some questions for you." Bree sat on a chair across the table from him.

Mason sat beside her. Handing the picture to Brian, he pointed out Abe. "This man look familiar?"

Brian paled a bit but met Mason's gaze bravely. "Never seen him before."

"Look again." Mason tapped the picture. "This is very important, Brian. We already know this is Neville. I just need you to confirm it."

He pushed the picture away. "If you already know, why are you trying to get me in trouble? You don't mess around with Neville."

"He's the brains behind the smuggling operation, right? When did you meet him?"

"Just a few weeks ago."

"What about Benjamin Mallory?" Bree had been wondering about that.

Brian slouched in his chair. "He's the dead guy, right? I saw it in the paper."

"You know more than that," Mason said. "Tell me what you know."

"I think I'd better talk to my dad." Brian bit his thumbnail and looked away.

Mason looked at Bree, and she could see the frustration in his eyes. He had no choice.

"Okay, but it would go easier for you if you were honest. Otherwise, we're going to wonder if you killed him."

"I didn't have anything to do with it!" Brian said. "Klepto found him—" He broke off, his face a mask of consternation. "I want my dad," he said woodenly.

"Klepto found him snooping around and killed him? Is that it?"

Brian's head stayed down, and he said nothing more. Mason motioned to Bree, and they left the room.

"What did you find out about your inquiry?" Bree asked him. "Is Neville Abe?"

"We don't know anything for sure yet. I don't have any fingerprints—not even a last name. But the photo is enough for me. My gut says it's him." Mason scowled. "Do you know how much I'm going to hate telling my wife her missing father is back in town? But not to see *her*—oh no—it's to head up a smuggling operation. And Anu, how is she going to take it? I hate this!"

"They have to know though. It's going to come out in the papers."

He sighed heavily.

"I'll come with you," Bree said.

$\mathcal{D}$r. Parker's car was in the lot as Kade swung his truck around and parked behind it. He strode into the office, past the startled receptionist who tried to stop him. "The doctor in here?" he asked his wide-eyed nurse.

"He's with a patient," she said.

Kade put his hand on the doorknob and twisted just as Dr. Parker opened the door from the other side. "What's going on out here?" he asked, a frown starting across his forehead.

Kade caught a glimpse of Steve Aster's curious face in the examining room. "I need to see you, Dr. Parker."

The doctor didn't argue. "I'll be right back, Steve," he said.

"No problem," Steve said.

Steve would ask him later what was up, but by then the whole town would know. He nodded to his friend and followed the doctor to his office.

"What's this about, Ranger? You have no right to come barging in here, disturbing my patients." The doctor lowered himself to his chair behind the desk.

Kade placed both palms on top of the desk and leaned toward the doctor. "Your son is in jail, Dr. Parker. And thanks to him, my sister is not only pregnant, she's in trouble with the law right along with him."

The doctor blanched and leaned forward. "What are you talking about?"

"I'm telling you that Brian is in jail for smuggling, and he's dragged Lauri down with him. And if that's not enough, she's due to have a baby in about seven and a half months. And don't even ask if it's Brian's."

"I wasn't going to," the doctor said mildly. "I have no doubt Lauri is not the kind of girl who would run around with a lot of different boys. In spite of your attitude today, I've always liked your sister." He reached for the phone. "Martha, cancel the rest of my appointments for the day. I'm going to be leaving."

"Is that all you have to say?"

"What do you want me to say? I need to go bail my boy out of jail."

"You don't seem surprised he's there."

Dr. Parker raised his eyebrows. "I'll make sure Brian doesn't implicate Lauri. As to the pregnancy, of course I'll take care of her and the baby. Brian will do what I say. I'll arrange a wedding as soon as possible."

"There will be no wedding!" Kade felt as if the ground had just opened up under his feet. Dr. Parker's reaction was unfathomable. Why wasn't he the least bit rattled?

Dr. Parker sighed. "Then what do you want, Kade? Blood? I'm sorry this has happened. But kids are kids. You love them anyway."

Kade stepped back as from a blow. Had he been guilty of everything Lauri had accused him of? He *did* love her, but she didn't seem to get it. Maybe he was just poor at talking about his feelings.

*L*auri's car was here. Kade parked behind it and strode toward the wildlife center. Zorro ran to greet him, but he had no time to spare. He burst into the nursery. Lauri sat on a gray metal chair with a baby raccoon in her arms.

Her smile died when she saw his face. "What is it?"

"I caught Brian and his friends smuggling stuff from Canada. Brian says you're involved too. I—I just want you to know I'm here for you. We'll face this together."

Lauri's head was bowed so her hair fell over her face. He wished he could see her expression.

"I'm sorry, Kade. I know I've disappointed you." She rubbed the raccoon's head, then finally looked up, and he saw tears in her eyes. "I was going to tell you. That's why I'm here."

"You could never disappoint me, Lauri. No matter what you did. I love you just like you are."

Her eyes widened, and a tear slid down her cheek. "I've never heard you say that before." She began to weep in earnest. "I'm in big trouble, aren't I? I was dumb." She swiped at the moisture on her cheek. "Well, I guess we'd better go. At least Bree didn't turn me in."

Kade froze. "Bree knew about this?" He didn't try to keep the incredulity from his voice. He felt like he'd been standing outside a party without a pass. Who else in town knew?

Lauri twirled a strand of hair around her finger and looked

away. "It's not so simple, Kade. Did Brian tell you about Neville? The ringleader? I was afraid he was going to hurt Bree or Anu. He had a bunch of stuff about the Nicholls family in a trunk. Bree saw one of the pictures, and it was of Neville. I guess he's really Anu's missing husband."

"*Abe Nicholls?* Are you telling me that Abe Nicholls is back in town and is involved in smuggling?"

"That's what Bree seems to think. She was going to talk to Mason about it."

Kade's sense of betrayal was complete. "I see," he said, trying to mask his intense hurt. "You'd better get a few things. You might have to spend the night in jail. I'll try to make bail, but it's pretty late in the day, and I might not be able to get a bondsman."

"But I'm pregnant!" Lauri wailed.

She was just a kid herself. Kade's heart wrenched, and he put his arm around her. "I know. You said you were ready to face the music. I don't like this tune either, but I'll do what I can."

Lauri left to pack an overnight bag, and Kade dropped onto the chair. He had never been so utterly weary in his life. Battered by the events of the past few days, he reached over and ran a finger over the downy head of a sleeping baby raccoon.

"I thought I'd find you in here." Gary Landorf advanced into the room. His face was twisted with anger. "I gave you express instructions there were to be no animals here except endangered ones. We don't have the funds to care for every deer and raccoon that gets dropped off here."

"Tell me what we're supposed to do with babies like this." Kade scooped the raccoon out of the cage and placed it in Landorf's hands. "Can you just let something that small and helpless die?"

Landorf glanced down at the raccoon, and his face clouded. "Don't try to change my mind. I have a budget to answer to."

"Then cut my pay!"

To Kade's surprise, Landorf's face softened. "I understand you've got a soft spot for the animals, Kade. But it's not possible to do everything you want to do. You have to take it in stages. Maybe next year." He started to thrust it back in Kade's hands when noises in the corridor made him swing around.

Dawn Anderson with KPTV—one of the reporters at Kade's press conference—came into the room with her camera entourage. "Perfect shot." A flash momentarily lit the room. "Ranger, I'd like your permission to do a special news story on the baby-wildlife center," she said, caressing the raccoon's head. "I'm hoping it might increase charitable giving, maybe even bring in some tourists to Rock Harbor. What do you say? This would make a great opening scene with you and the raccoon," she cooed.

In a daze Kade watched Landorf's scowl change to a smile as he reveled in the media attention. "I was just telling Ranger Matthews how precious these little animals are," he said. His hand stroked the tiny raccoon. "Let me tell you about our vision for the center."

Grinning, Kade tiptoed out of the room.

At last everyone was in bed. It had been hard keeping her thoughts from showing on her face. Bree didn't want to tell Anu about Abe until she was sure of her facts.

She paced the floor for a few minutes, then forced herself to sit back on the sofa. Her hand reached for the portable phone, then she pulled it back. Kade hadn't called for several days. There had been a couple of hang-ups on the answering machine, and she clung to the hope that he might have called and not left any message.

She sighed and curled back onto the sofa with her legs under her. Who was she trying to fool? She'd probably blown it with Kade. If anyone was to blame for the current situation of uneasy truce, it was her. Maybe it was best this way. Davy might never take to Kade, and he adored Nick. But the thought didn't put her heart to rest.

The ticking of the grandfather clock in the corner sounded louder than normal, and Bree realized she was holding her breath. How stupid. Quentin had been the one stalking her, and he was in custody. The danger to her was past. But Anu's heart was about to be broken.

Samson had joined her in the living room. She glanced at him. His ears stood up as he gazed at her with a question in his dark eyes.

"I know, I'm making you nervous," she told him. "I'm making myself a wreck as well. It's going to take some time to settle down and realize life is back to normal now." Whatever normal was. She didn't know anymore.

She should go to bed herself. Church was tomorrow, and she wanted to be fresh so she could really participate in worship, though lately she felt as if God wasn't listening. Would she ever forget the sound of Davy's accusations ringing in her ears? It was her fault his father was dead. *Her fault, her fault.* The knowledge echoed in her heart. If only she hadn't made that call the morning Rob was to fly home. If only she had waited until he got home and not picked a fight over the phone. If only . . .

She sighed. She wasn't the least bit sleepy, though she was tired from helping clean up the mess Quentin had made of Anu's house. Another day of work and Anu could go home.

She grabbed a pen and paper and began to write down what she knew about the murder of Peter Thorrington. The *Seawind* had been salvaged. Its cargo had allowed the survivors to realize a dream. Beulah had said she wished Peter was dead. Peter and Odetta's son, Benjamin Mallory, had been killed. Odetta claimed the hippo had ordered the killing. Hippo, what could that mean?

In her mind's eye, Bree saw the certificates on Dr. Parker's wall. The Hippocratic oath, the oath doctors take upon receiving their license. Blood rushed to her head. Could Dr. Parker be the Hippo? He'd gone away to college right after Peter's death, though his family had money and surely didn't need any ill-gotten gain. She tried to tell herself it couldn't be the doctor, but a sickening feeling in her stomach wouldn't go away. His son was involved in smuggling now too, just as the doctor had been in his younger days. Coincidence?

The lights flickered then came back on again. Samson got up and padded to the window. He seemed a little agitated, but Bree thought he sensed the jangled mess of her own nerves. It would take them all some time to settle down.

The wind rattled the slate shingles on the roof of the lighthouse, and Samson growled. "It's just the wind, boy," she assured him. A gust shook the big window in the living room, and the dog ran to it, the fur on the back of his neck raised. Rain came in driving sheets against the window. Samson began to pace, his tail straight out.

Bree grabbed a quilt and pulled it over her legs as the wind found entry into the room through the leaky walls of the old building. As far as she knew, there were no tornado or severe thunderstorm warnings out for the evening. She should unplug the television just in case.

She stood just as the lights went out. This time they didn't come back on. She walked carefully to the flashlight she kept on the fireplace mantel. When she clicked it on, she let its beam sweep the room. As it passed over the window, she saw a man's distorted face pressed against the glass. Bree's heart slammed against her ribs, and her breathing sounded loud in her ears. Samson lunged at the window, barking furiously. The man quickly stepped away.

She grabbed the phone and dialed 9-1-1. Nothing. No dial tone. Had the storm knocked out the phone, or had the man cut the wire? She clicked off the flashlight so he couldn't see in and tiptoed to the window that faced town. All the lights seemed to be on there, even the Blue Bonnet Bed and Breakfast at the end of the street.

Her fear heightened. Who was out there? Terror had her listening to every sound, imagining every shudder of the house was the man crashing through the door. She had to protect Davy. Her cell phone was in the Jeep, and there was no way to call for help without it. "Come!" she told Samson. She led Samson up the steps and checked on Davy. He was sound asleep. She pointed at the bed. "Guard," she told her dog.

She went across the hall to Anu's room. She awakened Anu and told her what was happening.

Anu pulled on her robe. "I will protect Davy. Call Mason."

That was her next mission. Bree pulled the bedroom door shut behind her, wishing she could lock it. The old doors had no locks, but Samson would defend "his" boy to the death. She went to the top of the stairs and listened, but the roar of the storm was too loud to make out much else. From the top of the stairs she could see the entry door. Still firmly shut. She went down the hall to the back stairway that led to the kitchen.

Carefully easing down the steps, she peered around the doorjamb. The kitchen was empty, and the door to the backyard was still shut. Whoever was out there hadn't forced his way in. Yet. She needed a weapon. What could she use?

The storm lashed its fury at a window, and she jumped at the clatter. She went down the hall to the entry. Maybe there was something she could use in the closet. She didn't dare flip on the flashlight for fear he might see.

Crouching in the darkness, she rooted through the mess on the floor of the closet. Boots, gloves, shoes—no help there. She found snow chains and hefted them in her hand for a moment, then tossed them aside. Too awkward.

She heard a noise at the door, a rattling. Was the man trying to come in, or was it the wind? Her hand at her throat, she decided it was the wind. Back in the closet, her questing hand touched something wooden. She grasped it and pulled it out. A baseball bat. That would have to do.

She stood and advanced to the door. Though her instincts screamed for her to run back upstairs and cower in the bedroom beside the dog, she knew she couldn't do that. She needed that cell phone.

The blood pounded in her veins with the same ferocity as the crashing thunder outside. If only the sound would die down long enough for her to listen, to make sure no one stood on the other side of that door. On her tiptoes, she peeked through the small window in the door but could see nothing in the darkness outside. The security light was out too.

Taking a deep breath, she prayed, then threw open the door. She made sure it was locked behind her, then dashed through the pelting rain to the Jeep. Luckily, it was unlocked, and she jumped inside and quickly locked the door. Just to be sure, she flicked on her flashlight and scanned the vehicle to make sure no one else was in the Jeep. She was alone.

Gripping the baseball bat with white knuckles, she punched in 9-1-1 and pushed send. Nothing. She stared at the screen and realized she hadn't recharged it for several days. The rain sluiced over the windshield in sheets.

She could drive for help, but not without getting Anu and Davy. Peering through the sheets of rain, she tried to see the front of the house, but it was impossible. Where was the man? Perhaps he had broken in the back door while she was out here.

She fumbled in her pocket for her house key and pulled it out. With the key in one hand and the bat in the other, she projected herself nearly three feet on her first bound. The wind drove the rain in her face, and she sputtered and squinted, trying to see through the sheets of water and the penetrating darkness.

Crossing that yard seemed to take hours. She finally stood at the front door. Jamming her key into the lock, she turned it and practically fell into the entry hall. She slammed the door behind her and threw the lock. Her chest heaving, she stopped and listened. *Please, God, let him not be in here with Davy.* She heard nothing and was just beginning to relax when a sound came from the direction of the kitchen.

A crash, and then an oath over the fury of the storm. The window. He was in. What if he went up the back stairway to Davy and Anu? She had to stop him. Samson was barking ferociously from upstairs, so that was good. Anu would know the danger level had heightened.

Gripping the bat with both hands, Bree advanced toward the door that led to the kitchen. It was hard to think, to plan, past the terror that dried her mouth. At the door to the kitchen she paused. Should she push the door open slowly and peek in or throw open the door and rush at the intruder?

Be bold, she told herself. She took a couple of deep breaths, then set her jaw. She could do this. She had to—there was no one else. Narrowing her eyes, she threw open the door and charged into the kitchen. A dark form threw up a hand and whirled to face her. His face was covered with a ski mask, and he had a gun in his right hand.

She planted her feet and brought the bat down on his wrist. The gun flew from his fingers, and he let out a gasp of pain or surprise or both and dived after the gun. He got there before she did. He whipped around and pointed it at her head.

"Drop the bat!" he ordered in a gruff voice. Bree maintained her grip on the bat and tried to decide if she could attempt to disarm him again.

"I said drop it!" He thumbed the hammer of the gun.

She had no choice. The baseball bat dropped from her suddenly nerveless fingers and clattered on the tile floor. He'd broken one of the six small panes in the door window, and wind gusted through the opening, but it wasn't the cold rain that chilled her.

"What do you want?" she demanded.

He motioned for her to precede him through the door to the basement. He marched her down the steps. She was trembling so hard she had to hang on to the railing to prevent herself from falling. This man wasn't Dr. Parker—he was too tall and slender. Her jolt of intuition had been all wrong.

His gun trained on her, he reached over and flipped a breaker. "Back upstairs," he ordered.

Back in the kitchen, he motioned for her to go through the kitchen door toward the front of the house. Walking slowly, her mind jumped from one possibility to another. As she entered the foyer, she saw Anu at the top of the stairs. The man behind her gave a hiss of recognition, and she realized with a sinking heart that he'd seen her too.

"Get down here," the man snarled.

Anu started slowly down the steps. Bree's chest felt like it might explode into a million fragments. *Davy, Davy.* She had to find a way to protect him. And Anu.

Her feet dragging, she led the way to the living room.

The man gestured for them to sit on the sofa. "Where is it?"

"Where is what?" Maybe they were finally going to find out what this was all about.

"The diamond."

Bree and Anu stared at one another. "We don't know anything about any diamond," Bree said.

"Don't play with me," he snarled. His eyes glowered behind the ski mask. "I don't have all day. Give me the diamond if you don't want to get hurt."

"We don't have any diamonds other than our engagement rings.

Is that what you want?" Bree couldn't think, couldn't focus. All this for a couple of rings? It didn't make sense.

The man began to pace, and she could feel his pent-up anger. It was like watching a storm building over Lake Superior while in a boat miles from shore.

He leaned forward and grabbed Anu's hand. "You were wearing it the other day, but it's not in your house and you don't have it on now. Where is it?"

Bree's eyes widened. "You mean the emerald ring?"

He gave a harsh laugh. "Sure, call it what you want. The green ring."

A green diamond—that's what he was talking about. Bree had heard of them, but she'd never seen one. Few people had. No wonder the color was so pale. It had to be worth millions.

She stared at the man. Something about his voice reminded her of someone.

The man squeezed Anu's hand, and she let out a gasp of pain. "I said where is it?"

"It's in my room upstairs." Anu met his gaze. "I'll go get it."

"We'll all go." He jerked Bree to her feet, then motioned for Anu to lead the way. They went up the steps to the door to the bedroom. From the other side of the door, she could hear Samson growling softly.

"Keep that dog in there, or I'll have to shoot him."

"He can't open the door by himself," she assured him.

Anu went to her room and approached the bedside table. She picked up a small ceramic bowl. She turned and offered it to the man.

He grabbed the bowl from her hands and looked inside. He swore. "Where is it? I don't have patience for tricks." The man's eyes narrowed behind the ski mask. "Who should I shoot first? Bree or the boy? Pick one."

$\mathcal{B}$ree cast her thoughts around for some way to get the gun away from the man, but all that she saw in the bedroom were stuffed toys and small pieces of Davy's fireman set. She clenched her hands and coiled to spring on him. She wouldn't allow him to hurt her son.

Anu took a step toward the man, and Bree gasped and turned to stop her.

"Abraham." Anu spoke the name softly. She held out her hand. The ring sparkled in her palm. "Is this what you're looking for, husband?"

Bree caught her breath and turned to stare at the gunman.

The man drew back as if he'd been struck. "Shut up," he said, his voice thick.

"I know it is you, my Abraham. I recognized your voice, though you tried to disguise it. And your walk is distinct."

The man's hand that held the gun began to shake. He took a step back. To Bree's astonishment, Anu took another step forward and took the gun from the man's unresisting hand. She reached up and pulled the ski mask from his face. A face lined and harsh appeared. Older than the picture she'd seen, but still recognizable. Abraham Nicholls, also known as Neville. Glints of blond and gray were beginning to show at the roots of his dyed hair.

Anu stepped back. "So, Abraham, you have returned. I admit our reunion is not quite as I'd pictured." Her faint smile was sad. She laid the gun on the bed.

Abe stared at her. "I can't believe you recognized me."

Anu's smile dimmed even further. "Your ways were etched on my heart," she said simply. "The way you walk, the tilt of your head, the sound of your voice."

Bree stepped closer to Anu and took her hand, nearly flinching at Anu's icy fingers.

Anu squeezed Bree's hand. "You do not seem surprised, *kulta*. Did you know of my husband's return?"

"I suspected it."

Bree turned to Abe. "You're the one who has been watching the house, right? Was it you who vandalized it?"

Abe scowled. "Give me the diamond, Anu." He held out his hand. "This is for your own good."

"You gave it to me, Abraham. If you wished it back, why did you not simply come to the door and ask?" Anu looked at the ring in her hand. "This diamond—it is worth a great deal of money?"

Abe's bark of laughter was bitter. "You have no idea."

"That is the only reason you've come back? I thought perhaps you'd come to seek—my forgiveness." Anu whispered the last two words.

He laughed again, a forced and harsh sound. "Just the diamond."

"Always I have prayed for you, Abraham. That God would speak to your heart and that you would turn to him."

How could she be so calm? Bree marveled at Anu's patient voice and wondered if she'd played out this scenario in her head over the years. Or maybe it was just God. Anu always seemed to know the right thing to say.

"I'm afraid I'm beyond redemption," Abe said. He tugged at his collar and looked everywhere but at his wife.

"There is nothing God doesn't forgive. You can stop this running now, Abraham. Face what you've done. Your daughter misses you." Anu cleared her throat, and her fingers tightened on Bree's. "I miss you too. God has brought you back to this place to force you to confront your past."

Abe shook his head slowly. "It's too late, Anu. No matter how much I might wish otherwise."

"I want to understand what happened, why you left us."

Abe grunted.

"I think I know," Bree said. "You were smuggling for a long time, weren't you? Why did it start?" Beulah had said the Do-Wrong Gang played poker. "Gambling debts?" It was a wild stab.

Abe sent her a glance of resentment. "Shut up. This isn't about you."

"You set fire to my house."

"I didn't," he growled.

Bree made another wild guess. "You used the *Seawind*, didn't you? For the bigger smuggling, the stuff that had to be shipped. What was it—gems, drugs?"

Abe turned around to face them again, and his blue eyes, so like Rob's, blinked slowly. "Give me the diamond and let me get out of here. I'm tired of both of you."

Bree's thoughts whirled. "Was Argie Hamel in on it?"

Abe slapped Bree and she gasped, sitting down hard on the edge of the bed.

"You're so stupid, and I'm tired of hearing you yap. There was a lot more money in prescription drugs and illegal booty from Canada than salvage on the boat."

"Argie Hamel shipped the stuff out on the *Seawind*," Bree said slowly, holding her hand to her cheek. "But why did you kill him?"

"I didn't!" Abe yelled, his face red as he stood over her. "Argie was into more big-time stuff than we were. He fell one day and broke his leg. Knocked over a box in the process, and all these gems fell out: rubies, emeralds, diamonds."

"And you didn't need to call a doctor, did you? Max Parker had been in med school." It was all falling into place for Bree. "Did he offer you a cut on the stones if you kept quiet?"

"Sounds like you've got it all figured out." In a quick move Abe snatched the ring out of Anu's hand and made for the door.

Bree drew a deep breath, the truth exploding in her. She stepped in front of Abe. "Dr. Parker was the brains behind the Do-Wrongs. The drug smuggling was his baby. He killed Argie."

"No!" Abe stopped with his hand on the knob. "Max took him home and bandaged him up. He was getting along just fine until some internal bleeding got him. There was nothing Max could do."

"And you swallowed that story?"

Abe's eyes widened. "Max said he bled to death. Said we might as well split those gems up among us."

"And you killed Peter in my basement for his share."

"Shut up! It wasn't like that." Abe let go of the door and clenched his hands as though he was trying not to strangle Bree. "We split up the gems, and I had the ring in my share. At first, we thought it was a poor-quality emerald."

"Which is why you gave it to Anu. She never expected much from you."

Abe shot her a fierce look from under his lowered brows. "Max found out what we really had and told me to give him the ring, that he'd sell it and we'd split the take. I said no. A deal was a deal. He came at me with Peter's wrecking tool, and Pete jumped in between at the wrong time. I lit out then and never went back."

He looked at Anu. "I always thought I'd be back for it before now, but I never really needed it. Then there was that picture of you in the newspaper article about the store's twentieth anniversary. I saw the ring on your finger and knew Max would go after it."

"You came back to protect Anu?"

He shrugged his shoulders.

"Oh, Abraham," Anu said softly. "Why didn't you go to the police when Max killed Peter?"

"They'd find out I was a smuggler and all the rest. Then you'd know too."

"Well, now we all know, don't we?" Dr. Max Parker shoved the door open and stepped in. He pointed a gun at Abe. "I'll take that ring now. You didn't think I'd let you get away with it, did you, Abe?" He snapped his fingers. "The ring."

Abe slowly dropped it into his hand. "I was getting it for you," he said.

"Sure, and there's a bridge I'd like to sell you." Dr. Parker's fist closed over the ring, and he smiled in triumph.

Anu's gaze lingered on the doctor's face in a way that would have touched anyone else's heart. "We've been friends a long time, Max," she said softly.

Dr. Parker ignored her. "Let's all go for a ride in my new yacht." He motioned to Bree. "Get the boy."

Bree was prepared to throw herself on the gun, anything to prevent his getting his hands on her son. She curled her fingers into her palms and raised a pleading gaze to Dr. Parker. "Please, leave him here. He's seen nothing and knows nothing." Bree knew what the boat ride meant. He'd toss them overboard and let Superior's cold water do the rest. Hypothermia would kill them in minutes.

Dr. Parker hesitated, then nodded curtly. "All right. I guess I don't really want the boy's death on my conscience. Maybe I'll make him my token charity of the day. Now move."

Bree walked slowly toward the door. She knew Anu was praying, and she prayed fervently too.

Bree could hear Samson pacing and snarling in Davy's room. They went down the stairs. She started toward the coat closet under the stairs.

"You won't need a jacket where you're going," the doctor said with a sneer.

"At least we can be more comfortable on the ride out there," she said, ignoring him and opening the closet door.

"Stop right there!"

"You're not going to shoot me. I'm going to get our jackets." Bree grabbed Anu's jacket and slung it to her, then took her own from the hanger. The heavy drape on the right side told her she wasn't mistaken. The new can of bear spray she'd bought was still in her pocket. She'd never transferred it to her ready-pack.

She slipped her arms into her jacket. The doctor gritted his teeth and grabbed her roughly by the arm. "Get in the car and don't give me any more trouble!" He marched them in a single file to his car, a new black Cadillac.

"You sit in the front with me. If either of you move, I'll shoot her," he told Anu and Abe.

Bree sat perfectly still in the passenger seat. She'd have to figure out when to make her move. She wouldn't let him put them on the boat. She stared at her house in the side mirror outside her window. *God, be with Davy.* Tears sprang to her eyes, and she swallowed hard. She had to live. For Davy's sake, she had to figure out how to defeat Max Parker.

"Why did the money matter so much?" She needed to keep him talking. "Your family has always been known as the richest in town."

He grimaced. "Well, appearances are deceiving, aren't they? My father came home from World War II with so many injuries, he became addicted to morphine. It took stronger drugs to keep the mental demons away. He squandered all our money on his drugs. When the money was gone, he introduced me to the trade of black-market painkillers. That's where the real money is." He waved the gun nonchalantly. "But I'm tired of it all. I don't want my boy messed up in this. Abe has already pulled him into enough trouble. And with the ring, neither of us will ever have to worry about money again." His eyes glittered.

"Even if you have to kill three more people. You're leaving Davy an orphan."

"He'll have Hilary and Mason. Your son will have a good home. I might even bestow some money on him." A trace of regret passed over his face. "I've always liked you, Bree. I'm sorry it had to end this way."

"It doesn't. You could let us go. Take the diamond and disappear."

He pursed his lips and shook his head. "And leave my comfortable spot in the community? No. It has to be this way. I'm sorry."

His inflexible voice made chills run up her spine. He drove to the marina. This early in the season, no one was around. Bree looked out at the inky black water, fear beginning to swamp her.

She forced her lips to move. "You trashed Anu's house, didn't you? And killed Benjamin Mallory. He worked with you, not Abe, like I thought, right? Mason said he'd heard that Benjamin had become a Christian. Did he get cold feet then and threaten to blow the whistle on you?"

He stared straight ahead.

"That's it, isn't it? You had him killed. I'm sure you didn't sully your hands with the killing yourself."

He shrugged.

"And you set fire to my house. I assume to cover any remaining evidence in the basement?"

"Forensics has come a long way. I wanted to make sure nothing down there might incriminate me."

"How can you think money is worth all those lives?" she asked.

He scowled and brought the car to a stop at a dock. "Enough talk."

Bree opened her door and stepped out. As she did, she zipped her jacket and slipped her hands into her pockets. "That wind is cold." Her fingers closed around the can of bear spray. She had to time this just right.

"Not as cold as the water," he said in a monotone voice.

She fumbled in frustration with the cap of the bear spray. At one point, her nails snapped against the plastic cap, and she froze, sure he'd heard. But the howling wind drowned out the noise. She finally succeeded in getting the cap off. Her finger on the trigger, she waited for the right moment. With her gaze she pleaded silently for Abe to do something, anything to distract the doctor.

Abe moved slowly. "I'm not feeling too good," he said.

"Pretty soon you won't feel anything at all," Dr. Parker said. "Move."

Abe shuffled forward with Anu helping him along.

"Can't you see he's sick?" Anu said sharply.

Abe groaned and sank to his knees. With the doctor's attention fully on the pair, Bree brought the can of bear spray out of her pocket. Holding it aloft, she shrieked at the top of her lungs. The doctor spun toward her in alarm. She pressed the nozzle of the spray and dosed his eyes with the pepper spray.

Screaming, Dr. Parker dropped the gun and dug at his eyes. He staggered along the pier, uttering high squawks of agony.

Abe grabbed the gun. "Stop!" he shouted at the doctor. Blinded by the bear spray, Dr. Parker reeled along the pier. A high board on the pier caught the doctor's shoe, and he toppled against one of the pier posts.

"Look out!" Bree shouted, running toward him.

He flung out his arms to try to regain his balance. Then, flailing wildly, he fell into the frigid water.

Bree glanced around for something to throw to him. Nothing. She'd seen a cell phone on the seat of the car. "I'll call for help," she shouted, running back to the Cadillac. "See if you can get him out." Scrabbling inside the car, she found the phone and dialed 9-1-1. The dispatcher promised to send someone to watch over Davy and to send aid to the dock.

She needed to get to Davy herself, make sure he was all right. She glanced at the ignition. The keys weren't there. Dr. Parker must have them. She got out and slammed the door behind her, then went running down the hill to the dock. If she could get the keys, she'd take the doctor's car and get to her son. The authorities could handle this mess.

Abe had managed to get the doctor out of the lake, though Dr. Parker still groped blindly. Gasping and shivering, he lay on the rocks with streaming red eyes.

"Where are the car keys?" she asked, kneeling beside him.

Coughing and sputtering, he turned his head away and didn't answer her. She patted his jacket and found the keys. When she pulled them out, the diamond ring came with them. She handed it to Anu. "Keep this for Mason." All she wanted was to get to her son.

Bree turned at the sound of a siren and saw Mason get out of the car. She saw her own relief echoed in Anu's face. Anu stayed close to Abraham, but Bree ran to Mason, and he hugged her in a tight, brotherly embrace.

"He was going to kill us," she said, her words muffled against his chest.

"You're safe now," Mason said. He patted her back, then released her. She turned to the doctor's car. "Wait, Bree," Mason said. "Hilary is with Davy. I need you here for a minute longer." Reluctantly, she followed him down the dock to where Abe stood guard over Dr. Parker.

Mason listened quietly to the explanation of all that had happened, his gaze lingering on Abe's face as Bree explained her father-in-law's part in everything.

"I'm afraid I'm going to have to arrest you as well, Mr. Nicholls," he told Abe.

"I know," Abe said. He held out his hands. "Can I see my daughter first?"

Mason's jaw twitched. "I'm sure she'd like to see you."

I'm in here," Hilary said.

Anu stopped Bree from entering the living room. "Wait, maybe I should prepare her," she whispered.

"How do you prepare someone for something like this?" Bree asked.

Anu's hand dropped, and she nodded. "Perhaps you are right."

They all stepped into the living room. Abe was beside Mason, though the sheriff had been thoughtful enough to remove the cuffs.

Hilary's face looked thin, drawn. She was curled up on the sofa with Bree's Bible in her hand. Her eyes were pink, and she wiped the moisture from them hastily.

"Is everyone is all right? I still can't believe the doctor would do something like this. I've been praying for him."

There was something different about Hilary, something Bree couldn't put her finger on. The worry about the baby had softened her sharp edges, but it wasn't just that.

Hilary's gaze went to Anu. "Are you okay, Mother?" She stood and embraced her.

Her shoulders shaking, Anu clung to her. Tears welled in Bree's eyes as well. This had to be so hard for Anu.

Hilary began to cry too, though Bree couldn't tell whether it was in sympathy for her mother or from her own emotional upheaval. Anu's shoulders straightened, and she began to soothe her daughter. Hilary finally pulled away. Her gaze touched Abe, then went to Mason, then back to Abe. Her eyes widened.

Anu took Hilary's hand. "You recognize this man, *kulta*? Look closely. He is your father."

Hilary put her hand to her mouth. "Daddy?"

"Hello, Hilly." Abe's arms hung slackly at his sides, then he rubbed his palms against his trousers as if he wasn't sure what to do with his hands.

Hilary gasped and her face paled.

"It's you, Daddy." She ran to her father, and Abe embraced her, tears trickling down his weathered cheeks.

Bree looked away. The moment was too private for her to stare. After a few minutes, the sound of weeping faded, and she peeked again at her family. Hilary had finally stepped back. She stood staring at her father as though she couldn't get enough of him.

"Why did you leave? All these years and not a word. And why are you here now?"

"I think we'd better all sit down. This is a story I want to hear as well," Mason said.

*B*ree reached out to take Hilary's hand. Hilary let her fingers lie in Bree's palm, but she didn't return the pressure. Stony-faced, she refused to look at her father as Mason stood to take him to jail.

"Hilly?" Abe said at the doorway.

Hilary turned her face away. "I don't ever want to see him again," she told her mother.

Anguish contorted Abe's features, and he turned slowly to go with Mason. The sound of the door closing seemed as final as a death.

"For your own sake, you must forgive him," Anu said.

Hilary said nothing, her face cold and white. She gathered her things and went to the door.

Bree followed Hilary to the door. "I'll be praying for you, Hilary."

"Don't bother," Hilary said, her voice clipped. "No amount of prayer will make me forgive him."

Bree stood on the porch and watched her leave. As she turned to go back inside, she saw the lights of a car approach, then stop. Nick got out and came running up the walk to her. "I just heard about it on the scanner." His face was drawn with concern, and when he held open his arms, she went to him. She allowed herself this moment of weakness. She was so tired of being the strong one, of holding everything together. For just a minute, it was good to let the tears flow.

K ade raced down Quincy Hill, gunning his engine as he made the curve and turned toward the lighthouse. Inperturbable Mason had sounded rattled when he called from the station. And no wonder, since he'd had to arrest his father-in-law. Kade still wasn't sure Mason knew what he was talking about when he said Bree was fine. How could she be fine when she'd nearly been killed?

Beside him, Lauri gripped the door handle to keep from being tossed around the truck. "Slow down!"

With all the evening's eventfulness, no one had been at the sheriff's office to question Lauri about her involvement in the break-ins and smuggling, so at least she hadn't had to spend the night in jail. Kade was grateful for that. He was frantic to get to Bree. She needed him. He wanted to wrap her in his arms and stand against anyone who would try to hurt her or Davy.

As he approached her home, he saw two figures on the porch, their arms wrapped around one another. His foot slipped from the accelerator as the porch light illuminated Bree's red hair. Bree was in Nick Fletcher's arms.

He heard Lauri gasp. The steering wheel went slack in his hands, and he narrowly missed a light pole. What a fool he'd been. He turned the truck and went back the way he'd come.

*B*ree held Davy's hand as they walked along the lakeshore. Davy stooped and picked up a piece of pink quartz, then they continued on their stroll. Bree lifted her face to the sun and relished the warmth on her skin. Her doubts behind her, the future looked as warm and sunny as the blue skies above her head.

Davy pulled his hand from hers and ran ahead of her to the edge of the water where a wave tossed a bit of flotsam onto his shoes. "Oh, it's cold, Mommy!"

Bree smiled and nodded. "It's always cold, remember? Even in the summer, it's cold."

"I remember."

She remembered too, so much that it brought her a bittersweet joy mixed with pain. The three of them had spent a lot of time here. Rob loved it as much as Davy. The hard rocks mixed with sand as fine and white as sugar reminded her of the way all sweet things are mixed with hard things that are sometimes difficult to endure. She would have to keep learning to thank God for them all.

There would be hard times ahead. Kade and Lauri would have to deal with Lauri's pregnancy and her trouble with the law, though Mason said he had talked with the district attorney and thought he could get Lauri probation. She was underage and penitent and had helped crack the smuggling ring wide open. All of them would have to forge new relationships with Abe and deal with the trauma caused by his greed. The consequences of what he'd done would reverberate for some time through their small community, which was still reeling from the discovery of Dr. Parker's murderous side.

Kade's struggle with his boss over the wildlife center had been solved by a grant that followed Dawn Anderson's favorable news report. Bree had stared longingly at the footage of Kade with the baby raccoons. He had avoided her for over a week now, and she was having to come to the realization that maybe it was over between them.

Watching her son, she tried to tell herself it didn't matter. What mattered was truth, love, and the future she and Davy would share together. She stooped and picked up a flat rock. "Watch, Davy!" She skipped the rock over the waves. It skimmed the water five times before a wave swallowed it up.

"Great, Mommy! Let me try." His tongue poking out of his mouth, he picked up a rock and tossed it. It sank on the first hit. "I'm not good at it like Daddy was. He was really good, wasn't he?"

"He sure was. And we'll always have him with us in our hearts. Someday we'll see him again."

"Yeah!" Davy ran down the beach with Samson barking and running at his side.

Bree smiled. She would let tomorrow's trouble take care of itself. She had this perfect day to savor. The wind blew through her hair as she raced after Davy and tackled him on the sand. They rolled over and over in the sand before coming to rest near Superior's cold spray.

Davy put his sandy palms on each side of her face and stared into her eyes. "I love you, Mommy," he said.

About the Author

RITA finalist Colleen Coble lives with her husband, Dave, in Indiana. She is the author of several novels including *Lonestar Sanctuary, Abomination, Alaska Twilight, Midnight Sea,* the Rock Harbor Series, and the Aloha Reef Series.

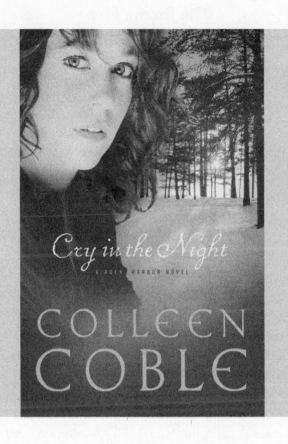

Cry in the Night

A ROCK HARBOR NOVEL

COLLEEN
COBLE

The New Rock Harbor Novel

AVAILABLE FEBRUARY 2009

THOMAS NELSON
Since 1798

An Excerpt from

A Cry in the Night

1

THE BABY IN THE CARRIER SLEPT PEACEFULLY, TINY FISTS thrust against her chubby cheeks blissfully unaware of her danger. Pia Westola clicked off the phone and sat back in her chair, gazing at the baby, sick with the awareness of this new, undesirable turn her life had taken. What had started out as a job she could believe in—even if it did sometimes drift into the law's gray areas—had just become clearly criminal. She would never have agreed to take this infant if what Florence had just told her was true.

One glance at the clock to her her boss would be here soon. Pia just had to keep the little one out of his reach. Adrenaline pulsed through her at the thought. Her decision made, she slipped on her coat, adjusted the insulating cover over the baby carrier that fit on her like a backpack, then grabbed the bottles and diapers and stuffed them in with the baby. If she could hide out long enough, maybe she could get the baby to safety.

Before she reached the garage door, she heard a car out front. Peeking through the curtains, she saw him get out. His car blocked Pia's getaway. Biting back panic, she realized she'd have to escape through the kitchen door.

She exited quickly with the baby and stood on the porch. She knew she had to hurry, but which direction? He'd see her on the road. Her only hope was through the thigh-high drifts across her backyard and into the woods. Her cross-country skis were propped against the side of the house. She shouldered into the baby backpack, slung the diaper bag over that, and then snapped on her skis.

She set out across the frozen landscape. Her muscles were warm by the time she reached the edge of the woods, and her breath fogged the frigid air. But she'd reached the path other skiers had used, and the going would be easier.

Her back aching from the weight of the carrier, she spared a glance behind her. Her spirits flagged when she caught a glimpse of him. He was on skis too. She'd forgotten he always carried them in his car. He wasn't burdened with the baby either. She was never going to make the sanctuary she'd hoped for. He hadn't seen her yet, though. She hoped he'd lose her tracks on the more highly trafficked trail.

Tension coiled along Pia's spine as she whirled and looked for a place to hide the baby. There—a fallen pile of logs had enough space under it to hide the infant. She slipped out of the backpack, and a crumpled piece of paper fell from her pocket. She wedged the carrier under the logs. She layered several insulated blankets around the tiny girl. At least the child was sheltered.

Picking up a branch, she erased the evidence of her tracks to the logs. She stared down the hill at the approaching figure, then retraced her steps. She met him at a bend in the trail. She'd never known him to be a violent man—maybe she could reason with him.

His narrowed gaze nearly cut her down. "Where's the baby?"

She tipped up her chin. "I'm not going to be part of this."

He grabbed her arm and twisted it. "Where is she?"

Reeling from the shock, Pia's shoulder shrieked with pain. Still she held his gaze defiantly. "Where you'll never find her."

"I saw you carrying her!" He slapped her, then slapped her

again. Both hands moved to her shoulders and he shook her. "Where is she?"

Pia's cheeks burned. Her head flopped with the violence of the shaking. Then he shoved her, and she was falling, falling toward a broken tree limb that jutted from the ground like a giant spear.

Return to the World of Rock Harbor!

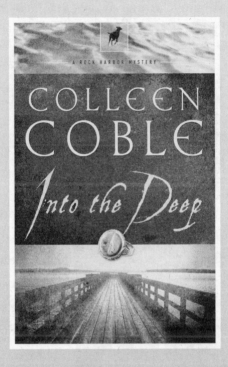

Bree Nichols and her beloved search-and-rescue dog, Samson, pitch in to help investigate the events disrupting their small community. But new discoveries soon throw her shaky love life into tilt, dredge up her painful past, and threaten her family. Bree must dive deep for the faith to keep going, the strength to defend those she cares about, and the courage to keep her fearful heart open to love.

Alaska Twilight

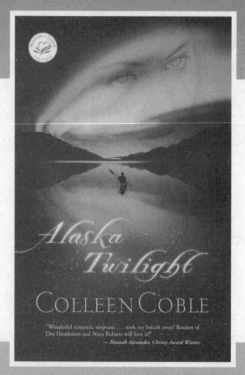

Wonderful romantic
suspense . . . took
my breath away!
Readers of Dee
Henderson and
Nora Roberts will
love it!

—HANNAH
ALEXANDER
Christy Award Winner

THOMAS NELSON
Since 1798

AVAILABLE NOW

"Colleen is a master storyteller."
KAREN KINGSBURY
Best-selling author of *Ever Now* and *Ever After*

LONESTAR SANCTUARY

COLLEEN COBLE

More Romantic Suspense
from Colleen Coble